FUNERAL
GAMES

Mary Renault

Introduced by Tom Holland

virago

VIRAGO

This edition published by Virago Press in 2014
First published in Great Britain by John Murray in 1981

3 5 7 9 10 8 6 4 2

A CIP catalogue record for this book
is available from the British Library.

ISBN 978-1-84408-959-8

Typeset in Goudy by M Rules
Printed and bound in Great Britain by
Clays Ltd, St Ives plc

Papers used by Virago are from well-managed forests
and other responsible sources.

MIX
Paper from
responsible sources
FSC® C104740

Virago Press
An imprint of
Little, Brown Book Group
Carmelite House
50 Victoria Embankment
London EC4Y 0DZ

An Hachette UK Company
www.hachette.co.uk

www.virago.co.uk

will feel for themselves the unsettling impact of Lowell's threnody on her hero:

> 'but if you wish to blackguard the Great King,
> think how mean, obscure and dull you are,
> your labors lowly and your merits less ...'

Tom Holland, 2014

practised enough in the arts of the bedchamber to satisfy him more fully than any woman. Men too, even Alexander himself, are tempted by the scope for reinvention offered by a spot of gender-bending. Smooth-cheeked, in pointed contrast to his hirsute father, and rumoured to possess 'a natural fragrance', the attributes of femininity only serve to enhance the potency of Alexander's world-conquering charisma. For women, though, it is very different. All attempts to escape 'claustral and stifling femininity' serve only to doom them. Even the most powerful are destroyed in the end by their ambitions. Olympias, who dares to stand up to her intimidatingly domineering husband, ends up permanently distanced from her son before finally being stoned to death; Eurydike, who bosses her own husband, goes hunting dressed in masculine clothing, and 'had known as long as she could remember that she should have been a boy', is incapacitated at the climactic moment of her career by the onset of her period. If the world of the Alexander trilogy is ultimately a tragic one, then it is especially so for women.

The paradox of Mary Renault, and the key to her greatness as a resurrectionist of antiquity, is that she was simultaneously ground-breaking and backward-looking, progressive and reactionary. With the Alexander trilogy, homoerotic fiction went mainstream for the first time; but in its scorn for democracy, its idealisation of the heroic, and its mistrust of the feminine, it was also profoundly true to the long-vanished age of Alexander. As the best historical fiction invariably does, it obliges readers to take a vanished world, not on their terms, but on its own. To us, in the shadow of repeated wars in the Middle East, the nobility of Alexander's ideals are liable, perhaps, to seem less self-evident than they did to Renault, and we may well find ourselves agreeing more readily with Robert Lowell, who declared in 1973, one year after the publication of *The Persian Boy*, that 'Terrible were his crimes'. Yet the American poet too felt the magnetism of Alexander's greatness – and all who have read Renault's trilogy contemporary sensibilities, does the challenge her trilogy represents to some of our most fundamental notions of what it means to be a female writer. Mary Renault, whose mother had always mocked her for her big feet and desire for a career, did not greatly like being a woman. 'Men,' she declared flatly, 'have more fun.' Perhaps, among her contemporaries, only Patricia Highsmith could rival her resentment at having been born female. Just as *Fire from Heaven* is alive with the excitement of being a man, so does it cast being a woman as a wretched second best. No taming of horses, no recording a first kill in battle for girls. Throughout the trilogy, they are described as twittering and flocking like birds, and sapping with their 'whispered confidences' the martial ardour of their menfolk. 'Women can't issue challenges to their enemies as we can,' Alexander observes to Hephaistion, 'they can only be avenged like women. Rather than blame them, we ought to be thankful to the gods for making us men.'

A declaration that in its ideological underpinnings is certainly true to what the historical Alexander would have believed – but one that also, authored as it is by a woman, is liable to strike the reader as just a trifle disorienting. Perhaps it is not surprising, then, that many of Renault's early readers should have believed her a male writer hiding behind a pseudonym. In reality, despite – or perhaps because of – the rigid contrast in Greek culture between the masculine and feminine spheres, her novels repeatedly explore what it might mean to blur the gender divide. 'There are eunuchs who become women,' declares Bagoas, 'and those who do not; we are something by ourselves, and must make of it what we can.' Indeed, so formidable is his commitment to self-invention that it marks him as both the most original of Renault's characters, and the most paradigmatic. Striking a balance between the twin ideals of hardiness and beauty, Bagoas is tough enough to accompany Alexander on even the most demanding of his campaigns, yet and his companions in *Fire from Heaven*. Her second ambition, to become a novelist, was pursued with a similarly unyielding resolve. Only she could write her novels, of course – but Renault, for all that, never lacked for support in her new career. In 1935, as a student nurse, she had met the woman who was destined to be at her side for the remainder of her life. In Julie Mullard she had found a yet further point of contact with Alexander. 'His emotional commitment to Hephaistion is among the most certain facts of his life.' So Renault wrote in the afterword to *Fire from Heaven*. It is hard not to feel that she was simultaneously paying tribute to the great love of her own life.

It is the measure of her achievement in the Alexander trilogy that we never find such a conceit ludicrous. So detailed and finely textured is her portrayal of Alexander's world, and so credible her evocation of his psychology, that the reader rarely pauses to take him on anything other than Renault's own terms. 'In grief more than in joy, man longs to know that the universe turns around him.' For most, such a yearning breeds only illusion; but with Alexander, Renault could explore a hero who had indeed moulded the world to his own ambitions, and made himself its pivot. The intoxicating pleasure of her trilogy is that it enables us to share in the glory and potency of such a man. 'In his presence,' declares Bagoas in *The Persian Boy*, 'I felt more beautiful.' All readers who find themselves seduced by Renault's fictionalisation of Alexander are liable to feel much the same.

Yet the figure of Bagoas, 'the elegant, epicene favourite', as he is described in *Funeral Games*, born a boy but looking like a girl, hints at the ambiguities which shadow the dynamics of the entire trilogy. It is not merely the dignity with which Renault endows same-sex relationships, at a time when suspicion of homosexuality remained rife, that marks her as a writer of fiction immeasurably more original than the vast majority of historical novelists. So too, and perhaps more disturbingly to an upsetting sight: that of his father packing in the dead of night, and leaving the family home for ever. 'After, when the passage of years had confused his memories of that night and overlaid them with later knowledge, what he remembered best was having known for the first time the burden, prison and mystery of his own uniqueness.' Laurie, growing up gay in a Britain that still criminalised homosexual acts, never manages to break free of mainstream society's contempt for his sexuality, and leads a life that is perpetually marked by compromise. Not so Alexander. He too, like Laurie, witnesses a profoundly disturbing scene in the dead of night, when his father bursts in on his mother, while Alexander is still sheltering in her bed. 'The child saw him rush upon them, like Polyphemos on his prey. He seemed to bristle all over; even the rod that hung in his black bushy crotch had risen by itself and was thrust forward, a sight of mysterious horror.' Alexander, however, does not allow himself to be dominated by the traumatic nature of the episode. Marked by it though his own sexuality certainly turns out to have been, he bends it, like everything else, to his will. Not for him what he sees as the priapic self-indulgence of his father. Instead, by committing himself enduringly to Hephaistion, he is able to cast himself as the new Achilles, bonded with a second Patroclus. The man who goes on to conquer the world is portrayed as a man who has first succeeded in conquering himself.

It is not hard to see, in the light of Renault's own life, what the significance of this exemplar might have been to her. Like Laurie, like Alexander, she was the child of a desperately unhappy marriage. Determined, in the face of strident opposition from both her parents, to make her own way in the world, she drove herself unflaggingly hard. Her first ambition, to become a nurse, saw her submit to a programme of training so redolent of the bleakest kind of boarding school that it surely influenced her portrayal of the literally Spartan regime endured by Alexander contemporary England, she embarked on the line of fictional evocations of ancient Greece that was to culminate in her Alexander trilogy. Like Bagoas, the castrated slave-boy who discovered in his submission to the great conqueror only liberation, Mary Renault associated Alexander above all with the joys of freedom.

Simultaneously, there was a measure of something else to be found in Renault's fascination with Alexander: self-identification. This is particularly evident in *Fire from Heaven*, where she had set herself an almost impossible task: not merely to animate the upbringing of the most charismatic conqueror who has ever lived, but to explore how the child had been father to the man. What sources there were for Alexander's youth Renault duly plundered; but these offered nothing like the detail that she required. Ancient biographers, by and large, took little interest in the childhoods of their subjects. Invariably, they would portray children merely as mini-versions of their adult selves. As a result, our sources for Alexander's early years are lacking in precisely the kind of psychological detail that a novelist tends most to prize. In her attempt to fill the gaps, Renault could draw on a knowledge of antiquity capable of satisfying even the sternest classicist; but it remained inadequate to her needs. Committed though she certainly was to meeting the highest possible standards of historical accuracy, she did not forgo the novelist's privilege of inventing what could not be known. As a result, *Fire from Heaven* is doubly a journey into the past: back to the fourth century BC, of course, but also to the well-springs of Renault's own career as a writer.

When Alexander, in the opening pages of the novel, slips into his mother's bed and demands that she tell him he is her favourite, he is echoing the behaviour of an earlier protagonist of Renault. In *The Charioteer*, her last work of contemporary fiction, the novel had opened in a very similar fashion, with its hero, the five-year-old Laurie Odell, leaving his bedroom and ending up in his mother's arms. He had sought refuge there from embarking on her fictionalisation of Alexander's life. Back in the 1920s, as a student at Oxford, she had discovered in the city's Ashmolean Museum a treasure-trove of ancient art so stunning that the memory of it never left her. Replicas from the bull-leaping civilisation of Minoan Crete; casts of golden youths from the heyday of classical Athens; portrait busts of philosophers, and poets, and tyrants: all would linger long in Renault's memory, and powerfully influence the fiction that she came to write. It was Alexander, though, who seems to have seduced her most enduringly: 'the amazing eyes,' as she wrote to Kasia Abbott, 'the way his hair springs from his brow, and what must already early in his twenties have been his weather-beaten beauty . . .' Something of how she came to write about him can be gauged, perhaps, from the structure of *The Persian Boy*. Although to Bagoas, the novel's narrator, Alexander's progress is only a faint rumour at first, the tremor of it grows inexorably ever more thunderous, until at last, brought before the great conqueror, he finds the rapture and the passion of the encounter overwhelming, and is smitten for life. So it was, perhaps, *mutatis mutandis*, for Mary Renault herself.

Not that she would ever have drawn the analogy herself. She had no illusions as to the chasm of difference that separated her from the world of Alexander. She was dismissive of any notion that people in the past were essentially just like those of the present. 'To pretend so,' she declared forthrightly, 'is an evasion and a betrayal, turning our back on them so as to be easy among familiar things.' It was precisely the contrast between antiquity and the world of her upbringing, which felt as vivid to her as that between an Aegean summer and the drizzle of an English February, which helps to explain her passion for Alexander. In 1948, oppressed by the grey drabness of post-war Britain, Renault had taken a steamer for South Africa, never to return. It was a bid for novelty, colour and excitement that she would replicate in 1953 when, after a series of novels set in

INTRODUCTION

'His face has haunted me for years.' This confession could have been made by any number of characters in Mary Renault's trilogy of novels about Alexander the Great. In *Fire from Heaven*, the greatest coming-of-age story ever to double as a work of historical fiction, it could have been spoken by Olympias, his predatory and implacable mother, or Hephaistion, his beloved friend, or the entire nation of Macedon, whose king by the end of the novel he has become. In *The Persian Boy*, it could have been whispered softly by Bagoas, the gazelle-eyed eunuch who first seduces Alexander, and then accompanies him on his campaign trail to the very ends of the earth. In *Funeral Games*, it could have been declared by numerous of the murderous cast of generals who, with the great conqueror dead before his time, struggle and fail to seize control of his legacy. Nowhere else in fiction have Alexander's beauty and charisma blazed with such potency as they do in Renault's trilogy. The entire landscape of her novels seems irradiated by their brilliance. Small wonder, then, in a world where the reality of the gods is never doubted, that her Alexander should indeed seem touched by the supernatural.

The confession, though, was Renault's own. She made it in a letter to an old university friend, Kasia Abbott, shortly before

'I foresee great contests at my funeral games.'

– *Reported deathbed words of Alexander the Great*

PRINCIPAL PERSONS

Invented characters are italicized; all those in roman type are historical. Persons marked * are dead before the story opens. Minor characters making a brief appearance are omitted.

ALEXANDER III   The Great. All further references to Alexander refer to him unless his son, Alexander IV, is specified.

ALEXANDER IV   His posthumous son by Roxane.

ALKETAS   Brother of Perdikkas, the general.

*AMYNTAS   Son of Philip II's elder brother, King Perdikkas. An infant when Perdikkas died, he was passed over in favour of Philip, after whose murder he was executed for treason. Husband of Kynna, father of Eurydike.

ANTIGONOS   General of Alexander; Satrap of Phrygia. Later a king, and founder of the Antigonid dynasty.

ANTIPATROS   Regent of Macedon during Alexander's years in Asia, and at the time of his death.

ARISTONOUS   A staff officer of Alexander; later loyal to Alexander IV.

ARRIDAIOS   See Philip III.

1

ARYBBAS	A Macedonian nobleman, designer of Alexander's funeral car. His real name was Arridaios; he is here given a rather similar Epirote name to distinguish him from Philip Arridaios.
Badia	*A former concubine of King Artaxerxes Ochos of Persia.*
BAGOAS	A young Persian eunuch, favourite successively of Darius III and Alexander. Though a real person, he vanishes from history after Alexander's death, and his appearance in this story is fictional.
*DARIUS III	The last Persian Great King; murdered by his generals after his defeat by Alexander at Gaugamela.
DEMETRIOS	Son of Antigonos. (Later known as The Besieger, he became King of Macedon after Kassandros' death.)
DRYPETIS	Younger daughter of Darius III; widow of Hephaistion.
EUMENES	Chief Secretary and general of Alexander; loyal to the royal house.
EURYDIKE	Daughter of Amyntas and Kynna. Her given name was Adeia; Eurydike was the dynastic name conferred on her at her marriage (or betrothal) to Philip III. She was the granddaughter of Philip II and of Perdikkas III, his brother.
*HEPHAISTION	Alexander's lifelong friend, who died a few months before him.
IOLLAS	Son of Antipatros the Regent of Macedon, younger brother of Kassandros; formerly Alexander's cupbearer.
KASSANDROS	Eldest son of Antipatros; lifelong enemy of

2

	Alexander. (Became King of Macedon after the murder of Alexander IV.)
Kebes	*Tutor to the boy Alexander IV.*
KLEOPATRA	Daughter of Philip II and Olympias, sister of Alexander. Married to King Alexandras of Molossia, which she ruled after his death in Italy. Her father, Philip, was assassinated in her wedding procession.
Konon	*A Macedonian veteran, attendant on Philip Arridaios.*
KRATEROS	Alexander's highest-ranking officer, absent on a mission to Macedon when Alexander died.
KYNNA	Daughter of Philip II by an Illyrian princess, from whom she learned the skills of war. Widow of Amyntas, mother of Eurydike.
LEONNATOS	Staff officer and kinsman of Alexander; betrothed to Kleopatra before his death in battle.
MELEAGER	(Greek spelling Meleagros.) A Macedonian officer, enemy of Perdikkas, supporter of Philip III.
NIARCHOS	Boyhood friend and admiral of Alexander.
NIKAIA	Daughter of the Regent Antipatros, married and divorced by Perdikkas.
NIKANOR	Brother of Kassandros; general in Eurydike's army.
*OCHOS	(King Artaxerxes Ochos.) Great King of Persia before the short reign of Darius III.
OLYMPIAS	Daughter of King Neoptolemos of Molossia; widow of Philip II; mother of Alexander.
PEITHON	Staff officer of Alexander, later of Perdikkas.
PERDIKKAS	Second in command to Alexander after Hephaistion's death. Betrothed to Kleopatra after death of Leonnatos.

3

*PERDIKKAS III	Elder brother of Philip II, who succeeded him after his death in battle. (See Amyntas.)
PEUKESTES	Staff officer of Alexander; Satrap of Persia.
*PHILIP II	The founder of Macedonian supremacy in Greece; father of Alexander.
PHILIP III	(Philip Arridaios.) His son by Philinna, a minor wife. The royal name of Philip was conferred at his accession.
POLYPERCHON	Staff officer of Alexander; Regent of Macedon after Antipatros' death.
PTOLEMY	(Greek spelling Ptolemaios.) Staff officer, kinsman, and reputed half-brother of Alexander. Later King of Egypt, founder of the Ptolemaic dynasty, and author of a history of Alexander extensively used by Arrian.
ROXANE	Wife of Alexander, married on campaign in Bactria. Mother of Alexander IV.
SELEUKOS	Staff officer of Alexander. (Later King of the Seleucid empire in nearer Asia.)
SISYGAMBIS	Mother of Darius III, befriended by Alexander.
STATEIRA	Daughter of Darius III, married in state by Alexander at Susa.
THEOPHRASTOS	Aristotle's successor as head of the Lyceum University at Athens, patronized by Kassandros.
THESSALONIKE	Daughter of Philip II by a minor wife; later wife of Kassandros.

323 B.C.

The ziggurat of Bel-Marduk had been half ruinous for a century and a half, ever since Xerxes had humbled the gods of rebellious Babylon. The edges of its terraces had crumbled in landslides of bitumen and baked brick; storks nested on its ragged top, which had once held the god's golden bedchamber and his sacred concubine in his golden bed. But this was only defacement; the ziggurat's huge bulk had defied destruction. The walls of the inner city by the Marduk Gate were three hundred feet high, but the ziggurat still towered over them.

Near by was the god's temple; this Xerxes' men had succeeded in half demolishing. The rest of the roof was patched with thatch, and propped on shafts of rough-hewn timber. At the inner end, where the columns were faced with splendid but chipped enamels, there was still a venerable gloom, a smell of incense and burnt offerings. On an altar of porphyry, under a smoke-duct open to the sky, burned in its bronze basket the sacred fire. It was low; the fuel-box was empty. Its shaven acolyte looked from it to the priest. Abstracted though he was, it caught his eye.

'Fetch fuel. What are you about? Must a king die when it

serves your laziness? Move! You were got when your mother was asleep and snoring.'

The acolyte made a sketchy obeisance; the temple discipline was not strict.

The priest said, after him, 'It will not be yet. Maybe not even today. He is tough as a mountain lion, he will die hard.'

Two tall shadows fell at the temple's open end. The priests who entered wore the high felt mitres of Chaldeans. They approached the altar with ritual gestures, bowing with hand on mouth.

The priest of Marduk said, 'Nothing yet?'

'No,' said the first Chaldean. 'But it will be soon. He cannot speak; indeed he can scarcely breathe. But when his homeland soldiers made a clamour at the doors, demanding to see him, he had them all admitted. Not the commanders; they were there already. The spear-bearers, the common foot-men. They were half the morning passing through his bedchamber, and he greeted them all by signs. That finished him, and now he is in the death-sleep.'

A door behind the altar opened to let in two Marduk priests. It gave a glimpse of a rich interior; embroidered hangings, a gleam of gold. There was a smell of spiced meats cooking. The door closed on it.

The Chaldeans, reminded of an old scandal, exchanged glances. One of them said, 'We did our best to turn him from the city. But he had heard that the temple had not been restored; and he thought we were afraid of him.'

A Marduk priest said stiffly, 'The year has not been auspicious for great works. Nebuchadrezzar built in an inauspicious year. His foreign slaves rioted race against race, and threw each other off the tower. As for Sikandar, he would still be fortunate, sitting safe in Susa, if he had not defied the god.'

One of the Chaldeans said, 'It seems to me he did well enough by the god, for all that he called him Herakles.' He looked round, pointedly, at the half-ruined building. He might as well have said aloud, 'Where is the gold the King gave you to rebuild, have you eaten and drunk it all?'

There was a hostile silence. The chief of the Marduk priests said, with emollient dignity, 'Certainly you gave him a true prediction. And since then have you read the heavens?'

The tall mitres bent together in slow assent. The older Chaldean, whose beard was silver against his dark face and purple robe, signed to the Marduk priest, beckoning him to the broken end of the temple. 'This,' he said, 'is what is foretold for Babylon.' He swept round his gold-starred wand, taking in the crumbling walls, the threadbare roof, the leaning timber-props, the fire-stained paving. 'This for a while, and then . . . Babylon was.'

He walked towards the entry and stood to listen; but the night noises were unchanged. 'The heavens say it begins with the death of the King.'

The priest remembered the shining youth who, eight years before, had come offering treasure and Arabian incense; and the man who had returned this year, weathered and scarred, the red-gold hair sun-bleached and streaked with white; but with the deep eyes still burning, still ready with the careless, reflex charm of the youth beloved, still terrible in anger. The scent of the incense had lasted long on the air, the gold much longer in the treasury; even among men who liked good living, half was in the strongroom still. But for the priest of Bel-Marduk the pleasure had drained out of it. It spoke now of flames and blood. His spirit sank like the altar fire when the fuel was low.

'Shall we see it? Will a new Xerxes come?'

The Chaldean shook his head. 'A dying, not a killing. Another city will rise and ours will wane. It is under the sign of the King.'

'What? Will he live, then, after all?'

'He is dying, as I told you. But his sign is walking along the constellations, further than we can reckon in years. You will not see it setting in your day.'

'So? Well, in his life he did us no harm. Maybe he will spare us dead.'

The astrologer frowned to himself, like an adult seeking words to reach a child. 'Remember, last year, the fire that fell from heaven. We heard where it fell, and went there, a week's journey. It had lit the city brighter than full moon. But we found, where it had struck, it had broken into red-hot embers, which had charred the earth around them. One had been set up by a farmer in his house, because that day his wife bore twin sons. But a neighbour had stolen it for its power; they fought, and both men died. Another piece fell at a dumb child's feet, and speech came back to him. A third had kindled a fire that destroyed a forest. But the Magus of the place had taken the greatest piece, and built it into the fire-altar, because of its great light while it was in the sky. And all this from the one star. So it will be.'

The priest bowed his head. A fragrance drifted to him from the precinct's kitchen. Better to invite the Chaldeans than let the meat spoil with waiting. Whatever the stars said, good food was good food.

The old Chaldean said, looking into the shadows, 'Here where we stand, the leopard will rear her young.'

The priest made a decent pause. No sound from the royal palace. With luck, they might get something to eat before they heard the wailing.

The walls of Nebuchadrezzar's palace were four feet thick, and faced with blue-glazed tiles for coolness; but the midsummer heat seeped in through everything. The sweat running down Eumenes' wrist blotted the ink on his papyrus. The wax glistened moistly on the tablet he was fair-copying; he plunged it back into the cold-water tub where his clerk had left it, with the other drafts, to keep the surface set.

8

Local scribes used wet clay; but that would have set hard before one could revise on it. For the third time he went to the doorway, seeking a slave to pull the punkah cord. Once again the dim hushed noises – soft feet, soft voices furtive or awed or grieving – sent him back behind the drawn door-curtain to his listless task. To clap the hands, to call, to shout an order, were all unthinkable.

He had not sought his clerk, a garrulous man; but he could have done with the silent slave and the waft of the punkah. He scanned the unfinished scroll pinned to his writing-board. It was twenty years since he had written with his own hand any letter not of high secrecy; why now was he writing one that would never go, short of a miracle? There had been many miracles; but, surely, not now. It was something to do, it shut out the unknown future. Sitting down again he retrieved the tablet, propped it, dried his hand on the towel the clerk had left, and picked up his pen.

And the ships commanded by Niarchos will muster at the river-mouth, where I shall review them while Perdikkas is bringing the army down from Babylon; and sacrifices will be made there to the appropriate gods. I shall then take command of the land force and begin the march to the west. The first stage . . .

When he was five, before he'd been taught to write, he came to me in the King's business room. 'What's that, Eumenes?' 'A letter.' 'What's the first word that you've written big?' 'Your father's name. *PHILIP*, King of the Macedonians. Now I'm busy, run back to your play.' 'Make me my name. Do, dear Eumenes. Please.' I gave it him written, on the back of a spoiled despatch. Next day he'd learned it, and carved it all over the wax for a royal letter to Kersobleptes of Thrace. He had my ruler across his palm . . .

Because of the heat he had left open his massive door. A brisk stride, half hushed like all other sounds, approached it. Ptolemy pushed aside the curtain and drew it to behind him. His craggy war-weathered face was creased with fatigue; he had been up all night, without the stimulus of action. He was forty-three, and looked older. Eumenes waited, wordlessly.

'He has given his ring to Perdikkas,' Ptolemy said.

There was a pause. Eumenes' alert Greek face – not a bookish one, he had had his share of soldiering – searched the impassive Macedonian's. 'For what? As deputy? Or as regent?'

'Since he could not speak,' said Ptolemy drily, 'we shall never know.'

'If he has accepted death,' Eumenes reasoned, 'we may presume the second. If not . . . ?'

'It's all one, now. He neither sees nor hears. He is in the death-sleep.'

'Do not be sure. I have heard of men who were thought already dead, and said later that they heard everything.'

Ptolemy suppressed an impatient gesture. These wordy Greeks. Or what is he afraid of? 'I came because you and I have known him since he was born. Don't you want to be there?'

'Do the Macedonians want me there?' An ancient bitterness pinched, for a moment, Eumenes' mouth.

'Oh, come. Everyone trusts you. We shall need you before long.'

Slowly the secretary began to put his desk in order. He said, wiping his pen, 'And nothing, to the last, about an heir?'

'Perdikkas asked him, while he could still get a whisper out. He only said, "To the best man. *Hoti to kratisto*."'

Eumenes thought, They say dying men can prophesy. He shivered.

'Or,' Ptolemy added, 'so Perdikkas told us. He was leaning over. Nobody else could hear.'

Eumenes put down the pen and looked up sharply. 'Or *Kratero*?

You say he whispered, he was short of breath.' They looked at one another. Krateros, the highest-ranking of all Alexander's staff, was on the march to Macedon, to take over the regency from Antipatros. 'If *he'd* been in the room . . .'

Ptolemy shrugged. 'Who knows?' To himself he thought, If Hephaistion had been there . . . But if *he'd* lived, none of this would have happened. He'd have done none of the crazy things he's dying of. Coming to Babylon in midsummer – boating about in the filthy swamps down river . . . But one did not discuss Hephaistion with Eumenes. 'This door weighs like an elephant. Do you want it shut?'

Pausing on the threshold, Eumenes said, 'Nothing about Roxane and the child? Nothing?'

'Four months to go. And what if it's a girl?'

They moved into the shadowy corridor, tall big-boned Macedonian and slender Greek. A young Macedonian officer came blundering towards them, almost ran into Ptolemy, and stammered an apology. Ptolemy said, 'Is there any change?'

'No, sir, I don't think so.' He swallowed violently; they saw that he was crying.

When he had gone, Ptolemy said, 'That boy believes in it. I can't yet.'

'Well, let us go.'

'Wait.' Ptolemy took his arm, led him back into the room, and dragged to the great ebony door on its groaning hinges. 'I'd best tell you this while we've time. You should have known before, but . . .'

'Yes, yes?' said Eumenes impatiently. He had quarrelled with Hephaistion shortly before he died, and Alexander had never been easy with him since.

Ptolemy said, 'Stateira is pregnant, too.'

Eumenes, who had been fidgeting to be gone, was struck into stillness. 'You mean Darius' daughter?'

'Who else do you suppose? She *is* Alexander's wife.'

'But this changes everything. When did ...?'

'Don't you remember? No, of course, you'd gone on to Babylon. When he came to himself after Hephaistion died' (one could not avoid the name for ever) 'he went to war with the Kossaians. My doing; I told him they'd demanded road-toll, and got him angry. He needed to be doing something. It did him good. When he'd dealt with them, and was heading here, he stopped a week at Susa, to call upon Sisygambis.'

'That old witch,' said Eumenes bitterly. But for her, he thought, the King's friends would never have been saddled with Persian wives. The mass wedding at Susa had gone by like some drama of superhuman magnificence, till suddenly he had found himself alone in a scented pavilion, in bed with a Persian noble-woman whose unguents repelled him, and whose only Greek consisted of 'Greeting, my lord'.

'A great lady,' said Ptolemy. 'A pity his mother was not like her. *She* would have had him married before he set out from Macedon, and seen that he got a son. He could have had an heir of fourteen by this time. *She'd* not have sickened him with marriage while he was a child. Whose fault was it that he wasn't ready for a woman till he met the Bactrian?' Thus, unofficially, did most Macedonians refer to Roxane.

'Done is done. But Stateira ... Does Perdikkas know?'

'That's why he asked him to name his heir.'

'And still he would not?'

'"To the best," he said. He left it to us, to the Macedonians, to choose when they came of age. Yes, he's a Macedonian at the last.'

'If they are boys,' Eumenes reminded him.

Ptolemy, who had been withdrawn into his thought, said, 'And if they come of age.'

Eumenes said nothing. They went down the dim corridor with its blue-tiled walls towards the death-chamber.

*

Nebuchadrezzar's bedroom, once ponderously Assyrian, had been Persianized by successive kings from Kyros on. Kambyses had hung its walls with the trophies of conquered Egypt; Darius the Great had sheathed its columns with gold and malachite; Xerxes had pegged across one side the embroidered robe of Athene, looted from the Parthenon. The second Artaxerxes had sent for craftsmen of Persepolis to make the great bed in which Alexander now lay dying.

Its dais was covered with crimson tapestries worked in bullion. The bed was nine feet by six; Darius the Third, a man seven feet tall, had had ample room. The high canopy was upheld by four golden fire-daimons with silver wings and jewelled eyes. Propped on heaped pillows to help him breathe, and looking small among all these splendours, the dying man lay naked. A thin linen sheet had been spread half over him when he had ceased to toss about and throw it off. Damp with sweat, it clung to him as if sculpted.

In a monotonous cycle, his shallow rattling breath grew gradually louder, then ceased. After a pause during which no other breath was drawn in the crowded room, it started again, slowly, the same crescendo.

Until lately there had been scarcely another sound. Now that he had ceased responding to voice or touch, a soft muttering began to spread, too cautious and muted to be located; a ground-bass to the strong rhythm of death.

Perdikkas by the bed's head lifted at Ptolemy his dark heavy eyebrows; a tall man, with the Macedonian build but not the colouring, and a face on which authority, long habitual, was growing. His silent gesture of the head signalled 'No change yet.'

The movement of a peacock fan drew Ptolemy's eye across the bed. There, as he had been for days, seemingly without sleep, seated on the dais was the Persian boy. So Ptolemy still thought of him though by now he must be three-and-twenty; with eunuchs it was hard to tell. At sixteen, he had been brought to Alexander by a Persian general involved in Darius' murder, to give exonerating evidence. This he was well placed to do, having been the King's minion, with inside knowledge of the court. He had stayed on to give his story to the chroniclers, and had never been far from Alexander since. Not much was on view today of the famous beauty which had dazzled two kings running. The great dark eyes were sunk in a face more drawn than the fever-wasted one on the pillows. He was dressed like a servant; did he think that if he was noticed he would be turned out? What *does* he think, Ptolemy wondered. He must have lain with Darius in this very bed.

A fly hovered over Alexander's sweat-glazed forehead. The Persian chased it off, then put down the fan to dip a towel in a basin of mint-scented water, and wipe the unmoving face.

At first Ptolemy had disliked this exotic presence haunting Alexander's living-quarters, encouraging him to assume the trappings of Persian royalty and the manners of a Persian court, having his ear day and night. But he was a fixture one had grown used to. Through Ptolemy's own grief and sense of looming crisis, he felt a stir of pity. Walking over, he touched him on the shoulder.

'Get some rest, Bagoas. Let one of the other chamberlains do all this.' A knot of court eunuchs, ageing relics of Darius and even of Ochos, advanced officiously. Ptolemy said, 'He won't know now, you know.'

Bagoas looked round. It was as if he had been told he was condemned to immediate execution, a sentence long expected. 'Never mind,' said Ptolemy gently. 'It's your right; stay if you wish.'

Bagoas touched his fingers to his forehead. The interruption was over. With his eyes fixed once more on the closed eyes of Alexander, he waved the fan, shifting the hot Babylonian air. He had staying power, Ptolemy reflected. He had weathered even the brainstorm after Hephaistion's death.

Against the wall nearest the bed, on a massive table like an

14

altar, Hephaistion was still enshrined. Enshrined and multiplied; here were the votive statuettes and busts presented by condolent friends, assiduous place-seekers, scared men who had once had words with the dead; commissioned by the best artists found at short notice, to comfort Alexander's grief. Hephaistion stood in bronze, a nude Ares with shield and spear; precious in gold armour with ivory face and limbs; in tinted marble with a gilded laurel crown; as a silver battle-standard for the squadron which was to bear his name; and as a demigod, the first maquette for the cult-statue of his temple in Alexandria. Someone had cleared a space to put down some sickroom object, and a small Hephaistion in gilded bronze had fallen over. With a quick glance at the blind face on the pillows, Ptolemy set it up again. Let them wait till he's gone.

The small sound drew Eumenes' eye, which quickly looked away again.

Ptolemy thought, You've nothing to fear now, have you? Oh yes, he could be arrogant now and then. Towards the end, he thought he was the only one who understood – and how far was he wrong? Accept it, Eumenes, he was good for Alexander. I knew when they were boys at school. He was somebody in himself and both of them knew it. That pride you didn't like was Alexander's salvation; never fawning, never pushing, never envious, never false. He loved Alexander and never used him, kept pace with him at Aristotle's lessons, never on purpose lost a match to him. To the end of his days he could talk to Alexander man to man, could tell him he was wrong, and never for a moment feared him. He saved him from solitude, and who knows what else? Now he's gone, and this is what we have. If he were alive, we'd all be feasting today in Susa, whatever the Chaldeans say.

A frightened physician, pushed from behind by Perdikkas, laid a hand on Alexander's brow, fingered his wrist, muttered gravely and backed away. As long as he could speak, Alexander had refused to have a doctor near him; and even when he was light-headed, none could be found to physic him, lest they should later be accused of having given him poison. It was all one now; he was no longer swallowing. Curse that fool quack, Ptolemy thought, who let Hephaistion die while he went off to the games. I'd hang him again if I could.

It had long seemed that when the harsh breathing changed, it could only be for the death-rattle. But as if the doctor's touch had stirred a flicker of life, the stridor took a more even rhythm, and the eyelids were seen to move. Ptolemy and Perdikkas each took a step forward. But the self-effacing Persian by the bed, whom everyone had forgotten, put down the fan and, as if no one else were in sight, leaned intimately over the pillowed head, his long light-brown hair falling around it. He whispered softly. Alexander's grey eyes opened. Something disturbed the silky cloak of hair.

Perdikkas said, 'He moved his hand.'

It was still now, the eyes shut again, though Bagoas, as if trans-fixed, was still gazing down at them. Perdikkas' mouth tightened; all kinds of people were here. But before he could walk up with a reprimand, the Persian had resumed his station and picked up his fan. But for its movement, he could have been a statue carved from ivory.

Ptolemy became aware of Eumenes speaking to him. 'What?' he said harshly. He was near to tears.

'Peukestes is coming.'

The huddled functionaries parted to admit a tall well-built Macedonian dressed as a Persian, even – to most of his country-men's shocked disapproval – down to the trousers. When given the satrapy of Persis he had adopted the native dress to please Alexander, not unaware that it suited him. He strode forward, his eyes on the bed. Perdikkas advanced to meet him.

There was a low buzz of talk. The eyes of the two men exchanged their message. Perdikkas said formally, for the bene-fit of the company, 'Did you receive an oracle from Sarapis?'

Peukestes bowed his head. 'We kept the night-watch. The god said at dawn, "Do not bring the King to the temple. It will be better for him where he is."'

No, thought Eumenes, there will be no more miracles. For a moment, when the hand had moved, he had almost believed in another.

He turned round looking for Ptolemy; but he had gone off somewhere to put his face in order. It was Peukestes who, coming away from the bedside, said to him, 'Does Roxane know?'

The palace harem was a spacious cloister built around a lily-pond. Here too were hushed voices, but differently pitched; the few men in this female world were eunuchs.

None of the women whose home the harem was had set eyes on the dying king. They had heard well of him; they had been kept by him in comfort and unmolested; they had awaited a visit that never came. And that was all, except that they knew of no male heir who would inherit them; in a little while there would even, it seemed, be no Great King. The voices were muted with secretive fear.

Here were all the women Darius had left behind him when he marched to his fate at Gaugamela. His favourites, of course, he had taken with him; these who remained were something of a mixture. His older concubines, from his days as a nobleman unplaced in line for the throne, had long been installed at Susa; here were girls found for him after his accession, who had failed to retain his interest, or had come too late to be noticed by him at all. As well as all these, there were the survivors of King Ochos' harem, who could not in decency be put out of doors when he died. An unwelcome legacy, they formed with one or two old eunuchs a little clique of their own, hating the women of Darius, that usurper they suspected of complicity in their master's death.

For Darius' concubines it was another matter. When brought

there they had been fourteen, fifteen, eighteen at most. They had known the real drama of the harem; the rumours and intrigues; the bribery to get first news of a royal visit; the long intricacies of the toilet, the inspired placing of a jewel; the envious despair when the menstrual days enforced retirement; the triumph when a summons was received in a rival's presence; the gift of honour after a successful night.

From a few such nights had come one or two little girls of eight or so, who were dabbling in the pool and telling each other solemnly that the King was dying. There had been boys too. When Darius fell, they had been spirited away with every kind of stratagem, their mothers taking it for granted that the new, barbarian king would have them strangled. Nobody, however, had come looking for them; they had returned in time and now, being of an age to be brought out from among women, were being reared as men by distant kindred.

With the long absence of any king from Babylon, the harem had grown slack. At Susa, where Sisygambis the Queen Mother lived, everything was impeccable. But here they had seen little even of Darius, nothing of Alexander. One or two of the women had managed to intrigue with men from outside and run away with them; the eunuchs, whom Ochos would have impaled for negligence, had kept it quiet. Some girls in the long idle days had had affairs with one another; the resulting jealousies and scenes had enlivened many hot Assyrian nights. One girl had been poisoned by a rival; but that too had been hushed up. The Chief Warden had taken to smoking hemp, and disliked being disturbed.

Then, after years in the unknown east, after legendary victories, wounds, perils in deserts, the King sent word of his return. The harem had aroused itself as if from sleep. The eunuchs had fussed. All through the winter, the Babylonian season of gentle warmth, when feasts were held, he was expected but did not come. Rumour reached the palace that a boyhood friend had

18

died – some said a lover – and it had sent him mad. Then he had come to himself, but was at war with the mountain Kossaians. The harem slipped back into its lethargy. At last he was on his way, but had broken his march at Susa. Setting out again, he had been met by embassies from all the peoples of the earth, bringing him golden crowns and asking him for counsel. Then, when late spring was heating up for summer, the earth had shaken under the horses and the chariots, the elephants and the marching men; and the palace had seethed with the long-forgotten bustle of a king's arrival.

Next day, it was announced that the King's Chief Eunuch of the Bedchamber would inspect the harem. This formidable person was awaited with dread; but turned out, shockingly, to be little more than a youth, none other than the notorious Bagoas, minion of two kings. Not that he failed to impress. He was wearing silk, stuff never seen within those walls, and shimmered like a peacock's breast. He was Persian to his fingertips, which always made Babylonians feel provincial; and ten years at courts had polished his manners like old silver. He greeted without embarrassment any eunuchs he had met in Darius' day, and bowed respectfully to some of the older ladies. Then he came to business.

He could not say when the King's urgent concerns would give him leisure to visit the harem; no doubt he would find in any case the perfect order which declares respect. One or two shortcomings were obliquely hinted at ('I believe the custom is so-and-so at Susa') but the past was left unprobed. The wardens were concealing sighs of relief, when he asked to see the rooms of the royal ladies.

They led him through. These rooms of state were secluded from the rest, and had their own courtyard, exquisitely tiled. There had been some dismay at their abandoned state, the dry plants and withered creepers, the clogged fountain with green scum and dead fish. All this had been seen to, but the rooms still had the dank smell of long disuse. Silently, just opening his delicate nostrils, Bagoas indicated this.

The rooms of the Royal Wife, despite neglect, were still luxurious; Darius, though self-indulgent, had been generous too. They led him on to the smaller, but still handsome rooms for the Queen Mother. Sisygambis had stayed here in an early year of her son's short reign. Bagoas looked them over, his head tilted slightly sideways. Unconsciously, over the years, he had picked up this tic from Alexander.

'Very pleasant,' he said. 'At any rate it can be made so. As you know, the lady Roxane is on her way here from Ekbatana. The King is anxious that she should have an easy journey.' The eunuchs pricked up their ears; Roxane's pregnancy was not yet public news. 'She will be here in about seven days. I will order some things, and send in good craftsmen. Please see they do all they should.'

In a speaking pause, the eunuchs' eyes turned towards the rooms of the Royal Wife. Those of Bagoas followed them, inexpressively.

'Those rooms will be closed at present. Just see they are well aired and kept sweet. You have a key for the outer door? Good.' No one said anything. He added, blandly, 'There is no need to show these rooms to the lady Roxane. If she should ask, say they are in disrepair.' He left politely, as he had come.

At the time, they had decided that Bagoas must have some old score to pay. Favourites and wives were traditional antagonists. The rumour ran that early in her marriage Roxane had tried to poison him, but had never again tried anything, so dreadful had been the anger of the King. The furniture and hangings now sent in were costly, and the finished rooms lacked nothing of royal splendour. 'Don't be afraid of extravagance,' Bagoas had said. 'That is to her taste.'

Her caravan duly arrived from Ekbatana. Handed down the steps of her travelling-wagon she had proved to be a young woman of striking, high-nosed beauty, with blue-black hair and dark brilliant eyes. Her pregnancy hardly showed except in opulent softness. She spoke fluent Persian, though with a Bactrian accent which her Bactrian suite did nothing to correct; and had gained a fair command of Greek, a tongue unknown to her before her marriage. Babylon was as foreign to her as India; she had settled without demur in the rooms prepared for her, remarking that they were smaller than those at Ekbatana, but much prettier. They had their own small courtyard, elegant and shady. Darius, who had held his mother in awe as well as in esteem, had always been attentive to her comfort.

Next day a chamberlain, this time of venerable age, announced the King.

The eunuchs waited anxiously. What if Bagoas had acted without authority? The King's anger was said to be rare, but terrible. However, he greeted them courteously in his scanty, formal Persian, and made no comment when shown to Roxane's rooms.

Through chinks and crannies known in the harem since the days of Nebuchadrezzar, the younger concubines glimpsed him on his way. They reported him handsome in countenance, for a westerner at least (fair colouring was not admired in Babylon); and he was not tall, a grave defect, but this they had known already. Surely he must be older than thirty-two, for his hair had grey in it; but they owned that he had presence, and awaited his return to see him again. They expected a lengthy vigil; but he was back in barely the time it would take a careful woman to bathe and dress.

This made the younger ladies hopeful. They cleaned their jewels and reviewed their cosmetics. One or two, who from boredom had let themselves get grossly fat, were derided and cried all day. For a week, each morning dawned full of promise. But the King did not come. Instead, Bagoas reappeared, and conferred in private with the Chief Warden. The heavy door of the Royal Wife's room was opened, and they went inside.

'Yes,' said Bagoas. 'Not much is needed here. Just there, and there, fresh hangings. The toilet-vessels will be in the treasury?'

Thankfully (they had tempted him more than once) the Warden sent for them; they were exquisite, silver inlaid with gold. A great clothes-chest of cypress-wood stood against the wall. Bagoas raised the lid; there was a drift of faded fragrance. He lifted out a scarf stitched with seed-pearls and small gold beads.

'These, I suppose, were Queen Stateira's?'

'Those she did not take with her. Darius thought nothing too good for her.'

Except his life, each thought in the awkward pause. His flight at Issos had left her to end her days under the protection of his enemy. Under the scarf was a veil edged with green scarab-wings from Egypt. Bagoas fingered it gently. 'I never saw her. *The loveliest woman of mortal birth in Asia* – was that true?'

'Who has seen every woman in Asia? Yes, it well may be.'

'At least I have seen her daughter.' He put back the scarf and closed the chest. 'Leave all these things. The lady Stateira will like to have them.'

'Has she set out from Susa yet?' A different question trembled on the Warden's lips.

Bagoas, well aware of it, said deliberately, 'She will be coming when the worst of the heat is over. The King is anxious she should have an easy journey.'

The Warden caught a sharp breath. Fat old chamberlain and slender glittering favourite, their eyes exchanged the immemorial communication of their kind. It was the Warden who spoke first.

'So far, everything has gone smoothly *there*.' He glanced towards the other set of rooms. 'But as soon as these apartments are opened, there will be talk. There is no preventing it. You know that as well as I do. Does the King intend to tell the lady Roxane?'

For a moment, Bagoas' urbane polish cracked, revealing a deep settled grief. He sealed it off again. 'I will remind him if I can. It is not easy just now. He is planning the funeral of his friend Hephaistion, who died at Ekbatana.'

The Warden would have liked to ask if it was true that this death had sent the King out of his mind for a month or more. But Bagoas' polish had hardened, warningly. Quickly the Warden smoothed away curiosity. They said of Bagoas that, if he chose, he could be the most dangerous man at court.

'In that case,' said the Warden carefully, 'we might delay the work for a while? If I am asked questions, without any sanction from the King . . . ?'

Bagoas paused, looking for a moment uncertain and still quite young. But he answered crisply, 'No, we have had our orders. He will expect to find them obeyed.'

He left, and did not return. It was reported in the harem that the funeral of the King's friend surpassed that of Queen Semiramis, renowned in story; that the pyre had been a burning ziggurat two hundred feet high. But, said the Warden to anyone who would listen, that was a little fire to the one he had had to face when the Royal Wife's rooms were opened, and news reached the lady Roxane.

At her mountain home in Bactria, the harem eunuchs had been family servants and slaves, who knew their place. The ancient dignities of the palace chamberlains seemed to her mere insolence. When she ordered the Warden a flogging, she was enraged to find no one empowered to inflict it. The old Bactrian eunuch she had brought from home, despatched to tell the King, reported that he had taken a flotilla down the Euphrates to explore the swamps.

When he got back she tried again; first he was busy, and then he was indisposed.

Her father, she was sure, would have seen to it that the Warden was put to death. But the satrapy conferred on him by the King was on the Indian frontier; by the time she could hear back from him, her son would have been born. The thought appeased her. She said to her Bactrian ladies, 'Let her come, this great tall flagpole from Susa. The King cannot abide her. If he must do this to please the Persians, what is that to me? Everyone knows that I am his real wife, the mother of his son.'

The ladies said in secret, 'I would not be that child, if it is a girl.'

The King did not come, and Roxane's days hung heavy. Here, at what was to be the centre of her husband's empire, she might as well be encamped in Drangiana. She could, if she wished, have entertained the concubines. But these women had been living for years in royal palaces, some of them since she had been a child on her father's mountain crag. She thought with dread of assured Persian elegance, sophisticated talk tossed spitefully over her head. Not one had crossed her threshold; she had rather be thought haughty than afraid. One day however she found one of the ancient crannies; it passed the time to lay an ear to it and hear them talking.

So it was that, when Alexander had been nine days down with marsh-fever, she heard a palace chamberlain gossiping with a harem eunuch. From this she learned two things: that the sickness had flown to the King's chest, and he was like to die; and that the daughter of Darius was with child.

She did not pause, even to hear them out. She called her Bactrian eunuch and her ladies, threw on a veil, brushed past the stunned Nubian giant who guarded the harem, and only answered his shrill cries with, 'I must see the King.'

The palace eunuchs came running. They could do nothing but run after her. She was the King's wife, not a captive; she stayed in the harem only because to leave it was unthinkable. On the long marches, out to India and back to Persia and down to Babylon, wherever the King pitched camp her baggage wagons had unpacked the wicker screens which had made her a travelling courtyard, so that she could leave her covered wagon and take the

24

air. In the cities she had her curtained litter, her latticed balconies. All this was not her sentence but her right; it was only whores whom men displayed. Now, when the unprecedented happened, to lay hands on her was inconceivable. Guided by her trembling eunuch, her progress followed by astonished eyes, she swept through corridors, courtyards, anterooms, till she reached the bedchamber. It was the first time she had entered it; or, for that matter, his own sleeping-place anywhere else. He had never summoned her to his bed, only gone to hers. It was the custom of the Greeks, so he had told her.

She paused in the tall doorway, seeing the high cedar ceiling, the daimon-guarded bed. It was like a hall of audience. Generals, physicians, chamberlains, stupid with surprise, stood back as she made her way to him.

The heaped pillows that propped him upright gave him still the illusion of authority. His closed eyes, his parted and gasping mouth, seemed like a willed withdrawal. She could not be in his presence without believing that everything was still under his control.

'Sikandar!' she cried, slipping back into her native dialect. 'Sikandar!'

His eyelids, creased and bloodless in sunken sockets, moved faintly but did not open. The thin skin tightened, as if to shut out a harsh glare of sun. She saw that his lips were cracked and dry; the deep scar in his side, from the wound he had got in India, stretched and shrank with his labouring breath.

'Sikandar, Sikandar!' she cried aloud. She grasped him by the arm.

He took a deeper breath, and choked on it. Someone leaned over with a towel, and wiped bloody froth from his lips. He did not open his eyes.

As if she had known nothing till now, a cold dagger of realization stabbed her. He was gone out of reach; he would no longer direct her journeys. He would decide nothing, ever again; would never tell her what she had come to ask. For her, for the child within her, he was already dead.

She began to wail, like a mourner over a bier, clawing her face, beating her breast, tearing at her clothes, shaking her dishevelled hair. She flung herself forward, her arms across the bed, burying her face in the sheet, hardly aware of the hot, still living flesh beneath it. Someone was speaking; a light, young voice, the voice of a eunuch.

'He can hear all this; it troubles him.'

There was a strong grasp on her shoulders, pulling her back. She might have recognized Ptolemy, from the triumphs and processions seen from her lattices; but she was looking across the bed, perceiving who had spoken. She would have guessed, even if she had not seen him once in India, gliding down the Indus on Alexander's flagship, dressed in the brilliant stuffs of Taxila, scarlet and gold. It was the hated Persian boy, familiar of this room she had never entered; he, too, a custom of the Greeks, though her husband had never told her so.

His menial clothes, his haggard exhausted face, conceded nothing. No longer desirable, he had become commanding. Generals and satraps and captains, whose obedience should be to her, who should be rousing the King to answer her, to name his heir – they listened, submissive, to this dancing-boy. As for her, she was an intrusion.

She cursed him with her eyes, but already his attention was withdrawn from her, as he beckoned a slave to take the blood-stained towel, and checked the clean pile beside him. Ptolemy's hard hands released her; the hands of her attendants, gentle, supplicating, insistent, guided her towards the door. Someone picked up her veil from the bed and threw it over her.

Back in her own room, she flung herself down in a furious storm of weeping, pummelling and biting the cushions of her divan. Her ladies, when they dared speak to her, implored her to spare herself, lest the child miscarry. This brought her to herself;

she called for mare's milk and figs, which she chiefly craved for lately. Dark fell; she tossed on her bed. At length, dry-eyed, she got up, and paced to and fro in the moon-dappled courtyard, where the fountain murmured like a conspirator in the hot Babylonian night. Once she felt the child move strongly. Laying her hands over the place, she whispered, 'Quiet, my little king. I promise you . . . I promise . . .'

She went back to bed, and fell into a heavy sleep. She dreamed she was in her father's fort on the Sogdian Rock, a rampart-guarded cavern under the mountain's crest, with a thousand-foot drop below. The Macedonians were besieging it. She looked down at the swarming men, scattered like dark grains upon the snow; at the red starry campfires plumed with faint smoke; at the coloured dots of the tents. The wind was rising, moaning over the crag. Her brother called to her to fit arrowheads with the other women; he rebuked her idleness, and shook her. She woke. Her woman let go her shoulder, but did not speak. She had slept late, the sun was hot in the courtyard. Yet the wind soughed on; the world was full of its noise, rising and falling, like its winter voice when it blew from the immeasurable ranges of the east . . . But this was Babylon.

Here it died down and there it rose, and now it came close at hand, the high wailing of the harem; she could hear now its formal rhythm. The women beside her, seeing her awake, at once began lamenting, crying out the ancient phrases offered to the widows of Bactrian chieftains time out of mind. They were looking at her. It was for her to lead the dirge.

Obediently she sat up, dragged at her hair, drummed with her fists on her breast. She had known the words since her childhood: 'Alas, alas! The light is fallen from the sky, the lion of men is fallen. When he lifted his sword, a thousand warriors trembled; when he opened his hand, it shed gold like the sands of the sea. When he rejoiced, it gladdened us like the sun. As the stormwind rides the mountains, so he rode to war; like the tempest that

27

fells great forest trees, he rode into the battle. His shield was a strong roof over his people. Darkness is his portion, his house is desolate. Alas! Alas! Alas!'

She laid her hands in her lap. Her wailing ceased. The women, startled, stared at her. She said, 'I have lamented; I have finished now.' She beckoned her chief waiting-woman and waved the rest away.

'Bring my old travelling-gown, the dark-blue one.' It was found, and dust shaken out of it from the Ekbatana road. The stuff was strong; she had to nick it with her paring-knife before it would tear. When she had rent it here and there, she put it on. Leaving her hair uncombed, she ran her hand over a dusty cornice and smeared her face. Then she sent for her Bactrian eunuch.

'Go to the harem, and ask the lady Badia to visit me.'

'Hearing is obedience, madam.' How did she know the name of Ochos' first-ranking concubine? But it was clearly no time for questions.

From her listening-place, Roxane could hear the fluster in the harem. Some were still wailing for the King, but most were chattering. After a short delay for preparation, Badia appeared, dressed in the mourning she had put on for King Ochos, fifteen years before, smelling of herbs and cedar-wood. For Darius she had not worn it.

Ochos had reigned for twenty years, and she had been a concubine of his youth. She was in her fifties, graceful once, now gaunt. Long before his death she had been left behind in Babylon while younger girls were taken along to Susa. But she had ruled the harem in her time, and did not forget.

Some minutes were passed in orthodox condolences. Badia lauded the valour of the King, his justice, his bounty. Roxane responded as was proper, swaying and keening softly. Presently she wiped her eyes, and made a few broken answers. Badia offered the immemorial consolation.

'The child will be his remembrance. You will see him grow to rival his father's honour.'

All this was formula. Roxane abandoned it. 'If he lives,' she sobbed. 'If Darius' accursed kindred let him live. But they will kill him. I know, I know it.' She grasped her hair in both hands and moaned.

Badia caught her breath, her lean face shocked with memory. 'Oh, the good god! Will those days come again?'

Ochos had achieved the throne by wholesale fratricide, and died by poison. Roxane had no wish to hear reminiscences. She flung back her hair. 'How can they not? Who murdered King Ochos when he lay sick? And the young King Arses and his loyal brothers? And Arses' little son, still at the breast? And when it was done, who killed the Vizier his creature, to stop his mouth? Darius! Alexander told me so.'

('I used to think so,' Alexander had told her not long before, 'but that was before I'd fought him. He'd not spirit enough to be more than the Vizier's tool. He killed him after because he was afraid of him. That was just like the man.')

'Did the King say so? Ah, the lion of justice, the redresser of wrongs!' Her voice rose, ready to wail again; Roxane lifted a quick repressive hand.

'Yes, he avenged your lord. But my son, who will avenge him? Ah, if you knew!'

Badia raised sharp black eyes, avid with curiosity. 'What is it, lady?'

Roxane told her. Alexander, still sick with grief for his boy-hood friend, had gone before, leaving her in safety at Ekbatana, to purge of bandits the road to Babylon. Then, weary from the winter war, he had stayed to rest at Susa, and been beguiled by Queen Sisygambis; that old sorceress who, if truth were known, had set on her son, the usurper, to all his crimes. She had brought to the King the daughter of Darius, that clumsy, long-legged girl he had married to please the Persians. Very likely she had drugged him, she was skilled in potions. She had got her grand-child into the King's bed, and told him she was with child by him, though who was to know the truth? And, since he had married her in state in the presence of the Persian and Macedonian lords, what could they do but accept her infant? 'But he married her only for show, for policy. He told me so.'

(Indeed it was true that before the wedding, appalled by Roxane's frenzy, deafened by her cries, and feeling remorseful, Alexander had said something to this effect. He had made no promises for the future, it being a principle of his to keep the future open; but he had dried her tears, and brought her some handsome earrings.)

'And so,' she cried, 'under this roof she will bear a grandchild to Ochos' murderer. And who will protect us, now that the King is gone?'

Badia began to cry. She thought of the long dull peaceful years in the quiet ageing harem, where the dangerous outside world was only rumour. She had outgrown the need of men and even of variety, living contentedly with her talking bird and her little red-coated monkey and her old gossiping eunuchs, maintained in comfort by the wandering, distant king. Now there opened before her dreadful ancient memories of betrayal, accusations, humiliation, the waking dread of the new day. It had been a cruel rival who had displaced her with King Ochos. The peaceful years fell from her. She sobbed and wailed; this time for herself.

'What can we do?' she cried. 'What can we do?'

Roxane's white, plump, short-fingered hand grasped Badia's wrist. Her great dark eyes, which had cast their spell upon Alexander, were fixed on hers. 'The King is dead. We must save ourselves as we best can.'

'Yes, lady.' The old days were back; once more it was a matter of survival. 'Lady, what shall we do?'

Roxane drew her near and they talked softly, remembering the crannies in the wall.

Some time later, quietly by the servants' door came an old eunuch from Badia's household. He carried a box of polished wood. Roxane said, 'It is true that you can write Greek?'

'Certainly, madam. King Ochos often called on me.'

'Have you good parchment? It is for a royal letter.'

'Yes, madam.' He opened the box. 'When the usurper Darius gave my place to one of his people, I took a little with me.'

'Good. Sit down and write.'

When she gave him the superscription, he almost spoiled the scroll. But he had not come quite ignorant of his errand; and Badia had told him that if Darius' daughter ruled the harem, she would turn all Ochos' people out in the street to beg. He wrote on. She saw that the script was even and flowing, with the proper formal flourishes. When he had done, she gave him a silver daric and let him go. She did not swear him to silence; it was beneath her dignity, and Badia would have seen to it.

He had brought wax, but she had not sealed it in his presence. Now she drew off a ring Alexander had given her on their wedding night. It was set with a flawless amethyst the colour of dark violets, on which Pyrgoletes, his favourite engraver, had carved his portrait. It was nothing like the royal ring of Macedon, with its Zeus enthroned. But Alexander had never been conventional, and she thought that it would serve.

She turned the stone in the light. The work was superb, and though somewhat idealized had caught a vivid look of him. He had given it her when they were at last alone in the bridal chamber; something to serve them in place of words, since neither could speak the other's tongue. He had put it on her, finding a finger it would fit at the second try. She had kissed it respectfully, and then he had embraced her. She remembered how unexpectedly pleasing his body was, with a warm freshness like a young boy's; but she had expected a harder grasp. He should have gone out to be undressed and have a wedding shift put on him; but, instead, he had just tossed off his clothes and stood there stark naked, in which state he had got into bed. She had been too shocked at first to think of anything else, and he had thought she was afraid of him. He had taken a good deal of trouble with her, some of it quite sophisticated; he had had expert tuition, though she did not yet know whose. But what she had really wanted was to be taken by storm. She had adopted postures of submission, proper in a virgin; for anything livelier on the first night, a Bactrian bridegroom would have strangled her. But she could feel he was at a loss, and had a dreadful fear that there would be an unstained bridal sheet for the guests to view next morning. She had nerved herself to embrace him; and afterwards all was well.

She dropped the hot wax on the scroll and pressed in the gem. Suddenly a piercing memory came to her of a day a few months ago in Ekbatana, one summer afternoon by the fishpool. He had been feeding the carp, coaxing the old sullen king of the pool to come to his hand from its lair under the lily-pads. He would not come in to make love till he had won. After, he had fallen asleep; she remembered the fair boyish skin with the deep dimpled scars, the soft margins of his strong hair. She had wanted to feel and smell him as if he were good to eat, like fresh-baked bread. When she buried her face in him, he half woke and held her comfortably, and slept again. The sense of his physical presence came back to her like life. At last, alone, in silence, she shed real tears.

She wiped them soon. She had business that would not wait.

In the bedchamber, the long days of dying were over. Alexander had ceased to breathe. The lamenting eunuchs had drawn out the heaped-up pillows; he lay straight and flat in the great bed, restored by stillness to a monumental dignity, but, to the watchers, shocking in his passiveness. A dead man, a corpse.

The generals, hastily called when the end was plainly coming, stood staring blankly. For two days they had been thinking what to do now. Yet, now, it was as if the awaited certainty had been some mere contingency with which their imaginations had been playing. They gazed stupefied at the familiar face, so finally untenanted; feeling almost resentment, so impossible did it seem that anything could happen to Alexander without consent of his. How could he die and leave them in this confusion? How could he throw off responsibility? It was quite unlike him.

A cracked young voice at the outer door suddenly cried out, 'He's gone, he's gone!' It was a youth of eighteen, one of the royal body-squires, who had been taking his turn on guard duty. He broke into hysterical weeping, which rose above the keening of the eunuchs around the bed. Someone must have led him away, for his voice could be heard receding, raw with uncontainable grief.

It was as if he had invoked an ocean. He had blundered, sobbing, into half the Macedonian army, gathered around the palace to await the news.

Most of them had passed through the bedchamber the day before; but he had known them still, he had remembered them; they, most of all, had good cause to expect a miracle. Now a huge clamour rose; of grief, of ritual mourning; of protest, as if some authority could be found to blame; of dismay at the uncertainties of the shattered future.

The sound aroused the generals. Their reflexes, trained to a hair by the dead man on the bed, snapped into action. Panic must be dealt with instantly. They ran out to the great platform above the forecourt. A herald, wavering at his post, was barked at by Perdikkas, lifted his long-stemmed trumpet, and blew the assembly call.

The response was ragged. Only yesterday, believing the call to be from Alexander, they would in silent minutes have sorted themselves into their files and phalanxes, each troop competing to get into formation first. Now, nature's laws were suspended. Those in front had to shout back to the rear that it was

Perdikkas. Since Hephaistion's death he had been Alexander's second in command. When he roared at them, it gave them some sense of security; they shuffled and shoved themselves into a semblance of order.

The Persian soldiers fell in with the rest. Their mourning out-cries had counterpointed the Macedonians' clamour. Now they grew quiet. They were – they had been – soldiers of Alexander, who had made them forget they were a conquered people, given them pride in themselves, made the Macedonians accept them. The early frictions had been almost over, Greek soldier slang was full of Persian words, a comradeship had begun. Now, suddenly, feeling themselves once more defeated natives on sufferance in an alien army, they looked at each other sidelong, planning desertion.

At Perdikkas' signal, Peukestes strode forward, a reassuring figure; a man renowned for valour, who had saved Alexander's life in India when he took his near-mortal wound. Now, tall, handsome, commanding, bearded in the fashion of his satrapy, he addressed them in Persian as correct and aristocratic as his dress. Formally he announced to them the death of the Great King. In due course, his successor would be proclaimed to them. They might now dismiss.

The Persians were calmed. But a deep muttering growl arose from the Macedonians. By their ancestral law, the right to choose a king belonged to them; to the Assembly of all male Macedonians able to bear arms. What was this talk of a proclamation?

Peukestes stood back for Perdikkas. There was a pause. For twelve years, both of them had watched Alexander dealing with Macedonians. They were not men who could be told to hold their peace and await authority's pleasure. They had to be talked to, and he had done it; only once, in all the twelve years, with-out success. Even then, once they had made him turn back from India, they were all his own. Now, faced with this disorder, for a moment Perdikkas expected to hear approaching the brisk impatient footsteps; the crisp low-spoken reprimand, the high ringing voice creating instant stillness.

He did not come; and Perdikkas, though he lacked magic, understood authority. He fell, as Alexander had done at need, into the Doric patois of the homeland, their own boyhood tongue before they were schooled into polite Greek. They had all lost, he said, the greatest of kings, the bravest and best of warriors, that the world had seen since the sons of the gods forsook the earth.

Here he was stopped by a huge swelling groan; no voluntary tribute, but an outburst of naked misery and bereavement. When he could be heard again, he said, 'And the grandsons of your grandsons will say so still. Remember, then, that your loss is measured by your former fortune. You out of all men, past or to come, have had your share in the glory of Alexander. And now it is for you, his Macedonians, to whom he has bequeathed the mastery of half the world, to keep your courage, and show you are the men he made you. All will be done according to the law.'

The hushed crowd gazed up in expectation. When Alexander had talked them quiet, he had always had something to tell them. Perdikkas knew it; but all he had to tell was that he himself was now, effectively, the king in Asia. It was too soon; they knew only one king, alive or dead. He told them to go back to camp and wait for further orders.

Under his eye they began to leave the forecourt; but when he had gone in, many came back by ones and twos, and settled down with their arms beside them, ready for night, to keep the death-watch.

Down in the city the sound of lamentation, like a brush-fire with a high wind behind it, spread from the crowded streets nearest the palace, on through the suburbs to the houses built along the walls. Above the temples the tall thin smoke-plumes, which had been rising upright in the still air from the sacred fires, one after

35

another dipped and died. By the heap of damp ashes in Bel-Marduk's brazier, the priests reminded each other that this was the second time in little more than a month. The King had ordered it on the day of his friend's funeral. 'We warned him of the omen, but he would hear nothing. He was a foreigner, when all is said.'

Theirs was the first fire quenched. In the temple of Mithra, guardian of the warrior's honour, lord of loyalty and the given word, a young priest stood in the sanctuary with a water-ewer in his hand. Above the altar was carved the symbol of the winged sun, at war with the dark, age after age till the last victory. The fire still burned high, for the young man had been feeding it extravagantly, as if it had power to rekindle the sinking life of the King. Even now, when he had been ordered to extinguish it, he put down his ewer, ran to a coffer of Arabian incense, and flung a handful to sparkle into fragrance. Last of the officiants, it was not till his offering had lifted into the summer sky that he poured the water hissing upon the embers.

On the Royal Road to Susa, a courier travelled, his racing dromedary eating the miles with its smooth loping stride. Before it needed rest he would have reached the next relay-post, whence a fresh man and beast would carry his charge on through the night.

His stage was halfway of the journey. The parchment in his saddlebag had been passed to him by the man before, without pause for questions. Only the first stage out from Babylon had been run by a rider unknown to his relief. This stranger, when asked if it was true that the King was sick, had replied that it might be so for all he knew, but he had no time for gossiping. Silent haste was the first rule of the corps; the relief had saluted and sped away, showing, wordlessly, to the next man in the chain, that his letter was sealed with the image of the King.

It was said that a despatch by Royal Messenger would outstrip even the birds. Winged rumour itself could not overtake it; for at night rumour stops to sleep.

Two travellers, who had reined in to let the courier past, were nearly thrown as their horses squealed and reared at the detested smell of camel. The elder man, who was about thirty-five, stocky, freckled and red-haired, mastered his mount first, wresting back its head till the rough bit dripped blood. His brother, some ten years younger, auburn and conventionally good-looking, took longer because he had tried to reassure the horse. Kassandros watched his efforts with contempt. He was the eldest son of the Regent of Macedon, Antipatros, and was a stranger in Babylonia. He had reached it lately, sent by his father to find out why Alexander had summoned him to Macedon and sent Krateros to assume the regency in his stead.

Iollas, the younger, had marched with Alexander, and till lately been his cupbearer. His appointment had been by way of an appeasing gesture to their father; Kassandros had been left behind on garrison duty in Macedon, because he and Alexander had disliked each other since they were boys.

When the horse was quiet, Iollas said, 'That was a Royal Messenger.'

'May he and his brute drop dead.'

'Why is he riding? Perhaps – it's all over now.'

Kassandros, looking back towards Babylon, said, 'May the dog of Hades eat his soul.'

For some time they rode in silence, Iollas looking at the road before him. At last he said, 'Well, no one can turn Father out now. Now he can be King.'

'King?' growled Kassandros. 'Not he. He took his oath and he'll keep it. Even to the barbarian's brat, if it's a boy.'

Iollas' horse started, feeling its rider's shock. 'Then why? Why did you make me do it? ... Not for Father? ... Only for hate! Almighty god, I should have known!'

Kassandros leaned over and slashed his riding-quirt down on the young man's knee. He gave a startled cry of pain and anger.

'Don't dare do that again! We're not at home now, and I'm not a boy.'

Kassandros pointed to the red weal. 'Pain's a reminder. You did nothing. Remember, nothing. Keep it in your head.' A little way further on, seeing tears in Iollas' eyes, he said with grudging forbearance, 'Like as not he took fever from the marsh air. By now he must have drunk dirty water often enough. The peasants down river drink swamp-water, and they don't die of it. Keep your mouth shut. Or you might die of it.'

Iollas swallowed and gulped. Dragging his hand across his eyes, and streaking his face with the black dust of the Babylonian plain, he said huskily, 'He never got back his strength after that arrow-wound in India. He couldn't afford a fever ... He was good to me. I only did it for Father. Now you say he won't be King.'

'He won't be King. But whatever name they call it, he'll die the ruler of Macedon and all Greece. And he's an old man now.'

Iollas gazed at him in silence; then spurred his horse and galloped ahead through the yellow wheatfields, his sobs catching their rhythm from the pounding of the hooves.

Next day in Babylon the leading generals prepared for the Assembly that was to choose a ruler of the Macedonians. Their law did not demand primogeniture as inalienable. It was the right of the men in arms to choose among the royal family.

When Philip had died, it had been simple. Almost all the fighting-men were still at home. Alexander at twenty had already made a name for himself, and no other claimant had been so much as named. Even when Philip, a younger brother, had been chosen before the child of King Perdikkas, lately fallen in battle, that had been simple too; Philip had been a tried commander, the child an infant in arms, and they were at war.

Now, Macedonian troops were scattered in strongpoints all

over central Asia. Ten thousand veterans were marching home for discharge under the command of Krateros, a youngish man, whom Alexander had ranked next after Hephaistion, and who was one of the royal kindred. There were the garrison troops in Macedon, and in the great stone forts which commanded the passes into southern Greece. All this the men at Babylon knew. But no one of them questioned that theirs was the right to choose a king. They were the army of Alexander, and that was everything.

Outside on the hot parade ground they waited, disputing, conjecturing, passing rumours on. Sometimes, as their impatience and disquiet mounted, the noise would surge like a breaker on a pebbled beach.

The generals inside, the high command known as the Royal Bodyguard, had been trying to get hold of the chief officers of the aristocratic Companions, with whom they wished to confer in their dilemma. Failing in this, they ordered the herald to blow a call for quiet, and summon them by name. The herald, knowing no army call for quiet alone, blew 'Assemble for orders'. It was received by the impatient men as 'Come to Assembly'.

Clamorously they poured through the great doors into the audience hall, while the herald shouted against the din the names he had been given, and the officers he named, those who could hear him, tried to shove themselves through the crowd. The crush inside grew dangerous; the doors were shut, in desperation, on everyone who had entered, authorized or not. The herald, gazing helplessly at the milling, cursing mob left in the courtyard, said to himself that if Alexander had seen it, someone would soon be wishing he'd never been born.

First to get in, because others had made way for them, were the men of the Companions, the horse-owning lords of Macedon, and any officers who had been near the doors. The rest of the crowd was a mixture of high and low, thrown anyhow together. The one thing they had in common was a deep unease, and the aggressiveness of worried men. It had come home to them that they were isolated troops in conquered country, half their world away from home. They had come here through faith in Alexander, in him alone. What they craved now was not a king but a leader.

The doors once closed, all eyes sought the royal dais. There, as often before, were the great men, Alexander's nearest friends, standing around the throne, the ancient throne of Babylon; its arms carved into crouching Assyrian bulls, its back recarved for Xerxes into the winged image of the unconquered sun. Here they had seen the small, compact, bright figure, needing a footstool, glowing like a jewel in too large a box, the spread wings of Ahura-Mazda above his head. Now the throne was empty. Across its back was the royal robe, and on its seat the diadem.

A low, sighing groan ran through the pillared hall. Ptolemy, who read the poets, thought it was like the climax of a tragedy, when the upstage doors are flung open, disclosing to the chorus that their fears are true and the king is dead.

Perdikkas stepped forward. All Alexander's friends here present, he said, would witness that the King had given him the royal ring. But, being speechless, he could not say what powers he was conferring. 'He looked at me fixedly, and it was clear he wished to speak, but his breath failed him. So, men of Macedon, here is the ring.' He drew it off, and laid it beside the crown. 'Bestow it as you choose, according to ancestral law.'

There were murmurs of admiration and suspense, as at a play. He waited, still downstage, like a good actor who could time his lines. So Ptolemy thought, glancing at the alert arrogant face, now set in impassive dignity; a well-carved mask; a mask for a king?

Perdikkas said, 'Our loss is beyond all measure, that we know. We know it is not to be thought of that the throne should pass to anyone not of his blood. Roxane his wife is five months with child; let us pray it will be a boy. He must first be born, and then

40

he must come of age. Meantime, whom do you wish to rule you? It is for you to say.'

The voices murmured; the generals on the dais looked restively at each other; Perdikkas had not presented another speaker. Suddenly, unannounced, Niarchos, the admiral, stepped forward; a spare, lean-waisted Cretan, with a brown weathered face. The hardships of the dreadful voyage down the Gedrosian coast had put ten years on him; he looked fifty, but still wiry and fit. The men quietened to hear him; he had seen monsters of the deep, and put them to flight with trumpets. Unused to public speaking upon the land, he used the voice with which he hailed ships at sea, startling them with its loudness.

'Macedonians, I put before you as Alexander's heir the son of Darius' daughter Stateira. The King left her pregnant when last he passed through Susa.' There were surprised, disconcerted murmurs; he raised his voice over them, as he would have done in a noisy storm. 'You saw their wedding. You saw it was a royal one. He meant to send for her here. He told me so.'

This wholly unexpected news of a woman who, barely glimpsed on her bridal day, had vanished at once into the recesses of the Susa harem, caused a surge of confusion and dismay. Presently a broad-spoken peasant voice called out, 'Ah, but did he say aught about the bairn?'

'No,' said Niarchos. 'In my belief he meant to bring up both sons under his eye, if both were sons, and choose the better one. But he's not lived to do it; and Stateira's child has right of rank.'

He stepped back; he had nothing more to say. He had done what seemed his duty, and that was all. Looking out over the sea of heads, he remembered how Alexander, lean as a bone and hollow-eyed from the desert march, had greeted him when he brought the fleet safe back, embracing him with tears of relief and joy. Since they were boys, Niarchos had been in love with him in an unsexual, undemanding way; that moment had been the climax of his life. What he would do with the rest of it, he could not begin to think.

Perdikkas' teeth were set with anger. He had urged the men to appoint a regent – who but himself? Now, they had been sidetracked into debating the succession. Two unborn children, who might both be girls. It was in the family; Philip had sired a horde of daughters, and only one son unless you counted the fool. The regency was the thing. Philip himself had started out as regent for an infant heir, but the Macedonians had not wasted much time in electing him King. Perdikkas himself had a good strain of the royal blood ... What had possessed Niarchos? There was no heading the men off now.

Their debate grew noisy and acrimonious. If, in their view, Alexander had had a fault, it was letting himself get Persianized. The Susa weddings, a serious manifesto, had caused much more unease than the campaign marriage with Roxane, the sort of thing his father used to do time and again. They had been indulgent towards the dancing-boy, as towards a pet monkey or dog; but why could he not have married a girl from a decent old Macedonian family, instead of two barbarians? Now this was what had come of it.

Some argued that any offspring of his must be accepted, half-breed or not. Others said there was no knowing if he would have acknowledged either; and you could be sure, if either of those women had a stillbirth or a girl, they would smuggle something in. They were crawling on their bellies to no Persian changeling ...

Ptolemy watched the scene with grief and anger, longing to be gone. From the time when Alexander's death had become a certainty, he had known where he wished to go. Ever since Egypt had opened its arms to Alexander as its liberator from the Persian yoke, Ptolemy had been entranced by it, its immemorial mellow civilization, its stupendous monuments and temples, the rich life of its sustaining river. It was defensible as an island, protected by sea and desert and wilderness; one had only to win the people's trust to hold it secure for ever. Perdikkas and the rest would gladly give him the satrapy; they wanted him out of the way.

He was dangerous, a man who could claim to be Alexander's brother, even though from adultery when Philip was in his teens. His paternity was unproved and unacknowledged; but Alexander had always had a special place for him, and everyone knew it. Yes, Perdikkas would be glad to see him off to Africa. But did the man think he could make himself Alexander's heir? That was what he was after; it was written all over him. Something must be done; and now.

The soldiers, when Ptolemy stepped forward, broke off their disputes to give him a hearing. He had been a boyhood friend of Alexander; he had presence without Perdikkas' arrogance; men who had served under him liked him. A group of them gave him a cheer.

'Macedonians. I see you do not wish to choose a king from the offspring of the conquered.'

There was loud applause. The men, who had all come armed – it was the proof of their voting right – beat their spears on their shields till the high hall echoed. Ptolemy raised a hand for quiet.

'We do not know if either wife of Alexander will bear a boy. If one or both should, when they come of age they must be brought before you and your sons, for Assembly to decide whom the Macedonians will accept. In the meantime, you await Alexander's heir. But who will act for him? Here before you are those whom Alexander honoured with trust. Lest too much power go to one man, I propose a Council of Regency.'

The voices were tempered. Reminded that in fifteen years or so they could still reject both claimants, they saw where the day's serious business lay. Ptolemy said into the new quiet, 'Remember Krateros. Alexander trusted him like himself. He sent him to govern Macedon. That is why he is not present now.'

That got home to them. They honoured Krateros next to

Alexander; he was of royal stock, capable, brave, handsome and careful of their needs. Ptolemy could feel the eyes of Perdikkas, red-hot in his back. Let him make the best of it; I did as I had to do.

As they buzzed and muttered below, Ptolemy thought suddenly, Only a few days back we were all alike the Friends of Alexander, just waiting for him to get up again and lead us. What are we now, and what am I?

He had never set great store on being Philip's son; it had cost him too much in childhood. Philip had been a nobody, a younger son held hostage by the Thebans, when he was born. 'Can't you make your bastard behave?' his father would say to his mother when he was in trouble. Philip had won him more than one boy's share of beatings. Later, when Philip was King and he himself a royal squire, his luck had turned; but what he had learned to care for was not being Philip's son, if indeed he was. He had cared, with affection and with growing pride, to be Alexander's brother. Never mind, he thought, whether it is the truth of my blood, or not. It is the truth of my heart.

A new voice broke his brief reverie. Aristonous, one of the Bodyguard, came forward to point out that whatever Alexander might have meant, he had given his ring to Perdikkas. He had looked around first, and knew what he was doing. This was fact, not guesswork; and Aristonous was for abiding by it.

He spoke simply and frankly, and carried the Assembly. They shouted Perdikkas' name, and many called to him to take back the ring. Slowly, scanning them, he took a few steps forward towards it. For a moment his eye met Ptolemy's, noting him in the way a man notes a newfound enemy.

It would not yet do, Perdikkas thought, to look over-eager. He needed another voice in Aristonous' support.

The hall, crowded with sweating men, was stiflingly close and hot. To the stink of humanity was added that of urine, where a few men had surreptitiously relieved themselves in corners. The generals on the dais were growing stupefied by their varied feelings of grief, anxiety, resentment, impatience and frustration. Suddenly, shouting something indistinct, an officer elbowed his way forward through the crowd. What, they all thought, can Meleager have to say?

He had been a phalanx commander since Alexander's first campaign, but had risen no higher. Alexander had confided to Perdikkas, one night at supper, that he was a good soldier if one did not stretch his mind.

He arrived below the dais, red-faced with the heat, with anger, and, by his looks, with wine; then lifted a harsh furious voice which stunned the crowd almost silent. 'That's the royal ring! Are you letting that fellow take it? Give it him now, he'll keep it till he dies! No wonder he wants a king who's not yet born!'

The generals, calling for order, were barely heard above the sudden roar. Meleager had aroused, from a kind of restless torpor, a mass of men who had not been heard before, the mental lees of the crowd. They took notice now, as they would of a knife-duel in the street, a man beating his wife, or a vicious dogfight; and shouted for Meleager, as if for the winning dog.

In the camp, Perdikkas could have restored order in minutes. But this was Assembly; he was not so much Commander-in-Chief as candidate. Repression might seem to forecast tyranny. He made a gesture of tolerant contempt, meaning 'Even such a man must be heard.'

He had seen the naked hatred in Meleager's face. The rank of their fathers had been much the same; they had both been royal squires to Philip; both had looked with secret envy at the tight-knit circle round the young Alexander. Then, when Philip was assassinated, Perdikkas had been the first to run down the fleeing assassin. Alexander had praised him, noticed and promoted him. With promotion came opportunity; he had never looked back. When Hephaistion died, he had been given his command. Meleager had remained an infantry phalanx leader, useful if not

45

too much was put on him. And, as Perdikkas saw, the knowledge that burned him was that they had started equal.

'How do we know,' Meleager shouted, 'that Alexander gave him anything? Whose word do we have for it? His and his friends'! And what are they after? Alexander's treasure here, which all of us helped to win! Will you stand for that?'

The noise turned to turmoil. The generals, who had thought that they knew men, saw incredulously that Meleager was beginning to lead a mob; men ready to sack the palace like a conquered town. Chaos broke out around it.

Perdikkas summoned, desperately, all his expert powers of dominance.

'Halt!' he thundered. There was a reflex response. He barked his orders; sufficient men obeyed them. Solid ranks with locked shields formed before the inner doors. The yelling sank to growls. 'I am glad to see,' said Perdikkas in his deep voice, 'that we still have here some soldiers of Alexander.'

There was a hush, as if he had invoked the name of an offended god. The mob began to lose itself in the crowd. The shields were lowered.

In the uncertain pause, a rustic voice, from somewhere deep in the press, made itself heard. 'Shame on you all, I say! Like the Commander says, we're soldiers of Alexander. It's his blood we want to rule us, not regents for foreign children. When we've Alexander's true-born brother, here in this very house.'

There was an astonished silence. Ptolemy, stunned, felt all his well-considered decisions shaken by a surge of primitive instinct. The ancient throne of Macedon, with its savage history of tribal rivalries and fratricidal wars, reached out its beckoning spell. Philip – Alexander – Ptolemy …

The peasant spearman below, having gained a hearing, went on with gathering confidence. 'His own brother which King Philip himself acknowledged, as every one of you knows. Alexander always cared for him like his own. I do hear say he was

46

backward as a boy, but it's not a month since the both of them were sacrificing for their father's soul at the household altar. I was on escort, and so were my mates here. He done everything right.'

There were sounds of assent. Ptolemy could barely repress the stare and dropped jaw of utter stupefaction. *Arridaios!* They must be mad.

'King Philip,' persisted the soldier, 'married Philinna lawful, which was his right to have more wives than one. So I say, pass by the foreign babes, and let's have his son, which is his rightful heir.'

There was applause from law-abiding men, who had been shocked by Meleager. On the dais, the silence was general and appalled. Simple or devious, not one of them had thought of this.

'Is it true?' said Perdikkas quickly to Ptolemy through the noise. '*Did* Alexander take him to the shrine?' Urgency overcame enmity; Ptolemy would surely know.

'Yes.' Ptolemy remembered the two heads side by side, dark and fair, the apprentice piece and the sculptor's. 'He's been better lately. He's not had a fit in a year. Alexander said he must be kept in mind of who his father was.'

'Arridaios!' came a growing shout. 'Give us Alexander's brother! Long live Macedon! Arridaios!'

'How many saw him?' said Perdikkas.

'The Companion escort and the foot-guard, and anyone looking on. He behaved quite properly. He always does ... did, with Alexander.'

'We can't have this. They don't know what they're doing. This must be stopped.'

The speaker, Peithon, was a short wiry man with a foxily pointed, rufous face and a sharp foxy bark. He was one of the Bodyguard, a good commander, but not known for the spirit of persuasion. He stepped out, forestalling Perdikkas, and snapped, 'Alexander's brother! You'd do better to choose his horse!'

The bite in his voice produced a brief, but not friendly silence;

47

he was not on the parade ground now. He went on, 'The fellow's a halfwit. Dropped on his head as a baby, and falls down in fits. Alexander's kept him like a child, with a nurse to tend him. Do you want an idiot for a king?'

Perdikkas swallowed a curse. Why had this man ever been promoted? Competent in the field, but no grip on morale in quarters. He himself, if this fool had not stepped in, would have recalled to the men the romantic winning of Roxane, the storming of the Sogdian Rock, the victor's chivalry; winning back their minds to Alexander's son. Now their feelings had been offended. They saw Arridaios as a victim of obscure intrigues. They had *seen* the man, and he had behaved like anyone else.

Alexander was always fortunate, thought Ptolemy. Already people wore his image cut on rings, for luck-charms. What spiteful fate inspired him, so near his end, with this kindly impulse towards a harmless fool? But, of course, there was a ceremony to come, at which he *must* appear. Perhaps Alexander had thought of that ...

'Shame!' the men were shouting up to Peithon. 'Arridaios, Arridaios, we want Arridaios!' He yapped at them; but they drowned his voice with boos.

Nobody noticed, till too late, that Meleager was missing.

It had been a long, dull day for Arridaios. No one had come to see him except the slave with his meals, which had been overcooked and half cold. He would have liked to hit the slave, but Alexander did not allow him. Someone from Alexander came nearly every day to see how he was, but today there had been no one to tell about the food. Even old Konon, who looked after him, had gone off just after getting-up time, saying he had to attend a meeting or some such thing, and hardly listening to a word he said.

He needed Konon for several things: to see he had something nice for supper, to find him a favourite striped stone he had mislaid, and to say why there had been such a terrible noise that morning, wailing and howling which seemed to come from everywhere, as if thousands of people were being beaten at once. From his window on the park, he had seen a crowd of men all running towards the palace. Perhaps, soon, Alexander would come to see him, and tell him what it was all about.

Sometimes he did not come for a very long time, and they said he was away on a campaign. Arridaios would stay in camp, or sometimes, as now, in a palace, till he came back again. Often he brought presents, coloured sweets, carved painted horses and lions, a piece of crystal for his collection, and once a beautiful scarlet cloak. Then the slaves would fold the tents and they would all move on. Perhaps this was going to happen now.

Meantime, he wanted the scarlet cloak to play with. Konon had said it was far too hot for cloaks, he would only make it dirty and spoil it. It was locked in the chest, and Konon had the key.

He got out all his stones, except the striped one, and laid them out in pictures; but not having the best one spoiled it. A flush of anger came over him; he picked up the biggest stone and beat it on the table-top again and again. A stick would have been better, but he was not allowed one, Alexander himself had taken it away.

A long time ago, when he lived at home, he had been left mostly with the slaves. No one else wanted to see him. Some were kind when they had time, but some had mocked him and knocked him about. As soon as he began to travel with Alexander, the slaves were different and more polite, and one was even afraid of him. It seemed a good time to get his own back, so he had beaten the man till his head bled and he fell down on the floor. Arridaios had never known till then how strong he was. He had gone on hitting till they carried the man away. Then, suddenly, Alexander had appeared; not dressed for dinner, but with armour on, all dirty and splashed with mud, and out of breath. He had looked quite frightening, like a different person, his eyes pale grey and large in his dirty face; and he had made Arridaios swear on their father's head never to do such a thing again. He had remembered it today when his food was late. He did not want his father's ghost to come after him. He had been terrified of him, and had sung with joy on hearing he was dead.

It was time for his ride in the park, but he was not allowed to go without Konon, who kept him on a leading-rein. He wished Alexander would come, and take him again to the shrine. He had held everything nicely, and poured on the wine and oil and incense after Alexander did, and had let them take the gold cups away though he would have liked to keep them; and afterwards, Alexander had said he had done splendidly.

Someone was coming! Heavy feet, and a clank of armour. Alexander was quicker and lighter than that. A soldier came in whom he had never seen before; a tallish man with a red face and straw-coloured hair, holding his helmet under his arm. They looked at one another.

Arridaios, who knew nothing of his own appearance, knew still less that Meleager was thinking, Great Zeus! Philip's face. What is inside it? The young man had, in fact, much of his father's structure, square face, dark brows and beard, broad shoulders and short neck. Since eating was his chief pleasure he was overweight, though Konon had never allowed him to get gross. Delighted to see a visitor at last, he said eagerly, 'Are you going to take me to the park?'

'No, sir.' He stared avidly at Arridaios, who, disconcerted, tried to think if he had done anything wrong. Alexander had never sent this man before. 'Sir. I have come to escort you to Assembly. The Macedonians have elected you their king.'

Arridaios stared at him with alarm, followed by a certain shrewdness. 'You're telling lies. *I'm* not the King, my brother is. He said to me, Alexander said, "If I didn't look after you, someone would try to make you King, and you'd end up being killed."'

He backed away, eyeing Meleager with growing agitation. 'I won't go to the park with you. I'll go with Konon. You fetch him here. If you don't, I'll tell Alexander of you.'

His retreat was blocked by the heavy table. The soldier walked right up to him, so that he flinched instinctively, remembering boyhood beatings. But the man just stared into his eyes, and, very slowly, spoke.

'Sir. Your brother is dead. *King Alexander is dead.* The Macedonians are calling for you. Come with me.'

Since Arridaios did not move, he grasped his arm and guided him to the door. He came unresisting, not heeding where he was led, striving to come to terms with a world which Alexander did not rule.

So expeditious had Meleager been that the crowd in the hall was still shouting 'Arridaios!' when he himself appeared upon the dais. Confronted by this sounding sea of men, he gazed in a numb astonishment, giving a brief illusion of dignified reserve.

Most of the dumbfounded generals had never seen him before; only a few of the men had glimpsed him. But every Macedonian over thirty had seen King Philip. There was a pause of perfect silence; then the cheers began.

'Philip! Philip! Philip!'

Arridaios sent a terrified look over his shoulder. Was his father coming, had he never been really dead? Meleager beside him caught the revealing change of countenance and whispered swiftly, 'They are cheering you.' Arridaios gazed about, slightly reassured, but still bewildered. Why did they call so for his father? His father was dead. *Alexander* was dead . . .

Meleager stepped forward. So much, he thought triumphantly, for that upstart Perdikkas and his unborn ward. 'Here, Macedonians, is the son of Philip, the brother of Alexander. Here is your rightful king.'

Spoken loudly and almost in his ear, it reached Arridaios with awful comprehension. He knew why all these men were here and what was happening. 'No!' he cried, his high plaintive voice issuing incongruously from his large hirsute face. 'I'm not the King! I told you, I can't be King. Alexander told me not to.'

But he had addressed himself to Meleager, and was inaudible beyond the dais, drowned by the cheering. The generals, appalled, all turned upon Meleager, talking across him. He listened with mounting fear to the loud angry voices. Clearly he recalled Alexander's large deep-set eyes, fixed upon his, warning him of what would happen if they tried to make him King. While Meleager was quarrelling with the tall dark man in the middle of the dais, he bolted for the now unguarded inner door. Outside, in the warren-like passages of the ancient palace, he wandered sobbing to himself, seeking the way back to his familiar room.

In the hall, new uproar began. None of this had precedent. Both the last two kings had been elected by acclamation, and led with traditional paeans to the royal palace at Aigai, whence each had confirmed his accession by directing his predecessor's funeral.

Meleager, wrangling with Perdikkas, had not missed his fugitive candidate till he was warned by sounds of derision from the floor. Feeling was swinging against him; the powerful presence of Perdikkas had appeal for men seeking some source of confidence and strength. Meleager saw that only instant resource would avail. He turned and ran, followed by boos, through the door Arridaios had used. The most vocal of his supporters – not the loot-hungry mob, but kinsmen and fellow-clansmen and men with grudges against Perdikkas – took alarm and hurried after.

Before long they ran down their quarry, standing where two passages met, debating with himself which way to turn. At sight of them he cried out, 'No! Go away!' and started to run. Meleager grasped his shoulder. He submitted, looking terror-stricken. Clearly in this state he could not appear. Gently, calmingly, Meleager changed his grip to a protective caress.

'Sir, you must listen. Sir, you've nothing to fear. You were a good brother to Alexander. He was the rightful king; it would have been wrong, just as he said, for you to take his throne. But now he is dead, and *you* are the rightful king. The throne is yours.' A flash of inspiration came to him. 'There is a present for you on it. A beautiful purple cloak.'

Arridaios, already soothed by the kindly voice, now brightened visibly. No one had laughed; things were too urgent and too dangerous.

'Can I keep it all the time?' he asked cannily. 'You won't lock it up?'

'No, indeed. The moment you have it, you can put it on.'

'And have it all day?'

'All night too, if you wish.' As he began to guide his prize along the passage, a new thought struck him. 'When the men called "Philip!" it was you they meant. They are honouring you with your father's name. You will be King Philip of Macedon.'

King Philip, thought Arridaios. It gave him confidence. His father must be really dead, if his name could be given away, like a purple cloak. It would be well to take them both. He was still buoyed by this decision when Meleager steered him on to the dais.

Smiling around at the exclamations, he saw at once the great swath of colour draped upon the throne, and walked briskly towards it. Sounds which he had mistaken for friendly greetings died; the Assembly, arrested by his changed demeanour, watched the drama almost in silence.

'There, sir, is our present to you,' said Meleager in his ear.

To a ground-bass of restless murmurs, Philip Arridaios lifted the robe from the throne, and held it up before him.

It was the robe of state, made at Susa for the marriage of Alexander to Stateira daughter of Darius, and of his eighty honoured friends to their Persian brides, with the whole of his army as his wedding guests. In this robe he had given audience to envoys from half the known world, during his last progress down to Babylon. It was of a wool as dense as velvet and soft as silk, dyed with Tyrian murex to a soft glowing crimson just tinged with purple, pure as the red of a dark rose. The breast and back were worked with the sunburst, the Macedonian royal blazon, in balas rubies and gold. A sleeveless dalmatic, it was clasped on the shoulders with two gold lion-masks, worn at their weddings by three kings of Macedon. The hot afternoon sun slanted down from a high window on the lions' emerald eyes. The new Philip gazed at it in rapture.

Meleager said, 'Let me help you to put it on.'

He raised it, and slipped it over Philip's head. Radiant with pleasure, he looked out at the cheering men. 'Thank you,' he said, as he had been taught when he was a child.

The cheers redoubled. The son of Philip had come in with dignity, looking like a king. At first he must simply have been abashed and modest. Now they were for the royal blood against the world.

'Philip! Philip! Long live Philip!'

Ptolemy felt almost choked with grief and anger. He remembered the wedding morning, when he and Hephaistion had gone to Alexander's room in the Susa palace to dress the bridegroom. They had exchanged the jokes which were traditional, along with private ones of their own. Alexander, who had been planning for weeks this great ceremony of racial concord, had been almost incandescent; one could have taken him for a man in love. It was Hephaistion who had remembered the lion brooches and pinned them on the robe. To see it now on a grinning idiot made Ptolemy long to spit Meleager on his sword. Towards the poor fool himself he felt horror rather than anger. He knew him well; he had often gone, when Alexander was busy, to make sure he was not neglected or ill-used; such things, it was tacitly agreed, were better kept in the family. Philip ...! Yes, it would stick.

He said to Perdikkas, who was beside him, 'Alexander should have had him smothered.'

Perdikkas, unheeding, strode forward, blazing with rage, trying vainly to be heard above the din. Pointing at Philip, he made a sweeping gesture of rejection and scorn.

Shouts of support came from just below him. The Companions, foremost by right or rank, had had the clearest view. They had heard of the fool; they had watched, in silent grief or sheer incredulity, the assumption of the robe. Now their outrage found vent. Their strong voices, trained in the piercing war-paean of the charging cavalry, overpowered all other sound.

It was as if the robe of Alexander had been a battle-standard, suddenly unfurled. Men started to put their helmets on. The hammering of spears on shields grew to a volume like the sound of onset. Nearer, more deadly, came the hiss and whisper of the Companions' unsheathed swords.

In alarm Meleager saw the powerful aristocracy of Macedon rallying in force against him. Even his own faction might fall off from him, unless forced to commit themselves beyond retreat. Each common soldier now shouting 'Philip!' was, after all, the tribesman of some lord. He must divide them from tribal allegiances, create new action. With the thought, the answer came to him. His own genius amazed him. How could Alexander have passed such a leader by?

Firmly, but imperceptibly, he guided the smiling Philip to the edge of the dais. The impression that he meant to speak procured a moment's quiet, if only from curiosity. Meleager spoke into it.

'Macedonians! You have chosen your king! Do you mean to stand by him?' The spearmen replied with defiant cheers. 'Then come with him now, and help him confirm his right. A king of Macedon must entomb his predecessor.'

He paused. He had real silence now. A ripple of shock could almost be felt, passing through the packed, sweat-stinking hall.

Meleager lifted his voice. 'Come! The body of Alexander awaits its rites. Here is his heir to perform them. Don't let them cheat him of his heritage. To the death-chamber! Come!'

There was confused, seething movement. The sounds had changed. The most determined of the infantry surged forward; but they did not cheer. Many held back; there was a deep mutter of opposing voices. Companions began to clamber on the dais, to guard the inner doors. The generals, all trying to protest at once, only added to the confusion. Suddenly, rising above everything, came the cracked new-broken voice of a youth, hoarse with passionate fury.

'Bastards! You bastards! You filthy, slave-born bastards!'

From a corner of the hall alongside the Companions, shoving through everyone regardless of age or rank, yelling as if in battle, came the royal squires.

The watch on duty had been with Alexander till he died, standing on after sunrise. They had been several years in attendance on him. Some of them had turned eighteen and had a vote, the rest had crowded into Assembly with them. They leaped and scrambled up on the dais, waving their drawn swords, wild-eyed, crop-headed, their fair Macedonian hair shorn raggedly almost to their scalps in mourning. There were nearly fifty of them. Perdikkas, seeing their fanatic rage, knew them at sight for the readiest killers in the hall. Unless stopped they would have Philip dead, and then there would be a massacre. 'To me!' he shouted to them. 'Follow me! Protect the body of Alexander!'

He ran to the inner door, Ptolemy neck-and-neck with him, the other generals close behind, and then the squires, so fierce in their rush that they outdistanced the Companions. Pursued by the angry cries of the opposition, they ran through the King's reception room, through his private sanctum, and on into the bedchamber. The doors were closed, not locked. The foremost men burst through them.

Ptolemy thought, with a shuddering realization, He has lain here since yesterday! In Babylon, in midsummer. Unconsciously, as the doors burst open, he held his breath.

56

There was a faint scent of almost burned-out incense; of the dried flowers and herbs which scented the royal robes and bed, mixed with the scent of the living presence which Ptolemy had known since boyhood. In the vast forsaken room he lay on the great bed between its watchful daimons, a clean fresh sheet drawn over him. Some aromatic sprinkled on it had cheated even the flies. On the dais, half propped against the bed with an arm thrown over it, the Persian boy lay in an exhausted sleep.

Roused by the clamour, he staggered dazedly to his feet, unaware of Ptolemy's touch upon his shoulder. Ptolemy walked to the bed's head and folded back the sheet.

Alexander lay in an inscrutable composure. Even his colour seemed hardly changed. His golden hair with its bright silver streaks felt, to the touch, still charged with life. Niarchos and Seleukos, who had followed Ptolemy, exclaimed that it was a miracle, that it proved Alexander's divinity. Ptolemy, who had been his fellow-student with Aristotle, looked down in silence, wondering how long a secret spark of that strong life had burned in the still body. He laid a hand on the heart; but it was over now, the corpse was stiffening. He drew the sheet over the marmoreal face, and turned to the ranks that were forming to hold the bolted doors.

The squires, who knew the room in detail, dragged up the heavy clothes-chests to form a barricade. But it could not last for long. The men outside were well used to pushing. Six or seven ranks deep, they leaned upon the doors as, ten years back, they had leaned with their fifteen-foot sarissas on Darius' levies; and, like the Persians at the Granikos, at Issos, at Gaugamela, the doors gave way. Grinding along the floor, the bronze-bound chests were heaved aside.

As the foremost thrust in, Perdikkas knew himself unable to cut them down, and be first with the shame of bloodshed in this room. He called back his men to bar the way to the royal bed. In a brief pause, the attackers looked about them. The ranks of the defenders screened the body, they saw only the spread wings of the gold daimons and their fierce alien eyes. They shouted defiance, but came no nearer.

There was movement behind them. Philip came in.

Though Meleager was with him, he was here of his own accord. When a person died, his family must see to him. All motives of policy had passed over Philip like unmeaning noise; but he knew his duty.

'Where's Alexander?' he called to the bristling barrier before the bed. 'I'm his brother. I want to bury him.'

The generals gritted their teeth in silence. It was the squires whose yells of wrath and spat-out insults broke the loaded pause. They had no reverence for the dead, because in their central consciousness Alexander was still alive. They shouted for him as if he were lying on a battlefield senseless with wounds, beset by cowards who would not have faced him on his feet. Their whoops and war-cries set off all the young men in the Companions, who remembered their own days as squires. 'Alexander! Alexander!'

From somewhere in the press, making a little whiffling sound as the spin-strap launched it, a javelin hurtled across and rang on Perdikkas' helmet.

In moments more were flying. A Companion knelt pouring blood from a severed leg-vein; a squire who had come helmetless had a slashed scalp and was masked in scarlet, his blue eyes staring through. Till it came to close quarters, the defenders were sitting game. They had brought only their short curved cavalry sabres, symbol of their rank, to what should have been a purely civil occasion.

Perdikkas picked up the javelin that had struck him and hurled it back. Others, plucking them from the bodies of the wounded, held them to serve as spears. Ptolemy, taking a step back to avoid a missile, collided with someone, cursed, and turned to look. It was the Persian boy, blood staining his linen sleeve from a gashed arm. He had thrown it up to ward a javelin from Alexander's body.

'Stop!' shouted Ptolemy across the room. 'Are we wild beasts or men?'

From beyond the doors, the hubbub still continued; but it trailed off, damped by the hush of those in front to a kind of shamefaced muttering. It was Niarchos the Cretan who said, 'Let them look.'

Grasping their weapons, the defenders made a gap. Niarchos uncovered Alexander's face and stood back, silent.

The opposing line fell still. The crowd behind, jostling to see, felt the change and paused. Presently in the front a grizzled phalanx captain stepped a pace forward and took his helmet off. Two or three veterans followed. The first faced around to the men behind him, lifted his arm and shouted, 'Halt!' Sombrely, in a kind of sullen grief, the parties looked at one another.

By ones and twos the senior officers unhelmed themselves and stood forth to be known. The defenders lowered their weapons. The old captain began to speak.

'There's my brother!' Philip, who had been elbowed aside, pushed forward. He still had on the robe of Alexander, pushed askew and crumpled. 'He has to have a funeral.'

'Be quiet!' hissed Meleager. Obediently – moments like this were familiar in his life – Philip let himself be hustled out of sight. The old captain, red-faced, recovered his presence of mind.

'Gentlemen,' he said, 'you are outnumbered, as you see. We have all acted in haste, and I dare say we all regret it. I propose a parley.'

Perdikkas said, 'On one condition. The body of the King shall be left inviolate, and every man here shall swear it by the gods below. I will take my oath that when a fitting bier is ready, I will have it taken to the royal burial ground in Macedon. Unless these vows are solemnized, none of us will leave this place while we can stand and fight.'

They agreed. They were all ashamed. Perdikkas' words about the royal burial ground had brought them sharply down to earth. What would they have done with the body if they had taken it? Buried it in the park? One look at that remote proud face had sobered them. A miracle he was not stinking; yet you would have thought he was still alive. A superstitious shiver had run down many backs; Alexander would make a powerful ghost.

On the terrace a goat was slaughtered; men touched the carcass or the blood, invoking the curse of Hades if they were forsworn. Owing to their numbers it took some time; as twilight fell they were still swearing by torchlight.

Meleager, the first to swear under Perdikkas' eye, watched, brooding. He had lost support and knew it. Only some thirty, the hard core of his partisans, still rallied round him; and even those because they were now marked men, frightened of reprisals. He must keep them, at least. While the sunset dusk hummed with the noises of an anxious fermenting city, he had been giving the matter thought. If he could separate the Bodyguard ... thirty to only eight ...

The last men had scrambled through their oaths. He approached Perdikkas with a sober placating face. 'I acted rashly. The King's death has overset us all. Tomorrow we can meet and take better counsel.'

'So I hope.' Perdikkas frowned under his dark brows.

'All of us would be ashamed,' went on Meleager smoothly, 'if the near friends of Alexander were kept from watching beside him. I beg you' – his gesture embraced the Bodyguard – 'return and keep your vigil.'

'Thank you,' said Niarchos, quite sincerely. He had hoped to do it. Perdikkas paused, his soldier's instinct indefinably wary. It was Ptolemy who said, 'Meleager has taken his oath to respect Alexander's body. Has he taken one for ours?'

Perdikkas' eyes sought Meleager's, which shifted in spite of him. All together, with looks of profound contempt, the

Bodyguard walked off to join the Companions encamped in the royal park.

Presently they sent messengers to the Egyptian quarter, summoning the embalmers to begin their work at dawn.

'Where were you all day, Konon?' said Philip, as his hot clothes were lifted off him. 'Why didn't they fetch you when I said?'

Konon, an elderly veteran who had served him for ten years, said, 'I was at Assembly, sir. Never mind, you shall have your nice bath now, with the scented oil.'

'I'm King now, Konon. Did they tell you I'm the King?'

'Yes, sir. Long life to you, sir.'

'Konon, now I'm King, you won't go away?'

'No, sir, old Konon will look after you. Now let me have this beautiful new robe to brush it and keep it safe. It's too good for every day ... Why, come, come, sir, you've no call to cry.'

In the Royal Bedchamber, as the evening cooled, the body of Alexander stiffened like stone. With a bloodstained towel round his arm, the Persian boy put by the bed the night-table of malachite and ivory, and kindled the night-lamp on it. The floor was strewn with the debris of the fighting. Someone had lurched against the console with the images of Hephaistion; they lay sprawled like the fallen after a battle. In the faint light, Bagoas took a long look at them, and turned away. But in a few minutes he went back and stood them up neatly, each in its place. Then, fetching a stool lest sitting on the dais he might sleep again, he folded his hands and composed himself to watch, his dark eyes staring into the dark shadows.

The harem at Susa was Persian, not Assyrian. Its proportions were elegantly balanced; its fluted columns had capitals sculpted with lotus-buds by craftsmen from Greece; its walls were faced with delicately enamelled tiles, and the sunlight dappled them through lattices of milky alabaster. Queen Sisygambis, the mother of Darius, sat in her high-backed chair, a granddaughter on either side. At eighty she kept the hawk-nosed, ivorine face of the old Elamite nobility; the pure Persian strain, unmixed with Median. She was brittle now; in her youth she had been tall. She was robed and scarved in deep indigo, but for her breast, on which glowed a great necklace of polished pigeon-blood rubies, the gift of King Poros to Alexander, and of Alexander to her.

Stateira, the elder girl, was reading a letter aloud, slowly, translating it from Greek to Persian. Alexander had had both girls taught to read Greek as well as speak it. From affection for him, Sisygambis had allowed him to indulge this whim, though in her view clerking was somewhat menial, and more properly left to the palace eunuchs. However, he must be allowed the customs of his people. He could not help his upbringing, and was never purposely discourteous. He should have been a Persian.

Stateira read, stumbling a little, not from ignorance but from agitation.

ALEXANDER KING OF THE MACEDONIANS AND LORD OF ASIA, to his honoured wife Stateira.

Wishing to look upon your face again, I desire you to set out for Babylon without delay, so that your child may be born here. If you bear a boy, I intend to proclaim him my heir. Hasten your journey. I have been sick, and my people tell me there is ignorant talk that I am dead. Do you pay no heed to it. My chamberlains are commanded to receive you with honour, as the mother of a Great King to be. Bring Drypetis your sister, who is my sister also for the sake of one who was dear to me as myself. May all be well with you.

Stateira lowered the letter and looked down at her grandmother. The child of two tall parents, she stood nearly six feet without her slippers. Much of her mother's famous beauty had passed to her. She was queenly in everything but pride. 'What shall we do?' she said.

Sisygambis looked up impatiently under her white brows. 'First finish the King's letter.'

'Madam grandmother, that is all.'

'No,' said Sisygambis with irritation. 'Look again, child. What does he say to *me*?'

'Madam grandmother, that is the end.'

'You must be mistaken. Women should not meddle with writing; I told him so, but he would have his way. You had better call a clerk, to read it properly.'

'Truly, there is no more writing on the paper. *May all be well with you.* See, it stops here.'

The strong lines of Sisygambis' face slackened a little; her years showed like sickness. 'Is the messenger still here? Fetch him, see if he has another letter. These men tire on the road and it makes them stupid.'

The rider was brought, gulping from his meal. He pledged his head he had received one letter only, one from the King. He shook out his wallet before them.

When he had gone, Sisygambis said, 'Never has he sent to Susa without a word to me. Show me the seal.' But her sight had lengthened with age, and even at arm's length she could not make out the figure.

'It is his likeness, madam grandmother. It is like the one on my emerald, that he gave me on my wedding day; only here he has a wreath, and on mine he wears a diadem.'

Sisygambis nodded, and sat awhile in silence. There were earlier royal letters in the care of the Head Chamberlain; but she did not like to let such people know that her eyes were failing.

Presently she said, 'He writes that he has been sick. He will be behindhand with all his business. Now he is overtaxing himself, as his nature is. When he was here, I saw he was short of breath ... Go, child, fetch me your women; you too, Drypetis. I must tell them what to pack for you.'

Young Drypetis, the widow of Hephaistion (she was seventeen) moved to obey, then ran back to kneel beside the chair. 'Baba, please come with us to Babylon.'

Sisygambis rested her fine-boned old ivory hand on the young girl's head. 'The King has told you to hurry on the road. I am too old. And besides, he has not summoned me.'

When the women had been instructed, and all the flurry had moved to the girls' bedchamber, she sat on in her straight-backed chair, tears trickling down her cheeks and falling upon King Poros' rubies.

In the Royal Bedchamber of Babylon, now redolent of spices and of nitre, the Egyptians who were the heirs of their fathers' art pursued the elaborate task of embalming the latest Pharaoh. Shocked at the delay which would surely undo their skill, they had tiptoed in by dawnlight, and beheld the corpse with awed amazement. As their slaves brought in the instruments, the vessels and fluids and aromatics of their art, the single watcher, a white-faced Persian youth, extinguished his lamp and vanished like a ghost in silence.

Before slitting the torso to remove the entrails, they remembered, far though they were from the Valley of the Kings, to lift their hands in the traditional prayer, that it might be lawful for mortals to handle the body of a god.

The narrow streets of ancient Babylon hummed with rumour and counter-rumour. There were lamps burning all night. Days passed; the armies of Perdikkas and Meleager waited in armed truce; the infantry around the palace, the cavalry in the royal park, beside the horse-lines where Nebuchadrezzar had kept his chariots for the lion-hunt.

Outnumbered four to one, they had discussed moving to the

plains outside, where there was room for horse to deploy. 'No,' said Perdikkas. 'That would concede defeat. Give them time to take a look at their booby king. They'll come round. Alexander's army has never been divided.'

On the parade ground and in the palace gardens, the men of the phalanx bivouacked as best they could. Stubbornly they clung to their victors' pride and their rooted xenophobia. No barbarian should rule their sons, they told each other across the campfires, where their Persian women, whom Alexander had induced them to marry lawfully, were stirring their supper-pots. They had long ago spent Alexander's dowries; not one man in a hundred meant to take home his woman when he was paid off.

They thought with confused resentment of the young bloods in the Companions, drinking and hunting beside the sons of Persian lords with their curled beards and inlaid weapons and bedizened horses. It was well enough for the cavalry; *they* could afford to Persianize without losing face. But the foot-men, sons of Macedonian farmers, herdsmen and hunters, masons and carpenters, owned only what the wars had won them, their little hoards of loot, and, above all, the just reward for all their toils and dangers, the knowledge that whoever their fathers might have been, they were Alexander's Macedonians, masters of the world. Clinging to this treasure of self-esteem, they spoke well of Philip, his modesty, his likeness to his great father, his pure Macedonian blood.

Their officers, whose affairs took them into the royal presence, came back increasingly taciturn. The enormous business of Alexander's empire could not come to a standstill. Envoys, tax-collectors, shipbuilders, officers of the commissariat, architects, disputing satraps seeking arbitration, still appeared in the ante-rooms; indeed, in augmented numbers, many having waited for audience through Alexander's illness. Not only had they to be dealt with; they had to find a visible, believable king.

Before each appearance, Meleager briefed Philip carefully. He

65

had learned to go, unled, straight to his throne, without wandering off to speak to some chance person who had caught his eye; to keep his voice down so that he was seen, but not heard to speak, enabling Meleager beside him to proclaim suitable replies. He had learned not to call while enthroned for lemonade or sweets, or to ask permission from his guard of honour when he wanted to go outside. His scratching himself, picking his nose and fidgeting could never be quite controlled; but if his appearances were kept short, he presented as a rule a quiet and sober figure.

Meleager had appointed himself to the post of Chiliarch, or Grand Vizier, created for Hephaistion and inherited by Perdikkas. Standing at the King's right hand, flamboyantly panoplied, he knew that he looked impressive; but he knew too, all too well, what a soldier thinks when the chief to whom he has come for orders speaks through an intermediary and never looks him in the face. His officers, all of whom had had free access to Alexander, could not be kept out; nor could the royal guard. And all of them, he felt it through his skin, were looking at the stout stocky figure on the throne, the slack mouth and wandering stare, and seeing in mind's eye the dynamic vanished presence, the alert responsive face, the serene authority, that now lay stilled for ever in the locked bedchamber, submerged in the embalmers' bath of nitre, preparing to abide the centuries.

Beyond all this, Persian officers appointed by Alexander could not be refused audience, and were not fools. The thought of a concerted rising, against a mutinous divided army, gave him waking nightmares.

Like other men who have indulged a long rancorous hate, he blamed all adversity upon its object, never considering that his hatred, not his enemy, had created his predicament. Like other such men before and after him, he saw only one remedy, and resolved to seek it.

Philip was still in his old apartments, which, having been chosen for him by Alexander, were pleasant and cool, at least for Babylon in midsummer. When Meleager had tried to move him into more regal quarters, he had refused with shouts so loud that the palace guard had come running, thinking murder was being done. Here Meleager sought him, taking with him a kinsman, a certain Duris, who carried writing things.

The King was occupied happily with his stones. He had a chest full, collected over thousands of miles of Asia as he trailed along after the army; pebbles he had picked up for himself, mixed with bits of amber, quartz, agate, old seals, and coloured glass jewels from Egypt, which Alexander or Ptolemy or Hephaistion had brought him when they happened to remember. He had arranged them in a long winding path across the room, and was on his hands and knees improving it.

At Meleager's entrance he scrambled guiltily to his feet, clutching a favourite lump of Scythian turquoise, which he hid behind his back lest it be taken away.

'Sire!' said Meleager harshly.

Philip, recognizing this as a severe rebuke, hastened over to the most important chair, carefully stuffing the turquoise under the cushion.

'Sir,' said Meleager, standing over him, 'I have come to tell you that you are in grave danger. No, don't be afraid, I will defend you. But the traitor Perdikkas, who tried to steal Alexander's body and rob you of the throne, is plotting to take your life, and make himself king.'

Philip jumped to his feet, stammering incoherently. Presently Meleager made out, 'He said . . . Alexander *said* . . . He can be King if he wants to. I don't mind. Alexander told me they mustn't make me King.'

With some trouble, Meleager freed his arm from a grip he had feared would break it. 'Sir, if he is King his first act will be to kill you. Your only safety is in killing *him*. See, here is the paper ordering his death.' Duris set it, with pen and ink, upon the table. 'Just write *PHILIP* here, as I taught you. I will help you, if you like.'

'And then you'll kill him before he kills me?'

'Yes, and all our troubles will be over. Write it here.'

The blot with which he began did not efface the writing; and he produced, after that, a quite tolerable signature.

Perdikkas' lodging was one of the grace-and-favour houses built in the royal park by the Persian kings, and bestowed on his friends by Alexander. Around it were encamped the royal squires. They had attached themselves to Perdikkas as Alexander's chosen regent. Though they had not offered to wait upon his person, and he had known better than to ask it, they rode with his messages, and guarded him in their accustomed rota by day and night.

He was consulting with Ptolemy when one of them came in. 'Sir. An old man is asking for you.'

'Thirty at least,' said Ptolemy flippantly. Perdikkas said crisply, 'Well?'

'He says, sir, he's the servant of Arridaios.' The honorific Philip was not used on the Companions' side of the river. 'He says it's urgent.'

'Is his name Konon?' said Ptolemy sharply. 'Perdikkas, I know this man. You had better see him.'

'So I intended.' Perdikkas spoke rather stiffly. He found Ptolemy too easygoing and informal, traits which Alexander had regrettably not discouraged. 'Bring him in, but search him for weapons first.'

Old Konon, profoundly ill at ease, gave an old soldier's salute, stood to attention, and said nothing till given leave.

'Sir, with permission. They've made my poor master sign a paper against you. I was in his bedroom, seeing to his things, they never thought to look. Sir, don't hold him to blame. They took

68

advantage of him. He never meant harm to you, not of his own accord.'

'I believe you,' said Perdikkas, frowning. 'But it seems that harm is done.'

'Sir. If he falls into your hands, don't kill him, sir. He was never any trouble, not in King Alexander's day.'

'Rest assured we have no such wish.' This man could be useful, his charge more useful still. 'When the army returns to duty, I will have your master well cared for. Do you want to stay with him?'

'Sir, yes sir. I've been with him nearly from a boy. I don't know how he'd go on without me.'

'Very good. Permission granted. Tell him, if he will understand you, that he has nothing to fear from me.'

'I will, sir, and God bless you.' He left, saluting smartly.

'An easy favour,' said Perdikkas to Ptolemy. 'Did he think we could afford to kill Alexander's brother? Meleager, now . . .'

Later, his day's business done, Perdikkas was sitting down to supper when raised voices sounded outside. From the window he saw a company of a hundred foot-soldiers. The squires on duty numbered sixteen.

He was too old a campaigner to have changed into a supper-robe. In moments, with the speed of two decades' practice, he had whipped his corselet from the stand and clasped it on. A panting squire dashed in, saluting with one hand while the other waved a paper.

'Sir! It's a summons from the rebels. A royal warrant they call it.'

'Royal, eh?' said Perdikkas calmly. The missive was brief; he read it aloud.

'PHILIP SON OF PHILIP KING OF THE MACEDONIANS AND LORD OF ASIA, to the former Chiliarch Perdikkas. You are hereby summoned to appear before me, to answer a charge of treason. If you resist, the escort has orders to use force.'

'Sir, we can hold them. Do you want a message sent?'

Not for nothing had Perdikkas served directly under Alexander. He laid his hand on the boy's shoulder, shaping his austere face into the needed smile. 'Good lad. No, no message. Guard, stand to arms. I will talk to this squad of Meleager's.' The squire's salute had the faint reflection of a remembered ardour. Perhaps, thought Perdikkas, I can show Acting Chiliarch Meleager why I, and not he, got promoted to the Bodyguard.

He had had twelve years to absorb a basic Alexander precept: Do it with style. Unlike Alexander, he had had to work for it, but he knew what it was worth. On his own account, needing instruction from no one, he could deliver a memorable dressing-down.

Striding bareheaded on to the porch, the summons in his hand, he paused formidably for effect, and began to speak.

He had recognized the officer – he had a good general's memory – and reviewed in detail the last campaign in which they had all served under his own command. Alexander had once spoken highly of them. What did they suppose themselves to be doing, disgracing themselves like this; they who had once been men, and even, God help them, soldiers? Could they face Alexander now? Even before he was King, the wittol bastard had been used in intrigue against him; anyone else would have had him put out of the way; but he in the greatness of his heart had cared for him as a harmless innocent. If King Philip had wished a fool to bear his name, he would have said so. King Philip! King Ass. Who would believe that men of Alexander's could come here as servants of Meleager, a man he had known too well to trust with a division, to sell the life of the man he himself had chosen to command them? Let them go back to their comrades, and remind them who they had been, and what they had sunk to now. Let them ask themselves how they liked it. They could now dismiss.

After an uneasy, shuffling silence, the troop captain rapped out gruffly, 'About turn! March.'

Meantime, the squires on watch had been joined by every squire in hearing. When the troop departed, they gathered round Perdikkas and cheered. Without effort this time, he returned their triumphant grins. Almost, for a moment, he felt like Alexander.

No, he thought as he went in. People used to eat *him* alive. They had to touch him, his hands, his clothes. I've seen them fighting to reach him. Those fools at Opis, when he'd forgiven them for rioting, demanded the right to kiss him . . . Well, that was his mystery, which I shall never have. But then, nor will anyone else.

Slowly, against the stream, the rowers' labour lightened sometimes by a flaw of wind from the south, the canopied barge meandered along the Tigris. On linen cushions stuffed with wool and down, waving their fans, the two princesses stretched like young cats, luxuriating in smooth movement and the cool air off the water, after the jolting heat of their covered wagon. Within the awning, their duenna was fast asleep. Along the towpath trundled the wagon and the baggage-cart, the escort of armed mounted eunuchs, the muleteers and the household slaves. When the caravan passed a village, all the peasants would gather on the bank to stare.

'If only,' sighed Stateira, 'he had not told us to hurry. One could go all the way by water, downstream to the Gulf, and up the Euphrates to Babylon.' She settled the cushions in her back, which had the ache of pregnancy.

Drypetis, fingering her dark-blue widow's veil, looked over her shoulder to be sure the duenna was sleeping. 'Will he give me another husband?'

'I don't know.' Stateira looked away at the riverbank. 'Don't ask him yet. He won't like it. He thinks you still belong to Hephaistion. He won't let Hephaistion's regiment ever have another name.' Feeling a desolate silence behind her, she said, 'If

I have a boy, I'll ask him.' She lay back in the cushions and closed her eyes.

The sun, splintering through tall clumps of papyrus, made shifting patterns in the rose-red light that filtered through her eyelids. It was like the sun-glowing crimson curtains of the wedding pavilion at Susa. Her face burned, as always when the memory came back to her.

She had been, of course, presented to the King before. Grandmother had ensured that she made the deepest curtsey, before he took his tall chair and she her low one. But the wedding ritual could not be evaded; it had followed the Persian rite. She had been led in by her dead mother's brother, a fine tall man. Then the King had risen from his chair of state, as the bridegroom must, to greet her with a kiss and lead her to the chair beside him. She had performed, for the kiss, the little genuflection Grandmamma had taught her; but then she had had to stand up, there was no way out of it. She was half a head taller, and ready to die of shame.

When the trumpets had sounded, and the herald announced that they were man and wife, it was Drypetis' turn. The King's friend, Hephaistion, had stood up and come forward, the most beautiful man she had ever seen, stately and tall – with his dark-gold hair, he could have been one of the fair Persians – and taken her sister's hand, matching her height to a hair. All the King's friends, the other bridegrooms, had given a kind of sigh; she knew that when the King had stepped out to meet her they had been holding their breath. At the end, he and she had had to lead out the procession to the bridal chambers. She had wished that the earth might swallow her.

In the crimson pavilion with its golden bed, he had likened her to a daughter of the gods (her Greek was quite good by then), and she had seen that he meant well; but since nothing could do away those dreadful moments, she would have preferred him to keep silence. He was a powerful presence, and she was shy;

though the defect was his, it was she who had felt like an ungainly tent-pole. All she had been able to think about in the marriage bed was that her father had run away in battle, and Grandmother would never speak his name. She must redeem the honour of her house by courage. He had been kind, and hardly hurt her; but it had all been so strange, so overpowering, she could hardly utter a word. No wonder she had not conceived, and that though he had paid her visits of compliment while still at Susa, and brought her gifts, he had never once had her to bed again.

To crown these miseries, she had known that somewhere in the palace was the King's Bactrian wife, whom he had taken along to India. A stranger to sexual pleasure, Stateira knew no sexual jealousy; but its fiercest torments could hardly have been more wounding than her thoughts of Roxane, Little Star, favourite and confidante. She pictured them lying side by side in tender love-making, intimate talk, amusing gossip, laughter – perhaps at her. As for Bagoas the Persian, she had heard nothing of him at her father's court, and nothing since. She had been carefully brought up.

The King's sojourn at Susa had gone by, its great political events dimly heard of and little understood. Then he had gone on his summer progress to Ekbatana. He had called to take leave of her (would he have done even that, except to see Grandmother?) without a word of when he would send for her or where. He had gone, taking the Bactrian woman; and she had cried all night from shame and anger.

But last spring, when he had come to Susa after the mountain war, it had all been different; no ceremony, no crowds. He had been shut up alone with Grandmother, and it almost seemed that she had heard him weeping. In the evening they had all dined together; they were his family, he said. He looked lean, weather-beaten and weary; but he talked, as she had never heard him do before.

73

At the first sight of Drypetis in her widow's veil, his face had frozen in a dreadful grief; but he had covered it quickly, and enthralled them with tales of India, its marvels and its customs. Then he spoke of his plans to explore the coast of Arabia, to make a road along north Africa and extend his empire westward. And he had said, 'So much to do, so little time. My mother was right; long before now, I should have begotten an heir.'

He had looked at her; and she had known it was she, not the Bactrian, who was the chosen one. She had come to him in a passion of gratitude, which had proved as efficacious as any other ardour.

Soon after he had gone, she knew that she had conceived, and Grandmother had sent him word. It was good that he had summoned her to Babylon. If he was still sick, she would tend him with her own hands. She would make no jealous scenes about the Bactrian. A king was entitled to his concubines; and, as Grandmother had warned her, much trouble could spring from quarrels in the harem.

The soldiers sent to arrest Perdikkas had seen, as he had advised, what had become of them, and did not like it. They went among their comrades, reporting his courage and their discomfiture; and relating, what he himself had first revealed to them, that Meleager had meant to have his head. They had been anxious, restless, volatile. While Meleager was still digesting failure, suddenly they were roaring at his doors like a human sea. The guards on duty abandoned their posts and joined them.

In a cold sweat, he saw himself dying, like a boar at bay, in a ring of spears. With the speed of desperation, he made for the royal rooms.

In a cheerful lamplight, Philip was seated at his evening meal, a favourite dish, spiced venison with pumpkin fritters. A jug of lemonade stood by him; he was not reliable if given wine. When Meleager burst in, he expressed annoyance with his eyes, since his mouth was full. Konon, who was waiting at table, looked up sharply. He was wearing his old sword; he had heard the noise.

'Sir,' panted Meleager, 'the traitor Perdikkas has repented, and the soldiers want him spared. Please go and tell them you have pardoned him.'

Philip bolted his mouthful to reply indignantly, 'I can't come now. I'm having my dinner.'

Konon took a step forward. Looking Meleager in the eye, he said, 'He was taken advantage of.' His hand rested, as if by chance, on his well-polished sword-belt.

Keeping his head, Meleager said, 'My good man, the King will be safer on his throne than anywhere else in Babylon. You know that; you were at Assembly. Sir, come at once.' A persuasive argument occurred to him. 'Your brother would have done so.'

Philip put down his knife and wiped his mouth. 'Is that right, Konon? Would Alexander go?'

Konon's hand fell to his side. 'Yes, sir. Yes, he would go.'

As he was steered to the door, Philip looked back regretfully at his dinner-plate, and wondered why Konon was wiping his eyes.

The army was placated for the time, but far from satisfied. Audiences in the Throne Room were going badly. The envoys' regrets for the late king's untimely death grew less formal and more pointed. Meleager felt his power increasingly unstable, and discipline crumbling by the day.

Meantime, the cavalry had taken counsel. Suddenly one morning they were found to have disappeared. The park was empty of everything but horse-droppings. They had made their way through the crumbling outer walls, and deployed to invest the city. Babylon was under siege.

Much of the terrain outside was swampy; it needed no great force to close the solid causeways and the firm open ground. As planned, the refugees were unmolested. At all the gates, with a hubbub of shouting men, wailing children, burbling camels, bleating goats and cackling poultry, the country people who feared war were pouring into the city, and the city people who feared famine were pouring out.

Meleager could have dealt with a foreign enemy. But he knew too well that he could no longer trust his troops for even the briefest contact with their former comrades. They were forgetting the threat of unborn barbarian heirs, and homesick for the familiar discipline of the old triumphant days, the officers who had linked them to Alexander. Less than a month ago, they had been limbs of a well-knit body directed by a fiery spirit. Now each man felt his isolation in a foreign world. Soon they would take revenge for it.

In this extremity, he went to consult Eumenes.

Throughout the turmoil since Alexander's death, the secretary had gone quietly about his business. A man of humble origins, discovered and trained by Philip, advanced by Alexander, he had been, and remained, uncommitted in the present strife. He had neither joined the Companions nor denounced them. His work, he said, was to carry on the kingdom's business. He had helped with replies to the envoys and the embassies, drawing on his records, and had drafted letters in the name of Philip, but without the title of King (it had been added by Meleager). When pressed to take sides, he would only say that he was a Greek, and politics were the concern of the Macedonians.

Meleager found him at his writing-table, dictating to his clerk, who was taking it down on wax.

Next day he bathed again, and sacrificed the appointed offerings, and after the sacrifice remained in constant fever. Yet even so, he sent for the officers, and ordered them to see that everything was ready for the expedition. He bathed again in the evening, and after that became gravely ill . . .

'Eumenes,' said Meleager, who had been standing ignored in the doorway, 'let the dead rest awhile. You are needed by the living.'

'The living need the truth, before rumour pollutes it.' He motioned to his clerk, who folded his tablet and went out. Meleager outlined his dilemma, aware as he went that the secretary had long since assessed it all, and was waiting impatiently for him to finish. He trailed to a lame conclusion.

Eumenes said without emotion, 'My opinion, since you ask it, is that it is not too late to seek a compromise. And it is too late for anything else.'

Meleager had already been driven to this view, but wanted to have it confirmed by someone else, whom he could blame if things went wrong. 'I accept your advice. That is, if the men agree.'

Eumenes said drily, 'Perhaps the King can persuade them.'

Meleager ignored the double edge. 'One man could do it: yourself. Your honour is unquestioned, your experience known. Will you address the Macedonians?'

Eumenes had long since taken his measure. His own sole loyalty was to the house of Philip and Alexander, who had lifted him from obscurity to prestige and power. Had Philip Arridaios been competent, he would have felt divided loyalties; but he knew what the elder Philip had thought about that, and was for the son of Alexander, unborn, unseen. Yet Philip was the son of Philip his benefactor, who had seen fit to acknowledge him; and Eumenes would protect him if he could. He was a dry, cool man, whose inward feelings few suspected; he had no taste for protestations. He said, 'Very well.'

He was well received. A man in his fifties, spare and erect, with the subtler features of the south yet a soldier's bearing, he said what was needed and no more. He made no attempt to emulate Alexander, whose sense of his audience had been an artist's gift. Eumenes' talent was for sounding reasonable, and keeping to

77

the point. Reassured by hearing their confused misgivings reduced to logic, the Assembly accepted his conclusions with relief. Envoys were sent to the camp of Perdikkas, to treat for terms. As they rode out at sunrise from the Ishtar Gate, crowds of anxious Babylonians watched them off.

They were back before noon. Perdikkas would raise the siege and reconcile the armies, as soon as Meleager and his accomplices gave themselves up to justice.

By now, any discipline still left among the troops in Babylon was self-imposed from dim feelings of dignity, depending chiefly on the popularity of any officer concerned. The returning envoys shouted back their message to anyone who stopped them in the street to ask. While Meleager was still reading Perdikkas' letter, the troops were pouring into the hall of audience, having called their own Assembly.

Eumenes in his business room listened to the rumble of conflicting voices, and the scrape of boot-nails continuing the ruin of the marble floor. A stair in the thickness of the wall had a window which overlooked the hall. He saw that the soldiers had not come armed only with token weapons; despite the heat, they had on their corselets; helmets were worn, not held. A visible division was starting; on one side the men who were for accepting the conditions; on the other, alarmed and angry, those who had committed themselves irretrievably to Meleager. The rest were waiting to have their minds made up for them. This, Eumenes thought, is how civil wars begin. He made his way to the royal rooms.

Meleager was there, standing over Philip and coaching him in a speech. Philip, more aware of his sweating desperation than of anything he said, was fidgeting, not taking in a word. 'What,' asked Eumenes bluntly, 'are you telling him to say?'

Meleager's light-blue eyes, always prominent, were now bloodshot too. 'To say no, of course.'

In the level voice to which even Alexander in anger had paid attention, Eumenes said, 'If he says that, swords will be out before you can take breath. Have you looked in the hall? Look now.'

A big, heavy hand clutched Eumenes' shoulder. He turned, startled. It had never occurred to him that Philip would be strong.

'I don't want to say it. I can't remember it. Tell him I've forgotten.'

'Never mind,' said Eumenes quietly. 'We will think of something else.'

The royal fanfare made a brief silence in the hall. Philip came forward, Eumenes just behind him.

'Macedonians!' He paused, reminding himself of the words the kind, calm man had taught him. 'There is no need for strife. The peacemakers will be the victors here.' He almost turned round for approval; but the kind man had told him not to.

A pleased murmur went round the hall. The King had sounded just like anyone else.

'Do not condemn free citizens ...' prompted Eumenes softly.

'Do not condemn free citizens, unless you wish for civil war.' He paused again; Eumenes, screening his lips with his hand, gave him his lines. 'Let us try again for reconcilement. Let us send another embassy.' He drew a breath of triumph. Eumenes whispered, 'Don't look round.'

There was no serious opposition. All welcomed a breathing-space, and argued only the ways and means; but as the voices grew louder, they brought back to Philip that dreadful day when he had run away from the hall, and they had given him a robe to make him come back again, and then ... Alexander had been lying dead, as if he were carved in marble. Alexander had told him ...

He felt at his head, at the gold diadem they always made him wear when he came out here. He took it off, and, holding it out, walked forward.

Behind him, Meleager and Eumenes gave a united gasp of dismay. He extended, confidingly, the crown to the staring soldiers. 'Is it because I'm King? It doesn't matter. I'd sooner not be King. Here, look; you can give it to someone else.'

It was a curious moment. Everyone had been at stretch, till the half-relief of borrowed time. Now this.

Always prone to emotion – a trait which Alexander had used with unfailing skill – the Macedonians were borne on a flood of sentiment. What a decent, good fellow; what a law-abiding king. Living under his brother's shadow had made him over-modest. No one laughed as he looked about for someone to take the crown. There were reassuring cries of 'Long live Philip, Philip for King!'

With happy surprise, Philip resumed his crown. He had got everything right, and the kind man would be pleased with him. He was still beaming when they shepherded him inside.

Perdikkas' tent was pitched in the shade of a tall palm-grove. He was settled back into surroundings so familiar that he seemed never to have left them; the light bed and folding chair, the armour-stand, the chest (there had been a pile of chests in the days of victorious loot, but that was over), the trestle table.

His brother Alketas and his cousin Leonnatos were with him when the new envoys came. Leonnatos was a long-boned auburn-haired man, who reminded the world of his connections with the royal house by copying Alexander's leonine haircut, even, said his enemies, reproducing its wave with the tongs. His ambitions, though high, were as yet inchoate; meantime he supported Perdikkas.

The envoys had been sent out while their message was considered. Peace was offered in King Philip's name, if his claim was recognized, and his deputy, Meleager, was appointed to share the supreme command with Perdikkas.

Leonnatos tossed back his hair; a gesture rarely used by

Alexander, which in his pupil had become a mannerism. 'Insolence! Do we need to disturb the others?'

Perdikkas glanced up from the letter. 'Here,' he said easily, 'I see the hand of Eumenes.'

'No doubt,' said Alketas, surprised. 'Who else would write it?'

'We will accept. Nothing could be better.'

'What?' said Leonnatos, staring. 'You can't take that brigand into the command!'

'I told you, I see the hand of Eumenes.' Perdikkas stroked the dark stubble on his chin. 'He knew what bait would draw the beast from his lair. Yes, let us have him out. Then we shall see.'

The barge on the Tigris was nearing the bend where the ladies must disembark, to join their caravan and proceed by land.

Dusk was falling. Their tent had been pitched on grass, away from the river-damp and the mosquitoes. They stepped ashore as the first torches were kindled about the camp; there was a smell of burnt fat as the lamb for supper sizzled over the fire.

The chief eunuch of the escort, as he handed Stateira off the gangplank, said softly, 'Madam. The villagers who came selling fruit are saying that the Great King is dead.'

'He warned me of it,' she answered calmly. 'He said there was this rumour among the peasants. It is in his letter; he said we should not heed it.'

Holding up her gown from the rushes heavy with dew, she swept on towards the lamplit tent.

To a spirited music of trumpets and double flutes, the foot-soldiers marched out under the towers of the Ishtar Gate, watched by the relieved Babylonians, to seal their peace with the Companions.

At their head rode Meleager, the King beside him. Philip made a cheerful and seemly figure, wearing the scarlet shoulder-cloak that Alexander had once given him, sitting a well-trained, solid horse that would walk half a length ahead of Konon with the leading-rein. He hummed to himself the tune that the pipes were playing. The air was still fresh with morning. All would be well, everyone was to be friends again. It would be no trouble, now, to go on being King.

The Companions waited on their glossy horses, restive from leisure; their bridles sparkling with gold pendants and silver cheek-rosettes, a fashion set by Alexander for Boukephalas. Dressed in the workmanlike panoply of campaign, plain Thracian helmet and stamped leather cuirass, Perdikkas watched with grim satisfaction the marching phalanx, the gaudy rider leading it. Meleager had had his parade armour adorned with a large gold lion-mask, and his cloak was edged with bullion. So! The beast was drawn.

They accorded Philip the royal salute. Well coached, he acknowledged it and reached out his arm; Perdikkas bore, with resolute affability, the crushing of his huge paw. But Meleager, with a look offensively familiar, had pushed up after, his own hand ready for the clasp of reconciliation. It was with far greater reluctance that Perdikkas returned that grip. He told himself that Alexander had once had to break bread with the traitor Philotas, biding his time; and if he had baulked at it, few of his advance force, including Perdikkas probably, would be alive today. 'It was necessary,' was what Alexander had said.

It was settled that the absent Krateros, considering his high rank and royal lineage, should be appointed Philip's guardian. Antipatros should keep the regency of Macedon. Perdikkas should be Chiliarch of all the Asian conquests, and, if Roxane bore a boy, should be joint guardian with Leonnatos. They were Alexander's kinsmen, which Meleager could not claim; but since he was to share the high command, the distinction did not trouble him. He had begun already to give them his views on the management of the empire.

When all this business was done, Perdikkas made a last proposal.

It was the ancient custom of Macedon, after civil war (another ancient custom) to exorcise discord with a sacrifice to Hekate. He proposed that all the troops in Babylon, horse and foot, should assemble on the plain for the Purification.

Meleager willingly agreed. He planned an impressive appearance, proper to his new rank. He would have his helmet topped with a double crest, like Alexander's at Gaugamela. Conspicuous; and a lucky omen.

Shortly before the rite, Perdikkas asked the Bodyguard to a private supper. He was back, now, at his house in the royal park. The generals rode or strolled over in the falling twilight, under the ornamental trees brought from far and wide by the Persian kings to adorn the paradise. A simple occasion, a meeting of old friends.

When the servants had left them with the wine, Perdikkas said, 'I have chosen the men and briefed them. I think that Philip – I suppose we must get used to calling him that – will have learned his part.'

Till Krateros, his new guardian, could take charge of him, Perdikkas was doing so. Since he lived in his accustomed rooms, with his accustomed comforts, he had scarcely noticed the change, except for the welcome absence of Meleager. He was getting new lessons; but that was to be expected.

'He has taken to Eumenes,' Ptolemy said. 'Eumenes doesn't bully him.'

'Good. He can help to coach him. Let us hope the noise and spectacle won't confuse him . . . There will be the elephants.'

'Surely,' said Leonnatos, 'he has seen elephants by now?'

'Of course he has,' Ptolemy said impatiently. 'He travelled from India with them, in Krateros' convoy.'

'Yes, true.' Perdikkas paused. There was a silence, a sense of more to come. Seleukos, to whose command the elephant corps belonged, said, 'Well?'

'King Omphis,' said Perdikkas slowly, 'had a certain use for them in India.'

There were sharply drawn breaths all round the supper-couches. It was Niarchos who said distastefully, 'Omphis maybe. Never Alexander.'

'Alexander was never in our dilemma,' said Leonnatos unwisely. 'No,' returned Ptolemy. 'Nor like to be.'

Perdikkas cut in, with brusque authority. 'No matter. Alexander knew very well the power of fear.'

The men were astir at cockcrow, to march to the Field of Purgation at break of day, and get the rite finished before the crushing heat of noon.

The rich wheatfields, which bore three crops a year, had been lately harvested. The sun, floating up from the flat horizon, slanted its first beams over miles of stubble, gleaming like golden fur. Here and there, scarlet pennants marked the limits of the parade ground, which were significant to the rite.

Thick and squat, their ancient Assyrian brick mortared with black bitumen, jagged and crumbling with the centuries and with the lassitude of a long-conquered race, the walls of Babylon, impassive, overlooked the plain. They had seen many deeds of men, and looked incapable of amazement. A wide stretch of their battlements had been flattened down into a new, smooth plat-form. Its smoke-blackened bricks still smelled of burning; streams of molten pitch had hardened down its sides. In the ditch below was a great pile of debris; half-charred timber with broken carvings of lions and ships and wings and trophies, still dimly picked out with gilding. It was the remains of the two-hundred-foot pyre on which, not long before his death, Alexander had burned the body of Hephaistion.

Long before dawn, the crowds had started to gather along the walls. They had not forgotten the splendours of Alexander's entry into Babylon; a free show, for it had surrendered peacefully, and he had forbidden his men to plunder it. They remembered the streets flower-strewn and wafted with frankincense; the procession of exotic gifts, gold-bedizened horses, lions and leopards in gilded cages; the Persian cavalry, the Macedonian cavalry; and the gold-plated state chariot with the slight, glittering figure of the victor like a transfigured boy. He had been twenty-five, then. They had hoped for more splendours when he came back from India; but he had given them only that stupendous funeral.

Now they waited, to see the Macedonian men of war march out in their pride, and offer their gods appeasement; the citizens, the soldiers' women and children, the smiths and tentmakers and sutlers and wagoners and whores, the shipwrights and seamen from the galley-slips. They loved a show; but under expectation was a deep unease. A time had gone, a time was coming; and they did not like the auspices of its birth.

Most of the army had crossed the river overnight, by Queen Nitokris' Bridge, or by the innumerable ferryboats of reed and pitch. They slept in the open, and polished their gear for the morrow. The watchers on the walls saw them getting up by torch-light, the sound of their stirring like a murmuring sea. Further away, the Companions' horses whinnied.

Hooves drummed on the timbers of Nitokris' Bridge. The leaders arrived, to direct the sacrifice which would cleanse men's hearts from evil.

The rite was very old. The victim must be dedicated, killed and disembowelled, its four quarters and its entrails carried to the boundaries of the field. The army would march into the space thus purified, would parade, and sing a paean.

The sacrifice was, as it had always been, a dog. The finest and tallest wolfhound had been chosen from the royal kennels; pure white, handsomely feathered. Its docility, as the huntsman led it forward to the altar, promised the good omen of a consenting sacrifice; but when its leash was handed to the sacrificer, it growled and flew at him. Even for its size, it was immensely strong. It took

four men to overpower it and get the knife to its throat; they finished with more of their own blood on them than the victim's.
To make things worse, in the midst of the struggle the King had
rushed up shouting, and only with trouble had been coaxed away.

Hastily, before there could be brooding on the augury, the four
horsemen, appointed to asperse the plain, galloped to its four corners with their bloody offerings. The lumps of white and scarlet
were flung outward with averting invocations to Triple Hekate
and the infernal gods; and the exorcised field was ready to receive
the army of Alexander.

The squadrons and the phalanxes were ready. The burnished
helmets of the horsemen gleamed; their crests of red or white
horsehair, the pennants on their lances, stirred in the morning
breeze. Their short sturdy Greek ponies whinnied at the tall
horses of the Persian troops. Most of the Persian foot had melted
away, trudging dusty caravan trails to their distant villages. The
Macedonian foot was present to a man. They stood in close order,
their whetted spear-tips making a glitter about them.

A square had formed on the wide stubbled plain. Its base was
the wall of Babylon; its left side was the infantry; its right, the
cavalry. Between them, making the fourth side, were the royal
elephants.

Their mahouts, who had come with them from India, and
knew them as a mother knows her child, had worked on them all
yesterday in the high thatched elephant-sheds among the palm-
trees; crooning and clucking and slapping, washing them in the
canal; painting on their foreheads, in ochre or scarlet or green,
sacred symbols enlaced with elaborate scrollwork; draping their
wrinkled flanks with tasselled nets brilliantly dyed and threaded
with gold bullion; fastening jewelled rosettes through slits in their
leather ears; grooming their tails and toes.

It was a year since the mahouts had had a chance to make
their children fine. They had had their schooling on the royal
maidan at Taxila; their children also. They had talked to them

softly, reminding them of old days beside the Indus, while they reddened their feet with henna, as the custom had always been for such occasions. Now in the pink early light they sat proudly on their necks, wearing their ceremonial silks and turbans with peacock feathers, their beards freshly dyed blue or green or crimson; each holding the gold-bound ivory goad, studded with gems, which King Omphis in his magnificence had presented with each elephant to King Iskandar. They had served two famous kings; the world should see that they and their children knew how things were done.

The generals, who had been pouring their libations at the bloody altar, went off to join their detachments. As Ptolemy and Niarchos rode side by side towards the ranks of the Companions, Niarchos rubbed a splash of blood from his bridle-arm, saying, 'The gods below don't seem disposed to cleanse us.'

'Are you surprised?' said Ptolemy. His craggy face was set in creases of disgust. 'Well, God willing, I shall be far away before long.'

'And I, God willing ... Do the dead watch us, as poets say?'

'Homer says the unburied dead do ... He never did let go easily.' He added, not altogether to Niarchos, 'I shall make him what amends I can.'

It was time for the King to take his time-honoured place at the right of the Companions. His horse was ready. He had been well rehearsed. Eager to produce him and get to business, Perdikkas was grinding his teeth in the effort to keep his temper.

'Sir, the army awaits you. The men are watching. You cannot let them see you cry. You are the King! Sir, compose yourself. What is a dog?'

'He was Eos!' Philip was scarlet-faced, tears running into his beard. 'He knew me! We used to play tug-of-war. Alexander said he was strong enough to look after himself. He knew me!'

'Yes, yes,' said Perdikkas. Ptolemy was right, Alexander should have had him smothered. Most of the crowd had thought he was assisting in the sacrifice; but all the omens had been disquieting. 'The gods required him. It is done now. Come.'

Obedient to authority and to a voice far more impressive than Meleager's, Philip wiped his eyes and nose with the corner of his scarlet cloak, and let a groom hoist him up on his embroidered saddle-cloth. His horse, a seasoned veteran of parades, followed each manoeuvre of the one beside it. Philip felt the leading-rein must still be there.

The troops awaited the final ceremony; the sound of the trumpet, giving the note of the paean for them to sing.

Perdikkas, the King beside him, turned to the officers strung out behind him, leading their squadrons. 'Forward!' he barked. 'Slow – march!'

The pipers struck up, instead of the paean, the cavalry walk familiar at parades. The sleek and glittering lines paced smoothly forward, rank upon rank, stepping delicately as they had done on triumphant days in the years of miracle, at Memphis, at Tyre, at Taxila, at Persepolis, and here on this very field. At their head rode Perdikkas, and, carried by his wise charger, the King.

The infantry, taken unawares by this manoeuvre, stood in their ranks and muttered. The decay of discipline showed; spears dipped or leaned askew. They were light parade spears, not the tall sarissas; suddenly their bearers felt half-armed. The advancing cavalry looked formal and ceremonious; had there been some muddle in the briefing? Such doubts, once unthinkable, were common nowadays. Under Meleager their morale was low, their bonding shaky.

Perdikkas gave an order. The left and centre wings reined to a halt; the right, the royal squadron, still advanced. He said to Philip, 'When we stop, sir, make your speech. You remember?'

'Yes!' said Philip eagerly, 'I'm to say—'

'Hush, sir, not now. When I have said "Halt!"'

Neatly, stylishly, the royal squadron advanced till it was fifty feet from the phalanx. Perdikkas halted it.

Philip lifted his arm. He was used by now to his comfortable horse. Set firmly on the embroidered saddle-cloth, in a loud and unexpectedly deep voice, surprising even to himself, he shouted, 'Surrender the mutineers!'

There was a moment of absolute, stunned silence. This was their own, their chosen Macedonian king. The front ranks, staring across incredulous, saw his face strained in the simple effort of a child getting his lesson right; and knew at last what they had done.

Voices broke out among the lines, suddenly raised, appealing for support. They came from Meleager's ringleaders. Among uncertain undertones, their own noise isolated them; it could be heard how few they were.

Slightly at first, looking almost accidental, spaces began to open around them. It was coming home to their former comrades that they themselves were not precisely threatened. And who, after all, had been to blame? Who had foisted on them this hollow king, the tool of anyone who, for the moment, owned him? They forgot the peasant spearman who had first called for Philip's son; remembering only how Meleager had dressed the fool in Alexander's robe, and tried to profane Alexander's body. What did anyone owe his creatures?

Perdikkas beckoned the herald, who rode up with a paper in his hand. In his trained, carrying voice, he read out the names of Meleager's thirty. Meleager's own name was not called.

In his station of honour before the right-wing phalanx, he felt, around him, the last lees of loyalty ebb away, leaving him high and dry. If he stepped forward, challenged Perdikkas' perfidy – that was the signal they were waiting for over there. He froze, the statue of a soldier, sweating cold under the brazen Babylonian sun.

Sixty men dismounted from Perdikkas' squadron. On foot they formed pairs; one holding a set of fetters, the other a coil of rope.

There was a crucial pause. The thirty turned here and there, protesting. Some spears were waved, some voices urged resistance. In the confusion, the trumpet spoke again. Quietly, seeming only to confer with him, Perdikkas had been rehearsing Philip in his next speech.

'Deliver them up!' he shouted. 'Or we will ride against you!' He began, unprompted, to gather up his reins.

'Not now!' hissed Perdikkas, to his relief. He had no wish to go any nearer the spears. They used to point all one way, when Alexander was there.

The spaces widened around the thirty as the fetter-men approached them. Some gave up and submitted; some struggled, but their captors had been picked for strength. All were soon standing, with fettered feet, in the space between the lines. They awaited they knew not what. There had been something odd in the faces of their captors, who had not met their eyes.

'Bind them,' said Perdikkas.

Their arms were trussed to their sides. The cavalry fell back to its first line, leaving once more a hollow square. The fetter-bearers pushed the bound men over; they fell forward helplessly, twisting in their bonds, alone under the sky in the field hallowed to Hekate.

From the far side came the shrilling of an eastern pipe and a roll of drums.

The hot sun flashed on the goads of gold and ivory, King Omphis' gifts. Gently the mahouts pricked the necks of their good children, shouting the old command.

Rising like one, fifty trunks curled backward. The troops heard with awe the high blare of their war-cry. Slowly, then at a steady thudding roll, their tread felt through the ground, the huge bedizened beasts moved forward.

The mahouts in their gleaming silks flung off their well-trained silence. They drummed with their heels, hallooing, slapping the necks of their mounts with their jewelled hands or the butts of the goads. They sounded like boys let out of school.

The elephants fanned out their great ears, and, squealing with excitement, began to run.

A kind of groan, of horror and a dreadful fascination, ran through the watching lines. Hearing it, the men on the ground writhed to their knees, staring about them. At first they looked at the goads; then one man, still struggling, saw the hennaed feet as they drummed closer, and understood. He screamed. Others tried to roll away in the thick grey dust. They had only time to move a yard or two.

With drawn hissing breath, the army of Alexander saw the treading of the human vintage; the bursting of the rind, the scarlet juices running from the pounded flattened flesh. The elephants moved with well-trained intelligence, catching the rolling bodies with their trunks, and steadying them while the feet came down, trumpeting as the war-smell steamed up from the ground.

From his station beside Perdikkas, Philip uttered little breath-less cheers. This was not like the killing of Eos. He was fond of elephants – Alexander had let him ride one – but nobody was hurting them. His eye was filled with their splendid trappings, his ear with their proud brayings. He hardly noticed the bloody mash below them. In any case, Perdikkas had told him that those were all wicked men.

The mahouts, seeing the work well done, calmed and praised their children, who willingly came away. They had done such things in battle, and several still bore the scars. This had been painless and quick. Following their leader, an elephant of great age and wisdom, they formed in line, red to the knees; paraded past Perdikkas and the King, touching brow with trunk in a grave salute; then went their way to the shady elephant-houses, the reward of palm-kernels and melons, the cool pleasant bathe which would sluice off the scent of war.

As indrawn breaths escaped, and the silence in the ranks was breaking, Perdikkas signed to the herald to blow again, and rode forward, a length ahead of the King.

'Macedonians!' he said. 'With the death of these traitors the army is truly cleansed, and fit again to defend the empire. If there is anyone among you who, deserving these men's fate, has today escaped it, let him thank his fortune and learn loyalty. Trumpeter! The paean.'

The stirring air sang out; the cavalry took it up. After a dragging moment, the infantry came in. Its ancient fierceness was reassuring as a lullaby. It took them back to days when they knew who and what they were.

It was over. Meleager left the ground, alone. His confederates were dead; out of all his hangers-on, not one came near him. He might have had the plague.

The servant who had held his horse seemed to look at him not with meant insolence, but with an inquisitiveness which was worse. Behind, in the vacant square, two covered wagons had appeared, and men with pitchforks were heaving the corpses into them. Two cousins and a nephew of his were there; he ought to arrange their funerals, there was no one else. The thought of searching that trampled meat for shreds of identity revived his nausea; dismounting, he vomited till he was cold with emptiness. As he rode on, he was aware of two men behind him. When he stopped they had drawn rein while one adjusted his saddle-cloth. Now they moved on.

He had fought in many battles. Ambition, comradeship, the bright fierce certainty radiated by Alexander, enemies on whom one could revenge and redeem one's fear, all these had carried him along and made him brave. Never before had he faced a lonely end. His mind began to run, like a hunted fox's, upon likely refuge. Above him, thick and ragged and pitch-black, sullen with the blood of worked-out slaves, loomed the walls of Babylon and the crumbling ziggurat of Bel.

He rode through the tunnelled gateway. The men were following. He turned off into narrow streets where women crushed themselves into doorways to give him room; filthy deep courts between eyeless houses, where huddles of thievish men stared at him dangerously. The pursuit was no longer in sight. Suddenly he came out into the wide Marduk Way, the temple just before him. A hallowed place, to Greeks as well as to barbarians. Everyone knew that Alexander had sacrificed there to Zeus and Herakles. Sanctuary!

He hitched his horse to a fig-tree in the weed-grown outer precinct. Through rank greenery a trodden path led to the ruined entry; from the gloom beyond came the universal temple smell of incense, burnt meat and wood-ash, the Babylonian smell of foreign unguents and foreign flesh. As he walked towards it in the dazzling heat, someone stood in the sunlight facing him. It was Alexander.

His heart stopped. Next moment he knew what he was looking at, but still he could not move. The statue was marble, tinted like life; a dedication eight years old from the first Babylonian triumph. It stood at ground-level, the plinth as yet unbuilt. Nude but for a red chlamys across one shoulder, grasping a spear of gilded bronze, Alexander calmly awaited the new temple he had endowed. His deep-set eyes, with their smoke-grey enamel irises, gazed out at Meleager, saying 'Well?'

He stared back, attempting defiance, at the searching face, the smooth young body. You were lean and sinewy and hacked about with scars. Your forehead was creased, you were drawn about the eyes, your hair was fading. What is that idol? An idea ... But memory, once invoked, conjured all too potently the real presence. He had seen the living anger ... He strode on into the temple.

At first the gloom almost blinded him after the harsh sun. Presently, by the light of a smoke-shaft high above, he saw looming in shadow the colossal image of Bel, Great King of Gods, enthroned with fists on knees. His towering mitre almost touched the roof; he was flanked by winged lions with the heads of bearded men. His sceptre was tall as a man; his robe, from which the gold leaf was peeling, glimmered dimly. His face was blackened with age and smoke, but his ivory-inlaid eyes glared fiercely yellow. Before him was the fire-altar, covered with dead ash. No one, it seemed, had told him there was a new king in Babylon.

No matter, an altar was an altar. Here he was safe. Content at first to get back his breath and enjoy the cool from the thick high walls, soon he started to peer about for signs of life. The place seemed deserted; yet he felt a sense of being observed, assessed, considered.

In the wall behind Bel, there was a door set in the dark-glazed tiles. He felt, rather than heard, stirrings of life behind it; but he dared not knock. Authority had drained from him. Time dragged by. He was a temple suppliant, someone should attend to him. He had not eaten since daybreak; behind the ebony door were men, food, wine. But he did not go to tell them he was there. He knew they knew it.

A rusty sunset light lowered in the courtyard. The shadows deepened round frowning Bel, drowning all but his yellow eye-whites. With the dark, he came into possession. The temple seemed peopled with the ghosts of men like stone, treading with stony feet the necks of their conquered enemies, offering their blood to this stone demon. More than for food, Meleager craved for the open skies of a mountain shrine in Macedon, the colour and light of a Greek temple, the gracious and human countenance of its god.

The last light-ray left the courtyard; there was only a square of dusk, and, within, thick dark. Behind the door, low voices sounded and went away.

His horse stamped and snorted outside. He could not stay here and rot; under cover of dark he could be gone. Someone would take him in ... but those who were safe were dead. Better to leave the city now, go west, hire out his sword to some satrap in nearer Asia. But he must get first to his rooms; he would need gold, he had taken bribes from scores of petitioners to the King ... The dusk in the courtyard moved.

Two shadows showed in the glimmering square. They came on, into the broken entry. They were not the shadows of Babylonians. He heard the rasp of drawn swords. 'Sanctuary!' he shouted. 'Sanctuary!'

The door beyond Bel's image opened a crack, lamplight bright in the darkness. He shouted again. The crack closed. The shadows approached, vanishing into blackness. He set his back to the unlit altar and drew his sword. As they came close, it seemed to him he knew them; but it was only the familiar smell and outline of men from home. He called their names aloud, recalling old friendships in the army of Alexander. But the names were wrong; and when they dragged back his head across the altar, it was remembering Alexander that they cut his throat.

Stripped of its banners and plumes, wreathed with cypress and weeping willow, the lamenting caravan paced slowly under the Ishtar Gate. Perdikkas and Leonnatos, warned by the forerunners of its coming, had ridden to meet the wife of Alexander and tell her that she was widowed. Bareheaded, their hair still cropped in mourning, they rode beside the wagon train, which had now the air of a cortège. The princesses sobbed, their women keened and chanted ritual threnodies. The keepers of the gate heard wondering these new tears, so long after the days prescribed.

In the harem, the rooms of the chief wife waited, perfumed and immaculate, as ordained by Bagoas two months before. The Warden had feared that after Alexander's death Roxane would demand them; but to his deep relief she seemed settled where she was. No doubt her pregnancy had quietened her. So far, thought the Warden, so good.

Perdikkas escorted Stateira there, concealing his surprise at her arrival; he had supposed her established in Susa to bear her child in quiet. Alexander, she said, had summoned her. He must have done so without informing anyone. He had done some very odd things, after Hephaistion's death.

Handing her down the wagon steps to the Warden, he thought her more beautiful than at the Susa wedding. Her features had purity of line, the Persian delicacy, fined down by pregnancy and fatigue, which had put smudges of faint cobalt under her large dark eyes; their lids with their long silky lashes looked almost transparent. The Persian kings had always bred for looks. Her hand on the curtain was long-fingered and smooth as cream. She had been wasted on Alexander; he himself, a good inch taller, could have stepped out with her very well. (His own Susa bride, a swarthy Median chosen for exalted birth, had greatly disappointed him.) At least, Alexander had finally had the sense to get a child on her. It should be certain of beauty, if nothing else.

Leonnatos, assisting Drypetis, noted that her face, though still immature, held distinguished promise. He too had a Persian wife; but this need not keep him from looking higher. He rode off in thought.

An obsequious train of eunuchs and waiting-women led the princesses through Nebuchadrezzar's devious corridors to the once-familiar rooms. As in childhood, they felt after the space and light of the Susa palace the frowning Babylonian strength. But then they came through to the sunny courtyard, the fishpool where they had floated their boats of split bamboo in lily-leaf archipelagos, or reached shoulder-deep after the carp. In the room that had been their mother's they were bathed and scented and fed. Nothing seemed changed since that summer eight years before, that watershed of time, when their father had brought them here before marching to meet the King of Macedon. Even the Warden had remembered them.

Their meal done, their attendants dismissed to be settled in their own quarters, they explored their mother's clothes-chest.

The scarves and veils still released their memory-stirring scent. Sharing a divan, looking out on the sunlit pool, they recollected that other life; Stateira, who had been twelve when it ended, reminding Drypetis, who had been only nine. They talked of their father whom Grandmother would never name, remembering him in their mountain home before he had been King, laughing as he tossed them eight feet in the air. They thought of their mother's perfect face, framed in the scarf with the seed-pearls and gold beads. Everyone gone – even Alexander – except for Grandmother.

They were growing sleepy when a shadow crossed the doorway. A child came in, with two silver cups on a silver tray. She was about seven years old, enchantingly pretty, with a blend of Persian and Indian looks, cream-skinned, dark-eyed. She dipped a knee without spilling a drop. 'Honoured ladies,' she said carefully. This, clearly, was all her Persian, learned by heart. They kissed and thanked her; she dimpled at them, said something in Babylonian, and trotted away.

The silver cups were misted with coolness, pleasant to touch. Drypetis said, 'She had beautiful clothes, and gold earrings. She wasn't a servant's child.'

'No,' said Stateira, worldly-wise. 'And if not, you know, she must be our half-sister. I remember, Father brought most of the harem here.'

'I'd forgotten.' Drypetis, a little shocked, looked around her mother's room. Stateira had gone out into the courtyard, to call back the child again. But she had gone, and no one was in sight; they had told their women they wished to rest undisturbed.

Even the palms seemed bleached in the dazzling heat. They lifted the cups, admiring their chased birds and flowers. The drink tasted of wine and citron, with a delicate bitter-sweet tang.

'Delicious,' said Stateira. 'One of the concubines must have sent it to make us welcome; she was too shy to come herself. Tomorrow we might invite her.'

The heavy air was still perfumed with their mother's clothes. It felt homely, secure. Her grief for her parents, for Alexander, grew dim and drowsy. This would be a comforting place to bear his child in. Her eyelids closed.

The shadow of the palms had barely slanted when pain awoke her. She thought at first that her child must be miscarrying, till Drypetis clasped her belly and screamed aloud.

Perdikkas, as Regent of Asia, had moved into the palace. He was seeing petitioners in the small audience room when the Warden of the harem appeared, unheralded, his clay-grey face and evident terror having passed him through the guards. Perdikkas, after one look, had the room cleared and heard him.

When the princesses began to cry for help no one had dared go near them; everyone in hearing had guessed the cause. The Warden, desperate to exculpate himself (he had in fact had no hand in it) had not waited for them to breathe their last. Perdikkas ran with him to the harem.

Stateira lay sprawled on the divan, Drypetis on the floor where she had rolled in her death-throes. Stateira drew her last gasp as Perdikkas entered. At first, transfixed with horror, he was aware of no one else in the room. Then he perceived that in the ivory chair before the toilet-table a woman was sitting.

He strode across and stared down at her, silent, hardly able to keep his hands from her throat. She smiled at him.

'You did this!' he said.

Roxane raised her brows. 'I? It was the new king. Both of them said so.' She did not add that, before the end, she had taken pleasure in undeceiving them.

'The King?' said Perdikkas furiously. 'Who will believe that, you accursed barbarian bitch?'

'All your enemies. They will believe it because they wish. I shall say that he sent the draught to me too; but when these fell sick I had not yet drunk it.'

'You . . .' For a while he vented his rage in curses. She listened calmly. When he paused, for sufficient answer she laid her hand over her womb.

He looked away at the dead girl. 'The child of Alexander.'

'*Here*,' she said, 'is the child of Alexander. His only child . . . Say nothing, and so will I. She came here without ceremony. Very few will know.'

'It was *you* who sent for her!'

'Oh, yes. Alexander did not care for her. I did as he would have wished.'

For a moment she felt real fear; his hand had dropped to his sword-hilt. Still gripping it, he said, 'Alexander is dead. But if ever again you say that of him, when your brat is born I will kill you with these hands. And if I knew it would take after you, I would kill you now.'

Growing cool again, she said, 'There is an old well in the back court. No one draws from it, they say the water is foul. Let us take them there. No one will come.'

He followed her. The well-cover had lately been loosened from its seal of grime. As he lifted it a smell of ancient mould came out.

He had no choice and knew it. Proud as he was, ambitious and fond of power, he was loyal to Alexander, dead as alive. His son should not, if Perdikkas could prevent it, enter the world branded as a poisoner's child.

He returned in silence, going first to Drypetis. Her face was soiled with vomit; he wiped it with a towel before he carried her to the dark hole of the well. When she had slipped from his hands, he heard her clothes brushing the brick till, about twenty feet down, she reached the bottom. He could tell, then, that the well was dry.

Stateira's eyes were staring open, her fingers clutched the stuff of the divan. The eyes would not close; while Roxane waited impatiently, he went to the chest for something to cover her face, a veil stitched with scarab-wings. When he began to move her, he felt wet blood.

'What have you done to her?' He drew back in revulsion, wiping his hand on the coverlet.

Roxane shrugged. Stooping, she lifted the robe of embroidered linen. It could be seen that Alexander's wife in her death-pangs had brought forth his heir.

He stared down at it, the four-month manikin, already human, the sex defined, even the nails beginning. One of the fists was clenched as if in anger, the face with its sealed eyes seemed to frown. It was still tied to its mother; she had died before she could pass the afterbirth. He drew his dagger and cut it free.

'Come, hurry,' said Roxane. 'You can see that the thing is dead.'

'Yes,' said Perdikkas. It hardly filled his hands, the son of Alexander, the grandson of Philip and Darius, carrying in its threadlike veins the blood of Achilles and of Kyros the Great.

He went again to the chest. A scarf trailed out, stitched with seed-pearls and gold beads. Carefully, like a woman, he wrapped the creature in its royal shroud, and gave it its own journey to the burial-place, before returning to send its mother after it.

Queen Sisygambis sat playing chess with the Head Chamberlain. He was an elderly eunuch with a distinguished past going back to King Ochos' reign. An expert survivor of countless court intrigues, he played a canny game, and offered more challenge than the waiting-ladies. She had invited him to relieve her boredom, and mere courtesy demanded that she should attend to him. She brooded over the ivory armies on the board. Now that the girls were gone with their young attendants, the harem seemed to have been left behind by time. Everyone here was old.

The Chamberlain saw her lethargy and guessed the cause. He fell into one or two of her traps and rescued himself, to enliven the game. In a pause, he said, 'Did you find, when the King was here, that he had remembered your instruction? You said, before he marched east, that he had promise if he would apply his mind.'

She said smiling, 'I did not test him. I knew he would have forgotten.' For a moment, reflected from the distance, rays of vitality seemed to surge through the muted room. 'I used to tell him it was called the royal war-game, and for my sake he pretended to care who won. But when I scolded him and told him he could do better, he said, "But, Mother, these are *things*."'

'He is not a man for sitting still, indeed.'

'He needed more rest. It was not the time to go down to Babylon. Babylon has always been to winter in.'

'It seems he means to winter in Arabia. We shall scarcely see him this year. But when he marches, for sure he will send Their Highnesses back to you, as soon as the child is born and the lady Stateira can travel.'

'Yes,' she said a little wistfully. 'He will want me to see the child.' She returned to the board, and moved an elephant to threaten his vizier. A pity, he thought, that the boy had not sent for her; she doted on him still. But, as she had said, it was no time to go down to Babylon, and she was turned eighty.

They had finished the game, and were drinking citron, when the Chamberlain was summoned, urgently, by the commander of the garrison. When he came back, she looked at his face, and grasped the arms of her chair.

'Madam . . .'

'It is the King,' she said. 'He is dead.'

He bowed his head. It was as if her body had known already; at his first word the chill had reached her heart. He came up quickly, in case she was going to fall; but after a moment she motioned him to his chair, and waited for him to speak.

He told her as much as he had learned, still watching her; her face was the colour of old parchment. But she was not grieving only; she was thinking. Presently she turned to a table near her chair, opened an ivory casket, and took out a letter.

'Please read me this. Not the substance only. Word for word.'

His sight was not what it had been; but by bringing it close he could see quite clearly. He translated scrupulously. At *I have been sick, and there is ignorant talk that I am dead*, he looked up and met her eyes.

'Tell me,' she said, 'is that his seal?'

He peered at it; at a few inches, the detail was sharp enough. 'It is his likeness, and a good one. But it is not the royal seal. Has he used this before?'

Without speaking, she put the casket into his hands. He looked at the letters, written in elegant Persian by a scribe; his eye caught one ending: *I commend you, dear Mother, both to your gods and mine, if indeed they are not the same, as I think they are.* There were five or six letters. All had the royal seal, Olympian Zeus enthroned, his eagle perched on his hand. She read the answer in his face.

'When he did not write to me ...' She took the casket and set it down beside her. Her face was pinched as if with cold, but without astonishment. All her middle years had been passed in the dangerous reign of Ochos. Her husband had had royal blood enough to be in danger whenever the King felt insecure. Trusting almost no one, he had trusted her and told her everything. Intrigue, revenge and treachery had been daily weather. In the end, Ochos had killed him. She had believed that he lived again in her tall son; his flight from Issos had almost killed her with shame. In the desolate tent, the young conqueror was announced, to visit the family his enemy had abandoned. For the children's sake, performing dignity like a well-trained animal its trick, she had knelt to the tall handsome man before her. He stepped back; everyone's dismay made her aware of a frightful error; she began to bow to the smaller man she had overlooked. He had taken her hands and raised her, and for the first time she saw his eyes. 'Never mind, Mother ...' She had had Greek enough for that.

The Chamberlain, the old survivor, almost as pale as she, was trying not to look at her. Just so someone had looked away when her husband had had his last summons to the court.

'They have murdered him.' She said it as something evident.

'This man says the marsh-fever. It is common at Babylon in summer.'

'No, they have poisoned him. And there is no word of my granddaughters?'

He shook his head. There was a pause while they sat silent, feeling disaster strike on their old age, a mortal illness, not to be shaken off.

She said, 'He married Stateira for policy. It was my doing he got her with child.'

'They may still be safe. Perhaps in hiding.'

She shook her head. Suddenly she sat up in her chair, like a woman thinking, Why am I idling like this, when I have work to do?

'My friend, a time is over. I shall go to my room now. Farewell. Thank you for your good service in all these years.'

She read new fear in his face. She understood it; they had both known Ochos' reign. 'No one will suffer. No one will be charged with anything. At my age, to die is easy. When you go, will you send my women?'

The women found her composed and busy, laying out her jewels. She talked to them of their families, advised them, embraced them and divided her jewels among them, all but King Poros' rubies, which she kept on.

When she had bidden them all farewell, she lay down on her bed in the inner room, and closed her eyes. They did not try, after her first refusals, to get her to eat or drink. It was no kindness to trouble her, still less to save her alive for the coming vengeance. For the first few days, they left her alone as she had ordered. On the fourth, seeing her begin to sink, one or other kept watch beside her; if she knew of them, she did not turn them away. On the fifth day at nightfall, they became aware that she was dead; her breathing had been so quiet, no one could be sure when it had ended.

Galloping day and night, by dromedary, by horse, by mountain mule as the terrain needed, man throwing to man the brief startling news, the King's Messengers had carried their tidings of death from Babylon to Susa, Susa to Sardis, Sardis to Smyrna, along the Royal Road which Alexander had extended to reach the Middle Sea. At Smyrna, all through the sailing season, a despatch-boat was ready to carry his letters to Macedon.

The last courier of the long relay had arrived at Pella, and given Perdikkas' letter to Antipatros.

The tall old man read in silence. Whenever Philip had gone to war he had ruled Macedon; since Alexander crossed to Asia he had ruled all Greece. The honour which had kept him loyal had also stiffened his pride; he looked far more regal than had Alexander, who had looked only like himself. It had been a joke of his among close friends that Antipatros was all white outside, with a purple lining.

Now, reading the letter, knowing he would not after all be replaced by Krateros (Perdikkas had made that clear) his first thought was that all south Greece would rise as soon as the news had broken. The news itself, though shocking, was a shock long half-expected. He had known Alexander from his cradle; it had always been inconceivable that he would make old bones. Antipatros had almost told him so outright, while he was preparing to march to Asia without begetting an heir.

It had been a false move to hint at his own daughter; the boy could hardly have done better, but it had made him feel trapped, or used. 'Do you think I've time now to hold wedding feasts and wait about for children?' he had said. He could have had a half-grown son, thought Antipatros, with our good blood in him. And now? Two unborn half-breeds; and meantime, a pride of young lions, slipped off the leash. He remembered, not without misgivings, his own eldest son.

He remembered, too, a scrap of gossip from the first year of the young king's reign. He had told someone, 'I don't want a son of mine reared here while I'm away.'

And that was behind it all. That accursed woman! All through his boyhood she had made him hate his father, whom he might have admired if let alone; she'd shown him marriage as the poisoned shirt of Herakles (that, too, a woman's doing!), then, when he'd reached the age for girls and could have had his pick, she was outraged that he'd taken refuge with another boy. He could have done far worse than Hephaistion – his father had, and got his death by it – but she could not live with what she'd brought about, had made an enemy where she could have had an ally; and all she'd achieved was to come second instead of first. No doubt she'd rejoiced to hear of Hephaistion's death. Well, she had another to hear of now, and let her make the best of it.

He checked himself. It was unseemly to mock a mother's grief for her only son. He would have to send her the news. He sat down at his writing-table with the wax before him, seeking some decent and kindly word for his old enemy, some fitting eulogy of the dead. A man, he reflected, whom he had not seen for more than a decade, whom he thought of still as a brilliantly precocious boy. What had he looked like, after those prodigious years? Perhaps one might still see, or guess. It would be something suitable with which to end his letter, that the body of the King had been embalmed to the likeness of life, and only awaited a worthy bier to begin its journey to the royal burial ground at Aigai. *TO QUEEN OLYMPIAS, HEALTH AND PROSPERITY* . . .

It was full summer in Epiros. The high valley on its mountain shoulder was green and gold, watered from the deep winter snows which Homer had remembered. The calves were fattening, the sheep had yielded their fine soft wool, the trees bent, heavy with fruit. Though it was against all custom, the Molossians had prospered under a woman's rule.

The widowed Queen Kleopatra, daughter of Philip and sister of Alexander, stood with the letter of Antipatros in her hand, looking out from the upper room of the royal house to the further mountains. The world had changed, it was too soon to know how. For Alexander's death she felt awe without grief, as for his life she had felt awe without love. He had entered the world before her, to steal her mother's care, her father's notice. Their fights had stopped early, in the nursery; after that they had not been close enough. Her wedding day, the day of their father's murder, had made her a pawn of state; him it had made a king. Soon he had become a phenomenon, growing with distance more dazzling and more strange.

Now for a while, the paper in her hand, she remembered the days when, boy and girl with only two years between them, their parents' ceaseless strife had brought them together in defensive collusion; remembered, too, how if their mother had to be braved in one of her dreadful weeping rages, it had been he who would always go and face the storm.

She laid Antipatros' letter down. The one for Olympias was on the table beside it. He would not face her now; she herself must do it.

She knew where she would find her; in the ground-floor state guest-room where she had been first received to attend the funeral of Kleopatra's husband, and where she had since remained. The dead king had been her brother; more and more she had encroached on the kingdom's business, while she pursued through a horde of agents the feud with Antipatros which had made her position in Macedon impossible.

Kleopatra set resolutely the square chin she had inherited from Philip, and, taking the letter, went down to her mother's room.

The door was ajar. Olympias was dictating to her secretary.

Kleopatra, pausing, could hear that she was drawing up a long indictment against Antipatros, going back ten years, a summary of old scores. '*Question him on this, when he appears before you, and do not be deceived if he claims that . . .*' She paced about impatiently while the scribe caught up.

Kleopatra had meant to behave, on so traditional an occasion, as a daughter should; to show the warning of a grave sad face, to utter the usual preparations. Just then her eleven-year-old son came in from a game of ball with his companion pages; a big-boned auburn boy with his father's face. Seeing her hesitating at the door, he looked at her with an air of anxious complicity, as if sharing her caution before the seat of power.

She dismissed him gently, wanting to hug him to her and cry, 'You are the King!' Through the door she saw the secretary busily scratching the wax. He was a man she hated, a creature of her mother's from long ago in Macedon. There was no knowing what he had known.

Olympias was a few years over fifty. Straight as a spear, and slender still, she had begun to use cosmetics as a woman does who means only to be seen, not touched. Her greying hair had been washed with camomile and henna; her lashes and brows were lined in with antimony. Her face was whitened, her lips, not her cheeks, were faintly reddened. She had painted her own image of herself, not enticing Aphrodite but commanding Hera. When, catching sight of her daughter in the doorway, she swept round to rebuke the interruption, she was majestic, even formidable.

Suddenly, Kleopatra was swept by a red surge of anger. Stepping forward into the room, her face like stone, making no gesture to dismiss the scribe, she said harshly, 'You need not write to him. He is dead.'

The perfect silence seemed deepened by each slight intrusive sound; the click of the man's dropped stylus, a dove in a nearby tree, the voices of children playing a long way off. The white cream on Olympias' face stood out like chalk. She looked straight before her. Kleopatra, nerved for she could not tell what elemental furies, waited till she could no longer bear it. Quiet with remorse, she said, 'It was not in war. He died of fever.'

Olympias motioned to the scribe. He made off, leaving his papers in disorder. She turned towards Kleopatra.

'Is that the letter? Give it to me.'

Kleopatra put it into her hand. She held it, unopened, waiting, dismissive. Kleopatra shut the thick door behind her. No sound came from the room. His death was something between the two of them, as his life had been. She herself was excluded. That, too, was an old story.

Olympias grasped the stone mullion of the window, its carvings biting, unfelt, into her palms. A passing servant saw the staring face and thought, for a moment, that a tragic theatre mask had been propped there. He hurried on lest her sightless gaze should light on him. She stared at the eastern sky.

It had been foretold her before his birth. Perhaps as she slept he had stirred within her – he had been restless, impatient for life – and it had made her dream. Billowing wings of fire had sprung from her body, beating and spreading till they were great enough to waft her into the sky. Still the fire had streamed from her, an ecstasy, flowing over mountains and seas till it filled the earth. Like a god she had surveyed it, floating on the flames. Then, in a moment, they were gone. From some desolate crag where they had abandoned her, she had seen the land black and smoking, sparked with hot embers like a burned-out hillside. She had started wide awake, and put out her hand for her husband. But she was eight months gone, he had long since found other bedfellows. She had lain till morning, remembering the dream.

When, later, the fire was running over the wondering world, she had said to herself that all life must die, the time was far off and she would not live to see it. Now all was fulfilled; she could only clench her hands upon the stone and affirm that it must not be. It had never been in her to accept necessity.

Down on the coast, where the waters of Acheron and Kokytos met, was the Nekromanteion, the Oracle of the Dead. She had gone there long ago, when for her sake Alexander had defied his father, and they had both come here in exile for a time. She remembered the dark and winding labyrinth, the sacred drink, the blood-libation which gave the shades strength to speak. Her father's spirit had stirred in the gloom and spoken faintly, saying her troubles would soon end and fortune shine on her.

It would be a long day's ride, she must set out at dawn. She would make the offering and take the draught and go into the dark, and her son would come to her. Even from Babylon, from the world's end, he would come ... Her mind paused. What if the first-comers were those who had died at home? Philip, with Pausanias' dagger in his ribs? His new young wife, to whom she had offered poison or the rope? Even for a spirit, even for Alexander, it was two thousand miles from Babylon.

No; she would wait till his body came; that, surely, would bring his spirit nearer. When she had seen his body, his spirit would seem less strange. For she knew that she feared its strangeness. When he left, he had been still a boy to her; she would receive the body of a man nearing middle age. Would his shade obey her? He had loved her, but seldom obeyed.

The man, the ghost, slipped from her grasp. She stood there empty. Then, uninvoked, vivid to sight and touch, came the child. The scent of his hair, nuzzled into her neck; the light scratches on his fine skin, his grazed dirty knees; his laughter, his anger, his wide listening eyes. Her dry eyes filled; tears streaked her cheeks with eye-paint; she bit on her arm to muffle her crying.

By the evening fire, she had told him the old family tales of Achilles handed down by word of mouth, always reminding him that it was from her side that the hero's blood came down to him. When schooldays began he had come eagerly to the *Iliad*, colouring it with the Achilles of the tales. Reaching the *Odyssey*, he came upon Odysseus' visit to the land of shades. ('It was in my country, in Epiros, that he spoke with them.') Slowly and solemnly, looking out past her at a reddening sunset sky, he had spoken the words.

'Achilleus,
no man before has been more blessed than you, nor ever will be. Before, when you were alive, we Argives honoured you as we did the gods, and now in this place you have great authority over the dead. Do not grieve, even in death, Achilleus.'

So I spoke, and he in turn said to me in answer, 'O shining Odysseus, never try to console me for dying. I would rather follow the plough as thrall to another man, one with no land allotted him and not much to live on, than be a king over all the perished dead.'

Because he did not cry when he was hurt, he was never ashamed of tears. She saw his eyes glitter, fixed on the glowing clouds, and knew that his grief was innocent; only for Achilles, parted from hope and expectation, the mere shadow of his glorious past, ruling over shadows of past men. He had not yet believed in his own mortality.

He said, as if it were her he was reassuring, 'But Odysseus did console him for dying, after all, it says so.'

So I spoke, and the soul of the swift-footed scion of Aiakos stalked away in long strides across the meadow of asphodel, happy for what I had said of his son, and how he was famous.

'Yes,' she had said. 'And after the war his son came to Epiros, and we are both descended from him.'

He had considered it. Then: 'Would Achilles be happy if I were famous too?'

She had bent and ruffled his hair. 'Of course he would. He would stride through the asphodel and sing.'

She let go of the window-column. She felt faint and ill; going to her inner room she lay down and wept fiercely. It left her almost too weak to stand, and at last she slept. At dawn, she woke to the recollection of great grief, but her strength was almost recovered. She bathed and dressed and painted her face, and went to her writing-table. TO PERDIKKAS, REGENT OF THE ASIAN KINGDOMS, PROSPERITY ...

On the roof of their house, a few miles inland from Pella, Kynna and Eurydike were practising with the javelin.

Kynna, like Kleopatra, was one of Philip's daughters, but by a minor marriage. Her mother had been an Illyrian princess, and a noted warrior, as the customs of her race allowed. After a border war against her formidable old father Bardelys, Philip had sealed the peace treaty with a wedding, as he had done several times before. The lady Audata would not have been his choice for her own sake; she was comely, but he had trouble remembering which sex he was in bed with. He had paid her attention enough to get one daughter on her, given them a house, maintained them, but seldom called on them till Kynna was of marriageable age. Then he had given her in wedlock to his nephew Amyntas, his elder brother's child, the same whom the Macedonians had passed over in his infancy, to make Philip King.

Amyntas, obedient to the people's will expressed in the Assembly, had lived peaceably through Philip's reign. Only when conspirators were planning the King's murder had he fallen to temptation, and agreed when the deed was done to accept the throne. For this, when it came to light, Alexander had put him on trial for treason, and the Assembly had condemned him.

Kynna, his wife, had withdrawn from the capital to his country estate. She had lived there ever since, rearing her daughter in the martial skills her Illyrian mother had taught her. It was her natural bent; it was an occupation; and she felt, instinctively, that one day it would be of use. She had never forgiven Amyntas' death. Her daughter Eurydike, only child of an only child, had known as long as she could remember that she should have been a boy.

The core of the house was a rugged old fort going back to the civil wars; later the thatched house had been built beside it. It was on the flat roof of the fort that the woman and the girl were standing, throwing at a straw man propped on a pole.

A stranger could have taken them for sisters; Kynna was only just thirty, Eurydike was fifteen. They both took after the Illyrian side, tall, fresh-faced, athletic. In the short men's tunics they wore for exercise, their brown hair plaited back out of their way, they looked like girls of Sparta, a land of which they knew almost nothing.

Eurydike's javelin had left a splinter in her palm. She pulled it out, and called in slave-Thracian to the tattooed boy who was bringing back the spears from the target, and who should have seen they were rubbed smooth. As he worked they sat to rest on a block of stone set for an archer, stretched and took deep breaths of the mountain air.

'I hate the plains,' said Eurydike. 'I shall mind that more than anything.'

Her mother did not hear; she had been looking out at the hill-road that led between the village huts to their gate. 'A courier is coming. Come down and change your clothes.'

They climbed down the wooden steps to the floor below, and put on their second-best dresses. A courier was a rare event, and such people reported what they saw.

His gravity and sense of drama almost made Kynna ask his errand before she broke the seal. But it would be undignified; she sent him off to be fed before she read Antipatros' letter.

'Who is dead?' asked Eurydike. 'Is it Arridaios?' Her voice was eager.

Her mother looked up. 'No. It is Alexander.'

'*Alexander!*' She spoke with disappointment more than grief. Then her face lightened. 'If the King is dead, I needn't marry Arridaios.'

'Be quiet!' said her mother. 'Let me read.' Her face had changed; it held defiance, resolution, triumph. The girl said anxiously, 'I needn't marry him, Mother? Need I? Need I?'

Kynna turned to her with glowing eyes. 'Yes! Now indeed you must. The Macedonians have made him King.'

'*King?* How can they? Is he better, have his wits come back?'

'He is Alexander's brother, that is all. He is to keep the throne warm for Alexander's son by the barbarian. If she has a son.'

'And Antipatros says I am to marry him?'

'No, he does not. He says that Alexander had changed his mind. He may be lying, or not. It's no matter which.'

Eurydike's thick brows drew together. 'But if it's true, it might mean Arridaios is worse.'

'No, Alexander would have sent word; the man is lying, I know it. We must wait to hear from Perdikkas in Babylon.'

'Oh, Mother, let us not go. I don't want to marry the fool.'

'Don't call him the fool, he is King Philip, they have named him after your grandfather ... Don't you see? The gods have sent you this. They mean you to right the wrong that was done your father.'

Eurydike looked away. She had been barely two when Amyntas was executed, and did not remember him. He had been a burden on her all her life.

'Eurydike!' The voice of authority brought her to attention. Kynna had set herself to be father as well as mother, and done it well. 'Listen to me. You were meant for great things, not to grow old in a village like a peasant. When Alexander offered you his brother's hand to make peace between our houses, I knew that it

113

was destiny. You are a true-born Macedonian and royal on both sides. Your father should have been King. If you were a man, they would have chosen you in Assembly.'

The girl listened in a growing quiet. Her face lost its sullenness; aspiration began to kindle in her eyes.

'If I die for it,' said Kynna, 'you shall be reigning Queen.'

Peukestes, Satrap of Persia, had withdrawn from his audience chamber to his private room. It was furnished in the manner of the province, except for the Macedonian panoply on the armour-stand. He had changed from his formal robe to loose trousers and embroidered slippers. A tall fair man, with features of lean refinement, he had curled his hair Persian-style; but at Alexander's death, conforming to Persian custom, had shaved it to the scalp, instead of cropping it as he would in Macedon. When exposed it still felt chilly; to warm his head he had put on his cap of office, the helmet-shaped kyrbasia. This gave him an unintended look of state; the man he had summoned approached him with downcast eyes, and prepared to go down in the prostration.

Peukestes looked at him startled, at first not knowing him; then he put out his hand. 'No, Bagoas. Get up, be seated.'

Bagoas rose and obeyed, acknowledging, with some gesture of the face, Peukestes' smile. His dark-circled eyes looked enormous; there was just enough flesh on him to display the elegance of his skull. His scalp was naked of hair; when it began to grow he must have shaved again. He looked like an ivory mask. Yes, something must be done for him, Peukestes thought.

'You know,' he said, 'that Alexander died leaving no will?'

The young eunuch made an assenting gesture. After a pause he said, 'Yes. He would not surrender.'

'True. And when he understood that the common fate of man had overtaken him, his voice had gone. Or he would not have forgotten his faithful servants ... You know, I kept vigil for him at the shrine of Sarapis. It was a long night, and a man had time to think.'

'Yes,' said Bagoas. 'That was a long night.'

'He told me once that your father had an estate near Susa, but was unjustly dispossessed and killed while you were young.' No need to add that the boy had been castrated and enslaved, and sold to pleasure Darius. 'If Alexander could have spoken, I think he would have bequeathed you your father's land. So I shall buy out the man who has it, and give it you.'

'The bounty of my lord is like rain on a dry river-bed.' A beautiful movement of the hand went with it, like an absent-minded reflex; he had been a courtier since he was thirteen. 'But my parents are both dead; so are my sisters, at least if they were fortunate. I had no brother; and I shall have no son. Our house was burned to the ground; and for whom should I rebuild it?'

He has made a grave-offering of his beauty, Peukestes thought; now he is waiting to die. 'And yet, it might please your father's shade to see his son restore his name with honour in the ancestral place.'

Bagoas' hollow eyes seemed to consider it, like something infinitely distant. 'If my lord, in his magnanimity, would give me a little time ... ?'

He wants only to be rid of me, Peukestes thought. Well, I can do no more.

That evening Ptolemy, on the eve of departing to the satrapy of Egypt, was his guest at supper. Since it seemed they might never meet again, their talk grew reminiscent. Presently it turned upon Bagoas.

'He could make Alexander laugh,' Ptolemy said. 'I have heard them often.'

'You would not think so now.' Peukestes related the morning's interview. The talk passed to other things; but Ptolemy, who had a mind that wasted nothing, pleaded tomorrow's press of business and left the party early.

Bagoas' house stood in the paradise a little way from the palace. It was small but elegant; often Alexander had spent an evening there. Ptolemy remembered the torches in their sconces by the door, the sound of harps and flutes and laughter, and, sometimes, the eunuch's sweet alto singing.

At first sight all was dark. Nearer, he saw a dim single lamp yellowing a window. A small dog barked; after a while, a sleepy servant peered through the grille, and said the master had retired. These courtesies over, Ptolemy went round towards the window.

'Bagoas,' he said softly, 'it's Ptolemy. I am going away for ever. Won't you bid me goodbye?'

There was only a short silence. The light voice said, 'Let the lord Ptolemy in. Light the lamps. Bring wine.'

Ptolemy entered, politely disclaiming ceremony, Bagoas politely insisting. A taper was brought, light shone on his ivory head. He was dressed, in the formal clothes he must have worn to call on Peukestes. They looked now as if he had slept in them; he was buttoning the jacket up. On the table was a tablet covered with score-marks; what was erased looked like an attempt to draw a face. He pushed it aside to make room for the wine-tray, and thanked Ptolemy for the honour of his visit with impeccable civility; peering at him blankly from deep hollow eyes, as the slave kindled the lamps, like an owl revealed in daylight. He looked a little mad. Ptolemy thought, Am I too late already?

He said, 'You have truly mourned for him. I too. He was a good brother.'

Bagoas' face remained inexpressive; but tears ran from his eyes in silence, like blood from an open wound. He brushed them absently away, as one might a lock of hair which has a habit of straying, and turned to pour the wine.

'We owed him tears,' Ptolemy said. 'He would have wept for us.' He paused. 'But, if the dead care for what concerned them in life, he may be needing more from his friends than that.'

The ivory mask under the lamp turned to a face; the eyes, in which desperation was tempered by older habits of gentle irony, riveted themselves on Ptolemy's. 'Yes?' he said.

'We both know what he valued most. While he lived, honour and love; and, after, undying fame.'

'Yes,' Bagoas said. 'So ...?'

With his new attention had come a profound and weary scepticism. Why not, thought Ptolemy; three years among the labyrinthine intrigues of Darius' court before he was sixteen – and, lately, why not indeed?

'What have you seen since he died? How long have you been shut up here?'

Raising his large dark disillusioned eyes, Bagoas said with a vicious quiet, 'Since the day of the elephants.'

For a moment Ptolemy was silenced; the wraith had hardened, dauntingly. Presently he said, 'Yes, that would have sickened him. Niarchos said so, and so did I. But we were overborne.'

Bagoas said, answering the unspoken words, 'The ring would have gone to Krateros, if he had been there.'

There was a pause. Ptolemy considered his next move; Bagoas looked like a man just waked from sleep, considering his thoughts. Suddenly he looked up sharply. 'Has anyone gone to Susa?'

'Bad news travels fast.'

'News?' said Bagoas with unconcealed impatience. 'It is protection they will need.'

Suddenly, Ptolemy remembered something said by his Persian wife, Artakama, a lady of royal blood bestowed by Alexander. He was leaving her with her family till, as he had said, the affairs of Egypt were settled. He had been uneasy with a harem, its claustral and stifling femininity, after the free-and-easy Greek hetairas. He meant his heir to be a pure-bred Macedonian, and had, in fact, offered for one of Antipatros' many daughters. But there had been some piece of gossip ... Bagoas' eyes were boring into his.

'I have heard a rumour – worth nothing I dare say – that a Persian lady came from Susa to the harem here, and was taken sick and died. But—'

Bagoas' breath hissed through his teeth. 'If Stateira has come to Babylon,' he said in a soft deadly voice, 'of course she has been taken sick and died. When first the Bactrian knew of me, I would have died of the same sickness, if I had not given some sweet-meats to a dog.'

Ptolemy felt a sickening conviction. He had been with Alexander on that last visit to Susa, been brought once to dine with Sisygambis and the family. Pity and disgust contended with the thought that if this had happened, and Perdikkas had con-doned it, his own design was justified.

'Alexander's fame,' he said, 'has not been very well served since the gods received him. Men who cannot match his great-ness of soul should try at least to honour it.'

Bagoas brooded on him, thoughtful, in a grey calm; as if he stood on the threshold of a door he had been going out of, and could not be sure it was worth while to turn back. 'Why have you come?' he said.

The dead are not respectful, Ptolemy reflected. Good, it saves time.

'I will tell you why. I am concerned for the fate of Alexander's body.'

Bagoas hardly stirred, but his whole frame seemed to change, losing its lethargy, becoming wiry and tense. 'They took their oath!' he said. 'They took it on the Styx.'

'Oath . . . ? Oh, all that is over. I'm not talking of Babylon.'

He looked up. His hearer had come in from the threshold; the door of life had swung to behind him. He listened, rigidly.

'They are making him a golden bier; nothing less is due to him. It will take the craftsmen a year to finish. Then, Perdikkas will have it sent to Macedon.'

'To *Macedon*!' The look of stunned shock quite startled

Ptolemy, his homeland customs taken for granted. Well, so much the better.

'That is the custom. Did he not tell you how he buried his father?'

'Yes. But it was *here* they . . .'

'Meleager? A rogue and a halfwit, and the rogue is dead. But in Macedon, that is different. The Regent is nearly eighty; he may be gone before the bier arrives. And his heir is Kassandros, whom you know of.'

Bagoas' slender hand closed in a sinewy fist. 'Why did Alexander let him live? If he had only given me leave. No one would have been the wiser.'

I don't doubt it, thought Ptolemy, glancing at his face. 'Well, in Macedon the King is entombed by his rightful heir; it confirms his succession. So, Kassandros will be waiting. So will Perdikkas; he will claim it in the name of Roxane's son – and, if there is no son, maybe for himself. There is also Olympias, who is no mean fighter either. It will be a bitter war. Sooner or later, whoever holds the coffin and the bier will need the gold.'

Ptolemy looked for a moment, and looked away. He had come remembering the elegant, epicene favourite; devoted certainly, he had not doubted that, but still, a frivolity, the plaything of two kings' leisure. He had not foreseen this profound and private grief in its priestlike austerity. What memories moved behind those guarded eyes?

'This, then,' he said inexpressively, 'is why you came?'

'Yes. I can prevent it, if I have help that I can trust.'

Bagoas said, half to himself, 'I never thought they would be taking him away.' His face changed and grew wary. 'What do you mean to do?'

'If I have word of when the bier sets out, I will march from Egypt to meet it. Then, if I can treat with the escort – and I think I can – I will take him to his own city, and entomb him in Alexandria.'

Ptolemy waited. He saw himself being weighed. At least there were no old scores between them. Less than delighted when Alexander took a Persian to his heart and bed, he had been distant to the boy, but never insolent. Later, when it was clear the youth was neither venal nor ambitious, simply a tactful and well-mannered concubine, their chance meetings had been unstrained and easy. However, one did not sleep with two kings and remain naive. One could see the assessment he was making now.

'You are thinking of what I stand to gain; and why not? A great deal, of course. It may even make me a king. But – and this I swear before the gods – never a king of Macedon and Asia. No man alive can wear the mantle of Alexander, and those who grasp at it will destroy themselves. Egypt I can hold, and rule it as he wanted. You were not there, it was before your time; but he was proud of Alexandria.'

'Yes,' said Bagoas. 'I know.'

'I was with him,' said Ptolemy, 'when he went to Ammon's oracle at Siwah in the desert, to learn his destiny.'

He began to tell of it. Almost at once the worldly alertness in his hearer's face had faded; he saw the single-minded absorption of a listening child. How often, he thought, must that look have drawn the tale from Alexander! The boy's memory must read like a written scroll. But to hear it from someone else would give some new and precious detail, some new sight-line.

He took trouble, therefore, describing the desert march, the rescuing rain, the guiding ravens, the serpents pointing as they lay, the sands' mysterious voices; the great oasis with its pools and palm-glades and wondering white-robed people; the rocky acropolis where the temple was, with its famous courtyard where the sign of the god was given.

'There is a spring in a basin of red rock; we had to wash our gold and silver offerings in it, to cleanse them for the god, and ourselves as well. It was icy cold in the hot dry air. Alexander of course they did not purify. He was Pharaoh. He carried his own divinity. They led him into the sanctuary. Outside, the light was all shimmering white, and everything seemed to ripple in it. The entrance looked black as night, you'd have thought it would have blinded him. But he went in as though his eyes were on distant mountains.'

Bagoas nodded, as if to say, 'Of course; go on.'

'Presently we heard singing, and harps and cymbals and sistra, and the oracle came out. There is not room for it inside the sanctuary. He stood there to watch it, somewhere in the dark.

'The priests came out, forty pairs of them, twenty before and twenty behind the god. They carried the oracle like a litter, with long shoulder-poles. The oracle is a boat. I don't know why the god should speak through a boat on land. Ammon has a very old shrine at Thebes. Alexander used to say it must have come first from the river.'

'Tell me about the boat.' He spoke like a child who prompts an old bedtime story.

'It was long and light, like the bird-hunters' punts on the Nile. But sheathed all over with gold, and hung with gold and silver votives, all kinds of little precious things swinging and glittering and tinkling. In the middle was the Presence of the god. Just a simple sphere.

'The priest came out into the court with Alexander's question. He had written it on a strip of gold and folded the gold together. He laid it on the pavement before the god, and prayed in his own tongue. Then the boat began to live. It stayed where it was, but you could see it quicken.'

'You saw it,' said Bagoas suddenly. 'Alexander said he was too far.'

'Yes, I saw. The carriers stood with empty faces, waiting; but they were like flotsam on a still river-pool, before the flow of the river lifts it. It does not stir yet; but you know the river is under all.

'The question lay shining in the sun. The cymbals sounded a

slow beat and the flutes played louder. Then the carriers began to sway a little where they stood, just as flotsam sways. You know how the god answers: back for no, forward for yes. They moved forward like all one thing, a skein of water-weed, a drift of leaves, till before the question they stopped, and the prow dipped. Then the trumpets sounded, and we waved our hands and cheered.

'We waited, then, for Alexander to come out from the sanctuary. It was hot; or we thought so, not having yet been in Gedrosia.' A shadowy smile replied to him. They were both survivors of that dreadful march.

'At last he came out with the high priest. I think more had happened than he had come to ask. He came out with the awe still in him. Then, I remember, he blinked in the sudden brightness, and shaded his eyes with his hand. He saw us all, and looked across and smiled.'

He had looked across at Hephaistion and smiled; but there was no need to say so.

'Egypt loved him. They welcomed him with hymns as their saviour from the Persians. He honoured all their temples that Ochos had profaned. I wish you had seen him laying out Alexandria. I don't know how far it has gone up now, I don't trust the governor; but I know what he wanted, and when I am there I shall see it done. There is only one thing he left no mark for: the tomb where we shall honour him. But I know the place, by the sea. I remember him standing there.'

Bagoas' eyes had been fixed upon a light-point on his silver cup. He raised them. 'What is it you want done?'

Silently, Ptolemy caught his breath. He had been in time.

'Stay here in Babylon. You refused Peukestes' offer; no one else will make you his concern. Bear with it if they take your house for some creature of Perdikkas'. Stay till the bier is ready and you know when it will set out. Then come to me. You shall have a house in Alexandria near where he lies. You know that in Macedon that could not be.'

In Macedon, he thought, the children would stone you in the street. But you have guessed that; there is no need to be cruel.

'Will you take my hand on it?' he said.

He held out his big-boned right hand, calloused from the spear-shaft and the sword, its seams picked out by the lamp as he held it open. Pale, slender and icy cold, Bagoas' hand took it in a precise and steady grip. Ptolemy remembered that he had been a dancer.

In a last fierce spasm, Roxane felt her infant's head thrust out of her. More gently, with swift relief, turned by a skilful midwife, the moist body slid after. She stretched her legs out, dripping with sweat and panting; then heard the child's thin angry cry.

Shrill with exhaustion, she cried out, 'A boy, is it a boy?'

Acclamation and praise and good-luck invocations rose in chorus. She gave a great groan of triumph. The midwife lifted the child to view, still on its blue-white cord. From the half-screened corner where he had vigilantly watched the birth, Perdikkas came forward, confirmed the sex, uttered a conventional phrase of good omen, and left the room.

The cord was tied, the afterbirth delivered; mother and child were washed with warm rose-water, dried, anointed. Alexander the Fourth, joint King of Macedon and Asia, was laid in his mother's arms.

He nuzzled for warmth, but she held him at arm's length to look at him. He was dark-haired.

The midwife, touching the fine fluff, said it was birth-hair that would fall away. He was still red and crumpled, his face closed up in the indignation of the newly born; but she could see through the flush an olive, not a rosy colouring. He would be dark, a Bactrian. And why not? Alone in a harsh alien element, missing the womb's blind comfort, he began to cry.

She lowered him to her body, to take the weight from her arms. He hushed; the slave-girl with the feather fan had come back to the bedside; after the bustle, the women with silence and soft feet were setting to rights the rooms of the Royal Wife. Beyond the door, the courtyard with its fishpool lay under the mild winter sun. Reflected light fell on the dressing-table, and on the gold and silver toilet-set that had been Queen Stateira's; her jewel-box stood beside it. All was triumph and tranquillity.

The nurse came fussing up with the antique royal cradle, plated with gold and time-yellowed ivory. Roxane drew the coverlet over the sleeping child. Under her fingers, almost disguised by the elaborate embroidery, was a smear of blood.

Her stomach heaved. When she had moved into this room it had all been refurbished and redraped. But the bed was a fine one and they had not changed it.

She had stood by while Stateira writhed and tried to clutch at her and moaned 'Help me! Help me!' and fumbled blindly with her clothes. Roxane had flung them back to see her beaten enemy, her son's rival, come naked into the world he would never rule. Could it be true that the thing had opened its mouth and cried? Disturbed by her tightened fingers, the infant wailed.

'Shall I take him, madam?' said the nurse timidly by her side. 'Would madam like to sleep?'

'Later.' She softened her grip; the child quietened and curled itself against her. He was a king and she was a king's mother; no one could take it from her. 'Where is Amestrin? Amestrin, who put this filthy cover on my bed? It stinks, it is disgusting, give me something clean. If I see it again, your back will know it.'

After panic scurryings, another cover was found; the state one, a year's work in Artaxerxes' day, was whisked out of sight. The baby slept. Roxane, her body loosening into comfort from its labour, sank into drowsiness. In a dream she saw a half-made child with the face of Alexander, lying in blood, its grey eyes staring with anger. Fear woke her. But all was well; he was dead and could do nothing, it was her son who would rule the world. She slept again.

322 B.C.

The army of King Philip was encamped in the Pisidian hills. Perdikkas, blood-spattered and smeared with ash, was picking his way down a stony path strewn with dead men and abandoned weapons. Above him, circling a cloud of stinking smoke, vultures and kites made exploring swoops, their numbers thickening as news of the banquet spread. The Macedonians, prompter than the birds, scavenged the charred ruins of Isaura.

Spared by Alexander because they had surrendered without a fight, the Isaurians had been left with orders to pull down the robber fort from which they had plagued their neighbors, and to live peaceably. In his long absence they had murdered his satrap and fallen back into old ways. This time, from bad consciences or from having less trust in Perdikkas than in Alexander, they had defended their craggy nest to the bitter end. When their outworks fell, they had locked into their houses their goods, their wives and children, set timber and thatch alight, and to the hellish music of the fires had hurled themselves on the Macedonian spears.

Some fifteen years of war had made Perdikkas almost nightmare-proof; in a few days he would be dining out on the story; but with the stench of burnt flesh still hanging in the air he had had enough for today, and had welcomed the news that a courier awaited him in his camp below. His brother Alketas, a hard man and his second in command, would oversee the raking of the cinders for half-melted silver and gold. His helmet was scorching hot; he took it off and wiped his sweating forehead.

From the royal tent of dyed and emblazoned leather, Philip came out and ran towards him. 'Did we win?' he asked.

He was armed in cuirass and greaves, a thing he had insisted on. In Alexander's day, when he had followed the army much as now, he had worn civil dress; but now that he was King, he knew what was due to him. He had in fact been eager to fight; but, used to obedience, had not insisted, since Alexander had never let him do it. 'You're all bleeding,' he said. 'You ought to see a doctor.'

'It's a bath I need.' When alone with his sovereign, Perdikkas dispensed with formality. He told him as much as it was good for him to know, went to his own tent, cleaned himself, put on a robe, and ordered the courier brought.

This person was a surprise. The letter he brought was reticent and formal; he himself had much to say. A hardy grizzled man in his early sixties, with a missing thumb lost at Gaugamela, he was a minor Macedonian nobleman, and not so much a messenger as an envoy.

With elation, tinged by well-founded misgiving, Perdikkas reread the letter to gain time for thought. *TO PERDIKKAS, REGENT OF THE ASIAN KINGDOMS, FROM KLEO-PATRA, DAUGHTER OF PHILIP AND SISTER OF ALEXANDER, GREETING.* After the usual well-wishings, the letter glanced at their cousinship, recalled his distinguished services to Alexander, and proposed a conference, to discuss *matters concerning the well-being of all the Macedonians.* These matters were not specified. The last sentence disclosed that the Queen had set out already from Dodona.

The envoy, affecting negligence, was toying with his wine-cup.

Perdikkas coughed. 'Am I to hope that if I should beg the honour of the lady Kleopatra's hand, my suit would be graciously received?'

The envoy gave a reassuring smile. 'So far, the Kings have been elected only by the Macedonians in Asia. Those in the homeland might like their own chance to choose.'

Perdikkas had had a gruelling and hideous, even though successful, day. He had come back for a bath, a rest and a drink, not to be offered at short notice the throne of Macedon. Presently he said, with a certain dryness, 'Such happiness was beyond my hopes. I feared she might still be mourning Leonnatos.'

The veteran, whom Perdikkas' steward had refreshed while he was waiting, settled into his chair. The wine was strong, with no more than a splash of water, Perdikkas having felt he needed it. The diplomat gave way visibly to the soldier.

'I can tell you, sir, why he was her first choice, for what it's worth. She remembered him from her childhood at home. He climbed a tree once, to get down her cat for her, when he was a boy. You know what women are.'

'And in the end I believe they did not meet?'

'No. When he crossed from Asia to fight the southern Greeks, he'd only time to raise his troops in Macedon and ride on down. Bad luck that he fell before our victory.'

'A pity that his troops were so cut up. I hear he fought while he could stand. A brave man; but hardly the stuff of kings?'

'She was well out of it,' said the soldier bluntly. 'All her friends tell her so. It was a fancy; she soon got over grieving. Lucky for her she has the chance to think better now.' He tipped back his cup; Perdikkas refilled it. 'If she had seen *you*, sir, at Gaugamela . . .'

This word of power diverted them into reminiscence. When they came back to business, Perdikkas said, 'I suppose the truth is, she wants to get away from Olympias.'

The envoy, flushed and relaxed, planked down his cup and

leaned his arm on the table. 'Sir. Let me tell you, between ourselves, that woman is a Gorgon. She's eaten that poor girl piece by piece, till she's hardly mistress of her house, let alone the kingdom. Not that she lacks spirit; but left as she is, without a man to stand by her, there's no fighting Olympias. She has the Molossians treating her like a queen. She *is* a queen. She looks like a queen; she has the will of a king. And she's Alexander's mother.'

'Ah. Yes ... So Kleopatra has a mind to leave her Dodona, and make a bid for Macedon?'

'She's Philip's daughter.'

Perdikkas, who had been thinking quickly, said, 'She has a son by the late king.' He had no wish to be caretaker for a stepson.

'*He'll* inherit at home, his granddam will see to that. Now Macedon ... No woman has ever reigned in Macedon. But Philip's daughter, married to a royal kinsman who's ruled like a king already ...' Abruptly, remembering something, he hitched at his belt-purse, and brought out a flat package wrapped in embroidered wool. 'She sent you this, seeing it's a long time since you had a sight of her.'

The portrait was painted with skill, in encaustic wax on wood. Even allowing for convention, which smoothed away personality like a blemish, it could be seen that she was Philip's daughter. The strong hair, the thick upswept eyebrows, the resolute square face, had defeated the artist's well-meant insipidity. Perdikkas thought, Two years younger than Alexander – about thirty-one, now. 'A queenly and gracious lady,' he said aloud. 'A dowry in herself, kingdom or no.' He found more of this kind to say, while he played for time. Danger was great; ambition also. Alexander had taught him long ago to assess, decide, and act.

'Well,' he said, 'this is serious business. She needs something more than a yes. Let me sleep on this. When you dine with us tonight, I'll tell them all you brought a letter from Olympias. She's forever writing.'

'I have brought one. She approves, as you may well suppose.'

Perdikkas set the thick roll aside, summoned the steward to find his guest a lodging, and, left alone, sat with his elbows on the rough camp-table and his head between his hands.

Here he was found by his brother Alketas, whose servants carried two rattling sacks filled with stained, smoked gold, cups and arm-rings and necklaces and coin; the Isaurians had been successful robbers. The slaves gone, he showed Perdikkas the loot, and was annoyed by his abstraction. 'Not squeamish?' he said. 'You were there in India, when the men thought the Mallians had killed Alexander. You should have a strong stomach after that.'

Perdikkas looked at him in irritation. 'We'll talk later. Is Eumenes back in camp? Find him, he can bath and eat later, I have to see him now.'

Eumenes appeared quite shortly, washed, combed and changed. He had been in his tent, dictating his memoir of the day's events to Hieronymos, a young scholar who, under his patronage, was writing a chronicle of the times. His light compact body was toughened and tanned from the campaign; soon he would be riding north to get his satrapy of Kappadokia in order. He greeted Perdikkas with a calm alert expectancy, sat down, and read the letter Perdikkas handed him. At the end, he allowed himself a slight lift of the brows.

Looking up from the scroll, he said, 'What is she offering? The regency or the throne?' Perdikkas understood him perfectly. He meant, Which do you plan to take?

'The regency. Or would I be talking to you now?'

'Leonnatos did,' Eumenes reminded him. 'And then decided that I knew too much.' He had, in fact, barely escaped with his life, having affirmed his loyalty to Alexander's son.

'Leonnatos was a fool. The Macedonians would have cut his throat; and they'd cut mine if I disinherited Alexander's boy. If they elect him when he comes of age, so be it. But he's the Bactrian's son; by that time, they may not be so fond of him.

Then we'll see. Meantime, I'll have been King in all but name for fifteen years or so, and I shan't complain.'

'No,' said Eumenes grimly. 'But Antipatros will.'

Perdikkas sat back in his leather-slung camp-chair, and stretched out his long legs. 'That's the crux. Advise me. What shall I do with Nikaia?'

'A pity indeed,' said the Greek, 'that Kleopatra didn't write a few months sooner.' He sat reflecting, like a mathematician before a theorem. 'You won't need her now. But you've sent her the betrothal gifts. She's the Regent's daughter. And she's on her way.'

'I offered for her too soon. Everything seemed in chaos; I thought I should make sure of an ally while I could ... Alexander would never have tied his hands like that. *He* always made alliances when he could dictate the terms.' It was rarely, now, that he was self-critical; he must be disturbed, Eumenes thought. He tapped absently at the letter. Perdikkas noted that even his nails were clean.

'Antipatros puts out his daughters as a fisherman puts out lines.'

'Well, I took the bait. What now?'

'You've bitten at the bait. The hook's not yet in your belly. Let us think.' His neat thin lips came together. Even on campaign, he shaved every day. Presently, looking up, he said crisply, 'Take Kleopatra. Take her now. Send an escort to meet Nikaia; tell her you're sick, wounded; be civil, but have her taken home. Act at once, before Antipatros is ready. Or he'll hear of it, you won't know how or when; and he'll act before *you're* ready.'

Perdikkas bit his lip. It sounded prompt and decisive; probably it was what Alexander would have done. Except that he would never have put himself in need of it. Among these doubts, a disturbing thought intruded: Eumenes hated Antipatros. The Regent had been snubbing him ever since he had been a junior secretary, advanced by Philip because of his quick mind. The old man had all the prejudices of his race against the effete, fickle, subtle men of the south. Eumenes' loyalty, his distinguished war record, had never made any difference. Even when he was in Asia as Chief Secretary to Alexander, Antipatros had tried often to go over his head. Alexander, whom it irritated, had made a point of replying through Eumenes.

Now that Perdikkas had been counselled to burn his boats, he felt a certain flinching. He said to himself that here was an old enmity, of the kind that warps a man's better judgement.

'Yes,' he said, affecting gratitude. 'You are right. I'll write by her envoy tomorrow.'

'Better use word of mouth. Letters can go astray.'

'. . . But I'll tell her, I think, that I've already married Nikaia. It will be true by the time it reaches her. I'll ask her to wait till I can decently get free. I'll put the palace of Sardis at her disposal, and ask her to consider us betrothed in secret. That will give me room to manoeuvre.'

Seeing Eumenes looking at him in silence, he felt the need to justify himself. 'If there were only Antipatros to consider . . . But I don't like what I hear of Ptolemy. He's raising too big an army down in Egypt. It only needs one satrap to make a kingdom of his province, and the empire will fall apart. We must wait a little and see what he means to do.'

A bland winter sun shone down through the columned window into Ptolemy's small audience room. It was a handsome house, almost a small palace, built for himself by the previous administrator, whom Ptolemy had executed for oppression. The slight rise commanded a view of new straight streets and handsome public buildings, their pale unweathered stone touched up with paint and gilding. New wharves and quays fringed the harbour; hoists and scaffolding surrounded a couple of nearly finished temples ordered by Alexander. Another temple, less advanced, but promising to be the most imposing, stood near the waterfront, where it would dominate the prospect for incoming ships.

Ptolemy had had a busy but congenial morning. He had seen the chief architect, Deinokrates, about the sculpture on the temples; some engineers, who were replacing insanitary canals with covered drains; and the heads of several nomes, to whom he had restored the right to collect taxes. This, to the Egyptians who had suffered under his predecessor, meant something like a fifty per cent tax reduction. A rapacious man, resolved to execute his commission and enrich himself as well, he had imposed forced levies and forced labour, extorted fortunes by threats to kill the sacred crocodiles, or to pull down villages for building-sites (which he would do in the end, when he had squeezed them dry). Moreover, he had done all this in the name of Alexander, which had so enraged Ptolemy that he had gone through the administration like a consuming fire. It had made him extremely popular, and he had remained so.

He was now busy recruiting. Perdikkas had only allowed him two thousand men when he took over the satrapy. He had found, when he got there, its garrison almost mutinous, the men's pay in arrears while the interest was being skimmed off it. Things were different now. Ptolemy had not been the most brilliant of Alexander's commanders; but he was reliable, resourceful, brave and loyal, all things Alexander valued; and, above all, he was good at looking after his men. He had fought under Philip before Alexander had his first command; the pupil of two great masters, he had learned from both. Trusted, sufficiently feared, and liked, he was apt with small touches of personal concern. Before his first year was out, thousands of active veterans settled in Alexandria were begging to re-enlist; by now, volunteers were arriving by land and sea.

He had not allowed this to inflate ambition. He knew his limits, and had no wish for the stresses of boundless power. He had what he had wanted, was content with it and meant to keep it; with luck, to add a little more. His men were well paid and fed; they were also well trained.

'Why, Menandros!' he said warmly as the last applicant came

in. 'I thought you were in Syria. Well, this is an easier climb than the Birdless Rock. You got here without a rope.'

The veteran, recognized at sight as a hero of that renowned assault, grinned with delight, feeling that after an uncertain year he had arrived where he belonged. The interview was happy. Ptolemy decided to take a break in his inner sanctum. His chamberlain, an Egyptian of great discretion, scratched at the door.

'My lord,' he murmured, 'the eunuch of whom you spoke has come from Babylon.'

The broken nose in Ptolemy's craggy face pointed like a hound's at a breast-high scent. 'I'll see him here,' he said.

He waited in the pleasant, cool, Greek-furnished room. Bagoas was shown in.

Ptolemy saw a Persian gentleman, soberly suited in grey, equipped for travel with a businesslike sword-belt, its slots well stretched by the weapons left outside. He had grown his hair; a modest length of it fringed his round felt hat. He looked handsome, lean, distinguished and of no particular age. Ptolemy supposed he must be twenty-four.

He made the graceful genuflection due to a satrap, was invited to sit, and offered the wine which had awaited the morning's leisure. Ptolemy made the proper enquiries about his health and journey; he knew better than to be precipitate with a Persian. It was clear that the midnight encounter in the paradise was to be remembered in substance only; etiquette was to be preserved. He remembered from old days Bagoas' infinite resources of tact.

The courtesies fully observed, he asked, 'What news?'

Bagoas set aside his wine-cup. 'They will be bringing him out from Babylon two months from now.'

'And the convoy? Who's in command?'

'Arybbas. No one has questioned it.'

Ptolemy sighed audibly with relief. Before marching south, he had proposed this officer to design and supervise the bier, citing his expertise; he had devised several important shrines for

Alexander, and could handle craftsmen. Not cited was that he had served in India under Ptolemy's command, and been on excellent terms with his commander.

'I waited,' said Bagoas, 'till I was sure of it. They would need him, in case of mishap, to see the bier repaired.'

'You have made good time, then.'

'I came up the Euphrates, and then by camel to Tyre. The rest by sea. Forty days in all.'

'You will be able to rest awhile, and still be in Babylon before they start.'

'If God permits. As for the bier, in a hundred days it could hardly reach the coast. The roadmakers are out already, smoothing the way. Arybbas reckons it will travel ten miles a day on level ground, or five over hills, if sixty-four mules pull it. To bring it from Asia into Thrace, they plan to bridge the Hellespont.'

The quiet madness of the house in the park was gone. He spoke with the concentration of a man going about his chosen calling. He looked lean and fit after his long journey.

'You have seen it then?' Ptolemy asked. 'Is it worthy of Alexander?'

Bagoas considered. 'Yes, they have done all that men can.'

Arybbas must have excelled himself, Ptolemy thought. 'Come to the window. There is something you must see.'

He pointed to the temple rising on the waterfront, the sea, pale blue under the mild sky, shining between the unfinished columns.

'There is his shrine.'

For a moment, the reticent face beside him lit and glowed. Just so, Ptolemy remembered from another life, the boy had looked when Alexander rode past in a victory parade.

'It should be ready in another year. The priests of Ammon would like him to go to Siwah; they say it would have been his wish. I have considered it, but I think this is his place.'

'When you have seen the bier, sir, you will know it could never go to Siwah. If once its wheels sank into sand, a team of elephants

134

could not drag it free ... That is a fine temple. They have worked quickly to get so far.'

Ptolemy had known that this must sometime be met. He said gently, 'It was begun before I came. Alexander approved the plan himself. It is the temple he ordered for Hephaistion ... He did not know how soon he himself would need it.'

Bagoas' face returned to agelessness. He gazed in silence at the sunlit shafts of stone. Presently he said calmly, 'Hephaistion would give it him. He would have given him anything.'

Except his pride, thought Ptolemy; that was his secret, it was why Alexander felt him as a second self. But it was only possible because they were boys together. Aloud he said, 'Most men would welcome Alexander as a guest, even in death. Well, let us come to ways and means.'

At the table he unlocked a silver-clasped document-box. 'This letter I shall give you when you leave, along with funds for your journey. Do not deliver it in Babylon. When the bier sets out, no one will wonder that you wish to follow it. Do nothing till it reaches Thapsakos – the Syrian border will be soon enough – and give it to Arybbas then. It commits him to nothing. It says I shall meet him at Issos, to do honour to Alexander. He will hardly suppose, I think, that I shall come alone.'

'I will see,' said Bagoas coolly, 'that he is prepared.'

'Don't lose the letter in Babylon. Perdikkas would send an army corps for escort.' Wasting no words, Bagoas smiled.

'You have done well. Tell me, have you heard anything of Roxane's child? He must be walking now. Does he favour Alexander?'

One of Bagoas' fine brows moved upward a very little. 'I myself have not seen him. But the harem people say he takes after his mother.'

'I see. And King Philip, how is he?'

'Very well in health. He has been allowed a ride on an elephant, which made him happy.'

'So. Well, Bagoas, you have earned my gratitude; trust in it from now on. When you are rested, see the city; it will be your home.'

Bagoas made the elegant half-prostration of the gentleman to the satrap, learned at Darius' court, and took his leave.

Later, as the sun declined towards the western desert, he walked down to the temple. This was the evening promenade of the Alexandrians, who would pause to notice the progress of the work; off-duty soldiers of Macedon and Egypt, merchants and craftsmen from Greece and Lydia and Tyre and Cyprus and Judaea; wives and children, and hetairas looking for trade. The crowd was not yet oppressive; the city was still young.

The workmen on the site were packing their tools in their straw bags; the nightwatchmen were coming with their cloaks and food-baskets. From the ships tied to the waterfront men were going ashore; the ship-guards on board kindled torches whose tarry smell hung over the water. As dusk fell, on the temple terrace a burning cresset was hoisted on a tall pole. It was not unlike the one Alexander used to have by his tent in central Asia, to show where his headquarters was.

The strollers drifted towards home; soon no one was about but the watchmen and the silent traveller from Babylon. Bagoas looked at Hephaistion's house, where Alexander would be his guest for ever. It was fitting, it was what he would have wished, and after all it made no difference. What was, was, as it had always been. When Alexander breathed his last, Bagoas had known who would be awaiting him beyond the River. That was why he had not killed himself; the thought was not to be borne of intruding on that reunion. But Alexander had never been ungrateful, he had never turned love away. One day, after faithful service done, there would be, as there had always been, a welcome.

He turned back towards the palace guest-house, where they

were lighting the lamps. Alexander would be served worthily here. Nothing else had ever mattered.

In the manor-house of the late Prince Amyntas, Kynna and Eurydike were trimming each other's hair. They were preparing for their journey. Till they were out of Macedon, they planned to travel as men.

The Regent, Antipatros, was besieging stubborn forts in the mountains of Aitolia, where the last of the Greek revolt still smouldered on. He had taken most of his troops. This was their chance.

'There,' said Kynna, standing back with the shears. 'Many young men wear it as long as that, since Alexander set the fashion.'

Neither of them had had to sacrifice much hair; it was strong and wavy, not long. A maid was called to sweep up the clippings. Eurydike, who had already prepared her mule-packs, went to the stack of spears in the corner, and chose out her favourite javelins.

'We shan't have much chance to practise on the road.'

'Let us hope,' said Kynna, 'that we may not need them in earnest.'

'Oh, robbers won't attack ten men.' They were taking an escort of eight retainers. She glanced at her mother's face, and added, 'You're not afraid of Olympias?'

'No, she is too far away, we shall be in Asia before she hears.'

Eurydike looked again. 'Mother, what is it?'

Kynna was pacing the room. On stands and tables and shelves were the family treasures, her dead husband's heritage from his royal father, and pieces from her dowry; her own father, King Philip, had given her a handsome wedding. She was wondering how much she dared entrust to such a journey. Her daughter could not go empty-handed, but . . .

'Mother, there is something . . . Is it because we've heard nothing from Perdikkas?'

'Yes. I don't like it.'

'How long since you wrote to him?'

'I did not. It was proper for him to write.' She turned to a shelf and picked up a silver cup.

'There is something else you've not told me. I know there is. Why is Antipatros against our going? Have they betrothed the King to someone else? ... Mother, don't pretend you don't hear me. I'm not a child. If you don't tell me, I won't go.'

Kynna turned round, with a face that would have meant a whipping a few years back. The tall girl, implacable, stood her ground.

Kynna put down the cup with its boar-hunt chasing. She bit her lip.

'Very well, since you will have it; I dare say it's better. Alexander said frankly it was an empty marriage. He offered you wealth and rank; I dare say you could have gone home after, for all he cared.'

'You never told me so!'

'No, because you were not meant to grow old in a village. Be quiet and listen. He never looked further than the reconcilement of our houses. That was because he believed what his mother told him. He believed that his brother was born a fool.'

'So are all fools. I don't understand.'

'Don't you remember Straton the mason?'

'But that was because a stone fell on his head.'

'Yes. He was not born stumbling in his speech, or asking for a tree when he wanted bread. That was done by the stone.'

'But all my life, I've heard Arridaios was a fool.'

'All your life he has been one. You are fifteen, and he is thirty. When your father was hoping to be King, he told me a good deal about Philip's house. He said that when Arridaios was born, he was a fine strong child, and forward. It is true your father was still a child himself, and it was servants' talk; but he listened, because it concerned another child. They said that

138

Philip was pleased with the boy, and Olympias knew it. She swore Philinna's bastard should not disinherit her son. The child was born in the palace. Maybe she gave him something, maybe she saw to it that something should hit his head. So your father heard them say.'

'What a wicked woman! Poor baby, I would not do it to a dog. But it's done; where is the difference now?'

'Only born fools beget fools. Straton's children are all sound.'

Eurydike drew a sharp, shocked breath. Her hands gripped defensively the javelin she was holding. 'No! They said I need not. Even Alexander said so. You promised me!'

'Hush, hush. No one is asking it. That is what I'm telling you. That is why Antipatros is against it and Perdikkas doesn't write. It is not what they want. It is what they fear.'

Eurydike stood still, absently passing her hand up and down the shaft of the javelin; it was a good one, of smooth hard cornel-wood. 'You mean, they are afraid I could found a royal line, to displace Alexander's?'

'So I think.'

The girl's hand tightened on the shaft so that the knuckles paled. 'If that is what I must do to avenge my father, then I will. Because he left no son.'

Kynna was appalled. She had only wanted to explain their dangers. Quickly she said that it had been only slaves' talk; there had always been gossip about Olympias, that she coupled with serpents, and had conceived Alexander by the fire from heaven. It might well be true that Philinna had borne a fool, and it had not shown till the child was growing.

Eurydike looked carefully at the javelin, and put it aside with the few she meant to take. 'Don't be afraid, Mother. Let's wait till we are there, and I can see what I ought to do. Then I will do it.'

What have I made, thought Kynna; what have I done? Next moment she reminded herself that she had made what she had planned, and done what she had long resolved. She sent word to the herdsman to bring an unblemished kid, for a sacrifice to dedicate their enterprise.

Arybbas, the creator of Alexander's bier, made his way to the workshop for his daily visit. He was a dandified but not effeminate man, soldier and aesthete, a remote kinsman of the royal house, and of course too aristocratic ever to have worked for hire. Alexander had made him lavish presents whenever he had created a shrine, a royal barge, or a public spectacle, but that had been just between friends. Alexander, who loved to give money away, took offence when it was stolen, and had valued his probity as well as his gifts. Ptolemy, when recommending him to Perdikkas, had stressed this virtue, so necessary in a man handling a great deal of gold.

He had in fact watched it jealously; not a grain had stuck to his fingers, nor anyone else's. Weighing was a daily rite. A sumptuous designer, used by Alexander when notable splendour was required, he had used with gusto the whole treasure entrusted to him, for Alexander's honour and his own. As the magnificent structure he had inspired took shape under the hammers and gouges and graving-tools of his hand-picked craftsmen, exultation mingled with solemnity; he pictured Alexander surveying it with approval. He had appreciated such things. Arybbas had never cared much for Perdikkas.

Outside the workshop he noticed that Bagoas the eunuch was loitering about again, and, smiling graciously, beckoned him up. Though hardly a person whose company one would seek in public, he had shown impeccable taste, and an eye for the finer points. His devotion to the dead was touching; it was a pleasure to let him view the work.

'You will find a change,' he said. 'Yesterday they mounted it on the wheel-base. So now you can see it whole.'

He rapped with his staff. Bolts grated; the little postern opened in the great door. They stepped into shadow surrounding a blaze of glory.

The broad matting on the roof, which kept out bad weather and thieves at night, had been rolled back to open the great working skylight. The spring sun shafted down dazzlingly on a miniature temple, sheathed all over with gold.

It was some eighteen feet long; its vaulted roof was of gold scales set with gems, glowing balas rubies, emerald and crystal, sapphire and amethyst. On its ridge like a banner stood a laurel wreath with leaves of shimmering sheet-gold; on its corners victories leaned out, holding triumphant crowns. It was upheld by eight golden columns; around the cornice was festooned a flower-garland in fine enamels. On the frieze were pictured the exploits of Alexander. The floor was of beaten gold; the wheels were sheathed with it, their axles capped with lion-heads. A net of gold wire half hid the inner sanctuary on three sides; on the fourth, two couchant gold lions guarded the entry.

'See, they have hung the bells.'

Those too were of gold; they hung from the tassels of the garland. He lifted his staff and struck one; a clear musical sound, of surprising resonance, throbbed through the shed. 'They will know of his coming.'

Bagoas swept his hand across his eyes. Now he had entered the world again he was ashamed of tears; but he could hardly bear that Alexander would not see it.

Arybbas did not notice; he was talking to the overseer about making good the dents and scratches caused by the hoisting. Perfection must be restored.

In a far corner of the shed gleamed, dimly, the sarcophagus, blazoned with the royal sunburst of Macedon. Six men could scarcely lift it; it was solid gold. Only at last, at the outset of his journey, would Alexander be brought out in his cedar coffin where, hollow and light, he lay in a bed of spices and sweet herbs, to be laid among more spices in his final resting place. Satisfied that it was undamaged, Arybbas left.

Outside, Bagoas offered unstinted praise, the price of admission,

willingly paid. 'It will be counted among the wonders of the world.'
He added deliberately, 'The Egyptians are proud of their funeral
arts; but even there I saw nothing to compare with it.'

'You have been to Egypt?' Arybbas asked, surprised.

'Since my service with Alexander ended, I have travelled a
little to pass my time. He spoke so much of Alexandria, I wished
to see it for myself ... You, sir, of course, were there at its foundation.'

He said no more, leaving Arybbas to ask questions. To these he
replied obligingly, leaving loose ends which prompted further
questions. These led to a modest confession that he had been
granted an audience with the satrap.

'As it happened, though officers and friends of Alexander had
come from most of nearer Asia to join his army, I was the only
one from Babylon, so he asked for news. He had heard, he said,
that Alexander's bier was to be a marvel, and asked who had been
charged with it. When he knew, he exclaimed that Alexander
himself could wish for no one better. "If only," he said, "Arybbas
could be here to adorn the Founder's temple." ... Perhaps, sir, that
is indiscreet of me.' Fleetingly, like a reflection upon water,
appeared the smile which had entranced two kings. 'But I don't
think that he would mind.'

They talked for some time, Arybbas having found his curiosity about Alexandria sharpened. Riding back to his house, he was
aware he had been delicately probed; but he did not pursue this
thought. If he knew what Ptolemy wanted, it might be his duty
to divulge it; and this, he suspected, might be to his disadvantage.

In the thick-walled palace of red stone on the red-rock citadel of
Sardis, Kleopatra and her women were settled in modest comfort
by the standards of nearer Asia; in luxury by those of Epiros.
Perdikkas had had the royal apartments refurbished and redraped,
and staffed with well-trained slaves.

To Nikaia his bride, during their brief honeymoon, he had

explained the arrival of the Molossian queen by saying she was in flight from her mother, who had usurped her power and threatened her life; a daughter of Antipatros would believe anything of Olympias. After some ceremonious festivities suited to her rank, he had despatched the lady to an estate of his near by, on the grounds that war continued and he would soon be taking the field. Returning to Sardis, he resumed his courtship of Kleopatra. His visits and costly gifts had all the conventions of betrothal.

Kleopatra had enjoyed her journey; the family restlessness had not passed her by. The sight of new horizons had consoled her even for leaving her son behind. His grandmother would treat him like a son of her own whom she could train for kingship. When she herself was married and living in Macedon, she could see him often.

She had assessed Perdikkas more as a colleague than a husband. He was a dominating man, and she had sounded him for signs that he would overrule and bully her. It seemed, however, he had the sense to know that without her support he could neither get nor keep the regency. Later, depending on how he behaved, she might help him to the throne. He would be a hard king; but after Antipatros a soft one would be despised.

With a certain detachment, she imagined him in bed with her, but doubted it would be of much importance to either of them once she had produced an heir. Clearly, it would be more valuable and more lasting to make a friend of him than a lover; this she was already doing with some success.

On this day of early spring he was to take the midday meal with her. Both preferred the informality of noon and the chance of undisturbed talk. The single dish would be good; he had found her a Karian cook. She studied his tastes against the time when they would be married. She did not mean to deal hardly with Antipatros' poor plain little girl, as her mother had done with rivals; Nikaia could go back safe to her family. The Persian wife from Susa had done so long ago.

He arrived on foot from his quarters at the other end of the rambling palace, whose buildings clambered about the rock. He had dressed for her with a jewelled shoulder-brooch and a splendid arm-ring clasped with gold gryphon heads. His sword-belt was set with plaques of Persian cloisonné. Yes, she thought, he would make a convincing king.

He liked to talk of his wars under Alexander, and she to listen; only fragmented news had reached Epiros, and he had seen the whole. But before they had reached the wine, her eunuch chamberlain coughed at the door. A despatch had arrived for His Excellency's urgent attention.

'From Eumenes,' he said as he broke the seal. He spoke rather too easily, aware that Eumenes called nothing urgent without good cause.

As he read, she saw his weathered tan go sallow, and sent out the slave who was serving them. Like most men of his time, he sounded the words he read (it was thought remarkable in Alexander to have suppressed this reflex); but his jaw had set; she heard only an angry mutter. Seeing his face at the end, she guessed that he would look like this in war. 'What is it?' she said.

'Antigonos has fled to Greece.'

Antigonos ... while he stared before him, she remembered that this was the Satrap of Phrygia, nicknamed One-Eye. 'Was he not under arrest for treason? I suppose he was afraid.'

He gave a snort like a horse's. 'He, afraid? He has gone to betray me to Antipatros.'

She saw that he wanted only to be thinking ahead; but there was more here than she had been told, and she had a right to know. 'What was the treason? Why was he being held?'

He answered savagely, 'To stop his mouth. I found out that he knew.'

She took this in without trouble; she was not a daughter of Macedon for nothing. My father, she thought, would not have done it; nor Alexander. In the old days ... must we go back to that? She only said, 'How did he come to know?'

'Ask the rats in the wall. He was the last man I'd have confided in. He was always close with Antipatros. He must have smelled something and sent a spy. It's all one now, the harm's done.'

She nodded; there was no need to spell it out. They must be married with royal ceremony before attempting Macedon. There was no time now; Antipatros would be marching north from Aitolia the moment he got the news. A scrambled wedding would bring them nothing but scandal. She thought, This will mean war.

He swung himself down from his dining-couch and began to stride the room; she had a stray thought that they might as well be married already. Wheeling round, he said, 'And I still have to deal with those accursed women.'

'What women?' She let her voice sharpen; he was keeping too much, lately, to himself. 'You've said nothing of women; who are they?'

He made a sound, compounded of impatience and embarrassment. 'No. It was hardly fitting; but I should have told you. Philip, your brother ...'

'Pray, don't call that wittol my brother!' She had never shared Alexander's tolerance of Philinna's son. Her only passage of arms with Perdikkas had taken place when he had wanted to install the King in the palace, as became his rank. 'If he comes, I go.' He had seen in her face a flash of Alexander's will. Philip had stayed in the royal tent; he was used to it, and had no thought of any other arrangement. 'What has *he* to do with women, in God's name?'

'Alexander betrothed him to Adeia, your cousin Amyntas' daughter. He even granted her the royal name of Eurydike, which she's made a point of using. I don't know what he meant by it. Shortly before he died, Philip took a turn for the better. Alexander seemed pleased. You'd not know, it's too long since you saw either of them. Alexander took him along in the first place to keep him safe out of the way, in case someone should use him in Macedon. Also, as he told me one night when he was drunk, because Olympias might have killed him if he was left behind. But he got a kind of fondness for him, after taking care of him all those years. He was glad to see him looking more like a man, and let him be seen with him, helping at the sacrifices and so on. Half the army saw it, that's why we've the trouble we have today. But there were no plans for any wedding. If he'd not fallen ill, he'd have marched to Arabia within the month. In the end, I expect, the marriage would have been by proxy.'

'He never told me!' For a moment her face was an injured child's; a long story was there, if Perdikkas had cared to read it.

'That was on account of your mother. He was afraid, if she knew, she'd do the girl an injury.'

'I see,' said Olympias' daughter, without surprise. 'But he should never have done it. Of course we must free her now, poor child.' He did not answer. In a new voice of authority, she said, 'Perdikkas, these are my kin. It is for me to say.'

'Madam, I know.' He spoke with studied respect; he could well afford it. 'But you have misunderstood. Antipatros cancelled the contract with my agreement, some months ago. In his absence, without his leave, her mother Kynna has brought the girl to Asia. They are demanding that the marriage shall proceed.'

His exasperation spoke for his truth. 'Shameless!' she cried. 'There you see the barbarian blood!' It might almost have been Olympias speaking.

'Indeed. They are true Illyrians. I hear that they travelled as far as Abdera dressed as men, and carrying arms.'

'What will you do with them? I can have no dealings with such creatures.'

'They will be dealt with. I have no time; I must meet with Eumenes, before Antipatros crosses to Asia. Krateros will be sure to join him, which is much worse. The men love Krateros . . . My brother will have to meet them, and keep them from making mischief.'

Presently he left to make his dispositions. One of these was to send to Ephesos, summoning Roxane and her child. He had known better than to quarter the Bactrian on the daughter of Philip and Olympias; besides, if she knew of their plans she would probably have him poisoned. But now it was time to move, and she must follow the army. At least, he thought, she was used to that.

On the high road to the Syrian coast, flashing in the sun and ringing all its bells, the bier of Alexander trundled towards Issos. The sixty-four mules drew it, four yoke-poles each hitching four teams of four. The mules wore gold wreaths, and little gold bells on their cheeks. Their tinkling, and the deep clear chime of the bells upon the bier, mingled with the shouts of the muleteers.

In the shrine, between the gold columns and the shimmering golden nets, the sarcophagus lay draped with its purple pall. On it was displayed Alexander's panoply of arms, his helmet of white iron, his jewelled sword-belt, his sword and shield and greaves. The cuirass was the parade one; the one he had used in battle was too worn and hacked to match the splendours around.

When the iron-bound felloes of the gold-sheathed wheels jolted on rough ground, the bier only swayed gently; there were hidden springs above the axles. Alexander would come whole to his tomb. Veterans in the escort said to each other that if he had been anywhere near as careful of his body while he was alive, he would be with them yet.

All along the road sightseers stood in expectant clusters, awaiting the sound of the distant bells. The fame of the bier had far outstripped its progress. Peasants had walked a day from mountain hamlets, and slept in the open to await it; riders on horses or mules or asses kept along by it for miles, unwilling to relinquish it. Boys ran themselves to a standstill, dropping like spent dogs when the escort struck camp at night, creeping to the cook-fires to beg a crust, and listening half in dreams to the soldiers' tales.

At each town on the way, sacrifices were offered to the deified Alexander; the local bard would extol his deeds, inventing marvels when his store of history failed. Arybbas presided calmly over these solemnities. He had had Ptolemy's letter, and knew what he would do.

Save for his one visit to Arybbas' tent, Bagoas made himself imperceptible. By day he rode among the changing sightseers; at night he slept among the Persian soldiers who formed the rear guard. They all knew who he was, and no one troubled him. He was keeping faith with his lord, as a true follower of Mithra ought. They respected his pious pilgrimage, and thought no more of it.

Kynna and her daughter had travelled as armed men, sleeping in their baggage-cart with their retainers in the open round them, till they could take ship from Abdera. There the people were Greek, there was plenty of merchant shipping, and the only question asked was whether they could pay. Kynna, who could deceive no one at close quarters, resumed female dress; Eurydike travelled as her son.

The ship carried hides on deck; the retainers found them a grateful bed at night, but their smell made Eurydike sick at the first flurry of wind. At last, they sailed into the green sheltering arms of the long gulf of Smyrna. From now on, their progress must be very different.

Smyrna consisted of ancient ruins, an old village, and a brand-new town refounded by Alexander, whom the harbour had impressed. The traffic had grown with his conquests, and it was now a busy port. Here they would be seen and spoken of; though Babylon was still far off, they must think about appearances. The old man who acted as their major-domo – he remembered Amyntas' father – went before them to seek good lodgings, and hire transport for the long journey overland.

He returned with startling news. The journey to the east was not required of them. Perdikkas, and King Philip with him, were no further off than Sardis, some fifty miles.

They felt a shock, as people do when a distant crisis leaps up close; then told each other that luck was speeding them. Eurydike went ashore with a long cloak over her tunic, and, in the lodging, assumed himation and robe.

They must travel at once with public consequence, a king's betrothed travelling to her bridal. They should of course have been met at the port by a kinsman or friend of the groom; but the greater their state, the less they would be questioned. They could afford lavishness for so short a journey; Amyntas' estates had never been confiscated, their quiet life had not been due to poverty.

When, two days later, they set out, their train was an imposing one. Thoas the major-domo, who had purchased them maids and porters, reported that according to people here they should have a eunuch chamberlain. Kynna, much outraged, replied that they were Greek, as was her daughter's bridegroom, and they had not crossed to Asia to adopt the disgusting customs of the barbarians. Alexander, she had heard, had been given too much that way.

The faithful Thoas, transacting all this business, made no secret of his ladies' rank, or of their purpose. It was no spy, but the eternal gossip of travellers on the road, that ran ahead of them with the news to Sardis.

The field of Issos still yielded up old weapons and old bones. Here, where Darius had first fled from Alexander's spear leaving mother and wife and children to await the victor, two armies sacrificed a milk-white bull before the golden bier. Ptolemy and Arybbas poured incense side by side. The escort had been much moved by Ptolemy's address, affirming the divine hero's wish that his body return to his father Ammon.

Each of Arybbas' men had been given a hundred drachmas, a bounty worthy even of Alexander. Arybbas himself had received, in private, a talent of silver, and in public the rank of general in the satrap's army, whither all his Macedonian troops had agreed to follow him. There was a feast at night in Alexander's honour; a whole spit-roast sheep and an amphora of wine to each camp-fire. Next morning, satrap and general riding either side the bier, the funeral cortège turned south towards the Nile.

Bagoas, whose name had been proclaimed in no citation, followed behind the rear guard. The other Persians had gone home; but the troops from Egypt made the column a very long one, and he was far, now, from the bier. When he topped a rise, he could just see its glittering crest. But he rode contented. His task was done, his god was served; and there would still be his fame to tend in his chosen city. A Greek might have seen in him the serenity of the initiate, fresh from a celebration of his mystery.

Kynna's caravan was within a day's journey from Sardis. They were not hurrying; they meant to arrive there next morning before the heat began. Its fame had reached even Macedon for wealth and luxury; the bride of a king must not be outshone by his subjects. Overnight they would prepare their entry.

Along the road, the stony heights were topped with old forts, newly repaired by Alexander to command the passes. They passed rock-slabs carved with symbols, and inscriptions in unknown writing. The travellers who passed them making for the port were all barbarians, strange to sight and smell; Phoenicians with blue-dyed beards, Karians with heavy earrings dragging down their lobes; a train of Negro carriers bare to the waist, their blackness strange and terrible to a northern eye used only to the red-haired slaves from Thrace; sometimes a trousered Persian, the legendary ogre of Greek children, with embroidered hat and curved sword.

To Eurydike all was adventure and delight. She thought with envy of world-wandering Alexander and his men. Kynna, beside her under the striped awning, kept a cheerful countenance, but felt her spirits flag. The alien speech of the passers-by, the inscrutable monuments, the unknown landscape, the vanishing of all she had pictured in advance, were draining her of certainty. Those black-veiled women, carrying burdens beside the donkeys their menfolk rode, if they knew her purpose would think her mad. The two-wheeled cart jolted over stones, her head was aching. She had known that the world was vast, that Alexander in ten years had never reached the end of it; but at home in her native hills it had no meaning. Now, on the mere threshold of the illimitable east, she felt like a desolation its indifferent strangeness.

Eurydike, who had been admiring the defences of the forts and pointing out their chain of beacons, said, 'Is it true, do you think, that Sardis is three times as big as Pella?'

'I dare say. Pella is only two generations old; Sardis ten maybe, or even more.' The thought oppressed her. She looked at the girl in her careless confidence, and thought, I brought her here from home, where she could have lived out her life in quiet. She has no one but me to turn to. Well, I am healthy and still young.

Night would soon fall. An outrider brought news that they were within ten miles of Sardis. Soon they must find a camping-place. A rocky turn shut off the westering sun, and the road grew dusky. The slope above them, dark against a reddening sky, was scattered with great boulders. Somewhere among them a man's voice called, 'Now!'

Stones and shale fell rattling on the road, dislodged by scrambling men. Thoas at the escort's head shouted out, 'Ware thieves!'

The men reached the road, thirty or forty or them, on foot, with spears. Among them the escort looked what it was, a troop of willing, confused old men. Those who had ever fought had done it in Philip's wars. But they were true Macedonians, with the archaic virtues of the liegeman. They shouted defiance, and thrust at the bandits with their spears.

The squeal of a wounded horse echoed against the rocks. Old Thoas fell with his mount; a huddle of men closed stabbing over him.

There was a high shout, a wordless 'Hi-yi!' of challenge. Kynna leaped down from the cart, Eurydike beside her. Their spears had been at hand; with practised speed they had kilted their skirts into their girdles. With their backs to the cart, which rocked with the shifting of the frightened mules, they stood to face the enemy.

Eurydike felt a shiver of exultation. Here at last was war, real war. Though she could guess the consequence of defeat if they were taken alive, it was mainly a good reason for fighting well. A man reached out at her, fair-skinned, with a week's red stubble on his chin. He had on a hide cuirass, so she went for his arm. The spear sank in; he leaped back crying out, 'You hell-cat!', grasping the wound. She laughed at him; then realized with a sudden shock that here, in Lydia, a bandit had spoken Macedonian.

One of the lead mules, hurt by a spear, suddenly squealed and leaped forward. The whole team bolted, the cart bucking and bouncing behind. It struck her, but she just kept her feet. There was a cry beside her. Kynna had fallen; she had been braced against the cart when it moved off. A soldier was leaning over her with a spear.

A man came forward with upheld hand. The men around her withdrew. It grew quiet, except for the struggling mules which had been pulled up by the soldiers, and the groans of three of the escort on the ground. The rest had been overpowered, save for old Thoas, who was dead.

Kynna moaned; the almost animal sound of a warm-blooded creature struggling in pain to breathe. Her breast was stained with red.

Eurydike's first impulse was to run to her, take her in her arms, entreat the bandits for mercy. But Kynna had trained her well. This too was war; there would be no mercy for asking, only for winning. She looked at the chief who had been at once obeyed, a tall dark man with a lean cold face. Knowledge was instant: not bandits, soldiers.

Kynna groaned again; the sound was fainter now. Pity and rage and grief lit like one flame in Eurydike, as they did in Achilles, shouting for dead Patroklos on the wall. She leaped to her mother's body and stood across it.

'You traitors! Are you men of Macedon? This is Kynna, King Philip's daughter, the sister of Alexander.'

There was a startled pause. The men all turned towards the officer. He looked angry and disconcerted. He had not told them.

A thought came to her. She spoke this time in the language of the soldiers, the peasant dialect of the countryside she had known before she was taught court Greek. 'I am Philip's grandchild, look at me! I am Amyntas' daughter, the grandchild of King Philip and King Perdikkas.' She pointed at the lowering officer. 'Ask him. *He* knows!'

The oldest soldier, a man in his fifties, walked across to him. 'Alketas.' He used the name without honorific, as a freeman of Macedon could do to kings. 'Is what she says true?'

'No! Obey your orders.'

The soldier looked from him to the girl, and from her to the other men. 'I reckon it's true,' he said.

The men drew together; one of them said, 'They're no Sarmatians, like he said. They're as Macedonian as I am.'

'My mother ...' Eurydike looked down. Kynna stirred, but blood was running from her mouth. 'She brought me here from Macedon. I am betrothed to Philip, your king, the brother of Alexander.'

Kynna stirred. She rose a little on one arm. Chokingly she said, 'It is true. I swear by ...' She coughed. A rush of blood came out, and she fell back. Eurydike dropped her spear and knelt beside her. Her eyes fixed, showing the whites.

The old soldier who had faced Alketas came over and stood

before her, confronting the rest. 'Let them alone!' he said. Another and another joined him; the rest leaned on their spears in a confused and sullen shame. Eurydike flung herself on her mother's body and wept aloud.

Presently, through the sound of her own crying, she heard voices raised. It was the sound of mutiny. Had she known, it was one with which Macedonian generals were growing over-familiar. Ptolemy had confided to close friends in Egypt that he was glad to hand-pick his men, and be rid of the standing army. It put one in mind of Alexander's old horse Boukephalas, liable to kick anyone else who tried to mount him. Like the horse, it had been too long used to a rider with clever hands.

More urgently now, Eurydike thought of throwing herself upon their mercy, begging them to burn her mother's body decently, give her the ashes to bury in the homeland, and take her back to the sea. But, as she wiped the blood from Kynna's face, she knew it for the face of a warrior steadfast to the death. Her shade must not find that she had borne a coward.

Under her hand was the gold pendant her mother always wore. It was bloodstained, but she slipped it over the lifeless head, and stood erect.

'See. Here is my grandfather King Philip's likeness. He gave it to my grandmother Audata on her wedding day, and she to my mother when she married Amyntas, King Perdikkas' son. Look for yourself.'

She put it in the veteran's cracked horny hand; they crowded round him, poring over the gold roundel with the square-boned, bearded profile. 'Aye, Philip it is,' the veteran said. 'I saw him many a time.' He rubbed it clean on a fold of his homespun kilt and gave it back to her. 'You should take care of that,' he said.

He spoke as if to a young niece; and it struck a chord in all of them. She was their foundling, the orphan of their rescue and adoption. They would take her to Sardis, they told Alketas; she had Philip's blood in her as any fool could see; and if Alexander had promised her his brother, wed they should be, or the army would know why.

'Very well,' said Alketas. He knew by now that discipline hung by a thread, and maybe his life. 'Then get the road cleared, and look alive.'

With rough competence the soldiers laid Kynna out in the cart, and covered her with a blanket; brought their own transport-cart for the dead and wounded guards, picked up the baggage which the porters had dropped when with the maids they fled to the hills. They settled the cushions for Eurydike, to ride beside her dead.

One of them rode off willingly with Alketas' despatch to his brother Perdikkas. On his way would be the main camp of Perdikkas' and Eumenes' armies, where he could spread the news.

So, when the last turn of the road showed her the red-rock citadel with the city around its feet, it showed her also a great throng of soldiers, crowding the road, and parting to make an avenue of honour, as if for a king.

As she came they cheered her. Close to her by the road she heard gruff murmurs: 'Poor maid.' 'Forgive them, lady, he told them wrong.' The strangeness, the dreamlike consummation of their long intent, made her mother's death dreamlike too, though she could have reached out and touched the body.

From her high window, Kleopatra looked down with Perdikkas, fuming, beside her. She saw his impotence, and struck her hand in anger on the sill. 'You are permitting this?'

'No choice. If I arrest her, we shall have a mutiny. Now of all times ... They know that she's Philip's grandchild.'

'And a traitor's daughter! Her father plotted my father's murder. Will you let her marry his son?'

'Not if I can help it.' The cart was coming nearer. He tried to descry the face of Amyntas' daughter, but it was too far. He must go down and make some gesture which would preserve his dignity and, with luck, gain time. Just then new movement below, from a new direction, caught his eye. He leaned out, stared, and, cursing, swung back into the room.

'What is it?' His rage and dismay had startled her.

'Hades take them! They are bringing Philip out to her.'

'What? How can—'

'They know where his tent is. You wouldn't have him here. I must go.' He flung out, without even the curtest apology. For a very little, she thought, he would have cursed her, too.

Down below in the thick outer walls the huge gates stood wide. The cart halted. A group of soldiers, pulling something, came running out of the gateway.

'Lady, if you'll please to step down, we've something here more fit for you.'

It was an old and splendid chariot, its front and sides plated with silver gryphons and gold lions. Lined with tooled red leather, it had been built for Kroisos, that legend for uncounted riches, the last Lydian king. Alexander had made a progress in it, to impress the people.

This moving throne made her sense of dream grow deeper. She came to herself to say that she could not leave her mother's body untended.

'She'll be watched with, lady, like she ought, we've seen to that.' Worn black-clad women came forward with eager pride; veterans' wives, looking from work and weather old enough to be their mothers. A soldier approached to hand Eurydike down. At the last moment Alketas, making a virtue of necessity, came up to do the office. For a moment she flinched; but that was not the way to take an enemy's surrender. She inclined her head graciously and took his offered arm. A team of soldiers grasped the chariot-pole, and pulled it forward. She sat like a king on Kroisos' chair.

Suddenly, the sound of the cheering altered. She heard the ancient Macedonian cries: 'Io Hymen! Euoi! Joy to the bride! Hail to the groom!'

The groom was coming towards her.

Her heart gave a lurch. This part of the dream had been blurred.

The man came riding, on a beautiful, slow-pacing dapple-grey. A grizzled old soldier led it by the rein. The face of the bearded rider was not unlike the one on the gold medallion. He was looking about him, blinking a little. The old soldier pointed towards her. When he looked straight at her, she saw that he was frightened, scared to death. Among all she had thought of, so far as she had allowed herself to think at all, she had not thought of this.

Urged by the soldiers, he dismounted and walked up to the chariot, his blue eyes, filled with the liveliest apprehension, fixed on her face. She smiled at him.

'How are you, Arridaios? I am your cousin Eurydike, your uncle Amyntas' daughter. I have just come from home. Alexander sent for me.'

The soldiers all around murmured approval, admiring her quick address, and cried, 'Long live the King!'

Philip's face had brightened at the sound of his old name. When he was Arridaios he had had no duties, no bullying rehearsals with impatient men. Alexander had never bullied, only made one pleased to get things right. This girl reminded him, somehow, of Alexander. Cautiously, less frightened now, he said, 'Are you going to marry me?'

A soldier burst into a guffaw, but was manhandled by indignant comrades. The rest listened eagerly to the scene.

'If you would like it, Arridaios. Alexander wanted us to marry.'

He bit his lip in a crisis of irresolution. Suddenly he turned to the old soldier who led his horse. 'Shall I marry her, Konon? Did Alexander tell me to?'

One or two soldiers clapped hands over their mouths. In the muttering pause, she was aware of the old servant subjecting her to a searching scrutiny. She recognized a resolute protector. Ignoring the voices, some of them growing ribald, which were urging the King to speak up for the girl before she changed her mind, she looked straight at Konon, and said, 'I will be kind to him.'

The wariness in his faded eyes relaxed. He gave her a little nod, and turned to Philip, still eyeing him anxiously. 'Yes, sir. This is the lady you're betrothed to, the maid Alexander chose for you. She's a fine, brave lady. Reach out your hand to her, and ask her nicely to be your wife.'

Eurydike took the obedient hand. Large, warm and soft, it clung to hers appealingly. She gave it a reassuring pressure.

'Please, Cousin Eurydike, will you marry me? The soldiers want you to.'

Keeping his hand, she said, 'Yes, Arridaios. Yes, King Philip, I will.'

The cheers began in earnest. Soldiers who were wearing their broad-brimmed hats flung them into the air. The cries of 'Hymen!' redoubled. They were trying to coax Philip into the chariot beside her, when Perdikkas, red and panting from his race down the steep and winding steps of the ancient city, arrived upon the scene.

Alketas met him, speaking with his eyes. Both knew too well the mood in which Macedonians grew dangerous. They had seen it in the time of Alexander, who had dealt with it at Opis by leaping from his dais and arresting the ringleaders with his bare hands. But such things had been Alexander's mystery; anyone else would have been lynched. Alketas met with a shrug of the shoulders his brother's furious stare.

Eurydike in the chariot guessed at once who Perdikkas was. For a moment she felt like a child before a formidable adult. But she stood her ground, sustained by strengths she was largely unaware of. She knew she was the grandchild of Philip and King Perdikkas, great-grandchild of Illyrian Bardelys, the old terror of the border; but she did not know they had bequeathed her more than pride in them; she had some of their nature, too. Her sequestered youth, fed upon legends, let her see in her situation nothing absurd or obscene. All she knew was that these men who had cheered her should not see her afraid.

Philip had been standing with one hand upon the chariot, arguing with the men who had been trying to hoist him into it. Now he grabbed her arm.

'Look out!' he said. 'Here comes Perdikkas.'

She put her hand over his. 'Yes, I see him. Come up here, and stand by me.'

He scrambled up; encouraging soldiers steadied the chariot as his weight rocked it. Grasping the rail, he stood rigid with scared defiance; she rose to her feet beside him, summoning her nerve. Briefly, they presented an uncanny semblance of a triumphant pair, remote in pride and power. Tauntingly, the soldiers flung at Perdikkas the marriage-cry.

He reached the chariot; there was a moment of held breath. Then he raised his hand in salute.

'Greeting, King. Greeting, daughter of Amyntas. I am glad that the King has been prompt to welcome you.'

'The soldiers made me,' mumbled Philip anxiously. Eurydike's clear voice cut in: 'The King has been very gracious.'

Philip gazed anxiously at these two protagonists. No vengeance from Perdikkas happened. The soldiers were pleased, too. He gave a conniving grin. Hiding with care her almost incredulous amazement, Eurydike knew that, for the present, she had won.

'Perdikkas,' she said, 'the King has asked for my hand with the goodwill of the Macedonians. But my mother, the sister of Alexander, is lying here murdered, as you know. First of all I must have leave to direct her funeral.'

Loud, respectful sounds of approval greeted this. Perdikkas agreed with as good a grace as he could. Scanning the sullen faces, thinking of Antipatros' forces making for the Hellespont, he added that the death of her noble mother had been a shocking error, due to ignorance and to the valour of her defence. The matter would of course be searched to the bottom shortly.

Eurydike bowed her head, aware that she would never know what Alketas' orders had really been. Kynna would at least meet the flame with all the honours of war; one day her ashes must return to Aigai. Meantime, her funeral offerings must be courage and resolve. As for her blood-price, that would be with the gods.

The funeral was barely over, when news reached Perdikkas that Alexander's bier was proceeding in state to Egypt.

It struck him like a thunderbolt. All his plans had been directed against the threat from the north, the outraged father-in-law to whom he had already despatched Nikaia. Now, from the south, came a clear declaration of war.

Eumenes was still in Sardis, summoned when danger came from the north alone. It had come, as they both knew, from neglect of his advice to marry Kleopatra openly, to send Nikaia still virgin home, and advance at once on Macedon. This was not spoken of. Like Kassandra, Eumenes was fated never to reap much good from being right. A Greek among Macedonians had no business to know best. He refrained, therefore, from pointing out that Perdikkas could now have been Regent of Macedon with a royal bride, a power against which Ptolemy could have attempted nothing; and merely voiced a doubt that he was planning war.

'All he has done so far in Egypt has been to dig in and make himself snug. He's ambitious, yes; but what are his ambitions? It was a fine piece of insolence to steal the body; but even that may be only to glorify Alexandria. Will he trouble us if he's let alone?'

'He's already annexed Kyrene. And he's raising a bigger army than he needs.'

'How does he know? If you march against him he'll need it.'

Perdikkas said with sudden venom, 'I hate the man.'

Eumenes offered no comment. He remembered Ptolemy as a gangling youth, hoisting the child Alexander up on his horse for a ride. Perdikkas had been a friend of the King's manhood, but it had never been quite the same. Alexander promoted on merit – even Hephaistion had started at the bottom – and Perdikkas had outstripped Ptolemy in the end. But it was Ptolemy who had suited Alexander like a well-worn, comfortable shoe; the trusted Perdikkas had never quite matched that ease. Ptolemy, by instinct and from watching Alexander, had a way with men; he knew when to relax discipline as well as when to tighten it; when to give, when to listen, when to laugh. Perdikkas felt the absence of that sixth sense as a man might feel short sight; and envy ate at him.

'He's like a vicious dog, that eats the flock it should be guarding. If he's not whipped back, the rest will be at it too.'

'Maybe; but not yet. Antipatros and Krateros will be marching now.'

Perdikkas' dark jaw set stubbornly. He has changed, thought Eumenes, since Alexander died. His desires have changed. They grow hubristic, and he knows it. Alexander contained us all.

Perdikkas said, 'No, Ptolemy can't wait. That asp of Egypt must be stepped upon in the egg.'

'Then we divide the army?' His voice was neutral; a Greek among Macedonians had said enough.

'Needs must. You shall go north, and refuse Antipatros the Hellespont. I will settle with Ptolemy, and settle for good ... But before we march, we must have this accursed wedding. The men won't move else. I know them too well.'

Later that day, Perdikkas spent an hour reasoning with Kleopatra. In the end, with flattery, cold logic, appeal, and as much charm as he could conjure, he persuaded her to act as Eurydike's matron of honour. The troops were set on the marriage; it must be done with a good grace. Any grudging would be remembered against them both, which they could not afford.

'The girl was a child at nurse,' he said, 'when they murdered

161

Philip. I doubt even Amyntas was more than on the fringe of it.
I was there when he was tried.'

'Yes, I dare say. But it is all disgusting. Has she no shame at all?
Well, you have dangers enough without my making more for you.
If Alexander was willing to give it countenance, I suppose I can
do the same.'

Eumenes did not await the feast. He marched at once to meet
the forces of Antipatros and Krateros (another of his sons-in-
law); leading the Macedonians with their loose and dubious
loyalty to the alien Greek. For Eumenes, that was an old story.
Perdikkas, whose business was less urgent, stayed on another week
to give his troops their show.

Two days before the wedding, a flustered maid announced to
Eurydike in her inner room – built for the chief wife of old
Kroisos – that the Queen of the Epirotes had come to visit her.

Kleopatra arrived in state. Olympias had not stinted her since
she left home; meanness had never been one of her sins. Her
daughter came dressed like a queen, and with queenly gifts: a
broad gold necklace, a roll of Karian embroidery stitched with
lapis and gold. For a moment, Eurydike was overwhelmed. But
Kynna had trained her in manners as well as war; she achieved a
kind of naive dignity which moved Kleopatra against her will.
She remembered her own wedding, to an uncle old enough to be
her father, at seventeen.

The compliments paid, the formal sweet cakes tasted, she went
dutifully over the wedding ritual. It was a dry business, since there
could be no question of the sly feminine jokes traditional at such
a conference. Careful correctness resulted. Kleopatra's sense of
duty nagged at her. This grave guarded girl, left alone in the world
at fifteen; what did she know? Kleopatra smoothed her gown over
her knees, and looked up from her ringed fingers.

'When you met the King' – how allude to so disgraceful an
occasion? – 'did you have time to talk with him? Perhaps you saw
he is a little young for his years?'

162

Eurydike's straight eyes met hers, deciding that she meant well and must be answered civilly. 'Yes. Alexander told my mother so; and I see it is so.'

This was promising. 'Then, when you are married, what do you mean to do? Perdikkas would give you an escort to your kin in Macedon.'

Eurydike thought, It is not quite a command, because it cannot be one. She answered quietly, 'The King has a right that I should be his friend, if he needs a friend. I will stay for a while and see.'

Next day, such ladies of standing as Sardis could supply – wives of senior officers and administrators, with a few timid ornate Lydians – paid their respects. Later, in the quiet afternoon, sacred since Kroisos' day to the siesta, came a different caller. A twittering maid announced a messenger from the household of the bridegroom.

Old Konon, when shown in, eyed the attendants meaningly. She sent them out, and asked what message he brought.

'Well, madam ... to wish you health and joy, and God speed the happy day.' Delivered of this set speech, he swallowed audibly. What could be coming? Eurydike, dreading the unknown, looked withdrawn and sullen. Konon, his nervousness increased, marshalled his words. 'Madam, he's taken a real liking to you, that's sure. He's forever talking of Cousin Eurydike, and setting out his pretty things to show you ... But, madam, I've cared for him man and boy, and I know his ways, which he sets store by, seeing he was ill-used before I came. If you please, madam, don't turn me off. You'll not find me taking liberties or putting myself forward. If you'll just keep me on trial, to see if I suit; I won't ask more.'

So that was all! In her relief she could have embraced him; but of course one must not show it. 'Did I not see you with the King? Your name is Konon, is it not? Yes, you will be welcome to stay on. Please tell the King so, if he should ask.'

'He's never thought to ask, madam. It would have put him in a terrible taking.' They eyed each other, a little relaxed, still cautious. Konon was reaching for words, even for the little that could be said at all. 'Madam, he's not used to big feasts, not without Alexander giving him the lead and seeing him through it. I dare say they told you, he has a bad turn sometimes. Don't be afraid, if you just leave him to me, he'll soon be right again.'

Eurydike said she would. Echoing silence engulfed them. Konon swallowed again. The poor girl would give anything to know what he didn't know how to tell her – her groom had no notion that the act of sex could be performed with a second party. At length, turning crimson, he managed, 'Madam, he thinks the world of you. But he'll not trouble you. It wouldn't be his way.'

She was not too naive to understand him. With as much dignity as she could summon, she said, 'Thank you, Konon. I am sure the King and I will agree together. You have leave to go.'

Philip woke early on his wedding morning. Konon had promised that he could wear the purple robe with the great red star. Besides, he was going to be married to Cousin Eurydike. She would be allowed to stay with him, and he could see her whenever he liked. Perdikkas himself had said so.

That morning, the bath-water came in a big silver ewer, carried by two well-dressed young men who stayed to pour it over him, wishing him good luck. This, Konon explained, was because he was a bridegroom. He saw the young men exchange a grin across him; but such things often happened.

A good many people were singing and laughing outside the door. He was no longer in his familiar tent, but had a room in the palace; he did not mind, he had been allowed to bring all his stones. Konon explained that there was no room in the tent for a lady, while here she could stay next door.

The young men helped him put on the beautiful robe; then he was taken by Perdikkas to sacrifice at the little temple of Zeus at the top of the hill. Alexander had built it there, where fire had fallen from heaven. Perdikkas told him when to throw incense on the burning meat, and what to say to the god. He got everything right, and the people sang for him; but nobody praised him afterwards, as Alexander used to do.

Perdikkas, indeed, had had trouble enough to plan a convincing ceremony. Thanks to Alketas, the bride had no family to give the marriage feast. He was grateful to Kleopatra for consenting to hold the torch of welcome in the bridal chamber. But what mattered most, because the troops would see it, was the wedding procession.

Then, to compound his troubles, at midday two forerunners announced the approach of the lady Roxane. Since this affair, he had entirely forgotten having sent for her, and had not even asked her to the wedding.

Lodgings were hastily prepared; her closed litter was carried up through the city. The Sardians crowded to see; the soldiers gave a few restrained greetings. They had never approved of Alexander's foreign marriages; but now he was dead, a kind of aura clung to her. Besides, she was the mother of his son. The child was with her. A Macedonian queen would have held him up for them to see; but Bactrian ladies did not show themselves in public. The child was teething and fretful, and could be heard whimpering as the litter passed.

Dressed in his wedding robe, and putting a good face on it, Perdikkas greeted her and invited her to the feast; prepared, he said, at short notice owing to the imminence of war.

'You told me nothing of it!' she said angrily. 'Who is this peasant girl you have found for him? If the King is to marry, he should have married me.'

'Among Macedonians,' said Perdikkas frostily, 'a dead king's heir does not inherit his harem. And the lady is granddaughter to two kings.'

A crisis of precedence now arose. Alexander and his officers had married their foreign wives by the local rites; Roxane, ignorant of Macedonian custom, could not be brought to see that Kleopatra was taking a mother's place and could not be removed from it. 'But I,' she cried, 'am the mother of Alexander's son!'

'So,' said Perdikkas, very nearly shouting, 'you are the kinswoman of the *bridegroom*. I will send someone to explain the rite to you. See to it that your part is properly done, if you want your son accepted by the soldiers. Don't forget they have the right to disinherit him.'

This sobered her. He had changed, she thought; grown colder, harsher, more overbearing. He had not forgiven Stateira's death, it seemed. She was unaware that others had noticed a change as well.

Philip had looked forward all day to the wedding ride. It did not disappoint him. Not since the time he rode an elephant had he enjoyed himself so much.

He wore the purple robe, and a gold diadem. Eurydike beside him had a yellow dress, and a yellow veil flung back from a wreath of gold flowers. He had thought they would have the car all to themselves, and had been displeased when Perdikkas got up on the other side. Eurydike was married to *him*, and Perdikkas could not marry her as well. Hastily people had explained that Perdikkas was best man; but it was Cousin Eurydike he listened to. Now he was married, he felt much less frightened of Perdikkas; he had been on the point of pushing him out of the car.

Drawn by white mules, they drove along the processional Sacred Way, which bent and turned to bring it downhill without stairs. It was adorned with old statues and shrines, Lydian, Persian, Greek. Flags and garlands were everywhere; as the sun sank they were starting to light the torches. People were standing and cheering all the way, climbing up on the house-roofs.

The tasselled, sequin-netted mules were led by soldiers wearing scarlet cloaks and wreaths. Behind and in front, musicians played Lydian airs on flutes and pipes, shook sistra with their little tinkling bells, and clanged great cymbals. Auspicious cries in mingled tongues rose like waves. The sunset glow faded, the torches came out like stars.

Full of it all, Philip turned and said, 'Are you happy, Cousin Eurydike?'

'Very happy.' Indeed, she had imagined nothing to compare with it. Unlike her groom, she had never before tasted the pomps of Asia. The music, the shouts of acclamation, elated her like wine. This was her element, and till now she had never known it. Not for nothing was she the daughter of Amyntas, a king's son who, when a crown was offered him, could not forbear to reach for it. And now,' she said, 'you must not call me cousin any more. A wife is more important than a cousin.'

The wedding feast was set out in the great hall, with a dais for the women in their chairs of honour, a flower-decked throne for the bride. Her gifts and her dowry were displayed on stands around her. With wondering and distanced eyes, she saw again the jewels and cups and vases, the bolts of fine dyed wool, which Kynna had brought with cherishing care from Macedon. Only one piece was missing, the silver casket which now held her calcined bones.

Kleopatra led her to the King's high table to take her piece of the bride-loaf, sliced with his sword. It was clear that he had never handled a sword before; but he hacked a piece off bravely, broke it in two when told, and, as she tasted hers – the central rite of the wedding – asked her if it was nice, because his own piece was not sweet enough.

Back on her dais, she listened to a hymn by a choir of maidens; Lydians mostly, mangling the words, a few Greek daughters trying hard to be heard. Then she became aware that the women round her were murmuring together, stirring with little fidgets of preparation. With a sudden clutch in her midriff, she knew that when the song ended, they would lead her to the nuptial chamber.

All through the ride, nearly all through the feast, she had over-leaped this moment, throwing her mind ahead to next month, next year, or living in the present only.

'Have you had instruction?'

She looked round with a start. The voice, with a strong foreign accent, came from just beside her. Not till this morning had she met the widow of Alexander. She had bowed to a small jewelled woman, stiff with embroideries of gold and pearl, rubies like pigeons' eggs hanging from her ears. Her surface had been so stunning that she had seemed hardly human, a kind of splendid adornment for the feast. Now, Eurydike met the gaze of two large black eyes, their whites brilliantly clear between eyelids dark with kohl, fixed on her in concentrated malice.

'Yes,' she said quietly.

'So, truly? I had heard your mother was a man, as well as your father. To look at you, one might think so.'

Eurydike gazed back, fascinated as the prey by the predator. Roxane, bright as a little shrike, leaned out from her chair of honour. 'If you know all you should, you will be able to teach your husband.' Her rubies flashed; the song, rising to its climax, did not cover her rising voice. 'To Alexander he was like a dog under his table. He trained him to heel, then sent him back to the kennel. It is *my* son who is king.'

The song was over. Along the dais there were agitated rustlings.

Kleopatra rose to her feet, as she had seen Olympias do it. The others stood up with her. After a moment Roxane followed, staring defiantly. In the formal, studied Greek of her father's court, looking down from her Macedonian height at the little Bactrian, she said, 'Let us remember where we are. And who we are, if we can. Ladies, come. The torches. Io, Hymen! Joy to the bride!'

'Look!' said Philip to Perdikkas, who had the place of honour beside him. 'Cousin Eurydike is going away!' He scrambled anxiously to his feet.

'*Not now!*' Grabbing him by his purple robe, Perdikkas thumped him back on his supper-couch. With savage geniality he added, 'She is changing her dress. We will take you to see her presently.'

The guests in hearing, even the elegant young Lydian servers who had picked up a bit of Greek, made stifled noises. Perdikkas, lowering his voice, said, 'Now listen to the speeches, and when they look at you, smile. We are going to drink your health.'

Philip pushed forward his wine-cup; an engraved gold Achaemenid treasure from the Persian occupation. Konon, standing behind his chair, got it quickly back from a too-zealous server, and filled it from a jug of watered wine, in the strength given to Greek children. He looked incongruous among the graceful Lydians and well-born Macedonian pages waiting at table.

Perdikkas rose to make the best man's speech, recalling the groom's heroic ancestry, the exploits of his grandfather whose name he had auspiciously assumed; the lineage of his mother, the noble lady of horse-loving Larissa. His compliments to the bride were adequate, though rather vague. Philip, who had been occupied in feeding someone's curly white poodle which had been sitting under the table, looked up in time to acknowledge the cheers with an obedient grin.

A harmless person, a distant royal connection, responded for the bride, uttering bland platitudes about her beauty, virtue and high descent. Once more the health was given, and honoured with ritual shouts. It was the time for serious drinking.

Goblets were emptied and briskly filled, faces reddened under tilting wreaths, voices grew louder. Captains still in their thirties argued and bragged about past wars and women; Alexander had died young with young men all about him. For the older men, a real Macedonian wedding brought back the feasts of their youth. Nostalgically, they roared out the time-honoured phallic jokes remembered from their family bridals.

The noble pages had slipped out to get their share. Presently one said, 'Poor fellow. Old Konon might let him have a mouth-ful he can taste, at his own wedding. It might put heart in him.' He and a friend came up behind Philip's couch. 'Konon, Ariston over there told me to say he pledges you.' Konon beamed, and looked about for his well-wisher; Perdikkas was talking to the guest on his other side. The second page filled up the royal cup with neat wine. Philip tasted his new drink, liked it, and tilted back his cup. By the time Konon noticed and angrily diluted it, he had had more than half.

Some of the men started to sing a skolion. It was not yet lewder than a wedding feast allowed, but Perdikkas pulled himself together. He had known all along that this could not be a long drinking-bout. A little time yet could be allowed for hospitality, but soon he must break it up. He stopped drinking, to keep alert.

Philip felt a surge of well-being, strength and gaiety. He banged the table in time with the skolion, singing loudly, 'I'm married, married, married to Eurydike!' The white poodle pawed at his leg; he picked it up and put it on the table, where it ran about, scat-tering cups, fruit and flowers, till someone hurled it off, when it fled yelping. Everyone laughed; some men far gone in drink bawled ancient encouragements to first-night prowess.

Philip gazed at them with blurred eyes, in which lurked a dim anxiety and suspicion. His purple robe felt too hot, in the stew of torch-warmed humanity. He heaved at it, trying to take it off.

Perdikkas saw that it was high time. He called for a torch, and gave the signal to conduct the bridegroom.

Eurydike lay in the great perfumed bed, in her night-robe of fine mussel-silk, the brideswomen gathered round her. They talked among themselves; at first they had dutifully included her, but none of them knew her, and the wait for the men was always tedious; the more since coy jokes were barred. Mostly the floor was held by Roxane, who described the far more splendid cere-monies of Alexander's day, and patronized Kleopatra.

Solitary in the little crowd, with its warm smell of female flesh, of the herbs and cedar-wood of clothes-chests, essence of orange and of rose, Eurydike heard the rising sounds of the men's revelry. It was warm, but her feet felt icy cold in the linen sheets. They had slept in wool at home. The room was huge, it had been King Kroisos' bedchamber; the walls were patterned in coloured marbles, and the floor was porphyry. A Persian lamp-cluster of gilt lotuses hung over the bed, bathing her in light; would anyone put it out? She had an overpowering memory of Philip's physical presence, his strong stocky limbs, his rather sweetish smell. The little she had eaten lay in her like lead. Supposing she was sick on the bed. If her mother were only here! The full sense of her loss came home to her; she felt, terrified, a surge of approaching tears. But if Kynna were here, she would be ashamed to see her cry in the presence of an enemy. She pulled in her stomach muscles, and forced back the first sob in silence.

Behind the matrons the bridesmaids clustered whispering. Their song sung, their small rite done of turning back the bride-bed and sprinkling it with perfume, they had nothing to do. Among a little set of sisters and cousins and friends, the tittering began; dying away if one of the great ladies looked round, rustling like a faint breeze in leaves. Eurydike heard it; she too had nothing to do. Then suddenly she knew that the sounds from the hall had altered. Supper-couches scraped along the floor, the slurred singing stopped. They were getting up.

Like a tense soldier released by the call to onset, she summoned up her courage. Soon all these people must go, and leave her alone to deal with him. She would talk to him, tell him stories. Old Konon had said he would not trouble her.

Roxane too had heard the sounds. She turned, clashing her intricate ruby earrings. 'Joy to the bride!' she said.

Surrounded and pushed on by laughing, drunken, torch-bearing men, stumbling over his robe on the shallow stately stairs with their painted murals, Philip made his way towards the royal bed-chamber.

His head swam, he sweated in his purple robe; he was angry about the dog being chased away. He was angry with Perdikkas for fetching him from the table, and with all the men for mocking him, as he knew they were; they had stopped even pretending. They were laughing at him because they knew he was scared. He had heard the jokes in the hall; there was something he was expected to do with Eurydike, so bad that one must not do it even by oneself, if anyone could see. He had been beaten long ago for being seen. Now, he believed – no one had thought to tell him otherwise – they would all stand and watch him. He didn't know how, and was sure Cousin Eurydike would not like it. Perdikkas was holding him by the arm, or he would have run away.

He said, despairingly, 'It's my bedtime. I want to go to bed.'

'*We'll* put you to bed,' they chorused. 'That's why we're here.' They roared with laughter. It was like the bad old days at home, before Alexander had taken him away.

'Be quiet.' Perdikkas' voice, suddenly unfestal, an angry martinet's, sobered everyone down. They led Philip to an anteroom, and started to undress him.

He let them take off the hot purple robe; but when they undid the girdle of his sweat-soaked tunic, he fought them, and knocked two flying. The rest all laughed; but Perdikkas, looming and awful, commanded him to remember he was King. So he let them strip him, and put him into a long white robe with a gold-embroidered hem. They let him use the chamber-pot (where was Konon?); then there was no more to stay for. They led him to the door. He could hear inside a murmur of women's voices. *They* would be watching, too!

The wide doors opened. There was Eurydike, sitting up in the great bed. A little brown slave-girl, laughing, ran before him with a long snuffer, ready to quench the hanging lamps. A great wave of anger and misery and fear built up in him. It hummed and boomed in his head, booom, booom, booom. He remembered, he knew that soon the white flash would come. Oh, where was Konon? He shouted, 'The light! The light!' and it flashed, a lightning that struck all through him.

Konon, who had been standing in shadow along the passage, ran in. Without apology he shoved aside the horrified group, shocked sober, which bent over the rigid figure on the floor; pulled from his belt-pouch a wooden wedge; prised Philip's jaws apart, so that his tongue should not fall back and choke him. For a moment, he looked up at the men with bitter reproach and anger; then his face settled back into the blank mask of the soldier confronted with stupid officers. He said to Perdikkas, 'Sir, I can see to him. I know what to do. If the ladies could leave, sir.'

Disgusted and ashamed, the men stood aside to let the women go first. In panic disregard for precedence, the bridesmaids ran at once, their slippers pattering on the stairs. The matrons of middle rank, obsessed all day with etiquette and protocol, clustered helplessly, waiting for the queens.

Eurydike sat in the bed, grasping around her the crimson goldfringed coverlet, looking for help. She had on only her thin wedding shift; how could she get up in the presence of men; of Konon, who was staying? Her clothes were on an ivory stool, at the far end of this great room. Would none of them remember her, stand to shield her, put something round her?

She heard a sound from the floor. Philip, stiff as a board till now, had begun to twitch. In a moment he was in the throes of the clonic spasm, his whole frame jerking and thrashing, his robe flung up by his kicking legs.

'Joy to the bride!' It was Roxane, looking down over her shoulder as she swept towards the door.

'Come, ladies.' Kleopatra gathered in a glance the huddled matrons, averting her face from scandal. Making for the door she paused, and turned back to the bed. Eurydike saw the long look of contempt, the unwilling pity. 'Will you come? We will find you something to wear.' Her eye moved to the clothes-stool; an offi-cious matron bustled over.

Eurydike looked after the widow of Alexander, whose gold embroideries gleamed beyond the door; she looked up at Alexander's sister, to whom she was like a beaten whore, whose shame must be covered for the house's honour. She thought, What do I know even of *him*, except that he killed my father? May the gods curse them all. If I die for it, I will make them kneel at my feet.

The matron brought her himation of dyed saffron, the lucky colour of fertility and joy. She took it in silence, and wrapped it round her as she rose. Philip's tremor was growing weaker; Konon was holding his head, to keep it from striking the floor. Standing between him and the watching faces, she said, 'No, lady, I will not come. The King is sick, and my place is with my husband. Please leave us and go away.'

She fetched a pillow from the bed, and laid Philip's head on it. He was hers now, they were both victims together. He had made her a queen, and she would be a king for both of them. Meantime, he must be put into bed and covered warmly. Konon would find her a place to sleep.

South down the ancient coast road that followed the eastern
shore of the Middle Sea, the army of Perdikkas marched with its
long following train: grooms and chandlers, smiths and carpenters and harness-makers, the elephants, the endless wagons, the
soldiers' women, the slaves. At Sidon, at Tyre, at Gaza, the
people looked down from the mended walls. It was eleven years
since Alexander had passed that way alive, whom they had just
seen on his last progress, going to Egypt with a chime of bells.
This army was no business of theirs; but it meant a war, and war
has a way of spreading.

Flanked by its guard of armed Bactrian and Persian eunuchs,
Roxane's wagon followed the march, as it had followed from
Bactria to India, to Drangiana, to Susa, to Persepolis, to
Babylon. Each part had been many times renewed as its journeys
lengthened, but it seemed the same, smelling as before of the
stamped dyed leather that roofed it, of the essences which at
each new city her eunuchs had brought for her approval; even
now, a drift of scent on a cushion could bring back the heat of
Taxila. Here were the heavy turquoise-studded bowls and trin-
kets of her dowry, the vessels of chased gold from Susa, a censer

from Babylon. It might all have been the same, except for the child.

He was nearly two, and seen to be small for his age; but, as she said, his father must have been so. Otherwise, it was clearly her looks he favoured; the soft dark hair, the bright dark eyes. He was lively, and seldom ill; curious and exploring; a terror to his nurses who must watch his safety at peril of their lives. Though he must be protected, she did not like him thwarted; he must learn from the beginning that he was a king.

Perdikkas called on her every few days; he was the King's guardian, as he reminded her whenever they fell out, which happened often. He was offended that the child shrank from him; it came, he said, of never seeing any other man. 'His father, you should remember, was not reared among eunuchs.'

'Among *my* people they leave the harem at five, and still make warriors.'

'However, he beat them. That is why you are here.'

'How dare you,' she cried, 'call me a captive of the spear! You who were our wedding guest! Oh, if he were here!'

'You may well wish that,' Perdikkas said, and left to visit his other ward.

When the army made camp, Philip had his tent just as before. Eurydike, as became a lady of rank, had her wagon; and in this she slept. It lacked Roxane's splendours; but, as she had not seen them, she found it comfortable, and even handsome when her dowry things were set out. It had a roomy locker; and in this, disguised in a roll of blankets, at the hour of departure she had concealed her arms.

Philip was quite happy with these arrangements. He would have been gravely disconcerted by her presence in his tent at night; she might even have wanted Konon to go. In the daytime he was delighted to have her company; would often ride beside her wagon, and point out the sights they passed. He had traversed this whole route in the train of Alexander, and from time to time something would jog an inconsequent flash of memory. He had been encamped for months before the huge walls of Tyre.

In the evening, she dined with him in his tent. She hated at first to watch him eat, but with instruction he improved a little. Sometimes at sunset, if the camp was near the shore, she would walk with him, guarded by Konon, helping him to look for stones and shells; and then she talked to him, telling the legends of the royal house of Macedon she had heard from Kynna, right back to the boy who took the sunbeam for his wages. 'You and I,' she said, 'will be King and Queen there soon.'

A dim anxiety stirred in his eyes. 'But Alexander told me . . .

'That was because he was King himself. All that is over. You *are* the King. You must listen to me, now that we are married. I will tell you what we can do.'

They had passed the Sinai, and in the lands of Egypt made camp by the flat green coast. A few miles ahead was the ancient port of Pelusion; beyond that, the spread-fingered Delta of the Nile, webbed with its intricate veins of canal and stream. Beyond the Nile was Alexandria.

Among the date-palms and little black irrigation canals and clumps of tall papyrus, the army spread itself restlessly. The warm dry wind from the southern sand was just beginning; the Nile was low, the crops stood deep in the rich silt, the patient oxen toiled at the wooden water-wheels. By the elephant-lines, the mahouts stripped off their dhotis to wash their children in the canal, gaily splashing them as they showered themselves with their trunks after the hot trudge across Sinai. The camels, drinking prodigiously, refilled their secret storage tanks; the soldiers' women washed their clothes and their children. The sutlers went out to find supplies. The soldiers prepared for war.

Perdikkas and his staff scanned the terrain. He had been here with Alexander; but that was eleven years back, and for the last two, Ptolemy had been making himself at home. The land's long vistas showed where, at vital points of access, where a mound or a rocky outcrop offered foundation, stout forts of brick or timber had appeared. He could get no further coastwise; Pelusion was well defended by the salt-marsh between. He must strike south, below the meshes of the Delta.

The main camp must stay here. He would take a mobile force, light and unencumbered. Alexander had taught him that. He rode back to his tent in the quick-falling dusk which the breath of the desert reddened, to make his plans.

Through the wide straggling camp, the cook-fires budded and bloomed; little fires of the women, big ones – for the nights were cold still – where twenty or thirty men would share their bean-soup and porridge, their bread and olives, with a relish of dates and cheese, washed down with rough wine.

It was in the hour between food and sleep, when men talked idly, told tales or sang, that the voices began to sound around the camp, just beyond the reach of the firelight. They called softly, speaking good Macedonian; uttering familiar names, recalling old battles under Alexander, old fallen friends, old jokes. First unrebuffed, then hesitantly welcomed, the speaker would come up to the fire. Just a jar together for old times' sake, seeing he'd brought one. Tomorrow, who could say, they might have to kill each other, but meantime, good health and no hard feelings. As for himself, he could only speak as he'd found; now Alexander was gone, Ptolemy was next best. He was a soldier and no one's fool; but he looked after you, he had time for your troubles, and where else would you find that today? What wage, by the way, was Perdikkas paying veterans? *What?* (A shake of the head, a long contemptuous whistle.)

'He promised you loot, I suppose? Oh, yes, it's *there*; but not so you'll ever get to it. This country's murder to those who don't know the waterways. Look out for the crocodiles; they're bigger than in India, *and* cunning.'

178

To a growing audience, he would go on to the comforts and pleasures of Alexandria, the shipping from everywhere, the good fresh food, the wineshops and the girls, the good air all the year round; and Alexander to bring the city luck.

The wine-jar emptied, his mission done, the visitor would slip away, his footfalls merging into the uncanny noises of the Egyptian night. As he threaded his way back to his fort, he would reflect comfortably that he'd not given them a word of a lie, and doing old friends a kindness was a very good way of earning a hundred drachmas.

Perdikkas made his last camp a little above the wrist of the Nile, from which the fingers of the Delta spread northwards. The non-combatants he had brought thus far would await him; among them the Kings, whom he wanted under his eye. From here he would make his march towards the river.

They watched him and his soldiers go into the shimmer of morning mist, horse and foot, the pack-mules with the rations, the camel-train with the parts for the catapults, the elephants plodding after. For a long time they grew smaller in the flat distance, vanishing at last into a low horizon of tamarisk and palm.

Pacing the royal tent, Eurydike waited restlessly for news. Konon had found an escort, and taken Philip riding. She too had liked to ride, free on the hills of Macedon, sitting astride; but she had to remember, now, what would be acceptable in a queen. Perdikkas had told her so.

Now that for the first time she was with an army in the field, all her training and her nature rebelled at being laid aside with slaves and women. Her marriage she had felt as a grotesque necessity, something to be managed, altering nothing of herself; even more, now, she felt women an alien species, imposing no laws upon her.

Over by her wagon, her two maids sat in its shade, chattering softly in Lydian. Both were slaves. She had been offered ladies-in-waiting, but had refused, telling Perdikkas she would not ask softly nurtured women to endure the hardships of the march. The truth was that she would not endure the tedium of female talk. To sex she was indifferent; in this respect she needed women even less than men. Her wedding night had killed the last of that. In adolescent dreams she had fought, like Hippolyta, at a hero's side. Since then she had become ambitious, and her dreams were otherwise.

By the third morning she was impatient even of ambition, which had no outlet. The day stretched before her, empty and flat as the land. Why should she endure it? She remembered the locker in the wagon which contained her arms. Her man's tunic was there as well.

She was the Queen; Perdikkas should have sent reports to her. If no one would bring her news, she would go and see.

All she knew of the expedition she had heard from Konon, who had many friends in the camp. Perdikkas, he had said, had started out without telling anyone his objective, neither the camp commandant nor the senior officers who were going with him. He had heard there had been spies about the camp. The officers had not liked it; Seleukos, who commanded the elephants, liked to know how they would be used. Konon kept to himself much more than he had told; they were saying in camp that Perdikkas was far higher-handed these days than Alexander ever was; Alexander had known how to talk you round.

He had confided, however, to Eurydike that with the stores and remounts they'd taken, he reckoned they would not be marching above thirty miles. And that was the distance to the Nile.

Eurydike changed into her tunic, clasped on her tooled-hide corselet, laced down the shoulder-pieces, put on riding-boots and greaves. Her breasts were small and the corselet hid their curve. Her helmet was a simple, unplumed Illyrian war-cap; her grandmother, Audata, had worn it on the border. The drowsy servants never saw her go. Down at the horse-lines the grooms took her for one of the royal squires, and at her imperious order led a sound horse out.

Even after three days, the spoor of the troops was plain: the ploughed-up grass, the bared dust, the horse and camel droppings, the trampled banks of the irrigation canals, the leaked water caking in the little fields. The peasants labouring to mend the dykes looked up with sullen hatred of all destructive soldiers.

She was only a few miles out when she met the messenger.

He was riding a camel; a dusty, drawn-faced man, who stared at her angrily for not making way for him. But he was a soldier; so she wheeled round and overtook him. Her horse shied from the camel; she called, 'What news? Has there been a battle?'

He leaned over to spit; but his mouth was dry, and only the sound came out. 'Get out of my way, boy, I've no time for you. I've despatches for the camp. They must get ready to take the wounded . . . what are left of them.' He switched his mount; it bobbed its scornful head and left her in its dust.

An hour or two later, she met the wagons. As they came nearer, she guessed their freight from the groaning, from the water-carriers on their donkeys, and the doctor leaning under one of the awnings. She rode down the line, hearing the humming flies, a curse or a cry when a wagon jolted.

The fourth of them had men talking and looking out; men with disabled limbs, not too weak to be alert. She saw inside a familiar face; it was the veteran who had first taken her part on the Sardis road, when her mother died.

'Thaulos!' she called, riding up to the tailboard. 'I am sorry to see you hurt.'

She was hailed with amazement and delight. Queen Eurydike! And they had taken her for some young blood in cavalry! What was she doing here? Had she meant to lead them into battle? A daughter of the house – her granddad would have been proud of her. Ah well, lucky she had been too late for yesterday's work. It did one good to see her.

She did not understand that it was her youth they found endearing; that had she been thirty instead of fifteen they would have made a barrack-room joke of her for a mannish termagant. She looked like a charming boy without having lost her girlishness; she was their friend and ally. As she walked her horse beside the cart, they poured out their discontents to her.

Perdikkas had marched them to a place on the Nile called Camelford. But of course the ford was guarded by a fort across the stream, with a palisade, a scarp, and the wall of the fort on top. Perdikkas' scouts had reported it lightly manned.

A younger veteran said resentfully, 'But what he forgot was that Ptolemy learned his trade from Alexander.'

'Perdikkas hates him,' said another, 'so he underrates him. You can't afford that in war. Alexander knew better.'

'That's it; of course the fort was undermanned. Ptolemy was keeping mobile, till he knew where the strike would be. Once he did know, he came like the wind; I doubt Alexander would have been much quicker. By the time we were half across, he was in the fort with a regiment.'

'And another thing I'll tell you,' Thaulos said. 'He didn't want to shed Macedonian blood. He could have lain low, and fallen on us as we crossed; for he'd come up out of sight. But up he stood on the walls, with a herald, and his men all shouting, trying to scare us back. He's a gentleman, Ptolemy. Alexander thought the world of him.'

With a grunt of pain, he eased himself over on the straw to favour his wounded leg. She asked if he needed water; but they were all in need of talk. The desperately wounded were in other carts.

Perdikkas, they said, had made a speech calling upon their loyalty. It was he who was guardian of the Kings, who had his appointment direct from Alexander. This they could not deny;

moreover he was paying them, and their pay was not in arrears.

Scaling-ladders had been carried by the elephants; and it was they, too, who had torn down the palisades on the river-bank, as their mahouts directed them, plucking out the stakes like the saplings whose leaves they fed on, their thick hides making little of javelins from above. But the defenders had been well trained; the glacis was steep; the men dislodged from the ladders had rolled down the broken palisade into the river, where the weight of their armour drowned them. It was then that Perdikkas had ordered the elephants to assault the walls.

'Seleukos didn't like it. He said they'd done their stint. He said there was no sense in a beast carrying two men up where they'd be level with a dozen, and exposing its head as well. But he was told pretty sharply who was in command. And he didn't like that either.'

The elephants were ordered to give their war-cry. 'But it didn't scare Ptolemy. We could see him up on the wall with a long sarissa, poking back our men as they came up. An elephant can scare any man down on the ground; but not when he's on a wall above it.'

The elephants had laboured up the scarp, digging their heavy feet into the earth, till Old Pluto, the one the others followed, started to pull at the wall-timbers. Old Pluto could shift a battering-ram. But Ptolemy stood his ground, threw off the missiles with his shield, reached out his long spear and got Old Pluto's eyes. The next elephant up, someone picked off the mahout. So there were these two great beasts, one blind and the other unguided, pounding and blundering down the scarp, trampling anyone in their way.

'And that,' said one man, 'is how I got a broken foot. Not from the enemy. And if I never walk straight again, it's not Ptolemy I'll blame for it.'

There was a growl of anger from every man in the cart. They

183

had seen little more of the action, having been wounded about this time; they thought it had gone on all day. She rode by them a little longer, offering sympathy, then asked them the way to Camelford. They urged her to take care, to do nothing rash, they could not spare their queen.

As she rode on, a dark moving bulk appeared in the middle distance, coming slowly from a palm-grove that fringed a pool. As it drew near, she saw two elephants in single file, the smaller going first, the bigger one holding it by the tail. Old Pluto was going home, led as he had been by his mother forty years ago in his native jungle, to keep him safe from tigers. His mahout sat weeping on his neck; his wounded eyes, dropping bloody serum, seemed to be weeping too.

Eurydike noted him, as proof of Ptolemy's prowess. At home her chief diversion had been the hunt; she took for granted that animals were put into the world for men to use. Questioning the other mahout, who seemed to have his wits about him, she learned that Perdikkas had abandoned the assault at evening, and marched after dark, the man did not know where. Clearly, if she rode on she risked falling among the enemy; so she turned back to the camp.

No one had missed her but old Konon, who recognized her as she came back; but, as she warned him with her eyes, it was not his place to rebuke her. He would not dare give her away. For the rest, Philip's wedding had been a nine days' wonder, and just now they had other concerns. It was she herself who began, dimly and gropingly, to see her way ahead.

The army of Perdikkas, what was left of it, came back next day.

Stragglers came first, unofficered, undisciplined, unkempt. Clothes, armour and skin were plastered with dried Nile mud; they were black men, but for their light angry eyes. They went about the camp, seeking water to drink and clean themselves, spreading each his tale of confusion and disaster. The main force followed, a sullen, scowling mass, led by Perdikkas with a face of stone, its tight-lipped officers keeping their thoughts to themselves. Her female dress and seclusion resumed, she sent out Konon to learn the news.

While he was gone, she became aware that round the small circle of the royal quarters a ring of men was gathering. They settled down in groups, not talking much, but with the air of men agreed upon their business. Puzzled and disturbed, she looked for the sentries who should have been somewhere near; but they had joined the silent watchers.

Some instinct dispelled her fear. She went to the entry of the royal tent, and let herself be seen. Arms went up in salute; it was all quiet, it had an air of reassurance, almost of complicity.

'Philip,' she said, 'stand in the opening there, and let those men see you. Smile at them and greet them as Perdikkas taught you. Show me; yes, like that. Say nothing, just salute them.'

He came in, pleased, to say, 'They waved to me.'

'They said, "Long live Philip." Remember, when people say that, you must always smile.'

'Yes, Eurydike.' He went to lay out with his shells some beads of red glass she had bought him from a peddler.

A shadow darkened the tent-mouth. Konon paused for leave to enter. When she saw his face, her eyes moved to the corner, where they kept Philip's ceremonial spear. She said, 'Is the enemy coming?'

'Enemy?' He made it sound like an irrelevance. 'No, madam ... Don't be in a worry about the lads out there. They've taken it on themselves, just in case of trouble. I know them all.'

'Trouble? What trouble?'

She saw his old soldier's stone-wall face. 'I can't say, madam. They say one thing and another in the camp. They were cut up badly, trying to cross the Nile.'

'I've seen the Nile.' Philip looked up. 'When Alexander ...'

'Be quiet and listen. Yes, Konon. Go on.'

Perdikkas, it seemed, had given his men a few hours' rest after

185

the assault upon the fort. Then he had ordered them to strike camp and be ready for a night march.

'Konon,' said Philip suddenly, 'why are all those men shouting?'

Konon too had heard; his narrative had been flagging. 'They're angry, sir. But not with you or the Queen. Don't fret about it, they won't come here.' He took up his tale again.

Perdikkas' men had fought through the heat of the day and on till evening. They were discouraged and dog-tired; but he had promised them an easy crossing, further south at Memphis, down the east bank of the river.

'Memphis,' said Philip, brightening. Long ago, from a window, he had watched the tremendous pageant of Alexander's enthronement as Pharaoh, Son of Ra. He had seemed to be made all of gold.

Konon was saying, 'Alexander, now; *he* knew how to make a man throw his heart into it.'

Outside, the voices of the encircling soldiers rose a tone or two, as if receiving news. The sound sank again.

In the dark before dawn, Konon went on, they had come to the crossing-place. Here the river was split by a mile-long island, breaking its force, and the forks were shallower. They were to cross in two stages, assembling on the island in between.

'But it was deeper than he'd thought. Half over from this side, they were chest-deep. With the current pulling at their shields, some of them keeled over; the rest had all they could do to keep their feet. So then Perdikkas remembered how Alexander crossed the Tigris.'

He paused, to see if she knew about this famous exploit. But she had encouraged no one to talk about Alexander.

'It's a fast stream, the Tigris. Before he sent the infantry across, he stood two columns of cavalry in the river, upstream and down of them. Upstream to break the current, downstream to catch any man carried away. He was the first man in on foot, feeling out the shoals with his spear.'

'Yes,' said Eurydike coolly. 'But what did Perdikkas do?'

'What *he* did was to use the elephants.'

'They didn't get drowned?' said Philip anxiously.

'No, sir. It was the men that drowned ... Where's that idle loafing Sinis? Trust a Karian to go off at a time like this. A moment, madam.' He took a taper to the little clay day-lamp which kept a source of fire, and kindled the cluster on the big branched lamp-stand. Outside, a red glow showed that the soldiers were making a cook-fire. Konon's shadow, made huge by the light behind him, loomed dark and manifold on the worn linen hangings of the tent.

'He put the elephants upstream, in line across, and the cavalry downstream; then he told the phalanx to advance. They went in, the phalanx leaders each with his men. And when they got to the middle, it was as if the Nile had come up in flood. It was over their heads; the horses downstream had to swim for it. It was the weight of the elephants did it; it stirred up the muddy bottom, which the Tigris didn't have. But the worst of all, they all say, was to see their mates being taken by crocodiles.'

'I've seen a crocodile,' said Philip eagerly.

'Yes, sir, I know ... Well, before it deepened too much, a good few men had scrambled up on the island. Perdikkas saw there was no going ahead; so he hailed them, and ordered them to come back.'

'Come *back*?' said Eurydike. She listened with new ears to the sounds outside; the muttering that rose and fell, a long keening from the bivouacs of the soldiers' women. 'He ordered them back?'

'It was that or leave them there. It meant throwing away their arms, which no Macedonian did as long as Alexander led them, and they don't forget it. Some of them shouted out they'd as soon take their chance in the west channel, and give themselves up to Ptolemy. No one knows what became of them. The rest went back in the water, which was deeper than ever, full of blood and crocodiles. A few got out. I've talked with them. One of them left his hand in a crocodile's mouth. The rest of his arm's in ribbons, he'll never live ... They lost two thousand men.'

She thought of the groaning hospital carts, a mere drop now in the ocean of disaster. A sweeping impulse, compounded of anger, pity, contempt, and ambition grasping at opportunity, lifted her out of herself. She turned to Philip.

'Listen to me.' He waited, attentive; recognizing as a dog would do the note of imperative command. 'We are going out to see the soldiers. They have been treated badly, but they know we are their friends. This time, *you* must speak to them. First return their salute; then say – now, listen very carefully – "Men of Macedon. My brother's spirit would grieve to see this day." Don't say anything more, even if they answer you. I will talk to them then.'

He repeated it after her; they went out into the falling dark, lit from behind by the lamps inside the tent, and from before by the soldiers' fire.

An instant cheer greeted them; the word ran round, men ran up crowding to hear. Philip did not falter; she had not charged him with more than he could retain. She saw him pleased with himself, and, lest he should be tempted to improvise, turned to him quickly with a show of wifely assent. Then she spoke.

They were all ears. The King's sense of their wrongs had amazed and pleased them; he could not be as slow as people said. A man of few words. No matter, the Queen would be worth hearing.

Roxane, near by in her wagon, had supposed the troop to have been posted for her own protection. Her eunuchs had told her there was trouble in the camp; but their Greek was poor, and no soldier had had time for them. Now with bewildered anger she heard the young ringing voice crying out against the waste of the gallant dead; promising that when the time came for the King himself to rule them, he would see to it that good men's lives were not thrown away.

Roxane heard the cheers. All her five years of marriage had been told with cheers; shouts of acclamation, the rhythmic roar as the victory parade went by. This sound was different; starting with indulgent affection, but ending with a chorus of revolt.

There, thought Roxane, was an unsexed virago! That bastard and fool the husband should never share *her* child's throne. Just then the child, who had been on edge all day, bumped into something and began to cry. Eurydike, the cheering over, heard the sound, and said to herself that the barbarian's brat should never reign in Macedon.

Perdikkas sat in his tent at his trestle table, stylus in hand, a wax diptych blank before him. He was alone. Before this he should have called his staff to a war council, to decide on his next move; but, he thought, he must give them time to cool. Seleukos had answered him in monosyllables; Peithon had looked foxily under his reddish brows and down his pointed nose, saying this or that, but none of what he thought; Archias, though known to be in camp, had not reported at all. Once more he regretted having sent Alketas north with Eumenes; there was nothing like a kinsman in treacherous times.

Round the double bowl of his tall-stemmed table-lamp, brittle bronze beetles and papery moths fluttered and fell in a ring of ephemeral death. Outside the tent, the squires on duty were talking softly together. It was a breach of discipline, but he was strangely reluctant to go out and deal with it. All he could hear was, now and then, a name. Through the slit of his tent-flap, like a fiery crack, shone the flame of the fire at which the rest were sitting. He had not – yet – the royal right to choose fresh boys from the noble houses of Macedon. One or two had died of fever, or fallen in war; the rest were all here still, his inheritance from the death-chamber in Babylon. He had not had much time for them lately, just taken for granted that they would be there at call. They had been with him at the Nile, ready with spare horses, waiting till he was ready to cross.

The soft voices buzzed, a little nearer now, or a little less careful. 'Alexander always used to …' 'Alexander would no more have …' 'Never! Remember how he …' The voices sank; voices not of protest but of intimate, private judgement. He got to his feet, then sat down again, staring at the tiny holocaust around the lamp. Well, he trusted me with his ring; do they forget that? But as if he had spoken aloud, he seemed to hear a murmur: 'But Krateros was in Syria. And Hephaistion was dead.'

Seeking warmth and comfort, his memory groped back to the days of youth and glory; further yet, to the moment of exultation when, the blood of Philip's assassin red on his sword, he had first looked into those searching intent grey eyes. 'Well done, Perdikkas.' (He knew my name!) 'When my father has had his rites, you will hear from me.' The long pageant of the short years unrolled. He rode in triumph through Persepolis.

There was a break in the sounds outside. The squires had fallen silent. New voices now; older, terser, more purposeful. 'You may dismiss.' A single, uncertain 'Sir?' Then, a little louder – Peithon surely – 'I said, dismiss. Go to your quarters.'

He heard the click of weapons and armour, the fall of departing feet. Not one had come in, to ask for orders, to give a warning. Two years ago, they had cheered him for defying Meleager. But then, they had only just come from the room in Babylon.

His tent-flap opened. For a moment he saw the bright leap of the fire, before the press of men blotted it out. Peithon; Seleukos; Peukestes with his Persian scimitar. And more behind them.

Nobody spoke; there was no need. He fought while he could, grimly, in silence. He had his pride; he had been, even though not for long, second to Alexander. His pride chose for him, when it was too late to think, not to die calling for help that would not come.

*

From the royal tent, Eurydike heard the rising confusion of rumour and counter-rumour, contention and savage cheers. Their protectors grew restless, seeking news. There was a sudden stir; a young man ran up, helmetless, red and sweating with excitement and the heat of the fire.

'King, lady. Perdikkas is dead.'

She was silent, more shocked than she would have supposed. Before she could speak, Philip said with simple satisfaction, 'Good. That's good. Did you kill him?'

'No, sir.' (Just as if, she thought subconsciously, a real man had asked.) 'It was the generals, as I understand. They . . .'

He paused. A new sound had pierced the vague fluctuant din: the roar of a lynch-mob for its prey. Soon it was mingled with the shrieks of women. For the first time she was afraid. A mindless thing was abroad, a thing that could not be spoken with. She said, 'What is it?'

He frowned and bit his lip. 'There's always some will go too far once they begin. They'll be after Perdikkas' people. Don't be afraid, lady; they won't harm the Kings'.'

She was startled by a strong voice just beside her. 'If they come here, I'll kill them.'

Philip had found his ceremonial spear, and was fiercely grasping it. The ornate blade was pointed. It took her a little time to coax it from his hands.

Ptolemy arrived in the camp next day.

He had been informed of Perdikkas' death as soon as it took place – some said before – and arrived with a cavalcade which, though impressive, had no appearance of threat. Relying on his informants, he chose to present himself as a man of honour trusting in his peers.

He was warmly welcomed, even cheered. The soldiers saw in this intrepid confidence a touch of Alexander. Peithon, Seleukos and Peukestes met and escorted him.

He had brought Arybbas, riding at his right hand. The bier of Alexander had been installed at Memphis, to await the completion of his tomb; Perdikkas from across the fatal river might almost have caught the gleam of its gold crest. Its architect now gave the generals a friendly salute. After the briefest pause they returned it; things had to be lived with as they were.

Ptolemy's terms had been agreed beforehand. The first of them was that he should address the army, to answer Perdikkas' accusation of treason. The generals had little choice. He had offered a gentleman's undertaking not to incite their own troops against them. The need for this reassurance spoke, after all, for itself.

The engineers, working at speed, had run up a rostrum. As Alexander had accustomed them to do, they put it near the royal quarters. Eurydike took it at first for a scaffold, and asked who was being put to death. They told her that Ptolemy was to make a speech.

Philip, who had been arranging his stones in an elaborate spiral, looked up alertly. 'Is Ptolemy coming? Has he brought me a present?'

'No, he is only coming to talk to the soldiers.'

'He always brings me a present.' He fondled a memorable lump of yellow crystal from central Asia.

Eurydike was staring at the tall dais, deep in thought. Now Perdikkas was dead, the only appointed guardian of the Kings was the distant Krateros, campaigning somewhere in Syria against Eumenes. There was no Regent of Asia, either. Was this the moment destiny had appointed? 'Men of Macedon, I claim the right to govern in my own name.' She could teach him that, and afterwards speak herself, as she had done last night. Why not?

'Philip. Put that away now.' Carefully she gave him his words. He was not to interrupt Ptolemy's speech; she would tell him when to begin.

A ring of soldiers cordoned the royal quarters. It was only to protect them from the crush of the Assembly; but it gave space, one could step out and be heard. She rehearsed her speech in her head.

Ptolemy, flanked by Peithon and Arybbas, mounted the steps to the rostrum, welcomed with cheers.

Eurydike was astounded. She had heard cheers already that day, but it had never occurred to her that they could be in honour of the recent enemy. She had heard of Ptolemy – he was, after all, a kind of left-handed kinsman – but had never seen him. She was young, still, in the history of Alexander's army.

However often told by Perdikkas that he was a traitor, the troops knew Ptolemy as a well-liked man, and one who led from the front. From the start, none of them had really wanted to go to war with him; when they met disasters, there had been no bracing hatred of the enemy to stiffen their morale. Now they hailed him as a revenant from better days, and heard him eagerly.

He began with an epitaphion for the dead. He mourned as they did the loss of brave former comrades, against whom it would have grieved him to lift his spear. Many had been cast up on his side of the river, whom, had they lived, he would have been proud to enroll under his command. They had had their due rites and he had brought their ashes. Not a few, he was glad to say, had reached shore alive. He had brought them back; they were here now at Assembly.

The rescued men led the cheering. All had been freed without ransom; all had enlisted with Ptolemy.

And now, he said, he would speak of him who, while he lived, had united all Macedonians in pride, victory and glory. Moving many to tears, he told them of Alexander's wish to return to the land of Ammon. (Surely, thought Ptolemy, he would have said so if he could have spoken at the last.) For doing Alexander right, he had been accused of treason, though he had never lifted sword against the Kings; and this by a man who had himself been reaching for the throne. He had come here to submit himself to the judgement of the Macedonians. Here he stood. What was their verdict to be?

The verdict was unanimous; it verged on the ecstatic. He waited, without anxiety or unbecoming confidence, till it had spent itself.

He was glad, he said, that the soldiers of Alexander held him in remembrance. He would subvert no man's loyalty; the army of the Kings could march north with his goodwill. Meantime, he had heard that through the late misadventures the camp was short of supplies. Egypt had had a good harvest; it would be his pleasure to send some victuals in.

Rations were indeed disorganized, stale and scanty; some men had not eaten since yesterday. There was a furore of acclamation. Seleukos mounted the dais. He proposed to the Assembly that Ptolemy, whose magnanimity in victory had equalled even Alexander's, should be appointed regent in Asia, and guardian of the Kings.

Cries of assent were hearty and unanimous. Hands and hats waved. No Assembly had ever spoken with a clearer voice.

For a moment – all the time he had – he stood like Homer's Achilles, this way and that dividing the swift mind. But he had made his choice, and nothing had really happened to change it. As regent, he would have had to leave prospering friendly Egypt, where he was as good as king already; to lead his troops, who liked and trusted him, into a cutthroat scrimmage where one could trust no one – look at Perdikkas, his body hardly cold! No. He would keep his own good land, husband it, and leave it to his sons.

Gracefully but firmly, he made his speech of refusal; the satrapy of Egypt, and the building of Alexandria, were a great enough charge for such a man as himself. But since he had been honoured with their vote, he would take it on himself to name two former friends of Alexander to share the office of guardian. He gestured to Peithon and Arybbas.

In the royal tent, Eurydike heard it all. Macedonian generals learned how to make their voices carry, and Ptolemy's soundbox was resonant. She heard him end his speech with some home-spun army anecdote, mysterious to her, delightful to the soldiers. With a sense of hopeless defeat she observed his height, his presence, his air of relaxed authority; an ugly, impressive man, talking to men. Philip said, 'Does your face hurt you?' and she found she had covered it with her hands. 'Shall I make my speech now?' he said. He began to step forward.

'No,' she said. 'Another day you shall make it. There are too many strangers here.'

He went back happily to play with his toys. She turned to find Konon just behind her. He must have been standing there quietly for some time. 'Thank you, madam,' he said. 'I think it's better.'

Later that day, an aide announced that Ptolemy would shortly pay his respects to the King.

He arrived soon after, saluted Eurydike briskly, and clapped Philip's shoulders in a fraternal embrace, to his beaming pleasure. It was almost as good as Alexander coming. 'Have you brought me a present?' he asked.

His face scarcely flickering, Ptolemy said heartily, 'Of course I have. Not here; I had to talk to all these soldiers. You'll get it tomorrow ... Why, Konon! It's a long time, eh? But I see you take good care of him; he looks as fit as a warhorse. Alexander used to say, "That was a good posting."'

Konon saluted with glistening eyes; no one since Alexander had commended him. Ptolemy turned to go, before remembering his manners. 'Cousin Eurydike, I hope that all goes well with you. Philip's been fortunate, I see.' He paused, and took a long second look at her. In a pleasant but different voice, he added, 'A sensible wife like you will keep him out of mischief. He's had enough in his life of people trying to use him. Even his father, if

195

Alexander hadn't . . . well, never mind. Now Alexander's gone, he needs someone to watch out for him. Well – health and prosperity, cousin. Farewell.'

He was gone, leaving her to ask herself what had possessed her, a queen, to bow to a mere governor. He had meant to warn, not praise her. Another of Alexander's arrogant kindred. At least she would never see *him* again.

Roxane received him with more formality. She still took him for her son's new guardian, and offered the sweetmeats kept for important guests, warning him against the intrigues of the Macedonian vixen. He disillusioned her, praising Peithon and Arybbas. Where, he wondered as he nibbled his candied apricot, would she be today if Alexander were alive? Once Stateira had borne a boy, would he have put up with the Bactrian's tantrums?

The child was clambering over him, clutching his clean robe with sticky hands. He had grabbed at the sweets, thrown down his first choice on the rug, and helped himself to more, with only the fondest of maternal chiding. None the less, Ptolemy took him on his knee, to see Alexander's son who bore his name. His dark eyes were bright and quick; he knew better than his mother did that he was being appraised, and put on a little performance, bouncing and singing. His father was always a showman, thought Ptolemy; but he had a good deal to show. What will this one have?

He said, 'I saw his father when he was as young as this.'

'He takes after both our houses,' said Roxane proudly. 'No, Alexander, don't offer a guest a sweet after you have bitten it . . . He means it for a compliment, you know.' He tried another, this time throwing it down.

Ptolemy lifted him firmly down and set him on his feet. He resented it (That's his father, Ptolemy thought) and started to howl (And that's his mother). It dismayed rather than surprised him to see Roxane picking him out his favourites from the dish, and feeding him in her lap. 'Ah, he will have his way. Such a little king as he is already.'

Ptolemy got to his feet and looked down at the child; who looked up, from the cosseting lap, with a strange uneasy gravity, pushing his mother's hands away.

'Yes,' he said. 'He is the son of Alexander. Do not forget that his father could rule men because he had first learned to rule himself.'

Roxane caught the child to her breast and stared at him resentfully. He bowed and saw himself out. At the entrance of the tent with its precious rugs and gem-studded hanging lamps, he turned to see the boy gazing after him with wide dark eyes.

In the palace of Sardis, seated in the same room where she had entertained Perdikkas, Kleopatra confronted Antipatros, the Regent of Macedon.

Perdikkas' death had shocked her to her roots. She had not loved him; but she had committed her life to him, and founded on him her future. Now she looked into a void. She was still trying to come to terms with her desolation when Antipatros arrived from his campaign in Kilikia.

She had known him all her life. He had been fifty when she was born. Except that his hair and beard and brows had turned from grizzle to white, he seemed unchanged, and as formidable as ever. He sat in the chair Perdikkas had often used, spear-straight, fixing her with a faded but fierce blue eye of inflexible authority.

It was his fault, she said to herself, that Olympias had come from Macedon to Dodona to make her life intolerable. It was his fault she was here. But the habit of youth still held; he was the Regent. It was she who felt in his presence like a child who has wickedly broken something old and precious, and awaits a well-earned chastisement.

He had not rebuked her; simply addressed her as someone whose deep disgrace could be taken for granted. What was there to say? It was she who had set the landslide moving. Through her, Perdikkas had rejected the Regent's daughter, after marrying her for policy; had planned to usurp his power, loyally wielded through two kings' reigns. She sat silent, twisting a ring on her finger, Perdikkas' betrothal gift.

After all, she thought, trying to summon up defiance, he is not the rightful regent. Alexander said he was too oppressive, Perdikkas told me so. By rights, Krateros should be regent now.

Antipatros said in his slow harsh voice, 'Did they tell you that Krateros is dead?'

'Krateros?' She stared, almost too dulled to feel it. 'No, I had not heard.' Handsome commanding Krateros, the soldiers' idol next to Alexander; never Persianized, Macedonian dyed in grain. She had adored him at twelve years old when he was one of her father's squires; she had treasured a strand of horsehair left in a tree by his helmet crest. 'Who killed him?'

'It would be hard to say.' He stared back under his white thatched brows. 'Perhaps he might think that you did. As you know, Perdikkas sent Eumenes north to hold the straits against us. He was too late for that; we crossed, and divided our forces, and it was he who met with Eumenes. The Greek is clever. He guessed that if his own Macedonians knew whom they were to fight, they would mutiny and go over; so he kept it from them. When the cavalry met, Krateros' horse went down. His helmet was closed, he was not recognized; the horses trampled him. When it was over they found him dying. I am told that even Eumenes wept.'

She was past tears. Hopelessness and humiliation and grief lay on her like black stones. It was grey winter with her; in silence she bore the cold.

He said drily, 'Perdikkas was unfortunate.' Was it possible, she thought, that there was more to come? He sat there like a judge counting the hangman's lashes. 'Eumenes' victory was complete. He sent a courier south to Egypt, to tell Perdikkas. If he had heard in time, he might have persuaded his men that his cause was still worth following. When it reached the camp he was dead.'

What did we do, she thought, to make the gods so angry? But she knew the annals of the throne of Macedon. She had the answer: We failed.

'And so,' Antipatros was saying, 'all Eumenes got for his trouble – and he is wounded too, I hear – was to be condemned in his absence, for treason and for the death of Krateros. Perdikkas' army condemned him in Assembly . . . also, when they mutinied, a mob of them murdered Atalante, Perdikkas' sister. Perhaps you knew her.'

She had sat in this room, tall and dark like her brother; rather grave, because of his other marriage, but civilly planning for the wedding; a woman with dignity. For a moment Kleopatra shut her eyes. Then she straightened. She was Philip's daughter. 'I am sorry for it. But they say, Fate rules all.'

He said only, 'And now? Will you go back to Epiros?'

It was the final stroke, and he must know it. He knew why she had left her dead husband's land, which she had governed well. He knew that she had offered herself to Leonnatos and then Perdikkas, not in ambition but in flight. No one knew more than he about Olympias. His wronged daughter was in his house in Macedon; and Olympias' daughter was wholly in his power. If he chose, he could pack her off like a runaway child, in custody to her mother. Rather than that she would die; or even beg.

'My mother is governing in Epiros till my son succeeds. It is her country; she is Molossian. There is no place for me in Epiros any more. If you will grant it me' – the words almost scorched her throat – 'I will stay here in Sardis and live privately. You have my word I shall do nothing more to trouble you.'

He kept her waiting, not to punish her but to think. She was still worth, to any well-born adventurer, what she had been to two dead pretenders. In Epiros she would be restless and resentful. It would be wisest to have her killed. He looked, and saw her father in her face. For two reigns he had kept his oath of loyalty to absent kings; now his pride was invested in his honour. He could not do it.

'These are uncertain times. Sardis has been fought for time out of mind, and we are still at war. If I do as you ask, I cannot ensure your safety.'

'Who is safe in this world?' she said, and smiled. It was her smile that for the first time made him pity her.

The army of the Kings had struck camp in Egypt. Generously victualled and politely seen off by Ptolemy, it was marching north to its rendezvous with Antipatros.

The guardians of the Kings, appointed after Alexander's death, were now both dead within two years of it. Their office was held, at present, by Peithon and Arybbas.

In the two royal households, only Roxane had known the fallen Krateros. He had convoyed her back from India with the noncombatants, while Alexander was shortening his life in the Gedrosian desert. She had greatly preferred him to Perdikkas, and looked forward to being in his charge again. She had had a new gown made to receive him in; her mourning for Krateros had been sincere. The new guardians were both unpromising. Peithon, fiercely devoted to Alexander, had always regarded her as a campaign wife who ought to know her place. Arybbas she suspected of preferring boys. Besides, they had only visited her both together; a precaution privately agreed between them.

To Eurydike, Krateros had been only a name. She had heard of his death with relief; his fame had threatened a powerful force; more powerful, she had been quick to sense, than the present guardians could command.

Soon after the mutiny she had felt the change of air. Morale had altered. These were now men who had successfully defied their leaders; some were men who had shed blood. They had won; but their inward certainty was wounded, not strengthened, by their victory. They had been led disastrously and did not repent rebellion; but a navel-cord that had nourished them had been broken, a common trust. Without it they felt restless and bereaved.

Peithon and Arybbas had not filled up their emptiness. Peithon they knew by repute, as all the eight Bodyguards were known; but few, as it happened, had ever served with him. His quality was untested, and in the meantime they found him uninspiring. As for Arybbas, his record under Alexander had been undistinguished except in the field of art, which did not interest them.

If either one had given signs of hidden fire, the army would have been his own; it was like a pack of powerful dogs missing a master's voice. But on both alike their office sat uneasily; both alike were anxious to avoid all occasion for disorder, all look of rivalry or of forming factions. Both went about their duties with sober competence.

Thus the drama dragged, the action sagged; the audience fidgeted, coughed and yawned, began fingering its apple-cores and half-bitten onions and crusts, but was not quite ready yet to throw them at the actors. The play was a gift to any talented supporting player who had the wit to steal it. Eurydike, waiting in the wings, felt the theatre pausing and knew that her cue had come.

Had Peithon had about him the wily veterans of his old command, some gnarled and canny phalanx-leader would have come to his tent and said, 'Sir, with respect. That young wife of King Philip's is going about among the men and making trouble ... Oh, not that kind of trouble, she's a lady and knows it too; but ... ' But Peithon's crafty old veterans had marched with Krateros, carrying the gold with which Alexander had paid them off. It was Eurydike who had her allies and her faithful spies.

Her chief problem was Philip. On the one hand he was indispensable; on the other, he could not safely be produced for more than minutes. To receive men without him would invite scandal; with him, disaster.

And yet, she thought, my blood is as good and better. What is he but the bastard of a younger son, even if his father did seize the throne? My father was the rightful king; what's more, I was born in wedlock. Why should I hold back?

She picked up her faction first from soldiers who already knew her; her saviours on the Sardis road, the men who had guarded the tent in Egypt; some of the walking wounded who had survived the battle on the Nile. Soon many found pretexts to approach her wagon on the march, give a respectful greeting, and ask if she or the King had need of anything. She had taught Philip, if he was riding beside her, to smile and salute and go a short way ahead. Thus sanctioned by her husband, the ensuing talk was relieved of any awkwardness.

Soon, by devious ways known to soldiers not keenly scrutinized, the King had his own unofficial guard, and his wife commanded it. It was proud of itself, and its unrostered numbers grew.

The march dragged on, at foot-pace with all its followers. A young officer of her troop, remembering Alexander (they were all prone to this, and she had learned better than to check them), told how he used to leave the sluggish column and go hunting with his friends. The idea delighted her. One or other of them would ask leave to ride out for the day and join the column at sunset, taking a few comrades; a common indulgence in a peaceful area. She would get into her men's clothes and, asking no one's leave, go with them.

Of course the news got round; but it did her no harm. She was played into her role by now, fed by her audience. A confiding gallant boy, a girl receiving gratefully their protection and support, a queen who was wholly Macedonian; in all these parts they loved her.

In upland pastures, sharing a breakfast of barley-cake and thin wine, she would tell them stories of the royal house, from her great-grandfather Amyntas down; of his gallant sons, Perdikkas and Philip, both kings and both her grandfathers, fighting the Illyrians on the border when Perdikkas fell. 'And because of Philip's valour they made him King. My father was a child and could not help them; so they passed him by. He never questioned the people's will, he was always loyal; but when Philip was murdered, false friends accused him falsely, and the Assembly put him to death.'

They hung on her words. All of them in their youth had heard old garbled tales around the family fire; but now they were getting the real truth, straight from a queen of the royal line; they were proud, impressed and deeply grateful. Her chastity, so evident to them, so natural to her as to be unconsidered, awed them. Each one of them would boast of her notice to a dozen envious comrades when the wineskin went round at night.

She talked, too, of Philip. He had been delicate, she said, in youth; when he grew strong, Alexander was in the full tide of his victories, and his brother felt abashed beside him. Now, he would be glad no longer to be ruled by guardians, but himself to be the guardian of the Macedonians, whose good he had at heart. But because of his modesty, Perdikkas had usurped his rights; and the new guardians did not know him, or care to know.

Philip was pleased, when he rode through the camp, to be so often and so warmly greeted. He would salute and smile; soon she advanced his instruction. He learned to say, 'Thank you for your loyalty,' and was happy to see how much the soldiers liked it.

Arybbas, going about, once or twice noticed these greetings, but saw no harm in them and did not report them to Peithon. Peithon for his part was paying the price for his own resentment of Perdikkas' overbearing ways. On the march to Egypt he had shrugged his shoulders and lost interest in administration. By the time catastrophe had prompted them to kill Perdikkas, Peithon was out of touch with the men. Mutiny had made them truculent; all he wanted was to get the army in one piece to the rendezvous with Antipatros. Once an Assembly could be mustered there, a permanent guardian could be elected. He would stand down with relief.

Discipline, meantime, he left to the junior officers, who in turn thought it wiser to take things easily. Eurydike's faction grew and fermented. When the army made camp at Triparadisos, the brew was ready.

Triparadisos – Three Parks – was in north Syria, the creation of some past Persian satrap who must have wished to emulate the Great King himself. Its small river had been channelled into pools and cascades and fountains, with marble bridges and whimsical stepping-stones of obsidian and porphyry. Rhododendron and azalea jewelled the gentle hills; specimen trees of great rarity and beauty, brought here by ox-train in a solid bed of their native earth, made laced or spreading patterns against a springlike sky. There were glades starred with lilies, whose green perspectives were overlooked by summerhouses with fretted screens, designed for harem ladies; and hunting-lodges of cedar-wood for the satrap and his guests.

During the years of war, the deer had been mostly poached, the peacocks eaten, and a good deal of timber felled; but to restless weary soldiers it was Elysium. Here was the ideal rest-camp in which to await Antipatros, reported a few days' march away.

The generals ensconced themselves in the chief hunting-lodge, built on a central eminence and commanding long man-made vistas. In the glades and clearings the army camped, bathing in the sparkling streams, cutting the trees for cook-fires, snaring conies and liming birds for the pot.

Arybbas found it delightful, and went off on long rambling

rides with a dear friend. Peithon so much outranked him that it seemed more graceful, as well as much more pleasant, to leave discipline to him.

Peithon, who thought him a lightweight, scarcely missed him, but thought uneasily that Alexander would have found the men something to do. Games very likely, with prizes big enough to keep them on their toes for a few days' practice ... He considered talking to Seleukos; but Seleukos, who thought he had a better claim to the guardianship than Arybbas, had been sulking lately. Well, thought Peithon, better leave it alone.

Philip and Eurydike were lodged in the summerhouse of the old satrap's chief wife. By now she had the remount officer among her partisans; a good horse was always hers for the asking. She rode about her business, wearing her man's tunic now all day. Peithon and Arybbas saw from their knoll, if they happened to look out, only a distant horseman like any other.

By now, most of the camp knew what was going on. Not everyone approved; but Philip was King, there was no getting past that; and no one loved either guardian well enough to risk the dangerous task of talebearing. No matter, the doubtful thought; any day now Antipatros would arrive.

As it happened, however, an inland cloudburst had brought the river Orontes down in flood, across Antipatros' line of march. Seeing no pressing need for haste in peaceful country, and preferring to keep his eighty-year-old bones dry, he made camp on rising ground and awaited the sinking of the waters.

In Triparadisos the weather was fresh and fine. Bright and early one day, when the dew lay on the spring lilies in crystal globes, and the birds were singing high in the fifty-year-old trees, Peithon was wakened by an aide who rushed into his room half dressed, still tying his girdle. 'Sir, the men ...'

His voice was drowned by a trumpet-call which brought Peithon to his feet, naked and staring. It was the royal fanfare which announced a king.

Arybbas came running in, a robe thrown around him. 'It must be Antipatros. Some fool of a herald . . . '

'No,' said Peithon. 'Listen.' He peered through the little window. 'What in the Furies' name . . . ? Get dressed! Get armed!'

It was quick work for Alexander's veterans. They came out on the veranda from which the satrap had aimed his arrows at driven game. The broad glade before them was filled with soldiers. At their head, mounted, were Philip and Eurydike. The trumpeter stood by them, looking defiant, and full of the importance of a man who is making history.

Eurydike spoke. She was wearing her man's tunic, and all her armour except her helmet. She was uplifted, glowing; her skin was clear and transparent; her hair shone; the vitality of great daring flowed through her and rayed out of her. She did not know, nor would have wished to know, that Alexander had glowed like this on his great days; but her followers knew it.

Young, clear and hard, her voice carried as far as Ptolemy's bass had done in Egypt. 'In the name of King Philip son of Philip! Perdikkas his guardian is dead. He has no need of new guardians. He is of age, thirty years old, and able to reign for himself. He claims his throne!'

Beside her, Philip threw up his hand. His shout, startlingly loud, unfamiliar to all his hearers, boomed out. 'Macedonians! Do you take me for your king?'

The cheers came crashing back, making the birds beat up from the tree-tops. 'Long live King Philip! Long live Queen Eurydike!'

A galloping horse thudded over to the lodge. The rider threw his bridle to a scared slave and strode up to the veranda. Seleukos, whose courage was legendary and who knew it, was having no one say he had skulked in his quarters during a mutiny. He was a well-liked general. In his presence, incipient shouts of 'Death to the guardians!' sank away. The cheers for Philip went on.

Through the din, Seleukos bawled in Peithon's ear, 'They're not all here. Play for time. Call for a full Assembly.'

It was true that about a third of the men looked to have stayed away. Peithon stepped forward; shouts sank to muttering. 'Very well. You're free Macedonians, you have your rights. But remember, Antipatros' men are only a few miles off, and they have *their* rights. This touches all the citizens.'

There was a surge of discontent. They were keyed-up, impatient. It needed only Eurydike's 'No! Now!' to set them off again.

Something made her look around. Philip was drawing his sword.

She had had to let him wear it if he was to look like a man, let alone a king. In another moment, by the look of his eyes, he would be charging at the lodge. For an instant she hesitated. Would they follow him ... ? But he would be helpless in combat, all would be lost. 'Let's kill them!' he said eagerly. 'We can kill them, look.'

'No. Put it back.' He did so, obedient though regretful. 'Now call out to the men, "Let Peithon speak."'

He was at once obeyed. Never before had he so impressed the soldiers. Peithon knew he could do no more. 'I hear you,' he said. 'Yes, you can call Assembly. Don't blame me when the Regent comes and it's all to be done again. Herald, you down there. Come up here and sound.'

The Assembly was held in the glade before the hunting-lodge. The men who had stayed aloof answered the summons; there were rather more than Eurydike had thought. But the glow of success was on her when, with Philip, she mounted the veranda which was to serve as rostrum. Smiling, she looked around the cheering faces. The silent ones she could do without well enough.

At the far end of the platform, Peithon was talking quietly to Seleukos. She ran over in her mind what she meant to say.

Peithon came up to her. 'You shall have the last word. A woman's privilege.' He was sure of himself, she thought. Well, let him learn.

He stepped forward briskly to the front of the platform. He got a few boos, but soon the sound died down. This was Assembly, and ancient custom held.

'Macedonians!' His crisp bark cut through the last murmurs. 'In Egypt, in full Assembly, you appointed me and Arybbas as guardians of the Kings. It seems that you've changed your minds, never mind why. So be it. We accept. No need to put it to the vote; we are both agreed. We resign the guardianship.'

There was complete, stunned silence. They were like men in a tug-of-war when the other team lets go. Peithon made the most of it.

'Yes, we resign. *But*, the office of guardian stands. That office was decreed in full Assembly when Alexander died. Remember, you have two kings, one of them too young yet to speak for himself. If you vote Philip to rule in his own right, you appoint him guardian of Alexander's son, till he comes of age. Before you vote, consider all these things.'

'Yes! Yes!' They were like the audience at a play when the actors are slow to enter. Eurydike saw it. It was for her that they were waiting; and she was ready.

'Here, then,' said Peithon, 'is Philip son of Philip, who claims his right to rule. King Philip, come here.' Meekly, with a look of faint surprise, Philip joined him at the head of the central steps. 'The King,' said Peithon, falling back a pace, 'will now address you and state his case.'

Eurydike stood frozen. The sky had fallen on her, and she had not seen that it was inevitable from the first.

She was crushed by the shock of her own folly. She sought no excuse, did not remind herself that she was only just turned sixteen. In her own mind she was a king, a warrior. She had blundered, and that was all.

208

Philip gazed around him, smiling vaguely. He was greeted with friendly, encouraging cheers. They all knew he was a man of few words, and over-modest. 'Long live Philip!' they called. 'Philip for King!'

Philip's head went up. He knew quite well what the meeting was about, Eurydike had told him. But she had told him, too, never to say a word she had not taught him first. He shot an anxious look at her, to see if she would talk instead; but she was looking straight before her. Instead, the voice of Arybbas just behind him, smooth and insistent, said, 'Sir, speak to the soldiers. They are all waiting.'

'Come on, Philip!' they shouted. 'Silence for the King!' He waved his hand at them; they hushed each other to hear.

'Thank you for your loyalty.' That was safe, he knew; yes, they all liked it. Good. 'I want to be King. I'm old enough to be King. Alexander told me not to, but he's dead.' He paused, collecting his thoughts. 'Alexander let me hold the incense. He told Hephaistion, I heard him, he said I'm not as slow as I'm made out to be.' There were indeterminate noises. He added, reassuringly, 'If I don't know what to do, Eurydike will tell me.'

There was a moment's stupefied pause, then confused uproar. They turned on one another, abusive, expostulating, wrangling. 'I told you, now you see.' 'He spoke to me like any man, only yesterday.' 'He has the falling sickness, it takes men so.' 'Well, he told us the truth, you can give him that.'

Eurydike stood as if bound to the execution post. Gladly she would have been dispersed in air. Everywhere, repeated as the joke was relished, she heard, 'Eurydike will tell me what to do.' Encouraged by his reception, Philip was still speaking. 'When I'm King, I shall always ride an elephant.'

Behind him, Peithon and Arybbas looked complacently at each other.

Something in the laughter began to give Philip doubts. It reminded him of the dreadful wedding night. He remembered the magic phrase, 'Thank you for your loyalty'; but they did not cheer, only laughed louder. Should he run away, would he be caught? He turned on Eurydike a face of panic appeal.

At first she moved like an automaton, carried by her pride. She gave the smug guardians a single look of scorn. Without a glance at the buzzing crowd below, she went on to Philip and took him by the hand. With ineffable relief and trust he turned to her. 'Was the speech right?' he said.

Holding up her head, for a moment she faced the crowd before she answered him. 'Yes, Philip. But it is finished now. Come, we can sit down.'

She led him to the benches by the wall, where once the satrap and his guests had sat with their wine to await the huntsman's call.

The Assembly continued without them.

It was involved and fretful. The factions had collapsed into absurdity. A few hundred voices urged Peithon and Arybbas to resume their charge, meeting a vigorous refusal. Seleukos in turn declined. While lesser names were being tossed about, a courier rode in. He announced that Antipatros with his army was crossing the Orontes, and would arrive within two days.

Peithon, giving out this news, reminded the men that ever since Perdikkas' death both the Kings had been on their way to Macedon, where they belonged. Who, then, was more fitted than the Regent to be their guardian, now Krateros was dead? Sullenly they settled for this solution, since no one had a better one.

Quietly, during the debate, Eurydike had led her husband away. Over their midday meal he repeated his speech to Konon, who praised it and avoided meeting her eyes.

She hardly heard them. Beaten to her knees, faced with surrender, she felt her blood remembering its sources. The shade of Alexander taunted her; he, at sixteen, had held Macedon as regent, and fought a victorious war. The fire of her ambition smouldered still under its embers. Why had she been humbled?

Not for reaching too high, but too low. I was mocked, she thought, because I did not dare enough. From now on, I will claim my rights for myself.

At evening, when the sun sank over Asia and the first smoke rose, she put on her man's tunic, called for her horse, and rode out among the watch-fires.

Two days later, riding ahead of the Regent and his army, Antigonos One-Eye reached the camp at Triparadisos.

He was the man who had escaped to Macedon to reveal Perdikkas' plot. Alexander had made him satrap of Phrygia; the grateful regent had appointed him Commander-in-Chief of all the troops in Asia. He was now on the way to take up his new command.

He rode a Persian 'great horse', being so tall that no Greek horse could carry him far. But for his eye-patch – he had lost the eye winning Phrygia for Alexander – he was still a handsome man. His even handsomer young son Demetrios, who went with him everywhere, worshipped him. Riding side by side, they made an impressive pair.

With the small column of his entourage, he entered the woodland fringes of the park. Soon, cocking his ear, he motioned his train to halt.

'What is it, Father? Is it a battle?' The boy's eyes kindled. He was fifteen, and had never yet fought in war.

'No,' said his father, listening. 'It's a brawl. Or mutiny. High time I came, by the sound. Forward.' To his son he said, 'What's Peithon about? He did well enough under Alexander. Never think you know a man whom you've only seen acting under orders. Well, he's a stopgap here. We'll see.'

The prospect did not displease him. His own ambitions were great.

Eurydike had rallied to her cause about four-fifths of the army. At the head of her troops, she had appeared before the generals' lodge, announced with the royal fanfare, demanding, this time, joint rule for Philip and herself.

The three generals gazed down with revulsion, not unmixed with fear, at the mob below. It looked worse than mutinous; it looked anarchic. Eurydike herself was half aware of this. Her training in weaponry had not included military drill, and she had not considered in advance that her following would be more manageable, as well as more impressive, if she drew it up in some kind of formation. A year ago, the junior officers (the seniors had held aloof) would have managed for her; but much had happened in a year, and most of it bad for discipline. So now an armed rabble followed her; men shouldered each other to get in front, and hurled insults at the generals.

It was as boos and jeers were drowning Peithon's voice that Antigonos and his suite had come into earshot.

After his first distant glimpse, he sent Demetrios to scout ahead; it was good training for the boy. He cantered gaily into the trees, coming back to report that there was a horde of men gathered in front of what looked like headquarters, but no one to speak of at the back.

Meantime, Eurydike felt, behind her, the mass begin to seethe. She must lead them on, now, or somehow hold them back. Inherited instinct told her she would not lead them long. They would surge past her and lynch the generals. After that, her frail authority would be swept away.

'Herald, blow halt!' She faced them with lifted arms; they swayed restlessly, but came no further. She turned again to confront the generals.

The veranda was empty.

During the uproar of the last few minutes, the generals had learned that their new commander-in-chief had arrived in camp. He was in the lodge behind them.

The room inside, with its dark wood and little windows, had an air of dangerous gloom, in which, peering, they made out the towering form of Antigonos, seated in the satrap's chair; glaring at them, like a Cyclops, with his single eye. The young Demetrios, a splinter of light picking out his dazzling profile, stood like a fierce attendant spirit behind him.

Antigonos said nothing. He pierced them with his eye, and waited.

As he heard out their lamentable tale, his face changed slowly from grimness to sheer incredulity. After a disturbing pause, he said, 'How old is this girl?'

Shouting against the impatient roar from outside, Seleukos told him.

Antigonos swivelled his head to sweep them with his eye, ending at Peithon. 'Thundering Zeus!' he said. 'Are you soldiers or pedagogues? Not even pedagogues, by God! Stay here.' He strode out on the veranda.

The apparition from nowhere of this huge, formidable and famous man, instead of the expected victims, startled the crowd into almost total silence. Eurydike, who had no idea who he was, stared at him blankly. Philip, whom she had forgotten, began, 'That's ...'

He was drowned by a boom from Antigonos' great chest. Soldiers in the front, despite themselves, straightened up and made vain shuffling efforts to dress their line.

'*Stand* back there, you sons of fifty fathers!' Antigonos roared. '*Get* back, Hades and the Furies take you! What do you think you are, a horde of naked savages? Stand up and let me look at you. Soldiers, are you? I've seen better soldiers robbing caravans. Macedonians, are you? Alexander wouldn't know you. Your own mothers wouldn't know you, not if they could help. If you want to hold Assembly, you'd better look like Macedonians, before some real ones come here and see you. That will be this afternoon. Then you can hold Assembly, if the rest agree. Clean yourselves up, curse you, you stink like goats.'

Eurydike heard, dismayed, defiant shouts change to an indeterminate grumbling. Antigonos, who had ignored her, seemed to see her for the first time.

'Young lady,' he said, 'take your husband back to his quarters, and look after him. It's a wife he needs, not a female general. Go about your work, and leave me to mine. I learned it from your grandfather before ever you were born.'

There was a wavering pause; the edges of the press began to fall away, the centre to loosen. Eurydike cried out, 'We will have our rights!' and some voices took it up, but not enough. The hateful giant had beaten her, and she did not know even his name.

Back in the tent, Konon told her. While she considered her next move, the smell of food reminded her that her young stomach was hungry. She waited till Philip had done – she hated to see him eating – and sat down to her meal.

Somewhere outside, a high imperious voice was arguing with the guard. Konon, who was pouring her wine, looked up. A youth came in; stunningly handsome, and hardly as old as herself. With his perfect features and clustering short gold curls, he could have posed for a Hermes to any sculptor. Like Hermes he entered lightly, and stood poised before her, fixing her with the gaze of a scornful god.

'I am Demetrios, son of Antigonos.' He sounded, too, like a deity announcing himself at the opening of a play. 'I am here to warn you, Eurydike. It is not my custom to make war on women. But if you harm a hair of my father's head, your life shall pay for it. That is all. Farewell.'

He was gone, as he had come, through the disorganized army; his speed, his youth and arrogance cleaving his way.

She stared after this first antagonist of her own age. Konon snorted. 'The insolent young dog! Who let him in? "Not my custom to make war on women"! Who is *he* used to make war on, I'd like to know? His father should take a strap to him.'

Eurydike ate quickly and went out. The visitation had spurred her flagging purpose. Antigonos was a force of nature with which she could not contend; but he was one man alone. The troops were still mutinous and ripe for revolt. She dared not assemble them, which would bring him down on her again; but she went among them, reminding them that Antipatros, who was coming, was not the rightful regent, that he feared being displaced by a rightful king. If he was allowed, he would seek out Philip and herself and all the best of their followers, to be put to death.

Antigonos, meanwhile, had sent one of his suite to meet the Regent and warn him to prepare for trouble. But the Regent and his escort had come by short-cuts over the hills; the messenger missed his way, arriving late at the tail-end of the column. There he was told that the old man had gone ahead with his bodyguard, long before noon.

Sitting straight on his easy-pacing charger, his stiff legs aching on the saddle-cloth, his face set in the harsh stare which was his mask for the pains and infirmities of age, the Regent rode to Triparadisos. His doctor had urged him to go by litter. But so had his son Kassandros, back in Macedon; who was only waiting to insist that his failing strength called for a deputy – naturally, himself. Antipatros neither trusted nor much liked his eldest son. Here in Syria, since Perdikkas' death anything might have happened; and he meant to arrive, the gods and physic helping him, looking like a man to be obeyed.

The main gate into the park was dignified with great columns topped with stone lotuses. Antipatros took the good road which duly led him there.

Noises came from beyond; but to his annoyed surprise no escort was there to meet him. He told his herald to announce him with a trumpet blast.

In the lodge, the generals knew, with dismay, that his main force could not have come so quickly. Their envoy had missed

215

him. Almost at once a rising commotion was heard; and a squadron leader, who had not joined the revolt, came galloping up. 'Sir! The Regent's here with no more than fifty horse, and the rebels are mobbing him.'

They ran for their helmets – the rest of their armour was on – and shouted for their horses. Neither Peithon nor Arybbas had ever lacked personal courage; they reached for their javelins briskly. Antigonos said, 'No, not you two. If you come they'll fall on all of us. Stay here, get anyone you can find and hold the lodge. Come, Seleukos. We'll go and talk to them.'

As Seleukos mounted, vaulting upon his spear, Antigonos on his tall horse beside him, he felt for a moment the old elation of the golden years. It was welcome after the squalid affair in Egypt, from which he did not yet feel clean. When, though, in those years had he ever felt in danger from his own men?

The Regent had reached an age when discomfort and fatigue bothered him more than danger. Expecting nothing worse than disaffection, he had come in a light riding tunic and straw sun-hat, armed only with his sword. Seleukos and Antigonos, galloping down between huge cedars and deodars and spreading planes, saw the tight knot of the bodyguard sway in the press around it, the broad-brimmed hat fly off among the helmets, the vulnerable gleam of silver hair.

'Try not to draw blood,' called Antigonos to Seleukos. 'They'll kill us then.' With a bellow of 'Halt, there!' he shoved down into the press.

Their firmness, their fame, Antigonos' great height and over-whelming presence, got them through to the Regent, glaring under his white brows like an ancient eagle beset by crows, and grasping his old sword. 'What's this, what's this?' he said. Antigonos gave him a brief salute (did he think there was time to chat? The old man must be failing at last) and addressed the soldiers.

Had they no shame? They claimed to respect the King; had

they no respect for Philip his great father, the maker of their nation, who had appointed this man and trusted him? He had never been deposed by Alexander, only summoned for a conference while a deputy relieved him ... Antigonos when he chose could persuade as well as dominate. The crowd sullenly parted; the Regent and his rescuers rode up to the lodge.

Eurydike had been preparing her speech for the coming Assembly, and knew nothing of the fracas till it was over. It shocked her that followers of hers might have butchered this ancient man. It offended her poetic image of war. Besides, they should be under her control and seen to be so. Only Athenian demagogues made speeches while others fought.

An hour before sunset, Antipatros' main force arrived. She heard, rumbling on into the dusk, the horse and foot filing into the parks, the shouting and creaking of the supply trains, the bustle of camp slaves pitching tents, the rattle of stacked arms, the whinnying of horses scenting their kind; and, lasting long after, the hubbub of men in animated talk, exchanging news and rumours and opinions. It was the sound of the agora, the wineshop, the gymnasium, the forum; age-long leitmotif of the lands by the Middle Sea.

After sundown, a few of her following came, to say they had been arguing her cause with Antipatros' men; one or two had cuts and bruises. But these had been little fights, stopped quickly by authority. She read the omens of discipline restored, and not wholly unwelcome. When a senior officer of the Regent's staff came to the tent, they all, to a man, saluted.

He announced that a full Assembly would be held next day, to decide the kingdom's affairs. King Philip would no doubt wish to attend it.

Philip had been building himself a little fort on the floor, and trying to man it with some ants who persisted in deserting. Hearing the message, he said anxiously, 'Must I make a speech?'

'That, sir, is as you wish,' the envoy said impassively. He turned to Eurydike. 'Daughter of Amyntas, Antipatros sends you greeting. He says that though it is not the custom of the Macedonians for women to address Assembly, you have his leave to do so. When he himself has spoken, they will decide if they wish to hear you.'

'Tell him I shall be there.'

When he had gone, Philip said eagerly, 'He promised I needn't make a speech if I didn't want to. Please don't make me.'

She felt she could have struck him; but she held back, fearing to lose her hold on him. Indeed, she had some fear of his strength.

The Assembly was held next day with ancient procedure. Foreign soldiers, the legacies of Alexander's catholic racial mix, were barred. An impressive rostrum was raised in the biggest clearing, with seats of honour below it. As Eurydike took her place, whispering to Philip a last order to keep still, she felt in the huge throng a new, impalpable change. Something was different, and yet somehow familiar. It was the feel of the homeland, the native hills.

Antigonos spoke first. Here, at Assembly, the angry general was gone. A statesman spoke, not without the skills of oratory. With dignity he reminded them of their heroic past under Alexander, urged them not to disgrace it, and introduced the Regent.

The old man stepped briskly up to the rostrum. His own army cheered him; no hostile sound was heard. As he looked about him, as with perfect timing he signed for silence, an unwanted voice said within Eurydike, This man is a king.

He had reigned over Macedon and Greece throughout Alexander's wars. He had crushed the sporadic risings of the south, imposed on its cities the rulers of his choice, exiled his opponents. He had defeated even Olympias. Now he was old and brittle, his height had begun to shrink, his deep voice to crack;

but still, given off from his inner core, the aura of power and command surrounded him.

He told them of their forefathers, he told them of Philip who had rescued their fathers from invasion and civil war, and begotten Alexander who had made them masters of the world. They had become a tree with wide and spreading branches – he gestured to the noble timber standing round – but the greatest tree will die if its roots are sundered from its native earth. Could they bear to sink down among the barbarians they had conquered?

He told them of the birth of Arridaios, the lackwit they had honoured with Philip's name; he told what Philip had thought of him, ignoring his presence in the seats below. He reminded them that in all their history, they had never had a woman ruler. Would they now choose a woman and a fool?

Philip, who had followed this peroration, nodded sagely. He found it somehow reassuring. Alexander had told him he ought not to be King, and now this forceful old man agreed. Perhaps they would tell him, now, that he could be Arridaios again.

Antipatros' own men had been for him from the start. For the rebels, it was like a slow awakening from restless dreams. All round her, like the sough of shingle on an ebb-tide beach, Eurydike felt the lapse of the withdrawing sea.

She would not, could not admit defeat. She would speak, it was her right; she had won them once and would again. Soon this old man would finish talking, and she must be ready.

Her hands had clenched, her back and her shoulders tightened; her stomach contracted, achingly. The aching turned to a cramp, a low heavy drag which, with dismay, she tried at first not to recognize. In vain; it was true. Her menses, not due for four days, had started.

She had always counted carefully, always been regular. How could it happen now? It would come on quickly, once begun, and she had not put on a towel.

She had been strung-up this morning; what had she failed to

notice in all the stress? Already she felt a warning moisture. If she stood on the rostrum, everyone would see.

The Regent's speech approached its climax. He was talking of Alexander; she hardly heard. She looked at the thousands of faces round her, on the slopes, in the trees. Why, among all these humans made by the gods, was she alone subject to this betrayal, she only who could be cheated by her body at a great turn of fate?

Beside her sat Philip, with his useless gift of a strong man's frame. If she had owned it, it would have carried her up to the rostrum and given her a voice of bronze. Now she must creep from the field without a battle; and even her well-wishers would think, Poor girl!

Antipatros had finished. When the applause subsided, he said, 'Will the Assembly now hear Eurydike, daughter of Amyntas, the wife of Arridaios?'

No one dissented. Antipatros' men were curious; her partisans were ashamed to vote against her. Their minds were made up, but they were prepared at least to listen. Now was the moment for a true leader to compel their hearts ... She had come, the morning being fresh, with a himation round her shoulders. Now, carefully, she slipped it down to her elbows, to drape in a curve over her buttocks, as elegant ladies wore it in fresco paintings. Getting to her feet, taking care over her draperies, she said, 'I do not wish to address the Macedonians.'

Roxane had kept her tent in a good deal of alarm, among scared eunuchs and terrified women; sure that if the mutiny succeeded, Eurydike's first action would be to kill her and her child; it was, as Roxane saw it, the natural thing to do.

It took her some time to learn the Assembly's decision, since only Macedonians had attended. At length her wagoner, a Greek-speaking Sidonian, came back to report that the wife of Philip had been quite put down without a word to say; that Antipatros the Regent had been made guardian of both the

Kings; and that, as soon as the great lords had agreed to divide the satrapies, he would take both royal households back to Macedon.

'Ah!' she cried, and threw off fear like a cloak. 'All will be well, then. It is my husband's kingdom. They know the fool Philip from his childhood days; of course they will have none of him. It is my child they will wish to see. Alexander's mother will be waiting.'

Alexander had never read her the letter Olympias had sent him when he had informed her of his marriage. She had advised him, if the barbarian girl should bear a boy, to have it smothered lest it should someday pretend to the throne. It was high time for him to visit the homeland and beget a Macedonian, as she had begged him to do before he crossed to Asia. This letter had not been placed in the royal archives. He had shown it to Hephaistion, and then burned it.

319 B.C.

Beside the great palace of Archelaos at Pella stood Antipatros' house. It was solid but unpretentious; scrupulously correct, he had always avoided a regal style. Its only adornments were a columned portico and a terrace.

The house was hushed and closed. Straw and rushes were laid on the terrace paving. Small groups of people stood at decent distances, to watch the comings and goings of the doctors and the kin: townspeople drawn by curiosity and the sense of drama; guest-friends awaiting the signal for condolence and funeral plans; dealers in mourning-wreaths and grave-goods. Hovering more discreetly, or represented by spies, were the consuls of client cities, who had the most at stake.

Nobody knew who would inherit power when the old man unclenched at last his grasp of life, or whether his policies would be continued. His last action, before he took to his bed, had been to hang two envoys bringing a petition from Athens, a father and son who he found had corresponded with Perdikkas. Neither age nor his wasting sickness had softened Antipatros. Now the watchers scanned, whenever it appeared, the set frowning face of his son Kassandros, trying to read the omens.

Near by in the palace, that famous wonder of the north, where both the Kings maintained their separate households, the tension was like the string of a drawn bow.

Roxane stood in her window, looking from behind a curtain at the silent crowd. She had never felt at home in Macedon. The mother of Alexander had not been there to receive her or admire her son, having vowed, it seemed, never to set foot in Macedon while Antipatros lived. She was still in Dodona. To Roxane the Regent had behaved with formal courtesy; but before they had crossed the Hellespont he had sent her eunuchs home. They would cause her, he told her, to be taken for a barbarian, and people would ill-use them. She was now fluent in Greek, and could be attended by Macedonian ladies. The ladies had instructed her, politely, in the local customs. Politely, they had dressed her suitably; and, very politely, made it clear that she spoiled her son. In Macedon, boys were made ready to be men.

He was now four, and in this foreign place inclined to cling to her; she in her loneliness could hardly bear him out of her sight. Soon Antipatros had reappeared – no doubt the women were his spies – and declared himself amazed that Alexander's son should have only a few words of Greek. It was time that he had a peda-gogue. This person arrived next day.

The customary sober slave, Antipatros had decided, was not enough. He had chosen a vigorous young patrician, already at twenty-five a veteran of the Greek rebellion. Antipatros had noticed the strictness of his army discipline. He had had no occa-sion to notice that he was fond of children.

It had been the dream of Kebes' life to fight under Alexander; he had been drafted to go with the contingent Antipatros would have brought to Babylon. He had borne in silence his shattered hopes, and performed his distasteful duty of fighting fellow-Greeks instead, though his men thought him rather dour. From habit rather than intent he had accepted his appointment dourly, betraying nothing to the Regent of the elation within.

The first sight of the dark-haired, soft-skinned, plump child had disappointed him; but he had not expected an Alexander in little. For the mother he had been prepared. She clearly supposed that once out of her care her son would be bullied and beaten; the child, seeing he was expected to be frightened, struggled and whined. Taken out firmly without fuss, he displayed a lively curiosity and swiftly forgot his tears.

Kebes knew the maxim of the famous Spartan nurses: never expose a small child to fear, let him enter confidently on boyhood. By small safe stages, he introduced his charge to horses, to large dogs, to the noise of soldiers drilling. Roxane, waiting at home to comfort her ill-used child, found him full of himself, trying to describe the delights of his morning, for which he knew only Greek.

He picked up the language quickly. Soon he was talking incessantly of his father. Roxane had told him he was the son of the world's most powerful king; Kebes related the legendary exploits. He himself had been a boy of ten when Alexander crossed to Asia; he had seen him in the height of his glowing youth, and imagined the rest. If the child was still too small to emulate, he could already learn to aspire.

Kebes had been happy in his work. Now, waiting with the rest before the straw-strewn terrace, he felt the uncertain future shadowing his achievement. Had the child, after all, any more in him than boys at home whom he had known at the same age? Had the great days gone for ever? What world would he and his like inherit?

He was brooding on this when the ritual wails began.

Roxane heard them from her window, saw the waiting people turning to one another, and went in to pace her room, pausing sometimes to clutch the child to her breast. Alarmed, he asked what was the matter, getting no answer but, 'What will become of us now?'

Five years before, in the summer palace of Ekbatana, Alexander had told her of Kassandros, the Regent's heir, whom he had left behind in Macedon from fear of treachery. When Alexander died he had been in Babylon; very likely he had had him poisoned. In Pella he had come to pay his respects to her, professedly on behalf of his sick father; really, no doubt, to look at Alexander's son. He had been civil, but unmeaningly, merely accounting for his presence; she had hated and feared his reddish freckled face, his harsh pale eyes, his look of undisclosed purpose. Today she was more frightened than during the mutiny in Syria. If only she could have stayed in Babylon, in a world she knew, among people she could understand!

Kassandros in the death-chamber stared with embittered anger at his father's shrunken corpse. He could not bring himself to lean and close his eyes; an old aunt, looking reproach, pressed down the withered lids and pulled up the blanket.

Across the bed from him stood stolid, fifty-year-old Polyperchon, his grey stubbled chin unshaven from the night-watch; making a matter-of-fact gesture of respectful grief, his mind already on his new responsibilities. To him, not to Kassandros, Antipatros had bequeathed the guardianship of the Kings. Thorough to the last, before he drifted into coma he had sent for all the chief noblemen to witness his intent, and elicited their oath to vote for it at Assembly.

He had been senseless since yesterday; the ceasing of the breath was a mere formality. Polyperchon, who had respected him, was glad to end the tiring vigil and get to business, which was in arrears. He had not sought his new charge; Antipatros had had to plead with him. It had been shocking and terrible, like seeing his own stern father grovelling at his feet.

'Do this for me,' he had wheezed. 'Old friend, I beg you.' Polyperchon was not even an old friend; he had been in Asia with Alexander until he rode back with Krateros. He had been in

Macedon when Alexander died, and made himself useful in the southern rebellion. While the Regent had been away in nearer Asia fetching home the Kings, Polyperchon had been left as deputy. That had been the start of it.

'I took my oath to Philip.' The dying man had cleared his throat, even that an effort. His voice rustled like dry reeds. 'And to his heirs. I will *not*' – he choked, and paused – 'be forsworn by my son. I know him. I know what ... Promise me, friend. Swear by the Styx. I beg you, Polyperchon.' In the end he had sworn, only to stop it and escape. Now he was bound.

As Antipatros' last gasps tainted the air, he could feel Kassandros' hatred flowing out at him across the body. Well, he had faced hard men under Philip at Chaironeia, under Alexander at Issos and Gaugamela. He had not risen above brigade commander, yet Alexander had picked him for the Bodyguard, and trust went no higher than that. Polyperchon, he had said, holds on.

Soon he must make himself known to the royal households, taking his eldest son; an Alexandros, he liked to think, who would bring no discredit on the name. Kassandros, who cared greatly what people thought of him, could at least be trusted to put on a handsome funeral.

Eurydike had been out riding when the Regent died. She had known the news was near; when she had had it, she would be pent in the dreary, stifling rites of mourning, which it would be indecent to neglect.

For company on her ride she had a couple of grooms, and a strapping young lady of her household, chosen only because she was a hill-woman and rode well. The days of her cavalry escorts were over; Antipatros had had her vigilantly watched for conspiracy with soldiers. Only Philip himself, by bursting into tears, had persuaded him to leave old Konon. Even so, she sometimes got salutes, and still acknowledged them.

Turning back towards Pella with a westering sun behind her, the hill-shadows creeping out over the lagoon, she felt a stirring of destiny, a change of pace in the wheel of fortune. It was not without hope that she had awaited the cries of mourning.

To her, as well as to Roxane, Kassandros had paid his respects during his father's illness. Formally speaking, he had paid them to the King her husband; but with some finesse had conversed respectfully with Philip, while making it clear that his words were meant for her. The looks which, to Roxane, had seemed fierce and savage, were to Eurydike those of a fellow-countryman; not notable for beauty, but engraved with resolution and strength. He would have, no doubt, his father's hardness; but also his father's competence.

She had assumed, since he clearly did so, that he would succeed his father. She had known what he meant when he said that the Macedonians were fortunate in having *one* king of the true blood, and a queen who was no less so. He had hated Alexander, he would never allow the barbarian's child to rule. It had seemed to her that they understood each other.

The news of Polyperchon's election had disconcerted her. She had never met him, barely knew him by sight. Now, when she came back from her ride, she found him in the royal rooms, talking with Philip.

He must have been there some time. Philip seemed quite at ease with him, and was telling him a rambling story about snakes in India. 'Konon found it under my bath. He killed it with a stick. He said the little ones were the worst.'

'Quite right, sir. They could get into a boot, a man of mine died of it.' He turned to Eurydike, complimented her on her husband's health, begged her to call on him if he could be of service, and took his leave. Clearly it was too soon, with the Regent still unburied, to ask him about his plans; but she was angry that he had told her nothing, and presented himself to Philip without regard for her absence.

All through the long pompous funeral rites, walking in the procession with shorn hair and ash on her black dress, adding her wail to the chant of lamentation, she scanned Kassandros' face, whenever he came in sight, for some hint of purpose. It was only solid, correct, shaped for the occasion.

Later, when the men went to the pyre to burn the body, and she stood apart with the women, she heard a loud cry, and saw some kind of stir beside the fire. Then Konon was running through all the men of rank towards it. Soon he came out, with a couple of the guard of honour, carrying Philip, with flaccid limbs and open mouth. Lagging, ashamed, she went over and walked with them towards the palace.

'Madam,' Konon muttered, 'if you could speak to the General. He's not used to the King, he doesn't know what upsets him. I had a word with him, but he told me to remember my place.'

'I will tell him.' With the back of her head, she could feel scornful Roxane looking after her. One day, she thought, you will not make light of me.

In the palace, Konon undressed Philip, washed him – in the fit he had wetted his robe – and put him to bed. Eurydike in her room took off her mourning dress and combed the soft wood-ash from her ritually dishevelled hair. She thought, He is my husband. I knew what he was before I took him. I did it from free choice; so I am bound to him in honour. My mother would tell me so.

She called for a warm egg posset with a splash of wine, and took it in to him. Konon had gone off with the dirty clothes. He looked up at her pleading, like a sick dog at a hard master. 'See,' she said, 'I have brought you something nice. Never mind that you were taken ill, you couldn't help it. Many people don't like to watch a funeral pyre.'

He looked at her thankfully and put his face to the bowl. He was glad that she asked no questions. The last thing he remembered, before the drumbeat in his head and the terrible white light, was the beard of the corpse blackening and stinking in the fire. It had brought back to him a day a long time ago, before he went journeying with Alexander. That had been the funeral of the King, so they had told him, but he had not known whom they meant. They had cut short his hair and put a black robe on him and dirtied his face, and made him walk with a lot of people crying. And there was his frightening father, whom he had not seen for years, lying on a bed of logs and brushwood, with a grand bedspread, grim-faced and dead. He had never seen a dead man before. Alexander was there. He too had had a haircut, the fair crop shone in the sun. He had made a speech, quite a long one, about what the King had done for the Macedonians; then, suddenly, he had taken a torch from someone who had been holding it, and stuck it in among the brushwood. Horrified, Philip had watched as the flames rushed up, roaring and crackling, running along the edges of the embroidered pall, then bursting through it; then the hair and the beard … For a long time afterwards, he would wake with a scream in the night, and could tell no one that he had dreamed of his burning father.

The polished marble doors closed on Antipatros' tomb, and an uneasy calm fell upon Macedon.

Polyperchon gave out that he had no wish for arbitrary powers. Antipatros had governed for an absent ruler. It was now proper that the chief men should share his counsels. Many Macedonians approved this sign of antique virtue. Some others said that Polyperchon was incapable of decision and wished to avoid too much responsibility.

The calm became easier. Every eye was upon Kassandros.

His father had not wholly passed him over. He had been appointed Chiliarch, Polyperchon's second in command, a rank to which Alexander had given high prestige. Would he be content with it? Men watched his rufous impassive face as he came and went in Pella, and said to each other that he had never been a man to swallow slights.

However, having buried his father he went quietly about his business through the mourning month. When it was up, he paid his respects to Philip and Eurydike.

'Greet him,' she said to her husband when he was announced, 'and then don't talk. It may be important.'

Kassandros' greetings to the King were brief. He addressed himself to the Queen. 'I shall be gone for a time; I am going to our country place. I have had a good deal to try me; now I mean to make up a hunting party of old friends, and forget public affairs.'

She wished him well with it. He did not miss the questioning in her eyes.

'Your goodwill,' he said, 'has been a solace and support to me. You and the King may count on me in these troubled times. You, sir' – he turned to Philip – 'are your father's undoubted son. Your mother's life was never a public scandal.' To Eurydike he said, 'As no doubt you know, there have always been doubts about the birth of Alexander.'

When he had gone, Philip said, 'What did he mean about Alexander?'

'Never mind. I am not sure what he meant. We shall find out later.'

Antipatros' country place was an old run-down hill-fort, overlooking a well-managed rich estate. He had lived at Pella, and run the land with a bailiff. His sons had used the place for hunting parties, such as this one had, till now, appeared to be.

In the upper room of the rude keep a fire was burning on the round hearth under the smoke-hole; autumn nights were sharp in the hills. Around it, on old benches or sheepskin-covered stools, sat a dozen or so of youngish men, dressed in the day's leather and tough-woven wool, smelling of the horses which could be heard stirring and champing on the floor below, where grooms speaking Thracian were mending and waxing tack.

Kassandros, a red man in the red firelight, sat by his brother

Nikanor. Iollas had died soon after he got home from Asia, of a quartan fever picked up in the Babylonian swamps; he had gone down quickly, showing little fight. The fourth brother, Alexarchos, had not been invited. He was learned, slightly mad, and mainly employed in inventing a new language for a Utopian state he had seen in visions. Besides his uselessness, he could not be trusted to hold his tongue.

Kassandros said, 'We've been here three days and no one's come spying. We can begin to move. Derdas, Atheas, can you start early tomorrow?'

'Yes,' said the two men across the hearth.

'Get fresh horses at Abdera, Ainos; Amphipolis if you must. Take care at Amphipolis, keep away from the garrison, someone might know you. Simas and Antiphon can start next day. Keep a day between you on the road. Two men aren't noticed, four make people look.'

Derdas said, 'And the message for Antigonos?'

'I'll give you a letter. You'll be safe enough if you don't draw notice. Polyperchon's a blockhead. I'm hunting, good, he can go to sleep again. When Antigonos reads the letter, tell him anything he wants to know.'

They had been hunting boar in the woods all day, to keep up appearances; soon afterwards the party went off to bed, at the far end of the big room behind a dressed hide curtain. Kassandros and Nikanor lingered by the hearth, their soft voices muted by the stable sounds below.

Nikanor was a tall, lean, sandy-coloured man; a capable soldier, who stood by the family loyalties and feuds and looked no further. He said, 'Are you sure you can trust Antigonos? He wants more than he has, that's plain.'

'That's why I can trust him. While he's stretching out in Asia, he'll be glad to have Polyperchon kept busy in Greece. He'll leave me Macedon; he knows Asia will take him all his time.'

Nikanor scratched at his head; one seemed always to pick up

231

lice on a hunting party. He caught one and dropped it in the fire. 'Are you sure of the girl? She'd be as dangerous as Antigonos, if she knew how. She made trouble enough for Father, and for Perdikkas before that. But for her, Philip would be a nothing.'

'M-m,' said Kassandros reflectively. 'That's why I asked you to watch her while I'm gone. I told her nothing, of course. She'll take our side, to keep out the barbarian's child. She showed me that.'

'Good so far. But she's the King's wife and she means to be reigning Queen.'

'Yes. With her descent, I dare say I shall need to marry her.'

Nikanor's pale eyebrows rose. 'And Philip?'

Kassandros made a simple gesture.

'I wonder,' said Nikanor thoughtfully, 'if she'd consent to that.'

'Oh, I dare say not. But when it's done, she won't settle down with the loom and the needle, it's not in her. She'll marry me sure enough. Then she can behave herself. Or ... ' He made the gesture again.

Nikanor shrugged. 'Then what about Thessalonike? I thought you'd settled for her. *She's* Philip's daughter, not his grand-daughter.'

'Yes, but the blood's only on the father's side. Eurydike first. When I'm King I can marry both. Old Philip would have made nothing of that.'

'You're sure of your luck,' Nikanor said uneasily.

'Yes. Ever since Babylon, I've known that my time has come.'

A half-month later, towards evening on a day of mist and rain, Polyperchon came to the palace, urgently demanding to see the King.

He barely waited to be announced. Philip, with Konon's help, was still gathering up an arrangement of his stones which he had been elaborating all day. Eurydike, who had been waxing the leather of her cuirass, had no time to hide that either. She looked resentfully at Polyperchon, who bowed formally, having first saluted the King.

'I've nearly put it away,' said Philip apologetically. 'It was a Persian paradise.'

'Sir. I must ask your presence at a council of state tomorrow.'

Philip looked at him in horror. 'I won't make a speech. I don't want to make a speech.'

'You need not, sir; only assent when the rest have voted.'

'On what?' asked Eurydike sharply.

Polyperchon, a Macedonian in the old tradition, thought, A pity Amyntas lived long enough to beget this meddlesome bitch. 'Madam. We have news that Kassandros has crossed to Asia, and that Antigonos has welcomed him.'

'What?' she said, startled. 'I understood he was hunting on his estate.'

'That,' said Polyperchon grimly, 'is what he wished us to understand. We may now understand that we are at war. Sir, please be ready at sunup; I will come and escort you. Madam.' He bowed, about to depart.

'Wait!' she said angrily. 'With whom is Kassandros at war?'

He turned on the threshold. 'With the Macedonians. They voted to obey his father, who had thought him unfit to govern them.'

'I wish to attend the council.'

Polyperchon jutted at her his grizzled beard. 'I regret, madam. That is not the custom of the Macedonians. I wish you good night.' He strode out. He was furious with himself for not having had Kassandros watched; but at least he need not put up with insolence from a woman.

The council of state considered the country's dangers and found them grave. Kassandros, it was clear, would only stay in Asia to get the forces he needed. Then he would make for Greece.

Since the last years of Philip's reign, and all through

Alexander's, the Greek states had been governed as Macedon ordained. Democrat leaders had been exiled, the franchise confined to men of property, whose oligarch leaders had to be pro-Macedonian. Alexander had been a long way off, and Antipatros had had a free hand. Since his supporters had enriched themselves at the expense of the many exiles, there had been violent consternation when Alexander, returning from the wilderness, had ordered them brought home and their lands restored. He had summoned the Regent to report to him in Babylon; Kassandros had gone instead. When Alexander died, the Greeks had risen, but Antipatros had crushed them. The cities, therefore, were still governed by his satellites, whose support for his son would be a matter of course.

All this time, the Greek envoys were hanging about in Pella, waiting, as they had done since the funeral, to learn the policy of the new regime towards their various states. They were now hastily summoned, and handed a royal proclamation. Much had been done in Greece, it said, which Alexander had never sanctioned. They could now with the goodwill of the Kings, his heirs, restore their democratic constitutions, expel their oligarchs, or execute them if desired. All their citizen rights would be defended, in return for loyalty to the Kings.

Polyperchon, escorting Philip from the council chamber, explained these decisions to Eurydike with punctilious care. Like Nikanor, he had reflected that she had a great capacity for mischief. She should not be idly provoked.

She listened without much comment. While the council deliberated, she too had had time for thought.

'A dog came in,' said Philip as soon as his mentor had gone. 'He had a great bone, a raw one. I said to them, he must have stolen it from the kitchen.'

'Yes, Philip. Quiet now, I must think.'

She had guessed right, then; when Kassandros came to see her, he had been offering her alliance. If he won this war, he would depose the child of the barbarian, assume the guardianship, enthrone Philip and herself. *He* had spoken to her as an equal. He would make her a queen.

'Why,' asked Philip plaintively, 'do you keep walking about?'

'You must change your good robe, you will get it dirty. Konon, are you there? Please help the King.'

She paced the room with its carved windows and great painted inner wall, covered with a life-sized mural of the sack of Troy. Agamemnon was carrying off Kassandra, shrieking, from the sanctuary; the wooden horse loomed between the gate-towers; in the foreground, at the household altar, Priam was lying in his blood; Andromache clasped to her bosom her dead child. All the background was fighting, flames and blood. It was an antique piece, the work of Zeuxis, commissioned by Archelaos when he built the palace.

About the hearth with its worn old stones clung faded aromatic odours, a fume of ancient burnings, and curious stains. It had been, for many years, the room of Queen Olympias. Much magic, people used to say, had been worked in it. Her sacred snakes had had their basket by this hearth, her spells their hiding-places. One or two were indeed still where she had left them, for she meant to return. Eurydike only knew that the room had a presence of its own.

Striding about it, she pondered her unspoken bargain with Kassandros, and for the first time thought, What then?

Only the child of the barbarian could beget a new generation. When he had been driven out, she and Philip would reign alone. Who would succeed them?

Who fitter than the grandchild of Philip and Perdikkas to carry on their line? To do that, she could put up with childbirth. For a moment she thought shrinkingly of teaching Philip; after all, there were women in every city who for a drachma put up with worse. But no, she could not. Besides, what if he should sire a fool?

If I were a man! she thought. On the hearth a bright fire of dry lichened apple-wood was burning, for winter was drawing on. The blackened stones under the fire-basket released drifts of old tainted incense in the heat. If I were a king, I could marry twice if I chose, our kings have often done so. A vivid recollection came to her of Kassandros' powerful presence. He had offered to be her friend … But then, there was Philip.

For a moment, recalling that moment of silent speech, she was on the edge of comprehension. To the last tenant of this room it would have been a simple thing, a matter of ways and means. Eurydike felt it loom, and flinched away from it. To see it must be to choose, yes or no, and she would not. She only said to herself that she must be able to depend upon Kassandros, and it was useless to think too far ahead. But the smell of the old myrrh in the stones was like the smoke of the hidden thought, buried under the smouldering embers, waiting its time.

Eumenes sat in his tent on the kindly coastland of Kilikia, looking across the sea towards Cyprus' distant hills. The warm fruitful
plain was a paradise after the cramped fort, perched on the high
Tauros, where Antigonos had kept him invested all through last
winter in the bitter mountain wind. A spring of good water,
plenty of grain, and precious little else. The men's gums had
started to rot from the lack of greenstuff; he had had hard work
to stop them from eating the horses, on which their lives might
yet depend; he had kept the beasts exercised by having their fore-
quarters hoisted up once a day in slings, and making the grooms
shout and hit at them, so that they thrashed about and got into
a sweat. He had almost made up his mind to slaughter them
when, of a sudden, Antigonos sent an envoy to offer terms. The
Regent was dead, it was every man for himself, and Antigonos
wanted an ally.

He had demanded an oath of loyalty before he lifted the siege.
To Antigonos and the Kings, the envoy said. Eumenes had
changed it, in the act of swearing, to Olympias and the Kings.
The envoy had let it pass. Antigonos had not liked it; but by the
time he knew of it, they had all got out. This was as well;

Eumenes had heard from Polyperchon, appointing him in the Kings' name to Antigonos' command; which, since Antigonos would certainly not resign it, he would have to get by force. Meantime, he was to take over the provincial treasury of Kilikia, and the command of its garrison regiment, the Silver Shields.

He was now in camp with them, while they made themselves snug with stolen comforts, won by every devious ruse known to campaigners who had been, many of them, fifty years under arms. None of them had been serving for less than forty; tough, wicked old sweats whom Alexander had thought himself well shot of, and whom even he had not rid himself of without a mutiny. They had been his legacy from his father Philip, men of the phalanx, wielders of the long sarissa, all of them hand-picked fighters. They had been young men along with Philip; many were older than he would have been if he were still alive. Now, when they should be living with their loot and Alexander's bounty on their homeland farms, here they still were, hard as their boot-nails, their discharge held up by the death of Krateros and their own obdurate resistance; never yet beaten, and ready to march again.

Not a man was under sixty; most of them were past seventy; their arrogance was a proverb; and Eumenes, a generation younger, and an alien Greek, had to take them over.

He had almost refused; but while, after the siege, he was salvaging his scattered forces, he had a letter brought by land and sea from Epiros. It was from Olympias.

I beg you to help us. Only you, Eumenes, are left, most loyal of all my friends, and best able to rescue our forsaken house. I entreat you, do not fail me. Let me hear from you; shall I entrust myself and my grandson to men who claim, one after another, to be his guardians, and then are found planning to steal his heritage? Roxane his mother sends me word that she fears for his life, once Polyperchon leaves Macedon to fight the traitor Kassandros. Is it best she flies to me here, bringing the boy; or shall I raise troops and go to Macedon?

The letter had deeply moved him. He had been still young when first he had met Olympias, and so had she. Often in Philip's absences the Regent, who loathed her, had sent Eumenes with messages to her, partly to slight her with his lower rank, partly to keep out of her way. During many domestic quarrels Philip had done the same. To the young Greek, she had a quality of archaic myth; a Bacchic Ariadne, awaiting the embrace of a Dionysos who never came. He had seen her in tears, in savage mirth, in blazing anger and sometimes in regal grace. He had no more desired her than one desires a splendid play of lightning over the sea; but he had adored her. Even when he had known well that she was in the wrong, and that he had to tell her so, he had never gone to face her without a thrill at the heart. In fact, she had often unbent to him. He had been a handsome young man; though she had never been able to make him her partisan or subvert his faith to Philip, she had enjoyed his admiration.

He knew she had harassed Alexander all through Asia, pursuing her feud with the Regent; he remembered how, handing him one such letter, her son had said, 'By God, she charges high rent for the nine-months' lodging she gave me!' But he had said it half laughing; he, too, had loved her through everything. He had left her still beautiful; and, like Eumenes, was never to see her old.

One thing he now knew at once: on no account must she go to Macedon, with or without an army. She knew moderation no more than a hunting leopardess; she would not be there a month before she destroyed her cause. He had written to her exhorting her to stay in Epiros till the present war was settled; meantime, she could count on his fidelity, to her and to Alexander's son.

He did not refer to Roxane and her fears. Who would say what fancies might scare the Bactrian? During his long campaign, followed by the winter siege, he had had little news from Europe. Since the wedding at Sardis, he had barely heard of Eurydike.

Soon Antigonos would be after him – clearly the man meant to make a kingdom for himself in Asia – and he must be moving, with his native levies and their stiffening, the battle-hardened Silver Shields. From his tent-opening, he could see them now, sitting in their groupings established over half a century, while their women made their breakfasts; Lydian women, Tyrian women, Bactrians and Parthians and Medes and Indians, the spoils of their long wanderings, with a few old hardy Macedonians who had come with them from home and somehow survived. The surviving children – a third, perhaps, of those begotten along the way – chattered softly round the cook-fires, wary of a clout from their fathers; brown and honey-coloured and fair, speaking their lingua franca. When camp broke, the women would pack the wagon train with all its world-wide pickings, and march once more.

On the next knoll, Eumenes could see the tents of the two commanders, Antigenes and Teutamos; crafty and stubborn old war-dogs, each old enough to be his father. Today he must call them to a war council; and would they defer to him without resentment? From wounded pride, he knew too well, comes treachery. He sighed wearily, his mind going back to the days when he and they had not been flotsam on the stream of history, but had proudly shaped its course. Those old sinners over there, he thought, even they must remember.

His mind had been suppled by years of precarious survival; now it took one of those leaps which had saved him in places tighter than this. The day was still young, the sunlight upon Cyprus fresh and tender. He shaved, dressed himself neatly without ostentation, and called the herald.

'Sound,' he said, 'for the officers to assemble.'

He had his slaves set out the stools and camp-chairs casually, without precedence, on the grass. As the leathery ancients, taking their time, approached, he waved them affably to be seated. From the chair they left for him, he rose and addressed them standing.

'Gentlemen, I have called you together to give you serious news. I have received an omen.'

As he had foreseen, dead silence fell. Old soldiers were as superstitious as sailors. They all knew what chance can do to a man in war.

'If ever the gods gave a man a powerful dream, they gave one to me at cockcrow. A dream more real than waking. My name was called. I knew the voice, it was Alexander's. He was in my tent, in that very chair that you, Teutamos, are sitting on. "Eumenes!" he said.'

They sat forward in their chairs. Teutamos' gnarled hands stroked the pinewood arms as if he touched a talisman.

'I begged his pardon for sleeping in his presence, as if he had been alive. He had on his white robe edged with purple, and a gold diadem. "I am holding a council of state," he said. "Are you all here?" And he looked about him. Then it seemed the tent was not mine but his, the tent he took from Darius. He was there on his throne, with the Bodyguard around him; and you too were there, with the other generals, waiting for his words. He leaned forward to address us; but as he began, I woke.'

Skilled in the arts of rhetoric, he had tried none here. He had looked and spoken like a man remembering something momentous. It had worked. They were looking at one another, but not in distrust, only wondering what it meant.

'I believe,' he said, 'that I divined Alexander's wish. He is concerned for us. He wants to be present at our councils. If we appeal to him, he will guide us in our decisions.' He paused for questions; but they hardly murmured.

'So let us not receive him meanly. Here we have the gold of Koyinda which you, gentlemen, have guarded for him faithfully. Let us send for craftsmen to make him a golden throne, a sceptre and a diadem, let us dedicate a tent to him, and lay the insignia on the throne, and offer incense to his spirit. Then we will confer before him, making him our supreme commander.'

Their shrewd, scarred faces considered him. He was not, it seemed, setting himself above them; he was not planning to steal the treasure; if Alexander had appeared only to him, after all he had known him well. And Alexander liked his orders obeyed.

The tent, the throne and the insignia were ready within a week. Even some purple was found, to dye a canopy. When it was time to march towards Phoenicia, they met in the tent to discuss the coming campaign. Before they sat down, each offered his pinch of incense at the little portable altar, saying, 'Divine Alexander, favour us.' All of them deferred to Eumenes, whose divination was manifest around them.

It did not matter that scarcely any of them had seen Alexander enthroned. They remembered him in old leather cuirass and burnished greaves, his helmet off for them to see him, riding along the line before an action, reminding them of their past victories and telling them how to win another. They did not care that the local goldsmith was not of the highest skill. The shining of the gold, the smoke of frankincense, wakened a memory long silted over by the weather and war and weariness of thirteen years; of a golden chariot driving in triumph through the flower-strewn streets of Babylon; the trumpets, the paean, the censers and the cheers. For a little while, standing before the empty throne, it seemed to them that they might become what they once had been.

317 B.C.

The spring sun warmed the hills, melting the snows; first filling, then tempering the streams. Roads deep in mud and silted with scree grew firm again. The land opened to war.

Kassandros, with the fleet and army Antigonos had lent him, crossed the Aegean and landed at Piraeus, the port of Athens. Before his father was dead, he had sent a man of his own to take command of the Macedonian garrison in the harbour fort. While the Athenians were still discussing the royal decree and the offer of their ancient liberties, they found that the garrison had come down and occupied the harbour. Kassandros had sailed in unopposed.

Polyperchon, getting this news, despatched advance troops under his son Alexandros. The campaign hung fire; he prepared to set out himself. When he began to mobilize, he came to the palace to see King Philip.

Eurydike received him with the offerings of formal hospitality; she was resolved to have her presence recognized. Polyperchon, as formally, asked after both their health, listened to Philip's account of a cockfight to which Konon had lately taken him, and then said, 'Sir. I have come to tell you that we shall soon be marching south together. The traitor Kassandros must be dealt with. We shall start in seven days. Please tell your people to have your baggage ready. I will see your man about your horses.'

Philip nodded cheerfully. He had been on the march for nearly half his life, and took it as a matter of course. He did not understand what the war was about; but Alexander had seldom told him. 'I shall ride Whitefoot,' he said. 'Eurydike, which horse will you ride?'

Polyperchon cleared his throat. 'Sir, this is a campaign. The lady Eurydike will of course remain at Pella.'

'But I *can* take Konon?' said Philip anxiously.

'By all means, sir.' Polyperchon did not look that way.

There was a pause. He awaited the storm. But in fact Eurydike said nothing.

It had never occurred to her that she could be left behind. She had looked forward to the escape from the tedium of the palace to the freedom of the camp. In the first moment of learning that she had been relegated to the women's rooms she had been as angry as Polyperchon had expected, and had been on the point of protest, when there came into her mind Kassandros' unspoken message. How could she influence affairs, trailing along with the army, watched at every turn? But here at home, with the guardian away at war ...

She swallowed her anger at being so belittled, and held her peace. Afterwards, she found a lingering hurt that Philip had found Konon more necessary than her. After all I have done for him, she thought.

Polyperchon meantime was at the other end of the palace. Here were the quarters where the elder Philip had moved, when he ceased to share the great bedchamber with Olympias. They were handsome enough to satisfy Roxane, and her son did not complain of them. They opened on to an old orchard where he liked to play now that the days grew warmer. The plum-trees were already budding, and the grass smelled of hidden violets.

'Considering his tender years and need of his mother,' Polyperchon said, 'I shall not expose the King to the hardships of the march. In any treaties I may sign or edicts I may issue, his name will of course appear with King Philip's, as if he were present too.'

'So,' said Roxane, 'Philip will go with you?'

'Yes; he is a grown man, it will be expected.'

'Then his wife will go to care for him?' Her voice had sharpened.

'No, madam. War is not women's business.' She opened her black eyes till the clear white showed all round. 'Then,' she cried, 'who will protect my son and me?'

What could the foolish woman mean? He brought down his brows in irritation, and answered that Macedon would be left well garrisoned.

'Macedon? Here, in this house, who will protect us from that she-wolf? She will only wait to see you gone before she murders us.'

'Madam,' he said testily, 'we are not now in the wilds of Asia. The Queen Eurydike is a Macedonian and will obey the law. Even if she wished otherwise, she would not dare touch the son of Alexander. The people would have her blood.'

He left, thinking, Women! They make war seem a holiday. The thought consoled him among his cares. Since the new decree, nearly all the Greek cities were in a state of civil war, or on the verge of it; the coming campaign promised every kind of confusion and uncertainty. Roxane's notion that he would add to his troubles by taking that termagant girl along was enough to make a man laugh.

A week later the army marched. From the balcony of the great bedchamber, Eurydike had watched the troops assemble on the great drill-field where Philip and Alexander had trained their men; had seen the long column wind slowly down alongside the lagoon, making for the coast road to the south.

As the lumbering baggage train began to follow the soldiers, she looked about her at the horizons of the land she still meant to rule. Over the near hills was her father's house where Kynna had taught her war. She would keep it for her hunting-lodge, her private place, when she was Queen.

She looked down idly at the grandiose front of the palace with its painted pediment and columns of coloured marble. On the broad steps the tutor Kebes came down, the child Alexander beside him, trailing a wooden hobby-horse by its scarlet bridle. The child of the barbarian, who must not reign. How would Kassandros deal with that? She frowned.

Roxane behind her curtains grew weary of watching wagons, a sight too long familiar. Her eyes wandered. There on a balcony, brazenly showing herself to the world like a harlot looking for trade, stood Philip's mannish wife. What was she staring at so fiercely? Roxane's ear caught the sound of her own child's piping chatter. Yes, it was at him that she was looking! Swiftly, Roxane made the sign against the evil eye, and ran to her casket. Where was the silver charm her mother had given her against the malice of harem rivals? He must put it on. A letter was beside it, with the royal seal of Epiros. She reread it, and knew what she must do.

Kebes proved easy to persuade. The times were doubtful; so was his own future. He could well believe that the son of Alexander was in danger, and not only from his mother's spoiling. He had softened to Roxane; she might need protection too. It was eleven years since her beauty had hit Alexander like a fiery arrow across a torchlit hall; but her looks had been tended, her legend lived in them still. It seemed to the young man that he too could enter the legend, rescuing the woman Alexander had loved, and his only child.

It was he who chose the litter-bearers and the armed escort of four; who swore them to secrecy, who bought the mules, who found a messenger to ride ahead with news of their coming. Two days later, just before dawn, they were on the mountain road making for Dodona.

The royal house had a steep-pitched roof to throw off the winter snows. Roofs in Molossia gave no platform for watchers. Olympias stood in the window of the King's bedchamber, which she had taken when her daughter left it. Her eyes were fixed on a curl of smoke from the nearest hilltop. On three heights in an eastward line she had had beacons laid, to signal the approach of her daughter-in-law and grandson. Now she sent for the captain of the palace guard, and ordered him to meet them with an escort.

Olympias had assented to her age. In the month of mourning for Alexander she had washed the paint from her face, and covered her hair with a dark veil. When the month was over, and she put the veil away, her hair was silky white. She was sixty, and lean where she had been slim. Her fine redhead's skin was brittle like pressed petals; but lacking colour the proud bone showed more. Under their white brows, the smoky grey eyes could still pale dangerously.

She had waited long for this day. As the emptiness of loss came home to her, she had craved to touch this last living vestige of him; but the child was unborn, there was no remedy for waiting. With the wars' delays, her longing dulled and earlier doubts returned. The mother was a barbarian, a campaign wife, whose son he had meant to pass over – in a secret letter he had told her so – if the Great King's daughter had borne a boy. Would anything remain of him in this stranger?

When the child reached Macedon, her feud with Antipatros had left her only two ways to go back there, submission or war. The first was unthinkable; against the second Eumenes, on whom she must depend, had warned her. Then Roxane had written begging for a refuge, and she had answered, 'Come.'

247

Next day the cavalcade arrived; the tough Molossian troopers on their shaggy ponies, two dishevelled waiting-women on stumbling donkeys, a covered litter with its mules. Her eyes on the litter, she did not see at first the young man who carried across his horse's withers a six-year-old boy. He lifted him down and spoke to him quietly, pointing. Resolutely, on legs more a boy's than a child's, he walked up the steps, gave her a soldier's salute, and said, 'May you live, Grandmother. I am Alexander.'

She took him between her hands while the company made respectful gestures, and kissed his brow, dirty with travel, and looked again. Kebes had fulfilled his trust. Alexander's son was no longer the podgy nursling of the harem tent. Olympias saw a beautiful young Persian, fine-boned and dark-eyed. The hair was cut sloping to the nape, as Alexander used to wear it, but it was straight, heavy, and raven-black. He looked up at her from under his fine dark brows and his blue-brown, thick-lashed eyelids; and though there was nothing of him anywhere that was Macedonian, she saw Alexander in his upward, deep-set gaze. It was too much, it took her a few moments to gather herself together. Then she took his pale slender hand. 'Welcome, my child. Come, bring me to your mother.'

The roads from Pella down into Greece had been smoothed since old Philip's reign for the swift march of armies. The roads to the west were rough. Despite the difference in distance, therefore, it was at about the same time that Polyperchon in the Peloponnese, and Olympias in Dodona, got news from Macedon that Eurydike had assumed the regency.

Polyperchon got, in addition, an order signed by her, directing him to hand over to Kassandros the Macedonian forces in the south.

Speechless for a while, the old soldier kept his head, offered the courier wine without disclosing the message, and asked for news. It seemed that the Queen had called Assembly, and addressed it with great spirit. The barbarian woman, she told them, had fled the land with her child, fearing the anger of the Macedonians; she would do well not to return. All who had known Alexander would testify that the child looked nothing like him. He had died before the birth, had never acknowledged the infant; there was no proof that he was the father. Whereas she herself had on both sides the Macedonian royal blood.

For a time, Assembly had been in doubt. But Nikanor, Kassandros' brother, had given her his voice and the whole clan had come in with him. That had carried the vote. She was now giving audiences, receiving envoys and petitioners, and in all ways acting as reigning Queen.

Polyperchon thanked the man, rewarded and dismissed him, cursed to relieve his feelings, and sat down to think. He quickly decided what he himself would do; and, soon afterwards, what to do with Philip.

He had had hopes of him, if he could be removed from his wife's control; but had soon learned better. At first, he had been so docile that it had seemed safe to produce him, set up impressively on a gold-canopied throne, for a delegation from Athens. In the midst of a speech he had guffawed at a rhetorical trope which, like a child, he had taken literally. Later, when Polyperchon had rebuked a speaker, the King had grabbed at his ceremonial spear; if Polyperchon had not grappled with him in front of everyone, the man would have been run through. 'You said,' he had protested, 'that he told lies.' The delegation had been dismissed too hastily, causing a political disaster and the loss of some lives.

It was now clear to Polyperchon that all Philip was good for was to hold the throne for Alexander's son, who had better come of age quickly. As for Eurydike, her claim was plain usurpation.

Konon came when sent for, saluting woodenly. His silent 'I told you so' had irked Polyperchon after the incident of the spear and several others. Good riddance to both of them. 'I have decided,' he said, 'to send back the King to Macedon.'

'Sir.' The general felt, reverberating from this blank surface, knowledge that the campaign had gone badly, that he had had to raise the important siege of Megalopolis, that Kassandros still held the Piraeus and might well get Athens, in which event the Greek cities would join him. But that was irrelevant now.

'I will give you an escort. Tell the Queen that I am sending back the King in obedience to her wishes. That is all.'

'Sir.' Konon left, relieved. He could have told them all beforehand, if he had been asked. Now, he thought, they would all have a chance to live in peace.

At a massive table of inlaid hardstone with lion-feet of gilded bronze, Eurydike sat in the royal study. King Archelaos, nearly a century ago, had designed this splendid sanctum when he built the palace to stun foreigners with its magnificence. From it, whenever they were at home, Philip the Second had ruled Macedon and his spreading conquests, and Alexander had ruled all Greece. Since Alexander had gone to rule the world from a moving tent, no king had sat at the table under Zeuxis' mural of Apollo and the Muses. Antipatros, rigidly correct, had governed from his own house. She had found everything swept, polished, scrupulously neat, and empty.

It had awaited a tenant for seventeen years, as long as she had lived. Now it was hers.

When she called Assembly to claim the regency, she had not told Nikanor of what she meant to do. She had guessed he would think it rash, but that confronted with the fact he would support her, sooner than hurt his brother's cause. She had thanked him afterwards, but had fended off his efforts to advise her. She meant to rule for herself.

Awaiting news from the south, she had spent most of her time on what she most enjoyed, exercising the army. She felt, at last, that she was fulfilling her true destiny when she rode along a line of cavalry, or took the salute of the phalanx presenting their great sarissas. She had seen a good deal of army drill and talked to many soldiers; she knew all the procedure. They were amused and delighted with her. After all, they thought, they were just a garrison army; if there was action the generals would of course resume command. Taking this for granted, they performed for her indulgently.

Her fame was spreading, Eurydike, the warrior Queen of Macedon. One day she would strike her own coinage. She was tired of seeing the eager long-nosed face of Alexander hooded in his lion-skin. Let Herakles give place to Athene, Lady of Citadels.

Each day she waited to hear whether Polyperchon had surrendered his command to Kassandros as she had ordered. So far she had heard from neither. Instead, unheralded, Philip returned to Pella. He carried no despatches and did not know where his guardian was going next.

He was delighted to be home, and ran on at length about his adventures on campaign, though all he knew of the debacle at Megalopolis was that the wicked people in the fort had put down spikes to hurt the elephants' feet. Even so, had she had patience to listen to his ramblings she might have learned something of value. He had been present, as a matter of form, at several councils from which Konon was excluded. But she was busy, and answered him with half her mind. She seldom asked where he was; Konon took him about and amused him. She had ceased to issue orders in his name, and used only her own.

Until just lately, everything had gone smoothly. She understood the disputes of Macedon, nearly all brought by petitioners in person. But suddenly, all at once, a flood of business was coming in from the south, even from Asia. It had not yet occurred to her that all these matters had been going to Polyperchon, who had dealt with them in Philip's name. Now, Philip was here; and Polyperchon, for good reasons, was no longer accessible.

She looked with dismay at petitions from towns and provinces she had never heard of, seeking judgements on land claims; reports on delinquent, distant officials; long obscure letters from priests of temples founded by Alexander, seeking guidance about rituals; reports from Asian satraps on the encroachments of Antigonos; passionate protests from pro-Macedonians of Greek cities, exiled or dispossessed under the new decree. Often she had trouble even in reading the script with its many contractions. Turning over in helpless bewilderment this heap of documents, she reflected unwillingly that it must be a fraction of what Alexander had dealt with in an army camp, in the rest-breaks of conquering an empire.

The chief secretary, who knew all this business, had gone south with Polyperchon, leaving only a subordinate at Pella. She would have to send for this underling and try to hide her ignorance. She rang the silver bell with which, long ago, her grandfather had summoned Eumenes.

She waited. Where was the man? She rang again. Urgent muttering voices sounded outside the door. The secretary came in, shaken, without apology for delay, without asking her what she wanted. She saw fear in his face, and the resentment of a frightened man towards someone who cannot help.

'Madam. There is an army on the western border.'

She sat up with brightening eyes. The border wars were the ancient proving-ground of the Macedonian kings. Already she saw herself in arms, leading the cavalry. 'The Illyrians? Where have they crossed?'

'Madam, no. From the southwest. From Epiros. Won't you see the messenger? He says Polyperchon is leading them.'

She straightened in her chair, her pride answering his fear. 'Yes, I will see him. Bring him in.'

It was a soldier, anxious and dusty, from a garrison fort on the Orestid hills. He begged pardon, his horse had gone lame, he had had to come on by mule, a poor beast, all he could get. It had lost him a day. He gave her the despatch from his commander, shocked to discover how young she was.

Polyperchon was on the border, announcing by heralds that he had come to restore Alexander's son. He was in the country of his clan and kindred, and many of them had joined him. From the fort itself there had, unhappily, been some desertions, and the post was gravely undermanned. Between the lines, she read the intention to surrender.

She sent the man out, and sat looking before her. On the far side of the room stood a bronze youth looking back, a Hermes, holding a lyre. He stood on a plinth of green marble, Attic, poised; his gravity seeming stern to an eye used to modern prettiness. A subtle melancholy in his face had once made her ask an old palace steward who he was. Some athlete, said the man, done by Polykleitos the Athenian; he had heard it was during the great siege when the Spartans won the war, and Athens was broken. No doubt King Archelaos' agents had picked it up cheaply afterwards; there was a great deal, then, to be had for very little.

The bronze face gazed at her with eyes of dark-blue lapis laid into white glass, between lashes of fine bronze wire. They seemed to say, 'Listen. I heard the footsteps of Fate.'

She got to her feet, confronting him. 'You lost. But I am going to win.' Presently she would give orders to raise the army and prepare to march. But first she must write to Kassandros and call him to her aid.

Travel to the south was quick. Her letter reached him in three days.

He was camped before a stubborn fort in Arkadia. That dealt with, he planned to reduce the Spartans, those relics of an outworn past. They had come down to walling their city, that proud open town whose only bulwark had been its warriors' shields. Their soul was cowed, they would soon be under his hand.

Athens had made terms and had let him appoint its governor. The officer who had taken the Piraeus for him had expected the post; but he had been looking too ambitious, and Kassandros had had him disposed of in a dark alley.

The new governor was a harmless, obedient client. Soon, thought Kassandros, he must visit the Lyceum. There was a great deal to be done there.

Eurydike's appointment of him as supreme commander, though too precipitate, had helped to sway many wavering Greek allegiances. Even some who had killed their oligarchs and restored democracy were now thinking again. He would be glad to finish with the south; he was interested in war only as an instrument of policy. He was not a coward, he could get his orders obeyed, he was a competent strategist, and that was all. Deep in his being, burned there since his youth, was a bitter envy of Alexander's magic. No one would cheer himself hoarse for Kassandros, no one be proud to die for him; his men would do what they were paid to do. That vain tragedian, he thought; let us see how he looks to the new age.

The news that Polyperchon was withdrawing his forces and heading north had been no great surprise. He was old and tired and a loser; let him go home with his tail between his legs, and bed down in his kennel.

Eurydike's despatch, therefore, had been a rude shock to him. The stupid, reckless girl, he thought. Had this been the time to denounce Alexander's brat? He fully intended, once Philip was out of the way, to govern at first as the boy's regent. There would be plenty of time before he came of age. Now, instead of biding the hour, as anyone would who had the beginning of statecraft, she had flung the country into a succession war. Did she know no history? One of her family should have remembered better than that.

Kassandros reached a decision. He had made a bad bargain and must get it off his hands, quickly, like an unsound horse. Afterwards, everything would be simpler.

He sat down to write a letter to his brother Nikanor.

*

254

With banners and standards streaming, with shrill flutes and the deep-toned aulos giving the time, the royal army of Macedon marched through the high western hills towards Epiros.

Summer had come. The thyme and sage bruised by the tramping feet censed them with aromatics; the uncurled bracken stood waist-high; heather and sorrel purpled the moors. The burnished helmets, the dyed horsehair plumes, the little bright pennants on the tall sarissas, glittered and glowed in long streams of moving colour, winding down through the passes. Herd-boys on the crags cried the warning that soldiers were coming, and called their little brothers to help drive in the sheep.

Eurydike in burnished armour rode at the head of the cavalry. The heady air of the hills exalted her; the wide prospects from the heights stretched before her like worlds to conquer. She had always known that this was her nature and her fate, to ride to victory like a king, her land behind her and her horsemen at her side. She had her Companions as a ruler of Macedon should. Before she marched she had made it known that when the war was won the lands of the western traitors would reward her loyal followers. Not far off, led by Nikanor, rode the clan of the Antipatrids, a hearteningly solid force.

Their chief had not appeared, nor sent her word. Clearly, as Nikanor said, some misadventure had overtaken her messenger. It would be better to send again, and she had done so. Then, too, the troops in the Peloponnese were often on the move, and that might have caused delay. At all events, said Nikanor, he himself was doing as he knew Kassandros would wish.

Philip on his big steady horse was riding near by; he, also, panoplied for war. He was still the King, and the troops would expect to see him. Soon, when they came near the enemy, he must be settled in a base-camp out of the way.

He was placid and cheerful, travelling with an army; he could hardly remember when this had not been his life. Konon was with him, riding as usual half a length behind. Philip had wanted him alongside, the better to talk about the sights upon the way; but Konon, as usual, had said it would not be proper before the men. Dimly, after the years, Philip still missed the days of strangeness and changing marvels, when his life had moved with the journeys of Alexander.

Konon had withdrawn into his thoughts. He, too, could have wished for Alexander, and for more urgent reasons. Ever since his young master Arridaios had become King Philip, he had known that the time would come which was coming now, had felt it in his bones. Well, he thought, it was an old proverb, not to look back at the end. He was nearly sixty, and few men lived longer.

A rider showed briefly on the crest of the ridge ahead. A scout, he thought; had the girl seen? He looked at Philip ambling along, a half-smile on his broad face, enjoying some pleasant fantasy. She ought to take more thought for him. Supposing . . .

Eurydike had seen. She too, long before this, had sent out scouts. They were overdue; she sent off two more. The army moved on, bright, burnished, the flutes giving the time.

Presently, when they reached the next ridge, she herself would ride up and survey the terrain. That, she knew, was the duty of a general. If the enemy was in sight she would study his dispositions, then hold a war council and dispose her troops.

Derdas, her second in command – a new promotion, so many of the higher ranks had marched with Polyperchon – rode up to her, young, lank-limbed, frowning with responsibility. 'Eurydike, the scouts ought to be back; they may have been taken. Shouldn't we make sure of the high ground? We may be needing it.'

'Yes.' It had seemed that the gallant march in the fresh morning would go on till she herself chose to end it. 'We will lead with the cavalry, and hold it till the infantry comes up. Form them up, Derdas; you take the left wing, and of course I shall take the right.'

She was issuing further orders, when a harsh, peremptory

cough sounded at her elbow. She turned, startled and put out. 'Madam,' said Konon. 'What about the King?'

She clicked her tongue impatiently; far better to have left him behind at Pella. 'Oh, take him back to the wagon train. Have a tent set up there.'

'Will there be a battle?' Philip had come up, looking interested and eager.

'Yes,' she said quietly, mastering her irritation before the onlookers. 'Go to the camp now, and wait till we come back.'

'Must I, Eurydike?' A sudden urgency disturbed Philip's placid face. 'I've never been in a battle. Alexander never let me. None of them let me. Please let me fight in this one. Look, here's my sword.'

'No, Philip, not today.' She motioned to Konon; but he did not move. He had been watching his master's face; now he looked into hers. There was a short silence. He said, 'Madam. If the King wishes. Maybe it would be best.'

She stared at him, at his sorrowful and sober eyes. Understanding, she caught her breath. 'How dare you? If there were time I would have you flogged for insolence. I will see you later. Now obey your orders.'

Philip hung his head. He saw that he had misbehaved, and everyone was angry. They would not beat him; but the memory of ancient beatings moved in his mind. 'I'm sorry,' he said. 'I hope you win the battle. Alexander always did. Goodbye.' She did not look after him as he went.

Her favourite horse was led up, snorting and tossing its head, full of high spirits. She patted the strong neck, grasped the tough mane on the withers, and vaulted with her spear on to the scarlet saddle-cloth. The herald stood near, his trumpet at the ready, waiting to sound the advance.

'Wait!' she said. 'First I will address the men.'

He gave the brief flourish for attention. One of the officers, who had been watching the ridge ahead, began to speak; but the trumpet drowned it.

'Men of Macedon!' Her clear voice carried as it had on the march from Egypt, at Triparadisos, at the Assembly where they had voted her the regency. Battle was near; let them only be worthy of their fame. 'If you were brave fighting against foreign enemies, how much more gloriously you will fight now, defending your land, your wives, your ...'

Something was wrong. They were not hostile; they were simply not attending, staring past her, speaking to one another. Suddenly, young Derdas, gravity changed to urgency, grasped her horse's headstall, wheeled it round to face forward, and shouted, 'Look!'

All along the crest of the ridge ahead, a dark dense bristle had sprouted. It was thick with spears.

The armies faced each other across the valley. Down at the bottom was a stream, low now in summer, but with a wide bed of stones and boulders bared by winter scour. The horsemen on both sides looked at it with distaste.

The western rise which the Epirote army commanded was higher than the Macedonian position. If their full strength was on view, however, they were outnumbered three to two on foot, though somewhat stronger in cavalry.

Eurydike, standing on an outcrop to survey the field, pointed this out to Derdas. The enemy flanks were on broken, brushy ground which would favour infantry. 'Yes,' he said, 'if they let our infantry get there. Polyperchon may be no' – he just stopped himself from saying Alexander – 'but he knows better than that.'

The old man could be clearly seen on the opposite slope, in a clump of horsemen, conferring. Eurydike's men pointed him out to one another, not feeling him a great menace in himself, but bringing the comfortless thought that they were about to fight old comrades.

'Nikanor.' (He had left his contingent to join the council of war.) 'There is still no signal from the beacon?'

He shook his head. The beacon had been laid on a peak behind them, commanding a view of the southern pass. 'Without a doubt Kassandros would be here, if something had not prevented him. Perhaps he has been attacked upon the march. You know the confusion in the Greek states, thanks to Polyperchon.'

Derdas made no comment. He did not like Nikanor's disposition of his men, but this was no time to say so.

Eurydike stood on the tall flat rock, shading her eyes to look across at the enemy. In her bright helmet and gold-studded cuirass, her knee-high kilt of scarlet wool above her shining greaves, she looked a gallant figure. Derdas thought to himself that she looked like a boy actor in a play, masked to enact the young Achilles at Aulis. It was she, however, who first saw the herald.

He emerged from the knot around Polyperchon, and rode down towards them; unarmed, bareheaded, with a white wool fillet round his grey hair, carrying a white rod bound with olive; a man with presence.

At the stream-bed he dismounted, to let his horse pick its way over the stones. Having crossed, he walked a few paces forward and waited. Eurydike and Derdas came down to meet him. She turned to Nikanor to join them, but he had disappeared into the mass.

The herald had voice as well as presence, and the curve of the slope threw up his words like the hollow bowl of a theatre.

'To Philip son of Philip, to Eurydike his wife, and to all the Macedonians!' He sat at ease on his strong stocky horse, a ward of the gods, protected by immemorial custom. 'In the name of Polyperchon, guardian of both the Kings.' He paused, just long enough for suspense. 'Also,' he added slowly, 'in the name of Queen Olympias, daughter of King Neoptolemos of Molossia; wife of Philip, King of the Macedonians; and mother of Alexander.'

In the silence, a dog could be heard to bark in a village half a mile away.

'I am charged to say this to the Macedonians. Philip found you pressed by enemies and torn with civil wars. He gave you peace, reconciled your factions, and made you masters of all Greece. And by Queen Olympias herself he was the father of Alexander, who made the Macedonians masters of the world. She asks you, have you forgotten all these benefits, that you will drive out Alexander's only son? Will you take up arms against Alexander's mother?'

He had thrown his voice past Eurydike and her staff, to the silent ranks of men. When he ceased, he wheeled round his mount, and pointed.

Another rider was coming from the group above. On a black horse, in a black robe and veil, Olympias paced slowly down towards the stream.

She rode astride, in a wide skirt that fell to the tops of her crimson riding-boots. The headstall of her horse glittered with gold rosettes and silver plaques, the spoils of Susa and Persepolis. She herself wore no ornaments. A little way above the stream, where she could be seen by everyone, and where Eurydike had to look up to her, she drew rein and threw back the dark veil from her white hair. She said nothing. Her deep-set grey eyes swept the hushed murmuring ranks.

Eurydike was aware of the distant gaze pausing upon her. A light breeze floated back the black veil, stirred the horse's long mane and ruffled the snowy hair. The face was still. Eurydike felt a shiver go through her. It was like being glanced at by Atropos, the third Fate, who cuts the thread.

The herald, who had been forgotten, now suddenly raised his loud voice again. 'Macedonians! There before you is the mother of Alexander. Will you fight against her?'

There was a pause, like the pause of a rearing wave before it topples to break. Then a new sound began. It was a slight rapping,

260

at first, of wood on metal. Then it was a spreading rattle, a mounting beat; then, echoing back from along the hillside, a thunderous drumming, the banging of thousands of spear-shafts upon shields. With a united roar the royal army cried, 'No!'

Eurydike had heard it before, though never so loudly. It had greeted her when she was voted Regent. For many long seconds, she thought they were defying the enemy, that the shouting was for her.

Across the stream, Olympias raised her arm in a regal gesture of acknowledgement. Then, with a beckoning movement, she turned her horse. She moved up the hill like a leader of warriors, who need not look back to be sure that they will follow.

As she went up in triumph, the whole prospect on the opposite slope fragmented. The royal army drawn up in its formations, the phalanx, the cavalry, the light-armed skirmishers, ceased to be an army, as a village struck by an earthquake ceases to be a street. There was just a mass of men, with horses heaving about among them; shouting to each other, gravitating to groups of friends or clansmen; the whole united only in a single disordered movement, going like landslide pebbles down towards the stream.

Eurydike was overwhelmed in it. When she began to shout orders, to exhort them, she was scarcely heard. Men jostled her unnoticing; those who saw her did not meet her eyes. Her horse grew restive in the crush and reared, she was afraid of being thrown and trampled.

An officer thrust through to her, held the horse and quieted it. She knew him, he was one of her partisans from the very first days in Egypt, a man about thirty, light-haired, with a skin still yellowed from some Indian fever. He looked at her with concern. Here at last, she thought, was a man in his right mind. 'How can we rally them?' she cried. 'Can you find me a trumpeter? We must call them back!'

He ran his hand over the horse's sweating neck. Slowly, like a man explaining something simple to a child, which even a child must see, he said, 'But, madam. That is Alexander's mother.'

'Traitor!' She knew it was unjust, her anger belonged elsewhere. She had seen, at last, her real enemy. Not the terrible old woman on the black horse; she could be terrible only because of him, the glowing ghost, the lion-maned head on the silver drachmas, directing her fate from his golden bier.

'There's no help for it,' said the man, forbearingly, but with little time to spare for her. 'You don't understand. You see, you never knew him.'

For a moment she grasped her sword; but one cannot kill a ghost. The jostling press below was beginning to cross the stream. Names were shouted, as the soldiers of Polyperchon welcomed back old friends.

He sighted a brother in the crush, and gave an urgent wave, before turning back to her. 'Madam, you were too young, that's all. You made a good try of it, but ... There's not a man wishes you harm. You've a fresh horse there. Make for the hills before her people cross over.'

'No!' she said. 'Nikanor and the Antipatrids are over there on the left. Come, we'll join them and fall back and hold Black Pass. *They'll* never make peace with Olympias.'

He followed her eyes. 'They won't do that. But they're off, you see.'

She saw, then, that the force on the heathery rise was moving. Its shining shields were facing the other way. Its head was dipping already over the skyline.

She looked round. The man had sought his brother, and vanished down the hill.

Dismounting, she held her horse, the only living thing that would still obey her. As the man had said, she was young. The despair she felt was not the grim resignation of Perdikkas, paying the price of failure. Both had played for power and lost; but Perdikkas had never put his stake upon love. She stood by the fretting horse, her throat choking, her eyes blinded with tears.

'Eurydike, come, hurry.' A little group, some of her court, had found its way to her. Wiping her eyes, she saw they were not defiant but afraid; marked men all of them, old allies of Antipatros, who had thwarted Olympias' intrigues, had intrigued against her, had crossed her will and wounded her pride and helped drive her out of Macedon. 'Quickly,' they said. 'Look, that cavalry there, those are Molossians, they're heading this way, it is you they will be looking for. Quickly, come.'

She galloped with them cross-country, cutting the corners of the rutted road, letting her horse pick its line over the heath; thinking how Nikanor had said that he was doing as he knew his brother would wish; remembering Kassandros' red hair and inflexible pale eyes. No messenger from her had fallen among thieves; he had had her cry for help, and decided she was expendable.

On the shoulder of the next hill they stopped to breathe their horses, and looked back. 'Ah!' said one of them. 'That was what they were after, to loot the baggage train. There they are at it; so much the better for us.' They looked again; and there was a silence which no one liked to break. In the distance they saw, among the wagons, a single tent with men surrounding it. A small far-off figure was being led outside. Eurydike realized that from the moment when Olympias had appeared and her army melted, she had forgotten Philip entirely.

They made their way east towards Pella, avoiding the look of fugitives as best they could, using for hospitality the mesh of guest-friendship that webbed every Greek land, excusing by their haste their lack of servants. They kept ahead of the news, pretending that a treaty had been signed upon the border, that they were hurrying to Pella to call Assembly and confirm the terms which the army in the west had agreed to. In this way they lodged for several nights, and left each morning aware of a cloud of doubt.

Nearing Pella, she glimpsed the tall keep of her father's house. With unbearable longing she remembered the quiet years with Kynna, the small boyish adventures and heroic dreams, before she entered the great theatre of history, to enact a tragedy in which no god came down at last from the machine to vindicate Zeus' justice. From her childhood on she had been given her role and taught her lines and shown the mask she must wear. But the poet was dead, and the audience had booed the play.

At Mieza, they passed an old manor whose overgrown gardens scented the warm air with roses. Someone said that this was the schoolhouse where Aristotle had taught many years ago. Yes, she thought bitterly; and now his boys were ranging the earth to pick up the leavings of their schoolfellow, who, grasping at power to serve a use beyond it, had put his stake upon love and swept the board.

They dared not enter Pella. They had only travelled at their own horses' pace; a courier with remounts on the way could have been there long before them, and they could not be sure of the garrison after the news from the western army. One of her suite, a certain Polykles, was brother to the commandant of Amphipolis, an old stronghold near the Thracian border. He would help them to get away by sea.

Henceforward they must try not to be seen. Their arms discarded, wearing homespun bartered for with peasants, they nursed their weary horses, skirting the great timeworn road that had carried Darius the Great towards Marathon, Xerxes to Salamis, Philip to the Hellespont and Alexander to Babylon. One by one, pleading sickness, or just disappearing in the night, her small company fell away. On the third day, there was only Polykles.

From a long way off they saw the great keep of Amphipolis, commanding the mouth of the Strymon River. There was a ferry there; troops were there also. They turned inland to seek the nearest ford. But at the ford, too, they were awaited.

When they brought her into Pella, she asked them to untie her feet, which were bound under the mule she rode, to let her wash and comb her hair. They replied that Queen Olympias had ordered her brought just as she was.

On the low hill above the town stood what looked at first like a thicket of stunted trees, laden with birds. When they came near, ravens and crows and kites rose, angrily cawing, from the branches. It was Gallows Hill, where the corpses of criminals were nailed up after execution, like vermin in a gamekeeper's larder. Philip's murderer had hung there once. The present corpses were no longer to be recognized – the scavengers had fed well – but their names had been painted on boards nailed at their feet. NIKANOR SON OF ANTIPATROS, one board said. There were more than a hundred crosses; the reek almost reached the town.

In the audience hall, on the throne where Eurydike had heard petitioners and envoys, Olympias was seated. She had changed her black robes and was dressed in crimson, with a gold diadem on her head. Beside her on a chair of state sat Roxane, the young Alexander on a stool at her knee. He stared with round dark eyes at Eurydike when she was led in, unkempt and dirty, with fetters on her legs and wrists.

The irons had been forged to restrain strong men. Her wrists with their dead weight hung down before her. She could only walk by sliding each foot in turn along the floor, and every step chafed her ankles. To keep the fetters from tripping her, she had to walk with an ungainly straddle. But she held her head high as she shuffled towards the throne.

Olympias nodded to one of the guards. He gave Eurydike a hard shove in the back; she toppled forward, bruising her chained hands. Struggling to her knees she looked up at the faces. Some had laughed; the child had laughed with them, but was suddenly grave. Roxane was still smiling. Olympias watched under dropped lids, intently, like the cat that waits for the caught mouse to move.

She said to the guard, 'Is this slut the woman who claims to be Queen of Macedon?' He assented, woodenly. 'I do not believe you. You must have found her in the harbour stews. You, woman. What is your name?'

Eurydike thought, I am alone. No one wishes me courage or will praise it. Any courage I have is for me, alone. She said, 'I am Eurydike, the daughter of Amyntas son of Perdikkas.'

Olympias turned to Roxane, and said conversationally, 'The father a traitor, the mother a barbarian's bastard.'

She stayed on her knees; if she tried to rise, her weighted wrists would pull her over. 'And yet, your son the King chose me to marry his brother.'

Olympias' face tautened with an old anger; the flesh seemed to grow dense. 'I see he did well. The trull is well matched with the fool. We will keep you apart no longer.' She turned to the guards and for the first time smiled. Eurydike could see why she did it seldom; one of her front teeth was black. The guards seemed to blink before they saluted. 'Go,' she said. 'Take her to the marriage chamber.'

When she had toppled twice trying to rise, the guards set her on her feet. She was led to the rear courts of the palace. Dragging her fetters, she passed the stables, and heard her horses whinny; the kennels, where the deep-voiced hounds she had hunted with barked at the foreign sound of her weighted footsteps. The guards did not hustle or harry her. They walked awkwardly at her dragging pace; once, when she tripped over a rut, one of them caught her to keep her from falling; but they did not look at her or speak to one another.

Today or tomorrow, or soon, she thought; what matter? She felt death present in her flesh, its certainty like a sickness.

Ahead was a low-walled stone hut with a pointed roof of

thatch. A stink came from it; a privy, she thought, or perhaps a sty. They steered her towards it. A muffled sobbing sounded from within.

They lifted the crossbar from the rough timber door. One of them peered into the fetid gloom. 'Here's your wife, then.' The sobbing ceased. They waited to see if she would go in without being forced. She stooped under the low lintel; the roof inside was hardly higher, the thatch pricked her head. The door closed behind her, the crossbar clattered back.

'Oh, Eurydike! I will be good! I promise I'll be good! Please make them let me out now.'

By the light of a foot-square window under the eaves she saw Philip, in fetters, hunched sideways against the wall. The whites of his eyes glittered in the tear-stained dirt of his face. He gazed at her pleadingly and held out his hands. The wrists were rubbed raw.

The room was furnished with a wooden stool, and a litter of straw like a horse's. At the further end was a shallow pit, reeking with excrement and buzzing with great blue flies.

She moved to the space under the high roof-peak, and he saw her fetters. He wept again, wiping his running nose. The smell of unwashed flesh repelled her as much as the privy. Involuntarily she drew back against the far wall; her head met the roof again and she had to crouch on the filthy floor.

'Please, please, Eurydike, don't let them beat me again.'

She saw then why he did not sit with his back to the wall. His tunic was stuck to his skin with dark stripes of clotted blood; when she came near he cried, 'Don't touch it, it hurts.' Flies were clustering on the yellow serum.

Fighting back her nausea she said, 'Why did they do it?'

He gulped back a sob. 'I hit them when they killed Konon.'

A great shame filled her. She covered her eyes with her chained hands.

He eased his shoulder against the wall, and scratched his side.

She had felt already the tickle of insects around her legs. 'I shouldn't have been King,' he said. 'Alexander told me I shouldn't be. He said if they made me King someone would kill me. Will they kill me?'

'I don't know.' Having brought him here, she could not refuse him hope. 'We may be rescued. You remember Kassandros? He didn't help us in the war; but now Olympias has killed his brother and all his kin. Now he must come. If he wins, he will let us out.' She sat down on the stool, holding her wrist-chains in her lap to ease their weight, and looking at the window-square, whose patch of sky was edged by a distant tree. A gull, seeking the pickings of the kitchen-midden, floated across from the wide free waters of the lagoon.

He asked her unhappily for permission to use the pit. When necessity drove her there, the flies flew up and she saw their crawling maggots.

Time passed. At length he sat up eagerly. 'Suppertime,' he said, and licked his lips. It was not only squalor that had changed him; he had lost several stone. A tuneless whistling was coming towards the hut.

A grimy, broken-nailed hand appeared in the window-hole, grasping a hunk of black bread smeared with greasy dripping. Another followed, then a crock of water. She could see nothing of the face but the end of a coarse black beard. The whistling receded.

Philip seized his bread and tore at it like a starving dog. It seemed to her she would never eat again; but her captors had fed her that morning. She had no need to ask if he had eaten that day. She said, 'You can have my piece today; I will eat tomorrow.'

He looked at her, his face illuminated, radiant. 'Oh, Eurydike, I'm so glad you've come.'

Afterwards he told her, rambling, the tale of his captivity. His sufferings had confused his mind, he was often hardly coherent. Far off and muted, as they might reach a sickroom, came the sounds of early evening, the lowing of cattle, horses returning to the stables, dogs barking, peasants hailing each other after work, the stamp and rattle of the changing guard. A cart lumbered near with a heavy load; she could hear the oxen straining, the driver cursing and beating them. It did not pass by, but creaked to a halt, and, rumbling and rattling, tipped its load. She listened dully, aware that she was exhausted, thinking of the crawling straw. She propped her back to the wall and fell into an unsleeping doze.

Footsteps approached. Is it now? she thought. Philip was stretched out and snoring. She waited to hear the bar withdrawn. But there came only the indistinct sounds of peasants at heavy work. She called, 'What is it? What do you want?'

The mutterings died into silence. Then, as if a stealthy sign had been made, the stirrings began again. There was a kind of patting and scraping against the door, then a thud, and another.

She went to the little window, but it did not overlook the door. All she could see was part of a heap of rough-dressed stone. She was tired, and slow to understand, but suddenly the sound came clearly: the slap of wet mortar, and the scraping of a trowel.

Kassandros was walking his siege-lines on the damp Arkadian plateau under the walls of Tegea; thick, dark, mossy, impacted brick, stuff that would only dent under a ram that could have loosened ashlar. The town had a perpetual spring inside; it was a slow business to starve them out. They had told his heralds that they were under the special patronage of Athene, who had promised in some oracle of remote antiquity that their city would never be taken by force of arms. He was resolved to make Athene eat her words.

He did not hurry to meet the courier from Macedon; it was sure to be another appeal from Eurydike. Then as he came near he saw the face of disaster, and took the man to his tent.

He was a servant who had escaped the massacre of the

Antipatrids. To the tale of death he added that Olympias had had the tomb of his brother Iollas battered down and his bones scattered for beasts to eat, claiming that he had poisoned her son in Babylon.

Kassandros, who had listened in rigid silence, leaped from his chair. There would be a time for grief; all he could feel was a blazing hate and rage. 'That wolf-bitch! That Gorgon! How did they let her set foot in Macedon? My father warned them against her with his dying breath. Why did they not kill her on the border?'

The messenger said, without expression, 'They would not fight the mother of Alexander.'

For a moment, Kassandros felt that his head would burst. The man looked with alarm at his staring eyes. Aware of it, he fought for composure. 'Go, rest, eat. We will speak again later.' The rider went off, not wondering that a man should be moved by such a slaughter of his kin.

When he had come to himself, he sent an envoy to make terms with the Tegeans. He excused them from allegiance to himself, if they would merely agree not to help his enemies. Face-saving formulae were exchanged; the siege was lifted; the Tegeans went in procession to the old wooden temple of Athene, to bring her thank-offerings for keeping her ancient promise.

Behind the walled-up door, time passed like the days of a slow fatal illness, bringing misery by small additions; more stink, more flies and lice and fleas, more festering of their sores, weakness and hunger. But still the bread and water came every day to the window-hole.

At first Eurydike had counted the days, scratching with a pebble on the wall. After seven or eight she missed one and lost count, and ceased to make the effort. She would have sunk into blank apathy, broken only by fighting with the insects, but for Philip.

His mind could not hold the sum of disaster long enough to be capable of despair. He lived from day to day. Often he would complain to the man who brought the food, and he would sometimes answer, not cruelly but like a sulky servant unjustly blamed, saying he had his orders and that was the end of it. She scorned to utter a word to him; but as time passed he grew a little more forthcoming, bringing out old saws about the ways of fortune. One day he even asked Philip how his wife was. He looked at her and answered, 'She says I'm not to tell.'

She drowsed away half the day but could not sleep at night. Philip's snores were noisy, the vermin as tormenting as her thoughts. One morning early, when they were awake and already hungry, she said to him, 'Philip. I made you claim the throne. It was for myself I wanted it. It is my fault you are shut up here, my fault that you were beaten. Do you want to kill me? I do not mind. If you like I will show you how.' But he only said with a whine like a sick child's, 'The soldiers made me. Alexander told me not to.'

She thought, I need only give up my bread to him. He would take it gladly if I gave it, though he will not rob me. I would surely die quickly, now. But when the time came she could not bear her hunger, and ate her share. To her surprise, she was aware that the portion had grown larger. Next day there was still more, enough to save for a frugal breakfast.

At the same time, they began to hear the voices of the guard outside. They must have been told to keep their distance – her record of subversion was well known – their comings and goings had been only measures of time. But discipline was relaxing, they talked and gossiped carelessly, weary perhaps of guarding a place without an exit. Then one night, as she lay watching through the window-hole a single star, there was a soft approach, the click of leather and metal; the opening was darkened for a moment, and when it lightened, there were two apples on the sill. The mere smell was ambrosia.

After that something came every night, and with less stealth, as if the officer of the watch were himself conniving. No one stayed to talk at the window, no doubt a hanging matter; but they talked to their relief, as if they meant to be heard. 'Well, we've our orders, like it or not.' 'Rebels or no, enough's enough.' 'And too much is hubris, which the gods don't like.' 'Aye, and by the look of it they won't wait long.'

Well versed in the tones of mutiny, she sensed something else. These men were not plotting; they were talking openly the common talk of the streets. She thought, We are not that woman's only victims; the people have sickened of her. What did they mean by the gods not waiting long? Can it be that Kassandros is marching north?

There had been cheese and figs in the night, and the jug had had watered wine in it. With better food her listlessness had left her. She dreamed of rescue, of the Macedonians staring with pity at their filth and wretchedness, clamouring for retribution; of her hour of triumph when, washed and robed and crowned, she resumed her throne in the audience chamber.

Kassandros' sudden departure for the north had left confusion behind him; his forsaken allies in the Peloponnese had to face alone the Macedonians led by Polyperchon's son. When their desperate envoys overtook his column, he only said he had business that would not wait.

Democrat Aitolians had manned Thermopylai against his passage. Such challenges had no romance for him. More practical than Xerxes, he commandeered everything that would float in the busy strait between Euboia and the mainland, and bypassed the Hot Gates by sea.

In Thessaly, Polyperchon himself awaited him, still faithful, despite Olympias, to Alexander's son. He too was sidestepped; some troops were detached to tie him up, while the main force pressed on northeast. Skirting Olympos, they were soon on the borders of Macedon.

The coastal fortress of Dion lay ahead. Kassandros' envoys promised an end to the unlawful tyranny of women and a return to the ancient customs. After a short conclave within, the gates were opened. Here he held court, receiving all who offered support or brought him intelligence. Many kinsmen of Olympias' victims, or men whom she had proscribed, came to join him, full of their wrongs and clamouring for vengeance. But others came by stealth who till lately would not have come; men who had refused to fight the mother of Alexander, and who said now that no one but Alexander could have held such a woman in check. These would go back, spreading news of Kassandros' pledges, and his claim to the regency on behalf of Roxane's son.

One day, he remembered to ask of such a visitor, 'And when they took Amyntas' daughter, how did she die?'

The man's face lightened. 'There at least I have good news for you. She was alive when I left, and Philip too. They are treated shockingly, walled up in a wretched sty; there is a great deal of anger among the people. I'm told they were in a very poor way, till even the guards took pity on them and gave them a little comfort. If you hurry, you can save them still.'

Kassandros' face had set in a moment's stillness. 'Shameful!' he said. 'Olympias should have borne her good fortune more becomingly. Can they have lived so long?'

'You can count on that, Kassandros. I had it from one of the guard.'

'Thank you for the news.' He leaned forward in his chair, and spoke with sudden animation. 'Let it be known I mean to right their wrongs. They shall be restored to all their dignities. As for Olympias, I shall hand over her person to Queen Eurydike, to punish as she sees fit. Tell the people.'

'Indeed I will; they will be glad to hear. I'll get word, if I can, to the prison. It will cheer them to have hope at last.'

He left, big with his mission. Kassandros sent for his officers, and told them he would delay his march for a few days more. It would give his friends time, he said, to gather more support.

Three mornings later, Eurydike said, 'How quiet it is. I don't even hear the guard.'

The first dawn was glimmering in the window-hole. The night had been cool, the flies were not yet awake. They had eaten well on what the night-guard had brought. The watch had changed just before dawn as usual; but the relief had been quiet, and now there was no sound of their movements. Had they deserted, mutinied? Or been called to help defend the city, which would mean Kassandros had come?

She said to Philip, 'Soon we shall be free, I feel it.'

Scratching at his groin, he said, 'Can I have a bath?'

'Yes, we shall have baths and good clean clothes, and beds to sleep in.'

'And I can have my stones back?'

'Yes, and some new ones too.' Often in their close quarters his nearness, his smell, the way he ate and belched and relieved himself, had been barely endurable; she would gladly have exchanged him for a dog; but she knew that she owed him justice. She must care for her mind, if she was to be fit again for ruling. So she seldom scolded him, and, if she did, gave him a kind word after. He never sulked, always forgave, or perhaps simply forgot.

'When will they let us out?' he said.

'As soon as Kassandros wins.'

'Listen. People are coming now.'

It was true, there were footsteps; three or four men by the sound. They were on the door side, where the window did not look. Their voices muttered but she could not make out their words. Then, suddenly, came a sound there was no mistaking – a blow of a pick on the wall that closed the door.

'Philip!' she cried. 'They have come to rescue us!'

He whooped like a child, and peered vainly through the

window. She stood up in the space under the roof-point, listening to the fall of rubble and thud of stones. The work went quickly; the wall had been a shoddy job, by men without their hearts in it. She called out, 'Are you Kassandros' men?'

There was a pause in the pick-strokes; then a thick foreign voice said, 'Yes, Kassans men,' but she could tell he had not understood her. His next words, to his workmates, were not in Greek, and now she recognized the sound.

'They are Thracians,' she said to Philip. 'They are slaves sent to knock down the wall. When that's done, someone will come to unbar the door.'

Philip's face had altered. He withdrew as far from the door as he could without falling into the privy. Old days, before the benevolent reign of Konon, were coming back to him. 'Don't let them come in,' he said.

She had begun to reassure him, when there was a laugh outside.

She stiffened. It was not the laughter of slaves, complaisant or discreet. She knew, with a crawling of the flesh, the nature of this archetypal mirth.

The last stones fell. The crossbar clattered from the door. It creaked open; the sunrise burst dazzling in.

Four Thracians stood on the threshold, staring across the rubble.

They choked, clapping hands to their mouths and noses; men bred in the clean hill air, with hundred-foot cliffs to receive the ordure of their villages. In this pause, she saw on their cheeks and foreheads their warrior tattoos, saw their pectorals of engraved bronze etched with silver, their cloaks with bands of tribal colours, the daggers in their hands.

Sickly she thought, The Macedonians would not do it. She stood straight, in the centre where the roof was high.

The leading Thracian confronted her. He wore an arm-bracelet of a triple-coiled snake, and greaves with women's faces

275

embossed upon the kneecaps. Spiral blue tattoos on his brow, and on his cheeks to his dark-red beard, made his expression impenetrable. 'Kill me then!' she cried, lifting her head. 'You can boast that you killed a queen.'

He put out his arm – not the right, with the dagger, but the left with the coiled bronze snake – and swept her out of his way. She lost her footing and fell.

'You slave, don't you dare hit my wife!' In a moment, the cowering form by the privy had hurled itself straight forward from a bent-kneed crouch. The Thracian, taken unawares with a butted midriff, had the breath knocked out of him. Philip, fighting like an ape enraged, using feet and knees and nails, struggled to get the dagger. He had sunk his teeth in the Thracian's wrist when the others fell on him.

Between his roars of pain as the knives went in, she thought that he called for Konon; then he gave a guttural choke, his head arched back gaping, he clawed at the dirt floor and lay still. One of the men shoved at him with a foot, but he did not move.

They turned to each other, like men whose task is done.

She rose on her hands and knees. A booted foot had trodden on her leg; she wondered that she could still move it. They were staring down at the body, comparing the bites and scratches Philip had given them. She caught in their unknown jargon a note of admiration; they had found, after all, a king.

They saw her movement and turned to look at her. One of them laughed. A new horror gripped her; till now she had thought only of the knives.

The man who had laughed had a round, smooth-skinned face and a pale scanty beard. He came towards her smiling. The leader who wore the greaves called something out, and the man turned away with a gesture which said he could do better for himself than this stinking drab. They looked at their red blades and wiped them on Philip's tunic. One of them threw it back to show the groin; the leader, rebukingly, pulled it down again. They went out, picking their way over the scattered stones.

She tottered to her feet, shaking and dazed and cold with shock. It had all taken, perhaps, two minutes from the time when the door gave way.

Clear early sun streaming through the doorway picked out the stale filth, the fresh scarlet blood on the body. She blinked in the unaccustomed light. Two shadows fell across it.

They were Macedonians, and unarmed, the second attendant on the first, for he stood half a pace behind and carried a bundle. The first came forward, a thickset middle-aged man in a decent drab tunic and shoulder-cloak. He gazed a few moments in silence at the scene, clicking his tongue in disapproval. Turning to the other he said, 'Mere butchery. A disgrace.'

He stepped into the entry, confronting the haggard, mat-haired woman with her grimy feet and black nails, and spoke in the flat, rather pompous voice of a minor functionary doing his office with regard for his own importance.

'Eurydike, daughter of Amyntas. I act under command, do you therefore hold me guiltless before the gods. Olympias, Queen of the Macedonians, says this by me. Because your father was born lawfully of royal blood, she does not condemn you to execution like the bastard your husband. She gives you leave to end your own life, and offers you a choice of means.'

The second man came forward, and looked for somewhere to put his bundle down. Seeming disconcerted to find no table, he opened it on the ground, and, like a peddler, set out the contents on the cloth: a short fine dagger, a stoppered flask, and a cord of plaited flax with a running noose.

Silently she considered them, then looked from them to the sprawling corpse beside her. If she had joined him as he fought, perhaps it would all be over. Kneeling she picked up the phial; she had heard that the Athenian hemlock killed with a creeping cold, giving no pain. But this came from Olympias, and if she asked what it was they might lie. The dagger was sharp; but she knew she was too weak to strike it home; half dead, what would they do to her? She fingered the rope. It was smooth, well made and clean. She looked up at the peak of the hut where the roof stood eight feet high, and said, 'This will do.'

The man gave a businesslike nod. 'A good choice, lady, and quickly over. We'll soon have it fixed, you've a stool there, I see.' When the servant mounted it, she saw there was even an iron hook, fixed to a little crossbeam, such as is found in places where tools or tackle are kept. No, they would not be long.

So, she thought, nothing at all remained. Not even style; she had seen hanged men. She looked down at Philip, left tumbled like a slaughtered beast. Yes, after all, something was still left. Piety remained to her. This was the King her husband, who had made her a queen, who had fought and died for her. As the executioner, his task done, stepped down from the stool, she said, 'You must wait awhile.'

The jug of watered wine, left by the night-guard for their comfort, stood untouched in the window. She knelt beside him, and wetting a corner of her tunic hem, washed his wounds as well as she could, and cleaned his face. She straightened his legs, laid his left arm on his breast and his right beside him, closed his eyes and mouth and smoothed his hair. Set in the gravity of death he looked a comely man. She saw the executioners looking at him with a new respect; she had done that at least for him. Scraping her hand along the earth floor, she strewed on him the ritual pinch of dust which would free him to cross the River.

There was one thing still, she thought; something for herself. It was not for nothing that her blood came down from the warring Macedonian kings and the chieftains of Illyria. She had her blood-feud; and if she could not pursue it, the powers whose work it was must do it for her. She stood up from the body, stretching her hands palms downwards over the trampled and bloodstained earth.

'Witness, you gods below,' she cried aloud, 'that I received these gifts from Olympias. I call upon you, by the waters of Styx, and by the power of Hades, and by this blood, to give her in her turn such gifts as these.' She turned to the men, saying, 'I am ready.'

She kicked the stool away for herself, not flinching or leaving them to take it, as they had seen strong men do many a time. All in all they thought she had shown a good deal of spirit, not unworthy of her ancestry; and when it seemed that her struggle might last longer than was needful, they dragged her down by the knees, to pull the noose tight and help her die.

Olympias, these needful things attended to, summoned her council. Few of the men about her were bound, now, by loyalty to her person. Some had blood-feuds with the Antipatrids; many knew they had given Kassandros cause for vengeance; others, she guessed, were loyal only to the son of Alexander. She sat at the great table of gilt and hardstone where her husband Philip had sat, a young king, in the old days of the civil wars which men of no more than sixty could still remember, and men of seventy had fought in. She did not ask them for advice. Her own will sufficed for her. The old men and soldiers sitting before her saw her impenetrable solitude, her enclosure in her will.

She did not mean, she told them, to sit at ease in Pella while rebels and traitors overran her frontiers. She would go south to Pydna; it was only some fifteen miles north of Dion where Kassandros had insolently set up his standard. Pydna had a harbour; it was well fortified; from there she would direct the war.

The soldiers approved. They thought of the bloodless victory in the west.

'Good,' she said. 'In two days I shall move the court to Pydna.'

The soldiers stared. This was another thing entirely. It meant a horde of women, servants and noncombatants taking up room, getting under the feet of the garrison, having to be fed. After a pause in which everyone waited for someone else to speak first, they told her so.

She said, unmoved, 'Our allies can join us by sea, without losses from fighting on the march. When we are in full strength, when Polyperchon has joined us, we will meet Kassandros.'

Agenor, a veteran of the east who had been given the chief command, cleared his throat and said, 'No one questions the honour of Polyperchon. But it is said he has had desertions.' He paused; everyone wondered if he would dare go on. 'And, as you know, we can expect nothing now from Epiros.'

She stiffened in her ivory-inlaid chair. The Epirotes who had followed her to the border had mutinied when ordered to fight in Macedon, and gone home. Only a handful of Molossians was left. She had shut herself up for two days to nurse her pride, and Kassandros' secret partisans had made the most of them. The councillors looked angrily at Agenor; they had seen her face harden. She fixed on him her inflexible dangerous eyes, looking out from her mask of will. She said, 'The court will move to Pydna. This session is closed.'

The men left, looking at one another, not speaking till they were in the open. Agenor said, 'Let her have her way. But she must be out before the winter.'

Kassandros had had good news from the officer he had sent to deal with Polyperchon. Avoiding battle, he had infiltrated the straggling camp with men who had a clansman or kinsman there. They spread the news that Olympias had shed the royal blood of Macedon, herself a foreigner and a usurper; and offered a bounty of fifty drachmas to any good Macedonian who would join Kassandros' force. Every morning the numbers in Polyperchon's camp were fewer; soon he and his faithful remnant were too few to consider more than their own defence. They dug themselves into the best of the local hill-forts, mended its walls, provisioned it, and waited upon events.

The corn and the olives ripened, the grapes were trodden, the women took to the mountains to honour Dionysos; in the dark before dawn the shrill Bacchic cry answered the first cockcrow. In Pydna, the watchers on the harbour walls scanned the sea, which the first autumn winds were ruffling. No sails appeared but those of the fisher-boats, already running for home.

Before the first gales began, Kassandros appeared from the passes he now commanded, and surrounded Pydna with a palisade.

316 B.C.

It was spring in the valleys. The peaks of Olympos still dazzled with winter snow under a clear pale sky. A single wreath of cloud hid the Throne of Zeus. His eagles had forsaken its lifeless purity to fend for themselves on the lower crags. Around the summits, only sheer cliffs that would not hold a snowflake slashed the white cloak with black.

In the foothills, the waters of the thaw scoured ravines and gullies in torrents that ground the boulders like thunder. Below, under the walls of Pydna, a mild sun warmed the corpses which the cold had stiffened, releasing their carrion reek, and the kites returned to them.

Olympias, pacing the walls, looked out beyond the siege-lines to the wild mountain ranges where the lynxes and wolves ran free, where the pines were shrugging the snow from their furry shoulders like awakening bears.

Her gaunt face looked out from a shapeless mass of clothing, layer upon layer. She had come in mild autumn weather, resolved that the war would be over in a month and Kassandros dead. Alexander had always done what he resolved, that she knew. He had seldom discussed with her the complex calculations which had preceded action. There was a sharp wind today; she was wearing even her state robe heaped over her shoulders like a wrap. With hunger one felt the cold.

The other women were huddled indoors over their tiny fire. The men upon the ramparts, skull-faced, glanced dully at her as she passed, their vitality too low to nourish a hot hate. All through the winter there had been no assault upon the walls; the corpses in the ditch were all dead of starvation. They had been flung there not from callousness but necessity; there was no room left in the fort to dig more graves.

Scattered among them were the huge bones of the elephants. The horses and mules had soon been eaten; but elephants were instruments of war, and, besides, no one had dared to slaughter them. They had tried to keep them alive on sawdust; for a time their complaining moans and forlorn trumpetings had disturbed the night, then one by one they had sunk down in their stalls, and what meat was left on them, all sinew, had been something to chew on for a while. The mahouts, who were useless now, had been taken off the ration list; they too were below the walls.

Somewhere in the fort a camp-woman's child was crying; new born, soon gone. The young Alexander was too old to cry. She had seen to it that he still had enough; he was a king and must not have the strength of his manhood crippled in his youth. Though the food was wretched he had been unexpectedly good, telling her that his father had gone hungry with his men. But often she would find herself looking through him, seeing the tall grandson she could have had if her son had obeyed her, and married before he rode to war. Why, she asked herself; why?

On the rampart that faced the sea the air was cleaner, with a sharp scent of spring. The Olympian massif with its snowy crests called to her like the trees to a captive bird. Last autumn's Dionysia was the first for forty years that she had not spent with her maenads in the mountains. Never again, said the caw from the kite-haunted bones. She refused it angrily. Soon, when it was sailing weather, Eumenes, whose loyalty had never failed, would cross with his troops from Asia.

There was a stirring along the ramparts. A little crowd was gathering and growing, coming towards her. She drew back from the brink and waited.

The band of emaciated men approached without sign of violence. Few looked to have strength for it. Their clothes hung on them like half-empty sacks; several leaned on a comrade's shoulder to keep their feet. Men of thirty could have been sixty. Their skin was blotched with scurvy and many had toothless gums. Their hair was falling. One, to whom still clung vestiges of command, came forward and spoke, lisping a little because his front teeth had gone.

'Madam. We request permission to leave.'

She looked at them, speechless. Anger surfaced in her eyes and fell away into their depths. The old, thin voice seemed not a man's but a Fate's.

Answering her silence, he said, 'If the enemy attacked he could lay us out barehanded. All we can do here now is share the last of the stores, and then go *there*.' He made a tired, economical gesture towards the ditch. 'Without us, what's left will last a little longer. Permission, madam?'

'But,' she said at last, 'Kassandros' men will butcher you.'

'As God wills, lady. Today or tomorrow, what's the odds?'

'You may go,' she said. He stood a few moments looking at her mutely as the rest began shambling away. She added, 'Thank you for your good service.'

She went in then, because of the cold; but a little later she went up again to watch them depart.

They had broken off branches from some scrawny pines that grew in the cracks of the stone, and as the gates creaked open they waved them in sign of peace. Slowly they eased themselves down the scarp, and plodded across no-man's-land towards the siege-works. The rough timber gate in the stockade was lifted open; they trickled through and stood in a clump inside. A single, helmeted figure came out to them, seemed to address them, and went away. Presently soldiers came among them with baskets and tall jars. She watched the bread and wine distributed, the stick-like arms reached out in eager gratitude.

She returned to her room in the gate-tower, to crouch over her little fire. A ribbon of ants was streaming along the hearth to a basket that stood beside it. She lifted the lid; inside, they were swarming over a dead snake. It was the last one left from the Thracian sanctuary of Dionysos, her oracle. What had killed it? The rats and mice had been trapped and eaten, but it could have lived on the creeping things. It was only a few years old. She gazed at the moving mass and shivered, then put the basket with its seething heap on to the fire.

The air grew mild, the breezes gentle. It was sailing weather; but the only sails were those of Kassandros' warships. The ration was down to a handful of meal a day, when Olympias sent envoys to ask for terms.

From the ramparts she saw them go into his tent. Beside her stood her stepdaughter Thessalonike, a legacy from one of Philip's campaign weddings. Her mother had died when she was born, and Olympias had tolerated her in the palace because she gave herself no airs, and was quiet and civil. She was thirty-five, tall and plain, but carried herself well. She had not dared confess that in Pella she had had an offer from Kassandros; she had come to Pydna letting it be thought it was her life she had feared for. Now, pale and lank-haired, she waited for the envoys, keeping her thoughts to herself.

The envoys came back, their lassitude a little lifted by the hospitality in the tent. Kassandros' envoy was with them.

He was a man called Deinias, who had done many secret errands for Olympias in the past and been well rewarded. How much had he told Kassandros? He behaved as if those days had never been, insolently bland. Florid, well-fleshed, his very body was an arrogance in that company. He refused a private parley, demanding to speak before the garrison. Having no choice, she met him in the central court where, while they were able, the soldiers used to exercise.

'Kassandros son of Antipatros sends you greetings. If your people give themselves up to him, they will be spared like those who have now surrendered. As for yourself, his terms are that you put yourself in his hands, without any conditions.'

She pulled herself upright, though a twinge reminded her that her back was stiffening. 'Tell Kassandros to come with better terms.' A whispering sigh ran through the ranks behind her. 'When Eumenes comes, your master will run like a hunted wolf. We will hold out till then.'

He raised his brows in overplayed surprise. 'Madam, forgive me. I had forgotten news does not reach you here. Do not set your hopes on a dead man.'

Her vitality seemed to drain, like wine from a cracked jar. She kept her feet but did not answer.

'Eumenes was given up lately to Antigonos. He was sold by the Silver Shields whom he commanded. By the chance of battle, Antigonos seized their baggage train. Their loot of three reigns was in it; also their women and children – one cannot tell how much that weighed with such men. At all events, Antigonos offered it back in exchange for their commander, and they struck the bargain.'

A rustling shudder passed through the brittle ranks. Horror perhaps, the knowledge that nothing was now unthinkable; or, perhaps, temptation.

Her face was parchment-coloured. She would have been glad of the stick she used sometimes to get about the rough places of the fort. 'You may tell Kassandros we will open the gates without condition, in return for our lives alone.'

Though her head felt icy cold, and a dazzle of darkness was

spinning in her eyes, she got to her room and shut the door before she fainted.

'Excellent,' said Kassandros when Deinias returned to him. 'When the men come out, feed them and recruit any who are worth it. Get a trench dug for the carrion. The old bitch and her household will stay here for the time.'

'And after?' said Deinias with feigned carelessness.

'Then ... well. She is still the mother of Alexander, which awes the ignorant. The Macedonians won't bear her rule again; but, even now ... I shall frighten her, and then offer her a ship to escape to Athens. Ships are wrecked every year.'

The dead were shovelled into their trench; the thin, pasty-faced women moved from the fortress into the town house reserved for royal visits. It was roomy and clean; they got out their mirrors, and put them quickly away; girdled their loose clothes round them, and ate cravingly of fruit and curds. The boy picked up quickly. He knew he had survived a memorable siege, and that the Thracian archers, in the secrecy of their guardroom, had made stew from the flesh of corpses. The inner defences of child-hood were making it like a tale to him. Kebes, whose fine physique had lasted him well, did not check this talk; the haunted ones were those who kept silent. All kings of Macedon were heirs to the sword; it was well to know that war was not all flags and trumpets. As man and boy gained strength, they began to exercise again.

It was Roxane who had changed most to the outward eye. She was twenty-six; but in her homeland this was matronhood. Her glass had showed it her, and she had accepted it. Her consequence was now a dowager's; she saw herself not as the last king's widow, but as the mother of the next.

Pella had surrendered, on Olympias' orders, dictated by Kassandros. This done, she sent to ask him if she might now return to her palace rooms. He replied that at present it was not convenient. At Pella he had things to do.

She would sit in a window that looked on the eastward sea, considering the future. She was exiled now from Epiros; but there was still the boy. She was sixty; she might have ten years or more to rear him and see him on his father's throne.

Kassandros held audience at Pella. The Epirotes made alliance with him; he sent an adviser to direct their king, the young son of Kleopatra. He buried his brother Nikanor, and restored his brother Iollas' desecrated tomb. Then he asked where were the bodies of the royal pair, so foully murdered. They led him to a corner of the royal burial ground, where in a little brick-lined grave Philip and Eurydike had been laid like peasants. They were hardly to be recognized, by now, as man and woman; but he burned them on a ceremonial pyre, denouncing the outrage of their deaths, and had their bones laid up in precious coffers while a handsome tomb was built for them. He had not forgotten that kings of Macedon were entombed by their successors.

There were many graves around Pella after Olympias' purge. The withered wreaths still hung upon the stones, tasselled with the mourners' hair. The kindred still came with tears and offering-baskets. Kassandros made it his business to go among them, commiserating their losses, and asking if time was not ripe for justice on the guilty.

Soon it was announced that the bereaved wished an Assembly called, to accuse Olympias of shedding without trial the blood of Macedonians.

She was sitting with the other women at the evening meal when a messenger was announced. She finished, drank a cup of wine, and then went down to him.

He was a well-spoken man with the accent of the north; a stranger, but there were many after her long absence in the west.

He warned her that her trial was to be demanded; then he said, 'I am here, you understand, at the instance of Kassandros. He pledged your safety when the siege was raised. Tomorrow at dawn, there will be a ship for you in the harbour.'

'A ship?' It was dusk, the lamps in the hall had not been lit yet. Her cheeks were hollowed with shadow, her eyes dark wells with a faint gleam in the depths. 'A ship? What do you mean?'

'Madam, you have good guest-friends in Athens. You have supported their democrats.' (It had been part of her feud with Antipatros.) 'You will be well received. Let Assembly try you in absence. No one yet died of that.'

Till now she had spoken quietly; she had not yet lost the lassitude of the siege. But her raised voice was full and rounded. 'Does Kassandros think I shall run away from the Macedonians? Would my son have done so?'

'No, madam. But Alexander had no cause.'

'Let them see me!' she cried. 'Let them try me if they wish. Say to Kassandros only to tell me the day, and I shall be there.'

Disconcerted, he said, 'Is that well advised? I was to warn you that some of the people wish you harm.'

'When they have heard me, we will see what their wish is then.'

'Tell her the day?' said Kassandros when this news was brought him. 'She is asking too much. I know the fitful hearts of the Macedonians. Call Assembly for tomorrow, and give out that she refused to come.'

The bereaved appeared before Assembly in torn mourning clothes, their hair newly shorn and strewn with ashes. Widows led orphaned children, old men bewailed the sons who had propped their age. When it was made known that Olympias would not appear, no one stood up to speak for her. By acclamation, Assembly voted for death.

'So far so good,' said Kassandros afterwards. 'We have authority. But for a woman of her rank, a public execution is unseemly. She would be able to address the people, a chance that she would not waste. I think we will make a different plan.'

The household at Pydna was busy with small mid-morning tasks. Roxane was embroidering a girdle; Thessalonike was washing her hair. (She had been told, on Kassandros' authority, that she was free to return to the palace; a distinction received with dread, and not responded to.) Olympias, sitting in her window, was reading Kallisthenes' account of the deeds of Alexander. He had had it copied for her by a Greek scribe somewhere in Bactria, and sent it her by the Royal Road. She had read it often; but today it had come into her mind that she would like to read it again.

There was an urgent tap on her door. Kebes came in. 'Madam. There are soldiers asking for you outside. They're here for no good; I have barred the doors.'

As he spoke, battering and clanging began, with shouted oaths. Roxane ran in with her sewing still in her hand. Thessalonike, a towel wound round her hair, said only, 'Is *he* with them?' The boy came in, saying sharply, 'What do they want?'

She had been putting her book aside; now she picked it up again. She gave it to him, saying, 'Alexander, keep this for me.' He took it with grave quiet eyes. The battering on the door grew louder. She turned to the women. 'Go in. Go to your rooms. And you too, Kebes. It is for me they are here. Leave them to me.'

The women withdrew. Kebes paused; but the boy had taken his hand. If he had to die, it would be for the King. He bowed and led him away.

The door was splintering. Olympias went to her clothes-chest, dropped to her feet the house-gown she was wearing, and put on the crimson robe in which she had given audiences. Its girdle was Indian cloth of gold, embroidered with bullion and rubies. She took from her casket a necklace of great pearls which Alexander had sent her from Taxila, clasped it on, and walking without haste to the stairhead, stood there waiting.

The doors gave way. A press of men stumbled in and stood staring about them. They began pulling out their swords, ready to ransack the house and seek such hiding-places as the sacking of towns had made them cunning in. Then, as they moved towards the stairs, they saw the silent figure looking down on them like an image on a plinth.

The leaders stopped. Those behind them, even those still at the gaping doors, saw what they saw. The clamour died into an eerie silence.

'You wished to see me,' said Olympias. 'I am here.'

'Did you run mad?' said Kassandros when the leader reported back to him. 'Do you tell me she was standing there before you, and you did nothing? Slunk off like dogs chased out of a kitchen? The old hag must have put a spell on you. What did she say?'

He had struck the wrong note. The man felt resentful. 'She said nothing, Kassandros. What the men said was, she looked like Alexander's mother. And nobody would strike first.'

'*You* were paid to do that,' said Kassandros tartly.

'Not yet, sir. So I've saved you money. Permission to withdraw.'

Kassandros let him go. Affairs were at a crux, commotion must be avoided. He would see the man got some dangerous mission later. At present, he must think of another plan. When it came to him, it was so simple that he wondered he could have been so slow to see it.

It was drawing towards evening. At Pydna they were looking forward to supper, not so much from hunger – their stomachs were still somewhat shrunken – as because it broke the tedium of the day. Alexander was being read to by his tutor from the *Odyssey*, the book where Circe changes the hero's men to swine. The women were making small changes in their toilet, to keep good manners alive. The sun hung over the high peaks of

Olympos, ready to sink behind them and plunge the coast in dusk.

The little crowd came quietly along the road, not with the tramp of army boots, but with the soft shuffling tread that becomes a mourner. Their hair was cropped, dishevelled and dusted with wood-ash, their clothing ritually torn.

In the last sunlight they came to the broken door, shored up by a local carpenter. It was ramshackle work. While passers-by stared, wondering what burial these people came from at such an hour, they ran up to the door and tore the planks apart.

Olympias heard. When the frightened servants ran up to her, she had already understood, as though she had known already. She did not change the homely gown she had on. She looked in the box where she kept the *Deeds of Alexander*. Good, the boy had it still. Walking to the stairs she saw the ash-streaked faces below, like masks of tragedy. She did not go through the farce of standing there, appealing to those unrelenting eyes. She went down to them.

They did not seize her at once. Each wanted his say. 'You killed my son, who never injured anyone.' 'Your people cut my brother's throat, a good man who had fought for your son in Asia.' 'You hung my husband on a cross and his children saw it.' 'Your men killed my father, and raped my sisters too.'

The voices rose, lost words, became a gabble of rage. It seemed they might tear her to pieces where she stood. She turned to the older men, steadier in their sternness. 'Will you not see that this is decently done?'

Though they felt no pity, she had touched their pride. One of them lifted his staff for quiet, and cleared a place around her.

Above in the house the womenservants were keening, Thessalonike moaning softly, Roxane wildly sobbing. She heard it like the noises of some foreign town which did not concern her. She cared only that the boy should not see.

The old man pointed his staff. They led her to a piece of wasteland near the sea, too poor for farming, where glaucous shore-plants grew in the stony ground, and a mat of flotsam edged the water. The stones that strewed it were smoothed by the sea's grinding, cast up in the winter storms. The people drew away from her, and stood round her in a ring, as children do in games. They looked at the old man who had appointed himself to speak.

'Olympias, daughter of Neoptolemos. For killing Macedonians without trial, contrary to justice and the law, we pronounce you worthy of death.'

Alone in the circle, she stood with her head up while the first stones struck her. Their force made her stagger, and she sank to her knees to prevent an unseemly fall. This offered her head, and soon a big stone struck it. She found herself lying, gazing upwards at the sky. A cloud of great beauty had caught the light from the sinking sun, itself hidden behind the mountain. Her eyes began to swim, their images doubled; she felt her body breaking under the stones, but it was more shock than pain; she would be gone before the real pain had time to start. She looked up at the whirling effulgent cloud, and thought, I brought down the fire from heaven; I have lived with glory. A thunderbolt struck from the sky and all was gone.

315 B.C.

The Lyceum stood in a pleasant suburb of Athens, near the plane-shaded Ilissos stream beloved of Sokrates. It was a new and handsome building. The humbler one, where Aristotle had set up his strolling university, was a mere annexe now. A long elegant stoa with painted Corinthian columns now sheltered the Principal and his students when they paced discoursing. Within, it smelled benignly of old vellum, ink and writing-wax.

It was all the gift of Kassandros, presented through his cultured Athenian governor. The Principal, Theophrastos, had long been eager to entertain their benefactor, and the auspicious day had arrived.

The distinguished guest had been shown the new library, many of its shelves consecrated to Theophrastos' works; he was a derivative but prolific author. Now they had returned to the Principal's rooms to take refreshment.

'I am glad,' said Kassandros, 'that you study history, and delighted that you compile it. It is for the scholars of each generation to purge it of its errors, before they infect the next.'

'Aristotle's philosophy of history ...' began Theophrastos eagerly. Kassandros, who had had an hour of learned garrulity, lifted a courteous hand.

'I myself sat at his feet, in my youth when he was in Macedon.' Hateful days, tasting of gall, seeing the charmed circle always from outside, exiled from the bright warmth by the centrifuge of his own envy. He said meaningly, 'If only the *chief* of his students had put his privilege to better use.'

Cautiously, the Principal murmured something about the corruption of barbarian ways and the temptations of power.

'You suffered a grievous loss when Kallisthenes met his end. A brilliant scholar, I believe.'

'Ah, yes. Aristotle feared, indeed predicted it. Some unwise letters ...'

'I am persuaded that he was falsely accused of inspiring his students to plot the death of the King. The voice of philosophy had become unwelcome.'

'I fear so ... We have no one here who accompanied Alexander, and our records suffer.'

'You have at least,' said Kassandros, smiling, 'a guest who visited the court at Babylon in its last weeks. If you would like to call a scribe, I can give you some account of what I found.'

The scribe came, well furnished with tablets. Kassandros dictated at a smooth, measured pace. ' ... *But long before this he had given way to arrogance and wantonness, preferring the godlike hauteur of a Persian Great King to the wholesome restraints of the homeland.*' The scribe would have no polishing to do; he had prepared it all in advance. Theophrastos, whose own career had been wholly scholastic, hung fascinated on this voice from the theatre of great events.

'*He made his victorious generals fall down to the ground before his throne. Three hundred and sixty-five concubines, the same in number as Darius had, filled his palace. Not to speak of a troop of effeminate eunuchs, used to prostitution. As for his nightly carouses ...*' He continued for some time, noting with satisfaction that every word was going down on the wax. At length the scribe was thanked, and dismissed to begin the work of copying.

'Naturally,' Kassandros said, 'his former companions will give such accounts of him as they hope will tend to their own glory.' The Principal nodded sagely, the careful scholar warned of a dubious source.

Kassandros, whose throat was dry, sipped gratefully at his wine. He, like the Principal, had looked forward to this meeting. He had never managed to humble his living enemy; but at least, now, he had begun to damp down the fame he had set such store by, for which he had burned out his life.

'I trust,' said Theophrastos civilly at parting, 'that your wife enjoys good health.'

'Thessalonike is as well as her condition allows at present. She has her father King Philip's good constitution.'

'And the young king? He must be eight years old, and beginning his education.'

'Yes. To keep him from inclining to his father's faults, I am giving him a more modest upbringing. Granted that the custom was an old one, still it did Alexander no good that all through his boyhood he had his Companions to dominate – a troop of lords' sons who competed to flatter him. The young king and his mother are installed in the castle of Amphipolis, where they are protected from treachery and intrigue; he is being reared like any private citizen of good birth.'

'Most salutary,' the Principal agreed. 'I shall venture, sir, to present you with a little treatise of my own, *On the Education of Kings*. When he is older, should you think of appointing him a tutor ...'

'That time,' said the Regent of Macedon, 'will certainly be in my thoughts.'

310 B.C.

The castle of Amphipolis crowned a high bluff above a sweeping curve of the Strymon, just before it reached the sea. In old days it had been fortified by Athens and by Sparta, strengthened and enlarged by Macedon, each of its conquerors adding a bastion or a tower. The watchmen on its ashlar walls could see wide prospects on every side. They would point out to Alexander, when the air was clear, distant landmarks in Thrace, or the crest of Athos; and he would try to tell them of places he himself had seen before he came here, when he was a little boy; but the years are long between seven and thirteen, and it was growing dim to him.

He remembered confusedly his mother's wagon, the women and eunuchs in her tent, the palace at Pella, his grandmother's house in Dodona; he remembered Pydna too well; he remembered how his mother would not tell him what had happened to Grandmother, though of course the servants had said; he remembered his aunt Thessalonike crying terribly although she was going to be married; and his mother crying too on the journey here, though she was settled now. Only one thing had been constant all his life: the presence of soldiers round him. Since Kebes had been sent away, they were his only friends.

He seemed never to meet other boys; but he was allowed out riding so long as soldiers went with him. It always seemed that as soon as he got to know them, to joke and race with them and get their stories out of them, they would be assigned somewhere else and he had a different pair. But in five years a good many turns had come round again, and one could pick up the threads.

Some of them were dour and no fun to ride with; but in five years he had learned policy. When Glaukias, the Commandant, came to see him, which happened every few days, he would say that these soldiers were most interesting people, who were telling him all about the wars in Asia; and soon after they would be transferred. When his friends were mentioned he looked glum, and they stayed on for some time.

Thus he had learned that Antigonos, the Commander-in-Chief in Asia, was making war on his account, wishing to get him out of Amphipolis and be his guardian. He had been two years old when Antigonos had come his way, and remembered only a huge one-eyed monster whose approach had made him scream with fright. He knew better now, but had still no wish to be his ward. His present guardian was no trouble because he never came.

He wished his guardian had been Ptolemy; not that he remembered him, but the soldiers said he was the best-liked of all Alexander's friends, and behaved in war almost as handsomely, which was rare these days. But Ptolemy was far off in Egypt, and there was no way of getting word to him.

Lately, however, it seemed the war was over. Kassandros and Antigonos and the other generals had made a peace, and agreed that Kassandros should be his guardian till he came of age.

'When *shall* I come of age?' he had asked his friends. For some reason this question had alarmed them both; they had enjoined him, with more than their usual emphasis, not to go chattering about what they'd said, or that would be the last he'd ever see of them.

There had always been two of them, until yesterday, when Peiros' horse had gone lame in the first mile, and he had begged Xanthos for one canter before they had to go home. So they had one while Peiros waited; and when they paused to breathe the horses, Xanthos had said, 'Never a word. But there's a lot of talk about you, outside of here.'

'Is there?' he said, instantly alert. 'No one outside of here knows anything about me.'

'So you'd think. But people talk, like we're talking now. Men go on leave. The word goes round that at your age your father had killed his man, and that you're a likely lad who should be getting to know your people. They want to see you.'

'Tell them I want to see them, too.'

'I'll tell them that when I want my back tanned. Remember; never a word.'

'Silence or death!' This was their usual catchword. They trotted back to the waiting Peiros.

Roxane's rooms were furnished from her long travels. The splendours of the Queen's rooms in Babylon, the fretted lattices and lilied fishpond, were twelve years away; all she had of them were Stateira's casket and jewels. Lately, she hardly knew why, she had put them away out of sight. But she had plenty of ornaments and comforts; Kassandros had allowed her a wagon-train to carry her things to Amphipolis. He was sending them both there, he had said, only for their protection after all the perils they had undergone; by all means, let her make her stay agreeable.

She had however been very lonely. In the beginning the Commandant's wife, and some of the officers' ladies, had made overtures; but she was the Queen Mother, she had not expected a long stay, and she had exacted her proper dignities. As months became years she had regretted this, and put out small signals of condescension; but it was too late, formality was coldly kept.

It distressed her that the King her son should have no company but women and common soldiers. Little as she knew of Greek education, she knew that he should be getting it; or how, when he came to reign, would he hold his own at court? He was losing his tutored Greek, and falling into the uncouth Doric patois of his escorts. What would his guardian think of him when he came?

And he would come today. She had just had word that he had arrived without warning at the castle, and was closeted with the Commandant. At least, the boy's ignorance should convince the Regent of his need for schooling and civil company. Besides, she herself should long since have been installed in a proper court with her ladies and attendants, not penned up among provincial nobodies. This time she must insist.

When Alexander came in, dusty and flushed from his ride, she sent him to bathe and change. In her long leisure she had worked beautiful clothes for both of them. Washed, combed, dressed in his blue tunic bordered with gold thread and his embroidered girdle, she thought that he had added to the grace of Persia the classic beauty of Greece. Suddenly the sight of him moved her almost to tears. He had been growing fast, and was already taller than she. His soft dark hair and his fine delicate brows were hers; but his eyes, though they were brown, had something in their deep-set intensity that stirred her memories.

She put on her best gown, and a splendid gold necklace set with sapphires which her husband had given her in India. Then she remembered that among Stateira's jewels were sapphire earrings. She found the casket in the chest, and put them on.

'Mother,' said Alexander as they waited, 'don't forget, not a word about what Xanthos told me yesterday. I promised. You've not told anyone?'

'Of course not, darling. Whom should I find to tell among these people?'

'Silence or death!'

'Hush. He is coming.'

Escorted by the Commandant, whom he dismissed with a nod, Kassandros entered.

He noticed that she had grown stout in the idle years, though she had kept her clear ivory skin and splendid eyes; she, that he looked older and thin to gauntness, and that his cheekbones had a flush of broken veins. He greeted her with formal civility, asked after her health and, without awaiting an answer, turned to her son.

Alexander, who had been sitting when he came in, got up, but only on reflection. He had long ago been told that kings should not rise for anyone. On the other hand, this place was his home, and he had a duty as host.

Kassandros, noting this, did not remark on it. He said without expression, 'I see your father in you.'

'Yes,' said Alexander, nodding. 'My mother sees it, too.'

'Well, you would have outgrown him. Your father was not tall.'

'He was strong, though. I exercise every day.'

'And how else do you spend your time?'

'He needs a tutor,' Roxane cut in. 'He would forget how to write, if I did not make him. His father was taught by a philosopher.'

'These things can be attended to. Well, Alexander?'

The boy considered. He felt he was being tested, to see how soon he would come of age. 'I go up to the ramparts and look at the ships and ask where they all come from, and what the places and the people are like, if anyone can tell me. I go riding every day, under guard, for exercise. The rest of the time,' he added carefully, 'I think about being King.'

'Indeed?' said Kassandros sharply. 'And how do you plan to rule?'

Alexander had given this thought. He said at once, 'I shall

find all the men I can whom my father trusted. I'll ask them all about him. And before I decide anything, I shall ask them what he'd do.'

For a moment, to his surprise, he saw his guardian turn quite white, so that the red patches on his cheeks looked almost blue; he wondered if he was ill. But his face grew red again, and he only said, 'What if they do not agree?'

'Well, I'm the King. So I must do what I think myself. He had to.'

'Your father was a—' Kassandros checked himself, greatly though he had been tempted. The boy was naive, but the mother had shown cunning in the past. He finished '. . . man of many aspects. So you would find . . . Well, we will consider these matters, and do what is expedient. Farewell, Alexander. Roxane, farewell.'

'Did I do well?' Alexander asked when he had gone.

'Very well. You looked truly your father's son. I saw him in you more than ever before.'

Next day brought the first frost of autumn. He rode out with Xanthos and Peiros along the shore, their hair blowing, tasting the sea-wind. 'When I come of age,' he shouted over his shoulder, 'I shall sail to Egypt.'

He came back full of this thought. 'I must see Ptolemy. He's my uncle, or partly. He knew my father from when he was born to when he died. Kebes told me so. And my father's tomb is there, and I ought to offer at it. I've never offered him anything. You must come too, Mother.'

Someone tapped at the door. A young girl slave of the Commandant's wife came in, with a jug that steamed spicily and two deep goblets. She set it down, curtseyed, and said, 'Madam brewed it for you, and hopes you will honour her by taking it, to keep out the cold.' She sighed with relief at having remembered it. She was a Thracian and found Greek hard.

'Please thank your mistress,' Roxane said graciously, 'and tell her that we shall enjoy it.' When the girl had gone, she said, 'She is still hoping to be noticed. After all, we shall not be much longer here. Perhaps tomorrow we will invite her.'

Alexander was thirsty from the salt air, and tossed down his cupful quickly. Roxane, who was at a tricky stage of her embroidery, finished the flower that she was stitching, and drank hers then.

She was telling him a story about her own father's wars – he must remember, after all, that there were warriors on her side too – when she saw his face tauten and his eyes stare past her. He looked urgently at the door, then rushed to a corner and bent over, retching and straining. She ran to him and took his head in her hands, but he fought her off like a hurt dog, and strained again. A little came up, smelling of vomit and spices; and of something else, that the spices had masked before.

It was from her eyes that he understood.

He staggered to the table, emptied the jug out on the floor, and saw the grounds at the bottom. Another spasm cramped him. Suddenly his eyes burned with pure rage; not like the tantrums of his childhood, but like a man's; like the blazing anger of his father which she had, once only, seen.

'You told!' he shouted. 'You told!'

'No, no, I swear!' He hardly heard her, clenched in his agony. He was going to die, not when he was old but now; he was in pain and afraid; but overwhelming even pain and fear was the knowledge that he had been robbed of his life, his reign, his glory; of the voyage to Egypt, of proving himself Alexander's son. Though he clung to his mother, he knew that he craved for Kebes, who had told him his father's deeds, and how he had died game to the last, greeting his men with his eyes when his voice was gone. If only Xanthos and Peiros had been here, to be his witnesses, to tell his story . . . there was no one, no one . . . The poison had entered his veins, his thoughts dissolved in pain and sickness; he lay rigid, staring at the roof-beams.

Roxane, the first qualms working in her, crouched over him, moaning and weeping. Instead of the stiffened face with the blue mouth, the white forehead sweating under the damp hair, she saw with dreadful clarity the half-made child of Stateira, frowning in Perdikkas' hands.

Alexander's body contracted violently. His eyes set. In her own belly the gripe became a stabbing, convulsive pain. She crept on her knees to the door and cried, 'Help me! Help me!' But no one came.

286 B.C.

King Ptolemy's book-room was on the upper floor of the palace, looking out over Alexandria harbour; it was cool and airy, its windows catching the sea-breeze. The King sat at his writing-table, a large surface of polished ebony which had once been crowded with the papers of his administration, for he had been a great planner and legislator. Now the space was clear but for some books, some writing things, and a sleeping cat. The business of Egypt went to his son, who was discharging it very capably. He had relinquished it by degrees, and with increasing satisfaction. He was eighty-three.

He looked over the writing on his tablet. It was a little shaky, but the wax was readably engraved. In any case, he hoped to live long enough to oversee the scribe.

Despite stiffness, fatigue and the other discomforts of old age, he was enjoying his retirement. He had never before had time to read enough; now he was making up for it. Besides, he had had a task saved up, to whose completion he had long looked forward. Many things had hampered it in earlier years. He had had to exile his eldest son, who had proved incurably vicious (the mother, married too soon for policy, had been Kassandros' sister) and it had taken time to train this much younger son for kingship. The crimes of the elder were the one sorrow of his age; often he reproached himself for not having killed him. But his thoughts today were serene.

They were interrupted by the entrance of his heir. Ptolemy the Younger was twenty-six, pure Macedonian; Ptolemy's third wife had been his stepsister. Big-boned like his father, he entered softly, seeing the old man so quiet in his chair that he might be dozing. But his mere weight on a floorboard was enough to dislodge two scrolls from one of the crowded shelves that lined the walls. Ptolemy looked round smiling.

'Father, another chest of books has come from Athens. Where can they go?'

'Athens? Ah, good. Have them sent up here.'

'Where will you put them? You've books on the floor already. The rats will have them.'

Ptolemy reached out his wrinkled freckled hand and scratched the cat's neck above its jewelled collar. Svelte and muscular, it flexed its smooth bronze-furred back and stretched luxuriously, uttering a resonant, growling purr.

'Still,' said his son, 'you do need a bigger book-room. In fact, you need a house for them.'

'You can build one when I'm dead. I will give you another book for it.'

The young man noticed that his father was looking as complacent as the cat. Almost he had purred too.

'What? Father! Do you mean that *your* book is finished?'

'In this very hour.' He showed the tablet, on which was written above a flourish of the stylus, HERE ENDS THE HISTORY OF ALEXANDER. His son, who had an affectionate nature, leaned down and embraced him.

'We must have the readings,' he said. 'In the Odeion of course. It's nearly all copied already. I'll arrange it for next month, then there will be time to give out word.' To this late-born child, his

306

father had been always old, but never unimpressive. This work, he knew, had begun before he himself was born. He was in haste to see his father enjoy the fruits of it; old age was fragile. He ran over in his mind the names of actors and orators noted for beauty of voice. Ptolemy pursued his thoughts.

'This,' he said suddenly, 'must kill Kassandros' poison. I was there, as everyone knows, from the beginning to the end ... I should have done it sooner. Too many wars.'

'Kassandros?' Dimly the young man recalled that king of Macedon, who had died during his boyhood and been succeeded by disastrous sons who were both dead too. He belonged to the distant past; whereas Alexander, who had died long before his birth, was as real to him as someone who might now walk in at the door. He had no need to read his father's book, he had been hearing the tales since childhood. 'Kassandros ... ?'

'In the pit of Tartaros, where he is if the gods are just, I hope he learns of it.' The slack folds of the old face had tightened; it looked, for a moment, formidable. 'He killed Alexander's son – I know it, though it was never proved – he hid him through all his growing years, so that his people never knew him, nor will he be known by men to come. The mother of Alexander, his wife, his son. And not content with that, he bought the Lyceum, which will never be the same again, and made a tool of it to blacken Alexander's name. Well, he rotted alive before he died, and between them his sons murdered their mother ... Yes, arrange the readings. And then the book can go to the copy-house. I want it sent to the Lyceum – the Academy – the school at Kos. And one to Rhodes, of course.'

'Of course,' said his son. 'It's not often the Rhodians get a book written by a god.' They grinned at each other. Ptolemy had been awarded divine honours there for his help in their famous siege. He gently stirred the cat, which presented its cream belly to be tickled.

The younger Ptolemy looked out of the window. A blinding

flash made him close his eyes. The gold laurel-wreath above the tomb of Alexander had caught the sun. He turned back into the room.

'All those great men. When Alexander was alive, they pulled together like one chariot-team. And when he died, they bolted like chariot-horses when the driver falls. And broke their backs like horses, too.'

Ptolemy nodded slowly, stroking the cat. 'Ah. That was Alexander.'

'But,' said the young man, startled, 'you always said—'

'Yes, yes. And all of it true. That was Alexander. That was the cause.' He picked up the tablet, looked at it jealously, and put it down.

'We were right,' he said, 'to offer him divinity. He had a mystery. He could make anything seem possible in which he himself believed. And we did it, too. His praise was precious, for his trust we would have died; we did impossible things. He was a man touched by a god; we were only men who had been touched by him; but we did not know it. We too had performed miracles, you see.'

'Yes,' said his son, 'but they came to grief and you have prospered. Is it because you gave him burial here?'

'Perhaps. He liked things handsomely done. I kept him from Kassandros, and he never forgot a kindness. Yes, perhaps ... But also, when he died I knew he had taken his mystery with him. Henceforward we were men like other men, with the limits that nature set us. Know yourself, says the god at Delphi. Nothing too much.'

The cat, resenting his inattention, jumped into his lap and began kneading itself a bed. He unhooked its claws from his robe and set it back on the table. 'Not now, Perseus, I have work to do. My boy, get me Philistos, he knows my writing. I want to see this book set down on paper. It is only in Rhodes that I am immortal.'

When his son had gone, he gathered the new tablets together with shaky but determined hands, and set them neatly in order. Then he waited at the window, looking out at the gold laurel-wreath that stirred as if alive in the breeze of the Middle Sea.

Author's Note

Among the many riddles of Alexander's life, one of the strangest surrounds his attitude to his own death. His courage was legendary; he consistently exposed himself in the most dangerous part of any action; if he believed himself to be god-begotten, this did not in Greek belief make men immortal. He had had several dangerous wounds and nearly fatal illnesses. One might have supposed that a man so alert to the contingencies of war would have provided for this obvious one. Yet he ignored it totally, not even begetting an heir till the last year of his life, when after his severe wound in India he must have felt his dynamic vitality begin to flag. This psychological block, in a man with immense constructive plans meant to outlast his life, will always be an enigma.

Had Hephaistion survived, he would presumably have been left the regency as a matter of course. His record reveals, besides a devoted friend and, probably, lover, an able intelligent man, sympathetic to all Alexander's ideas of statecraft. His sudden death seems to have shattered all Alexander's certainties, and it is clear that he had not yet recovered from the shock when, partly as a result of it, his own life ended. Even so, during his last illness he continued to plan for his next campaign till he could no longer speak. Perhaps he held the view Shakespeare gives to Julius

Caesar: *Cowards die many times before their deaths; The valiant never taste of death but once.*

His responsibility for the murderous power struggle which followed does not lie in his personality as a leader. On the contrary, his standards were high in terms of his own day, and he demonstrably checked in his chief officers the unscrupulousness and treachery which surfaced when his influence was gone. In so far as he was to blame, it was in not making a good dynastic marriage, and begetting an heir, before he crossed to Asia. Had he left a son of thirteen or fourteen, the Macedonians would never have considered any other claimant.

As it was, the earlier history of Macedon makes it plain that his successors simply reverted to the ancestral pattern of tribal and familial struggles for the throne; except that Alexander had given them a world stage on which to do it.

The deeds of violence which this book describes are all historical. It has indeed been necessary, for the sake of continuity, to omit several murders of prominent persons; the most notable being that of Kleopatra. After Perdikkas' death, she lived quietly in Sardis till she was forty-six, refusing an offer of marriage from Kassandros. In 308, probably from sheer ennui, she made overtures to Ptolemy. It seems unlikely that this prudent ruler meant to repeat Perdikkas' rash adventure; but he agreed to marry her, and she prepared to set out for Egypt. Her plans became known to Antigonos, who, fearing an obstacle to his own dynastic aims, had her murdered by her women, afterwards executing them for the crime.

Peithon allied himself with Antigonos, but became powerful in Media and seemed to be planning revolt. Antigonos killed him too.

Seleukos outlived even Ptolemy (he was a younger man) but when nearly eighty invaded Greece to attempt the throne of Macedon, and was killed by a rival claimant.

Aristonous, at the time of Olympias' surrender to Kassandros, was garrison commander of Amphipolis. Kassandros lured him out under a pledge of safety and had him murdered.

Pausanias says of Kassandros, *But he himself had no happy end. He was filled with dropsy, and from it came worms while he was still alive. Philip, his eldest son, soon after coming to the throne took a wasting disease and died. Antipatros, the next son, murdered his mother Thessalonike, Philip's and Nikasepolis' daughter, accusing her of being too fond of Alexandros, the youngest son.* He goes on to relate that Alexandros killed Antipatros his brother, but was killed in turn by Demetrios. This extirpation of the entire line reads like the vengeance of the Furies in some Greek tragedy.

Antigonos strove for years to conquer Alexander's empire for himself, till Ptolemy, Seleukos and Kassandros made a defensive alliance and killed him at the battle of Ipsos in Phrygia, before his son Demetrios, who was always loyal to him, could come to his help.

The remarkable career of Demetrios cannot be summarized in a note. A brilliant, charming, volatile and dissipated man, after notable achievements, which included the Macedonian throne, he was captured by Seleukos, in whose humane custody he drank himself to death.

The strange phenomenon of Alexander's uncorrupted body is historical. In Christian times this was considered the attribute of a saint; but there was no such tradition in Alexander's day to attract hagiographers, and allowing for exaggeration it does seem that something abnormal occurred, which the great heat of Babylon made more remarkable. The likeliest explanation is of course that clinical death took place much later than the watchers supposed. But it is evident that someone must have taken care of the body, protecting it from the flies; the probability being that this was done by one of the palace eunuchs, who had no part in the dynastic brawls going on outside.

Alexander's eight chief officers were known as the Bodyguard; this is a literal translation of the Greek, but it would be wrong to suppose that they were in constant attendance on his person. Many held important military commands. They have therefore been described as staff officers in the list of Principal Persons. The title of Somatophylax, or Bodyguard, is probably rooted deeply in Macedonian history.

Principal Sources

Quintus Curtius, Book X, for events immediately after Alexander's death: thereafter, Diodorus Siculus, Books XVIII and XIX. Diodorus' source for this period is a good one: Hieronymos of Kardia, who followed the fortunes first of Eumenes, afterwards of Antigonos, and was close to many of the events he describes

FIRE FROM HEAVEN
A Novel of Alexander the Great

Mary Renault

Introduced by Tom Holland

In the first novel of her stunning trilogy, Mary Renault vividly
imagines the life of Alexander the Great, the charismatic leader whose
drive and ambition created a legend.

Alexander's beauty, strength and defiance were apparent from birth,
but his boyhood honed those gifts into the makings of a king. His
mother, Olympias, and his father, King Philip of Macedon, fought
each other for their son's loyalty, teaching Alexander politics and
vengeance from the cradle. His love for the youth Hephaistion taught
him trust, while Aristotle's tutoring provoked his mind and Homer's
Iliad fuelled his aspirations. Killing his first man in battle at the age of
twelve, he became regent at sixteen and commander of Macedon's
cavalry at eighteen, so that by the time his father was murdered,
Alexander's skills had grown to match his fiery ambition.

THE PERSIAN BOY
A Novel of Alexander the Great

Mary Renault
Introduced by Tom Holland

In the second novel of her stunning trilogy, Mary Renault vividly imagines the life of Alexander the Great, the charismatic leader whose drive and ambition created a legend.

The Persian Boy traces the last years of Alexander's life through the eyes of his lover, Bagoas. Abducted and gelded as a boy, Bagoas is sold as a courtesan to King Darius of Persia, but finds freedom with Alexander the Great after the Macedon army conquers his homeland. Their relationship sustains Alexander as he weathers assassination plots, the demands of two foreign wives, a sometimes mutinous army, and his own ferocious temper. After Alexander's mysterious death, we are left wondering if this Persian boy understood the great warrior and his ambitions better than anyone.

THE CHARIOTEER

Mary Renault

Introduced by Simon Russell Beale

Injured at Dunkirk, Laurie Odell, a young corporal, is recovering at a rural veterans' hospital. There he meets Andrew, a conscientious objector serving as an orderly, and the men find solace in their covert friendship. Then Ralph Lanyon appears, a mentor from Laurie's schooldays. Through him, Laurie is drawn into a tight-knit circle of gay men for whom liaisons are fleeting and he is forced to choose between the ideals of a perfect friendship and the pleasures of experience.

First published in 1953, *The Charioteer* is a a tender, intelligent coming-of-age novel and a bold, unapologetic portrayal of homosexuality that stands with Gore Vidal's *The City and the Pillar* and James Baldwin's *Giovanni's Room* as a landmark work in gay literature.

virago

To buy any of our books and to find out more
about Virago Press and Virago Modern Classics,
our authors and titles, as well as events and
book club forum, visit our websites

www.virago.co.uk
www.littlebrown.co.uk

and follow us on Twitter

@ViragoBooks

To order any Virago titles p & p free in the UK,
please contact our mail order supplier on:

+ 44 (0)1832 737525

Customers not based in the UK should contact
the same number for appropriate postage
and packing costs.

ARE YOU A *JACKIE* OR A *MARILYN?*

TIMELESS LESSONS ON LOVE, POWER, AND STYLE

PAMELA KEOGH

GOTHAM BOOKS

GOTHAM BOOKS

Published by Penguin Group (USA) Inc.
375 Hudson Street, New York, New York 10014, U.S.A.

Penguin Group (Canada), 90 Eglinton Avenue East, Suite 700, Toronto, Ontario M4P 2Y3, Canada (a division of Pearson Penguin Canada Inc.); Penguin Books Ltd, 80 Strand, London WC2R 0RL, England; Penguin Ireland, 25 St Stephen's Green, Dublin 2, Ireland (a division of Penguin Books Ltd); Penguin Group (Australia), 250 Camberwell Road, Camberwell, Victoria 3124, Australia (a division of Pearson Australia Group Pty Ltd); Penguin Books India Pvt Ltd, 11 Community Centre, Panchsheel Park, New Delhi—110 017, India; Penguin Group (NZ), 67 Apollo Drive, Rosedale, Auckland 0632, New Zealand (a division of Pearson New Zealand Ltd); Penguin Books (South Africa) (Pty) Ltd, 24 Sturdee Avenue, Rosebank, Johannesburg 2196, South Africa

Penguin Books Ltd, Registered Offices: 80 Strand, London WC2R 0RL, England

Published by Gotham Books, a member of Penguin Group (USA) Inc.

Previously published as a Gotham Books hardcover edition

First trade paperback printing, November 2011

1   3   5   7   9   10   8   6   4   2

Gotham Books and the skyscraper logo are trademarks of Penguin Group (USA) Inc.

Copyright © 2010 by Pamela Keogh
All rights reserved

The Library of Congress has cataloged this book as follows:

Keogh, Pamela Clarke.
Are you a Jackie or a Marilyn? : timeless lessons on love, power and style / Pamela Keogh.
p. cm.
ISBN 978-1-592-40569-5 (hardcover)   978-1-592-40677-7 (paperback)
1. Beauty, Personal. 2. Feminine beauty (Aesthetics)   3. Monroe, Marilyn, 1926–1962.
4. Onassis, Jacqueline Kennedy, 1929–1994. I. Title.
HQ1219.K46 2010
646.7'042—dc22   2010015286

Printed in the United States of America
Set in Sabon • Designed by Spring Hoteling • Illustrations by Meg Hess

While the author has made every effort to provide accurate telephone numbers and Internet addresses at the time of publication, neither the publisher nor the author assumes any responsibility for errors, or for changes that occur after publication. Further, the publisher does not have any control over and does not assume any responsibility for author or third-party Web sites or their content.

For Lauren Marino, who saw this book before I did,
and
Terri Austin Keogh—
a great friend who is both Jackie and Marilyn.

Contents

Introduction

"Are you a Jackie or a Marilyn?"

Jacqueline Kennedy Onassis and Marilyn Monroe are two of the most memorable women to have graced our cultural—and visual—landscape in modern times. Both were legendary, but in completely different ways, and they represent opposite possibilities for modern women to aspire to, even today.

Jackie or Marilyn—at first glance, it seems so simple, doesn't it?

The first lady versus the Hollywood starlet. The Vassar girl versus the teenager who dropped out of Hollywood High after six months. The woman from a "good family" (and all that entails) from Washington, D.C.; Newport, Rhode Island; Southampton, New York—with occasional forays to Europe—versus the woman from the Los Angeles Orphans Home and a hundred film sets, scrapping her way up the ladder.

Are they alike? Are they different? And more important, how do they speak to us today?

Jacqueline Bouvier Kennedy Onassis was born on July 28, 1929, in Southampton, New York, where her parents spent the summer. While the Kennedys might be described as "American royalty" by well-meaning journalists, Jackie and the Bouvier clan were (on technical points) several rungs up the social ladder and far more royal than her future in-laws. Born into the *Social Register* and (although Catholic) part of the elite, regimented and very restricted WASP aristocracy, Jackie was first introduced to the American public in 1953, after marrying Senator John F. Kennedy, and became widely known while campaigning for her husband's bid for presidency.

When he won the election in 1960 (by the slimmest margin in the 20th century), Jackie—stylish, chic and very much the anti–Mamie Eisenhower (her predecessor)—burst onto the world stage as the wife of the thirty-fifth president of the United States, and the media breathlessly followed her every move.

When Jackie wore a sleeveless sheath dress and bare legs (a teenage girl or woman not wearing stockings in public just wasn't done in those days) to Sunday Mass in Palm Beach, it caused an uproar, and millions of women quickly followed suit. Her bouffant hairdo and her habit of wearing jodhpurs as sportswear and a triple-strand pearl necklace tucked into the neckline of her dress were all instantly copied.

Among the first celebrities not based on the stage or screen, Jackie and her husband lifted the curtain on the American upper class and disseminated East Coast style throughout the country and the world.

After John F. Kennedy was assassinated on November 22, 1963, Jackie rebuilt a life for herself and her children, Caroline and John Junior, in New York City. In 1968, she married the Greek shipping magnate Aristotle Onassis, earning the ire of the world. After his death in 1975, she settled permanently in Manhattan and began working as a book editor at Doubleday publishers. As the most famous woman in the world, Jackie made news with every move.

*G*rowing up and throughout her life, Jackie had every imaginable advantage—gracious homes with staff and her own horse, the best education possible, a father who doted on her and husbands who protected her. But perhaps the most important thing Jackie had was a center, a clear identity: She knew who she was and her place in the world.

Marilyn, on the other hand, had none of these advantages. For starters, not even the name "Marilyn Monroe" was originally her own. Instead, it was a studio invention.

Three years older than Jackie, Marilyn was born Norma Jeane Mortenson on June 1, 1926, in Los Angeles, California, to Gladys Baker, an unmarried woman with deep psychological problems who worked as a film cutter at RKO studios. The identity of Marilyn's father was never made known to her (in later life, she claimed to remember a photograph of a handsome man with a mustache), and she was later baptized Norma Jeane Baker.

Unlike Jackie's, Norma Jeane's childhood was uncertain and, at times, harrowing. She had a clear memory of her mother having a fit and being taken out of the house in a straitjacket, and for the rest of her life, she feared that she might end up the same way.

On June 19, 1942, she wed her twenty-one-year-old neighbor, Jimmy Dougherty, whom she barely knew. It is said that Norma Jeane was weeping when her husband left, having been drafted during World War II. A few months later she was discovered while working in a wartime factory and found an even greater love: the camera.

Marilyn's will was formidable; her desire, immense. She wanted, she wanted, she wanted.

She wanted respect. She wanted love. She would marry and divorce twice more. She wanted a home and a loving husband, children even. She wanted to be a world-famous movie star; she fought for decent scripts. In retrospect, when she was recognized all over the world—our blonde bombshell goddess, Marilyn—it all seemed inevitable.

Perhaps it was.

And yet. . . . While Jackie had every societal advantage and Marilyn so many strikes against her in her birth, they were more than equal in the fame game. Although Jackie lived a longer life, Marilyn is perhaps more beloved today because people all over the world connect with her on an emotional level. Her desire to be known, to be loved, is as much a part of her appeal as her innocent sexuality.

Jackie and Marilyn came of age in the 1950s, when socially acceptable roles for women were limited: wife and mother (the best), and if you had to work, schoolteacher or nurse. Or maybe waitress or secretary. That's about it.

Yet they both moved beyond the strictures of their time and became icons—the free-spirited movie star and the cosmopolitan first lady. If Jackie symbolized well-bred propriety, Marilyn *was* sex.

Jackie and Marilyn, it seems, ascribed to their public personas. It is no wonder that in the second season of *Mad Men,* where all of the women in Don Draper's world are either Madonnas or whores, the ad campaign they came up with for Playtex included photos of two models side by side in their brassieres. One was a "Jackie." The other was a "Marilyn"— and you can guess which was which.

While this limited way of thinking dictates that women are one or the other, the fact is that most of us, really, are a mixture of both.

The question "Are you a Jackie or a Marilyn?" seems simple enough, but like the two women it is based on—Jacqueline Kennedy Onassis and Marilyn Monroe—the answer is often far more complex and not so obvious as might first appear.

The Jackie Woman we envision is strong, intelligent, socially impeccable, well married, probably a mother and can take care of herself and others. The Marilyn Gal is vulnerable, emotionally unbalanced, enjoys sex immensely, with lots of beauty, sorrow, pills, high living, celebrity, glamour, black eyeliner, fake eyelashes and champagne in her day-to-day existence. Plus, you know she's got some beautiful, beautiful photographs of herself stashed away.

In today's celebrity world, the comparison might be Jennifer Garner versus Kate Moss, or Reese Witherspoon compared to, say, Amy Winehouse.

Among women we love, let's take Tina Turner as an example. With her perfect legs, fringed miniskirts (that she has been rocking since about 1967) and daunting sexual energy, she might appear to be a Marilyn. But looking beyond first impressions to her courage, strength and personal work ethic, she is actually a Jackie.

Her heir apparent of today, Beyoncé Knowles, is the rare pop icon who combines discipline, talent and a wholesome sexual energy to present herself as a combination of both Jackie and Marilyn.

On the other side of the spectrum, classic style icon Grace Kelly was extremely Marilyn-esque before her marriage, but as she settled into an almost suburban existence as Her Royal Highness Princess Grace of Monaco, she became more and more personally conservative until she was even less a Jackie than the real Jackie herself.

*B*ut like so many things in life, the answer to whether one is a Jackie or a Marilyn is not black and white. Human beings are complex creatures (especially *you*), and there is a broad spectrum within which one can fall; we are not necessarily one or the other—the Jackie/Marilyn hybrid, if you will. And at the risk of becoming too schizophrenic, this option could very well be the best of both worlds, because clearly, the choice between being a Jackie or a Marilyn depends on the situation.

(And here's something else we've noticed: Whether you are a Jackie or a Marilyn, you are always a bit of an actress. You might be studying at the Actors Studio, or you might work at the Genius Bar of the Apple store or as a teller in a bank. You could be a stay-at-home mom or married to the president of the United States. In your mind, it's all shades of the same inherently fabulous "look at me!" energy—just the venue is different.)

For the J+M Gal of today, it's all about style, attitude and behavior . . . and then channeling (if only in your mind) your favorite icon. You might even mix it up a little. If you are going on a job interview: Jackie. Going to Vegas: Marilyn. Going on a job interview *in* Vegas? More Marilyn with a touch of Jackie.

Meeting your future mother-in-law for the first time? Definitely Jackie.

Going to Paris for a long weekend with the new beau? Jackie with a soupçon of Marilyn (and if you are staying at the Georges V, feel free to pour on the Marilyn with abandon).

The mind boggles. Which is why you need this handy primer to make your way in the world. After studying the underlying habits, belief systems, fashion advice and sexual energy (oh, you knew we'd get there eventually) of both JKO and MM, we will determine whether you are a Jackie or a Marilyn (or somewhere in between). So consider this your go-to guide for being a retro-modern woman. It's all here, from finding your style to feathering your nest. From courtship to sex and beauty, we have advice on how to write a love letter, how to stock a bar, how to ask for a raise, even what books, CDs and DVDs the Jackie or Marilyn Gal—i.e., *you*—might favor. We cover all the bases, from soup to nuts. We're in your boudoir, we're in your office and we're on your first date—and the third. We have recipes, historical references, real-life situations, diet tips and even some great gossip.

Finally, we know that the Jackie/Marilyn Woman has courage and style in spades. Even better, we can show you how to recognize it in yourself and bring out your inner Jackie or Marilyn in any situation.

So—*are* you a Jackie or a Marilyn? By the time you finish reading this book, you might find that there is less than you might imagine separating the two. And whether you favor ballet flats, kitten heels, marabou mules, Converse sneakers or sky-high stilettos, we will show you how to throw the dice, take chances and sashay down the sidewalk of life with more style than you can imagine.

*J*ust like our girls Jackie and Marilyn. And now you.

THE JACKIE OR MARILYN QUIZ

In pondering the essential differences between the Jackie and the Marilyn Gal (with their attendant lifestyles, first husbands, lingerie and heel choices), it is first vital to ascertain whether you are a Jackie or a Marilyn.

Herewith a test.

And in case you are wondering, the Jackie among us is a test taker nonpareil, who would fill this out very fast, with perfect concentration and a perfectly sharpened No. 2 Ticonderoga pencil. And the Marilyn? Distractedly (no doubt wearing a sheer peignoir), with an eyebrow pencil fished out from the bottom of her purse—but she would look *adorable* mulling it over.

1. Who said, "All men are rats and cannot be trusted"?

   a) Jackie's father, John "Black Jack" Bouvier

   b) Gloria Steinem

   c) Marilyn Monroe in *Some Like It Hot*

2. Who said, "Just give me champagne and good food and I'm in heaven and love"?

   a) Oprah Winfrey

   b) Ina Garten

   c) Marilyn Monroe

3. Of these modern-day celebrities, who is the least Marilyn-esque?

   a) Madonna

   b) Scarlett Johansson

   c) Lindsay Lohan

4. During times of stress, do you—

    a) go for a walk on the beach.

    b) meditate.

    c) pour gin in your tea.

5. For you, sex is—

    a) uncomplicated and fun!

    b) a way of saying "thank you."

    c) a means to an end.

6. Before you meet a man for dinner, you—

    a) shave your legs

    b) run a Dun & Bradstreet on the guy.

    c) break out your tippy-tallest Manolos and hope for the best.

7. You wake up every morning—

    a) with your day completely planned.

    b) and do whatever you feel like.

    c) turn to the person next to you and say, "Hello, dear."

8. Your childhood is something—

    a) not discussed.

    b) to be celebrated.

    c) you've been running from your whole life.

9. Your father—

    a) loved you and gave you confidence.

    b) was Clark Gable.

    c) taught you to throw a football.

10. Your mother—

    a) scares the hell out of you.

    b) left you all of her Balenciaga and Schlumberger.

    c) secretly loves your little sister (you know, the "pretty one") more.

11. After you sleep with someone for the first time, he—

    a) offers you the lead in his movie.

    b) asks you to marry him.

    c) has a Cartier bibelot on the breakfast tray.

12. In your opinion, money is—

    a) everything.

    b) no, we mean it—*everything*.

    c) not that important—as long as you have a roof over your head and Veuve Clicquot in the fridge, you're cool.

13. Meeting your future mother-in-law for the first time, you—

    a) convert to Judaism.

    b) brush up on your French.

    c) eschew underwear.

14. Former beaux keep up with you—

    a) on Facebook.

    b) on the front page of the *New York Times*.

    c) They don't. They're still devastated by the breakup. They'll never get over it. Never.

15. You best friend is—

    a) your roommate from prep school.

    b) your hairdresser, makeup artist, stand-in, publicist, housekeeper, majordomo, Peggy Siegal—or some varying combination of the above.

    c) just you, baby. Just you.

16. Questions for general discussion—Is it better to be a Jackie or a Marilyn—

if you are in the running for first lady of the United States?

in bed with a handsome stranger you will never see again?

in bed with a French couturier?

lunching at Bailey's Beach?

on the proverbial (or not so proverbial) casting couch?

applying to Vassar?

on a photo shoot with Bert Stern, a case of champagne and immortality?

Answers—1) a—Black Jack Bouvier; **2)** c—Marilyn Monroe; **3)** a—Madonna—while she may have looked like MM in her youth, her MO is pure JKO; **4)** a—Jackie; b—Jackie; c—Marilyn; **5)** a—Marilyn; b—Marilyn; c—Jackie; **6)** a—Marilyn; b—Jackie; c—Marilyn; **7)** a—Jackie; b—Marilyn; c) either; **8)** a—Marilyn; b—Jackie; c—Marilyn; **9)** a—Jackie; b—Marilyn; c—neither; **10)** a—either; b—Jackie; c—Jackie; **11)** a—Marilyn; b—Marilyn; c—Jackie; **12)** a—Jackie; b—Jackie; c—Marilyn; **13)** a—Marilyn; b—Jackie; c—Marilyn (of course); **14)** a—neither; b—either; c—Marilyn; **15)** a—Jackie; b—Marilyn; c—Marilyn.

To Determine Scoring—Tally up your responses, giving yourself one "Jackie" point for each question you answered about her correctly and one "Marilyn" point for each correct Marilyn answer. Whichever score is highest corresponds to your predominant archetype. In case of a tie, you are either kidding yourself or are Uma Thurman.

1 Becoming a Woman of Mystery

"No one ever told me I was pretty when I was a little girl. All little girls should be told they're pretty, even if they aren't."

—MM

. . . .

"I like to use the word original in describing Jacqueline. . . . She was very intense and felt strongly about things. . . ."

—JANET LEE AUCHINCLOSS, JKO'S MOTHER

The number-one rule for living like a Jackie or a Marilyn (or some combination thereof) is to create yourself in your own (best) image.

Infamous paparazzo Ron Galella (who bugged the heck out of stars like Jackie, Robert Redford and Marlon Brando but has some amazing photographs to show for it) described the transformation of Jackie and Marilyn. "They were both actresses—they both created themselves. Jackie created an aura, and she kept people at a distance with her whispery voice. She really wasn't out there as much. She was a mystery. Marilyn was more obvious, straightforward. As far as being sexy—she had it over Jackie. *Way* over Jackie."

And don't let something as minor as a lack of education (MM), social background (MM) or a challenging childhood (JKO/MM) deter you from your particular vision. F. Scott Fitzgerald had it wrong when he said, "There are no second acts." This is America after all, where people straining the outer boundaries of late middle age are capable of saying "sixty is the new forty" with a straight face (and meaning it). We practically invented the third, fourth and fifth act.

In fact, we encourage you to be whatever you want—it can change from day to day, even from hour to hour. The most important thing is, you're in control.

J+M LIFE LESSONS

The Jackie Life Lesson—Remake Your Past
The Marilyn Life Lesson—Run from Your Childhood. Fast.

*W*hile Jackie had the typically strict (and somewhat neglected) upbringing of her upper-class milieu (noted for its emphasis on horseback-riding skills, attracting suitable beaux, attention to clothes and maintaining slimness), Marilyn Monroe's childhood was so bereft it was Dickensian.

Unlike Jackie, Marilyn was raised on the outskirts of society in foster homes and orphanages until 1937, when she moved in with a friend of her mother's, Grace McKee Goddard. Her time with Mrs. Goddard and her husband was happy—Grace loved the movies, and she and Norma Jeane would spend afternoons in the theater watching Jean Harlow. She also encouraged Norma Jeane to wear powder and makeup and took her to the hair salon to get her hair done. Unfortunately, when Grace's husband was transferred to the East Coast in 1942, the couple could not afford to bring the sixteen-year-old Norma Jeane with them, and Norma Jeane was given two options: return to the orphanage (a place she hated) or get married.

With a mentally unstable mother, a history of sexual abuse and a succession of increasingly negligent foster-home situations, Marilyn was born so far behind the eight ball, one cannot help but root for her.

Almost through dint of will, both Jackie and Marilyn remade themselves in the image of they wanted to be—and again, Marilyn's childhood experience was exponentially worse than Jackie's—but the lesson is that whether you are a Jackie or a Marilyn, you can, too.

Let's start at the beginning, and that is—

RECAST YOUR CHILDHOOD

When reordering your childhood under the Jackie/Marilyn model, you have several different options on how to present yourself. You might decide to be like Jackie and stick to your story or, perhaps, be like Marilyn and tell lots of different stories about your childhood (or really, like any good actress, just the one that serves your purpose at the moment). If all else fails, you can always fall back on the perennial celebrity favorite—lie.

Bob Dylan, for example, claimed to be an orphan (always a favorite among the future famous) who ran away and joined the circus. In actuality, he was born Robert Zimmerman and grew up in stable, middle-class surroundings in Hibbing, Minnesota, and yes, both of his parents were very much alive when they read the whole orphan/circus thing.

Jackie's father, John "Black Jack" Bouvier, presented by her as a glamorous roué, was—when seen in another light—a crippling alcoholic with father/daughter boundary issues, as well as a dissolute spendthrift incapable of remaining faithful in a marriage, who got so intoxicated the night before Jackie's wedding, he was unable to walk her down the aisle.

Overlooking all of this, Jackie adored him and placed him on a pedestal—in direct opposition to her strict, spoilsport mother. One of her prized possessions that she kept her entire life was his French Empire desk.[1] When he died in 1957, she had her husband, then Senator Kennedy, hand deliver his obituary (which she wrote) to the *New York Times* so that her father would be properly recognized.

She even planned his funeral. "I want everything to look like a summer garden. Like Lasata in August,"[2] she told her baffled aunts, going so far as to blanket his coffin with bachelor's buttons at the gravesite. Considering that Bouvier's funeral service, held at Saint Patrick's Cathedral in New York City, featured not one but several rows of mysterious weeping women fully draped in black widow's weeds, this gesture was perhaps appropriate.

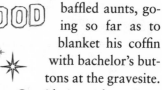

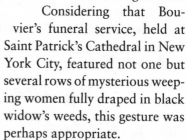

During her early years, because of her mother's mental instability and the fact that she grew up without a family, Marilyn was a ward of the state and raised by several foster families. Some were well intentioned, others abusive.[3] (In later years, she would confide in her psychiatrist, Dr. Ralph Greenson, that a boarder at one of her foster homes had sexually abused her beginning at the age of seven, and that when she told her foster mother about it, she did not believe her.) Between stints at

1 It was sold at a Sotheby's auction after her death for $70,000.
2 Lasata was the name of the Bouvier estate in the Hamptons. It was purchased in 2007 by Reed Krakoff, president and CEO of Coach, for $24,000,000.
3 As Marilyn was a child of the Depression, it was also intimated that several families took in children purely for financial gain, rather than for any altruistic reasons.

foster homes, she also spent time at the Los Angeles Orphans Home (later renamed Hollygrove), a place she hated. (Some biographies say that she was treated with love and respect there, so it is difficult to figure out what is the truth and what is Marilyn's perception of the situation.)

In her own words, "I had—let's see—ten, no, eleven families. The first one lived in a small town near Los Angeles—I was born in Los Angeles. I stayed with them until I was around seven. They were terribly strict. They brought me up harshly, and corrected me in a way I think they never should have—with a leather strap. That finally came out, and so I was taken away and given to an English couple. Life with them was pretty casual and tumultuous."

As a child Marilyn developed a bad stutter that continued to adulthood. "In the orphanage I began to stutter. The day they brought me there, after they pulled me in, crying and screaming, suddenly there I was in the large dining room with a hundred kids sitting there eating, and they were all staring at me. So I stopped crying right away. Maybe that's a reason along with the rest: my mother and the idea of being an orphan. Anyway, I stuttered."

REVISIONIST HISTORY. WAY REVISIONIST HISTORY

All people, celebrities especially, recraft their personal stories to one degree or another.[4] Jackie came by this instinct naturally. At the time of her marriage to JFK, her Bouvier relatives spun the fanciful story that they were descended from Charlemagne and were vastly superior to the bootleggin', knockabout, who-knows-where-the-money-came-from Kennedys. "It was a fairy

4 See Madonna, who somehow ended up with a posh English accent by way of Rochester Hills, Michigan.

tale history," said her cousin John Davis. They were actually descended from a French cabinetmaker named Michel Bouvier who came to America in 1815 and settled in Philadelphia.

Jackie's great-grandfather, Dr. James Lee, was a superintendent of the New York City public school system, although Janet Bouvier preferred to tell people that he was a Maryland-born veteran of the U.S. Civil War and peripherally related to Robert E. Lee. By the end of her life, she came to believe this was actually true and wondered why her name was not included in official genealogies of the Lee family.

Now, in thinking about your own background and wondering where it fits into the Jackie or Marilyn scenario—

Did you have a truly crazy childhood? And not just "My parents didn't buy me a BMW on my sixteenth birthday"? We mean Oprah Bad. Chances are you are a Marilyn.

Did it propel you to "make" something of yourself, almost to the exclusion of all else? Again, Marilyn.

At the other end of the spectrum, do you feel the urge to take your family's history—which is fine the way it is, really—and with a nip and tuck here, a bit of polish there, make it even better? Then you are a Jackie.

*I*n this age of Google, it is difficult, if not impossible, to pretend to go to Harvard or Spence when you did not, but cast off those nutty cousins or aunts and uncles! Forget those Irish forebears in favor of French aristocracy (much chicer, anyway)! Bag Catholicism and join the Episcopal Church!

Like Jackie, you can choose to be above it all. Ignore the haters. Admit nothing. Work behind the scenes with a family flunky (in her case, Mary Van Rensselaer Thayer) and have her ghostwrite your biography while you are in the White House, as Jackie did. (Unknown to the public at the time, Thayer "wrote" *Jacqueline Bouvier Kennedy*, "a warm, personal story of the First Lady illustrated with family pictures" with a strong editorial assist from Mrs. K, who gave her pages and pages of handwritten notes on yellow legal paper.)

Toward the end of your life, when you are truly famous because of your own accomplishments, embrace your formerly spurned ethnic heritage in a big way. Jackie made a point of watching the Saint Patrick's Day Parade from her Fifth Avenue balcony, and JFK Junior had a shamrock tattooed on his backside.

Marilyn, on the other hand, had none of the lyrical childhood memories of Jackie to look back on and enjoy . . . books, her own horse, the rose gardens at Lasata. Instead, she escaped to the movies at Grauman's Chinese Theatre or looked out her window at the water tower of RKO Pictures and dreamed of someday being a star.

"The world around me then was kind of grim," she recalled. "I had to learn to pretend in order to . . . I don't know . . . block the grimness. The whole world seemed sort of closed to me. . . . (I felt) on the outside of everything, and all I could do was to dream up any kind of pretend-game."

SHOULD YOU PLAY THE DAMSEL IN DISTRESS?

No matter what Jackie's upbringing was like (her mother had a fierce temper—"high strung" in yesterday's kinder parlance—and used to slap her or hit her with a hairbrush when she was frustrated.[5] "Nothing we ever did was good enough," recalled Jackie's younger sister, Lee.), there was no way she was going to complain about it to anyone. Ever. She just wasn't built that way.

Marilyn's childhood, on the other hand, was tragic. Perhaps

---

5 In one memorable incident, she threw a knife at a maid for not folding towels properly.

because of her unstable upbringing, Marilyn often felt alone, uncared for. During times of stress or pressure, she felt (rightly or wrongly) that she was alone in the world, without anyone to help her or rely upon. In speaking with journalists, lovers, psychiatrists or close friends, she would talk about her childhood, about what had happened to her in the past, and change the details of the stories around just a bit. Was she really raped at the age of eleven? Did she have sixteen abortions? Was she forced to subsist on $1 a day (and take acting classes) as a struggling starlet? Was she a streetwalker on Hollywood Boulevard?

And finally, did the facts of her story matter so much as the essential truth she told—and believed—herself? As a friend of hers noted, "Marilyn had the talent to make people feel sorry for her and she exploited it. Even people who had been around and around and around, they fell for this: help me."

This vulnerability and the need to shade her life story (depending on who she was speaking with) also became an essential part of the Marilyn myth.

J+M FIELD NOTES: DECIDE WHO YOU WANT TO BE

"I'm going to be a great movie star some day."

—MM

. . . .

"I could be a sort of Overall Art Director of the Twentieth Century, watching everything from a chair landing in space. . . ."

—JKO

While Marilyn's early rise in Hollywood was not swift, once she saw how much she loved being in front of a camera, she had found her beacon, her calling. She was tenacious. She saw a path. She moved to Hollywood, divorced her first husband, took acting lessons, dyed her hair blonder and blonder to emulate her favorite, Jean Harlow. She went on auditions, dieted ruthlessly, lived on a dollar a day and posed for practically any photographer who asked.

She got around, freshening drinks and clearing ashtrays at studio president Joe Schenck's Sunday-night poker parties. She got a contract at 20th Century Fox for $126 a week.

Even before they hit their stride, Jackie and Marilyn both presented themselves to the world in the way they wanted to be perceived—Marilyn as a Hollywood movie star and Jackie . . . well, she did not know exactly what she wanted to be (in later years, she said that she might have liked to be a writer or a journalist, before her life took a different path), but she wanted to get out there and lead an interesting life.

At the risk of getting too metaphysical, the first secret in discovering your essential Jackie-ness or Marilyn-ness is to *decide* who you want to be, and then move forward from there. This ability to "know yourself" does not just work for being more like Marilyn or Jackie; it can be applied to any creative field you want to be successful in—from Wall Street or politics to the fashion biz.

THE JACKIE, THE MARILYN: JUDGING CHARACTER

Jackie—or the Jackie-esque Gal—adores history, the telling story or anecdote that reveals character. She is drawn to the great man (or woman, but more likely the man), to her possible place in the scheme of things and how she might be part of something greater than herself. Politics interest her in the purely Shakespearean sense—the characters involved, the actions they take, or don't, when they think no one is looking.

Jackie believes that adversity reveals character. She abhors weak men, people who complain (*Get on with it!* she practically wants to shake them[6]), as well as bullies, fatties, those

....

6 But doesn't.

without style (or those with a masculine style that reveals itself in wide lapels and goofy ties). She really doesn't like high-pitched voices—in men or women.

Out in the real world, she loves four-year-olds but is very suspicious of grown men who dress like them (a baseball cap, cargo shorts and T-shirt in the city). If a grown man is wearing clogs, Crocs or running shoes outside of a gym or professional kitchen—well, that says all one needs to know about him, in the Jackie's mind.

For her part, the Marilyn of today is far more understanding of the foibles of human nature. She has seen more of the world—both its glamorous and unseemly side—than her sister in style, the Jackie. She tends to take people and situations as they are: hoping for the best in people, not that surprised when it does not work out. *Que sera sera* and all that.

In this sense, she is far more vulnerable than Jackie.

A PSYCHOLOGICAL TIME-OUT FOR LES GALS

In recasting her childhood, her father, her relationship with her mother and (as we will see) both of her marriages, Jackie was enormously disciplined about looking at her life and seeing it the way she wanted it to be. Perhaps an early proponent of *The Secret,* she once admitted, "I always push unpleasant things out of my head on the theory that if you don't think about them they won't happen."

Marilyn, on the other hand, was psychologically looser. Emotionally, she was all over the map—giddy, glowing, charismatic one moment, then depressed the next. She was much freer with her emotions than Jackie (probably freer than most people in general) and not afraid to show them.

On some level Marilyn must have also known that the ability to do whatever the hell she wanted at any time—and get away with it—was part of what made her attractive to people and was no small part (along with her talent and her beauty) of what made her a star.

Because any true star deserving of her fans is a bit of a diva, isn't she?[7] We expect it of them.

"I'm selfish, impatient and a little insecure," Marilyn once admitted. "I make mistakes, I am out of control and at times hard to handle. But if you can't handle me at my worst, then you sure as hell don't deserve me at my best."[8]

Is one better than the other? In a perfect world, it might be good to be a mixture of both. Psychologists are now learning that it is actually healthier to focus on what you want and ignore what you don't. In fact, opponents of marriage counseling say that focusing on a couple's problems and endlessly talking talking talking talking about them can actually make them worse, rather than leading to any kind of a resolution.

On the other hand—don't you think it would be fun to just blow off steam once in a while and not be so *conscientious* about everything?

---

7 Liz Taylor, Sharon Stone in her heyday, Winona Ryder, Mariah Carey . . .
8 Which, you have to admit, is kind of the perfect diva statement.

GOSSIP GIRLS

Although she is often the subject of some speculation in her group (whether she lives in the city or a one-stoplight town), the Jackie of today is Queen Bee in any group and *lives* for gossip.[9] In the midst of society, she appears to float above it, not to care (and on a certain level she doesn't; she has her own thing going on). But on the other hand, there is nothing—nothing—she likes better than a tête-à-tête with a girlfriend (or even better, a guy).

Having said all this, the Jackie is wildly discreet, almost to the point of Ice Princess-dom about what is going on in her own life. Possibly because she grew up as the daughter of divorce, possibly because at a very young age, when she confided in the adults in her life, they had a habit of throwing it back at her in a moment of rage, but the Jackie has a lot of secrets.

This is part of what gives her power—her ability to hold people's confidences and not reveal them. And to keep her own. She collects anecdotes and stories about famous people—Pamela Harriman, Hillary Clinton, Keith Richards—and reads thick biographies for insight into how they did it. She likes to learn as much as she can about people—whether in history or real life.

She also knows, if she knows anything, that "discretion is the better part of valor," quoting Falstaff as only a Jackie-esque Gal can.

But what the heck, it works.

And what sort of gossip does the Jackie like? Anything. Everything. But she can't be bothered scrolling the Internet or (god forbid) watching television—too obvious, too public, too known. She likes the really good stuff you hear at dinner parties (dessert has just

---

9 We're sorry, she does.

been put out, the table of twelve is polishing off its fourth or fifth bottle of wine, and the conversation keeps getting louder and rowdier), that—if printed— would get the *US Weekly* editor tossed in jail. The kind of stuff you can't wait to tell your lunch date the next day, strictly sotto voce.

The Marilyn, on the other hand, does not gossip. She has been on the receiving end too often and heard too many lies, half-truths and innuendos about herself. It's too painful to think about, all the slush swirling around her.[10]

THE J+M QUICKTEST:

To begin to ascertain your essential Jackie-ness or Marilyn-ness, read the following statement and ask yourself: Does this ring true for me right now? For best results, be like Marilyn—don't overthink things, and follow your first instinct.

The Marilyn Quicktest: People give you things. You don't know why.

The Jackie Quicktest: With the exception of your mother, people tend to do what you say. You don't push it.

---

10 Oh and BTW, the Jackie Gal has no compunction about gossiping about the Marilyn. None whatsoever. She figures: It's a tough world out there.

FACE IT: SECRETS = MYSTERY

You can look at it any way you want, but both Jackie and Marilyn were women of mystery even at a very young age, because they had a lot to hide. And in this age of the twenty-four-hour news cycle, the ubiquitous Internet, and bloggers intent on sharing Every. Little. Thing, keeping one or two secrets of your own can be sort of empowering.

Think of it—why is Don Draper so darn seductive? Secrets. (Like, a *lot* of them.) And who cares if it is causing him great internal struggle and tearing him up inside (well, this season anyway)—he looks fantastic! Daniel Craig as James Bond? Secrets. Angelina Jolie? Secrets!

And why is someone like Heidi Pratt so blessedly uninteresting? No secrets.

KEEPING TO YOURSELF = MYSTERY

Marilyn's grade-school science teacher, Mrs. Nash, remembers her as being "a good child, but a little set apart." After her parents' vituperative divorce (that went on for four years and remained an ongoing skirmish for the rest of Jack Bouvier's life), Jackie withdrew into herself. As early as high school, Jackie was known among her schoolmates for being self-contained and keeping her own counsel. At Vassar, she studied hard but disappeared most weekends.

MYSTERY = MYSTERY

And finally, don't give away the ball game. While Marilyn might *appear* nude onscreen in her conversation-stopping, flesh-colored tulle and satin evening gowns (in *Bus Stop,* for example), she was never actually unclothed. It was the 1950s, after all, and Marilyn knew how to work the striptease of what is shown and not shown to her advantage.

Same thing with Jackie. Once she had been admitted into

the rambunctious, wily, competitive inner sanctum of the Kennedy dining room early in her marriage, JFK turned to her and said, "A penny for your thoughts."

"But they're my thoughts," she responded. "And they wouldn't be my thoughts anymore if I told them, now would they?"

Touché.

SECRET SECRETS—THE JACKIE: THINGS YOU MIGHT NOT KNOW ABOUT HER

Whether she admitted it or not, Jackie always wanted to lead a big life. Always. In her high school yearbook, she wrote that one of her ambitions was "to not be a housewife."

SECRET SECRETS—THE MARILYN: THINGS YOU MIGHT NOT KNOW ABOUT HER

In school, Marilyn's favorite subjects were English and art. "I hated math, and numbers. . . . I would just stare out the window and daydream."

2 Emulating Jackie Style and Marilyn Style

> "I never leave my house unless I'm suitably dressed."
>
> —JKO

. . . .

> "I don't know who invented high heels, but all women owe him a lot."
>
> —MM

In terms of style, Jackie and Marilyn are opposite sides of the coin—light and dark. Day and night. Acceptability and sex. Sophistication and playful naïveté.

If Jackie was French couture and the sleeveless shift, Marilyn was the white silk dress slipping off her shoulders as she laughed, pretending not to notice.

The intriguing thing about both Jackie's and Marilyn's style is that they knew what worked for them and used this to their advantage. Nothing was an accident. As a young model trying to break into Hollywood, Marilyn soon found out that if she was a blonde, she got more work from photographers. It took her sixteen tries to get the right shade that would transform her from brown to bombshell, but once she was as blonde as Harlow, she never looked back. Shortly thereafter, in true diva mode, she even made a point of surrounding herself with as much white as possible—from the outfits she chose to the furnishings in her apartment.

It is also said that Marilyn shaved one-quarter inch off the right heel of her shoes (always, always heels—never loafers, ballet flats or, god forbid, sneakers) so that she would walk with a bit of an awkward gait, making her hips even more noticeable. And if you think of her opening entrance in *Some Like It Hot,* when she transfixed us (along with Tony Curtis and Jack Lemmon) with her mesmerizing stroll down the station platform, you know that Marilyn knew exactly what she was doing.

> *"I learned to walk as a baby and I haven't had a lesson since."*
>
> —MM

Both Marilyn and Jackie developed their own very distinct visual presentations. With slight modifications, Jackie (like Audrey Hepburn) found a style early on that worked for her and kept it—more or less—for the rest of her life.

And because their style sense was so strong and unique, both Marilyn and Jackie developed identifiable looks that the rest of us, whether we are in the mood to be a classic or a sexpot (or a classic sexpot), have been riffing on ever since.

FOR JACKIE, FOR MARILYN, FOR YOU: STYLE IS EVERYTHING

When it comes to achieving Jackie or Marilyn mystique, 98 percent of the endeavor hinges on having a signature style—a style that you might actually possess at the moment or one that you aspire to.

Think of someone like Coco Chanel, one of Jackie's favorite designers. No surprise, JKO, like Coco, was also a Leo, and

although she always claimed to be wearing Oleg
Cassini in the White House, she actually wore a
lot of Chanel and Hubert de Givenchy (passed
off as American made Cassini). In addition to the
material and cut of her suits, Jackie must have
admired Chanel's gumption. Chanel's sense of
self was so acute, her talent so unquestioned,
her ego so vast, that we are still wearing—
and coveting—her designs more than half a
century later.

In fact, Chanel's personal style was
so essential to who she was that she
founded a fashion empire based
entirely on her own whims.

Although they came from
opposite sides of the social
scale, Jackie and Marilyn shared
Chanel's belief that more than a
mere dress, style was essential—style defined
who you were. In fact, if you were to look at the
silhouette of either Jackie or Marilyn (Jackie—
classic, Marilyn—fitted to within an inch of her
life, and then some), you would be able to tell,
instantly, who was who.

THE LOOK

Interestingly, in terms of their style, the looks that "worked"
for them were almost polar opposites—MM favored softer,
shinier fabrics that clung to her body and celebrated her awe-
inspiring curves, while JKO was more tailored. She did not
wear revealing styles or fabrics. Jackie's shape was always suggested, not overtly revealed. As a young wife to John F. Kennedy
shuttling between the Cape and Georgetown, on the campaign
trail and in the White House, and up until the mid-1960s, she
favored spare outfits that hid her body. Her bouffant hairdo,

boxy sheaths and three-quarter-inch heels were very much a public uniform, hiding the woman within.

Once Jackie shed her state wear (and the baggage and expectations that went along with being the wife of a president), she looked decades younger. A photographer friend who took her picture in the 1970s when she was working as an editor at Doubleday thought she looked younger in her fifties than she did while in the White House.

Jackie dressed herself within a certain classic framework but added her own individual twist to reveal her personality, while Marilyn (when not being stupefyingly attractive in capri pants and a simple T-shirt) was pure Hollywood glamour.

 RX—THE JACKIE LOOK

When going for the Jackie, think East Coast sophistication with a soupçon of Paris style and a dash of the tomboy (okay, okay, we'll stop with the Julia Child metaphors). The look is clean, classic, somewhat spare without being minimal or overly Comme des Garçons. Very American. As shorthand, we might say Ralph Lauren, except that (as a Jackie) you know that RL is aping *your* style.

That said, there are a few rules in acquiring Jackie Style.

You wear your clothing; your clothing never wears you.

This is a hard thing to teach,[1] but it has to do with being comfortable in your own skin. This is why JKO (or someone like Audrey Hepburn or even Elvis Pres-

---

1 As a Jackie, we know you know it already!

ley) never used or needed a stylist. Through trial and
(very little) error, she knew what worked for her.

You know when you see an actress or singer on the
red carpet and she looks really uncomfortable, like she's
playing dress-up or wearing a costume? Well, that's not
what you want. Ideally, as a Jackie, your style will be a
reflection of your life, your experiences, your (dare we
say) background. It's also why you want to nab well-
made pieces from your mom, dad, grandfather, one of
your brothers, your current boyfriend. Not only is the
older stuff generally better made, but it's your history—
wear it!

Make sure your clothing fits you.

We cannot stress this enough. If you do nothing else,
make sure your damn clothing fits! (Please, no trousers
puddling on the floor or jacket cuffs that are too long.)
It takes minutes to go to a tailor and have everything
fitted at the waist, the hemline, the cuff.

Get the best stuff you can afford.

To be honest, we're not wild about buying tons and
tons of cheap clothing. Well, maybe a piece or two every
few years from H&M, but even then, it's sort of a goof,
right? As a Jackie, you are going to shop more like the
French or a *Vogue* editor—know what you want, buy
the best stuff you can afford, take care of it, wear the
heck out of it, and at the end of your life, either leave
it to the Costume Institute (á la couture goddess Nan
Kempner[2]) or your fortunate nieces.

Besides, here's something we learned from the men

---

2 Who was so insane about couture that she basically kicked her own children out of her
NYC apartment and converted their bedrooms into several walk-in closets for herself.

in our lives who have their suits "built" (as they say) on Savile Row—we know of no other incentive to keep your waistline in shape than buying good clothing. As an added benefit, you will also hang it up properly and not drop it on the floor.

Keep it loose.

This is a hard thing to impart, but once you have decent clothing, wear it lightly. Don't wear a single designer all at once. Don't wear anything that screams label label label. Mix the high and the low—jeans and a pair of Vivier shoes. The main thing is this: You don't want to seem as if you are trying too hard. Wear Schlumberger on the subway (the chances of anyone knowing what it is are pretty much nil, and besides, it's insured). You know you are in the Jackie Zone when you can wear a ball gown or a bathing suit as effortlessly as jeans and a T-shirt (or vice versa).

 JACKIE'S STYLE FAVORITES

Jackie's style favorites were a compendium of high-end European designers mixed in with some classic American sportswear. First, the big boys (or girls): Chanel, Valentino, Givenchy, YSL, Gucci, Giorgio Armani, Carolina Herrera, Hermès handbags. Then, moving on to her more casual, everyday favorites: Lacoste, Lily Pulitzer, Zoran, Roger Vivier buckled flats, Jack Rogers sandals, Manolo Blahnik, Ferragamo, Creed Fleurissimo perfume, Tretorn sneakers, Dunhill cigarette lighter, cotton T-shirts from the Gap, Schlumberger enameled bracelets (pricey!), the occasional jodhpurs worn indoors. And as far as riding in style, she gave a Jaguar as a gift to JFK when he was a senator (and it had to be exchanged for an American car), and in later years she drove a BMW.

And where did Jackie like to shop? Um, anywhere on earth? In New York City, her number-one primo spot was probably Bergdorf Goodman, but she also favored the exclusive emporiums on Madison Avenue—Armani, David Webb, Porthault for linen. In Paris, there were the usual suspects—Hermès, Givenchy and Fogal, where she got her stockings.

RX—THE MARILYN LOOK

When you're channeling Marilyn, you're asking for the ultimate va va voom and then some. But remember, part of the reason we are still drawn to MM is her combination of sexual knowingness and innocence—and that particular alchemy is important. When making wardrobe choices, the right decision can mean the difference between being in the Marilyn Zone and looking like Pamela Anderson or Anna Nicole Smith.

It's all about the waist.

The basic premise of Marilyn Style is this: No matter your dress size (which, if you know what you are doing in terms of fashion, does not really matter that much), if you have a waist, we want to see it. And that means one thing: Cinch it.

If you are less than thrilled with your figure, take a

tip from the ladies of *Mad Men* and utilize some under-garments that can give you the figure you want.

Show some skin!

Listen—you're gorgeous, you're fabulous in the sack, you love champagne, everyone in the world wants to go out with you—what the heck—own it! If you have legs, we want to see them. If you have gorgeous arms, a beautiful neck, perfect hands . . . you get the idea. The Marilyn is never afraid to show some skin. What she doesn't want to do is show too much of it—no belly button (unless she is—lucky world—wearing a bikini). No tramp stamp.

Have a sense of humor.

And again, as we said with Jackie, the best thing about Marilyn Style is that you don't have to take it (or yourself) too seriously. As a Marilyn Gal, you won't—this is part of your appeal, after all. Men (and many women and children and dogs) especially hate it when it seems as if someone is trying too hard. So you can be on a first date. You can be walking the red carpet or dripping in diamonds (borrowed from Winston, natch), but it's always good to take yourself lightly.

MARILYN'S STYLE FAVORITES

Marilyn's style was more eclectic than Jackie's. Rather than automatically falling into the classic column, she was a Hollywood starlet who reveled in being photographed. Hence, she took more risks with skintight satin, bright colors, strategically placed bows and polka dots, plunging halter dresses, dangling rhinestone earrings, white fur wraps, peep-toe shoes and some serious (god-given) décolletage.

Like most modern American women, Marilyn mixed casual sportswear with some pricey, one-of-a-kind showstoppers. Although she did not have a ton of clothing for a celebrity of her stature (especially compared to the übershopper Jackie), she took her pieces and, by the very fact that she was wearing them, made them her own. She tended to wear her clothing a good deal and then duck into the wardrobe room at Fox if she needed to borrow something for an awards show or a night out at Romanoff's.

When she was not in costume on a movie set, Marilyn wore a lot of pure American sportswear—JAX (also favored by Audrey Hepburn and Patricia Kennedy Lawford), Madcap, Geistex, John Moore and Levi's, Lee or J.C. Penney denim. In terms of designers we might know today, Emilio Pucci was her absolute favorite, as well as Billy Travilla, who designed her iconic white cocktail dress from *Seven Year Itch,* as well as the hot pink gown she wore while singing "Diamonds Are a Girl's Best Friend" in *Gentlemen Prefer Blondes.* Marilyn favored Ferragamo heels (in case you were wondering, those were Ferragamo white slingbacks worn while cavorting over the subway grate in the *Seven Year Itch*). In addition to wearing off-the-rack cocktail dresses, she also had some pricey couture—Norman Norell, Ceil Chapman, Galanos.

When she was in Manhattan, she favored a camel hair coat or a Blackglama mink that was a gift from Joe DiMaggio.

Marilyn did not have much real jewelry—she owned a 16-inch strand of Mikimoto pearls given to her on their honeymoon in Japan (she gave it to the teenaged Susan Strasberg and Strasberg later returned it to Mikimoto in 1998). She had her platinum and diamond eternity wedding band from Joe DiMaggio. (The ring with thirty-five baguette-cut diamonds—one was missing—was later sold at auction for $772,500.)

J+M FIELD NOTES—THE FIVE ESSENTIALS

JACKIE'S FIVE STYLE ESSENTIALS

Sheath dress—Although she didn't wear them much past 1972, the sleeveless sheath dress still worked when Jackie was having a Camelot redux moment, and the sheath still works today (hello, Mrs. Obama!). Some advice? Your arms have to be in very good shape to pull off this look, so don't neglect those push-ups.

White jeans, or navy blue—JKO was one of those lucky women who looked great in boyishly trim jeans (see also Audrey Hepburn, Kate Moss and Amanda Burden) well into her sixties. Must have been all the speed walking she did around the island of Manhattan, trying to escape the long lens of paparazzo Ron Galella. Although she wore blue jeans in her twenties, nothing says upper class like the white jeans she wore later in sunny Greece or Martha's Vineyard.

T-shirt—JKO (like her future daughter-in-law Carolyn Bessette) favored Petit Bateau in white, navy blue or striped. Although you can now pick them up stateside, she got hers by the dozen in Paris.

Killer jewelry—And when we say killer, we mean some killer, *crazy* jewelry—like the gold and ruby ear clips that Jackie's second husband, Greek shipping magnate Aristotle Onassis, got her in 1969 to commemorate man's landing on the moon. They were a literal representation of the lunar landing, complete with gold spaceships and ruby craters. Made especially for Ari by his jeweler in Greece, of course. But beyond the nutty bibelots, he also got her some extremely serious diamonds from Harry Winston and Van Cleef & Arpels.

Hermès scarf—Tie it under your chin, then put your oversized sunglasses on. Everyone will know it is you, but you can still pretend you are going incognito. Also useful after getting your hair done at Kenneth Salon or Thomas Morrissey's.

MARILYN'S FIVE STYLE ESSENTIALS

Since Marilyn was so physically compelling, she could wear pretty much anything and look amazing. Hence, the basic Marilyn style MO is: "If you've got it, flaunt it."

Devastating evening dress—Billy Travilla (known simply as Travilla) created some of MM's most iconographic evening dresses. They first met in 1950, when she asked if she could borrow his fitting room to try on a costume.

They worked together on eight movies—and what movies they were: *Monkey Business* (1952), *Don't Bother to Knock* (1952), *Gentlemen Prefer Blondes* (1953), *How to Marry a Millionaire* (1953), *There's No Business Like Show Business* (1954), *River of No Return* (1954), *The Seven Year Itch* (1955) and *Bus Stop* (1956). He was nominated for an Oscar for his work on two Marilyn movies, *There's No Business Like Show Business* and *Bus Stop*.

Travilla designed most of Marilyn's most memorable costumes and helped to sew her into the sheer gold lamé dress she wore (briefly—it was deemed too revealing to pass the censors) in *Gentlemen Prefer Blondes*.

Not surprisingly, MM recognized his talent, too. Lifelong friends, she autographed a nude calendar for him with the words "Billy Dear, please dress me forever. I love you, Marilyn."

Daytime/cocktail dress—Marilyn had such a great figure that she could rock a white halter dress and look amazing. For daytime, she liked color in casual West Coast styles—Pucci or a lime green dress in a soft silhouette. For night, her preferred color was (no surprise) black in either drapey wool or velvet.

Bikini (oh, what the heck)—The string bikini was not in evidence in Marilyn's day, so hers tended to be fairly high waisted and somewhat prim by today's standards, although they did reveal her belly button. We have never seen a bathing-suit shot of MM where she was not smiling and looking very happy. So the moral is this: If you are going to wear a bikini, make sure you have gotten a pedicure and *own it*.

White terry cloth bathrobe (nude underneath)—For relaxing at home or on set between takes while having your hair/makeup done. It has to be thick white terry cloth, tied closure in front. You can be like a real star and nab yours from the Chateau Marmont or the Beverly Hills Hotel.

Beautiful silk slip with lace inserts—This can also double as negligee. (We know that the Marilyn doesn't actually wear a nightgown.)

A fashion time-out from *Mad Men*'s Joan Holloway that Jackie or Marilyn would agree with: "Make sure your slip shows just a tiny, tiny bit when you're sitting down because that's alluring."

Herewith some advice based on Marilyn's shoe collection. For starters, the shoe, and the foot itself, cannot be underestimated in Marilyn World. (Fashion strivers, fetishists and Louboutin wannabes, take from that what you will.)

The heel (much like the red-toed pedicure) is so vital in and of itself to the Marilyn psyche that were the Marilyn Gal ever to write her autobiography (and what the heck, we are sure she will be asked), it would probably be titled *A Heel. Always.*

MM wore Ferragamos, although if she were here today, she would no doubt be wearing Manolo, Louboutin or Jimmy Choo. Jackie wore Blahniks when they were very much the insider's shoe—you could only get them at one shop off King's Road in London and then in one tiny shop in NYC.[3]

What shoes would they wear? Marilyn had more leeway in terms of style. Unlike Jackie, she *always* wore heels. Her shoes (for lack of a better term) were sexier—she might wear peep-toe stilettos or rope-heeled espadrilles with a striped shirt and a little pair of shorts, T-straps, even cowboy boots.

TO FUR OR NOT TO FUR

Let's tackle the animal rights question. How would Jackie and Marilyn come down on this one?

To begin, we have to say that when they were both alive (right up until the early 1990s), wearing a fur was a badge of success, a sign that you had made it (and in a lot of places, it still is). Wearing a fur was also a decidedly romantic gesture—since a spouse or admirer had often given the pricey fur as a gift.

Plus, Marilyn is the (and we mean *the*) iconic blonde in a dark mink.

On the other side of the argument is the fact that Jackie and Marilyn were devoted animal lovers. They both had dogs as pets,

. . . .

3 As a bachelor, JFK Junior was known to go to the Manhattan shop with a page torn out of *Vogue* and buy shoes for his current girlfriend.

while Jackie owned several horses throughout her life, and her children owned goldfish, hamsters, etc. After JKO wore a leopard-skin coat as first lady (a gift from the emperor of Ethiopia), so many were killed by Jackie wannabes trying to copy her that they almost became extinct, and this did not make her happy.

So they would probably be pro–animal rights in theory.

But on the other hand, Jackie and Marilyn were each extremely individualistic free thinkers who did exactly what they wanted, regardless of what others thought they should do.

So, fur? No fur? They both certainly owned and wore a lot of fur during their lifetimes.[4] Were Jackie or Marilyn alive today, our instinct is that they would have come down on the side of individual rights and done whatever they felt like.

MM AND JEANS

Marilyn *owned* denim.

And while Jackie looked cute in jeans (particularly cropped white jeans in the summer), she didn't cause people to stop dead in their tracks when she walked by, and people aren't still discussing how great her, ahem, figure looked in them.

Marilyn's jeans were so iconic that when they were auctioned off by Christie's, New York, in 1999, designer Tommy Hilfiger bought three pairs worn in her 1954 movie *River of No Return* for $42,550.[5]

At the same sale, he also bought her boots from 1961's *The Misfits* for $85,000.

He gave one pair of MM's jeans to Britney Spears and another to Naomi Campbell as gifts. And if you are ever fortunate enough to visit him, he has one pair enshrined in his office.

. . . .

4 MM, in particular, owned several mink coats, a fox stole, rabbit muffs . . . all kinds of fur. And you know what? Who knows what she would choose to do if she were alive today (probably follow the Stella McCartney route), but she wore it well.

5 The inside tag reads "J.C. Penney 24 waist"

THE MARILYN RX—CARING FOR YOUR JEANS

Here is the skinny on caring for your jeans.

Unless you are out mucking around in the mud or work in a coal mine, you don't need to wash your jeans all that often; depending on how often you wear a particular pair, once or twice a month should be enough.

Fashion experts believe that jeans, worn correctly, are as revealing of your identity as a fingerprint. To that end they advise—no kidding—that you should not wash your new jeans for at least six months. Or longer. Unless you are a college freshman or in a rock band,[6] we don't know how realistic this is, so we advise a happy medium . . . wear your jeans for as long as you can before washing them.

If you are trying to keep your jeans dark (much chicer), turn them inside out before tossing them into the washing machine. And separate your light and your dark clothing before washing so your favorite white T-shirts don't turn light blue.

If your jeans fit perfectly, turn them inside out and wash them in cold water so they keep the same shape and the color doesn't run. Personally, we like to wash our jeans in warm or even hot water if we are trying to shrink them a bit.

Finally, the dryer. Some denim fashionistas advise that you take your newly washed jeans, put them on and (we kid you not) sit in a bathtub filled with water for a while so the denim will mold to your shape. They then (and this is the truly insane pièce de résistance) suggest that you walk around in your wet denim until you have a perfect fit.

Wow.

We love our jeans, and we love to be fashionable (sort of), but this is beyond the pale, even for us. So please, no—unless you want to court walking pneumonia (*very* un-Jackie or Marilyn), don't do this. Use the dryer.

And finally, never send your jeans to the dry cleaner (where

. . . .
6 Or, you know, you have to go out and interact with other human beings.

they will give them the dreaded center crease) unless you are a European investment banker or a German aristo.

MARILYN MONROE: STUNNING IN A POTATO SACK

Let's put it this way: There is a reason she was a world-famous movie star and one of the most recognized women to this day.

Do you know that phrase "She would look good even in a potato sack?" (Okay, maybe not, it's an oldie, but ask your parents or grandparents.) In 1952, the publicity department at 20th Century Fox decided to make a fringed minidress out of an Idaho potato burlap sack and put the twenty-six-year-old Marilyn Monroe in it. Predictably, the results were stunning. With her Monroe-perfect hair, glorious smile and T-strap sandals, Marilyn looked as glamorous as if she were wearing a Patou gown.[7]

JACKIE KENNEDY: EVERYONE'S FAVORITE DEB

When she made her society debut in 1947, Hearst columnist Igor Cassini dubbed her "Debutante of the Year." By the time her daughter, Caroline, came of age, Caroline refused to even consider being presented to society. And as for Caroline's daughters coming out? Forget it.

QUICKTESTS

The Marilyn Quicktest: You never have a bad hair day. Ever. Plus, you look pretty amazing in anything you wear.

The Jackie Quicktest: Sunglasses, day or night: non-negotiable.

---

7 For some reason, celebrity fitness expert Denise Austin re-created this same look to promote the Idaho Potato Commission in 2005. Let's just say there is only one Marilyn.

WAS MARILYN A SIZE 16?

In a word, no. But for some reason, women today are obsessed with Marilyn's weight and dress size. Back in the day, they were obsessed with her shape more than her size, because she was so curvaceous.

For the record, MM was 5 feet 5.5 inches and throughout her life weighed between 116 and 140 pounds (during the Joe DiMaggio years, when she was eating lots of Italian food and had several pregnancies that were not brought to term).[8] Her measurements were 36-23-35.

Without seeing her clothing in person, determining her size by today's standards is difficult. For starters, all of her costumes were custom designed and fitted for her specifically. Having seen her dress dummy, Marilyn had a very narrow back and rib cage, with a bust size of 36C. What made her figure so extraordinary was the 13-inch difference between her bust and hips and her waist, which resulted in an extreme hourglass shape. (Think of the cartoon character Jessica Rabbit, but entirely natural.)

According to designer Jeffrey Banks, "Sizing in the 1950s was much more generous than today. It was not until about 1967 that Anne Klein starting sizing to flatter women—what would have been a 12 in the 1950s was now an 8." In today's world, Jeffrey thinks that MM would have nominally been a size 10 (and with a 23-inch waist, clothing would have seriously been taken in at the midsection), going to perhaps a 12, but with alterations.

So don't kid yourself. Marilyn was a physically compelling woman. While she wasn't the boyishly skinny runway model that seems to pass for beautiful today,

8 At her death in 1962 (at the age of thirty-six), she weighed 117 pounds.

she certainly had (and still does have) her own appeal and millions of fans. There is a reason she was a movie star, perhaps one of the greatest icons (and certainly one of the sexiest) of the 20th century.

JACKIE AS MATERIAL GIRL

We have to hand it to Jackie. When it came to shopping, she was world class.

As one Ari associate described her (and not in a good way), she was "a speed shopper. She could be in and out of any store in 10 minutes or less, having run through $100,000 or more." Truman Capote once recalled accompanying her on "one of those shop-till-you-drop sprees. She would walk into a store, order two dozen silk blouses in different shades, give them an address and walk out." Once she bought two hundred pairs of shoes in a single foray, running up a tab of $60,000.

Part of Jackie's rationale might have been that she was married to one of the richest men in the world, so she should be able to do what she wanted, right? Plus, it helped Onassis's business mystique to be married to one of the most glamorous women in the world, so she couldn't exactly shlub around. Jackie never cut down on her shopping; she simply had the bills sent directly to Ari, or raised cash by selling her clothes—many never worn—on consignment to New York City thrift shops, such as Michael's or Encore.

And she kept right on shopping.

IF JACKIE AND MARILYN
WENT SHOPPING TODAY

JKO:

> Michael Kors
> Lisa Perry (post-1967)
> The Town Shop or Le Petite Coquette for lingerie
> J.Crew
> Bergdorf Goodman
> Lanvin
> Charvet, Paris (for the lucky man in her life)
> Roger Vivier (NYC outpost on Madison only)
> JKO would stop by Red Mango for dessert while
>   shopping
> Tory Burch
> D. Porthault
> Jason Wu
> Petit Bateau
> Van Cleef & Arpels
> MIHO flowers (under the premise: It is better to re-
>   ceive, than to give.)

MM:

> Juel Park Lingerie (Los Angeles—MM had lingerie
>   made there, still in business)
> MM would completely, *completely*, rock out the DVF
>   wrap dress
> MM would wear a *Paris Review* T-shirt and drive all
>   the lit boys mad. (Available only online. They run
>   very small, so order accordingly.)
> La Petite Coquette
> J. Mendel, Paris
> Barneys New York
> Oscar de la Renta for big events
> Harry Winston
> Camel hair coat from Brooks Brothers

They would both nab shirts/cashmere/blazers from
their husband's/boyfriend's closet

SECRET SECRETS—THE JACKIE:
THINGS YOU MIGHT NOT KNOW ABOUT HER

Although she had a wardrobe to rival the second floor of Bergdorf's (and the designer duds to prove it), Jackie wore jeans and a T-shirt 90 percent of the time.

SECRET SECRETS—THE MARILYN:
THINGS YOU MIGHT NOT KNOW ABOUT HER

Although known for her glamorous image, MM disliked wearing makeup or jewelry, wearing little of either in her off hours.

3 *Cultivating Beauty*

"I want to feel blonde all over."
—MM, WHEN ASKED WHY SHE STAYED
PALE AND DID NOT SUNBATHE

. . . .

"I am a woman above everything else."
—JKO

*B*oth Marilyn and Jackie understood the power of beauty. And yet curiously (but perhaps not so surprisingly), neither thought she was pretty growing up. In Jackie's family, her sister, Lee, was considered the "pretty one," while Jackie was considered the "brains."[1]

For better or worse, Marilyn *was* her beauty, was sex. This was both empowering—the control she had over men—but also debilitating because, Jesus, what would happen when she lost her looks or wanted to be taken seriously as something other than a sex object?

A child of Hollywood, Marilyn knew the transience of physical beauty—and in her world, its absolute necessity. "Gravity

. . . .

1 This was similar to the dynamics of Grace Kelly and her family, where her older sister, Peggy, was considered the "star," and Grace (if it can be imagined) the plain Jane. Continuing this theme, Audrey Hepburn (unbelievably) also thought that she was "funny" looking.

catches up with all of us," she said. And this, perhaps, is why it was even more important for her to leave something of lasting value—her own image on the screen.

In terms of their individual beauty, Jackie and Marilyn were almost opposite archetypes—Marilyn lush and light, Jackie darker and more angular. While Marilyn wore Chanel No. 5 perfume to bed, Jackie wore Chanel suits to White House functions. They each made the most of what they had—as a child, Jackie's face was so broad that she had to have her glasses custom made. As the first lady, millions of women around the world copied her style, as she brought the look of French couture from the runways to suburban housewives. Marilyn brought a sense of humor to relations between the sexes, avoided the sun, preferred her clothing skintight, and didn't like to wear underwear.

And each, in her own way, became a style icon.

"BEAUTY IS TRUTH, TRUTH BEAUTY. . . ."

No matter how they chose to present themselves to the world (Jackie in white jeans, T-shirt and Jack Rogers sandals, stepping off a boat in Greece; Marilyn in full movie star regalia—white silk shantung gown and matching fur stole, dripping in diamonds on the red carpet), Jackie and Marilyn were both keenly aware of how they looked and how they appeared in public. Both were great dressers with natural style whether by way of Southampton or Hollywood. Both had an innate aesthetic sense honed from pedigree, interest or necessity.

It may have looked carefree—Marilyn grinning beneath a sheet, being photographed for *Vogue*, Jackie wearing a thin sweater and jeans on a city street, turning to smile for the camera. But don't kid yourself; Jackie and Marilyn took care of themselves. Yes, they were both extremely fortunate in the genetic lottery, but they also pampered their skin, hair and bodies as much as their respective budgets allowed.

JACKIE: TAILORED PERFECTION

As the daughter of Jack Bouvier, a debutante, a Vassar girl, first lady, the wife of a rich man (on two separate occasions), the "most famous woman in the world," Jackie was expected to keep it together. There was no way you would ever see her slouching off to the supermarket in a velour sweat suit with lettering on her backside. Or (god forbid) wearing flip-flops on a city sidewalk. Or with stringy hair. Like the Kennedy women of their generation, the Bouvier gals—Jackie and Lee—were fierce dieters. If Jackie gained as little as 4 pounds, her mother (no slouch in the slim department herself) let her know she had noticed.

MARILYN: BEAUTY WAS SEX

Marilyn's beauty was, literally, her ticket out of a miserable anonymous existence—the kind she had seen her mother endure. Making her way up the Hollywood ladder without a protector, without family connections or the liberal arts education that Jackie had enjoyed, Marilyn almost had to be beautiful to make her way to the head of the line; to get the hell out of where she came from. And even with her considerable physical assets, Marilyn studied her features and highlighted them to give herself even more of an advantage. With Marilyn, nothing was left to chance. When it came to her own self-presentation, she (like Jackie in her own way) was a perfectionist.

Photographer David Conover, who "discovered" Marilyn during an early photo session, said that he could not remember another model "so self critical," nor one who so acutely scrutinized every contact sheet, every negative and print for the tiniest flaw: "What's happened to me here?" she asked, or "This is awful, where did I go wrong?"

It took her one and a half to three hours to turn herself into "Marilyn," which was one of the reasons she was so chronically late for a film set, a meeting or even a cocktail party.[2] She wanted to be perfect. She knew what her audience expected from her (a look that she herself created), and she worked to give it to them. She had to, because she believed that "If I'm a star, then the people made me a star."

- -

JKO AND MM SKIN CARE SECRETS
- -

As a young woman, Jackie cornered Hollywood starlet Zsa Zsa Gabor on a plane coming back from London (where she had covered Queen Elizabeth's coronation for *The Washington Times-Herald*) to ask about her skin care secrets. Gabor clued her in to Erno Laszlo—a Hollywood skin care specialist little known to the general public whose products were used by Marilyn Monroe, Audrey Hepburn and Ava Gardner, among others. JKO got on the Laszlo bandwagon, too. (Zsa Zsa Gabor also, oddly, advised Jackie to "eat a piece of raw green pepper every single day in order to achieve and maintain beautiful skin." There is no word as to whether JKO ever actually tried this.)

Laszlo's system, still available today, was famously complex, involving many stages—skin was "clocked" depending on level of dryness or oiliness, then there was a whole system of sea mud soap, thirty splashes of lukewarm water, Active pH-elityl Oil, astringent with white powder mixed in for overnight, a different-colored astringent for daytime, various moisturizers for day or night, a loose powder to go over it all. . . .

But both Marilyn and Jackie swore by his methodology.

FIELD NOTES: THE DIET PLAN

Marilyn loved food, and she particularly loved to drink champagne—any time of the day or night. "Just give me champagne and good food and I'm in heaven and love," she said. To

- - - - - - - - - - - - -
2 This did not include hours spent in the bath or her habit of washing and rewashing her hair if she was unhappy with the way it looked.

loosen her up for a memorable 1962 *Vogue* photo shoot, Bert Stern had a case of Dom Pérignon delivered to their bungalow at the Hotel Bel-Air.

And boy, did it work. By the middle of the shoot, Marilyn had shed all of her clothing and was frolicking beneath the white sheets of a rumpled bed, her white-blonde hair blending into the pillow, smiling slyly at the camera, her lips a riotous red, one beautiful bare arm revealed.

Jackie, on the other hand, was fastidious about her weight, her diet, how she looked in clothes, how she appeared in public—there was no *way* she would ever end up nude at the Bel-Air with a case of champagne and Bert Stern shooting away for *Vogue*.

To deal with stress, Jackie smoked two packs of cigarettes a day her entire life, starting from the age of fifteen, and bit her nails to the quick (the yellowing of her fingertips and her nail-biting habit were part of the reason she wore gloves in public, thereby starting a fashion trend). When in the White House, if she felt she had gotten above her goal weight of 120 pounds, she subsisted on little more than broth and fruit for a day or so until she got it down. (For his part, JFK fretted about his midlife weight gain, taking Metamucil before meals in a 1960s-inspired way to lose weight, and he was self-conscious about his "jowls"—worried that no one would vote for him in the next election.)

It continued to the next generation. When their daughter, Caroline, was a teenager and having lunch with her mother at the Ritz in Boston, Jackie delivered the ultimate mom put-down—"You'd better not have dessert, because you'll get fat and no man will want you."

Ouch.

. . . .

THE BOMBSHELL DIET

. . . .

Perhaps because she came of age in the middle of the 20th century, Marilyn's diet was, well, pretty 1950s. The way she ate reflected the most advanced thinking at the time (mainly veggies and protein, avoiding carbs), but it was also grounded in much of the same sound advice we might follow today.

As a struggling actress, Marilyn was poor, often subsisting on a dollar a day (granted, that was in 1940s money), on things like raw hamburger, peanut butter, hot dogs, chili, crackers, oatmeal and orange juice.

A neglected child of the Depression, Marilyn was not a foodie. When she cooked, she kept things very simple . . . and by simple, we don't mean an egg white omelet or skim cappuccino, we mean cooking peas and carrots together because she liked the color combination. At the age of twenty-six, she spoke of her "bizarre eating habits" in a magazine interview (accompanied by a stunning photograph of her in bed with full hair and makeup, seemingly nude beneath a sheet—risqué!— smiling gloriously at the camera), saying that for breakfast she warmed a cup of milk on a hot plate in her hotel room, broke two raw eggs into it, whipped it up with a fork, and drank it while she dressed. And then she had a multivitamin.

During the day she went to acting class, or auditions, or maybe over to the studio lot to see if she could scare up some work as an extra. Occasionally she would stop off at Wil Wright's ice cream parlor for a hot fudge sundae on the way home (interestingly, Audrey Hepburn used to do the same thing in the afternoons). "I'm sure that I couldn't allow myself this indulgence were it not that my normal diet is composed almost totally of protein foods."

"My dinners at home," she said, "are startlingly simple. Every night I stop at the market near my hotel and pick up a steak, lamb chops or some liver, which I broil in the electric oven in my room. I usually eat four or five raw carrots with my meat, and that is all. I must be part rabbit; I never get bored with raw carrots."

Later on in life, even after she had had success, Marilyn still kept things fairly basic. Joe DiMaggio exposed her to Italian food, and after their marriage, she ate pasta on and off for the rest of her life. When married to Arthur Miller, she also tried her hand at Jewish food.

When she wasn't dieting for a film role, she enjoyed hot dogs, caviar, Mexican food, steak (her favorite) and vanilla ice cream (her favorite dessert).

While filming *Let's Make Love* in the late 1950s, she ate a lot of spaghetti and lamb stew, washing it down with vodka and champagne (she considered Dom Pérignon 1953 the best). Like every starlet and socialite of note in the 1950s and '60s (Babe Paley, Jackie Kennedy, legendary *Vogue* editor Diana Vreeland, most people's moms), she often had grapefruit for breakfast (Grace Kelly had hers broiled).

Never heavy by today's standards (where more than half of Americans are overweight), Marilyn's weight generally stayed in the 115- to 120-pound range, although she went up to 140 pounds during her marriage to Joe DiMaggio and her tumultuous years with Arthur Miller, from 1956 to 1961. Although it is difficult to say why she gained so much weight at that time, some theorize that it might have been caused by her three (unsuccessful) pregnancies, the strain of Miller being investigated by the House Un-American Activities Committee, domestic bliss when first settling down with Miller or the strain of the marriage collapsing a few years later.

When she had to lose weight for a role, Marilyn followed what would today be considered the Atkins Diet. A typical breakfast might consist of egg whites poached in safflower oil, toast, hard-boiled eggs or a grapefruit. Lunch might be a broiled steak and some greens. While she cut down on her drinking when she was in "training" (as she put it), she still enjoyed vodka. In 1962 she shed 20 to 25 pounds in preparation for *Something's Got to Give,* and she reported to work thinner and fitter than she had been in years.

· ·

JACKIE'S TRICKS FOR STAYING SLIM

· ·

At 5 feet 7 inches Jackie stayed slim through the extremely effective socialite regime of exercise, smoking, and watching what she ate. Oh, and genetics (her sister, Lee, was also exceptionally thin). Having said that, she didn't eat a lot of junk or processed food. There was the occasional chocolate ice cream, but she wasn't rocking it out at McDonald's or anything. She did snack between meals, but it would be sliced carrots or celery sticks.

A MORNING STAPLE: "THE GREEN SMOOTHIE"

Every model, actress and healthy person we know swears by this. Plus, if you are in a hurry, it is an easy way to get your greens. While JFK Junior was a protein shake aficionado, here is an updated recipe Jackie or Marilyn would have followed. It is a great way to start your day.

A green smoothie can be made with any combination of raw greens (lettuce, celery, spinach, kale), water, and some fruit for sweetness (and to make it palatable). If you want it thicker, you can add a few ice cubes at the end. To improve it even more, add a scoop of protein powder and flaxseed.

THE J+M GAL'S GREEN SMOOTHIE

A handful of raw spinach

2 stalks of celery

½ cucumber

Handful of kale (remove stems)

½ apple

1–2 bananas

4–5 frozen whole strawberries

1–2 cups water, depending on thickness

There are a million variations of this smoothie available online. Adding pineapple (canned is fine) is really good. Adding frozen blueberries to *anything* blended is also terrific. Add enough water so it is not too thick.

Make sure you rinse all raw greens to clean them. Frozen fruit (bananas, strawberries, mixed berries) are fine. For best results, you need a strong blender like a Vitamix.

J+M—FOOD RULES

Here is another question to ponder: What the heck did Jackie and Marilyn eat to look so darn terrific?

For starters, they knew their bodies pretty well, and they knew what they could and could not get away with. Marilyn, for example, knew that if she ate too many croissants or a lot of processed food (Lay's Potato Chips, ice cream—basically, all the fun stuff), the back of her thighs would start looking shlubb-o (at least to her extremely discerning eye).

Jackie, for her part, was almost comically disciplined in terms of what she ate, even more so than Marilyn. By the time she got to the White House, her strict diet was second nature. Not only did she have the knowledge base of a nutritionist, she also kept up to date on the most recent health and medical news (both mainstream and the more outlandish claims) and would have been happy to answer any questions you might have about the importance of getting vitamin D, having some protein for breakfast and how addictive carbs and white sugar can be. After her favorite aunt, Edith Bouvier Beale, and her mother began showing signs of Alzheimer's, she became obsessed with the thought that she might be losing her memory (she wasn't). And she tossed out all the nonstick pans in her kitchen.

Quicktests

The Jackie Quicktest: You can actually put down the breadbasket. Like, forever.

The Marilyn Quicktest: You might say you are dieting, but really, you like yourself better with curves.

JACKIE TODAY: REAL-LIFE ADVICE

Don't kid yourself. Although there is an element of genetics involved, the Jackie and Marilyn Gals of today don't look that good without taking care of themselves. They—and particularly the Jackie (who might gleefully eat french fries for lunch but has carrot juice for the rest of the day)—watch what they eat. In real life, Jackie was perfectly capable of surviving on skinless chicken or fish and a lightly dressed salad for dinner. Her regime rivaled that of a Ford model's (well, without the endless coffee and vitamin C powder).

Similarly, if the Jackie-esque gal of today knows she is going to an amazing restaurant that night, she eats lightly during the day. If she spends New Year's Eve at a house party in Gstaad, she makes sure she gets back on the treadmill or the yoga mat when she gets home. You can be certain that when she's in Paris she is going to eat all the croissants she wants—because, after all, isn't France where all the great croissants come from? But she will stay away from carbs once she gets home.

If she is invited to a dinner party or (even better) if a man cooks for her, the Jackie will eat everything on her plate and seconds. If there is homemade dessert—particularly something she does not normally make for herself (Profiteroles! Crème brûlée! Rice Krispies treats!), she is having it.

The real Jackie never turned down an opportunity to have real whipped cream. Ever. She was not a fan of low-fat, pro-

cessed, diet or fake food. When she was on the Vineyard, she made a point of stopping by Mad Martha's Ice Cream shop and having a cone because she knew you needed some fat in your diet to keep your hair and skin looking good.

With her innate sense of what worked for her (as well as an extremely fortunate metabolism), Jackie never got too far off-kilter. And neither does the Jackie Gal of today.

J+M FIELD NOTES: AT THE GYM

Although she looked softer and relatively more fleshy when compared to the angular Jackie, Marilyn was an early proponent of physical exercise. She lifted 5-pound weights during her early years as a young starlet to maintain her bust line and jogged in the morning. Following her masseuse Ralph Robert's instruction, she also took ice baths sprinkled with Chanel No. 5 to highlight her already luminous skin and minimize cellulite.

There was a reason Jackie stayed a perfect size 6 her entire life—she was almost addicted to exercise. She rode horses and also water-skied, jogged, did yoga, went hiking and kayaking and was a member of two health clubs in New York City.[3]

*B*ut what were their particular exercise regimes? For starters, Marilyn would probably have caused a riot if she had shown up at an actual gym the way we would today. She could barely cross the studio lot without men hounding her. But having said that, she was not averse to lifting weights in the privacy of her own home, and when she was just starting out as an aspiring (read: starving) Hollywood starlet, she asked a military instructor who had been a weight-lifting champion to teach her how to use barbells and other gym equipment.

He agreed.

Like Cary Grant, Marilyn put together her own rudimentary workout routine (Grant's home gym was in his garage), which was almost unheard of for a female in the late 1940s, early 1950s. Visitors would find gym equipment in the corner of her living room. At a time when hardly anyone ran for exercise (men or women), she regularly took early-morning jogs through the backstreets of Beverly Hills.

In terms of a regime, here is Marilyn's, in her own words: "Each morning, after I brush my teeth, wash my face and shake off the first deep layer of sleep, I lie down on the floor beside my bed and begin my first exercise. It is a simple bust firming routine using 5-pound weights. . . . I lie on my back and lift my arms as long as I can. I then move the weights in circles until I am tired.

. . . .

3 There was a reason her son, John, looked so good, too. He was a member of four gyms dotted around Manhattan so he could duck in and work out whenever the mood struck. JFK Junior also smoked two cigarettes a day, just to prove that he could.

I don't count rhythmically like the exercise people on the radio. I couldn't stand exercise if I had to feel regimented about it."

And although Marilyn loved romping on Malibu Beach (especially if there was a *LIFE* photographer around) or being out in nature, she was not much for organized sports, such as golf or tennis. "I'll leave those things to the men."

Jackie, on the other hand, was so athletic, she practically could have tried out for the Olympics. Here, the social differences in their upbringing showed. While Jackie's favorite sports were foxhunting, jogging, skiing, flirting, fine dining and competitive shopping, she certainly knew her way around a tennis court and loved sailing, too.

When Jackie was in New York City, she went for a late-morning jog around the Reservoir in Central Park (now renamed after her), occasionally pursued by her nemesis, Ron Galella. Twice a week she used a personal trainer at the Vertical Club on East 56th Street. For the last seventeen years of her life, Tillie Weitzner, a well-regarded yoga instructor, visited her twice a week. When Jackie's non-air-conditioned prewar New York City apartment got overheated, she said that Jackie, wearing "an old black leotard with holes in it," never complained. "Jackie remained very serious about yoga. She was always pushing herself to get better."

During summer months on Martha's Vineyard, Jackie's routine was no less strenuous. After breakfast, mornings were for kayaking, and the hours after lunch might be spent swimming or water-skiing. (During the White House years, Jackie encouraged Joan Kennedy to use flippers when swimming out on the Cape to trim her thighs.)

Fall found Jackie out in Bernardsville, New Jersey, riding horses. She often spent the week before November 22 (the anniversary of JFK's assassination) riding with the Orange Hunt in Middleburg, Virginia, where she stayed at a cottage on Mrs. Paul "Bunny" Mellon's estate.

During the winter—are you still with us?—Jackie was out walking practically every day in Central Park or running errands on Madison Avenue. After Christmas, she recuperated from the holiday hubbub by flying down to Antigua and staying at Curtain Bluff.

THE JACKIE RX

If you are a Jackie, you are a bit of a jock. You are also more high end when it comes to working out. (And you know that today's Jackie can't just go to any gym—she would have a personal trainer come to her home, or she'd join the Reebok Sports Club in Los Angeles or New York City or the East Bank Club in Chicago.) Plus, the Jackie needs lots of gear—a private lake, a private island with its own security force, yachts, a stable, running shoes, proper riding gear, even a worn leotard.

THE MARILYN RX

If you are a Marilyn, you're probably a bit more low key, do-it-yourself when it comes to exercise. And really? Unless you are up for a film role or about to shoot a magazine spread, let's be honest—you really don't like exercise anyway. So get some beauty rest (hey, you were probably out late last night), go for a walk on the beach in the late afternoon and lift weights once in a while—*but only if you feel like it.*

Besides, as a Marilyn, you know that it almost doesn't matter what you do in terms of exercise or working out, because you will always—and let's be honest here—*always* be more physically compelling than the Jackie.

JACKIE AND MARILYN: THE EXHIBITIONISTS

"I'm only comfortable when I'm naked," said Marilyn, and given their druthers, the Marilyns of today get out of their skivvies as soon as possible, too. They love being naked. And even fully dressed, they give off the vibe—somehow—of being half dressed.

Marilyn was, if possible, even more beautiful nude than wearing any article of clothing she owned—any bathing suit, sable, jeans, T-shirt, Travilla gown. As her acting teacher Lee Strasberg put it, "Her quality when photographed is almost of a supernatural beauty."

Jackie went topless in public, but only situationally, say, in the south of France or in Greece, where she knew it was very unlikely that she would run into friends of her parents or anyone she knew from the club.

Like many American women even today, Jackie went a little bonkers in Europe. Losing her virginity in an old-fashioned lift in a *pensione* in Paris. ("Is that all there is to it?" she wondered.) Skinny-dipping off Skorpios. Going braless under a T-shirt in the late 1960s. With her puritan forefathers at her back, the Jackie Gal of today will wear beautiful lingerie that costs a week's salary and towering heels overseas—cobblestones be damned!

Today's Marilyn goes much, much further. She has no problem with sex or nudity—she loves her body and feels happiest when she is naked. She also loves taking baths; she loves the water and the beach.

PLASTIC SURGERY?

In 1950, Marilyn had her nose thinned by a plastic surgeon. Details about the procedure are scarce. Other than that, she seems to have been antisurgery. And she certainly never had breast implants, lip implants, liposuction, Botox, Restylane, or any of the other assists that seem common among most twentysomething starlets (or aspiring Playboy bunnies) today in Southern California. "I want to grow old without face-lifts," she declared. "I want to have the courage to be loyal to the face I have made."

Jackie, on the other hand, had no problem with plastic surgery (as was common with her social set). In the spring of 1989, she had a very subtle face-lift performed by Dr. Michael Hogan, a Park Avenue plastic surgeon.

J+M FIELD NOTES: BODY TYPE

Freud wasn't kidding: Anatomy *is* destiny. Determining whether your body type is more Jackie or more Marilyn, and thus figuring out your attendant decorating, wardrobe, career, spouse and lifestyle choices, it's pretty simple.

In the Jackie/Marilyn worldview, there are only two options: the hourglass or the tomboy. Don't let women's fashion magazines or hectoring "how to dress" cable television shows complicate the issue—it doesn't matter how tall (or short) you are. It doesn't matter what your waist size, your dress size or your shoe size is, or what you weigh when you step on the scale on any given morning. If you have curves, you are a Marilyn, and if not, you are a Jackie.

. . . .

THE MARILYN RX

. . . .

You have curves, so flaunt them. Simple as that. Cinch in that waist. Wear your clothing just a *bit* too small, and cherish the hobble skirt. Get your jeans tailored so that they nip in at the waist (a style-setter trick that the seamstress at your dry cleaner can do for about $10). Better yet, toss your just-washed jeans in the dryer and set it on high so they really shrink. Leave the top three or four buttons on your sweater undone. Don't wear anything underneath said sweater; show some skin. For the Marilyn Gal, a white T-shirt is not a friend.

The basic premise in Marilyn World is that if you can walk

too quickly or too comfortably (or, god forbid, run without twisting your ankle), you are not doing it right. Take it easy. Slow down. Walk away from him and break his heart. Sashay down the Boulevard of Life, and let the world enjoy the view while you are at it.

. . . .

THE JACKIE RX

. . . .

If you have a boyish figure, emphasize that, too. Wear all the things your fuller-figured sisters wish they could (and thereby assuage your guilt at not having to wear a bra when you are home alone). The basic MO is prep with a twist—cropped trousers with no socks. White jeans or corduroy in December. Because your legs are good, set the bar high with a miniskirt. (And if you wear heels, wear tights of a similar shade to continue the line.)

Shop in the boy's department at a place like Brooks Brothers for great quality at a better price. With your straight silhouette, you can be classic with a kick—cowboy boots in the city, a peacoat, sunglasses in the rain, a goofball furry hat (real or faux) picked up at Harvey Nicks in London.

Now, the Jackie Girl—the Jackie Girl strides. No matter what decade she currently occupies, one imagines her, easily, as a nineteen-year-old sophomore dashing across the quad, late for class. Whether in the big city or suburbia, she walks fast as if to outrun the paps (real or imagined) that invariably follow her every move.

THE HAIR GUY—

If conspiracy theorists had their acts together, they would have figured out that hair maestro Kenneth Battelle is the true missing link between Jackie and Marilyn, as he created both of their iconic hairstyles.

In 1954, Kenneth, working at the Helena Rubenstein salon in New York City, made over newlywed Jacqueline Kennedy, softening and lengthening her hair from the Audrey Hepburn in *Roman Holiday* style she previously had.

In 1958, Marilyn, just finishing up *Some Like It Hot,* sought out Kenneth's help on the advice of designer Norman Norell, as her hair was falling out from overbleaching and perming. Kenneth made Marilyn even more *Marilyn* by creating the iconographic blonde goddess hair we associate her with. From then on, she made a point of visiting his salon every time she was in New York. The following year, he traveled with her to Chicago for the world premiere of *Some Like It Hot.*

In 1960, Kenneth created the tousled bouffant for Jacqueline Kennedy, causing something of a stir among old-line socialites (like her mother, Mrs. Auchincloss, who considered it too "casual" and modern looking—and inappropriate).

In 1961, Kenneth did all of the Kennedys' hair for Inauguration Day.

The following year, Kenneth did Marilyn's hair for JFK's forty-fifth birthday rally at Madison Square Garden. A few months later, over the summer, Kenneth styled her hair for what ended up being her final photo session with Bert Stern for *Vogue.* On November 21, 1963, Kenneth cut Jackie's hair at 7:00 a.m., just before she left with her husband for Dallas.

In 1963, Kenneth fulfilled a longtime dream by opening his own salon on East 54th Street, in a 17,000-square-foot townhouse that had been a former Vanderbilt residence. Society decorator Billy Baldwin (a favorite of JKO's) decorated it. For the next thirty years, Kenneth was the go-to guy for society women like Babe Paley, Diana Vreeland, and Happy Rockefeller, as well as styling for *Vogue, Glamour* and *Harper's Bazaar* cover shoots.

Today, Kenneth still works at his salon (now ensconced in the Waldorf) every day. Overseen by artistic director Kevin Lee, it is still flourishing and catering to a new generation of style setters.

THE JACKIE, THE MARILYN HAIR RX

Whether you favor Jackie or Marilyn, your hair is talismanic. Although you don't give it much thought after you brush it in the morning, your hairstyle is so vital to your persona that it almost has its own character. No matter your age, you have the soft hair of a child. If you have it colored—even if it is platinum blonde—you never admit to it.

Of the two, the Jackie is more natural looking. You would never know that she dyes her hair. With the exception of Carmen Dell'Orefice, our favorite model in the entire world, neither the Jackie nor the Marilyn will ever go gray. Ever.

Some of the best advice we've gotten is not to wash it too often. One of the most recent comebacks in beauty tricks is the use of dry shampoo, a very fine powder that was big in the late 1960s. Marilyn got the same effect by sprinkling her roots with Johnson's Baby Powder that had been sifted to give it an even finer consistency. Terrific for travel or when you've gotten your hair done and it has to "last" a few more days. Today, there are even better formulations available.

THE MM LOOK: HOW-TO

We think that if most women had to choose between Jackie Hair and Marilyn Hair, they would choose the latter (if only for the riotous effect it had on the opposite sex).

To get true Marilyn hair, it helps to have Kenneth (New

York) or Gladys Rasmussen (California)—two of Marilyn's longtime hair stylists—on call. But if not, what can today's modern gal do? We spoke with Kevin Lee, artistic director of Kenneth's salon, for advice.

And he said, "To get Marilyn's look, you need a true set. You can get some life with hot rollers on your own, but that really isn't a strong enough hold. You also have to find someone who is talented at setting up a pattern with rollers. Then you have to sit under a hood dryer. Or, you could air dry your hair, but that could take six or seven hours!"

He also advised using setting lotion. But the main thing he said was, "There are modern versions of it. You don't want it to look exactly the way Marilyn's did, but you can tweak it and make it look modern. . . . For Marilyn-type hair—you want it to be touchable, loosened up, because that's what's sexy. You want it almost to look like 'bed head,' the morning after. If it is too stiff or too perfect—that can come off as a little icy."

. . . .

MM: THE EVOLUTION OF A BLONDE

. . . .

While it is commonly perceived that Marilyn's hair was always platinum, her hair actually evolved through the spectrum of blonde possibilities as her career progressed. As a young model just starting out, she was told by Emmeline Snively, owner of the Blue Book Agency, that she would get more work as a blonde, because photographers could work with lighting to change her look. As a young girl, Marilyn also idolized 1930s film star Jean Harlow, and this also fueled her desire for perfect, high-maintenance, almost otherworldly (and really, isn't that the definition of a legendary Hollywood star, too?) platinum blonde.

Marilyn first hit the bottle at Hollywood's Frank Joseph Salon in 1946, where her hair was bleached to a golden blonde and chemically straightened. As her career progressed, she tried out practically every blonde that Clairol invented, among them golden blonde, ash blonde, champagne blonde, honey blonde, bleached blonde, strawberry blonde and platinum blonde, until she reached the apotheosis of pure Marilyn-ness—white blonde. She was also fond of bleaching her pubic hair, as she "liked to feel blonde all over."

By the time she was a world-famous starlet, her hair was so high maintenance that she had to have it highlighted every three weeks to maintain her look. This left her naturally fine hair very brittle and prone to breakage (fortunately, a visit to Kenneth and his magical unguents brought it back to life). By the time of her death in 1962, her hair was completely stripped of pigment to a shade she fondly referred to as "pillow case white."

WHAT YOU CAN TELL FROM A WOMAN'S HANDS

Both the Marilyn and the Jackie Gals of today have beautiful hands that they emphasize by taking care of them, since they know that (even unconsciously) people notice your hands. As first lady, Jackie claimed to use Johnson's Baby Lotion as a moisturizer and later, One & All Hand Cream.

The Jackie wears clear nail polish or a sheer pink color.

Since she uses her hands a lot, she keeps them to a manageable length—no Barbra Streisand talons for her!

The Marilyn will often get away with colored nails—opaque pink to match her evening dress or even red.

SIGNATURE SCENTS

Marilyn Monroe—Chanel No. 5, Fracas, Joy

Jackie—Jicky by Guerlain (also worn by her future daughter-in-law, Carolyn Bessette), Joy, Fleurissimo, Jean Patou 1000

To Tan or Not to Tan?

"Despite its great vogue in California, I don't think sun tanned skin is any more attractive than white skin."

—MM ON TANNING

JKO was the exact opposite. When we think of Jackie, or any of the Kennedys for that matter, we think of summers on the Cape (or Skorpios) and tan, golden skin. Clearly, this was not someone who spent long days in an office cubicle.

THE JACKIE AND MARILYN REGIME

Both Jackie and Marilyn had their own personal regimes, tricks of the trade that helped them look so memorable.

Also, perhaps because they were of the same generation, they actually shared some beauty secrets (Erno Laszlo, Kenneth for hair).

Marilyn had massages and occasional colonics to lose weight quickly.

In the late 1950s and early 1960s, Jackie got B_{12} shots from Max Jacobson, a.k.a. Dr. Feelgood, which were basically amphetamines and vitamin B. He was the go-to guy for New York society and the New Frontier. "I don't care if it's horse piss, it works!" said JFK after Jacobson's ministrations helped his back pain. Anyone who was anyone went to him at one time or another—Marlene Dietrich, Truman Capote, photographer Mark Shaw, Leonard Bernstein. A socialite remembered that "you would run into *everyone* in the waiting room!"

MARILYN'S BEAUTY SECRETS

Like a true diva, MM was very reluctant to share her secrets, but we have unearthed a few. Writing to a fan, she said she had very few beauty tricks, but that she put her face in a sink filled with hot water—as hot as she could stand—morning and night.

As a devotee of the Erno Laszlo skin care system, she also rinsed her face thirty times after every wash.

When not wearing makeup, she might apply Vaseline, cold cream, lanolin, olive oil or hormone cream to her face as a protective agent.

Marilyn was famous for her seductive eyes. She once admitted that she lowered her eyelids a little just before the picture was snapped to make them look mysterious.

Marilyn wore false eyelashes and was one of the first women to meticulously cut them in half and apply them only to the outer edges of her eyelids.

Like JKO, she was a fan of Pond's Cold Cream. (Or we should say, because of the timing issue, that Jackie was following Marilyn's lead here—she used to slather it on her face and then sit outside on the porch and read manuscripts when she was on the Vineyard. Houseguests of her son John be damned!)

JACKIE'S BEAUTY SECRETS

Jackie never got stuck in a certain "look" and was always on the lookout for the latest beauty tips.

She used foundation by Elizabeth Arden.

Prior to a gala event hosted by the American Ballet Theatre in the 1980s, Jackie had her makeup done at her New York City apartment by a professional makeup artist a week before, to see how it would look. She wore a white dressing gown to match the color of the dress she intended to wear. Every time the makeup artist did something, Jackie took out her own hand mirror to see what she had done and then wrote it down, meticulously, on a yellow legal pad, so she could learn to do it in the future.

Left alone, her hair was somewhat kinky. To get that perfect "ladies who lunch" look, she had her hair blown out twice a week by Thomas Morrissey on the Upper East Side.

Like Marilyn, Jackie was also big on getting massages.

J+M: GETTING THE LOOK

We asked our favorite makeup guru, Darac, to give us some tips for getting the Jackie or Marilyn Look. Both women loved experimenting with makeup, so we say, "Go for it!"

JACKIE

According to Darac, the Jackie look is Classic Elegance—softly sculptured, approachable beauty and satin skin.

Brow

The brow should have a natural look with rounded arches; nothing in nature has a 45-degree angle. The brown should have a soft start, and then it should curve and end at the corner of the eye.

Eyes

Create soft and smoky eyes using neutral beige, taupe and dark brown eye shadow, soft pencil liner and thickening mascara.

Cheeks

Focus on the apples of the cheeks, and blend in cheek color with the rest of the face.

Use tapped-on and blended cream color.

Face

Dust the entire face with a soft veil of pink/peachy powder.

Lips

Apply lipstick or lip gloss first, then softly use liner to strengthen but not define the lip line.

MARILYN

Here, we are going for the Femme Fatale, definitely provocative! Aim for a more finished look and structured application, with eggshell skin.

Brow

Go for a severe arch that is full and defined. Definition is everything!

Eyes

Shadow should match skin tone to intensify the impact of the lash line.

Use lengthening mascara for intense lashes, with false lashes on the outer ends and liquid liner that curves up and away at the ends to match lashes.

Cheeks
Use very little color on the apples of the cheeks. Focus on defining the cheekbones.

Face
Porcelain-like; clean and even all over.

Lips
First line the lips, defining the top lip in a bow shape. Then apply lipstick, blot with tissue, apply powder over a tissue, and then reapply lipstick.

BOMBSHELL RED

Marilyn *owned* red lipstick. Owned it.

Red lipstick is a beauty trend that is currently, happily, back in style and emulated by everyone from Madonna and Gwen Stefani to Scarlett Johansson and Christina Hendricks. Back in the day, MM wore Shiseido in a color that is no longer available. But today's formulations are so much improved over those from the 1950s that you will barely notice.

Here is some advice to make red lipstick your own.

Skin tone. The most important thing in determining which red is right for you is your skin tone. Are you a warm red or a cool red?

If your skin has pink undertones, you should stick to reds that have a pink base. If you have warm yellow tones, look for a red with a golden or tawny base. If you are the classic pale and pink coloring, lipsticks with a touch of blue will be the best match.

Be prepared. When you are moisturizing your face, don't forget your lips, as you want them to be well cared for.

Conceal and protect. Using lip liner is essential with red lipstick. It helps to seal the color and prevents the ultimate red lipstick faux pas: bleeding. Liner also acts as great base for lipstick, so use it all over the lips. Try to use the same shade as the lipstick so it doesn't alter the finished look, or go with a shade that matches your natural lip color.

Brush strokes. When applying reds, always use a lip brush. It gives you much more control over where and how much color you are putting on. Apply lip color, blot with tissue, then reapply color and *don't* blot. This way, you'll get long-lasting color.

Some red lipsticks we like:

Lancôme, Chris and Tell (inspired by MM)

Jemma Kidd

Makeup School

Collection, Scarlett

Chanel Rouge Allure Laque, Dragon

Secret Secrets — The Jackie:
Things You Might Not Know About Her

Jackie could do ten push-ups at will, anytime, anywhere—real ones, not girl push-ups.

Secret Secrets — The Marilyn:
Things You Might Not Know About Her

When she first began modeling, Marilyn had the widow's peak on her forehead removed with electrolysis.

4 *That Certain Something: Sex Appeal*

"I'm only comfortable when I'm naked."

—MM

. . . .

"There are two kinds of women, those who want power in the world and those who want power in bed."

—JKO

For Jackie and Marilyn, *this* was the ball game—for they both understood a fundamental law of life: Sex is power.

Jackie and Marilyn reveled in being female and the advantages it gave them—because let's face it, the reality is that in dating or marriage, women have a great deal of leverage because they have the ability to say yes (or no).

And everyone knows that the right woman can vastly improve a man's life—or make it really, really bad.

Having said that, Jackie and Marilyn approached sex—and quite possibly viewed sex—in two fundamentally different ways.

Marilyn put it out there. If you saw Marilyn—in real life (please god), in a photograph, on the screen—it wasn't subtle. You knew what she was about and what she was offering you.

Jackie, on the other hand, was the exact opposite. She was sexy, but it was hidden. You might get there eventually (or you might not, ever), but she was going to make you work for it. And Jackie knew this about herself. Of her romantic life with JFK, she compared them to two icebergs and said, "The public life is above the water—the private life is submerged."

Marilyn's sexuality was present, obvious, very much in the forefront: She *was* sex.

Jackie revealed herself by withholding herself. Was it an upper-class thing? A 1950s thing? Maybe. (We think of Grace Kelly, a notorious sexpot in her youth.)

*M*arilyn fully embraced her sexuality and had no qualms or apologies about it. Once, famously, when asked what she wore in bed, she quipped, "Why, Chanel No. 5, of course." (Which was an amazingly risqué thing to say in 1955. The fact that it was true made it even more so.)

If Jackie was part of the Eastern establishment, that rapidly disappearing outpost of decorum, good manners and where you summer, Marilyn was all about escape. Release. "Who gives a damn?" Marilyn knew her appeal and worked it. "Men like happy girls," she noted and made a point of appearing light and carefree on a date no matter what was going on in her personal life. She might be privately heartbroken, she might be broke and half-starving, but boy, you were not going to hear about it.

While Jackie was far more publicly disciplined, with her enigmatic smile, whispery voice and ballet posture (who knew *what* she was thinking behind all that decidedly good form), there is the opposite sense that Marilyn would do anything, be anyone you wanted. This was especially powerful in the 1950s, when "good girls didn't," or at least not without the imprimatur of marriage.

And even then they might not.

Marilyn always gave the impression that she was up for anything—"Ever notice how 'What the hell' is always the right answer?" she once observed.

Jackie might be up for anything . . . eventually. But she was not known for giving it away. In college, the young men in her social set (using a term then popular) described Jackie as a "hold your meter, driver" type. They knew to have the taxi wait with the meter running when they walked her to the front door, because nothing was going to happen that night.

MARILYN COULD MELT YOU WITH HER EYES

Don't ever underestimate the power of sex and beauty. As photographer Lawrence Schiller observed, "Marilyn was very sensual. She knew how to handle her body. She knew how to handle her lips. With Marilyn, when everything was working, there was no one single element. She was in perfect harmony. She knew how to look into your eyes, and that was very, very powerful."

Combining a sense of humor with some measure of vulnerability—and Marilyn was far more publicly vulnerable than Jackie—she was almost irresistible to men.

> *"A sex symbol becomes a thing, and I just hate to be a thing. You're always running into people's unconscious. It's nice to be included in people's fantasies, but you also like to be accepted for your own sake. I don't look at myself as a commodity, but I'm sure a lot of people have. . . . If I'm sounding 'picked on,' I think I have been."*
>
> MARILYN ON BEING A SEX SYMBOL

JACKIE WAS THE BETTER KISSER. SHE WAS ALSO THE BETTER POKER PLAYER

While the Jackie Gal and the Marilyn Woman of today are both sensualists, the Jackie Gal is more guarded, less obvious in her sexual energy. Still, the sophisticated male knows it is there.

Surprisingly, the Jackie is the better kisser, if only because she grew up with a sister everyone considered prettier, while she was the smart one. Plus, she went to highly restrictive, all-girls' schools, so there were months, years even, to get very good at necking.

While Marilyn was very upfront and open in her dealings with the opposite sex, Jackie—having been caught in the cross-fire of her parents' divorce (when divorce was both stigmatized and a rarity) and tutored in the ways of men and women by her oh-so-cynical father—realized that it was, on one level, a game. And man, could she play it.

The Jackie MO in dealing with men is this: Accept the premise that a relationship is almost like a poker match (at least in its early stages). You have to be able to walk away, leaving your cards on the table at any time.

Another JKO corollary is that men get bored pretty easily, so you have to mix it up. For example:

1. Don't throw yourself at him.

2. Be very, very present.

3. Disappear for a while.

4. Oh, okay—throw yourself at him.

Pretend you're a major-league pitcher—mix up your game a bit. Call him first thing in the morning just to say hello, then accept a lot of dinner invites from other friends and ignore him for a week or so. Whatever you do, *don't* be an open book.

. . . .

How Was Jackie Sexy?

. . . .

Jackie was sexy in that you didn't expect it from her. In this way, she was almost the opposite of Marilyn—where Marilyn revealed (in a big way), Jackie withheld.

Like her romantic nemesis Grace Kelly, she appeared deeply conventional, but then she would say something to an aging dinner-partner (say, at a state dinner at the White House) and "his eyes would practically pop out of his head."

Aristotle Onassis (a man who certainly knew how to seduce a woman) called it when he said of Jackie, "She is a totally misunderstood woman. Perhaps she even misunderstands herself. She's being held up as a model of propriety, constancy and so many of those boring American female virtues. She's now utterly devoid of mystery. She needs a small scandal to bring her alive—a peccadillo, an indiscretion. Something should happen to her to win over fresh compassion. The world loves to pity fallen grandeur."

Less than a year later, they were wed.

. . . .

*H*ave No Problem with Nudity—Love your body, whatever its shape. When you get right down to it, most men are so thrilled to see a nude woman in any shape or form and at any time of the day or night that you don't need to be a perfect size 6 to be loveable. It's all about energy and how you view yourself, something our European counterparts have known for centuries.

It also helps to have a sense of humor about the whole thing. Once, asked what she had on during a nude calendar shoot she had posed for as a starving model/actress, the Real Marilyn quipped, "The radio."

"35-22-35"[1]

Whether you are planning to seduce someone or (god forbid) you get hit by a bus and end up in the emergency room, you want to look fabulous in your lingerie.

To get the expert's opinion on beautiful undergarments, we went to the source—Rebecca Apsan, owner of La Petite Coquette, the insider's lingerie shop favored by Cindy Crawford, Sarah Jessica Parker, Angelica Huston, Uma Thurman and sophisticated gals (and the men who love them) from all over.

To begin with, Apsan believes that 85 percent of women are wearing the wrong bra because "they're wearing the same size bra that their mother told them they should be wearing when they were fourteen years old!" Add that to the fact that there is no standardized sizing for brassieres, and it's no wonder most women's bras are not doing them any figure favors.

Instead, Apsan suggests that a woman go to her local lingerie shop and spend about forty-five minutes trying

[1] Marilyn's measurements.

on different sizes to see what fits her best. Apsan believes that an intimate wardrobe should contain four to six key pieces: everyday bras that are rotated, including basic T-shirt bras. You should also have two or three demi-cup or push-up bras in lace or a special color to "jumpstart your day" when you need it. Finally, you should have two strapless bras.

Bras should generally be nude or black, as white stands out too much.

More fun facts: Apsan confided to us that "the more sophisticated, classy women—the Jackies—are usually kinkier in bed. They'll push the envelope. The most proper looking girls are the ones wearing garter belts and stockings. The Marilyn types—the ones that are really obvious about putting it out there—want sex the least. . . ."

Finally, Apsan concludes, "A good bra is like a good man—good looking, supportive and never lets you down. . . ." Having experienced both, we agree.

THE SPANX SECRET

In case you are wondering how every woman between the ages of twenty and eighty has created a masterful MM/Joan Holloway silhouette for herself this season, we introduce you to Spanx®, the genius, genius undergarment that Sara Blakely invented.

If you don't know about these, you should.

Spanx fans range from Oprah to Gwyneth, from stylists to size-2 Upper East Side socialites. All swear by them to smooth out their figures. Beginning with a surprisingly comfortable body shaper, the line has been expanded to include camisoles, leggings to be worn under pants, and even brassieres. (We have heard, anecdotally, that some women wear two pairs at once for the ultimate in midsection control. But wow, even we can't imagine being this committed to looking a size smaller.)

In addition to inventing—on her own, on her living room floor—one of the most necessary contributions to modern feminine beauty since the lipstick (and we promise, we are not on the take here), Sara is also intensely cool and has started her own charitable organization to support and empower women around the world. She says, "I feel very blessed to have had my 'aha' moment in America, where women are free to start their own business."

Wow, *talk* about a Jackie/Marilyn Gal . . .

MARILYN KNEW HOW TO TURN IT ON (AND OFF)

Sex appeal was something that Marilyn, along with most women, could turn on or off. In fact, to her, "Marilyn Monroe" was almost a character that she created.

In New York City she once turned to a friend and said, "I can put on a polo coat and no makeup and get along pretty well. . . . Want to see me be her?"

And then she did.

Lawrence Schiller said that Marilyn "was really an actress. The 'dumb blonde' image was a total performance. She could turn it on and she could turn it off."

As he recalled, "I remember once I was walking with her from the parking lot to the dressing room. She had on this big black and white cardigan sweater. Her voice was very quiet and we were just talking about what she was going to do that afternoon. A couple of guys came around the corner, walking in the opposite direction towards her. And all of a sudden she became Marilyn Monroe, the dumb blonde. Her shoulders changed, her face changed. When they walked by, she turned her head over her shoulder and flashed that coquettish smile of hers—she was playing to them because she knew they wanted to see 'Marilyn Monroe.'"

THE MARILYN MIEN: ADORABLE DISHABILLE

In terms of style and manner—and dress—the Marilyn Gal is just a little bit looser than the Jackie Gal, on a lot of levels.

And even though her clothes are extremely fitted, there always seems to be a strap falling off her shoulder. (And if not actually slipping off her shoulder at this moment, there is always the impression of a strap *about* to fall off.)

Fully dressed (sitting in the midst of a major board meeting, for example), she seems as if she is about to fall out of her clothing, even if, in a nod to respectability (or the fall season), she is wearing a cashmere button-down cardigan.

Unlike the Jackie, the Marilyn is rarely still. The air around her is charged. Even sitting still (a thing to behold), she is always imperceptibly moving. This keeps everyone in her vicinity off balance.

Which is precisely the point.

Even her hair is sexy. While it might be "done," it was done for a date the night before, and here we are now, the following day. But even a bit dishabille, she still looks amazing.

She wears heels, naturally, 99.9 percent of the time and has an adorable habit of falling out of her slingbacks. Like a *Vogue* editor, the Marilyn rarely wears stockings, even in February. But if she does, they are Fogal up to the thigh (bought at Bloomingdale's or a little shop in the 7th Arrondissement she happened upon), sheer black, occasionally fishnet, never patterned or opaque—why waste the beautiful gams with too much window dressing, she figures. Should she go to the effort of the whole garter/merry widow routine, it is for a man she truly loves.

If the Marilyn is not in heels, she is barefoot at home or on a beach in Malibu, wearing bright red nail polish.

Alone or with company, she is the rare woman who can pull off marabou mules unironically.

And yet there is nothing untoward about our Marilyn—in some ways, she *was* America—the fun, sexy, childlike, trusting, noncynical part of America.

She was so open, so obvious, that there was nothing hidden about her desire, about what she might do for you. This is part of her charm, after all.

> *"Marilyn is a kind of ultimate. She is uniquely feminine. . . . She makes a man proud to be a man."*
>
> —CLARK GABLE

THE JACKIE MIEN: STRAITLACED. SORT OF.

The Jackie woman is "acceptable." We've established that. If you are up for an ambassadorship, partner at the law firm or have to close a business deal, you want her at your side.

Because of the breadth of her experience, Jackie can go high or low.

Speak French? She can do that better than you.

Get on a horse and ride (English or western)? Fine.

Head down to some juke joint in the Mississippi Delta (where they have never seen anyone like her before) and drink beer out of a bottle? No problem. She can do that *and* dance with the locals.

The great thing about the Jackie Gal is that she can roll with it. A Valentino gown or T-shirt and jeans, she can wear either with equal aplomb.

The true Jackie keeps her cards close to her chest. She can be ironic, quietly sarcastic among those she trusts. In this way, she is as great an actress as the Marilyn. After all, it was JKO who famously said, "Sex is a bad thing because it rumples the clothes." (She was *kidding*—we think.)

And what is she like in bed?

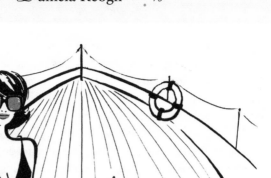

Memorable. Possibly because once you get her there and she trusts you, anything is possible.

Like most women, she equates sex with love. But she is no pushover. Like a true Leo, she is proud. She expects to be treated properly because she knows her worth. (If her father taught her nothing else, he taught her this.) She will not say a word, but ignore her or get her a crappy present for Christmas, and it will take some effort to regain her trust.

And by then, she is gone.

MARILYN'S POWER OVER MEN (AND SOME WOMEN)

While Jackie might be socially acceptable (for what that was worth in those days) or have gone to better schools (ditto), Marilyn held sway (sexual, emotional, obsessive, psychic) over men. Some people say this control over the opposite sex is what really matters, where all other success comes from.

"I don't mind being burdened with being glamorous and sexual," Marilyn said. "Beauty and femininity are ageless and can't be contrived, and glamour, although the manufacturers won't like this, cannot be manufactured. . . . We are all born sexual creatures, thank God, but it's a pity so many people despise and crush this natural gift. Art, real art, comes from it, everything."

Marilyn's power sprang from one essential fact. She could look into a man's eyes, smile (or not—it didn't matter), and get what she wanted. And she knew it. Her seductive powers, her *need* to be loved, worked with women, too. Her first drama coach, Natasha Lytess, devoted herself to Marilyn for years, proclaiming her love for her and almost becoming obsessed with her, as did another acting coach, Paula Strasberg, and (for some reason) her housekeeper, Eunice Murray.

Not knowing any better (one imagines her on the cusp of thirty or forty), she feared it could leave her with age, but it never did. Beauty is only part of Marilyn's sexual energy, that great Nile—but not all of it.

Unlike Jackie, Marilyn needed an audience—needed to be seen, to be recognized. She wanted to get the hell out of where she was from, not to be anonymous, to make her mark on the world. *Love me,* she seemed to say. Unlike Jackie, Marilyn needed her work. She needed to be known in a very public sphere (the only kind that matters, after all).

But still, it was never enough. And if the Marilyn Gal of today has not learned this yet, she will.

JACKIE'S POWER OVER MEN

How did Jackie do it? Well, she liked men, for starters. And this is a huge advantage. (You would be surprised at the number of women out in the world who don't.) She also knew that if a man had her by his side, she was an asset. She had that skill of the courtesan (that both of her husbands also had, actually): When she looked into your eyes and listened to you, there was no one else in the room. She listened. She heard. She remembered what you had said.

Like most professional wives, she was exceedingly thoughtful and really good on the follow-through, at perceiving what might make one's life easier (or just improved), without being told. When she visited London for Queen Elizabeth's coronation and had been dating JFK for a year with no sign of an engagement,[2] she lugged home a heavy suitcase full of rare hardcover books for him, paying $100 in extra charges—when $100 meant something—to get it on board.

Similarly, when she was married to Onassis, for some reason he loved Duncan Hines chocolate cake made from the box. Sure, he had a French chef on Skorpios, his private island, but he just really, really liked the way the Duncan Hines cake tasted. So Jackie made sure there were always several boxes on hand, flown in specially from New York.

It is this kind of attention to detail, the little things that matter, that made JKO a keeper.

On the other hand, Jackie did not have a ton of girlfriends. She went to all of those single-sex girls' schools through college, and frankly, large groups of women sort of drove her up the wall. She didn't know why, they just got on her nerves. Today's Jackie Gal has to be careful—she has such a strong personality that she tends to attract followers (the weaker willed are quickly turned into glorified secretaries or assistants). She knows she has this tendency. Which is why she prefers men.

BEING MARILYN: WHEN EVERYONE WANTS TO SLEEP WITH YOU

The Marilyn Gal of today has sex. A lot.

And when she isn't, she has lots of sexual energy—beaux,

---

2 What can we say? The Kennedys, being Irish, liked long engagements. JFK's sister, Eunice, subjected poor Sarge to a seven-year courtship.

admirers, some guy she met two years ago on a plane coming back from the Vineyard over the Fourth of July weekend. He, of course, has been thinking about her since the morning they met. And wondering, *praying,* how he might run into her again. He even remembers her perfume, her hair, the dress she wore and exactly what she said to him. She doesn't remember him.

Some women get crushes on her, too. She pretends not to notice; she doesn't want to deal with it. It has happened before and will happen again. Eventually, it blows over.

As a side note, people tend to get obsessed with the Marilyn in a far more intense way than they do with the Jackie. It has always been like this.

Men do mad things to get her attention—write poetry (even if they can't write),[3] invite her to London to go to a matinee, give her a puppy as a gift.[4]

The Marilyn knows that she is the person they are all so attracted to, of course. But sometimes she almost feels as if all the attention has nothing to do with her. Like "Marilyn" is a construct she has created that she can turn off or on at will.

When she is in a funny mood she thinks, of course everyone wants to sleep with her—they can't help it! Heck, *she* sleeps with her and almost can't believe her good fortune.

She's kidding.

(Sort of.)

She has found herself in these situations since she was fifteen years old, and as a result, the Marilyn likes being around women and gay men because she can relax and let her guard down. She also loves children and animals; she loves their innocence and the fact that they don't want anything from her. For this reason, she is a big supporter of the ASPCA. She cannot

. . . .

3 In another life, the Marilyn would have hung with Carl Sandburg. Today, it is just as likely to be Russell Simmons and his Def Jam poetry.
4 And for the M, it really is the thought that counts . . . forget diamonds—give her a puppy or a hardcover book she has not read yet, and see how she reacts.

bear to even walk by a pet store with puppies in the window; she wants to adopt them all.

Crowds of men frighten her the most.

AND WHICH ARE YOU?

In assessing your own situation—in determining whether you are a Jackie or a Marilyn—it is important to realize that although the Marilyn appears outwardly more sexual, the Jackie does not enjoy sex any less. She is simply less obvious about it.

What we are saying is this: Look beyond the first, obvious appearances. The Marilyn of today can go to Harvard; the deeply aspirational Jackie might work at Starbucks.

J+M—THE BARE ESSENTIALS

Although sex appeal is (of course) indefinable, for Jackie and Marilyn, it can be broken down into a few essentials.

. . . .
THE VOICE
. . . .

In real life (no matter how they presented themselves in public and on screen), both Jackie and Marilyn spoke in low, dulcet tones. Friends who knew Jackie said that her "real" voice was low and even a bit masculine; in fact, meeting her for the first time over a late-night dinner at P. J. Clarke's, one female friend said she was surprised at how direct and outspoken Jackie was. The fey, whispery voice was something she put on when she was anxious about speaking in public. (If you really want to hear what she sounded like, listen to JKO speak in a foreign language—either French or Spanish.)

Similarly, Marilyn's "movie voice" was a bit of a fake. Lawrence Schiller observed that MM's voice was "an octave or two lower" than what you would expect. The movie Marilyn voice was almost an extreme example of seduction: breathy, languid, with a hint of uncertainty behind it. Even when ordering a cup of coffee, she seemed to be whispering promises in your ear.

THE WALK

While their voices were similar, Jackie and Marilyn each had very distinctive walks. While JKO glided as subtly as a geisha through official state functions in the White House, revealing little,[5] and her private years away from Washington were characterized by a very fast, athletic gait, Marilyn (often hours late) made an entrance when she walked into a room and always made a point of wearing clothing that emphasized her assets.

Jackie withheld while Marilyn revealed.

WORDS HAVE POWER

Jackie, perhaps taking a page from Marilyn's *Some Like It Hot* playbook, would say the most outlandish thing to world leaders, who were mostly old men and used to being catered to. And it worked. Upon being introduced to JFK during the very stressful Vienna summit, Nikita Khrushchev said, "I want to shake *her* hand first."

Later, speaking with Khrushchev during a formal dinner, Jackie said, "Oh Mr. Premier—don't bore me with your silly statistics. . . ."

As Jackie knew, you can say some pretty outrageous things if there is a smile in your voice (which is why email can get you in so much trouble; it doesn't convey the tone of what you are saying).

---

5 The White House press office was instructed by JKO: "I want minimum information given with maximum politeness."

SECRET SECRETS—THE MARILYN:
THINGS YOU MIGHT NOT KNOW ABOUT HER

Marilyn knew that the way a man can really get to a woman is through her brain: "If you can make a girl laugh, you can make her do anything."

SECRET SECRETS—THE JACKIE:
THINGS YOU MIGHT NOT KNOW ABOUT HER

From all reports, JFK was not a very attentive lover. Ari was.

5 : Dating and Courtship

"No serious interests, but I'm always
interested. . . ."
— MM, WHEN ASKED IF SHE WAS DATING OR IN LOVE

. . . .

"Jackie had more men per square inch than
any woman I have ever known."
— LETITIA BALDRIGE

Jackie and Marilyn both instinctively played to men, but in a
different way. "Marilyn's supposed helplessness was her greatest strength," said Arthur Miller, while Jackie also worked the
"little girl lost" thing (although not to the degree Marilyn did).

JKO's father adored her and instilled in her the knowledge
that she was special (among other things, he counseled her
on dating, telling her that "all men are rats"), while MM's
father was absent, and her difficult childhood set her up for
a lifetime where it was impossible for her *not* to play up to a
man. (She turned men on with this act and enjoyed the power
of it).[1]

. . . .

1 Intriguingly, MM had a childhood fantasy that Clark Gable was her father, while JKO's actual father really did look like Clark Gable. In 1960, MM filmed *The Misfits* with Gable.

Both were attracted to powerful men and had powerful older protectors—Marilyn was discovered by Hollywood superagent Johnny Hyde, while Jackie had the patriarch Joseph P. Kennedy in her corner. Marilyn Monroe was married three times—to James Dougherty, Joe DiMaggio and Arthur Miller. Jacqueline Onassis was married twice, to John F. Kennedy and Aristotle Onassis, a man twenty-three years her senior. (It is said that she "stole" him from her sister, Lee Radziwill, who was originally dating him before he turned his attention to Jackie. In an infamous anecdote, Janet Auchincloss once stormed into Onassis's suite at Claridge's Hotel in London, looking for her daughter. Dressed in a bathrobe and smoking a cigar, Onassis drawled, "And who is your daughter?" "The Princess Radziwill!" Mrs. Auchincloss huffed. "In that case, Madame," Onassis said, "she just left.")

After Onassis's death, Jackie had a longstanding relationship with diamond merchant Maurice Tempelsman.

*W*ith the Jackie and Marilyn Gals of today, relating to men is perhaps a matter of degree and circumstance. There are times in life when it is more advantageous to be more Jackie (when meeting your possible future mother-in-law, for example), and other times when it is better to be a full-on Marilyn (say, the proverbial third date).

But in any event, neither Jackie nor Marilyn ever fell into the demeaning *He's Just Not That Into You* single-gal construct that has been created today. Whether dating, dealing with a director, married, or meeting Nikita Khrushchev, Marilyn and Jackie always had the upper hand with the opposite sex.

In earlier chapters, we explored two pillars of the essential Jackie or Marilyn appeal—sex and beauty. (The third, in case you're wondering, is intelligence.) But between sex and beauty, well, there is the really fun stuff of men, dating and courtship.

THE JACKIE AND THE MARILYN REAL-WORLD DATING TIPS

(Sort of like _The Rules,_ but hipper and more life-enhancing.)

_B_etween the two of them, Jackie and Marilyn knew pretty much everyone worth knowing in the latter part of the 20th century. Name a man of talent or stature on either the East or West Coast (or Paris, London, Skorpios and Dublin, for that matter), and Jackie or Marilyn had met, dated, knew, worked with, admired, flirted with, befriended, bedded or possibly been engaged and/or married to him.

Winston Churchill? Check. Bill Holden? Check. Hubert de Givenchy, Walter Winchell, Darryl Zanuck, Marlon Brando, the maitre d' of the Stork Club, the Kennedy boys? Joe DiMaggio? Truman Capote? (And in Jackie's case, since she lived longer, Valentino, Bill Clinton, Mikhail Baryshnikov, Mick Jagger and Deepak Chopra? Check, check and check.)

And what does this mean for you, oh J+M Gal? Well for starters, get out there and meet people! It doesn't matter how you do it—travel, volunteer, take a friend who is having a bad day out to lunch, just get out of the house—you never know what might happen out there.

Flirt Like Hell—Both the Jackie and the Marilyn Gal flirt like hell with pretty much everything that moves—men, women, puppies, babies, senior citizens, the downstairs neighbor. They can't help it; it's just the way they are.

The world is a stage, and once the Marilyn walks out her front door, she is _on._ And it should be the same for you. Every day is an audition. Every waking moment is full of verdant, romantic possibilities. The way the Marilyn sees it, if she walks past a construction site and no one notices her, she's doing something wrong. If she walks out her front door and the doorman doesn't instinctively smile at her—_what?_

She knows that men are visual creatures, and for whatever reason, they like to look at her. In the Marilyn's view, that's okay, because life is hard enough, and if someone can make you laugh or lift your spirits (or vice versa), that's always a good thing.

In our grandmothers' day, they called it charm. Take our word for it: It still works. But keep it light—gather some pointers from how well MM flirted with grumpy Larry Olivier in *The Prince and the Showgirl*.

Jackie, on the other hand, goofs around with men, keeps them on their toes, kind of makes fun of them, almost in spite of their worldly success and power. In 1957, she and Senator Kennedy were invited on Aristotle Onassis's yacht to meet Winston Churchill, one of JFK's idols. The former prime minister was quite elderly and seemed to ignore JFK or not quite know who he was. After they left, Kennedy was bereft at having failed to connect with his idol.

"Maybe he thought you were a waiter," said Jackie mischievously, taking note of his white dinner jacket.[2]

Keep a Lot of Men Hanging Around—Seventy-year-old confirmed bachelors, couturier designers, former beaux still pining away, the seventeen-year-old delivery boy from the butcher shop downstairs—who cares? Whether you are married, dating or single,[3] what you want is masculine energy. That way, you are happy and it keeps everyone (yourself included) from getting complacent. Some happy hunting grounds include major league baseball games, the Dartmouth Winter Carnival and the gym.

One of our best friends met the man she married (yes, married) on a subway. And he's terrific. Another

. . . .

2 Another anecdote: JKO's private nickname for Onassis (after their marriage) was "Goldfinger" after the extremely rich Bond baddie.
3 And, some would say, especially if you are married.

(we kid you not) met the handsomest man in New York in an elevator. They worked on completely different floors, but he tracked her down on Valentine's Day by sending one of his officemates to her door with a handmade card.

Or heck, if you are a Marilyn, just going down to the local Starbucks any given morning can work just fine.

And forget expensive moisturizers and dubious plastic surgery—what is it the French say? *"Elle doit être amoureuse, elle a arrêté de porter la fondation."*[4] If nothing else, both the Jackie and the Marilyn know that having a lot of admirers keeps them looking young and everyone on their toes.

Mum's the Word—And yet, be wildly discreet about the specifics of who you are actually dating. No matter what the papers intimated, Marilyn always referred to Joe DiMaggio and Arthur Miller (husbands number two and three) as "Mr. DiMaggio" and "Mr. Miller." Jackie was engaged to John Husted the entire time she was being courted by JFK. "Don't believe all that stuff you hear about Jack Kennedy," she assured Husted.

When it comes to your personal life, a bit of mystery never hurt anyone, and besides, the person you are really involved with knows who he is—and that's all that matters, right?

Absence Really Does Make the Heart Grow Fonder— If you're not getting the attention you feel you deserve in the romance department, split. Take a break. Hit the road and ignore his emails. Tell him your iPhone ran out of batteries or something. Better yet, leave the country.

. . . .

4 "She must be in love, she's stopped wearing foundation."

A BRIEF TIME-OUT—MM HAD HER OWN DATING RULES: NONE

Okay, as J+M Gals, we have shared some rules, but here's the thing we have to admit—Marilyn was so desired by *everyone* that she had no rules. She did whatever the hell she wanted at all times.

Even she admitted it—"When I was 11, the whole world suddenly opened up. Every fellow honked his horn. The world

became friendly. . . ." She walked out her door and had men literally following her down the street. (Which, now that we think of it, actually sounds kind of scary in real life.)

After ending her first marriage to James Dougherty and moving to Hollywood, she began to have some small success in minor roles and got even more attention from powerful studio heads Jack Warner and Joseph Schenck, producer Darryl Zanuck and others.

But even then, among the hotshot agents and studio presidents who could further her career, MM was an equal-opportunity dater. A reporter from *LIFE,* doing an early piece on her, tells of being with her at the Chateau Marmont and some poor guy showing up at her door with a dozen roses— a day early for their date . . . or maybe Marilyn got the date mixed up and thought it was the next night. But at any rate, the poor shlub left the roses and went sadly on his way.

But you know what? It didn't matter—do you think he was back the next night with a new bouquet hoping she would be there? Absolutely.

Because let's face it: If you are pretty enough to whomever you are dating, every rule gets tossed out the window.

THE J+M LIFE LESSON—BELIEVE WHAT HE TELLS YOU

A man will always tell you who he is, where he is in the world and what he has on his mind (especially in regard to you). The smart Marilyn or Jackie listens. In real life, it never took Jackie long (say, about thirty-five seconds) to get the lay of the land in any situation, particularly when it came to possible romantic partners. And then she did what was best for her.

After she graduated from college, she began dating a very nice guy, John Husted.[5] His family was in the *Social Register.* He was a friend of her father, Jack Bouvier, and the Auchin-

. . . .
5 And, ladies, with the description "very nice guy," you know where this is going. . . .

closses. He was a stockbroker. He went to Yale and summered in Nantucket. In short: He was very acceptable.

After a few months, he and Jackie got engaged, as was the custom in 1951. Shortly thereafter, there was an announcement in the *New York Times*.

In May 1951, prior to the engagement, Jackie met then–Senator John F. Kennedy at a Georgetown dinner party hosted by their friends Charles and Martha Bartlett—who had been trying for months to get the two of them together. There was a brief overlap between Husted and JFK, with Jackie (admitting nothing to either man) eventually returning the engagement ring and her mother placing a small "calling off the engagement" notice in the newspapers.

At the time, Jackie admitted to friends that Husted was too "immature" and "sedate" for her taste (well, he was a stockbroker). In later years, Husted felt that Jackie's mother got between them, intimating that he did not earn enough money to support Jackie—although in the 1950s, $17,000 a year was an extremely good salary.[6]

Marilyn, for her part, never looked at her dating life so strategically—or, well, strategically at all. While she went to poker nights at Joe Schenck's home (he was the powerful studio head of 20th Century Fox) on Sunday night and laughed and joked and emptied ashtrays with the best of the up-and-coming starlets, she was just as comfortable—probably more so—getting chili at Howard Johnson's in Times Square with a fellow student from the Actors Studio.

Marilyn's opinion of relations between the sexes was much less prosaic than Jackie's. More than anything, she believed in love, and she would not sell out for it. "It's often just enough to be with someone. I don't need to touch them. Not even talk. A feeling passes between you both. You're not alone."

. . . .

6 Ever the gentleman, Husted never spoke to the press about his time spent with Miss Bouvier.

MARILYN MONROE: (LITERAL) HEARTBREAKER

Johnny Hyde was a powerful older agent (fifty-three years old to Marilyn's twenty-three) who is credited with discovering Marilyn Monroe. Best friends with all of the studio bosses in Hollywood, he was a man who could—and did—do a lot for Marilyn in the early years of her career. He paid for her slight rhinoplasty and encouraged her to go platinum blonde. He also got her a screen test and hired at 20th Century Fox after they had turned her down two years earlier.

Hyde was not only powerful and respected, he was also madly in love with Marilyn and begged her to marry him repeatedly. But she knew that she was not in love with him and turned him down.

Hyde begged her.

He even moved out of his home and left his wife and three children to show Marilyn how serious he was about being with her. He was sick, with a heart condition, and was convinced that he would not live long. He assured Marilyn that as his widow, he would leave her a wealthy woman, respected in the small company town. Marilyn refused. She loved him as a friend, sure. But not in that way.

Shortly thereafter, Joe Hyde died of a heart attack, and his family closed ranks, refusing to allow Marilyn to attend the funeral. She was devastated.

YOU DON'T CHANGE ANYONE!

In Date World (as in friendships), choose who you spend your time with wisely. A man is not a car—you can't remake him or turn him into your personal project. Oh, sure, you can change minor things like getting him a better haircut or eyeglasses, or a preference for cashmere or suede loafers, but you can't teach him thoughtfulness, grace, kindness, style or a sense of humor.

If You're Not Happy, Dump His Sorry A**—Tough but

true. Not to get too Oprah here, but love is supposed to make you feel happy. It is supposed to be positive. We are not saying there won't be a few bumps along the road, but not while you are dating! The entire dating/courtship phase is supposed to be fun.

While a perfect set of washboard abs is nice,[7] look at his character. Keep an eye out for gambling problems, addiction, abusive behavior—see how he treats the waitstaff. Does he raise his voice to you? Is he dismissive of your opinion when you try to broach sensitive subjects? If he is divorced, how does he treat his children? His former wife? Does he fulfill his commitments or expect them to live on $17 a month?[8]

THE SEVEN-YEAR ITCH. IN REAL LIFE.

"Husbands are chiefly good as lovers when they are betraying their wives."—MM

To hit the historical reset button here, both Jackie and Marilyn were involved with married men at various times in their lives. (If it matters, Jackie more publicly than Marilyn, although never while she was married.)

For Jackie, maybe it had something to do with her history, as both her father and her husbands were noted philanderers. After JFK's assassination, the men Jackie publicly dated were described as "very married, very old, or very queer." Not seeming to mind that many of her escorts were married, she went out with Mike Nichols, Peter Duchin, Gianni Agnelli and Frank Sinatra, among others. Her relationship with Ros Gilpatric, who served as Kennedy's deputy secretary of defense, became publicly known after a romantic letter

7 Extremely.
8 And then bitch about it to you. Charming.

she wrote him while on her honeymoon with Aristotle Onassis (explaining her recent, as-secret-as-possible marriage to Ari) was stolen and leaked to the press, causing Gilpatric's third wife, Madelin, to file for divorce shortly thereafter.

And Marilyn? Well, she *was* Marilyn Monroe, possibly the most desired female in the entire world—then and now—and had everyone from T. S. Eliot to Orson Welles to Yves Montand (her costar in *Let's Make Love*) to Arthur Miller (whom she eventually married and later divorced) to JFK and RFK after her.[9]

And how is this applicable today? As true Jackie/ Marilyn Gals, we have very few rules when it comes to affairs of the heart—want to send him flowers? Go right ahead. (We have one friend who sent a bouquet to her beau on a construction site. Now *that* made a statement among all the guys, who then wanted to meet her.) Sex on the first date? Sex on the seventieth date?

We don't care. We really don't.

But when it comes to dating, we have one no-kidding-around rule: Don't get involved with a married man. (And if you are a guy, the same goes for a married woman.)

Maybe it's deeply confident, maybe it's wildly egotistical (okay, we cop to both), but whether you are seriously dating someone or just palling around, you are top dog. No scraps, no second place.

Besides, with all of your life experience and inherent Jackie/Marilyn fabulousness, you know there are a lot of fish in the sea. All you have to do is walk out the door to meet people. Lots and lots and lots of terrific, handsome, wonderful men who are insane about your fabulous self. And if he is that enamored with you, he can take care of business and get a proper divorce before you get involved in his life.

9 As well as Marlon Brando, Frank Sinatra, Richard Burton and Elia Kazan.

If all the married people want to run around like they're in a badly cast Updike novel, that's their deal. You're not the one breaking up a family.

(And if nothing else, think of the heavy, heavy karma on that last decision.)

THE JKO DATING MO

When she first began dating, Jackie seemed to want to present herself as *less than*. Was it something girls were taught in the 1950s, so as not to intimidate possible beaux? Was it in the water? According to *Time* magazine, Jackie almost seemed to fear scaring her friends away by being both beautiful and bright and often hid her intelligence behind a mask of school-girl innocence.

Recalled her friend, socialite Jonathan Isham, "She was so much smarter than most of the people around her that she sublimated it. . . . She sometimes came across as a wide eyed, sappy type. It's pure defense. When I'd take her to the Yale Bowl, and it'd be fourth down and five to go, she'd say to me, 'Oh, why are they kicking the ball?' I'd say, 'Come on, Jackie, none of that.' She felt she ought to play up to the big Yaleman. The truth is, she probably knew more about football than I did."

And yet JFK (no slouch in the brain department himself) recognized Jackie's intellectual gifts early on and was attracted to her for them. She never acted like a lightweight for him.

A friend of JFK's said that Jackie was unlike any of his other girlfriends, who tended toward the "Dallas cheerleader, glamour girl type. . . . Jackie had substance." His secretary, Anne Lincoln, noticed that JFK always called Jackie himself to ask her out, instead of relegating the duty to her.

The Big Three:

1. Drug/alcohol abuse

2. Demeaning behavior

   This includes putting you down in public, cheating, being dismissive toward you, checking out other women in front of you, or any kind of weird sexual stuff you are uncomfortable with.

3. Dishonesty

   Lying, not keeping his word. Because frankly, life's too damn short to put up with such nonsense. It's one thing if a guy is shy or takes too long to get to the punch line of a joke. It's another thing if he is less than truthful . . . or makes promises that he has no intention of keeping.

There are also the satellite transgressions—

Forgetting Your Birthday. As a Leo, Jackie loved her birthday. She thought of it as "Christmas in July." Frankly, we can't imagine anyone forgetting our birthday—or yours—but if he does . . . out.

Being Mean to Your Dog—This is not even worth discussing. On par with (well, worse than) forgetting your birthday. Even the slightest transgression in this category and you are O.U.T. out!—ciao, lose my number, darling.

Not Tipping; Dissing the Help—We shouldn't even have to spell this one out for you, oh intrinsically fabulous one. Even when she was a struggling model/actress, the real Marilyn always tipped. If he doesn't, you should. And let that be the last you see of him.

General Jerkiness—There are several character traits we don't like in a man or woman—prejudice, small-mindedness, pessimism, grumpiness, complainers, warmongering, any kind of drama, watching FOX television (Kidding! Kidding!).

It is all about energy. Any relationship you have, whether it is with your mom, the butcher, your trainer, the accountant, your agent, the hairdresser, should be uplifting and positive. If not, it's time to do some rethinking and consider culling the inbox. (More difficult to do with your parents and close family members, granted.)

And not to get too metaphysical (oh, what the heck, the rest of the world is), but you can't meet the one you are *supposed* to be with if Mr. Negative is taking up so much of your space and time. But the real question, whether you are a Jackie or a Marilyn, is this: Why would you want to share your terrific life with a guy like this, anyway?[10]

And do you really think you are going to maintain your essential Jackie/Marilyn gorgeousness surrounded by such negative energy?

Exactly.

JKO CONVERSATIONAL GAMBITS

Jackie said very little about herself on a date. She knew that men love to talk about themselves, and if a woman encourages this, she quickly gains a reputation for being a great conversationalist.

There were two secrets to the JKO conversational arsenal that apply even today. The first is focus, focus, focus, and allow the person speaking to you to feel as if he is the only person in the entire world. (Supreme seducers like JFK, Pamela Harriman, Peter Duchin and Bill Clinton used this to great effect.)

· · · · · · · · · · · · · ·
10 No one is that good in bed.

Second, Jackie paid attention to everything someone said and used even the simplest conversation to gain insight into a person. So if you say *one thing,* the Jackie Gal of today is going to remember it forever and bring it up—if she has to—at an opportune time. She wouldn't throw it in your face during an argument (she is both too kind and too smart for that) or bring it up after you've had a hard day at work (she knows the brutal Darwinism of the office), but in some ways, the Jackie is like a four-year-old . . . you say one thing, make one promise, one offhand remark, and she is going to remember it forever.[11]

QUICKTESTS

The Marilyn Quicktest: The man says "I love you" first. Always.

The Jackie Quicktest: You think that what goes on between a man and a woman is the most fascinating game of all. And you are very good at it.

---

11 And with her almost scary recall, she will probably be able to tell you what you were wearing, where the conversation took place, what she was wearing . . . (you get the idea).

J+M FIELD NOTES: HOW TO WRITE A LOVE LETTER

Hard as it is for the younger set to believe, in Jackie and Marilyn's day, there were three options for getting a hold of someone to let them know what was going on in your life. First, **the telephone,** which was expensive for anything other than local calls. Plus, there was generally one phone per household, and you did not pick up the phone every three minutes and call someone to discuss something trivial, like *American Idol.* A long-distance call usually meant bad news; i.e., someone had died or gotten drafted into the Korean War. **Second, the telegram** (again, bad news). These were transmitted to the local Western Union office, and a messenger showed up via bicycle on your doorstep to deliver it. Or, third, you sent **a letter or postcard.**

So, slightly off topic, but if you were going to meet someone, you had to make plans well in advance, make them very specific and *not change them.* If you were late, if the train was delayed, if you spaced and "forgot" you were supposed to meet your friend, he or she could wait hours for you to arrive. Or you might miss one another by showing up at the wrong spot, or he or she might be waiting for you (in the old days, people seemed to have less trouble simply waiting) and meet someone else and fall in love with *that* person—hence setting up the plot of practically every single 1940s heartbreak movie.

While it might surprise no one that Jackie was an inveterate letter writer, so was Marilyn. But first, the stationery. Both Jackie and Marilyn wrote their letters on really great stationery—Marilyn's (befitting her station as a world-famous actress) was simply embossed with her name on the top and on the back of the envelope, while Jackie's bore the address of her residence (3307 N Street; 1095 North Ocean Boulevard, Palm Beach, Florida; The White House).

Both wrote their letters by hand. Marilyn had the invented, dramatic penmanship of someone who had grown used to signing autographs, while Jackie bore the well-bred backward slant of a Farmington girl—the sort of handwriting seen in Diana Vreeland, Babe Paley and Princess Diana.

Both letter writers were inventive and showed insightful—if humorous—analysis of events of the day. Face it: If you got a letter from either Jackie or Marilyn, you were going to keep it. (And most did.)

Now, on to your own *billets doux*. How to write a love letter à la Jackie or Marilyn?

Okay, right off the bat, with all of the forgettable cell phone, email, Twitter and IM nonsense going back and forth, if you take the time to write anything longer than two sentences, put it in an envelope and send it via U.S. mail, you are way ahead of the pack. In the old days (forget your parents' generation—say, five years ago) people still wrote letters. Now, only those with an eye toward posterity do.

Type it so that he can read what you are saying. Be like Marilyn and scrawl your name at the bottom with great abandon, as if you are a Hollywood star. Give the impression that this is no big deal: You send dozens of these notes to your admirers. (Which you probably do.)

Regarding content, in some ways, it almost does not matter what the note says. It can be four sentences; it can be two and a half typed pages (single spaced) of whatever is on your mind. You can discuss Descartes. You can discuss a great pair of shoes you saw in a shop window. If you are entertaining enough, it does not matter.

Whatever you do, do not mention the word "love" in the letter. Do not tell him how great he is (that is for him to tell you), do not tell him you miss him, do not thank him for being in your life, do not ask him where the "relationship is going" (zzzzzzzzzzzzzzzzzzzz).

If you are feeling warmhearted, thank him for his friendship. This will keep him off balance. (Friendship? He will read it and think to himself, and then start to get very, very worried.)

Other topics include: You are packing to leave for Paris but wanted to get this in the mail; you are en route to Paris; you are in Paris *at this very moment*; the Red Sox made the playoffs.

Similarly, do not sign "love" unless you are engaged. In that case, all bets are off, and you can do whatever you want.

Be sure to write "PERSONAL" on the back flap so that his secretary/assistant does not open it by mistake. Marilyn spritzed her letters with perfume, but personally (unless he is serving in the armed forces overseas), we think this is a bit much.

Send it to the office. Men find the combination of business-like (his typed address on the front) and personal (your note inside) particularly compelling.

And let's face it: Most guys working in offices are bored out of their minds and just looking for something to break up the monotony of the day. If he gets an actual letter in the mail and realizes it's from you, forget it—he can close the door, ask his assistant to hold his calls, open it carefully with a letter opener (remember those?), put his feet up on the desk and take his time reading it.

Once he has read it a few times (with his feet still up on the desk), he will fold it back up carefully, look out the window at the sky for a while and think of what a lucky S.O.B. he is to have you in his life. He might then take the letter from his desk again, carefully reread it, and have a very Cary Grant moment.

Anything you can do to make a man feel like Cary Grant in this day and age is not to be underestimated.

· ·

An Apocryphal Pickup Line

· ·

We have no idea if this is true, but what a great story.

Albert Einstein and Marilyn sat next to each other at a dinner party. After a few flutes of champagne, she cooed in his attentive ear, "I want to have your child. With my looks and your brains, it will be a perfect child!"

Einstein replied, "But what if it has my looks and your brains?"

We don't think this story is true because 1) there is no evidence that AE and MM ever met, and 2) the same story is often told of George Bernard Shaw and Isadora Duncan. But still— what if they *had*?

J+M FIELD NOTES: WHO PAYS FOR DINS?

On a date, the Marilyn could (maybe hypothetically *perhaps*) pay for dinner, especially when seated across from a starving but exceptionally cute artist.[12] After all, she knows what it is to be hungry.

The Jackie? Never.

Never. Never. Never. Never. Never. Never.

To say that it might even enter her mind to pay for a man in a date situation is beyond the realm of comprehension— like walking off the roof and flying. It is a matter of personal respect, after all.

Plus, the guy has the distinct privilege of sitting across a table from her while she focuses her attention on him (and is seen in public doing so). Having said this, the Jackie Woman of today is careful not to order anything too expensive if she thinks it might be an issue with her man. As long as he is understandably half in love with her, she is just as happy sitting with him on a park bench and eating an ice cream cone as she is having dinner at Daniel.

J+M FIELD NOTES: HOW TO SEND A MAN FLOWERS

Sending a man flowers is sort of like kissing him (bear with us). In the same way that you kiss the way you want to be kissed, only send flowers that you would like to receive. Both the Jackie and the Marilyn have been the recipient of so many bouquets that they could practically open their own flower shop with their expertise. (And on Valentine's Day—

. . . .

12 And we mean really cute—like (generationally speaking) Robert Pattinson or James Dean cute.

forget it!—the Marilyn gets so many arrangements that her home begins to resemble a hospital room or a mobbed-up funeral parlor, albeit with good design sense. She compensates by anonymously leaving them on the doorsteps of several of her neighbors the next morning and never admitting where they came from.[13])

In the same way that you would send what you would like to receive, we are also of the personal opinion that you only send flowers to a guy you know really well (i.e., your boyfriend, brother or husband). And even then, sparingly, say, once a year (if that).

Of course, the man can send you flowers as often as he wants—once a month, once a week. When he is in the doghouse. We have one friend who was being courted by someone she didn't really want to go out with. He sent progressively larger and larger bouquets to her place of work every day for almost a month. It got so bad that the receptionist and her coworkers were taking bets on what the next day's floral cavalcade might bring.

Wanting to bring an end to the petal-tastic onslaught, she finally agreed to go out with him.

They were married in less than a year.

*O*kay, back to basics. In general, we like compact arrangements. They are less fussy. You don't want to get too dramatic with the floral arrangement (no excessive height, no stalky things that no one knows where they came from and please—no baby's breath). In short, nothing that might embarrass the guy.

We also like a tight grouping of the same flower, and generally the same color—roses, tulips, daffodils in the spring, daisies, even. Again, you want to make a statement, but you also want it to look natural, unobtrusive and sort of cool, like you know what you are doing. In terms of color, about the only thing we

13 Oh, they can probably figure it out.

would not do is send a man a dozen red long-stem roses. We don't even like them for ourselves—too Miss America—and they have far too many romantic 1950s-ish overtones to ever send to a man.

When you call the florist, let them know what you have in mind and where it is going. If they ask, describe the recipient to them. See what is in season or in the market that day, but make sure you express what you envisioned. For example, if we were sending a bouquet to a man, we would see what they had in shades of blue—light blue, purple (maybe), lilac even, with some smaller white flowers for accents. Freesia always smells terrific. Never yellow, pink or (with rare exceptions) white.

If you don't feel like having a florist send them, another option would be to gather a bunch of flowers from your garden and make a bouquet of your own, again keeping them low and tight and tying a wide ribbon around the neck of the vase to give it a little personality.

And the note? Nothing too mushy. The flowers are enough of a statement.

At the end of the day we want to make one thing clear, whether you are sending or receiving flowers—it truly does not matter what you send; it is the thought that counts. And the fact that you were thoughtful enough to send a bouquet of flowers is what he will remember.

Really.

A REALLY GREAT MM DATE STORY

While Jackie was the queen of America, Marilyn could have been Princess of Monaco. In the early 1950s, Aristotle Onassis cooked up the idea of polishing the fading fortunes of Monaco (described by Somerset Maugham as "a sunny place full of shady people") by having Prince Rainier marry an American film star. Onassis thought Marilyn Monroe would be perfect for the role (as it were) and suggested the idea to her representatives.

At first, Marilyn thought the whole thing was a goof ("Prince

Reindeer," she dubbed Rainier, giggling, to her girlfriends) and wasn't even sure where Monaco was. In Africa, perhaps?

For his part, Onassis wondered whether Rainier would want to marry Monroe.

Marilyn—no slouch when it came to gauging her own desirability—said, "Give me two days alone with him, and of course he'll want to marry me."

Eventually cooler heads prevailed, and Rainier was introduced to Grace Kelly, and the rest, as they say, is history.

Grace, interestingly, had her own connection to Jackie and the Kennedys. Growing up in Philadelphia, the daughter of a self-made bricklayer millionaire, the Irish Catholic Kellys were—if possible—even more photogenic and athletic than the Kennedys. Of course, the families knew one another, and JFK and Grace dated. After JFK and Jackie were married, Jack had to endure a brutal back operation at the Hospital for Special Surgery in New York. To cheer him up, Jackie (who had run into Grace at a dinner party) had Grace dress up as a nurse and surprise him.

Jack was so groggy and in pain that he didn't seem to recognize her. About twenty minutes later, Grace left his hospital room, despondent. "I must be losing my touch," she said.

After Grace married Rainier, Marilyn sent her a congratulatory telegram: "So glad you've found a way out of this business."

JFK, perhaps not the most thoughtful husband in the world, said to Jackie as they watched the newsreel of Grace's wedding, "*I* could have married her."[14]

THE J+M LIFE LESSON—MAINTAIN YOUR CENTER

When it came to men, when it came to almost anything, Jackie was a pretty cool customer—which was largely to her advantage. She maintained her center while dating, while Mari-

. . . .

14 To wrap up: Years later, when JFK was in the White House, Princess Grace of Monaco and her husband came to visit, and boy, did Jackie not like that idea. For starters, she downgraded her visit from a dinner to a luncheon (considered a dis). Pictures of the day show GK looking on quite adoringly at JFK.

lyn had a tendency to go off the deep end a bit (well, she was an actress) or at least to fall madly in love with the wrong guy.

Marilyn, unlike Jackie, wore her heart on her sleeve and then some. If she was upset over something, the world was going to know about it, and she was perfectly capable of taking to her bed for days on end.

When Johnny Hyde died, she managed to push her way into his funeral—against the wishes of his family—and threw herself over his coffin, weeping.

Wow. A young, beautiful twentysomething MM (perfectly coiffed and dressed in black, of course) draping herself over your coffin. Most men would dream of a send-off like that. Only in Hollywood, right?

But she was authentically bereft at the loss of her dear friend.

Jackie, on the other hand—like the Kennedy and Onassis families—watched the angles. She was far more capable of looking analytically at any situation, even *l'affaire d'amour*. If she was in a situation where the ship was about to go down, she wasn't going to be on it.

THE END OF THE AFFAIR

For whatever reason, you and Mr. Wonderful have decided to call it quits. Now is the time that you really want to channel Jackie and do a slow (if elegant) fade-out. Your heart may be broken, you might have a million questions you *must* ask him. You miss him and all the fun times you had together. . . .

So what (as JKO would advise with her usual brand of soigné toughness).

The main thing is this: Do not turn into Stalker Chick. Do not ask him to "explain himself." Boring. If you aren't happy, that is enough of a reason to leave.

Do not send him emails.

Take him off your Facebook friend list (not that he should have been on it in the first place).

Delete his number from your cell phone.

Do not send him news articles you think he might be interested in.

The fact that he is never going to see you again is enough of a psychic price to pay. You don't need to inflict any more drama or heartache on the guy.

Gone is gone.

SECRET SECRETS — THE JACKIE:
THINGS YOU MIGHT NOT KNOW ABOUT HER

Perhaps it was the supersocial world she grew up in, but Jackie always loved going on dates. She also made each of her escorts feel as if he was the most fascinating man on earth.

SECRET SECRETS — THE MARILYN:
THINGS YOU MIGHT NOT KNOW ABOUT HER

As a young Hollywood starlet, MM had no problems scheduling three dates in an evening (with three separate admirers): cocktails, dinner and après-dinner late-night clubbing.

6 Marriage

"I don't think there are any men who are faithful to their wives."

—JKO

. . . .

"Marriage is my main career from now on."

—MM

In marriage, Jackie and Marilyn aimed high. Although Jackie seemed far more interested in the social aspects of marriage (as compared to Marilyn), since that was the world she was raised in, she did not go for the typical WASP stockbroker who played golf on the weekends and bitched about paying taxes. They both went for the smartest, most creative, best-looking man in the room.[1] Marilyn, for her part, conjured up the near impossible in her last marriage—a Pulitzer Prize–winning play-wright/tough guy from Brooklyn who could also use his fists and look good in a white T-shirt (in a craggy, Lincoln-esque sort of way).

When push came to shove, neither Jackie nor Marilyn[2] set-

. . . .

1 Or more likely, the smartest, most creative, best-looking man in the room went for them.
2 With the exception of MM's first marriage, when she had no other options.

tled. Simple put: They married the man at the top of the heap whom they were madly in love with. And remember Joan's ultimate put-down of a guy on *Mad Men?* "He reminds me of a *doorman.*"

That was not the man they chose.

In thinking about who they married, Jackie probably went for power (in the social, political and financial field), while Marilyn went for talent (in writing, in baseball), although the distinction may be somewhat moot, since talent often brings power, and power can come from talent. At any rate, Jackie and Marilyn (and again, it may have been more unconscious on her part) went for the name brand when choosing a life partner.

MARILYN'S STARTER MARRIAGE

Her first, to James Dougherty, was literally a child bride situation. Married off just days past her sixteenth birthday, because it was either that or go back into yet another foster home, the marriage was—like Marilyn at that time—nebulous from the start.

Marilyn and Jimmy, officially husband and wife, lived almost like brother and sister. When he went away to the war, leaving her alone—and there are some women you simply do not leave alone—Marilyn was discovered by Army photographer David Conover while working in a parachute factory in 1945, and the die was cast.

From the start, the camera loved Marilyn. A lonely child, docile, well behaved, "pretty good" at school (but nothing exceptional like Jackie), with an absent mother and shunted from foster home to foster home, she came alive in front of a camera. Looking at her early test shots before she became the Marilyn of millions of men's dreams, even in her struggling anonymity, it is no small thing to say that the camera loved her.

And it did.

Marilyn came alive for the camera in a way that she rarely did for her first husband. Years later, after she had moved into the stratosphere of celebrity far, far past him, Dougherty turned bitter, remembering the simple, loving girl who now sang for a president, had married one of the gods of baseball. "Marilyn had no problem being married as long as I could do something for her," he recalled. He was small-minded and petty, something MM (for all of her faults) never was.

MARILYN AND THE YANKEE CLIPPER

Her second marriage captured America's imagination.

At first, she did not even want to meet baseball great Joe DiMaggio—knowing nothing about sports, she wondered what they would even talk about. But he had seen her photograph in the newspaper and insisted on an introduction.

When they first met in a restaurant, Marilyn found him quiet, respectful, not at all the athlete show-off she expected. They grew close, and after dating for two years were married by a San Francisco justice of the peace on January 14, 1954, surrounded by a scrum of reporters and fans, although they tried to keep it quiet.

Like the rest of America, Marilyn's bosses at Fox were delighted with the union. "We didn't lose an actress," they said, "we gained a center fielder."

In spite of the inherent romance of their union—the baseball star and the pinup girl—there were fundamental problems from the start. DiMaggio's career was winding down, and he wanted Monroe to stay home and be less Marilyn and more Mrs. Joe DiMaggio. And for a time, it seemed, she tried.

DiMaggio was supposed to be remarkable in bed, which always helps. Unfortunately, there was the life they had to lead outside the bedroom—it always comes to that eventually, doesn't it? They loved each other. They just could not live together. Marilyn wanted to be an ordinary housewife, she really did—to stay home nights and watch television, the way Joe liked. Now that she was Mrs. Joe DiMaggio, he expected her to tone down her "Marilyn-ness"—that thing that attracted him to her in the first place. Don't dress so sexy, don't drive other men wild. Give up your career. She learned to cook a good Italian red sauce from his mother. She befriended, even loved, his son from his first marriage, Joe Junior. (Years later, he remembered that she used to write him letters posing as one of the family dogs, saying that she had been chewing things up.)

But still, demure cotton blouses buttoned up to her chin and Italian red sauce aside, she was *Marilyn,* and the cameras and the studios and her future beckoned. What did he expect? What did any husband of hers expect?

The famous sidewalk scene in *The Seven Year Itch* was the nail in their marital coffin (so to speak).

It was a night shoot in New York City, Lexington and 52nd. The Fox publicists had alerted the newspaper columnists that Marilyn would be wearing something that "would really stop traffic," and somehow the entire city seemed to know that Marilyn was in town, shooting a movie on the East Side. There was Marilyn, luminous, in a plunging, deeply cut V-neck dress, no stockings and two pairs of white panties, it was said, to get around the censor. The crowd—thousands of anonymous men, it seemed, hovering, as ravenous as any wolf pack, waited on Marilyn's every move.

It was a scene Joltin' Joe—famously jealous to begin with—never should have seen.

The lights were ready. The cameras were in place. The wind machine, sadistically positioned under the subway grating, too, was in place. Marilyn and her costar, Tom Ewell, walked over it again and again and again.

The crowd howled. Marilyn smiled and held the hem of her dress down the best she could, then turned and posed prettily. She almost couldn't help herself. If the men loved her (and there was no doubt that they did), the camera loved her more.

She laughed, she giggled. She threw back her head and held the word's attention as she struggled (but not really) to keep her dress from blowing above her waist. You could also tell: She *loved* it.

Joe was seething. He and Walter Winchell had begun the evening at Toots Shors . . . and now this disgrace?—god-*dammit!* No wife of his should ever behave like this!

Seemingly unable to separate life from art (and who could blame him, really?) Joe had words with Marilyn, had words with Billy Wilder, had a fit and stormed off the set.

Later that night, he and Marilyn argued at their hotel and, it is said, he hit her.

They went back to California and tried to rebuild their marriage, but it was no use. Less than nine months later, on October 27, 1954, they were divorced.

MARILYN AND THE MAN WHO SOLD HER OUT

On June 29, 1956, Monroe married her third husband, playwright Arthur Miller, whom she had first met in 1950. Raised nominally as a Christian Scientist, she converted to Judaism for the ceremony.

Just prior to their marriage, Miller was called before the House Un-American Activities Committee (HUAC), a congressional committee that was investigating supposed communists working in Hollywood. Marilyn accompanied Miller to his testimony, putting her own career in jeopardy, and was beside him the entire time. Although it was not known at the time, she also paid for Miller's lawyers, as well as his alimony and child-support payments to his first wife, Mary Slattery.

Although we are sure there must have been love at the beginning of their relationship, maybe Marilyn was just too much for Miller to handle . . . or maybe it was the difficulties of two very creative people trying to live together. At any rate, Miller was mean to Marilyn, putting her down, mostly, for her lack of intellectual heft, versus his intellectual plaudits as the playwright of his generation. Shortly after their marriage, he began work on what would become *The Misfits,* and in spite of her extraordinarily compelling performance, Miller said that working on that project was the "lowest point" of his life. Shortly after the film commenced shooting, the pair separated.

Marilyn went to Mexico and got divorced from him on the day of Kennedy's inauguration on the advice of her publicist, Pat Newcomb, who thought the news of the world would be focused on Washington, D.C. It was.

Nineteen months later, Marilyn was dead from an apparently accidental drug overdose.

In the coming years, Miller really went to town on his relationship with one of the most famous women in the world. In 1964, he published *After the Fall,* a play about MM. And although it was known that he would not discuss his relationship with Marilyn, he wrote about her in great detail in his 1987 autobiography, *Timebends.* In each case, his characterization of MM was thought to be unnecessarily cruel.

But what was it Joan Didion wrote? "[There] is one last thing to remember: writers are always selling somebody out."

JACKIE AND JFK

"God, she loved Jack."

—C.Z. GUEST

Jackie and Senator John F. Kennedy were introduced at a dinner party at the home of their mutual friend Charles Bartlett in Georgetown. "We were introduced over the asparagus," Kennedy recalled. "They didn't serve asparagus," Jackie replied.

Although attracted to each other, they had what Jackie described as a "spasmodic" courtship and did not even see each other until six months after that first meeting.

Still, they both knew—on some level—that they had met their match.

Later, writing of herself in an authorized biography published when she was in the White House, Jackie described meeting Kennedy: "She knew instantly that he would have a profound, perhaps disturbing influence on her life. In a flash of inner perception, she realized that here was a man who did not want to marry. She was frightened. Jacqueline, in the revealing moment, envisaged heartbreak, but just as swiftly determined that heartbreak would be worth the pain."

And so it began.

Jack and Jackie were almost two halves of the same whole; even their names matched. Equally intelligent, ambitious, seductive, funny and hidden, both shied away from public displays of affection, and they were two of the most emotionally reserved people their mutual friend Ben Bradlee had ever met. At the same time, neither was a shrinking violet (though Jackie could be shy around people she did not know), and each was used to getting his or her own way.

So there would be sparks in their relationship.

As a rich man's son (and an Irish man with no interest in navel gazing or introspection), JFK probably did not foresee this possibility, but Jackie knew their similar personalities would cause some friction. "Since Jack is such a violently independent person, and I, too, am so independent, this marriage will take a lot of working out."

In retrospect, it is incredible how much they experienced together in their ten years of marriage. Almost immediately after their honeymoon, JFK returned to politics and threw himself into running for higher office. After serving in the Senate, his name was unexpectedly put on the ballot for vice president during the 1956 Democratic convention. While he did not win, he began to have national appeal. Running for reelection in the Senate and then for the presidency was grueling. When he won the 1960 election against Richard Nixon, Kennedy was, at forty-three, the youngest man ever elected president.

During these years, Kennedy also underwent a horrific back operation that almost killed him, authored a book (with Jackie's help), *Profiles in Courage,* that won a Pulitzer, and traveled the country, giving hundreds of speeches.

During his administration, he dealt with conflicts including the Bay of Pigs invasion, the Cuban missile crisis, the cold war, the construction of the Berlin Wall, and the beginning of what would become the Vietnam War. JFK also started the Peace Corps, introduced the importance of the arts to American society, and—with Jackie's help—elevated America's status abroad.

In their personal lives, there was tragedy and joy—Jackie gave birth to four children, Arabella (who died at birth), Caroline, John Junior, and Patrick (who lived just two days before dying of a lung ailment). Jackie's beloved father died, and JFK's father, the patriarch of the Kennedy family, suffered a crippling stroke.

And all of these events played out very much in the public sphere, with newsmen, and the world, watching their every move.

So yes, Jackie was right in thinking that meeting John F. Kennedy would have a "profound" influence on her life.

By the time they celebrated their ten-year anniversary, in September 1963, Jack and Jackie had been through so much together. As Jackie's mother put it, "I can't think of two people who had packed more into ten years of marriage than they had. And I felt that with all their strains and stresses . . . [they] had eased to the point where they were terribly close to each other. . . . He appreciated her gifts and she worshipped him and appreciated his humor and kindness, and they really had fun together."

In the end, no one really knows what goes on between two people, particularly two people so much in the public eye, but this much is undisputed: Jackie loved her husband. In later years, after the trauma of his death had faded—although it probably never did, she just learned, on some level, to live with it—she would sometimes tell anecdotes about "Jack," keeping his memory alive.

But it is known that Jackie could never bear to look at his picture after his death, and much later she admitted that she had difficulty remembering his voice.

NOVEMBER 22, 1963

JFK's assassination was the 9/11 of our parents'—or grandparents'—generation. After his death, Camelot was over. Jackie left Georgetown for the relative anonymity of New York City—too many memories of N Street and her "crooked little house." Grown men walked around shattered for months. Some—his brother, Bobby, his best friend, Lem Billings—never got over it. Marriages blew up, friendships ended. Some people never spoke to otherwise close friends again. It was as if JFK—the center of it all—was gone. And there was nothing holding them together anymore.

THE MYTH OF THE KENNEDY-MONROE ROMANCE

In one of the most famous (or infamous) love triangles of our time, there was Jackie, Marilyn and at the center, JFK.[3]

As one woman who knew him said, "Some men give off light and some men give off heat. He gave off light." Everyone loved JFK: old people, young people, dogs (although he was allergic to dogs and horses), egghead intellectuals, nuns. Everyone.

He was one of those men, largely neglected in childhood in favor of an overbearing older brother, Joe Junior, who had to depend on his personality and intellect to get attention. (Even now, men who knew him and worked in his administration get upset thinking about the loss. "Oh Christ, we loved Jack," one admits, finally, trying to explain it all.)

JFK—even his nickname, redolent of the can-do optimism of the 1960s, moved fast. He walked fast. His mind worked fast. He was a known speed reader who almost seemed to be in a race against time, against some future he could not imagine. He rarely planned ahead. He hated to be kept waiting on a date—or for anything.

The number, the scope and range of the women he dated was notable. Just in Hollywood, there was Angie Dickinson, Audrey Hepburn, Gene Tierney, Jayne Mansfield, Gypsy Rose Lee, his sister-in-law Lee Radziwill (if gossips are believed). Not to mention any num-

---

3 And, as these famous-person romantic roundelays go, JFK was not the only man they shared, but he was the only one in which there was obvious overlap. In the Jackie/Marilyn love connection, there was also Marlon Brando (Marilyn had gotten involved with him first) and Frank Sinatra (again, Marilyn); but decades separated Jackie's involvement with the two men who had romanced Marilyn in her younger days.

ber of secretaries, stewardesses, starlets and New York City society girls from nice families.

Jackie and Marilyn: Is it possible that each wanted (on some level) what the other possessed?

In a perfect world, Jackie could loan Marilyn class and "a good background," which we know in today's PC world sounds *awful*. Marilyn could impart Jackie with some sex appeal (and perhaps confidence), a more public sense of humor and a general loosening up.

Tabloid historians say that Marilyn dreamed of becoming the next Mrs. Kennedy and moving into the White House. With Jackie's radar instinct, we have no doubt that she knew all about MM. She knew, in the abstract and often in the specific, about all her husband's women.

In reality, though, JFK and MM met only four times in their entire lives, always in the company of others. Jack had a soft spot for actresses going through a hard time. As president, he used to call Judy Garland and ask her to sing "Somewhere Over the Rainbow" for him once in a while. So the myth of a great Kennedy-Monroe romance is largely that: a myth. As someone who traveled in that world said, "The Secret Service would have known about it—the Secret Service knew *everything*."

THAT DRESS

"Happy Birthday, Mr. Pre-s-i-*dent*. . . ."—MM

"I can now retire from politics after having had 'Happy Birthday' sung to me in such a sweet, wholesome way."—JFK

Let's pause for a moment to discuss the iconographic public moment JFK and MM shared that made people stop and wonder: *What?*

Imagine this happening today: a fund-raiser for the president of the United States, ostensibly celebrating his birthday, attended by more than 15,000 supporters at Madison Square Garden in New York City. Hosted by Jack Benny, the entertainment includes Peter Lawford, Marilyn Monroe, and a host of stars, including Maria Callas, Ella Fitzgerald, Jimmy Durante, Shirley MacLaine and Peggy Lee.

Putting Marilyn aside for the moment, the JFK birthday bacchanal is notable for its high jinks. And you realize that in the days before CNN, YouTube, twitter and 24/7 surveillance, *these people had fun.*

And best of all, they (the richies, Hollywood people, celebrities, Kennedys) didn't care who knew it.

Perhaps the largest political stag party in history, the event was actually televised on CBS, and it is wild to watch now. Picture it: Late night, May 19, 1962, we see the president of the United States smoking a cigar with his feet up on the parterre, clapping appreciatively to an actress—well, one of the actresses—he was rumored to be having an affair with, not caring who saw.[4]

JFK's "I don't give a damn" attitude is pretty fabulous. He is totally old school—sort of like everyone's dad of a previous generation. He just doesn't care, especially when you consider that his seventy-two-year-old mother and two sisters are in the audience with him. (Jackie is nowhere to be seen, having taken the children and decamped to Virginia and her horses in a snit.) It's very *Mad Men.* Actually, it is beyond *Mad Men*—it is how Don Draper would behave if he were

---

4 A fact not known by the general public at the time, obviously. (Not that anyone would have believed it anyway.)

the most powerful man in the world and not just a square-jawed ad exec.

Now, the dress. Monroe's dress (designed and made by Hollywood couturier Jean Louis at a cost of $11,000) was flesh colored with 2,500 rhinestones sewn into it. Adlai Stevenson described it as "skin and beads."

So form fitting that she had to be sewn into it, Marilyn did not (as was her wont) wear anything underneath it. She walked onstage and dropped the white fur coat, her hair, skin, gown and very much in evidence body bathed in an aura of light, and people gasped.

"Happy birth . . . day . . . to you . . ." she began tentatively. The children's tune turned into a seduction. The crowd—sounding like mostly men at a fight match—roared with disbelief at what they were seeing. It was such a blatant display of sexual pandemonium manifested in one woman.

Having paid $1,000 for her own ticket, it was Marilyn's last public performance.

For JFK's next (and final) birthday the following year, the anti-Marilyn, Audrey Hepburn, sang "Happy Birthday" to him.

And the dress? Marilyn's dress was sold at auction in 1999 for $1.3 million, one of the highest amounts of money ever paid for an article of clothing.

JACKIE AND ARISTOTLE ONASSIS

Aristotle Onassis, like JFK, like Joseph P. Kennedy, like "Black Jack" Bouvier, was a pirate. One of the original jet-setters (when the term meant something), he roamed the world, bending it to his will. As Napoleon said, "Circumstances— what are circumstances? I create circumstances."

One might say Jackie had a type.

. . . .

*B*orn in 1900, he made his first million importing tobacco in Argentina and quickly got into the oil and shipping business. From there, he became one of the wealthiest men in the world, going on to own more than seventy vessels, as well as stock in oil companies in the United States, the Middle East, and Venezuela. He also owned an airline (Olympic Airlines), a yacht (the *Christina*), two islands (Scorpios and Sparta), a gold-processing plant in Latin America, and lots of real estate—with apartments in Paris, London, Monte Carlo, Athens and Acapulco, and a castle in the south of France. In Manhattan, although he generally stayed at his suite at the Pierre, he owned a fifty-two-story high-rise called Olympic Tower, as well as a building on Sutton Place.

Onassis was not conventionally handsome, and did not photograph well. Yes, there was the money (which no doubt attracted Jackie, but there are a lot of rich guys in the world). But there was something about his energy. He had the world's dark magic. He was devastating to women. He had that trick of the professional seducer: He focused all of his attention on a woman, remembering everything she said, as well as her favorite flower, favorite perfume, favorite style of jewelry. Hélène Arpels, a Parisian socialite who knew him in the 1940s, well before he ascended to billionaire status, said that he was one of the most charismatic men she had ever met in her life.

He picked up the telephone, and things happened.

In many ways, Onassis was the anti-JFK.

He had considerable charm, but he was not an establishment smoothie. He was not formally educated but a genius in business; and you knew going into it, if you had any sense at all, that he was going to gain the upper hand in any dealings you might have with him. Like all great businessmen (like all those who hold our attention), he had the essential capacity for heartlessness.[5] He could be dismissive of his children. He ran

. . . .

5 What was it Balzac said? "Behind every great fortune there is a crime."

through people, treating Maria Callas, the great love of his life, abominably, tossing her aside, quite publicly, for Jackie.

*W*hen Jackie married Onassis on October 20, 1968, it was almost as if she had offended the world's sensibilities. "Jackie, How Could You?" read the headline of one newspaper, as Mrs. Kennedy, the beloved widow of JFK, became "Jackie O," the most famous woman in the world. For her part, Lee Radziwill probably called it right when she commented on the snobbishness by saying: "If Jackie's new husband had been blond, rich, young, and Anglo-Saxon, most Americans would have been much happier."

In the beginning (like so many things), all was fine in the House of Onassis. Jackie was a wonderful spouse. She learned Greek, refurbished Scorpios, doted on Ari as they traveled the world together. By all accounts, he took very good care of her and had a wonderful relationship with her children.

Then, cracks began to appear in their relationship. Onassis balked at Jackie's incessant spending. The accountants in his office began to call her "the supertanker" as the financial demands of maintaining her lifestyle cost Ari as much as one of his ships. (But still, said an associate of Onassis's, "I'm sure he was no picnic to live with either.") They grew apart as Jackie spent more time in New York City and Ari in Greece, Paris or London.

The end of the relationship occurred on January 24, 1973, when Onassis's only son, Alexander, was killed in an airplane crash. He was twenty-five years old. His son's tragic death dealt Onassis a shattering blow from which he never recovered. Although Jackie tried to be supportive, Onassis's grief was so intense, so unrelenting, that he went a little mad. Veering wildly between bouts of depression and rage, he spoke of divorce and spent hours obsessively reworking his will. Before any of this could take place, he died, in Paris, on March 15, 1975.

MRS. O'S SHOPPING ALLOWANCE

For all the men who gripe about their wives' extravagant spending; well, it could be a lot worse. You could have been married to Jackie—who had no qualms about spending ten minutes in a store and running up a $50,000 tab. Every day.

And although he had a fortune estimated at $500 million to $1 billion (in 1969 dollars) and had no problem buying Jackie some major baubles (among his gifts to his wife were a $1.25-million heart-shaped, ruby-and-diamond engagement ring and a $1-million 40.42-carat diamond ring from Cartier for her fortieth birthday), Onassis eventually became enraged by Jackie's prodigious shopping.

The couple's arguments over money escalated, their differences grew more apparent, and the two spent less and less time together. "They started with separate beds in the same bedroom," Onassis's colleague said, "and ended with separate beds on separate continents."

THE JACKIE LIFE LESSON—LEARN TO OVERLOOK THE SMALL STUFF

If there is anything Jackie learned in her marriages to two high-powered men, it was to overlook the small stuff.

During her ten-year marriage to JFK, there had been so much real drama: being drawn into the very public Kennedy family whirlwind, a life she did not grow up aspiring to lead; two miscarriages and the sorrowful deaths of two babies, Arabella and Patrick; JFK's hidden illnesses (he was given the Last Rites of the Catholic Church three times before the age of forty); JFK's run for the presidency and winning by one of the smallest margins in U.S. history; the death of her beloved father at the age of sixty-six; and on and on and on. It almost didn't make sense to bitch about the things most couples squabbled about, like: What are we going to watch on television tonight?

Between JFK's death and her marriage to Aristotle Onassis in 1968, there were the assassinations of Robert F. Kennedy and Martin Luther King, Jr., the escalation of the war in Vietnam, the increasing violence in the streets of America. And while her marriage to Onassis brought her unimaginable material comforts, she lost most of her privacy and, at times, could barely walk out her front door without being besieged by paparazzi.

By the time she hit her sixties, she had been through so much trauma and heartbreak that she became very zen about her experiences.

Jackie was more apt to laugh at people's foibles or the sense that one "should" do something, which made her clash with her mother, Janet Auchincloss (who felt very strongly about what "should" be done and made sure Jackie knew it[6]) and mother-in-law, Rose Kennedy. In one famous instance, Rose told Jackie that they were expecting important guests for lunch and to make sure that she was at the table on time. Jackie did not come downstairs at all. Instead, she remained in bed and, in fact, had a maid bring her lunch up on a tray.

In spite of her regal public demeanor she was, inside, a free spirit—much like her father, "Black Jack" Bouvier, or her nutty aunt and cousin "Big Edie" and "Little Edie" Beale.[7] John H. Davis, a cousin who wrote *The Bouviers* in 1993, described her as a young woman who outwardly seemed to conform to social norms. But he wrote that she possessed a "fiercely independent inner life which she shared with few people and would one day be partly responsible for her enormous success."

What we're saying is this: Pick your battles. Don't make everything into World War III. Occasionally, you can pull a Jackie and sulk (which drove JFK nuts), or if your man's done something that really annoys you, either put it on the table and discuss it or disappear for a while.

That will get his attention.

. . . .

6 When she was in the White House, Mrs. Auchincloss was always telling her daughter that her hair was too "messy" and "windblown."
7 Of *Grey Gardens* fame.

In today's world, we would suggest that you learn to let things slide once in a while. When your significant other says (or does) something really irritating but excusable, be like JKO and ignore it. He might be testing you, or he might just be bored.

THE ART OF CONVERSATION

There was one thing both Jackie and Marilyn were experts at, and that is holding a man's attention through the art of conversation . . . although to be honest, they each had to say very little in terms of actual *sentences* to get someone's attention—it was more the *way* they might say something.

(One thinks, here, of a famous dinner party at Peter and Pat Lawford's home in Santa Monica in 1962, where Marilyn met then–Attorney General Robert F. Kennedy. She wanted to have a conversation about civil rights and pulled out a piece of paper with her questions written out in lipstick—which, you have to admit, for an opening gambit was pretty original, even for Marilyn. Kennedy was charmed and spent the rest of the evening speaking to her.)

One of the first things that attracted JFK to Jackie was her intelligence. During their courtship, when she was put through the ringer of a Kennedy family weekend (word games: yes; touch football: not so much), JFK soon learned to get her on his team during hard-fought battles of charades, as her side invariably won. After they were married, many of the best lines from his speeches (whether from George Bernard Shaw or Yeats) were often supplied by the more literary Jackie.

. . . .
A Touch of Reality That No MM Movie Ever Touched Upon
. . . .

Has anyone noticed that American society fetishizes the wedding day without placing enough emphasis on the fact that now you are married to the guy and have to stay married?

Just saying.

CLOSING THE DEAL

. . . .

"WILL YOU . . . ?"

. . . .

If you're a Jackie, Don't Say Yes Right Off the Bat. If You're a Marilyn, Don't Say Yes at All. The Luckiest Guy in the World has just proposed, and you might decide to burst into tears and start screaming, "Yes! Yes! Yes!" right away (like *The Bachelor*), or you might decide to go on a cruise and tell him you will consider it. In either event, it is a story you are going to have to tell your children (or, maybe, his children—your stepchildren), so make sure you maintain your dignity.[8]

*W*hen JFK asked Jackie to marry him after a year-long courtship, she agreed in principle, but then took off to cover Queen Elizabeth's coronation in London, letting him know that she needed to consider the reality of the whole Marrying a Kennedy thing.

Her coverage of the coronation appeared on

. . . .

8 It's not so much a delaying tactic as an "I need to think about it" tactic. If nothing else, it will show him (and the world) that you recognize the seriousness of what is about to take place.

the front page of the Washington newspapers, and JFK wired her: "article great but you are missed." When she returned to America, he surprised her by meeting her plane in Boston. And when they saw each other again in person, she officially agreed to become Mrs. Kennedy.

THE CEREMONY

If it is your first wedding, do whatever you want, and don't let your mother run the show—she had her day.[9] If it's your second, think tasteful. A Valentino daytime dress should do the trick.

Because of her celebrity and innate personal shyness (yes, really), Marilyn's second (to Joe DiMaggio) and third (to Arthur Miller) marriages were small small small. If you are a Marilyn, you want your marriage service as small as possible without offending your in-laws, whether it is your first or your third trip down the aisle. While there is no shame in a justice of the peace ceremony, don't go to Vegas.

COMPARING JKO'S AND MM'S FIRST WEDDINGS

"More than anything in the world," a friend remembered during Jackie's engagement to JFK in 1953, "Jackie wanted to be Mrs. John F. Kennedy."

Jackie's first wedding was not what she had in mind (tasteful, Newport chic), but instead was a giant Kennedy-palooza masterminded for maximum publicity by family patriarch Joseph P. Kennedy with twenty-four bridesmaids, a blessing from the cardinal and 1,200 in attendance, with the entire U.S. Senate invited.

9 Not incidentally, JKO agreed with this. When her daughter, Caroline, married Edwin Schlossberg in 1986, she did not even want to see the wedding dress that Carolina Herrera designed, saying, "It's Caroline's day, whatever she wants."

It was a great society bash as guests sat at tables on the lawn, dined on creamed chicken, viewed the wedding gifts displayed in the house and danced to the Meyer Davis Orchestra on the terrace of Hammersmith Farm, the Auchincloss estate in Newport.

The night before, JFK gave a toast and joked that he had to marry Jackie to remove her from the Fourth Estate, because she was becoming too big a risk to his political fortunes. For her part, Jackie held up a postcard that Kennedy, "a Pulitzer Prize–winning author," had sent her—his lone romantic missive throughout their courtship—and read it to the crowd: "Wish you were here. Jack"

En route to their honeymoon in Acapulco, Jackie wore a gray Chanel suit and a diamond feather brooch that was a wedding gift from her husband.

Marilyn's first wedding was a slapdash, almost haphazard affair. Her mother did not attend, and she did not know who her father was. At 8:30 on the evening of June 19, 1942, the ceremony was performed by a non-denominational minister named Benjamin Lingenfelder at the home of Mr. and Mrs. Chester Howell (friends of Grace's) at 432 South Bentley Avenue, West Los Angeles. Everything seemed slightly surreal and improvised. A girl Norma Jeane/Marilyn knew only slightly at University High was her matron of honor; Jim's brother Marion was best man. The groom recalled that Marilyn "was shaking so much she could hardly stand."

A modest reception was held at a nearby restaurant, where a showgirl entertaining another wedding party dragged Dougherty onto a makeshift stage for a dance. But when he returned to his table, he found his bride "not very happy." She thought he had "made a monkey" out of himself.

At about four in the morning, the newlyweds returned home to Sherman Oaks. There was no honeymoon.

Are DIAMONDS A GIRL'S BEST FRIEND?

To be honest, the Kennedys were not big on what they considered extraneous expenses. They would spend money—lots of it—to get one of the boys elected to the presidency or the Senate, but they didn't spend much on antiques, artwork, jewelry, fixing the roof or paying the help a decent wage. Jackie had a very nice 2.8-carat emerald and diamond engagement ring from Van Cleef & Arpels (picked out and paid for by Kennedy père, Joseph P. Kennedy) and a Schlumberger brooch that her husband bought her after their son, John, was born. But mostly she wore costume jewelry—pearl necklaces bought at Bergdorf Goodman for about $35 in the 1950s[10] and faux diamond earrings.

Jackie didn't have any real jewelry prior to the go-go Onassis years—and what years they were, jewelry-wise. In the early, happy years of their courtship and marriage, Onassis got into the habit of giving JKO a little something on her breakfast tray. There was a 40-carat diamond engagement ring (later bought by Irish millionaire Tony O'Reilly for his wife for $2.5 million at the Sotheby's auction after her death) that JKO wore twice and otherwise kept in a safe deposit box in New York, a 20-carat ruby ring, a pair of cabochon ruby and diamond ear clips and matching pendant—which were a wedding gift from Onassis in 1968.

As Maria Callas said of Onassis, "Anything he learned about women he learned from a Van Cleef & Arpels catalogue."

Which, you have to admit, is not a bad way to go.

THE END GAME

After a marriage had ended (through tragedy and death in each of Jackie's two marriages, and divorce in Marilyn's), Jackie and Marilyn always spoke lovingly of their husbands.

---

10 After her death, two faux pearl necklaces worn by JKO were sold for $112,500 at the Sotheby's auction.

In spite of JFK's rumored infidelities (which never became public during his lifetime), Jackie never spoke of him less than lovingly. "Now he is a legend when he would have preferred to be a man."

After Onassis's death, regardless of the fact that the jet set was buzzing with rumors that the Kennedy-Onassis marriage was on its last legs, Jackie remembered her time with him gracefully: "Aristotle Onassis rescued me at a moment when my life was engulfed with shadows. . . . He brought me into a world where one could find both happiness and love. We lived through many beautiful experiences together which cannot be forgotten and for which I will be eternally grateful."

To friends, she told funny stories about how Ari was an insomniac and would go for walks up Park Avenue at all hours of the night and drag friends home with him.

After her divorce from Arthur Miller, Monroe spoke of the split with dignity, saying to reporters, "It would be indelicate of me to discuss this. I feel it would be trespassing. Mr. Miller is a wonderful man and a great writer, but it didn't work out that we should be husband and wife. But everybody I ever loved, I still love a little."

Ending a marriage or a long-term relationship is always painful. From Jackie and Marilyn's example, we have one thing to say: Take the high road. Always. Because at one point, you loved him enough to marry him. And there may be children involved, and if not children, then in-laws and a whole constellation of friends and family members surrounding you.

And besides (as Jackie and Marilyn knew), the way you speak of someone says more about you than him.

· ·

POSTSCRIPT

· ·

At the very end, Joe DiMaggio tried to be Marilyn's protector. At the time of her death, on August 5, 1962, she and Joe DiMaggio were planning on remarrying just four days later. Joe DiMaggio hated Hollywood, hated the hustlers and the agents and the schemers and the yes men who (he felt) had all contributed to Marilyn's death.

The day after her death, her body—desired by millions—lay at the Los Angeles County Morgue, with no family member to claim it. DiMaggio stepped in. He called Allan "Whitey" Snyder, Monroe's friend and longtime makeup man, to make sure that Marilyn looked her best. Ten years earlier, she had secured a promise from him: "Promise me that if anything happens to me—please, nobody must touch my face but you. Promise me you'll do my makeup, so I'll look my best when I leave."

"Sure," he said, laughing, kidding around, "but bring the body back while it's still warm and I'll do it."

A few weeks later, Allen received a gift from Marilyn in a sky blue Tiffany box—a gold money clip with the engraving: "Whitey dear—While I'm still warm—Marilyn."

And so he fulfilled his last promise to her.

DiMaggio took control of her funeral, allowing only thirty relatives and friends to attend—no studio executives, no producers, no Hollywood stars (and god knows, no newsmen, photographers or reporters). Her acting coach, Lee Strasberg, spoke briefly: "We knew her as a warm human being, impulsive, shy and lonely, sensitive and in fear of rejection, yet ever avid for life and for reaching out for fulfillment. The dream of her talent was not a mirage."

Years earlier, Marilyn had told DiMaggio the story of William Powell's pledge to the dying Jean Harlow—that he would deliver flowers to her grave and not forget her. Knowing how moved Marilyn was by this story, he had a bouquet of roses delivered to her crypt three times a week for the next twenty years. He never wrote or spoke publicly of their relationship. Nor did he remarry. According to his son, he never got over her death. It is said that his final words were, "I'll finally get to see Marilyn."

WOULD SHE DO IT AGAIN?

Twice widowed by the age of forty-five, Jacqueline would not marry again. "I have always lived through men," she confided to a friend after Onassis's death. "Now I realize I can't do that anymore." In the 1970s, as an editor at Doubleday involved in an extremely settled and happy relationship with Maurice Tempelsman, Jackie once said that if she had to do it all over again, she might have stayed single and been a globe-trotting journalist like her friend Gloria Emerson.

SECRET SECRETS — THE MARILYN: THINGS YOU MIGHT NOT KNOW ABOUT HER

Although their marriage ended badly, Marilyn kept every letter that Arthur Miller ever wrote her.

SECRET SECRETS — THE JACKIE: THINGS YOU MIGHT NOT KNOW ABOUT HER

Prior to her marriage, Jackie (like all of her family and pretty much every single member of her social set) was a Republican. Marrying into the Kennedy clan, she knew she had to switch her allegiance to the Dems. And she did.

7 | The Life of the Mind

"He [Arthur Miller] wouldn't have married me if I had been nothing but a dumb blonde."

—MM

. . . .

"I always wanted to be some kind of a writer. . . . Like a lot of people, I dreamed of writing the Great American Novel."

—JKO

*S*expots read Nietzsche, too, you know. Diana Vreeland, the legendary style maker and *Vogue* editor (and friend of both Jackie's and Marilyn's) had it right when she said, "The only real elegance is in the mind; if you've got that, the rest really comes from it."[1]

And while they were both stylish and visually compelling women, Jackie and Marilyn took this insight to heart, knowing that no matter how pretty one might be, it was what went on inside that made her memorable.

. . . .

1 DV was friends with both Jackie and Marilyn. She advised JBK on her inaugural ensembles in 1961 and also commissioned a famous *Vogue* shoot with Bert Stern and MM in 1962.

JACKIE'S SCHOOL DAYS

As a young woman of privilege, Jackie received the best education in the country. Able to read before grammar school, she attended Miss Chapin's School on East End Avenue in New York City. Bright, rambunctious and sometimes bored, she acted up and often found herself in the office of headmistress Ethel Stringfellow. Miss Stringfellow got her to focus and direct her talent by comparing her to a thoroughbred, saying that "without self-discipline and training, the horse's abilities would serve no use." She later recalled that "I mightn't have kept Jacqueline, except that she had the most inquiring mind we'd had in the school in thirty-five years." The headmistress's redirection worked.

From there, Jackie went to Miss Porter's School, an all-girls' boarding school in Farmington, Connecticut. Jackie was well liked at Farmington (in the preppie parlance of the day) and made some lifelong friendships—among them Nancy Tuckerman ("Tucky"), who would not only work with her in the White House but for most of the remainder of her adult life. Well liked and popular, her teachers regarded her as an outstanding student, but she once fretted to a friend, "I'm sure no one will ever marry me, and I'll end up being a housemother at Farmington."

Jackie attended Vassar for two years, and while she loved it intellectually, she began to chafe at being stuck up in Poughkeepsie, referring to it as "that damn Vassar." When the opportunity arose to study at the Sorbonne in Paris during her junior year, she jumped at it. Later, she recalled that it was "the happiest time of my life." Since there was no way that she was going back to Vassar, she ended her college career at George Washington University in Washington, D.C., graduating with a bachelor's degree in French literature.

Although she might have hidden it during her early dating forays, Jackie was smart. Jackie was always smart. She knew a lot, and then she wanted to know more.

Unlike the typical mind-set that led to a calcified worldview as one gets older, Jackie was always, always pushing for new books, new experiences, new people, new thoughts. A friend who knew her says, "Jackie wasn't an intellectual, but she made the effort to find out what was going on in the world." When she was in the White House, she made Oleg Cassini show everyone how to do "the twist," a new dance craze that was sweeping New York City. Throughout her life, if there was a painter, a poet or a writer she admired, she might write him or her a fan letter, and they often became friends. In the 1970s, she met *New Yorker* cartoonist Charles Addams this way.

Moving beyond the casual, comfortable prejudices of the 1940s Newport she grew up in (against the blacks, Jews, Catholics, Irish—pretty much any non-WASP), by the end of her life Jackie was doing yoga and meditating, working at a "real" job, and mixing with people from all kinds of backgrounds.

Once on the beach at Skorpios, she had a conversation with her friend Vivian Crespi. "Do you realize how lucky we are, Vivi? To have gotten out of that world we came from. . . . Going every day to that club with the same kinds of people. . . . You and I have taken such a big bite out of life."

MARILYN'S EDUCATION

Marilyn's education (much like her upbringing) was the complete opposite of Jackie's. She got none of the praise that went with being the brightest girl in the class. She did not spend hours in her beautiful yellow and white bedroom overlooking Narragansett Sound, reading Shakespeare.

Instead, Marilyn (then Norma Jeane) went to local public schools in Los Angeles. She attended Emerson Junior High School in West Los Angeles, between Wilshire and Santa Monica boulevards. At school she was mostly anonymous and did not really stand out as a student. Her courses were designed for girls not on the college track—science, office practice, English, bookkeeping. She received mostly B's and C's. As she recalled,

"I loved English. I hated arithmetic. I was always staring out the window."

"She was very much an average student," recalled Mabel Ella Campbell, who taught the life sciences class. "But she looked as though she wasn't well cared for. Her clothes separated her a little bit from the rest of the girls. . . . Norma Jeane was a nice child, but not at all outgoing, not vibrant."

She went to Van Nuys High School, where her report card was even less distinguished than at junior high. For the second half of her sophomore year, she attended University High School at the corner of Westgate and Texas avenues. By this time, the fifteen-year-old had begun to date Jim Dougherty, a handsome neighbor five years her senior. In mid-March, she shocked her teachers and classmates by informing them that she was quitting school to get married in June 1942. After that, she was not seen in class again, and her formal studies officially ended in the middle of her second year of high school.

In spite of her abysmal education, Marilyn, in her own way, also yearned to know. Although she did not have Jackie's impressive pedigree, she was always reading and going to art galleries when she could and attending the occasional college course. Having already appeared in a few small but memorable roles in *Love Happy* (1949) with the Marx brothers and *The Asphalt Jungle*, directed by John Huston, she signed a seven-year contract with 20th Century

Fox the following year. It is telling that even at this early stage of her career, in 1951, she took evening courses at UCLA in "art appreciation and literature."

Later, as her career skyrocketed, it would be impossible for her to sit in a college classroom anonymously. In 1955 (after she became a star), she attended the famed Actors Studio in New York City and studied with Lee Strasberg.

Unlike most 21st-century Americans, she had a great desire for self-improvement. She kept a list of words that she was unfamiliar with and looked them up when she had a chance.

Marilyn had a touching belief in Merriam-Webster and the power of education.

ZEN AND THE ART OF ABSOLUTE FABULOUSNESS

. . . .
THE JACKIE PHILOSOPHY
. . . .

Jackie was outwardly religious and privately spiritual. Practicing her own highly individual form of Zen Catholicism, she often lit a candle in church for friends going through a tough time but then might also bake them a chocolate cake. Well versed in the tenets of the Catholic Church from the tragedies she endured—the untimely deaths of John F. Kennedy and Robert F. Kennedy, her miscarriages and the death of her son, Patrick, who lived only a few days, she thought "the Catholic Church understands death. . . . If it weren't for the children, we'd welcome it."

From JFK she learned to have (as he did) an almost fatalistic view of life that pushed against the Kennedy ethos that believed with enough money, enough power, enough hard work, enough juice, you could bend the outcome of events to your will. "It is not reality that counts," Joseph P. Kennedy counseled Jackie and his children, "it is the appearance that counts." Instead, JFK thought that whatever was going to happen was going to happen—and there was very little you could do about it. As

Jackie said, "From my husband I learned to do the best you can and then the hell with it."

From the Kennedys, Jackie also gained a sense of their fundamental joy in life, its lightness and humor; but also the senselessness of trying to control it and even the ridiculousness of planning for the future. So one should take whatever joy one might come across, whatever beauty or laughter, because there was often heartbreak lurking around the corner.

For Jackie to be able to fashion some sort of life for herself after November 22, 1963, she had to let a lot of things go: ignore them, not discuss them. Although she went to a psychiatrist once a week in the 1970s, she had no interest in reading the *Warren Report,* or finding out who killed her husband or following conspiracy theorists. "None of it will bring him back, will it?"

While Jackie was Catholic, she was also very drawn to India (which might have something to do with the fact that when she visited in 1961, crowds followed her, calling, "Ameriki Rani").[2] An interest in myths was furthered when she edited

2 "Queen of America"

a book written by Bill Moyers, *The Power of Myth*.[3] In the 1980s, she meditated every evening from 7:00 to 7:30 and befriended Deepak Chopra. When he was in town, they even meditated together. "She had no ego," Chopra recalled. "She was very natural. She had a great sense of humor! She was a lot of fun, the way she joked and kidded around."

There was nothing mean-spirited about Jackie (well, only a little, in the service of a good punch line or to illustrate a point). She was a great conversationalist; the ability to tell a story, to hold a room, to make another human being laugh was no small thing. While her charm was as real as her smile, she also believed strongly in the adage "Never let the facts get in the way of a good story."

THE MARILYN PHILOSOPHY

Marilyn was more purely spiritual. If she had an ethos, it might have come from the Dalai Lama: "My religion is very simple. My religion is kindness."

Growing up, she had an "Aunt Grace," a friend of her mother's who helped raise her, named Grace McKee Goddard. She had an interest in Mary Baker Eddy and was one of the few people who were good to Marilyn. Goddard gave her a copy of *Science and Health With Key to the Scriptures*, and Marilyn kept it with her and read it throughout her life.

But Marilyn was fairly ecumenical. She also had a beautiful rosary made of large garnet beads and an oversized cross. It was a gift to her from Joe DiMaggio and had belonged to his mother. Marilyn used it often—the beads were worn down, like worry beads.[4]

Marilyn, far more than the emotionally circumspect Jackie, wore her heart on her sleeve. A true actress, her heart was sometimes a roller coaster of emotions—from laughter to tears,

3 That nobody at Doubleday wanted to publish, BTW. It became a huge best seller.
4 It was mysteriously sold to a private collector for $50,000 in 2006.

often within minutes. She saw beauty in a sunset, a flower, one person's kindness to another, a child's laughter.

And just when you thought you had our two women figured out—that Jackie was the cool one and Marilyn the sexpot; Jackie the brains and Marilyn the beauty, there is this:

> *"I believe that everything happens for a reason. People change so that you can learn to let go, things go wrong so that you appreciate them when they're right, you believe lies so you eventually learn to trust no one but yourself, and sometimes good things fall apart so better things can fall together."*

> —MM

Not bad, right?

And the take-away (other than having this sentiment taped to your bathroom mirror so that you can read it every morning) for today's Marilyns? Take a tip from MM (as seen in some of her more memorable comedic screen roles like the *Seven Year Itch* and *Gentlemen Prefer Blondes*): When in doubt, say less than necessary.

JACKIE AND MARILYN DIDN'T JUDGE

In any event, both Jackie and Marilyn were extremely liberal when faced with the personal peccadilloes of others. They had certainly seen enough of the world and all of its vagaries not to judge. (Which is not to say that Jackie or Marilyn did not have opinions about people, about situations—in fact, Jackie believed, along with one of her favorite writers, Ernest Hemingway, that "action revealed character," and she *loved* hearing the inside scoop on all the people she knew. When she was in the White House, she saved her favorite Hollywood gossip she had heard and shared it with JFK to entertain him and take his mind off the complexities of the day.)

Jackie and Marilyn were each extremely open-minded when it came to the life choices of others. Her Vassar classmate Selwa Roosevelt remembered that Jackie "was discriminating in her tastes, not discriminatory towards people. In fact, she was always open to new ideas, new people and new ways of thinking."

JACKIE AND MARILYN STAY HOME WITH A GOOD BOOK

ON JACKIE'S BOOKSHELF

Jackie was always a reader. In an autobiographical essay about her childhood, she recalled, "I read a lot when I was little, much of which was too old for me. There were Chekhov and Shaw in the room where I took naps and I never slept but sat on the windowsill reading, then scrubbed the soles of my feet so the nurse would not see that I had been out of bed. My heroes were Byron, Mowgli, Robin Hood, Little Lord Fauntleroy's grandfather, and Scarlett O'Hara."

Her entire life, Jackie read everything—old stuff, new stuff, French existentialists, the *New York Post*. Between her various homes, she owned thousands of books, some bought, many that were gifts and signed by the author, first editions. Traveling across the country on the Kennedy family plane, the *Caroline,* on the campaign trail in 1961, she put her feet up and read a battered paperback copy of Jack Kerouac's *On the Road*. In India, she discovered the love poetry of Rumi, the brilliant 13th-century Persian mystic (a favorite of Audrey Hepburn's, too). At her place on Martha's Vineyard, one wall in her bedroom had a floor-to-ceiling bookcase filled exclusively with French literature.

She was also friendly with writers, and like a fan, invited such authors as Robert Lowell, William Styron and Mary Hemingway to the White House.[5]

Also on Jackie's bookshelf:

In the Russian Style (edited and with intro by JKO)

The White House: An Historic Guide (authored by JBK)

Unseen Versailles, Deborah Turbeville and Louis Auchincloss (edited by JKO)

Grand Central Terminal, Deborah Nevins (edited by JKO)

Present Indicative, Noël Coward

White House Nanny, Maud Shaw

Rose: A Biography of Rose Fitzgerald Kennedy, Gail Cameron

House of Splendid Isolation, Edna O'Brien (inscribed)

The Land of the Firebird, Suzanne Massie (inscribed)

Bound copies of *The Paris Review*

The Sunset of the Romanov Dynasty, inscribed by Suzanne Massie

Selected Poetry and Prose of William Blake

The Prodigal Rake, William Hickey

Pigeon Feathers and Other Stories, John Updike

Six Plays, Lillian Hellman

---

5 Lowell first met JKO at a 1962 White House state dinner with his wife, author Elizabeth Hardwick. Prone to manic episodes, Lowell later became convinced that Jackie wanted to marry him and sent her long, rambling letters. This was quickly discouraged by the Secret Service.

The Feminine Mystique, Betty Friedan

Anna Karenina, Leo Tolstoy

The Age of Napoleon, Katell Le Bourhis

A Woman's Life in the Court of the Sun King, Duchess d'Charlotte-Elisabeth Orléans (gift from Michael of Greece)

The Roosevelt Family of Sagamore Hill, inscribed by Joseph P. Lash

Preface à Sumer, André Malraux

ON MARILYN'S BOOKSHELF

Contrary to popular perception, MM was a wide and varied reader and had more than four hundred books in her personal library, covering art history, psychology, philosophy, literature, religion, poetry and gardening. In 1945, she had a library card from the Westwood Public Library and opened her first charge account at a bookstore in 1946. In 1951, Marilyn even took a night course at UCLA, "Backgrounds in Literature."

After she became famous, she had friendships with literary greats such as T. S. Eliot (they had a long-running correspondence), Carl Sandburg and Marianne Moore.

Some of her favorite authors included Fyodor Dostoyevsky, J. D. Salinger, George Bernard Shaw, Walt Whitman, Thomas Wolfe, John Keats. After her acting teacher Michael Chekhov died, she bought his library on an installment plan when she was just starting out as a contract player at Fox Studios.

Browsing among her library would make any English major's heart beat just a little faster (well, more than a little).

Among the first editions was her own copy of the beat-generation classic *On the Road* by Jack Kerouac, Ralph Ellison's *The Invisible Man* and William Styron's *Set This House on Fire*. There was also F. Scott Fitzgerald's *The Great Gatsby*, Lewis Carroll's *Alice's Adventures in Wonderland*, James Joyce's *Dubliners*, Ernest Hemingway's *The Sun Also Rises*, and *The Fall* by Albert Camus. Her library also contained her bibles and children's books, including (our personal favorite) *The Little Engine That Could*.

Other books in MM's library included:

Psychology of Everyday Life, Sigmund Freud

Life Among the Savages, Shirley Jackson

The Importance of Living, Lin Yutang

Goodnight, Sweet Prince, Gene Fowler

Greek Mythology, Edith Hamilton[6]

The Course of My Life, Rudolf Steiner

Stanislavsky Directs, Michael Gorchakov

Lust for Life, Irving Stone

To the Actor, Michael Chekhov

The Thinking Body, Mabel Elsworth Todd

The Web and the Rock, Thomas Wolfe

An Actor Prepares, Kostantin Stanislavski

---

6 Interestingly, JKO gave RFK this book after JFK died to try to help him make sense of the tragedy.

Autobiography of Lincoln Steffens

Science and Health with Key to the Scriptures, Mary
    Baker Eddy

Biography of Eleanora Duse, William Weaver

Your Key to Happiness, Harold Sherman

J+M GALS—LIBRARY OF TODAY

The Jackie of today is literary in the old-fashioned sense: She knows her Shakespeare, Yeats, F. Scott Fitzgerald, and Edna St. Vincent Millay (she knows, too, that Edmund Wilson was Fitzgerald's literary champion since their days at Princeton and that "Bunny" Wilson was madly in love with Edna Millay for years). Today, she would probably prefer real books to Kindle, although she sees the use of an e-reader when traveling abroad.

The Marilyn of today is also a great reader, but she wears her bookishness less obviously than the Jackie. Instead, beaux and admirers are surprised when they visit her home and see the piles of hardcover books (mostly heavy tomes on art, psychology and biography) strewn about. Sometimes, when she is having her picture taken, she will be reading a book, and this will surprise people, too.

HEREWITH, THE ABRIDGED (AND HIGHLY ARBITRARY) J+M
LIBRARY OF TODAY . . .

One Special Summer—A reprinted scrapbook that Jackie and Lee made for their mother and stepfather of their 1951 trip to Europe. Jackie was twenty-two and Lee was eighteen. Needless to say, they had the time of their lives: think *The Talented Mr. Ripley* without all the scary stuff.

The Prince by Niccolò Machiavelli—The JKO Gal has to learn to navigate the ways of the world somehow.

Reporting Back by Lillian Ross—On one level, JKO really wanted to live a life of adventure and write for the *New Yorker*.

History of Art by Anthony F. Janson—A doorstop; the Marilyn is working her way through it.

Anything written by Pema Chödrön—It might not help, but the JKO Gal is willing to give it a try.

The Gospel According to Coco Chanel by Karen Korbo—Of course she already knows most of this stuff by heart, but the JKO Gal would read this to gild the lily, as it were.

The Best and the Brightest by David Halberstam—One of the few books that both the Jackie Gal and the Marilyn Gal would read. Those who do not know the sins of the past are condemned to repeat them.

Pools by Kelly Klein—Since the Marilyn Gal looks so great in a bikini. Or just in a bikini bottom if it is midnight and the pool lights are off.

The Official Preppy Handbook, edited by Lisa Birnbach—The Jackie Gal will skim this to see how "right" the authors got it, and all the inside stuff she already knows. Will then put it aside and never open it again, silently blessing the gods that got her away from that life . . . and those people. Very well written.

Anything by James Salter, Joan Didion, Stephen Colbert or Evelyn Waugh—Jackie, Jackie, Jackie, although MM will drop Salter's name to test her dates.

Angela's Ashes by Frank McCourt—The MM finds comfort in a childhood worse than her own.

The March of Folly by Barbara Tuchman—The JKO on a history kick.

The Happy Summer Days by Fulco—JKO, def. A society memoir, Verdura palled around with Chanel and Doris Duke *and* is the designer of some of the most gorgeous jewelry in the world—what more does a gal want?

Life at the Marmont by Raymond Sarlot and Fred E. Basten—The MM is visualizing herself poolside, getting discovered.

My Life With The Saints by James Martin, SJ—The Catholic Church is routinely battered and, well, the JKO (no surprise) is friends with Fr. Martin.

The Odyssey translated by Robert Fagles—The MM reads this one for self-improvement, etc.

Zelda by Nancy Milford—Poor Zelda. This one makes the MM cry every time.

Extremely Loud and Incredibly Close Jonathan Safran Foer—JKO, def.

Mastering the Art of French Cooking by Julia Child, Louisette Bertholle and Simone Beck—The Jackie would have this in her kitchen, just to show off.

The Secret History by Donna Tartt—For the MM, a book *everyone* was reading one season.

Napoleon & Josephine by Evangeline Bruce—Sigh. The Jackie would move to France in an *instant*.

Sophie's Choice by William Styron (signed)—JKO met him once at a party and never recovered. . . . and have you seen his sons?

Collected Poems by Robert Penn Warren (signed)—MM met *him* at a party and instantly fell in love.

Dead Poet's Society (script)—Memorized by the Marilyn Gal. Carpe diem and all that.

The Estate of Jacqueline Kennedy Onassis, April 23–26, 1996, Sotheby's—As if she needs more inspiration, the Jackie Gal uses it for future reference.

The Marilyn will also read tons of movie books—bios of Billy Wilder, James Dean, Barbara Stanwyck, Joe Eszterhas, *You'll Never Eat Lunch in This Town Again* by Julia Phillips, *Inside "Inside"* by James Lipton, *The Last Tycoon* by F. Scott Fitzgerald, *The Kid Stays in the Picture* by Robert Evans, *Vanity Fair: The Portraits* by Graydon Carter.

Lovingkindness by Sharon Salzberg—The Marilyn, because she's *got* to start being kinder to herself and stop being such a perfectionist. (She's trying, but honestly, it's not really working.)

The Balthazar Cookbook by Keith McNally—The Jackie's. Spine has never been cracked.

J+M MIND-SET: HEAD GAMES

When the situation called for it, Jackie was very disciplined, while Marilyn was, shall we say, whimsical.

If something was bothering JKO (whether it was her husbands' infidelities, a situation she did not like, a person who was bothering her), her basic MO would be to ignore it. Or them.

When Martha Stewart got herself invited to have lunch with Jackie and a Doubleday coworker in Los Angeles in the mid-1980s, Martha (for whatever reason) was almost an hour late.

An hour late. For lunch. With Jacqueline Kennedy Onassis.

Did Jackie say anything? Did she ask why the then-largely unknown Martha Stewart was late? Did she care?

No. Instead, Jackie never could remember Martha's name when it came up after that, referring to her as "that pretty girl. . . ." And she made it clear that she could never figure out what the heck Martha did for a living, anyway—didn't people already know how to put cookies on a decent plate or flowers in a vase?

Both Jackie and Marilyn presented themselves to the world as they wanted to be seen. When she was dating, Marilyn quickly realized that men liked a "happy" girl; they didn't want to hear her troubles. So the "real" Marilyn—the public Marilyn—was a bit of a subterfuge. But this is how she decided to be.

Similarly, Jackie's strength of mind helped her to consciously create herself as she wanted to be; for example, as a woman in a loving, solid marriage to JFK. While he may have loved her in his own way (he admitted, "I'm just not a flowers and candy guy"), they never did have a middle class, monogamous,[7] "Honey, I'll be home for dinner at six," kind of relationship.

Jackie, like Marilyn, was essentially an actress. Priscilla Mc-Millan, a friend of JFK's, once said of Jackie: "I always felt from the first moment I met her that I was in the presence of a great actress." JFK was a bit of an actor himself. He portrayed himself as robust and athletic, but in reality, he was a sickly child and as an adult suffered from Addison's disease, a chronic condition characterized by the withering away of the adrenal glands.

With the Kennedys, there were always boxes within boxes, secrets within secrets, and situations some knew about but others did not. Typical of the Irish, quite a bit was never discussed.

Interestingly, both Marilyn's and Jackie's favorite movie was *Gone With the Wind*. One thinks of Scarlett O'Hara's overall head-in-the-sand mentality and her mantra: "Tomorrow is another day."

IT'S ALL IN THE HAND: JACKIE VS. MARILYN

Although Jackie and Marilyn never met, Jackie was no dummy and certainly knew that her husband was infatuated with Marilyn Monroe (like the rest of the world). As an inquiring photographer for the *Washington Times-Herald* (before she even knew JFK), Jackie asked bystanders, "If you had a date with Marilyn Monroe, what would you talk about?"

But what if Jackie and Marilyn *had* met—and there is no evidence that they ever did, except in some *Weekly World News* alternative universe. Would they get along? What would their interaction be like?

To find out, we asked world-famous graphologist Arlyn Imberman to analyze Jackie's and Marilyn's handwriting.

· · · · · · · · · · · · · · ·

7 On JFK's part, anyway. There was never any marital scandal associated with JKO in this regard. Ever.

According to Imberman's assessment, "Jackie was a woman of mystery and great subtlety—a person of fortitude and discipline. Marilyn would, no doubt, be effusive and long for approval, which Jackie would delight in denying.

"Marilyn was a woman of spontaneity, anxiety and self-indulgence. Unlike Jackie (whose career was perfecting her persona), Marilyn had no insulation. They each had a separate public self, but Marilyn often blurred the lines between the two.

"Jackie's disdain would lower the room temperature, and with the movement of an eyebrow, reduce Marilyn to Jell-O.

"Marilyn believed elegance was excess; Jackie believed elegance was refusal. They were both canvases one could project one's fantasies upon."

 JACKIE'S FAVORITE MUSIC

Jackie loved all kinds of dance music and loved to dance—the twist, the cha-cha. In the 1960s, she took lessons in the frug and the watusi (ask your parents or grandparents) from society dance instructor Frank "Killer Joe" Piro. Jackie also liked Broadway musicals like *Candide* and *Camelot,* as well as anything by Leonard Bernstein.

Other favorites:

Meyer Davis Orchestra

1950s jazz

Miles Davis

Elvis Presley's "Blue Suede Shoes"

"The Girl from Ipanema"

"On a Clear Day You Can See Forever" by Alan Jay Lerner

Paul McCartney and Wings—JKO went to a concert and apparently loved it(!)

Carly Simon

In later years, taking a cue from her son John, she also liked the Rolling Stones and the Grateful Dead.

 MARILYN'S FAVORITE MUSIC

Marilyn loved music of all kinds—jazz and the blues particularly. She also, famously, personally integrated the Mocambo (a well-known Los Angeles club) in the 1950s by lobbying the owner to book Ella Fitzgerald and promising to sit at a front table every night for a week if he did so.

Frank Sinatra

Gertrude Lawrence

Gertrude Niesen

Janice Mars

Ella Fitzgerald

Charlie "Bird" Parker

J+M CHARACTER-BUILDING EXERCISE: GET OFF THE WWW ONCE IN A WHILE

Some words of advice to you, oh Jackie or Marilyn-esque Gal. Were they alive today, we think that both JKO and MM would be in the throes of a nascent (or not-so-nascent) Internet obsession because they both had somewhat addictive personalities.

We imagine that Jackie would be more of a www gal for her love of shopping (hello, giltgroupe.com!) and continuing interest in politics and world events, as well as reading books and trending somewhat toward excessive exercise habits.

Marilyn favored champers and daytime indolence; we think she would be more technology-averse. Today she would rarely read or send emails (and take pride in this) and would probably pay one of her assistants to program her iPod with her favorite music.

And then leave it in the back of a limo somewhere.

FUNNY GIRL(S)

Both Jackie and Marilyn were funny. We're not talking slapstick comedy, but funny enough that people commented on it.

(For some reason, people are always surprised when a beautiful woman is funny.)

Their humor—that most personal thing—reflected their personalities. Jackie was wry, a little bit cutting. Once, commenting to another friend about Pamela Harriman, who was part of their social set and made a point of only becoming involved with rich, powerful men who underwrote her lifestyle, Jackie described her as "a bit of a feeder fish." She also did devastating imitations of famous people after she had met them (Charles de Gaulle was apparently a favorite). In the White House, Tish Baldrige remembers, "She imitated people, heads of state, after everyone had left a White House dinner. Their accents, the way they talked. She was a cutup. Behind the closed doors, she'd dance a jig."

Marilyn was more winsome. Ambushed by reporters after she returned from Mexico, having gotten a secret-ish divorce from Arthur Miller, she said, "I am upset and I don't feel like being bothered with publicity right now," and then realizing that the reporters needed something quote-worthy, smiled and continued, "but I would love to have a plate of tacos and enchiladas—we didn't have time for food in Mexico."

Jackie scared you a bit with her humor. The head girl at school, she was that smart and unafraid and let you know it. Marilyn, with little guile, just wanted you to love her.

THE JACKIE PSYCHE: KEEP YOUR EYE ON THE PRIZE

Jackie kept her eye on the prize. Always. She was the kind of a gal who asked for a prenup and got the best attorney in town (or her former brother-in-law) to negotiate it for her, and then read the fine print. She noticed what gifts she received from her significant other on birthdays and Christmas (Valentine's Day, like Saint Patrick's Day and New Year's Eve, is for pikers). And while homemade gifts were encouraged from her nephews and nieces and her own children, the man in her life had better come up with something major in a small leather box—say, Van Cleef & Arpels or Harry Winston. Securities, land and Impressionist paintings also made good gift ideas.

For Jackie, money, and the security it brings, was paramount.

A true Leo, the Jackie Gal is a winner. This is how she was raised. This is what is expected of her and, truth be told, how she sees herself. In Jackie's case, perception is reality, and she does not suffer too many bouts of uncertainty or self-pity. In general, the Jackie thinks she is pretty terrific and is not surprised to find that the world does, too.

THE MARILYN PSYCHE: YOU ARE DESTINED TO BE A STAR

Marilyn was noticeably more vulnerable than Jackie (who had the essential tough-guy nature needed to thrive during life with the Kennedys). With the exception of abandoned puppies and kittens, she was practically more vulnerable than anyone.

For Marilyn, respect was more important than status, fame or money. She was more apt to take lost stragglers under her wing, fall for a sob story, loan money to her maid, give money to good causes (particularly those that helped homeless animals or orphans) and rework her will, leaving everything to her acting coach.

In her mind (regardless of her current celebrity or status), she was still the underdog. She would always be the underdog. And yet, she was a *star* with a capital *S,* and she knew it. She had beauty, talent and the desire to move beyond her humble beginnings to become her own glorious creation: *Marilyn.*

Whether an actress, accountant,[8] fashion editor or studying for the bar exam, the Marilyn Gal of today is always appearing in her own screenplay. A romantic comedy, a tragedy, a love story or somewhere in between, the Marilyn is always the star of that production called *My Life.*

As children, both the Marilyn and the Jackie Gals wanted to lead a big life, to be "someone." (Or at least create an impression while they are here.)

---

8 An unlikely Marilyn-esque occupation, we admit.

Surprising to those who know her, the Jackie Gal goes to a shrink and actually enjoys it. She is so closemouthed about pretty much everything going on in her life that her friends can't imagine her confiding in anyone about anything. But she gets a secret kick out of her 50-minute, once-a-week session—she thinks of it like being on the *Charlie Rose Show* (sort of) and tucks away interesting stories and observations to share with the doctor.

Overall, the Jackie finds the whole process (i.e., herself) pretty fascinating.

She considered asking him to sign a confidentiality agreement (if she is not famous now, she is confident she will be in the near future) but decided against it; she didn't want to offend him.

The Marilyn (not surprisingly) is an enthusiastic proponent of psychiatry, and visits to her shrink are more like performance art. She loves going. To her, it's like a date, only without the dinner and candlelight (and the whole sex thing afterward, obviously). She loves being listened to with any kind of intensity and even plans what she is going to wear in advance (see? the perfect date). She would go five times a week, for hours at a time, if she could. She loves talking and thinking about herself. With all kinds of boundary issues (sometimes troubling, gen-

erally charming), the Marilyn practically wills her psychiatrist (Jewish, male, intellectual, happily married) to fall in love with her.

He might, but nothing ever comes of it.

YOU DON'T NEED AN IVY-LEAGUE DEGREE TO SHINE

Face it: After you are out of school for a year, it is sort of loser-ish to still be name-dropping about where you got your degree—*who cares!* If you were fortunate enough to ace the SAT and get a scholarship or have parents who underwrote the operation, that's great. We are all for higher ed, but frankly, some of the coolest people we know didn't even finish college.[9]

And Marilyn? No—Marilyn is not someone who went to college. She is someone who left home as soon as she could (whether literally or metaphorically).

Never stop learning.

Don't be afraid to ask questions.

Do your research. In this age of Google and the Internet, it's easier to check a historical figure, a fact, or the correct meaning of a word without having to haul yourself to a library and pull out an actual book. So there are no excuses for "not knowing" something.

Be taken seriously. Even if you are deeply sexy (and the Marilyns of today are), you should know your stuff. Because for even the prettiest supermodel, dumb gets old fast. If you are looking for a role model, think Christy Turlington—a supermodel of the 1980s and '90s who went on to become a human rights advocate, businessperson and graduate from NYU and Columbia University.

---

9 Bill Gates, Steve Jobs, Jann Wenner, three-quarters of Hollywood . . .

Secret Secrets—The Jackie:
Things You Might Not Know About Her

For such a famous person, Jackie actually loved being alone and relished her privacy. There was no entourage for her.

Secret Secrets—The Marilyn:
Things You Might Not Know About Her

In 1999, Marilyn's private library was sold in a record-breaking Sotheby's auction. The proceeds from this specific sale benefited Literacy Partners in New York City.

8 | *Jackie and Marilyn at Work: Professional Demeanor and Achievements*

"What matters is what you get up on the screen—the art."

—MM

. . . .

"My name is Jacqueline Kennedy Onassis, I am an editor, and I am now working on a book."

—JKO

$\mathcal{R}$egardless of how frothy she appeared on-screen, Marilyn was deeply intent on being an actress, a star—on having her own career and being taken seriously. As she put it, "My work is the only ground I've ever had to stand on." Unlike Jackie, she was not interested in money, per se, but the respect of her peers and the audience. "I want to be an artist and an actress with integrity. . . . I don't care about the money," she admitted. "I just want to be wonderful."

Perhaps because she was the wife of a beloved president or born on the right side of the tracks, Jackie (except for a slight dip in public opinion during her free-spending Onassis years) always had respect. Whether overseeing the restoration of the White House while first lady or working as a book editor in the mid-1970s until her death, she was as conscientious as a schoolgirl. She did not miss deadlines, and as an editor, she coddled her writers with the attention that most writers dream about.

Marilyn's one great dream was to be a movie star, to become famous, because it would put an end—once and for all—to the indignities she had suffered in her youth. Unlike Jackie, she did not marry for security (as she could have any number of times). But the possibility—that necessity of being an actress, of greatness, of being *known*—really drove her.

Both Jackie and Marilyn wanted a stable home life, and both dreamed of having children (because of gynecological problems, Marilyn was unable to bear children and suffered because of this), but both Jackie and Marilyn (on some level) also wanted to live a big life—an exciting life, too.

The Marilyn Gal of today would set her sights on what she wanted and go after it with the tenacity of someone with nothing to lose. While Jackie might be subtler in her direct dealings with power (as she could afford to be), at the end of the day, both Marilyn and Jackie would get what they wanted.

*M*arilyn needed to be a success. Even at the beginning, when she was just starting out on her first modeling shoots, she took it very, very seriously. David Conover, one of the first photographers who discovered her in 1944, said that he had never met anyone so driven.

"There was a luminous quality to her face," he recalled years later, "a fragility combined with astonishing vibrancy." He also said that he could not recall any other model so self-critical. Dissatisfied with anything less than perfection, Marilyn wanted every image of herself to be brilliant.

THE FAME GAME

"Fame will go by, and, so long, I've had you fame . . . it's something I experienced, but that's not where I live."

— MM

. . . .

"The sensational pieces will continue to appear as long as there is a market for them. One's real life is lived on another private level."

— JKO

Did either Jackie or Marilyn trust fame? Both of them, having known celebrity and its price and rewards, certainly knew the cost of it. As Marilyn observed, fame at the level she (and Jackie) experienced it almost turns a person into a thing. "It stirs up envy, fame does. People . . . feel fame gives them some kind of privilege to walk up to you and say anything to you—and it won't hurt your feelings—like it's happening to your clothing."

If a comparison were made, Marilyn was probably more purely ambitious for her own sake. She had to be. Having come from nowhere, she needed fame far more than Jackie, if only to give herself definition as well as a sort of stand-in currency for love and acceptance. A child of Hollywood, she remade herself more thoroughly than Jackie—from a neglected little girl named Norma Jeane Baker to the sexy, platinum goddess Marilyn Monroe.

In spite of the fact that she was "the most famous woman in the world," Jackie never considered what she did as particularly important; instead, she felt that what she had was almost reflected glory (whether these were her true thoughts or merely good WASP breeding, it is hard to say). As the daughter and wife of two famous men, Jackie never really felt that she came into her own until she worked as an editor in publishing. Once, swimming on Martha's Vineyard with her friend Carly Simon, there were helicopters overhead, and Jackie looked up and said, "Look, Carly—they must know you're here!"

But putting aside her disingenuousness—this is a woman, after all, who sent her maid out to buy copies of the *New York Post* and the *National Enquirer* and savored any mention of herself[1]—Jackie used her fame for her own ends, like when she wanted to restore the White House, for example, or save Grand Central Terminal from the wrecking ball. In other words, she wanted it both ways. She wanted to control her image and be able to move freely in the world, taking photographer Ron Galella to court (and winning) when he harassed her children, donning dark sunglasses—or using wigs, fake accents and disguises—to walk around New York City unmolested. But she also wanted to be able to use her fame when it counted, from attending a press conference to save Saint Bartholomew's Church from having an office tower built over it to her campaign to preserve Grand Central Terminal.

The first victims of the paparazzi era (and god knows what Marilyn would have been subjected to today, when lesser Monroe doppelgängers like Lindsay Lohan or Paris Hilton are endlessly harassed), both Jackie and Marilyn were exceedingly aware of the public "self" they presented, and they took pains to preserve it the way they wanted to. Sporty Jackie with her brown bob and dark sunglasses, mysterious as she smiled and walked quickly away. Marilyn in a white silk dress cut deep in front, bare legged, laughing over a subway grate, her skirt billowing up, thrilled by the sexual havoc she caused.

Whether wanting to become a movie star or save a historical monument, both Jackie and Marilyn used fame to their own ends.

. . . .

1 Once, when he was a boy, JFK Junior asked his mother to buy him an ice cream cone. She said no, she did not have any money. Throwing a slight tantrum, he said, "What do you mean? You're the richest woman in the world!" So yes, even her children knew of her reputation. [BTW, the tantrum didn't work.]

When Your Name Is on the Front Door, Everything Matters—
Jackie took her duties seriously. After JFK was assassinated, she was obsessed with the thought that America and the world would forget her husband. She devoted herself to protecting and promoting his legacy by building the JFK Library (originally supposed to be on the Harvard campus, it is now in Columbia Point, overlooking Boston Harbor), and by encouraging everyone in his administration, from heavies like National Secretary of Defense Robert McNamara to Larry Arata, the White House upholsterer, to submit to an oral history about their time in the White House. Currently housed in the archives of the JFK Library, these interviews are a vital research tool used to this day.

After choosing I. M. Pei, a then-unknown architect, to design the soaring building, Jackie devoted herself to fund-raising for the library. To everyone who donated $1,000, she sent a personal thank-you note.

And, of course, being Jackie, she would not really be involved in the library if she did not get involved in the aesthetics—and she was, down to the placement of the stones and sea grass around the building and even the recipe for the New England clam chowder served in the restaurant. When Jackie made site visits, workers were known to try to hide, she could voice her opinions so strongly. But then, if you visit the JFK Library today, the hand of JKO is everywhere—from the delicious chowder, to the beautiful grounds and even the small flower arrangements on each table in the café.

*P*rotect the Brand—MM was so proprietary about her own look that when she started filming *Bus Stop,* she became convinced that lesser costar Hope Lange's (in one of her first major roles) hair was competing with her own. The producer, director and her makeup team tried to convince her that she, Marilyn, was the true platinum blonde and Hope was a lesser blonde and therefore no competition, but MM was having none of it.

The Divine Miss M (in true diva style) shut down production for three days as the fair-haired Lange was progressively dyed darker and darker until she was a more earthbound brown.

The lesson? *Nobody* messes with the blonde.

Don't Sell Yourself Short—In work situations, take yourself seriously. In Monroe's day, movie stars did not appear on the small screen, except for a brief appearance she made in 1953 on *The Jack Benny Show,* when she was a rising star.

As her agent said to a producer pitching a TV idea for her, "Marilyn doesn't do television. If you want to see Marilyn Monroe, look at the big screen."

Although she may have had the very polite WASP manner of making sure other people's accomplishments were mentioned ahead of her own, Jackie was not a pushover. She always took herself seriously and generally accomplished what she set out to. Jackie was single-minded in her intention to make the JFK Library a world-class library and museum near a major research center at a time when there were only four other presidential libraries, located in mostly out-of-the-way American towns.

Behind her feminine veneer, she could be relentless in seeing that her vision was fulfilled. According to Charles Daly, director of the Kennedy Library Foundation in Boston, "She was not at all above giving very direct criticism when warranted." He recalls the day she visited the library building when it was under construction. She saw an asphalt driveway where lawn and trees should have been. "She called one of I. M. Pei's guys out and pointed to the asphalt," says Daly. "She nearly ate the guy for lunch. She could be very tough."

Today, thanks to Jackie's foresight and determination, the JFK Library is a renowned presidential museum and library that allows open access to researchers and also contains Ernest Hemingway's papers.

Stick to Your Guns—Jackie quit her publishing job at Viking Press in 1977 when they published a book titled *Shall We*

Tell the President? A political thriller, its plotline included an attempted assassination of Ted Kennedy.

Marilyn brought 20th Century Fox to its knees when she got them to agree to her unprecedented creative demands. It is a story worth telling in full.

Marilyn Monroe first met Milton Greene in 1953 when he photographed her for *Look* magazine. When they were first introduced, she could not get over how young he was. "Why, you're just a boy," she said to him.

"And you're just a girl," he replied. Something of a boy wonder, Greene had been taking photographs since he was fourteen years old and was renowned for his fashion and celebrity images.

Rather than the usual sexy, cheesecake images that other photographers took of her, Greene produced compelling, classic images that revealed her inner beauty. Marilyn and Milton became close friends, and when she told him of her troubles with her most recent 20th Century Fox contract (her salary for *Gentlemen Prefer Blondes* amounted to $18,000, while freelancer Jane Russell was paid more than $100,000), he agreed with her that she could earn more by breaking away from Fox.

They formed a new company: Marilyn Monroe Productions.[2] He gave up his job in 1954, mortgaged his home and even allowed her to live with his family as they reassessed Monroe's career.

By 1955, Marilyn had left Hollywood and moved east, where she studied at the Actors Studio and ignored the studio's entreaties to re-sign her for such marginal terms.

Needless to say, the suits at Fox were not happy, particularly when *The Seven Year Itch* was released and was a huge hit—and they realized that Monroe was the studio's biggest asset, and in fact had generated most of its box-office income for the past two years.

The deal that Marilyn's lawyers and Milton Greene worked

. . . .

2 They would go on to produce *Bus Stop* and *The Prince and the Showgirl*.

out was groundbreaking for any actor, male or female. She received story and director approval, as well as approval of the cinematographer. Her contract also stipulated that she would appear in only top-notch productions, or "A-films." In addition, her salary was boosted to $100,000 per film *and* she was allowed to make films with independent producers and with other studios. It was a long way from the struggling contract player paid $125 per week.

Marilyn signed her fourth and final contract with 20th Century Fox on December 31, 1955.

Her contract was unprecedented, and Hollywood took notice.

No longer seen as just a bubbly blonde, Marilyn's victory over the ever-powerful studios made her a force to be reckoned with. Suddenly, everyone began taking her more seriously. In January of 1956, a year after some reporters had laughingly dubbed her "Bernhardt in a bikini," the Los Angeles *Mirror News* noted that "Marilyn Monroe, victorious in her year-long sit-down strike against 20th Century Fox, will return to the studio next month with a reported $8,000,000 deal. Veterans of the movie scene said it was one of the greatest single triumphs ever won by an actress."

"I feel wonderful. I'm incorporated."

—MM

MAKE SURE YOUR HEART IS IN IT

Marilyn took her work seriously, and because of this, she suffered to get it right. She was insightful enough to know she had this predilection. She admitted to Richard Merryman of *LIFE* magazine that she wasn't just punching a time clock, no matter what the studio thought best for her, "Successful, happy and on time—those are all the glib American clichés. I don't want to be late, but I usually am, much to my regret. Often,

I'm late because I'm preparing a scene, maybe preparing too much sometimes. But I've always felt that even in the slightest scene the people ought to get their money's worth. And this is an obligation of mine, to give them the best. When they go to see me and look up at the screen, they don't know I was late. And by that time, the studio has forgotten all about it and is making money."

So if Marilyn was dissatisfied with the production or the studio's support, if she threw the script on the ground in disgust or showed up on set hours late (if at all) and kept the leading man, and the director, and the set dressers, and the cameramen all waiting . . . it is not because she was thoughtless (she was not) but because she was almost too thoughtful. It meant too much to her. She wanted to do a good—no, a great—job. She wasn't phoning it in. It is *her* image, her face up there.

And that scared the heck out of her.

Whether it's writing a blog or learning her lines for acting class (or that big marketing presentation on Monday), the Marilyn of today cares.

As Marilyn Monroe said, "I used to think as I looked out on the Hollywood night, 'There must be thousands of girls sitting alone like me, dreaming of becoming a movie star.' But I'm not going to worry about them. I'm dreaming the hardest."

JACQUELINE KENNEDY ONASSIS, EDITOR

> "*Lady, you work and you don't have to? I think that's great!*"
> —NEW YORK CITY CAB DRIVER TO JKO

Although Jackie is most publicly known as the first lady of the United States or by her marriages to JFK and Aristotle Onassis, in reality, she spent the longest—and least publicized—part of her life as a book editor in New York City. For close

to twenty years, from 1975 through 1994, Jackie worked as an editor, first at Viking and then (from 1978 to 1994) at Doubleday.

Going back to work at the age of forty-six must have been daunting but ultimately satisfying for Jackie. For the first time since her school days and early work as a newspaper photographer in Washington, D.C., before her marriage, Jackie was not in anyone else's shadow. And although she was expected to use her renown to persuade other celebrities to write their autobiographies (some did, some didn't), she was also able to leave her public self at the door and be judged for her own abilities.

Having spent so many years in the public eye and never really wanting to be there, this must have come as a relief. As she admitted, "One of the things I like about publishing is that you don't promote the editor—you promote the book and author." To that end, she worked closely with proofreaders, designers and marketers. She even wrote personal notes to booksellers to help promote her titles.

No surprise to those who knew her, Jackie was a collegial coworker. She made coffee, went on company picnics, sat on the stairwell during fire drills and was accessible to everyone within the company. She created her own family within Doubleday, sending her assistant, Scott Moyers, to her doctor when he wasn't feeling well and scolding him for coming to work with wet hair and not wearing a hat in the winter—even getting him Theraflu and leaving it on his desk when he was sick.

But still, no matter how she tried to be just one of the gang (and she was, most of the time, bringing sliced-up carrots and celery wrapped in foil to snack on), let's be honest: She was still Jackie O. An editor from *Rolling Stone* was visiting her office, as the magazine was thinking of serializing one of her authors. She opened her desk drawer, and there were about a dozen pairs of dark sunglasses in it. After Jackie called a publishing friend and left a voicemail on his phone, he saved it for years and played it for all his friends. When she visited a national magazine, she was the only person who did not have to sign the receptionist's log, as people stole the page she signed on.

Jackie was a natural editor. Intellectually curious, widely read and with an impeccable eye for what worked on the printed page, she had always loved books and authors. According to a friend, JKO had "an unrelenting desire to observe new things." Now she was paid to share her interests with others.

"What I like about being an editor," she admitted, "is that it expands your knowledge and heightens your discrimination. Each book takes you down another path."

For her writers, Jackie was a dream editor. She photocopied pages of research, tracked down hard-to-find books and delivered them to her authors to help with the manuscript. She called John Loring, a friend and design director at Tiffany, late at night to see how he was holding up, knowing he was on deadline. She did meticulous line edits, knowing that the copy editors would catch any glaring mistakes, but she wanted the manuscript to be perfect. If possible, she cared about her authors' books as much as they did, and maybe more.

Ultimately, Jackie seems to have gotten as much out of working as her writers, coworkers and Doubleday got out of her. If anything, she almost seemed grateful to have been given the opportunity to use her mind and expand her horizons even further. "This is the definition of happiness," she said of being an editor, " 'complete use of one's facilities along the lines leading to excellence in a life affording them scope.' . . . We can't all reach it, but we can try to reach it to some degree."

Jackie continued working at Doubleday until the spring of 1994, just weeks before she died. "I think that people who work themselves have respect for the work of others."

JACKIE AND JACKO

Yes, Jackie knew Michael Jackson. Although the media (for some reason) never made much of it at the time.

Part of her job at Doubleday was asking celebrities who might never otherwise consider an autobiography to write one for her.

Considering that she ran away from any reporter or journalist who tried to get her thoughts down on paper, Jackie was pretty shameless—pitching Diana, Princess of Wales, her nemesis Camilla Parker Bowles, her former flame Frank Sinatra, even Oprah Winfrey.[3]

In 1984, MJ was riding high from the success of *Thriller* and agreed to write an autobiography for Doubleday. Well, he agreed to write a book specifically for Jackie Onassis, as he was a collector of celebrities himself. "Jackie was the only person in

---

3 Oprah countered by asking JKO to appear on her show. She said no (of course). Slightly off topic, Oprah once said that her two dream interviews were Jackie and Princess Diana.

America who could get him on the phone," a publishing friend recalled.

The manuscript came in, and "it was pretty bland stuff," another editor recalled, "almost a press release." Jackie the editor, the woman who loved gossip, wanted more concrete information—What was it like being a child in the entertainment business? What were his struggles? Had he encountered any prejudice? She wanted to see the real-life challenges behind his success.

Another draft came back. Still, pretty dull.

Jackie knew what she had to do. Rolling up her sleeves and doing her best, "Okay, now Mom's annoyed but we're on deadline so let's get going" routine, she flew to Los Angeles (a city she disliked, as she associated it with starlets and considered it a kind of playpen for the Kennedy men of her generation) and went directly to Neverland.

After a tour of the house (we would have given anything to be a fly on the wall for that experience), Jackie sat at Michael's baronial dining room table and went over the manuscript, clarifying her points and, again, asking for him to reveal more of himself.

For some reason, Jackie was obsessed with Michael's sexuality. Driving back to her hotel, she grilled her coworker— "What do you think he's like?" "Who does he date?" She even asked the limo driver—"Do you think he likes girls?"

The book was published in 1988 and was a great success, spending weeks at number one on the *New York Times* bestseller list.

Still, there was some annoyance with Michael on Jackie's part. He had agreed to publish the book with Doubleday only if Jackie wrote a glowing and lengthy introduction. Jackie did not want to do it and felt backed into a corner by him.

Taking one for the team, Jackie wrote a very perfunctory three-paragraph intro.

When it came time for the book to go back to press for another printing and later to go into paperback (where publishers stand to make most of their money with a successful book), Michael refused to allow it on both counts, really ticking off Jackie, who did not consider him a team player. After all, she had written that silly introduction he had insisted upon.

She rarely spoke of him again.

> *"Like everyone else, I have to work my way up to an office with a window."*
>
> —JKO

QUICKTESTS

The Marilyn Quicktest: Okay, okay, you do keep people waiting. But you're absolutely worth it. (And besides, no one has ever *not* waited for you, right?)

The Jackie Quicktest: You've never missed a deadline. Ever.

MARILYN KNEW WHO HER FRIENDS WERE

MM was very instinctive when it came to trusting people—whether directors, makeup men or photographers . . . or some guy who wanted to take her to dinner.

In 1962, Marilyn's lawyer arranged for her to have a new secretary, Cherie Redmond, to help with her business affairs. They had traveled together to Mexico to help MM buy furniture for her new house in Los Angeles and then to New York City. There must have been some sort of a personality clash in New York, because when she came back, Marilyn told her housekeeper, Eunice Murray, that Cherie was never to be allowed in her home. "She might be a good secretary . . . but she can't be one of my close friends."

Although Cherie was extremely capable of taking care of

the details of Marilyn's financial arrangements, MM did not want her getting too close. When Cherie needed Marilyn to sign checks, Marilyn would do the paperwork and have her housekeeper give Cherie any papers or checks at the gate of her home. For some reason, there was something Marilyn did not like about her.

"I don't want her advice on anything but business matters," she said. "Besides," Marilyn said, only half joking, "she drank up the last of my Dom Pérignon."

SO YOU WANT TO BE AN ACTRESS

Marilyn, even more so than Jackie, was one of a kind. Billy Wilder, who directed her in *The Seven Year Itch* and *Some Like It Hot,* said, "She had flesh which photographed like flesh. You feel you can reach out and touch it. Unique is an overworked word, but in her case it applies. There will never be another one like her, and Lord knows there have been plenty of imitations."

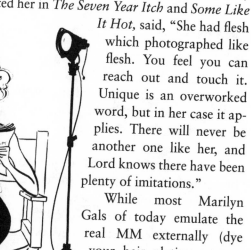

While most Marilyn Gals of today emulate the real MM externally (dye your hair platinum, wear red lipstick), some might actually want to *be* an actress. And although we know we can never dream of surpassing or even equaling Marilyn, here is some advice.

You need god-given

talent, and no one can give that to you. But desire is also essential. The problem today, of course, is that people want to be famous without really working for it, or they want to be famous for the sake of being famous (see most reality TV participants). According to her acting teacher Lee Strasberg, "Marilyn always dreamt of being an actress. She didn't, by the way, dream of being just a star. She dreamt of being an actress. And she had always lived somehow with that dream."

For Marilyn, the work is what mattered.

Study. Know your craft. Of course, the great thing about becoming an actor is that, like Buddhism, there are many paths to enlightenment—or Hollywood, as the case may be.

If all else fails, date a producer.

ON YOUR DAY OFF, DO SOMETHING OUT OF CHARACTER

Perhaps because they are so responsible (well, Jackie more than Marilyn, although Marilyn delivered the goods when she had to), we suggest that the Jackie and Marilyn Gals of today do something out of character once in a while.

Disappear

In this age of email, cell phones, Facebook and all-around Twitter ubiquity, it is cool to sometimes just disappear, if only for the weekend or a day. In a world where you are never untethered (and this is considered a good thing), it's not a bad idea to shut off all of your electronic devices and just think sometimes.

Flâneur

For the generally type A Jackie (with all of those demands placed on you), why not just go for a walk and do something you would not generally do for yourself?

Sit in a café.
Go for a stroll in the park.
Buy yourself a little something.
Make a dinner reservation for you and a friend.

Get yourself a manicure and a pedicure. This always
cheers people up.

For some reason, we think it would be funny for the Jackie
Gal to play "The Beatles: Rock Band" in her underwear (Hanro,
of course) or eat ice cream out of the container with a spoon.
Tell someone you love him (or her).
Expect nothing in return.
Iron your sheets yourself. Then enjoy them.

THE JACKIE GAL AS STEVEN SPIELBERG

The current-day Jackie Gal has a strong point of view
about pretty much everything. She can't help it; she just *sees*
things . . . the chair that is out of place in the living room, that
thread hanging off the hem of your blazer, the ice tray in the
freezer that needs refilling. Like, now.

And Jesus—don't even get her started on men who leave
the seat up. It is so far beyond her comprehension that she can't
even . . . (we imagine her sputtering here) . . . she can't even
deal with it. For her, this is very close to a deal breaker. She has
ended relationships over less.

Perfect Jackie career choices include movie producer, dicta-
tor and running a five-star hotel. A pure Leo, it is hard for her
to take a backseat to anyone. In spite of her cursory shyness,
she is not—has never been—anonymous. If she is in a room
with a group of people and there is a Q&A, she is going to get
her hand up and ask a question.

THE MARILYN SIREN AS QUINTESSENTIAL
ABOVE-THE-TITLE TALENT

Our Marilyn of today, on the other hand, is almost pure
emotion. An actress (even if she works as a partner in a law
firm), she feels things so intensely, it can almost seem painful
to an outsider. She reads books, certainly, studies art and music

and goes to museums to look at art. (The Marilyn observing a perfect nude sculpture as everyone observes her observing the nude sculpture is something to behold.) She has a flawless French accent that charms everyone, even as she barely speaks the language.

Almost unavoidably, the most successful Marilyn careers involve the arts: actress, painter, best-selling author, muse . . . and although she might work at her craft with great assiduity, it is not for the Marilyn to be stuck in a garret, alone all the time—after a certain point, she has to get out and see her people!

(Which she does.)

The Marilyn Gal has such an active imagination that you are not sure if some of the stories she tells you (about her childhood, her second husband) are 100 percent true, but on the other hand, you are in her company, so it almost doesn't matter.

To be the Marilyn's friend, to be her confidante (and possibly more), is a thrilling thing, something not soon forgotten. If you are with her, she shares great intimacies. Her beauty is one thing, her vulnerability is another. She weaves a web and allows you inside.

But regardless of her chosen profession, the Marilyn has whims, flights of fancy, mild obsessions—and then moves on. If you are a friend of the Marilyn, you must know this: Once she leaves you, she is gone. On to the next thing, the next experience.

The Marilyn (our Marilyn) doesn't take too many people with her. She can't afford to.

FACING THE CAMERA

No matter how easy—or hard—they make it look, being an actor has got to be terrifying. Especially if you take it seriously and are a perfectionist like MM was. Before she walked on set and faced the cameras, Marilyn would ask her makeup man to wish her luck and "save a happy thought for me."

JACKIE'S INTERPERSONAL RELATIONSHIPS

If you tell the Jackie something, if you mention a line even in passing, she remembers it forever (or at least for as long as you are in her life). If you give her a minute, she'll quote what you said back to you. Which is both impressive and annoying if you happen to be one of her siblings or married to her.

She doesn't flaunt it (well, not really), but the Jackie has an almost photographic memory. She reads something once, and it sticks in her head.

So you don't want to get in an argument with her. Not unaware of her power, she generally pulls her punches, unless she comes up against any kind of prejudice or small-mindedness—which drives her up the wall. Then the Jackie has zero compunction about giving it to someone higher up on the food chain if she thinks he or she deserves it.

MARILYN'S INTERPERSONAL RELATIONSHIPS

For her part, the Marilyn is more likely to use guile than a strictly linear thought process to win an argument. As a corollary, she has two fallback positions in response to any emotionally taxing situation: "cute" and "tragic"—as well as the less well regarded (in her mind) "flirtatious" and "sexual" (because that's just too easy for the Marilyn). In all honesty, the Marilyn knows she doesn't need to do much to get what she wants—aside from her sheer physical presence, we mean. When the going gets tough, all she has to do—really—is raise her eyebrow to get a response.

If all else fails, both the Jackie and the Marilyn know that they can burst into tears. This is especially useful if they get stopped for a speeding ticket.

DEALING WITH SUCCESS: DOES IT CHANGE THEM?

JACKIE—FOR A TIME, YES

Although Jackie was always her essential self and had a very strong core, it has to be admitted that she went a little bit off the deep end during her marriage to Onassis. Perhaps it was the freedom from America, from the Kennedys and their almost puritan expectations of her. Perhaps it was the ability to pick up the phone and get whatever she wanted at any time: a plane, her hair done, a massage, a necklace from Van Cleef, Robert Lowell over for lunch. But Jackie, it seemed, turned into Queen Jackie for a spell . . . with, perhaps, less regard for the millions of other "real" people in the world.

Once Onassis died and she returned to the rough-and-tumble workaday world of New York City, she righted herself and used her celebrity not purely for her own sybaritic enjoyment but for the good of others through her friendships, her work in historic preservation and the JFK Library.

MARILYN—NO

For better or worse, success changed the essential Marilyn very little. "I'm the same person," she once said. "It's just a new dress."

If anything, she was a bit suspicious of fame, seeing it as a burden. "I mean—they're going to take pieces out of you. I don't think they realize it—grabbing pieces out of you, and you—you want to stay intact. . . . They think they can walk up and ask you anything—I guess they think it's happening to your clothing or something." And while she enjoyed the attention of her fans, knowing it went part and parcel with being a movie star, it also frightened her at times. "The public scares me, like mobs—they scare me, but people individually, they react and you react to them. That's something you can trust."

If anything, she was aware of the cost of success and once admitted, "If I had a child, I wouldn't want a child of mine to go through what I went through. . . . Fame is fickle. It stirs up envy—'Who does she think she is—Marilyn Monroe?'"

MARILYN AS GIFT GIVER

Having grown up poor, Marilyn appreciated a small, velvet-lined box. She was not "crafty" (other than a stunning ability to put on her eye makeup herself), did not do needlepoint or scrapbooking or bake apple pies.

However, she was exceedingly generous—almost excessively so—with those closest to her. She was capable of handing over a Mikimoto pearl necklace (a gift from the emperor of Japan when she was on her honeymoon with Joe DiMaggio) on the spur of the moment to Lee Strasberg's twelve-year-old daughter, Susan, who was feeling ugly that day. Or, in her will, leaving one-quarter of her estate to her psychoanalyst, Dr. Marianne Kris, "for the furtherance of the work of such psychiatric institutions or groups as she shall elect" and the bulk of her estate to her acting coach, someone she barely knew.

Like her acting choices, Marilyn made decisions based on instinct, however she was moved.

Above all, the Marilyn Gal of today longs to be loved, of course. She wants to be remembered. (Don't we all?)

> *"I think love and work are the only things that really happen to us, and everything else doesn't really matter."*
>
> —MM

MONEY, MONEY, MONEY

Jackie and Marilyn had very idiosyncratic—and opposing—attitudes toward money.

For all of her high-toned upbringing, Jackie was a bit crafty when it came to cash in ways that MM never was.

For starters, her mother ingrained in her the absolute importance of marrying "big time money," and by that we mean it wasn't enough to have a nice upper-middle-class married life but millionaire (or billionaire) status.

There were other ways she differed from Marilyn. She bought her New York City apartment, 1040 Fifth Avenue, in 1964 for $200,000, but everyone (it seems) kicked in the cash to help her buy it. Without knowing that others were also contributing to the apartment fund, RFK, Aristotle Onassis (he and Jackie were secretly seeing each other, but it was still on the DL), and even financier André Meyer all contributed hundreds of thousands of dollars to "help" her buy the apartment.

Marilyn, who was *poor* (and we mean cook-on-a-hot-plate-in-your-little-single-room poor), never accepted money from anyone.

Jackie also haggled with tradesmen, cooks, chefs, housekeepers and secretaries who worked for her. One favorite technique was to pay men who worked on her apartment (painters, for example) by check, knowing that they would never cash it but instead keep it because it had her signature on it. She would also offer to "pay" by giving them a signed photograph of herself. Eventually, word got around, and they asked to be paid in cash.

Like many women of her social class, Jackie raised "pin money" by selling her gently worn or extra designer duds to resale shops on the Upper East Side.

Although she was devoted to the JFK Library and did an amazing job bringing it to fruition, Jackie—like most of the Kennedys—was not known to give much money to charity.

Marilyn, as we have seen, grew up truly poor, but having money was not her overriding concern. Instead, she wanted to develop as an actress, to be taken seriously by the creative community, and help her friends (all of which she did). In fact, although she had less money than Jackie, she was far more generous. She donated $25,000 to JFK's presidential campaign. Pre–campaign financing laws, that was a lot of money in 1960 (when $10,000 a year was a very good salary for a white professional male) and a lot of money now.

She was also generous to those she loved. It is a little-known fact that when she was married to Arthur Miller, she paid for all of his legal fees when he had to testify before the House Un-American Activities Committee (HUAC), as well as his wife's alimony and child support for his two children.

Although it never appeared that Marilyn had any real inclination toward excessive personal luxury for herself, especially given how famous she was, toward the end of her life, it was said that she "spent money like a drunken sailor."

Jackie also liked to spend money—lots and lots of it—but it was always other people's money.

LAST WILL AND TESTAMENT: THE FINAL FRONTIER

JACKIE'S WILL

To those who know their estate planning, Jackie's thirty-six-page last will and testament is described as "elegant." She obviously gave her final affairs a great deal of thought. She made Maurice Tempelsman, her friend and companion of some fifteen years, the executor of her estate, and she left him a Greek alabaster head of a woman. To Caroline and John, she left $250,000 apiece in cash, her Fifth Avenue apartment and other property and personal effects, and money in a trust that she inherited from her first husband.

With an estimated $200 million in wealth, Jackie, with the aid of her attorneys at the New York law firm Milbank, Tweed, Hadley & McCloy, planned wisely.

According to *Fortune* magazine, Jackie's will made smart use of estate-planning vehicles like trusts to pass money on to heirs and charities while reducing the bite from the tax man. In the beginning of her will, she made specific bequests. Valuable items with sentimental attachment for particular people were duly assigned, such as a copy of John F. Kennedy's inaugural address signed by Robert Frost to her lawyer, Alexander Forger. Personal friends, maids and the butler got cash gifts ranging from $25,000 to $250,000. Property went to those who would get the most out of it—her kids got the New York apartment, but Hammersmith Farm, the Newport, Rhode Island, property she inherited from her mother, went to her stepbrother Hugh Auchincloss Jr. She also thought ahead and not only left her maid $50,000 but also arranged to pay the taxes on it.

In writing her will, Jackie covered all the bases and had the final word in her affairs. For example, she asked her children to respect her desire to keep her papers private.

And they did.

MARILYN'S WILL

Compared to Jackie, Marilyn's will was far more quixotic (shall we say) and not as well thought out.

When she died in 1962 at age thirty-six, she left an estate valued at $1.6 million. In her will, Monroe bequeathed 75 percent of that estate to Lee Strasberg, her acting coach, and 25 percent to Dr. Marianne Kris, her psychoanalyst. A trust fund provided her mother, Gladys Baker Eley, with $5,000 a year. When Dr. Kris died in 1980, she passed her 25 percent on to the Anna Freud Centre, a children's psychiatric institute in London. Since Strasberg's death in 1982, his 75 percent has been administered by his widow, Anna, and her lawyer, Irving Seidman.

Marilyn asked that her personal effects be distributed to her friends, but Lee Strasberg never fulfilled her wishes.

It is interesting—if a bit tragic—that Marilyn, who had no real family, left money for the care of her mother, to her psychoanalyst and her acting coach. And, ironically for a woman who cared little for money or material possessions, her image spins off millions of dollars in royalties every year.

But in truth, Marilyn Monroe (perhaps even more than Jackie) transcends any will or legal instrument.

SECRET SECRETS—THE JACKIE: THINGS YOU MIGHT NOT KNOW ABOUT HER

Jackie took her work very seriously. After all, her name is associated with it.

SECRET SECRETS—THE MARILYN: THINGS YOU MIGHT NOT KNOW ABOUT HER

Marilyn loved her work and felt lucky as hell to have it. She needed it.

9 : *Jackie and Marilyn at Home*

"I have too many fantasies to be a housewife. I guess I am a fantasy."

—MM

. . . .

"Jackie's house was such a refuge, so private, so beautifully done, simple . . . just perfectly in tune with the surroundings."

—HILLARY CLINTON

On the home front, Jackie and Marilyn are complete opposites.

Growing up rootless and on the outskirts of society, in an orphanage and in foster homes, Marilyn did not have much of a sense of what constituted a happy home life. Married three times, it almost seemed as if she was playing at being a wife and always searching for a home—finding it briefly with James Dougherty, Joe DiMaggio and Arthur Miller. After her final divorce, she created her own life with her makeup man, hairdresser and secretary (as do many stars), but it seems she was always searching, and she died without heirs and direct descendants.

Jackie's family meant everything to her. She was very proud of being a Bouvier—even more so, certainly, than marrying into the rowdy Kennedy clan—and she drew great strength from the fact that she "came" from somewhere.

Whether her "crooked little brick house" on N Street in Georgetown, the White House, her place on Fifth Avenue, or her getaway on Martha's Vineyard, Jackie's home was deeply important to her. Because of the extremely public life she was forced to lead, her home was a place of great solace where she could be with her children and those she loved.

While Marilyn could truly be described as a desultory housekeeper who was an anxious dinner party hostess, Jackie was a legendary hostess who regularly planned state dinners for two hundred guests as well as birthday parties for her children. And although she was not personally doing the ironing, JKO was a great homemaker who insisted on having her sheets changed twice daily in the White House, French wine at dinner, and fresh flowers in every room.

HOME NOTES

. . . .

JACKIE LOVED TO REDECORATE

. . . .

Jackie was a fastidious housekeeper—not that she physically did the housework herself, mind you—but she knew how to get a proper nurse's corner on a bed or the best way to hand wash delicate china.

Typical of a woman of Jackie's background, she expressed her true personality in the home through decorating. She had fun decorating (and decorating, and decorating) the first home she shared with JFK at 3307 N Street in Georgetown. According to her mother, Janet Lee Auchincloss, she redid the front living room three times in the first four months they lived there. "And how wildly expensive it was to paint things and upholster things and have curtains made," her mother recalled.

While JFK generally begrudged his wife nothing, he finally grew so tired of coming home and continuously seeing his home being repainted, repapered, the furniture rearranged or covered in canvas, that he had a fit—wondering why there wasn't one damn chair to sit down on!

But still, he had a sense of humor about it. When his in-laws came to the newlyweds' for their first dinner party (an event Jackie obsessed over as if Queen Elizabeth were attending), JFK asked his mother-in-law, "Mrs. Auchincloss, do you feel we're prisoners of beige?"

Until she became successful, Marilyn had none of the beautiful homes that Jackie did. Instead, her living situations were more weigh stations than proper homes—a succession of hotels and (when she was growing up) foster homes. After she became a star, she bought a beautiful apartment on Sutton Place in New York City and a home in Hollywood.

Interestingly (like JKO), she was very particular about whom she allowed into her homes.

Marilyn Loved Her Bed

Like many Hollywood starlets—well, like most of us in general—Marilyn loved her sleep. (Ava Gardner, for example, once attributed her beauty to fifteen hours of sleep a night. We think she was kidding.) As for Marilyn, "I suppose I have a languid disposition," she once said. "I hate to do things in a hurried, tense atmosphere, and it is virtually impossible for me to spring out of bed in the morning."

"On Sunday, which is my one day of total leisure, I sometimes take two hours to wake up, luxuriating in every last moment of drowsiness. Depending on my activities, I sleep between five and ten hours every night. I sleep in an extra-wide single bed, and I use only one heavy down comforter over me, summer or winter. I have never been able to wear pajamas or creepy nightgowns; they disturb my sleep."

As a miscellaneous beauty tip, Marilyn slept on satin pillowcases to preserve her hairstyle.

THE J+M WAKE-UP CALL

Neither JKO nor MM was a morning person. They came to life, really, after dark—think of hanging at Bemelmans Bar at the Carlyle, nightcaps, wearing a white silk evening gown by twinkling candlelight.

After she became a star, Marilyn suffered from insomnia and, toward the end of her life, often depended on prescription drugs—sometimes mixed with champagne or vodka, the only liquor she could tolerate—to help her sleep. She used blackout drapes to block the light and would often talk on the phone for hours with friends deep into the night if she was lonely.

While Jackie was much healthier than Marilyn, sleepwise, she, too, liked to stay up late. When she was a newlywed, living with JFK in Georgetown or in the White House, she had breakfast in bed and then had her secretary come in to give her notes and go over the day. If she got up earlier than usual to have breakfast with her children, she took a nap in the afternoon.

SLEEP RX

Can't sleep? No need to resort to the old-school starlet regime of an endless supply of Seconal and vodka. Instead, follow a few simple rules.

Make sure your bedroom is cool and dark. Use blinds or drapes to block the light.

No caffeine. No heavy meals late in the day. No alcohol.

Don't exercise at night, either. Experts say it will give you a burst of energy (good) and keep you awake (bad).

Get the television out of the bedroom. Your bedroom should be used for only sex and sleeping. Some experts say that you should not read in bed, but we disagree—your bed is one of the best places to read!

On a related note, get your laptop out of the bedroom. One friend's spouse taps taps taps away at it all night—extremely unseductive. Same thing with the BlackBerry. If you must keep it near, TURN IT OFF! Otherwise that blinking light will keep you up all night, wondering what important news/information/trivia/endless gossip you are missing.

Don't watch the evening news—too depressing—or read a scary book that will freak you out before bed.

Take a hot bath with some sea salts and a few drops of lavender oil to help you relax.

If you must take meds, try some natural sleep remedies from the health-food store, such as valerian and/or magnesium.

JKO FLOURISHED IN THE DRAWING ROOM

Although you might eventually end up in the bedroom, with her obvious intellectual strengths, the dining room or the library are equally compelling in the JKO lair. When she could, Jackie liked nothing better than lazing on the couch and reading, ignoring the phone. She also loved hosting dinner parties for friends or get-togethers prior to attending the theater or ballet.

Although Jackie knew how to give instructions to the cook, the kitchen was not her particular province. She once told an *I Love Lucy*–type story of attempting to cook a meal early in her marriage one Thursday night (cook's night off) and completely burning the roast. The kitchen was in shambles. She burst into tears, and her husband came home and wisely took her out to dinner.

Quicktest

The Marilyn Quicktest: Your home is the one place you feel safe. You could spend hours in your bedroom. And often do.

The Jackie Quicktest: Whether you live in a studio or a mansion, your home reflects your personality, and people love visiting and seeing how you live.

J+M LOUNGEWEAR

Although Marilyn couldn't bear to wear an actual nightgown to bed, she had lots of very beautiful negligee "sets," as they used to be called. Many of them were handmade and embroidered by Juel Park Lingerie in Hollywood (a shop that still exists).

Jackie preferred delicate white cotton nightgowns in Irish linen or very fine Hanro Swiss cotton.

Today's J+M Gals can wear your (current or former) boyfriend's V-neck T-shirt (white only)—either Hanes or Brooks Brothers three-pack. As with a pearl necklace, the more you wear it, the better it looks. Plus, any future beaux will wonder about its provenance.

In real life, Marilyn had the most beautiful feet imaginable and even got away with wearing those goofy marabou slippers at home. She took such good care of her feet, they were almost as graceful as her hands.

For Jackie at Home, there are moccasin slippers from L.L. Bean (on her, they actually look sort of chic). Delman ballet slippers. She had large-ish feet that she took very good care of but still was somewhat self-conscious about.[1]

The Jackie/Marilyn Gal of today will often go barefoot at home, great for her foot health and also rendering her vulnerable to those who don't know her too well (a rarely expressed sentiment for the Jackie Gal). Her pedicure (either red or the newly chic nude nail polish) will quietly intrigue male visitors, since she rarely takes her shoes off in public.

JACKIE AND MARILYN IN THE KITCHEN

Here's a little J+M secret—the fact that you are even allowing him into your home means you don't really need to cook anything. With Marilyn, especially, all she had to do was appear—she was the kind of gal who men didn't expect to slave away in the kitchen. She brought enough to the table by just showing up. So if she tried to do something—anything—culinary, they thought it was adorable.

But you know what? Having said that, here's another little-known fact: Marilyn was actually a pretty good cook. Compared to Jackie, she was actually a *very* good cook (which is not saying much).[2] Her typical fare was 1950s—meat and

. . . .

1 Prior to her marriage to JFK, her future sister-in-law, Ethel Kennedy, once made fun of her size-10 feet, calling them "clodhoppers." Not nice.
2 In later years, when JKO stayed at Mrs. Mellon's cottage in Middleburg during fox-hunting season, she discovered Lean Cuisine and raved about it.

some vegetables on the side, Mexican sometimes, nothing too exotic, something our parents might have grown up on. As a *People* magazine reporter observed, "She was a good cook. It was hard for her to go out so she cooked." She even had a twelve-piece Le Creuset pot set, which is something only real foodies would own.[3]

For a dinner party at Marilyn's, there might be scrambled eggs on toast and shrimp with cocktail sauce from a jar (ladled into a nice china bowl, obviously). Although fancy cooking is not her main forte, Marilyn is really great at presentation, in much the same way that she puts outfits together with such élan.

We have also seen her handwritten recipe book, filled with recipes from (among others) her masseure, Ralph Roberts. She loved Mexican food, and we tracked down one of her cookbooks—*Elena's Favorite Mexican and Spanish Recipes* (1950), a much-used, wire-bound paperback version. Unfortunately out of print, it can be picked up online at places like alibris.com.

FIELD NOTES: HOSTING A DINNER PARTY: JACKIE VS. MARILYN STYLE

When it comes to floating through life with the social graces, Marilyn had Jackie beat, because frankly, she didn't *care* about social graces. Marilyn knew that even in the stuffiest situations, she could rely on her sex appeal to get her out of a jam.

Compared to the doldrums of post–World War II America, Marilyn was an inventive homemaker. In the late 1950s, when she was Mrs. Arthur Miller and lived with him in Connecticut, she made homemade pasta, hung the noodles on the back of a wooden chair in the kitchen, and dried them with a blow-dryer. We have seen a photo of MM and Gina Lollobrigida "cooking dinner at home in Los Angeles." Lollobrigida looks as if she is actually checking a pot and manning the stove while MM is

3 It was later sold at a 1999 auction for $25,000 ($800 estimate).

posed in the doorway in a beautiful black cocktail dress. (The way we always imagine her.)

Similarly, as a Marilyn Gal, if you are hosting a dinner party and the duck a l'orange is charred to a crisp, take everyone's focus off the mishap and direct it toward *you*! For starters, slip on your marabou mules, turn up the music and do the rumba (or a mock striptease if things are looking really grim) in the middle of the living room. Then crack more ice and freshen everyone's drink.

*N*ow, on to the dinner party. For the Jackie Gal or the Marilyn Gal, the optimum dinner party male/female ratio is 6 to 1. Actually, we're kidding (a bit). Jackie was more of a stickler for arranging the table and would definitely have seated her guests boy, girl, boy, girl. But she would be certain to separate all the married couples, who are probably bored out of their minds with each other anyway.

Marilyn prepared for a dinner party the way she might for a date (or a job interview, or an audition—in her mind, they were all about the same thing), except on a slightly larger stage. This means the single most important thing is you, then your outfit. After that, it's the usual drill: manicure, pedicure and three days before the event, dye your hair platinum. All of it.

To prepare MM style, empty the ice trays into a bucket and refill. Put champagne on ice (you get three bottles to yourself).

Make sure the music is set. Arrange flowers in their vases a day or so earlier so the buds can open up. In the realm of housekeeping, Marilyn loved to vacuum, so you might want to do that for the heck of it, although, honestly, no man will notice if you vacuum or not.

Not surprisingly, Jackie was a perfectionist when it came to planning a dinner party. To her, it was all about details, details, details. Whether in the White House or in her private home, she planned above and beyond which course to serve first. The china: She had so many sets of china, she could have opened a shop, with everything from antique Chinese porcelain to English bone china to Belleek, given to President Kennedy when he visited Ireland in 1961, to Limoges. And then there was the Simon Pearce glassware she preferred at her home on the Vineyard, along with the more casual blue and white country Spode. The linen: She favored colorful Porthault or subtle Irish linen. Even which candles to use: dripless Cape Cod candles, generally white tapers, although red candles were used on the dining room table on Christmas morning.

If you were fortunate enough to be invited to Jackie's for a meal, you know she put more than a little thought into it.

She was equally exacting when it came to communications with the kitchen. Often she would write a note on lined yellow legal paper with items that needed improvement or had been overlooked. We have seen these communiqués, and they are genius in their randomness—"Sanka not hot enough!" "Please get the soufflé out early . . ." "Fresh orange juice—not frozen—for the children's breakfast."

If a dinner party went particularly well, she also wrote a thank-you note (again, handwritten on yellow legal paper) before she went to bed.

JACKIE'S DINNER PARTY MENU

For a buffet dinner in New York City during the winter, Jackie might serve poached salmon with green sauce, jambon persillée (a spicy ham dish), a Russian salad of grated celeriac or some other root vegetable, slices of paté, and a basket of good chewy bread.

She was also not averse to suggesting that someone in the kitchen pick up "a paper thin apple tarte from Zabar's" that would then be warmed and served with vanilla ice cream for dessert.

JACKIE'S DINNER PARTY MENU— MIDWINTER BUFFET IN NEW YORK CITY

Salade Russe

Sliced Pâté de Foie Gras

Jambon Persillée

Poached Salmon with Green Sauce

Chilled white burgundy, such as Puligny-Montrachet, or a California chardonnay, such as Kistler

GREEN SAUCE

For the sauce to work, all the ingredients should be at room temperature.

Mayonnaise

3 egg yolks
1 tablespoon lemon juice or wine vinegar
Salt and white pepper
Powdered mustard
2½ cups olive oil (or canola oil, if you prefer)

Greens

½ cup minced fresh spinach
½ cup minced watercress leaves
Minced parsley
2 tablespoons minced fresh chives
1 teaspoon minced fresh tarragon

In a warm, medium-sized bowl, beat the yolks with a wire whisk for a minute or two until they are sticky. Stir in the lemon juice or vinegar and salt, pepper and mustard to your taste, then beat just to incorporate (less than a minute).

Start adding the oil. Don't stop beating once you begin this process. Keep adding the oil bit by bit until half a cup of oil has been incorporated and the mixture is the consistency of a medium gravy. Then you can begin adding more oil, a tablespoon or two at a time.

Keep adding and beating until the sauce is the consistency you want. If it gets too thick, you can add more lemon juice or vinegar. To thicken, keep adding oil. You might not need to add the entire amount called for. Recipe will yield about 2½ cups.

Blanch the spinach, watercress, a little parsley for color, the chives and the tarragon in ¼ cup water, covered in a small pan. Simmer about 3 minutes, then press into a fine sieve briefly to drain.

Stir the minced greens into the mayonnaise. Serve with poached salmon.

MARILYN'S DINNER PARTY MENU

Marilyn's dinner party fare did not differ much from what she would eat on an average night. For a dinner party at home in Los Angeles, Marilyn would start with a simple green salad with sliced tomatoes and a vinaigrette dressing. She would then have a male guest (like her makeup artist, Allan "Whitey" Snyder) fire up the grill and cook either steak or lamb chops, served with creamed spinach and baked potatoes. When in doubt, be like Julia Child and put an extra dab of butter—real butter, not faux-healthy oleo-substitute—on everything.

MARILYN'S DINNER PARTY MENU— TWILIGHT SUPPER IN LOS ANGELES

Simple Green Salad with Sliced Tomatoes and Vinaigrette

Lamb Chops with Creamed Spinach

Baked Potatoes

Homemade Tangerine Ice Cream

Dom Pérignon or chilled vodka on the rocks with a twist

MARILYN'S FAVORITE TANGERINE ICE CREAM

1 cup sugar
1½ cups water
Grated rind of 4 tangerines
4 cups tangerine juice
Juice of 1–2 lemons

> *Boil the sugar and water for 10 minutes. Add the grated tangerine rind to the syrup while hot. Let cool slightly, and add the tangerine juice and lemon juice. Taste for sweetness and acidity, as the tangerines vary. Chill thoroughly, strain and freeze.*

MM's Hors D'oeuvres

For all of you aspiring Marilyns out there, her favorite hors d'oeuvres were cherry tomatoes filled with cream cheese and caviar. No matter how culinarily challenged you might be, surely you can try this at home and serve it at your next cocktail party.

A Typical Dinner at Home

Unlike Jackie, MM was a pretty simple eater. If you've ever watched *Mad Men,* you've seen what Marilyn might have for a typical "at-home" dinner with a friend. Out in Los Angeles, it might be charcoaled steaks, baked potatoes and a salad. Ralph would have a vodka tonic, and Marilyn would have champagne with a strawberry in it.

And actually, now that we think of it, Marilyn's very American culinary tastes were quite close to JFK's, whose favorite lunch, even in the White House, was grilled cheese and Campbell's tomato soup. As an antidote to Jackie's overly Frenchified outlook, he preferred Boston clam chowder (the cook in every one of his houses was instructed to always have a fresh batch in the refrigerator, ready to be heated), chocolate ice cream for dessert and a Heineken to go with it.

Jackie always had a cook and a housekeeper,[4] or in later years, a former nanny of her children's (Marta Sgubin) who

---

4 During the Onassis years, she had two round-the-clock French chefs onboard the *Christina.*

could cook, so she always had lovely, lovely meals cooked precisely to her specifications.

A Simple Dinner on Martha's Vineyard

When JKO was dining alone on the Vineyard, here are a few wonderful things that Marta whipped up for dinner.

Grilled Dover sole with chive sauce and lemon wedges, or veal chop without the bone.

To cook the veal, Marta would cut a pocket in it and fill it with finely chopped aromatic vegetables sautéed in butter. She then deglazed the pan with port or marsala and poured the sauce over the chop. If JKO was alone, she did not want a starch, so Marta made two vegetables (like many rich people, Madame liked her vegetables petite)—often julienned vegetables or cabbage and carrots sautéed in sesame oil or steamed broccoli and cauliflower.

And yes, this was JKO dining alone on the Vineyard.

The Jackie's Sweet Tooth

Today's Jackie Gal has a sweet tooth and is addicted to Fran's sea salt caramels and dark chocolate. She also picks up See's Candies when she passes through LAX. When campaigning with JFK, the real Jackie always carried a chocolate bar (in her case, Hershey's with almonds) in her pocketbook, in case they went hours between meals.

JACKIE AND MARILYN STOCK THE BAR

The first thing to remember is that neither Jackie nor Marilyn ever had to walk up to the bar and physically mix a drink herself—that was for the man hovering around, wondering how to make himself useful. Here are some bar essentials that JKO and MM would have kept around: vodka, gin, rye, whiskey, vermouth, bourbon, single-malt scotch, lots of white wine, fresh mint (for the southsides Jackie remembered from her deb years spent in Locust Valley), simple syrup, lemons and limes, club soda.

Incidentally, JKO liked to drink Perrier in small individual bottles. During parties on the Vineyard, they were kept in low wooden buckets filled with ice (one filled with Perrier, the other with Beck's beer for John and his friends), next to the buffet table.

. . . .

JKO + MM—Okay, They Drank . . .

. . . .

Although she occasionally drank vodka, Marilyn preferred champagne—practically daily, as it did not upset her stomach. Her favorite was Dom Pérignon.

After the German consulate general sent her a bottle of champagne, she sent him a typed note: "Dear Mr. Fuehlsdorff: Thank you for your champagne. It arrived, I drank it, and I was gayer. Thanks again. My best, Marilyn Monroe."

Jackie favored slightly more complicated drinks such as daiquiris, mojitos, and southsides, although white wine with ice—and cigarettes to help take the edge off—did in a pinch. JFK, who drank very little, nursed a scotch all night and enjoyed a daiquiri (the Kennedy family recipe was taped to the wall in the White House kitchen) or Heineken (the beer was not yet imported into the country, but his father brought it in specially from Holland). For this reason, Jackie and the rest of the Kennedys were—and still are—partial to Heinekens and daiquiris (served on ice in proper silver cups).

For the man in her life? A really good single-malt scotch (the most expensive you feel comfortable buying, or ask friends traveling in Scotland or Ireland to pick up a bottle for you). And for the nondrinkers? Perrier or Coca-Cola.

THE MARILYN CHAMPAGNE COCKTAIL

Both of these drinks are courtesy of our favorite bartender (and when we say bartender, we mean that he is a real, old-style mixologist) Dale DeGroff, James Beard winner and author of *The Craft of the Cocktail* and *The Essential Cocktail*. Jackie or Marilyn would have loved having this guy over for a party.

BIG SPENDER

Ingredients

> 1 ounce of your favorite añejo tequila
> 1 ounce Clément Liqueur Créole or Orange curaçao
> 1½ ounces blood orange juice
> Rosé champagne

Preparation

Assemble the first three ingredients in a bar glass with ice, and stir to chill. Strain into a chilled champagne flute, add champagne, and garnish with spiral of orange peel and a flamed orange zest.

 THE JACKIE DAIQUIRI

DAIQUIRI

Ingredients

> 1½ ounces light rum
> ¾ ounce simple syrup
> ¾ ounce fresh lime juice
> Thin lime wheel garnish

Preparation

Shake all ingredients with ice, and strain into a small cocktail glass. Float a thin wheel of fresh lime on top of the drink for garnish.

MARILYN DRANK WHEN SHE GOT BLUE

Marilyn got blue sometimes—it just came over her. It could be because it was raining, or because she saw a child crossing the street, or because it's Tuesday, or because of something she read in the newspaper—or for no reason at all.

Jackie drank when something really awful happened to her but then straightened out pretty quickly for three reasons:

1. **Incipient Alcoholism**—Jackie didn't want to end up like her nutty aunt (Big Edie) and cousin (Little Edie) Beale (every family's got 'em), who practically let their East Hampton estate, Grey Gardens, once the pride of the Bouvier family, fall down around them, causing a great public scandal. The neighborhood children called it "the witch house" for good reason. Local grocery deliveries (sardines, toilet paper, Ritz crackers, peanut butter, no real food) were left at the front door. It was beyond charming— the house was in such bad shape that documentary filmmakers wore flea collars around their ankles while shooting on the premises. Indoors.

   After her aunt's death (and yes, contrary to rumor, Jackie paid to have the roof replaced), the house was bought for millions by the celebrity media couple Ben Bradlee and his wife, Sally Quinn, taken down to the studs, and lovingly restored to its pre–personal income tax splendor. You can still smell the cat pee when it rains.[5]

2. **Vanity**—Have you seen those women in Florida who smoke and drink too much and sit out in the sun, and then they get age spots and those little lines

---

5 A little-known fact: JKO sent a monthly check to her aunt Edith Ewing Bouvier Beale (Big Edie) and cousin Edith Bouvier Beale (Little Edie). After her death, JFK Junior continued to do so.

around their lips (that you can see even when they're not smiling)? They look like they're well over eighty (and not in a good way) when they're barely pushing forty. Jackie didn't want to end up like them.

3. **Bum, Busted**—It's very easy to fall off a horse if you've had too much too drink. Not that Jackie knew about this from experience.

. . . .

THE MEDICINE CABINET

. . . .

In the realm of artificial stimulants, cigarettes, white wine over ice and B_{12} shots is Jackie, while the typical 1960s "Mother's Little Helper" triple play of Seconal, vodka and sleeping pills (sadly) is Marilyn. Champagne is both Jackie (who favored Veuve Clicquot) and Marilyn (Dom Pérignon '53).

JACKIE AND MARILYN AS HOUSEGUESTS

The Marilyn as Houseguest—First of all, even having the Marilyn of today in your home for the weekend would be a coup, so it wouldn't matter if she attempted to "help out." Although she could be counted on to get on the floor and play with the children or a new puppy, she would look at the dishwasher almost as if it were a foreign object.

However, the Marilyn will dress and look stunning for dinner (even if she has zero interest in clearing the table).

The Jackie as Houseguest—The Jackie Gal is a great houseguest in that she can do extremely specific things very well—things that generally have to do with her and/or will garner her some praise. She can make a mean cappuccino, bake chocolate chip cookies that everyone raves about or an amazing three-layer cake for friends' birthdays. If called upon, she can recite poetry at the spur of the moment, give a toast or head up a team for Pictionary.

After dinner, the Jackie will sit with the men and regale them with great stories of books she just read.

The Jackie wakes up every day with a plan, a schedule. In fact, she wakes up every day with a plan not only for herself but for those in her circle: her children, her husband, the kid who works in the Starbucks down the street. She can't help it—she's a Leo.

Having married a powerful man (or intending to), she is more attuned to history and her place in it. Being the behind-the-scenes overseer of a presidential library, for example, makes perfect sense to her.

The Jackie wakes up with a checklist practically next to her bed. There is staff to oversee, children to attend to, dinner menus to approve.

Today's Marilyn, on the other hand, is ruled almost entirely by whim. She wakes up practically every day and thinks: *What do I want to do today?* And then she does it.

Or not.

A midnight person, the Marilyn is a firm believer in black-out drapes, sleeping potions and eye masks. She takes her sleep seriously, claims to suffer from insomnia, and a perfect day is one in which she is not expected on set (or in the office) so she can wake up around noon.

Although she means well, somehow, one never imagines the Marilyn of today with children—it's too much! She is far too childlike herself to consider taking on an actual child. The Marilyn is not a morning person by any stretch of the imagination, and children, well, they like to wake up and be fed and bathed and clothed and spoken to sometime before noon. (Or so we have heard.)

Plus, children cannot be sent to the store to pick up cigarettes and French shampoo when you run out.

The Marilyn is circumspect about her own upbringing. She

may have had an unhappy childhood. There might be some vague, unnamed tragedy in her past that is never discussed in her presence (but which she uses to bring pathos to the screen and take to her bed when feuding with her director). She may suffer from unnamed "women's problems" that render her unable to bear children. She compensates by being overly protective of small, fluffy dogs, and she cannot stand unkindness (or prejudice) in any of its forms.

The Jackie, on the other hand, *loves* children. She lives for children. In some ways, it is a bid to repair her own childhood—which featured an overly strict mother and a generally absent father. The Jackie sees her relationship with her own children[6] as a way to correct this.

If Marilyn Had Been a Mother

While we have no doubt that the Marilyn loves her children, their upbringing will be a bit *lax*, especially when compared with our 21st-century, helicopter-mom upbringings of today. And while we are sure that the Marilyn loves the concept of having her own progeny (much as she loves the idea of being a brunette, cooking a four-course meal, or wearing eyeglasses in public), as a maternal figure, she is not so much neglectful as distracted. There are just so many other things vying for her attention: that new script delivered from the studio, a vase

6 And yes, she might be seen as a bit controlling by others, but nothing like her own mother.

of yellow roses on the windowsill, the Mexican bullfighter she met last weekend in Las Brisas.

Perhaps she is between roles, or trying out some new lipstick, or about to embark on her fourth marriage with The One! And there is such hope! Such optimism! Who has time—really—to think about permission slips and juice boxes?

Still, the Marilyn loves loves loves *loves* babies—and they love her, too. Babies are so cute and so photogenic—sort of like her.

Should the Marilyn decide to take the plunge of motherhood, she needs a large support staff. There is always a nanny (or two) standing offstage ready to attend to the little darling. Either that or the children, once they reach the age of reason (say, five or six), end up being the "mom." (See Judy Garland's children, Liza Minnelli and Lorna and Joey Luft.)

If you wonder what sort of a mom the Marilyn will honestly be, see how she treats her pets. None of her dogs are housebroken. They bark incessantly and sleep on the bed. If a dog causes too much trouble, it is given away to her makeup man or secretary. Among the pets, turnover is high, so it is better not to get too attached. (This causes underlying anxiety among her children because it sends the distinct message: "Shape up or you are out of here!" And they might be right.)

If Junior asks where Buddy went, the party line is: "He went to live in the country."

As a rule, the Marilyn's kids are shipped off to boarding school at an early age, say, four. The British had the right idea ("Just look what Choate did for Michael Douglas!"). If the school has a high celebrity-parent quotient and dauntingly high tuition,[7] even better.

. . . .

JACKIE AS A MOTHER TODAY

. . . .

The Jackie Mom of today is a great mother, just as—in real life—the actual JKO was.

. . . .

7 Le Rosey, for example.

The Jackie Mother is the cool mom, the one whose house all the other kids want to hang out at. (In fact, if they are having adolescent difficulties at home, they often do.)

A few minor quibbles with the JKO Mom of today—she can be strict with her kids. She does not mess around. You stand when she enters the room (old style!). You had better remember to write thank-you notes for Christmas and birthday gifts—and by that we mean on proper stationery and mailed to her, even if you are living in the same house, and oh yeah, you know she is going to be checking on the penmanship and commenting on it. She will read the note slowly, carefully, to make sure you manage the proper balance of being loving, witty and respectful (even if you are ten years old) all at the same time.

As the offspring of the JKO Mom, there is no free ride. You are expected to get good grades, dress properly for public events (Mass, memorial services, etc.), shake hands and look guests in the eye when you are introduced to them. If you gain more than four pounds, slouch, or—god forbid—don't use proper manners at the dinner table, you are going to hear about it.

But on the other hand, don't think that the JKO Mom demands any less of herself.

But most of all, as a child, you are aware of your place in the stratosphere as the offspring of a JKO Mom. ("To whom much is given, much is expected," etc.) So if you screw up— total the car, get caught in some nefarious act, end up on the front page of the *New York Post*—it is not so much the public humiliation or even possible police record that will cause you to think twice about your actions, but more strongly, "Wow— Mom is going to be ticked off when she hears about *this*," that will keep you in line.

In real life, Jackie was a great mother. She encouraged her two children, Caroline and John, to follow their own interests, but then also had high expectations of them both. She tried to shield them from the psychic weight of being the offspring of two famous people, and in particular a beloved American president. After the death of JFK, she considered being a mother her most important calling, saying, "If you bungle raising your children, I don't think whatever else you do matters very much."

According to Ted Kennedy, "Her love for Caroline and John was deep and unqualified. She reveled in their accomplishments, she hurt with their sorrows. At the mere mention of their names, Jackie's eyes would shine brighter and her smile would grow bigger."

JFK Junior loved his mother deeply and knew that she loved him. But still, he needed to blow off steam once in a while, away from the far-reaching (but very well intended) gaze of his mother.

He did this by dating supermodels—lots of them.

Or by hopping on a plane to Memphis, renting a car and heading down to the Delta where nobody knew him. There, he hung out in exceptionally divey juke joints, stayed in a crummy motel in Clarksdale, danced (he was an exceptionally cool dancer, not like some prepster from Brown), drank beer from the bottle and listened to the blues.

No one bothered him there. No one looked at him twice. Most didn't know who he was. He loved it.

While she had expectations for her children (she frowned on John's vague plans of becoming an actor and did not approve of his dating Daryl Hannah or Madonna; for her, it was law school, and then he could figure out what he wanted to do with his life), Jackie also wanted her children to be their own people. When Caroline married Edwin Schlossberg in 1986, she did not make a move to influence her choice in a wedding gown. According to Carolina Herrera, a friend who designed the gown, "Jackie did not interfere with Caroline's wedding dress—'I'm not going to get involved because Caroline is the one who will wear it. I want her to be the happiest girl in the world.' "

According to her friend Charles Whitehouse, Jackie was a great mom because "she never said anything bad about someone else. Never even suggested things in a subtle or snide way . . . she was completely unjudgmental when discussing other humans and their difficulties. It was clear when she disapproved of an action, but she sympathized with people with problems."

J+M: LES CHIENS AND OTHER PETS

"I like animals. If you talk to a dog or a cat it doesn't tell you to shut up."

—MM

Jackie and Marilyn both loved animals, perhaps because animals were loving and depended on their humans. Perhaps because they would never ask for an autograph or sell them out to the *National Enquirer*.

Both, incidentally, were dog people.

Jackie owned a lot of animals throughout her life. A *lot*. As a two-year-old, she owned Hootchie, a black Scottish terrier (and showed her at the East Hampton dog show). There was the beloved Danseuse, her first horse, that she brought with her to boarding school, now buried on the grounds of the Auchincloss "farm" in Newport. In the White House, there was a menagerie of animals—Charlie, a Welsh terrier; Tom Kitten, a cat; and Robin, a canary. There were two parakeets, Bluebell and Marybelle, and Caroline's pony, Macaroni. There were also ponies, Tex and Leprechaun, and hamsters, Debbie and Billie. There were lots of other dogs, among them Clipper, a German shepherd (once, asked what he ate, Jackie grinned and said, "Reporters"); Pushinka (a gift from Khrushchev), Shannon and Wolf, which were gifts from friends in Ireland. As well as the puppies of Pushinka and Charlie—Butterfly, White Tips, Blackie and Streaker.

In New York City, the pet population was cut back considerably; Shannon, the Irish spaniel, stayed on, and his son Whiskey also joined the household.

Marilyn had her own share of pets throughout her life, mostly dogs.

Tippy was a black-and-white dog given to Norma Jeane/

Marilyn by her foster father, which accompanied her to school each day. When Norma Jeane lived with the Goddard family in the 1940s, she had a pet spaniel. Marriage to Jim Dougherty brought her a pet collie named Muggsie. At the time she was signed by Columbia Pictures in 1948, Marilyn owned a pet Chihuahua. When she moved to New York City in the mid-1950s, she had a white Persian cat named Mitsou.

Marriage to Arthur Miller brought Hugo, a basset hound who lived with them at their East 57th Street apartment in New York. Once, playwright Norman Rosten and Marilyn spoon-fed straight scotch to Hugo to cheer him up. When Marilyn and Arthur split up, Arthur retained possession of Hugo. Butch was a parakeet owned by the Millers who also lived at the 57th Street apartment.

Ebony was a horse that the Millers purchased for their Connecticut farm. MM only rode Ebony a few times.

Finally, there was Maf, a little white French poodle that was given to Marilyn by Frank Sinatra. Sinatra had purchased the dog from Natalie Wood's mother, and Marilyn named the dog Maf (as a joke) because of Frank Sinatra's alleged mafia connections. To spite Arthur Miller—boy, this is when you know things are not going well in a marriage—Marilyn used to let Maf sleep on an expensive white beaver coat that Miller had given her. When Marilyn returned to live in Hollywood, Maf went with her. Following her death, Maf was inherited by Frank Sinatra's secretary, Gloria Lovell.

MARILYN'S MARIAH'S WHITE PIANO

As a young girl, Marilyn's mother, Gladys, owned a white baby grand piano. After Gladys was institutionalized, the piano was sold, and Marilyn was separated from her mother. Unlike Jackie, Marilyn (and her mother) did not have many possessions, so the piano obviously had great sentimental value for her. Once she became famous, she took over the care of her mother and hired detectives to track down the piano and buy it back for her.

It took them years to find it, but once they did, Marilyn kept it for the rest of her life (most recently in her New York City apartment on Sutton Place).

After her death, it was bought at auction in 1999 by Mariah Carey, who owns it today, for $662,000.

J+M HOUSEKEEPING TIP

Jackie and Marilyn were both pack rats—they kept everything. Jackie, perhaps more than Marilyn, was mindful of her place in history, and before she died of cancer at the age of sixty-four in 1994, sat in front of a roaring fire in her New York City apartment with her friend Nancy Tuckerman, reading personal letters she had received from friends and former lovers, then burned them one by one.

Fortunately for us, Marilyn did not have Jackie's same foresight. In 2009, almost forty years after her death, two metal filing cabinets belonging to her surfaced, containing receipts from places like JAX, the Ritz Fur Shop on West 57th Street in New York City, Bloomingdale's, letters, old checks, mash notes from T. S. Eliot.

On the plus side, both Jackie and Marilyn had historic sales of their extraneous stuff after their deaths. Jackie's took place in April 1996 and allowed a rare glimpse into her personal world. With more than one thousand lots, there was a ton of items ranging from Greek antiquities to silver "JBK"-engraved ashtrays. And all of it sold. The four-day sale raised an astonishing $34.5 million and showed the sentimental connection many people still felt for Jackie and JFK—JFK's golf clubs, for example, went for $1,160,000. A triple-strand faux-pearl necklace went for $211,500.

In October 1999, in what it billed as the "Sale of the Century," Christie's auctioned off about five hundred items that Marilyn left to Lee Strasberg, her late acting teacher, which then passed on to his wife, Anna. The sale was controversial because Marilyn intended for her personal effects to be distributed by Strasberg to her friends. Instead, they had been in storage since 1962. Many fans were offended because they believed that Marilyn's things belonged in a museum rather than sold for Strasberg's personal gain. Still, fans came out for Marilyn, and prices, while not in the Jackie stratosphere, were high. Tommy Hilfiger, Demi Moore, supermodel Linda Evangelista all bid. Massimo Ferragamo, chairman of the design company, bought a pair of red stiletto Ferragamos for $42,000. "A bargain," he declared. All told, the sale brought in $5,030,000.

SKORPIOS FOR SALE?

At the time of Jackie's marriage to Onassis in 1968, society scuttlebutt was that "she married him for the island." (And she did, in a way, to remove herself from the increasingly turbulent and violent American society at that time.)

In 2009, one wild rumor hit the real-estate world that Skorpios, Onassis's private island, was for sale for $170 million—and that Bill Gates, Madonna and Russian billionaire Roman Abramovich were interested in buying it.

While island owning is somewhat de rigueur for celebrities today—Marlon Brando, Leonardo DiCaprio and movie pirate Johnny Depp have their own islands (Depp privately refers to his as "F**k Off Island"), as do Faith Hill and Tim McGraw and even Tony Robbins—Ari started the whole "Billionaire owning an island" thing.

And you might think, okay, an island . . . big deal . . . until you go on Google Earth and see how big it is. We mean, check it out—it's an entire *island*. Skorpios even has its own Wikipedia entry (and, in 2001, a census record of two people living there, which sort of kills us). Besides Onassis's house, the island has a pink house

(Jackie's villa), tennis courts, parks, two lovely beaches, a beautiful chapel where Onassis and JKO were married and a cemetery where Onassis, his son Alexander and daughter Christina are also buried.

Athina Onassis, granddaughter of shipping magnate Aristotle, finally ended speculation by releasing a statement saying that she has no plans to sell Skorpios.

SECRET SECRETS—THE JACKIE: THINGS YOU MIGHT NOT KNOW ABOUT HER

JKO did not have a photograph of JFK publicly displayed in her New York City apartment. She kept a small funeral mass card photo of RFK in a silver frame in her bedroom.

SECRET SECRETS—THE MARILYN: THINGS YOU MIGHT NOT KNOW ABOUT HER

Marilyn's favorite photograph of herself was in a jeep, wearing a flack jacket and great smile, from when she entertained the troops in Korea. She carried it in her pocketbook wherever she was. On the back she wrote, "I like this one the best."

10 ⎪ *Diva Behavior*

> *"Well-behaved women rarely make history."*
> —MM

. . . .

> *"I think I'm more of a private person. I really don't like to call attention to anything."*
> —JKO

O-kay—diva behavior.

On this topic, Jackie and Marilyn could school us all and then some (unless Mariah Carey happens to be reading this). In their prime, they were each prima donnas in their own sphere—Jackie as the political/first lady/society babe and Marilyn as the world-famous superstar.

Both Jackie and Marilyn were divas, but MM, being of Hollywood, was the more extreme, *fabulous,* West Coast example. She had no compunction in leaving cast, crew and directors on film sets waiting for hours while she washed her hair three times, practiced her lines, or just sat and looked out the window.

Why? Because she could. Because. That's. What. Divas. Do.

Her costar Clark Gable suffered a heart attack just three

days after they finished filming *The Misfits* in 1960 and died eleven days later. And although he smoked three packs of unfiltered cigarettes a day his entire adult life (as well as cigars and a pipe, and drank copious amounts of whiskey) and insisted on doing his own stunts during a very arduous shoot (being dragged by a pickup truck in horrific desert heat, for example), rumor had it that his wife, Kay, put the blame squarely on Marilyn's unprofessional behavior. (In reality, Kay did not blame Marilyn. She was well aware of Gable's health issues—and invited Marilyn to the baptism of Gable's only son, John Clark Gable, born four months after his death.)

But these were the kinds of rumors that trailed Marilyn.

And although Jackie was perhaps more socially adroit than Marilyn (which manifested itself in some pretty passive-aggressive behavior when she was unhappy with a person or situation), don't kid yourself—she was equally adept at starring in her own diva-esque scenarios.

Although she did many good, even admirable, things while first lady, if she wasn't in the mood or didn't see the point, Jackie could—in true Leo style—just as easily become The First Lady Who Wouldn't.

She feigned illness and left congressional wives cooling their heels while she went horseback riding in the Virginia countryside because she could not be bothered with *yet another* boring White House tea. Or she might say that she was "indisposed" and then be photographed shopping and attending the ballet in New York City.

In one instance, there was a White House reception for Dean Rusk, and word got around that Mrs. Kennedy would not be attending, as she was not feeling well. When one European ambassador shook hands with the president, he conveyed his regrets that the first lady was "under the weather," and he wished for her speedy recovery.

When the president was out of earshot, the ambassador's socially alert wife asked her husband, "How is it, if Mrs. Kennedy is 'under the weather,' that I heard on the radio just one hour ago that she is in New York being fitted for a new gown by Oleg Cassini?"

The Kennedys were noted tightwads, and JFK hated it when anyone sulked or spent too much money. In 1961, Jackie reportedly spent more than $110,000 on "incidentals" (which was more than the president's salary of $100,000[1]). During the campaign, a reporter got a hold of the story that Mrs. Kennedy was spending a ton of money to look so good. She said, famously, in response, "A newspaper reported that I spent $30,000 a year buying Paris clothes and that women hate me for it. I couldn't spend that much unless I wore sable underwear."

But guess what? She *was* (spending that much on her wardrobe, we mean—we don't know about the wearing-sable-underwear thing). The beauty is that Joseph P. Kennedy—always able to spot a possible political liability a mile away—was actually picking up the tab. And what a tab it was. At a time when a very good upper-middle-class salary for a man—say an Ivy-educated lawyer or Wall Street banker—was $11,000 a year, Jackie was spending some serious coin to look so good. And further, to put the whole *how much did Jackie spend?* question in concrete terms, her secretary, Mary Gallagher, who worked full time, plus nights and weekends, was paid $4,800 a year (with the Kennedys bitching the whole way about having to pay that much).

But Jackie thought nothing of spending $3,000 on a single Givenchy blouse, hand embroidered, French couture, the whole nine yards. (And a very good copy of one of Hubert's blouses could be had at the New York City department store Russek's for $10.95.)

During the high-octane Onassis years, Jackie thought nothing of emptying out the entire first-class cabin of Olympic Airlines when she was traveling on it. Or sending a plane back to New York to pick up a forgotten antique footstool. This was,

1 Kennedy donated his salary to the Boy Scouts and Girl Scouts of America.

of course, decades before one worried about a carbon footprint—or even knew what one was.

WHY THEY GOT AWAY WITH IT

Looking to our world, the Jackie and Marilyn Gals of today might be divas, but in varying degrees. For our money, the Marilyn Gal is always far more entertaining, far more of a risk taker and far more exciting to watch in action—since you don't know *what* is going to happen next.

But the real lesson for us today is that whether they were divas or not, both Jackie and Marilyn had the goods to back it up. They were not famous for the sake of being famous or for having been on some ersatz reality show or involved in a scandal that ended up on the front page of the *New York Post*—they were famous because they had talent, they accomplished something.

Jackie was first lady of the United States and held the country together during some of our nation's darkest days in November 1963, then went on to raise her children, contribute to society and lead a productive life. With energy, resilience and the ability to take the historical long view, she burnished JFK's legacy to a high gloss—without her, there would be no Camelot. Today, JFK is *the* president most Americans would like to see added to Mount Rushmore. Her work in historical preservation, starting with saving Lafayette Square when she was in the White House and continuing with Grand Central Terminal and Saint Bartholomew's Church in Manhattan in the 1980s, showed us that our own architecture was actually worth saving decades before most people had an appreciation for this kind of thing.

Marilyn was a renowned actress who held the world in her thrall—and still does to this day—every time she appears on a movie screen. (As director Billy Wilder said of her, "I don't care if it takes her ten hours to get on the set. No one can do what she does—when she arrives—it's magic.") More specifically (if we want to be hard-nosed and talk dollars and cents), she was one of the top-earning actresses of her time. In fact, after *The Seven Year Itch* was released, it earned an unexpected $8 million and was credited with keeping Fox afloat that year. Marilyn's magic still holds with the public—in 1999, she was ranked as the sixth-greatest female star of all time by the American Film Institute.

J+M FIELD NOTES: THE DIVA'S PERSONAL PRESENTATION

Although they were both fastidious in terms of personal mise-en-scène—the way they presented themselves to the world—Marilyn was a bit of a mess in private. But she tended to have people around her (housekeeper, secretary, hairdresser, dog walker, current husband or boyfriend hoping to move up to the front position) who kept things tidy. Plus, she looked so amazing when she walked out the front door that who cared if her bedroom was in shambles?

We think (for example) of the priceless bit of stagecraft after she and baseball god Joe DiMaggio announced their divorce and left the home they shared together for the last time. Clutching the arm of her attorney, surrounded by photographers and newsmen who had been camped out on her front lawn for the previous two days, Marilyn looked both dignified and distraught. Wearing a black turtleneck dress that hugged her curves and impeccable hair and makeup (while she still wore her sorrow like a mantle), she was every inch the heartbroken leading lady.

Jackie, like Marilyn, had a keen sense of her visual self, but she did not share MM's laissez-faire approach to housekeeping. In fact, she was the exact opposite. In Jackie Land, if you did something Not Our Kind Dear, like leave the top off the toothpaste (*really?*) or—god forbid—didn't put the toilet seat down, it was, to her, the same as murdering kittens.

Today, for the sake of familial peace, it is probably best to opt for separate bathrooms. The Jackie in particular hates slobs. She takes it as a personal affront to her Jackie-esque worldview.

And you know—she's probably right.

JKO — Dealing with the Paps

Jackie's relationship with the paparazzi was complex. On the one hand, they annoyed her, and she even took Ron Galella to court in 1972 for harassing her and her children (the court ruled that he had to stay 150 feet away from Jackie and her children).[2] On the other hand, she had a great eye and appreciated fine photography. White House photographer Cecil Stoughton became a good friend, creating several private photo books for her (that she loved) and always made sure to edit her selections so that she looked good in all of her photos.[3]

So it seems that Jackie wanted to control the press, control the situation. Although she sent her housekeeper out to buy newspapers like the *Star,* the *Enquirer* or the *New York Post* whenever she was mentioned in them, Jackie also fired a maid working for her who was being courted by a paparazzo hoping to get inside information on her.

MM's Relationship with the Camera

Marilyn loved the camera. Always did. Always, always, always. In fact, it could be said that the camera made Marilyn the iconic star that she became—and kept her in the celestial firmament. Even more than a movie camera, the still camera created the Marilyn that we know and love, even today.

Every photographer who was fortunate enough to work with Marilyn attested to the fact that she "came alive" for the camera. Douglas Kirkland, who shot her at the age of twenty-

---

2 After JKO's death, John Junior lifted the restraining order and allowed Galella to take photos of him in public.
3 Interestingly, Ron Galella also tried to take only "good" shots of JKO.

seven for *Look* magazine, recalled that when Marilyn arrived for the session, she seemed "very white, almost luminescent—this white vision drifted in as if in slow motion into the studio. She seemed to give off a glow."

Two days later, after the shoot, Kirkland brought the contact sheets over to Marilyn's house so that she could select the images she liked and reject those not up to her standards. Marilyn selected ten photographs that she liked and cut up the ones she did not with scissors.

Kirkland was left with the impression of a woman in love with the camera who was also a consummate professional.

And the paps? Although the paparazzi were not the aggressive mob they are today, Marilyn was clearly hounded by the press. And they could, at times, be almost frighteningly intrusive, like when she tried to marry Joe DiMaggio in a quiet civil ceremony in San Francisco, or when their divorce was announced several months later. It is almost scary to see the mob surrounding her.

Still, unlike Jackie, Marilyn was always gracious and took the time to pose (when at a movie premiere, for example) and stop and speak to her fans and photographers when she could, even in her "private" time.

IN POPULAR CULTURE

Although they might not be carbon copies, gals with the mojo of JKO and MM are all around us. A few of today's more notable examples—

. . . .

THE JACKIES

. . . .

Amanda Burden, Tory Burch, Michelle Obama, Natalie Portman, Jennifer Garner, Kate Spade, Diane Sawyer, Marina Rust, Susan Fales-Hill, Marjorie Gubelmann, Cate Blanchett, Iman, Tina Fey, Cynthia Rowley, Anna Wintour, Amanda Brooks, Katie Holmes, Cornelia Guest, Patricia Duff, Diane Von Furstenberg (with MM overtones), Patricia Clarkson, Minnie Mortimer, Sandra Bullock, Plum Sykes, Nicole Kidman

. . . .

THE MARILYNS

. . . .

Scarlett Johansson, Angelina Jolie, Penelope Cruz, Jennifer Lopez, Goldie Hawn, Pink, Christina Hendricks, Kate Moss, Jessica Simpson, Naomi Campbell, Mariah Carey, Rihanna, Mary J. Blige, Megan Fox, Drew Barrymore, Kelly Ripa, Christina Aguilera

THE DIVINE MISS M: BEHIND THE CURTAIN

Still, in spite of her charms, Marilyn could be quite trying at times. It wasn't all sweetness and light. For one thing, she followed her own internal time clock in regard to pretty much everything. With the eyes of the room and sometimes (it seemed) the world upon her, she was not going to walk on that stage until she was good and ready. As she herself admitted, "I am invariably late for appointments—sometimes as much as two hours. I've tried to change my ways but the things that make me late are too strong, and too pleasing."

If you were not already in love with her (rare, you probably just hadn't met her yet) or on the verge of falling in love with her (everyone else), she could be exhausting to be with. Unlike Jackie, Marilyn had no filter. This was both exciting and scary. Although honestly? Some men like The Crazy the same way they insist on chasing models and actresses who are way out of their league. Why do some men go for this? Probably because they think crazy outside of bed equals crazy in bed (however you define that).

But fast-forward to today—why deal with a woman who is, quite frankly, a pain in the ass? It has always been our theory that if she is pretty enough, a man will put up with just about anything to be with her. *Anything.* Or maybe he likes a challenge or is going to be the one to "fix her." Of course, he won't be.

Even we know that.

"I've been on a calendar but never on time."

—MM

FRIENDSHIP WITH JKO / MM: IS IT WORTH IT?

To be honest, Jackie (somewhat a product of her generation) did not have much use for female friends until later on in life.

When she was growing up and in the White House, her sister, Lee, was her confidante. (Truman Capote, for his part, called them "the whispering sisters.") Once, when Lee's first husband, Michael Canfield, was courting her, he took the Bouvier gals on a rowboat ride in Central Park. He grew concerned as he watched them discussing what seemed to be a matter of great importance. Was there a family illness? Some great tragedy in the wings?

Later, he asked and was told, "Gloves."

Marilyn, on the other hand, truly loved and depended on the company of women. Growing up without a sister or a mother she could depend on, she surrounded herself with older, maternal figures, such as her mother's best friend, Grace McKee.

On film sets, she befriended her stand-in, Evelyn Moriarty, and the script girl. During the last weekend of her life, she invited her publicist, Pat Newcomb, to stay over in her guest room and rest because Pat was suffering from bronchitis, and Marilyn thought it might make her feel better to lie in the sun and use her pool.

In the last interview she gave to Richard Merryman of *LIFE* magazine, she showed him around her new house and said she wanted to have a small guest suite, "A place for any friends of mine who are in some kind of trouble. Maybe they'll want to live here where they won't be bothered till things are okay for them."

In later years, Jackie and Lee grew apart. Perhaps it was because Lee was an indifferent mother (when her daughter, Christina, was a teenager, she even went to live with Aunt Jackie for a spell). Perhaps it was because the balance of power shifted from the pretty Lee to the bookish Jackie, who grew up to be one of the most influential women in the world, while Lee floundered with what to "do" with herself (trying acting, writing, interior decorating and finally fashion PR for Giorgio Armani in the 1980s).

After Jackie died, she left nothing in her will to her sister ("I have made no provision in this my Will for my sister, Lee B. Radziwill, for whom I have great affection because I have already done so during my lifetime"), a telling sentiment from someone as thoughtful as Jackie. She did, however, leave $500,000 to each of Lee's two children.

On a broader note, in regard to friendship in general, Jackie and Marilyn were on different wavelengths. Jackie, perhaps because of the very public tragedy she had to endure with the assassination of JFK, was very adept at ending close relationships and moving on. Maybe too adept. Perhaps this was how she kept her sanity. If she felt that you had "dissed" her in some way—whether you were a former best friend of JFK's[4] or a Bouvier family member[5]—you were out.

Marilyn, on the other hand—once you were in her life, you were in it for keeps. As she put it, "I've never dropped anyone I believed in." After her divorce from Joe DiMaggio, she remained close with his son, Joe Junior, giving him advice on his love life and even buying him a car. After her divorce from Arthur Miller, she remained close with his seventy-year-old father, Isidore ("Izzy"), sending him airplane tickets and inviting him to visit her in California, something his own son never did. He was her escort when she sang for JFK's birthday celebration at Madison Square Garden. When he accompanied her to the after party (where she dodged the attentions of John Kenneth Galbraith and both Kennedy brothers), she was mainly concerned that he was comfortable and looked after.

FRIEND OF MARILYN'S

Seemingly more vulnerable that Jackie, Marilyn was a lovely friend. Betty Grable, who worked with her on *How to Marry a Millionaire,* remembers Marilyn's thoughtfulness. As the up-and-coming star being groomed to take Grable's place, studio photographers wanted to take Marilyn's picture in front of Grable's old dressing room (that was now hers). Marilyn refused.[6] One day during shooting, Grable had to leave early because her son was sick. Marilyn called later that night to see

4 After Ben Bradlee published an extremely loving memoir of his friendship with JFK (he was the Washington editor of *Newsweek* and became friends with JFK when they were neighbors in Georgetown in 1958), *Conversations With Kennedy*, in 1975, Jackie took offense to it and never spoke to him again.

5 Ditto for John H. Davis, Jackie's cousin who published *The Bouviers* in 1969 and exposed the reality that the Bouviers were not descended from French nobility but just regular folk. JKO never spoke to him or his mother again. He had to personally call and beg Jackie's assistant to allow his mother—her aunt Maude—to attend Jackie's funeral at Saint Ignatius Loyola in New York City (where she was a parishioner) or risk standing out on the sidewalk. Jackie's assistant relented.

6 For her part, BG was sanguine about MM taking her place in the Hollywood constellation. "Go and get yours, honey, I've had mine," she famously said.

how he was doing. Grable remembered that she was the only one from the studio to do so.

In today's world, as a friend of a Marilyn, you probably know some of the downsides—the teary 3 a.m. phone calls, the *beyond* dramatic love life, the missed airplane flights, impossible mornings, harrowing near-death experiences, endless Sturm und Drang (and that's just on a Tuesday).

But the question for you is: Is it worth it? Is *she* worth it? Absolutely. No doubt about it.

FRIEND OF JACKIE'S

Like Bobby Kennedy, like all the Kennedys, like the Irish for that matter, Jackie had a very black and white view of friendship: You were on the team or you were not. If she felt that you had betrayed her in some way, there was no forgiveness, no looking back, no understanding for any sort of human transgression. One mistake, and you were voted off the island—one need only remember her absolute ability to cut off employees, relatives and formerly close friends who had transgressed her zone of privacy.

Having said that, once you proved your faithfulness and that you could be trusted, Jackie was a great friend. Every August, she lent her home on Martha's Vineyard to Provi Paredes and her son, Gustavo. Provi had been her maid when she was first married to Senator Kennedy and later Jackie's personal assistant while she was in the White House, and had remained close to the Kennedy family.[7] When her sister Lee Radziwill's daughter, Christina, was not getting along with her mother, she went and lived with Jackie for several years as a teenager.

Jackie always seemed to know the right thing to say. When Robert McNamara was going through a tough time in the press, she encouraged him, saying, "Just remember what Eleanor Roosevelt said—nobody can make you feel bad about yourself unless you give them permission."

7 Jackie also remembered her in her will, leaving her $50,000.

Guys, at this point in the game, knowing as much as we do about the Marilyn Gal and the Jackie Gal, we are going to give you some advice. When in doubt, it is easier to fall on the sword and simply apologize for what happened.

Whatever it is.

We know! We know! We hear what you are saying—why are you always the one who has to make the first move, capitulate, come in from the rain, send flowers. We get that. And again, we're not saying it is fair—we're just saying . . . if you want to be with a Jackie or a Marilyn (and especially a Marilyn), well, let's just say that there are sacrifices you will occasionally have to make to keep the peace.

And yet we know—as you do—that it's a fine line because both the Jackie Gal and the Marilyn Gal abhor weaklings (of the male variety, especially). They just don't like woosy men—guys who own cats, wear flannel shirts, are thinner than they are, have nicer skin or hair,[8] do yoga.

We get that. They like a strong man who can also cook, play the piano, recite poetry and make them laugh. Plus, get their parking tickets taken care of.

(For her part, the Marilyn—dreamer that she is—ups the ante by envisioning a Pulitzer Prize–winning author who looks nice in khakis and a white T-shirt. And he must be taller than she is and fix her computer when it breaks down.)

So, yes—walking this emotional tightrope is a pretty tall order. But on the other hand, the payoff is that you get to have the diva in your life.

· · · · · · · · · · · · ·

8 If that's even possible.

MM — DIVA-*fantabulous!*

In case you are trying to picture what it might really be like to be part of MM's inner circle, here's one especially memorable story.

Marilyn was at her apartment in New York City, getting ready for JFK's birthday bash at Madison Square Garden. At one point, she was reclining on a white lounge chair, having her hair and makeup done. When she stood up and walked away, there was a perfect (nude) outline of Marilyn, her shoulders, back and legs running down the length of the chair. It seems that her full-body makeup had left an impression on the chair, ruining it.

Or rendering it priceless.

HELLO/GOOD-BYE DIVA

Sure, Marilyn and Jackie could be divas, but then—in true diva fashion—they could be *anti*-divas and exceedingly generous at the drop of a hat. It all depended on their whim at the moment.[9]

And again, in true diva style, you did not know what you might get from one moment to the next . . . like the weather, like rain falling in London, you had *no idea* what would crop up on the horizon, so you had to be prepared for any possibility.

This is what kept things exciting in Diva World.

MARILYN COULD BE EXTREMELY THOUGHTFUL

On her last movie, *Something's Got to Give,* Marilyn was at her most tenuous (and diva-esque). But it wasn't her fault, not really. Preproduction went well, with wardrobe and hair and makeup tests. The night before the first day of shooting, she called in sick, explaining that she had gotten a severe sinus

9 Just like Elvis Presley, Elizabeth Taylor, Karl Lagerfeld, Steve Jobs . . .

infection after she had traveled to New York City to go over her role with her acting coach, Lee Strasberg. The studio doctor examined her and said that yes, she was sick and would be out for a month.

A *month*? The studio and the producer must have had heart attacks when they heard this . . . a leading lady off the set of a major motion picture (that was supposed to refill the coffers after Liz Taylor and Richard Burton's *Cleopatra* debacle filming on the other side of the world) was not good.[10]

In spite of this, the studio and George Cukor, the director, decided to begin production and shoot around her. Which they did for the next month as MM recovered, stopping by the set only occasionally.

An additional wrinkle was added to the timeline of *Something's Got to Give* when Marilyn was invited to sing at President Kennedy's Madison Square Garden birthday party, an event she had gotten permission from the studio to attend well before the picture began production. Given her late start, no one expected her to take a week off to go to New York City to sing for the president.

But she did.

So by the time she returned to the set, they were behind schedule, rewriting parts of the script almost daily—something Marilyn hated, as it made it difficult for her to learn her lines to her satisfaction, and Marilyn was not getting along with Cukor (who was supposedly a very "female friendly" director—for what that was worth). Given this chaos, the studio was also threatening (in the press) to shut down the picture, claiming that Marilyn's tardiness and decision to fly to New York City to sing for the president was the reason (although we know now, of course, that the studio was aware of all of it and perhaps just looking for an excuse to pull the plug on an ill-fated movie).

All of this made Marilyn very unsettled, feeling that neither

. . . .

10 BTW, Cleopatra (with a budget of $44,000,000—$307,000,000 in today's dollars) would eventually cause Fox to have to sell off most of its back lot to real-estate developers.

the studio nor the director was in her corner. As she put it, "An actress is not a machine, but they treat you like a machine. A money machine." She fought back with one of the tools in her arsenal: showing up later and later on set, hiding out in her dressing room, flubbing her lines and requiring take after take after take. Which exhausted the crew, the cameramen, her director and even the other actors.

Finally, late one night, her friend Larry Schiller, the photographer on set, asked her, "Marilyn, when is this going to end?"

"What are you worried about?" Marilyn wondered.

"I'd like to get home," he said. "I've got a new 7-month-old little girl."

"I didn't know you were married . . ."

"I've been bar mitzvahed too," Schiller said. "What else do you want to know about me?"

Marilyn laughed, and they sat on the steps of her trailer and talked. Schiller told Marilyn of his recent success as a photographer, how an assignment from *Playboy* allowed him to buy a little house for his family with a backyard and a swimming pool. "Look what tits and ass can do for you. Now I got a house with a backyard and a swimming pool."

"So do I," said Marilyn with a quiet little giggle.

Much later that night, Schiller drove home to find his wife up, waiting. What was going on, he wondered. His wife, Judi, said that someone had come to the door and woken her. It was a deliveryman with two dozen roses and a note from Marilyn Monroe: "Sorry for keeping him so late," she had written.

After that, Marilyn and Schiller were even better friends. He no longer had to knock upon entering her dressing room; if the door was ajar, he just went in. The next day, he brought a single rose to the set and presented it to Marilyn.

She laughed and put it between her teeth.

SECRET SECRETS—THE JACKIE: THINGS YOU MIGHT NOT KNOW ABOUT HER

Jackie never felt sorry for herself. "If you get out into the world, and move around a little bit, you begin to see that there are people who have been through much worse things than I have."

SECRET SECRETS—THE MARILYN: THINGS YOU MIGHT NOT KNOW ABOUT HER

Here's MM, speaking like a true diva (who, like all true divas, knows her worth): "If you can't handle me at my worst, then you sure as hell don't deserve me at my best."

"I think my biggest achievement is that after going through a rather difficult time, I consider myself comparatively sane."

—JKO

. . . .

"If you want the girl next door, you should go next door."

—MM

JACKIE AND MARILYN HAD COURAGE

*P*erhaps the most admirable thing about Jackie and Marilyn, knowing their lives as we do now—beyond the first blush of their obvious beauty, style or fame—is their courage. Each in her own way had a great deal to overcome (and yes, by any measure, Marilyn's internal emotional challenges were far more difficult than Jackie's). And each rose to meet those challenges.

If nothing else, Jackie and Marilyn persevered in spite of what lay in front of them on the road ahead. Marilyn overcame a bleak childhood to become one of the most famous actresses in the world. And beyond that, she moved past her status as a Hollywood pinup girl to be taken seriously as a "real" actress. As one of the youngest first ladies of the 20th century, Jackie revitalized the White House and added a cultural sheen to America. She held this country together in the grim days following her husband's assassination, and then went on to not only raise her children successfully but also to find a measure of peace and personal satisfaction as a book editor in New York City.

Overcoming heartbreak, grief, uncertainty, discouragement and occasional loneliness, Jackie and Marilyn rose above their circumstances and what society expected of them.

And they did it with no small measure of courage, style and élan, which we could certainly use more of today.

As Marilyn said (describing Chérie, her character in *Bus Stop*, though she might have been describing herself): "She was a girl who knew how to be happy even when she was sad. And that's important, you know."

Absolutely.

THE POWER OF FEMININITY

Jackie and Marilyn were deeply, inherently feminine; they knew the power of being a woman and were unafraid to use it. Marilyn's entire career, in fact, rested on her ability to project the feminine ideal.[1] However, like the powerful men surrounding them, Jackie and Marilyn were intelligent, savvy and ambitious; they knew how to navigate the politics of the workplace and how to persevere in attaining their goals.

Were they feminists?

Although the word barely existed in their adulthood (and MM died before the women's

---

1 As does her posthumous career, for that matter.

movement blossomed in the late 1960s), Marilyn fought to be taken seriously in Hollywood, pushing for both creative and financial independence from the studios. And, famously, she won, becoming one of the first actors to put a chink in the studio system. Jackie, for her part, was a friend of Gloria Steinem's and donated money in 1972 to help found *Ms. Magazine*.

But they were also, in many ways, traditional. They both longed for marriage and a family, children even, and wanted to create a warm, private, comfortable home for themselves and those they loved. And they saw this as a woman's role.

Ultimately, Jackie and Marilyn can, in many ways, serve as role models for us today, because they did not compromise when it came to their goals and their dreams, and they did it by being women, not by trying to act like men.

ALWAYS DRINK THE WINE

As Jackie and Marilyn's mutual friend Frank Sinatra so famously put it, "I will drink the wine." And Jackie and Marilyn did, living their lives to the fullest. We have almost reached the end of our time together, so whether you have decided you are a Jackie or a Marilyn (or more likely, a combination of the two), we have one final piece of advice: Live a big life. In other words, roll the dice. Leave a trail. Be memorable.

If you're not sure whether to write that encouraging letter to a friend, write it and send it.

Laugh out loud. And if you can make someone else laugh, even better. That's a rare gift—don't take it for granted.

Look up and smile, just for the heck of it. You never know, you might be encouraging someone else to keep going.

Don't keep your heart in trust. Tell him you love him. Whether you hear it in return is almost beside the point.

And if you can give a child some confidence, that's always a good thing. He or she just might remember that moment (and you) longer than you can imagine.

Stay up and watch the sun rise every once in a while. And if you happen to find yourself on the deck of a boat moored in Vineyard Haven in August, even better.

When in doubt, order the champagne. And wear your highest heels—you never know.

You only go around the track once, but with some self-awareness and the right attitude, we guarantee: It will be more than enough.

MM CONNECTS WITH PEOPLE. STILL.

"It's all make believe, isn't it?"

—MM

While Jackie is respected in many circles and might even remind a certain stratum of American society of their mothers, she does not have the cultural resonance (along with James Dean, Audrey Hepburn, or Elvis Presley) of Marilyn. For some reason, Marilyn, far more than Jackie (with the bulwark of the Kennedys and her husband's presidency, her self-sufficiency and her Vassar education behind her), captures our imagination.

We think we could have saved her, been her friend, *understood* her—and thereby protected her.

There is something in Marilyn (her vulnerability? her beauty? her tragic Hollywood story?) that causes people to connect with her on a deeply personal level even today. Even though she died in 1962 (close to fifty years ago) at the age of thirty-six, fans travel from around the world to make a pilgrimage to her gravesite. More psychics claim to contact her from beyond the grave than almost any other celebrity. Elton John wrote "Candle in the Wind," a haunting song about his boyhood crush on her and how he would have liked to have known her, but he was just a kid. . . .

As a celebrity, her spirit is so present in the current American media mix that it is almost as if she never left.

JACKIE AND MARILYN: THEIR LEGACY IN CELEBRITY WORLD TODAY

Jackie and Marilyn never met, but they are connected in Celebrity World (think of it as "six degrees of separation" but without the Kevin Bacon factor). They were both involved with JFK, Marlon Brando and Frank Sinatra. Before his marriage, Jackie's son, John (much to his mother's chagrin), dated Madonna, who has a full-blown Marilyn obsession.[2] In fact, with her too-toned body and deal-making prowess, she might be considered Marilyn without the vulnerability factor (Marilyn 2.0).

The Jackie/Marilyn connection came full circle when, in a totally metacelebrity media conflagration (or just a way to sell more magazines), JFK Junior put Drew Barrymore on the September 1996 issue of *George* maga-

2 See the "Material Girl" music video, also *True Blue* and other album covers.

zine, done up as Marilyn Monroe, with the headline "Happy Birthday Mr. President."[3]

And the Michael Jackie-Marilyn-Madonna connection continued when Michael Jackson and Madonna attended the 1991 Oscars. Walking into the after party at Spago, Madonna channeled the full-blown "Diamonds Are a Girl's Best Friend" Marilyn, with platinum hair, 20 million dollars worth of borrowed Harry Winston gems and a white satin evening dress cut on the bias, while MJ wore a white dinner jacket, his own massive diamond brooch and white gloves.

One cannot help but wonder: What would Jackie and Marilyn have said?

THE TAKEAWAY

Now that you've read the book, here is the abridged version of the J+M ethos . . .

Lose the ego.

Take the high road.

When in doubt, wear lipstick.

If someone calls your name when you are out walking, turn and smile—it could be Ron Galella. And possibly posterity.

WHAT NEXT

We've given you the ground rules. Now it's up to you to take your utterly fabulous Jackie or Marilyn self out into the world and see how *you* can shake things up.

---

3 One can only imagine how this would have gone over had his mother been alive.

"I've had a great run."

—JKO

SECRET SECRETS — THE JACKIE:
THINGS YOU MIGHT NOT KNOW ABOUT HER

It is said (among historians) that JKO kept a diary. And it still exists.

SECRET SECRETS — THE MARILYN:
THINGS YOU MIGHT NOT KNOW ABOUT HER

Marilyn collected poetry. After her death, the following snippet of Yeats (written in her own hand) was found among her papers: "That only God, my dear, / Could love you for yourself alone / And not your yellow hair."

Although Yeats's love poem was to Maud Gonne, he might have been speaking of MM.

*F*requently Asked Questions

. . . .

*C*an *anyone* be like Jackie or Marilyn?

Absolutely! All it takes is vision and determination (much like Jackie and Marilyn had themselves).

On second thought, it helps to be female and, barring that, "creative."

*M*y mother is making me insane! What can I do?

Jackie and Marilyn both had fraught relationships with their mothers—Marilyn because her mother was mentally unstable and had to be institutionalized; Jackie because her mother was an Irish Catholic passing for French in a WASP world (when this mattered), with insanely high standards for both of her daughters, a very sharp tongue, no compunctions about making her views known and overall wasn't very nice to Jackie.

However, both Jackie and Marilyn chose to take the high road in regard to their mothers. Marilyn supported her mother and made sure her care continued after her death by writing it in her will. (In fact, Marilyn's mother outlived her daughter, never knowing how famous her daughter was when she died in 1984.)

Jackie also made sure that her mother was well cared for, setting up a trust fund for her and making sure that she had household staff, nurses and the best medical treatment available. In her inimitable style, JKO "overlooked" her mother's earlier treatment of her. And Mrs. Auchincloss, in her own style, always spoke very highly of Jackie to others—but never to her directly.

I don't have a perfect figure. Can I still be like Jackie or Marilyn?

Please—neither did Jackie! Not to be impolite, but go back and read chapter four—and then get back to us.

I have a date with this guy I really like. Advice?

Heels, always. And lipstick and mascara. Lower your voice. Don't talk too much. Make him come to you.

I would like to encourage my seven-year-old daughter to be like Jackie and Marilyn. What should I give her?

Confidence. A sense of history. A library card.

*W*hat would Jackie and Marilyn think about social networking—Facebook? Twitter? Email?

Email, yes. BlackBerry, def (but they would not be wed to it). Marilyn would repeatedly lose her BB, thereby giving obsessed fans even more reason to track her down.

Facebook and Twitter? Jackie—no, TMI! Marilyn would have her publicist or one of her fans take care of this for her.

Both Jackie and Marilyn would have shopped extensively online. Late at night when she couldn't sleep, Marilyn would probably respond to her fans' blogs and comments. The mean stuff would hurt her feelings, though.

*H*ow can we continue this conversation?

Online, of course. www.jackieormarilyn.com or www.pamelakeogh.com

Acknowledgments

$\mathcal{I}$ would like to thank my editor, Lauren Marino, who saw this book before I did. I would also like to particularly acknowledge associate editor Jessica Sindler and thank her for her creative and much needed (*much* needed) editorial guidance. I think she has a great future ahead of her as the Max Perkins of her generation.

Enormous kudos to my agents, who are such a great team because they combine both Jackie and Marilyn Style in their own inimitable way—Linda Chester (a Jackie) and Alexandra Machinist (a definite Marilyn).

Thanks, too, to Gary Jaffe (a Cary Grant, but that's another book) of LCA for keeping the ship afloat.

I would like to thank all the people I interviewed and who were of assistance during the research and writing of this book—Carl Sferrazza Anthony, Hélène Arpels, Rebecca Apsan, Yusha Auchincloss, Peter Bacanovic, Letitia Baldrige, Jeffrey Banks, Deepak Chopra, Darac, James de Givenchy, C. Z. Guest, John H. Davis, Dale DeGroff, David Fairchild, Ron Galella, Renée and Suzette Guercia, Alexander Haas, Victoria Haas, William A. Henry, III, Arlyn Imberman, Lorrie Ivas, Kevin Lee, John Loring, James Martin, S. J., Beth Mendelson, Joseph Montebello, Pamela Needham, Caroline Sharp, Stacey Smoker, Dr. Amy Weschler, James T. Curtis, Bob Willoughby, Susan Zummo.

I would also like to give a special shout out to Fitzwilliam Anderson, who loves to read and is deeply entertained by, and immersed in, modern American culture.

Jacqueline Onassis and Marilyn Monroe are two of the most well documented women of our time. I would like to recognize the journalists and biographers who came before me—Christopher Anderson, Letitia Baldrige, George Barris, Ben Bradlee, Jim Bishop, Oleg Cassini, Marie Clayton, Fleur Cowles, Rita Dallas, Nigel Dempster, Mike Evans, Paul B. Fay, Jr., Kim France and Andrea Linett, Mary Barelli Gallagher, Karen Karbo, Sam Kaschner, Barbara Leaming, Evelyn Lincoln, Lynne McTaggart, Arthur Miller, Jan Pottker, Mini Rhea with Frances Spatz Leighton, Cynthia Rowley and Ilene Rosenzweig, Raymond Sarlot and Fred E. Basten, Lawrence Schiller, Maud Shaw, Marta Sgubin, Fred Sparks, Donald Spoto, Gloria Steinem, Laren Stover, Anthony Summers.

One of my favorite parts of writing is the research. In addition to all the people I interviewed, I would like to thank Kathryn Felde and Mark Ekman at the Paley Center for Media in New York City—an amazing place to do research—as well as the New York Society Library (another gem). And 71 Irving—the best coffee in the city. Additional research was done at the JFK Library, particularly the oral histories, as well as the AMPAS library in Los Angeles.

At Gotham, I would like to thank publisher Bill Shinker, who leads the crew with a personal élan and vision that Jackie and Marilyn would admire. Lisa Johnson and Anne Kosmoski did great work getting this book out into the world. And tremendous gratitude to the most talented illustrator, Meg Hess, who brought our Jackie and Marilyn-esque Gals to life.

Finally, I would like to thank my friends who were with me when I wrote this book—the pizza, dark chocolate, occasional Heineken, flowers, late-night phone calls, encouragement and moral support were all greatly appreciated.

Also by Pamela Keogh

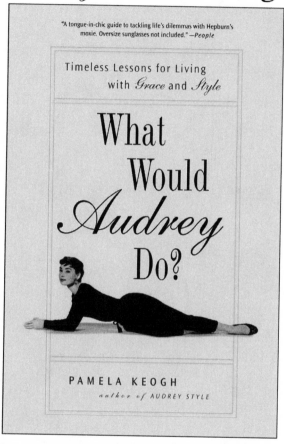

"A tongue-in-chic guide to tackling life's dilemmas with Hepburn's moxie. Oversize sunglasses not included." —*People*

Timeless Lessons for Living
with *Grace* and *Style*

What Would *Audrey* Do?

PAMELA KEOGH
author of AUDREY STYLE

The *New York Times* bestselling author provides a charming guide to Audrey Hepburn–inspired living for the modern woman.

On sale now.

GOTHAM BOOKS a member of Penguin Group (USA) | www.penguin.com